PRAISE FOR

Hula Girls: A Novel

"*When Joe tried to strangle her, she did what any woman would do. She crossed him off her list.*" This character-driven novel explores the social and psychological terrain of a gorgeous, American military housewife in Hawaii in the 1940s. Every plot turn is thought-provoking. . . . This novel is an emotional journey with great storytelling and a satisfying ending. It can inspire readers to contemplate gender roles and conflicts arising from World War II that have left an impact on our world today." —US Review of Books, Recommended

"Eric B. Miller's *Hula Girls* delivers an engrossing epic about a young Navy wife who grapples with her life in Honolulu amidst the outbreak of WWII. . . . A superb storyteller. . . . This is an immersive novel that examines how one reconciles with the past, while providing insight into American women's changing roles in the mid-twentieth century." —BlueInk Reviews, Starred Review

"A debut novel tracks a brave and resourceful woman from right before the Pearl Harbor attack through the next thirty years. . . . The tale's point of view is Claudia's, and Miller loves to play with clichés ("Claudia thought her can of worms was nothing like Annette's kettle of fish") and delightful figurative language (at Adm. Harris' reception and dance, "the presence of a powder room had eddied a flotsam of ladies"). The author also provides nostalgic period touches . . . so that readers get the sense of being enveloped in a long-ago era. Though it covers only three decades, this story has the feel of a saga and is as satisfying as one. A wonderful evocation of a time and place and a woman's indomitable spirit." —Kirkus Reviews

Little Known Stories: Prose in Format

"A collection of poetic vignettes detailing a lifelong love, a terminal illness, and an unbearable absence. These detailed poems provide readers with a nonlinear voyage through the author's memories, jumping between his present solitary state and the relationship he shared with his late wife, Lisa. . . . To combine simplicity with artistry is a demanding task, and it's one that few works can accomplish. Such a balance pulses throughout these stories, which are as stark and complex as loss itself. A beautiful and piercing look at grief handled with delicacy." —Kirkus Starred Review

Also by eric b. miller

Hula Girls, A Novel
Little Known Stories: Prose in Format

Tidewater

A Novel

eric b. miller

MILBROWN PRESS
Denver
www.ericbmiller.com

© 2024 by Eric B. Miller

All rights reserved. No part of this book may be reproduced in any form or by any electronic or mechanical means, including information storage and retrieval systems, without written permission from the publisher, except by a reviewer who may quote passages in a review.

Cover illustrations: Photo of cliff-side view across the Sassafras River at Sassafras Natural Resources Management Area in Kennedyville, Maryland © Erin Gifford (*front*); © Yvonne Navalaney (*back*). Author photo by Larry J. Cohen.

Published by Milbrown Press
An imprint of JBM Publishing Company
1265 South Columbine Street
Denver, Colorado 80210
(303) 503-1739

Printed in the United States of America

ISBN: 979-8-9859113-2-9 (paperback)
ISBN: 979-8-9859113-3-6 (ebook)

Publisher's Cataloging-In-Publication Data
(Provided by Cassidy Cataloguing Services, Inc.).

Names: Miller, Eric B., 1948– author.
Title: Tidewater : a novel / Eric B. Miller.
Description: Denver, Colorado : Milbrown Press, [2024]
Identifiers: ISBN: 979-8-9859113-2-9 (paperback) | 979-8-9859113-3-6 (ebook)
Subjects: LCSH: Landowners—Maryland—Fiction. | Families—Maryland—Fiction. | World War, 1914–1918—Fiction. | Interpersonal relations—Fiction. | Love—Fiction. | Coastal plains— Maryland—Fiction. | United States—History—1865–1921—Fiction. | LCGFT: Domestic fiction.
Classification: LCC: PS3613.I5361 T54 2024 | DDC: 813/.6—dc23

Front-cover concept by Jeff Miller
Cover and page design by Pratt Brothers Composition

To Whitehall as it was,
and to those who were young in its finest days.

CONTENTS

AUTHOR'S NOTE
ix

PART ONE
Chapters 1–18
3

PART TWO
Chapters 19–30
179

PART THREE
Chapters 31–46
291

PART FOUR
Chapters 47–58
365

PART FIVE
Chapters 59–77
429

PART SIX
Chapters 78–83
539

ACKNOWLEDGMENTS
575

ABOUT THE AUTHOR
577

AUTHOR'S NOTE

This book began with a memory of my father crouching in the sand in his bare feet with his old army khaki trousers rolled up to the knees, showing us where to look for arrowheads along the shore of the Sassafras River. I wish the younger ones of the family had known him then.

TIDEWATER

PART ONE

CHAPTER ONE

MARYLAND, SEPTEMBER 1919

The Big Train, as Elijah Brown called it, came through overnight with sheets of rain, followed by a roaring wind, and suddenly summer was gone. Right behind it was a noticeable drop in the temperature when he slipped quietly out of the bed he shared with Viola, his wife of thirty years. He got dressed, turned on a light downstairs in the kitchen, took a piece of bread out of the breadbox, and walked across the way to the milking barn. At four o'clock in the morning, the stars were out in a clear black sky with no sign as yet of light over the east. There was a light on in the Banks' kitchen, one in the Eldridges' kitchen, and another in the Coopers', so Kenneth, Lamont, and Earling would be over before long.

He was right about the look of the sky yesterday, as he had been every year since he came up with a name for it, but he had an apprehension that Lamont and Earling wouldn't be talking about the weather.

The old gray-and-white flannel shirt felt right for the chill in the air, as did Danforth's velvet fedora, shabby though it was after fifteen years of him being dead and gone. Elijah held no ill will against Danforth. No, sir. When the good Lord lay his hand on a man, time to take yours off—as the man says. Just the same, he knew the old master might be turning over in his grave to see a black man wearing his hat. Not that Elijah ever had his eyes on it; it was just there on the pile for anyone to take when the Crofts took over the farm and tore down the Danforth place.

New hay in the loft and sixty cows in for the night made it warm and smelling of grass and summer inside the long barn. The stock stirred up when Elijah swung back the big doors and let the cold air in. He found the switch box in the dark and turned on the electric. All at once, forty clear-glass bulbs went on, frosted over with barn dust, one every ten feet, mounted to each six-by-six oak upright.

"Time to git up, you cows. Nother day."

Elijah nudged through the cows to the other end of the barn and opened up the doors there. Then to the grain bin, fishing in his pocket for the key ring. The cows raised their noses to the cross breeze, but they settled down and lined up by habit to the stalls with their heads to the hayrack waiting for grain. As Elijah walked the other side of the stalls, up one end of the barn and down the other, spreading bucket after bucket into the trough, the cows tossed their heads and snorted the grain over the edge, fighting over it as far as their necks could reach in both directions.

"Hey, hey. Quit throwin' that grain 'round," he said, gently batting their noses as he went back and forth to the grain bin.

Grain was costly. Elijah didn't know why Captain Croft wanted it put out all year, but that was his business. It was his farm, and he could do what he wanted with it. At least he came into dairy farming with money. Whether he cared about money or not was still in question for maybe everybody living on the farm. For one thing, there was the retirement pasture. In fifteen years, Elijah had never known Captain Croft to send a used-up cow to the knackers. The old ones got turned out to pasture and lived out their lives in a pretty meadow. Used-up cows got the grain too.

In the beginning, Elijah thought the captain was just too tenderhearted for farming right. Too much blood on the hands. Rabbits caught in the reaper, knocking gophers on the head with a shovel, setting out poison for foxes, and butchering your own meat. Too much for city sensibilities. But the first time one of the retired cows went into decline, Captain Croft said he'd take care of it himself. He and Mr. Thompson came out on horseback to the retirement meadow, where Elijah was told to hold the cow. They had leather cases across the pommels of their saddles and rode off to the line of woods a quarter mile distant. While Elijah was stroking her sides and talking to her like the good old days, the old cow suddenly dropped stone dead at his feet.

At first Elijah didn't know what had happened. The report from the woods was so far off that he wasn't sure if he had heard anything at all. But looking the cow over, he found two bullet holes in her head. Then the captain and Mr. Thompson came out of the woods with some kind of rifles slung over their shoulders. Elijah didn't think he ever saw the same rifles twice, and every one was some kind of gun Elijah had never seen on the Eastern Shore.

Anytime a cow ate some bailing twine, got thin and sickly from getting into the thistles, or couldn't stand up anymore for one reason or another, he'd let the captain know, and that's what would happen.

When he was done with the grain, Elijah tapped his empty buckets out on the metal trough and put them back in the bin.

"No more grain till evenin', ladies," he said. "Better eat that hay now 'fore it gits cold."

He stood at the swung-out doors of the barn, waiting for the men. He turned to look down the row of thirty cows on one side of the barn and thirty more on the other, all swishing their tails. It was the biggest dairy herd in Maryland, as far as he knew, and he was in charge. But it was a lot of work for four men. He could hear the cows munching on the hay in the racks, and their steamy breath rose to the electric light like it was already winter.

Kenneth Banks, Lamont Eldridge, and Earling Cooper came straggling in still buttoning up their shirts, a little late after the push yesterday to get the hay in before the storm. They strapped on their stools and got started. Elijah and Kenneth worked down one row of cows, Lamont and Earling down the other. As Elijah pressed his head and shoulder into the flank of his first cow, he could hear Lamont and Earling talking about Captain Croft coming out to help in the field yesterday. He was going to have to make a rule about that, first thing after the milking.

Elijah considered Lamont and Earling not yet grown up, though both were married with little children, living in their own houses. They inclined to excitement like the young always do. They just looked grown up. Lamont was tall. That was why he was prone to the collapsed lung he had when he was younger. That's what the doctor said. Tall and thin made him prone. They got him to Chestertown in time in the Crofts' fastest car, the Silver Ghost. What a ride that was. Captain Croft did the driving himself and cut the time it took in half. Earling was tall too but never had that trouble. They were just two tall young men you'd see anywhere—working on docks, fields, or factories—young men who had yet to find what they were prone to besides collapsed lungs.

It wasn't hard for Elijah to remember himself as a young man and how much like Lamont and Earling he was in his own youth. Without a doubt, he was glad to be almost the last one alive who had known his young self. There seemed to be more old men around back then, before machines came in. Old men had a way of looking at you. They must have been thinking what he was thinking about Lamont and Earling now.

Elijah and Kenneth never talked as they went along their row and always stayed ahead of the other two. Elijah had come to a conclusion about why that was and came up with three reasons that stood the test of time. Number one, he was boss. Number two, Kenneth was a white man. And number three, he and Kenneth had a good deal of age on Lamont and Earling. Each reason was probably good enough all by itself.

They milked twice a day. Early morning and early evening. When Elijah and Kenneth finished their row, Elijah went to the glass-enclosed office to start his paperwork. Kenneth usually pitched in on the other side so Lamont and Earling could get home and go back to bed for a few hours. Kenneth was from the mountains, and true to mountain people, as Elijah had occasion to observe, he never shrank back from work that needed to be done. Another thing about Kenneth was never showing his feelings one way or the other about anything. He worked the same dogged way when he found out his three boys were killed in the war, one after the other, in the same order they were born. There was just nothing to say about it, like the late frost last year that did in the apple blossoms. Elijah took that to be a mountain trait, though he had never seen such an extreme case as Kenneth.

The sun was up by the time the milking was done. The men rolled the tall metal cans to the back door just as the truck from Abbotts was coming around the corner. Elijah guided the motor truck as it backed up to the dock, and they all helped the driver take the empties off and load on the full cans. Elijah tallied up his cans, the driver tallied up his, and they signed each other's papers. Then the driver got up in the cab, grumbled thanks for the help loading, and was off. Elijah gave him a wave and turned to his men.

"I know you gotta get your girls up, Kenneth," he said, "so you can go. But you two," turning to Lamont and Earling with his hands up to hold them, "we got to talk private in the office."

"What about?" Lamont asked.

"I got to make a rule today."

Elijah nodded to Kenneth, and he turned to go.

"Won't keep you long, men. Git the heater goin' in the glass room, and I'll get Viola over with some coffee."

Elijah went to the front doors of the barn and called across to his house. Before long, Viola came out on the porch in her housecoat with a pot of coffee. She was a big, round woman, but short, with white hair pulled back in a bun, and a natural smile that drew along its lines all the features of a good-natured face. Elijah met her halfway and took the heavy pot.

"Thank you for using my name this morning," she said, with an unmistakable hint in her voice that she shouldn't have to bring it up.

"You sayin' you don't like how I call cross the yard?"

"Elijah! You call the cows with that wup wup. And why can't you come get the coffee yourself?"

"The boys like to see a pretty face, Viola. You can't blame me for that. None a' they wives up yet. Anyway, it look bad for an old man like me—and 'specially me bein' boss—pourin' coffee for young men like they is."

"Only thing putting lines in your face is talking that way," said Viola, frowning.

"Well, if it ain't that, then must be the company I keep," said Elijah, pondering as they walked over. "Maybe I should get a younger woman, Viola, but I know you don't want me doin' that. You funny that way, don't you know."

Viola laughed. "You think any young woman crazy enough to have you?"

"Don't think there ain't some young crazy ones around, girl."

Viola thought that was very funny, but all she could say as they entered the warm dark of the barn was, "Oh, dear Lord, Elijah, you got no idea how much trouble I saved you from."

Elijah held the glass door of the office open for her. There was condensation hazing the glass on all three sides of the office where Elijah had his big wooden desk. Lamont and Earling stood up from two chairs around the kerosene heater and at the same time said, "Good morning, Mrs. Brown."

"Nice and warm in here," she said. She poured out their coffee and looked askance at their mugs. "You boys ever wash those things out?"

"Oh, no need for that," said Lamont. "We got our names on 'em."

"Well, that puts my mind at ease," Viola said, lowering her eyebrows.

After a pause, she shook her head.

"No, no, I can't sit down. I got to get Delphina out of bed."

Then, looking from Lamont to Earling and back to Lamont, she said, without disturbing the good humor of her face, "I know your wife don't like you smoking, Lamont. Well, you're going to do it anyway, aren't you? So I'll address my comments to Mr. Brown. Don't be too long in here smoking, Elijah," she chided. "I don't want you still shaving when me and Delphina ready to go."

Earling and Lamont thanked her for the coffee as she topped off their mugs.

"I'm only giving you this much," she said frowning. "Then you go home and get back to bed."

"You're not going to say nothing are you, Mrs. Brown?"

"Lamont, you're a grown man now, and what you do is a private matter between you and your wife. I imagine she give you a lot of leeway, but my advice is don't you take advantage." She ended smiling all around.

Lamont and Earling got up out of politeness, and when Viola went out the glass door with the coffeepot, they moved the chairs around to better get their boots toward the heater. Elijah sat down at the desk and got out the cigarettes. When they were settled with their coffee and blowing smoke up in the air, Lamont spoke up.

"Abbotts's man in a bad mood today."

"I'd say he was," said Earling with a nod.

"Hard to tell," said Elijah. "You never know. Well, he up more early than anybody else, drivin' that truck 'round. But then you might say that a'sessery to the point." Elijah took a long draw on his cigarette. "He just quiet. Like Kenneth. Mountain people like that. But you two young fellas wouldn't know that. Not many mountain people 'round here now. You too young to remember, but we seen a lot a' them comin' down from the mountains through here few years back lookin' for factory work they hear about. Men mostly. A dollar a day they lookin' for. That about five in today's money. Imagine that."

"Nothing like that around here," said Lamont, leaning with his elbows on his knees, and his hands holding the coffee mug and cigarette between them, looking sideways over at Earling.

"Not to my knowledge," said Earling.

"Well," said Elijah, taking a draw on the stub of his cigarette, "evidently mountain people not so good on direction once they come to flat land, so we point 'em the right way, and they go on. But Kenneth an' a few like the fella in the feed store and Abbotts's man stay on. Maybe they jus' tired a' walkin' sideways to the horizon. That land give them people a lot a' trouble you know. Can't use no chinery. Once I seen a tractor tip over side a' hill in West Virginia, and Lord, don't they go over quick. Ain't no time to jump off. You get your legs crushed right smart. So they farm old-fashion manual like we used to do. But that don't necessary explain how they quiet like they is either. Mountain people just got some strange ways that might raise wonder around here."

He leaned back in his chair and reached for the piece of tin with crimped sides they used as an ashtray.

"I remember when Kenneth first come here. They move in the cabin where your house now standin', Lamont. They come with nothin' but a roll-up on his back and a roll-up on hers, and them three young boys. I believe I never saw white people lookin' so impoverished as they was lookin' at that time. So naturally we took notice to see white people in bad straights that way."

He remembered how Liza Banks brought to mind a toothpick when he first saw her. And Kenneth looked like a brick. A brick and a toothpick.

"I remember," he said, after thinking that over. "I remember every mornin' Liza Banks come out on her porch and whack a fryin' pan gainst the side a' the cabin. It turn out that how she clean her cook pans. You could tell which cabin be the Banks by the grease down the sides a' the front door. An' you never know from the cookin' smells that they ever ate but fried potatoes. They a sorry bunch back then all right."

Lamont and Earling started to smirk. They had never known any white people without money. Elijah suspected that, in their minds, only colored lived poor, and the other side of that coin was the conviction that there was no excuse but a lack of character for white people to live that way.

"Kenneth might laugh about that now, hisself," he said. "Truth is, hard not to look up to the man. He took to farmin' on flat land and learned workin' with that reaper and the tractors, an' havin' more an' one cow to look after. He a smart man, for all that he might not look it. And that Liza Banks smart, too. When the Crofts come in an' Kenneth start makin' decent money, she go into town and bring back rolls a' cloth and go to work puttin' Kenneth an' her boys in good work clothes. All hand-stitched, you know, cause she never use a machine before. Then she start cookin' more than fried potatoes. You wouldn't know it now, but that Liza, she knew how to come up in the world when she saw a chance. Pretty soon the Banks start to look like a credit to they race."

He had not said it to be funny, but Lamont and Earling laughed. Elijah paused for a draw on another cigarette and a swallow of coffee, and added, "As the man says."

"As the man says," said Lamont.

Earling nodded.

"Well," said Elijah, snuffing out his cigarette in the ashtray and sliding it over toward Lamont and Eldridge, "we all come up in the world when the Crofts come in. A pity to see the Banks goin' backward now. A shame them boys got killed. You 'member, Ty, Will, and—what's the other one?"

"Robert," said Lamont.

"That right. Robert. He the one died of the influenza on the boat home. That after the war over with." Elijah shook his head and looked at the steam on the windows. "They say the other two got killed but a day apart, in that big woods where them Germans holed up. News come in about 'em one by one. Would a' been kinder hearin' it all at once. They was good to you two, weren't they, them Banks boys?"

"Yes, they were," said Lamont in a reverent way.

Earling nodded.

"Hard to shake off bad luck when it stuck to you like pine tar," said Elijah. "Well, I got to get down to business now."

Turning sideways to his desk, Elijah leaned forward on his elbows toward Lamont and Earling, as if he were drawing them into a confidence.

"I heard you two talkin'," he said. "And I think I got to make a rule. I don't want any stories goin' around."

"What about?"

"About Captain Croft, yesterday, when we was gittin' the hay in."

"Why just us?" said Lamont. "What about Kenneth and the Johnson boy? They were there too."

"Don't have to talk to Kenneth," said Elijah shaking his head. "To my knowledge, nobody ever got nothin' in the nature a' speculatin' outta Kenneth. And the Johnson boy, well, he outta my juristicki'n—so that right—it jus' you two."

Elijah looked at Lamont, then at Earling.

"We all seen the captain yesterday with his shirt off. Nobody from the house ever come out to help in the field. That's all need be said about it. You know what I'm sayin'?"

Lamont turned to Earling. "I'd say, it looks like the captain got shot up bad at one time," he said.

"I'd say so," said Earling. "Cut across his middle right smart too."

"Now, that jus' what I don't want goin' round."

Lamont and Earling looked at each other, waiting.

"Can't say nothin' to you wives neither."

Elijah gave the men a good stern look and raised his eyebrows until he got a nod of assent from each. He was going to tell Viola, but that was only because she never gossiped.

"All right. We got that settled. Next thing, it look to me like number forty-two gonna freshen this week. So we'll call 'em in early. If forty-two don't show up to the barn, Earling, I want you take a horse out lookin' for her. Don't want her havin' that calf out in the field with all them foxes in the woods. Don't want to lose another calf since only two out a' six took this time."

"Something wrong with that old bull," said Lamont gravely.

"He's just too old, I'd say," said Earling.

"No, no," said Elijah, "nothin' wrong with Toby far as I can tell. Five years ain't nothin' to a good dairy bull like he is. He look pretty strong on them gals. We just pick the wrong gals."

"Well, you the one that picked 'em," said Lamont.

"No accountin' for it," said Elijah.

It was really not a laughing matter. And Elijah knew there should be someone called to account for it. He had to figure out what the problem was on his gestation charts. He learned them from his father, who kept them for Danforth when they had the Jerseys, and there would have been hell to pay under Danforth for these last two years of poor performance. They had a regular herd in the retirement pasture now, a meadow full of washed-up cows that cost as much to keep as the milking ones, and not many young ones coming up in the herd.

Lamont's oldest boy, Jake, came back to the glass room looking for everybody. Elijah sent Lamont and Earling home for breakfast and back to bed for a few hours. Then he turned the wick down on the kerosene heater until it went out, moved the chairs back, and had Jake start turning the cows out. Almost too late he remembered the cats, went to the office door, and shouted down to the end of the barn.

"Hold them last two, Jake. Strip 'em for the cats. Got a bowl right here." Elijah held up the milk bowl over his head in case Jake didn't hear. He thought he should start down toward Jake, but the boy was already half the distance to the glass room. Elijah remembered when he could run that fast and wondered if he could run at all now. He thought he could if he had to, but he didn't want Jake to see him try and go away swearing he'd never get so old as to run that bad.

"An' you may as well put out some a' that meal from the tin," he said, when Jake came up to him. He reminded the boy to keep his eye on the clock in the glass room and not be late for the school wagon. "An' after you done sweeping out the barn and hosing off the concrete, make sure you clean them shoes off good," he said. "I don't want Miss Berrigan comin' 'round here."

"Yes sir, Mr. Brown," said Jake.

"You puttin' away them silver dollars like you s'pposed to, boy?"

"Yes sir, Mr. Brown," he said. "I got four now."

"That's good. You keep at it, and you be a rich man like me someday."

Then he laughed as he turned to leave the boy to his work. He propped the doors of the milking barn wide open for the nice air going through and walked around to the shed in back, flipping through the keys on his ring for the one to the padlock on the door. Inside was the new Ford Model T.

He could not help feeling pride in all the keys he held and figured that must have been the idea behind it. Working people like holding keys to what they work with. Nobody had keys before the Crofts came. At the house, Mr. Thompson and all the help, Viola, Delphina, Cassie, and Lilly had keys to one thing or another—the wine cellar, the pantry, the laundry building, the housekeeping closets, and whatever else. Not that the captain and Mrs. Croft seemed to want so much locked up, but they must have known how good it makes people feel holding keys.

On the ring hanging from his belt were keys to the silo, the sheds and equipment, the gas pumps on the farm and at the river, the big greenhouse where they kept the palm trees over the winter, and the sawmill down in the woods. The smaller ring had the key to the mail pouch and the key to the post office box.

The Model T fired right up. Elijah liked to give it plenty of time to warm up. First, he had to get Viola and Delphina to work at the chateau. Then he had to run to Cecilton for the mail. By the time he got back, Viola would have his breakfast ready.

The captain had the good idea to pay the young ones in silver dollars. It took a long time to earn one, but it was harder money to spend. Captain Croft gave them out himself. Delphina still had every one of them from when she helped Mrs. Croft in the greenhouse when she was little. All the other little girls from the farm who helped tend the garden got silver dollars too, and he had heard that the silver dollars had already gone as dowry for some of them.

He knew Delphina was in no hurry to tie herself down. She had been turning boys away since she was twelve or thirteen, and ever since she outgrew the school in Cecilton and the Crofts let her in the library at the chateau, all she cared about was reading books. Smart books, she said they were, not stories like Viola read in her magazines. She had the idea to go up to the Johns Hopkins one day for more school. Delphina had given him the idea that the Crofts had a mind to see to it. She said Mrs. Croft wanted her to be the first colored girl to go there, and Mr. Croft gave his wife free rein.

Elijah thought he understood this much of his daughter—that only a boy with some brains in his head had any chance with her. He tried to explain it to Viola, but now that Delphina was seventeen and every boy she had turned down had gone off and married someone else, the issue brought him into contention with his wife whenever it came up. Viola said Delphina was too proud and haughty. She thought that a husband and three or four babies to look after was the best remedy for proud and haughty. Even as they watched Delphina mature into a graceful young lady, it was all Elijah could do to bring Viola around to agreeing with him that it would be a shame to see her silver dollars swooped up by any boy they knew currently residing between Cecilton and Galena.

CHAPTER TWO

Kenneth Banks was forty-five and square in the face, with thin lips that he kept tight together, as if he were enforcing a rule about his face that his mind had decided to stick to. He usually looked down when anyone spoke to him and kept his thoughts to himself. One of his eyes was cloudy, and with the other one usually looking down, they appeared to be matched most of the time under the wide brim of his beaten-up old hat. In the first years on the farm, working for Danforth, he wore the same long coat every day, whatever the weather, and the shirt under it looked just as moth-eaten as the coat, shot through with holes and wear. The coat only had two buttons, so in winter he turned up the collar, tied a rag of a scarf around it, and pulled the hat still lower on his head.

Liza Banks shared with her husband the lean, gaunt look of having come from the mountains. She had fret, care, and poverty lined into her face so deeply that it made a hard plot of ground for a smile to take seed. But when the Crofts took over and built them a house with a kitchen, electric, running water, and bedrooms upstairs, it changed everything; she sprang up like a flower that only blooms when the sun and the temper of the soil are right. It was not long before she was talking across the porches with the neighbors, Viola Brown, Ginny Cooper, and Ramona Eldridge.

She was taller than Kenneth by an inch and wore her hair in a long, thin braid down her back. She was as lean as Kenneth was square, but they looked like they belonged together and made a fair picture of a man and woman who had lived some time in the weather.

When the three Banks boys got old enough, they worked a few years for Danforth, tending the split-rail fences that separated the fields and bordered the twelve hundred acres of farm and woods. Then each one in turn by age went to seek his fortune elsewhere.

Annabelle Banks did not know her brothers because they left before she was born. But she remembered how proud her mother was of them. The eldest had gone into the army and had become a sergeant. The next had gone to New York, where he cooked for a restaurant, and the youngest went for logging in the Northwest. Her mother brought up their success in life when her father was low. Annabelle could see that her mother wanted him to feel they had raised their boys well and that it was a natural consequence that boys from such an upbringing would achieve heights beyond the reach of their parents. Whether or not that sufficed to better her father's outlook, Annabelle was unable to tell, for she knew him to be a quiet man, and to such efforts toward him as her mother often made, he was likely to respond with little more than a tight smile and a nod that the encouragement had been duly noted.

Annabelle was a chubby little girl with a nose that looked too small for her face and eyes that could hardly be seen for her plump cheeks and puffy eyelids. When one of the elder churchwomen of Galena suggested that her mother could afford to go easier on the corn bread and bacon with Annabelle, her mother curtly told her off, then bent down to adjust the ribbons on Annabelle's little straw hat and told her how proud she was to have such a pretty little girl. Baby Emma came when Annabelle was two years old.

When it came time for Annabelle's first day of school in Cecilton, it was a great occasion. Liza finished the new dress she had made for Annabelle and produced a pair of white gloves she had ordered from the Sears catalog. She had the idea to make something special for the teacher, but when she told Annabelle, they revised the plan to include surprising the other children as well. Annabelle got so excited that she went to the woods right away to carry out the first part of the plan by bringing home a basket full of pretty fall leaves—oak, poplar, elm, yew, chestnut, maple, and linden in all colors, each one a perfect specimen of its kind. Liza told Annabelle that this would make it easy for the teacher to remember her name because she would stand out in the class, and it would make the other children want to be friends with her.

On the stove, Liza heated up an old saucepan and placed in it six or seven white candles. When the wax was melted and clear, they took turns dipping the leaves into the wax, one by one, and laying them out to cool on a clean cloth on the kitchen table. It took some time, but they ended up with a fine assortment of pretty wax leaves from which they chose the twenty-eight best.

The next part of the plan was for Kenneth to get Annabelle to school early, before the school wagon. They kept a pony in the shed behind the house and an old phaeton carriage they used once a week to go shopping at the store in Cecilton and church in Galena on Sundays. Liza made sure the seat was cleaned off and didn't have any spiders under it before she helped Annabelle up with her new dress and white gloves. Then she said she had the perfect thing and ran back to the house. She returned with pink ribbons to tie around the ends of Annabelle's plain brown braids, and a pocket mirror so Annabelle could see how pretty she was.

When they got to the schoolhouse, her father helped her down from the carriage while she held up her dress. She kissed him on the cheek and sent him off and then hurried into the old brick building with her brown paper bag of leaves. It was easy to tell which room she belonged in because each of the doors along the hallway had a drawing on it of children of different heights.

In the classroom, there were individual desks with seats attached to them. There were three rows of these in front of the teacher's big desk, and Annabelle went up and down the aisles between them placing a waxed leaf on every desk. There were four left over, so she left them on the teacher's desk arranged as if they had just fallen from the sky, and then she hurried to sit down in the front row because she heard the other children coming in the outside door. She was so pleased with the plan having worked so well and sat with her white-gloved hands folded on top of her desk in a way she deemed ladylike.

The only thing Annabelle remembered from her first day at school were the first words Miss Berrigan said to the class after she said, "Good morning. I am Miss Berrigan, and I will be your teacher."

Miss Berrigan looked at the wax leaves indifferently, took the trash basket out from under her desk and brushed the leaves off the desk into it. Then she looked along the rows of desks in front of her, saw the other wax leaves and said, "I don't know where they came from, but they don't belong in the classroom." She handed the trash basket to a boy in the first row and had him walk up and down collecting the wax leaves.

Annabelle felt herself get very hot and flushed. Perspiration came out on her upper lip, and then she broke into a sweat all over. She thought everyone must be looking at her, and she kept her eyes down as she dropped her waxed leaf into the trash basket.

When the children were dismissed after school, Annabelle hid behind the building until the others were picked up by the school wagon and the teacher left. She went back to the room and picked the leaves one by one out of the trash basket and put them in her paper bag. Then she started walking home. After a mile or so she thought there would not be a good reason she could give for bringing them home, so she went off in the grass under the trees and found a shallow depression at the base of an oak tree. There she tenderly placed her wax leaves and covered them over with the fallen leaves around the tree trunk.

Her father in the pony phaeton met her on the road. She said she missed the school wagon because she was telling her teacher how she had made the wax leaves. When they got home, Annabelle showed her mother how the teacher held up each of her leaves and marveled at how pretty it was, and how she made a number of new friends that day. They all took their leaves home to show, she said.

Annabelle got carried away with her story of the success of their wax leaves as she saw how happy it made her mother. They held hands and danced around little Emma in her crib until her father came in the back door of the kitchen from putting up the pony and the carriage and wanted to sit down to dinner.

That night in bed, Annabelle cried into her pillow. Her new dress wasn't that pretty. The pretty girls in the classroom were not in homemade dresses and did not bother with ribbons in their hair or white gloves. They were pretty all by themselves. She cried for thinking herself pretty and thinking other children would want to be friends with her, and for her mother's folly. She could not tell her mother anything she had learned in school that day, and her mother had thought that very queer. She cried from vanity and shame, and she was too young to tell which was which.

A year later, Mrs. Croft brought the news to the Banks house that their son Ty was killed. A month after that, she came with news that Will was killed also, and a longer time later, the news that Robert was dead.

What Annabelle knew of it was from overhearing people talking. They said at least Robert's body was not across the ocean in France or blown to pieces. She didn't know what the word remains meant, but the remains of Robert were sewn up in canvas on a ship in New York harbor.

The Crofts arranged for the body to be brought down to the farm, and they buried Robert in the woods over the river and put up a stone with the names of all three of the Banks boys on it. At the funeral, Liza fell down in a dead faint, and from all appearances, Annabelle thought her mother had just died too and fell upon her, crying.

Kenneth kept silent and worked every day as if nothing had happened. Ginny Cooper, Viola Brown, and Ramona Eldridge came over and sat with their needlework and their handkerchiefs and cried with Liza Banks. Mrs. Croft came and talked with her. The pastor from Galena came by many times as well, but Liza Banks had what people said was a breakdown. It left her quiet and detached, and seemed a quiet in keeping with one who had lived most of her life poor in the mountains.

In the months that followed, Liza absented herself from cooking, cleaning, mending, and tending the garden. She spent most of the day walking around the back of the house in a long oval path through the grass, trooping around it by day and by night in all weather.

Annabelle took care of Emma, but being only ten, she had not spent enough time at her mother's side to learn the skills that were now lacking in the house. She tried to keep Emma and her clothes pretty and did not forget to hold hands and dance with her. It was her best memory of their lost mother, and she wanted Emma to have it too. Despite Annabelle's efforts, as the months went by and Liza fell into a sluggish despondency incapable of moving itself in any worthwhile direction, the household and its occupants began to drift irretrievably into neglect.

One day, months after Robert's funeral, Kenneth confided to Elijah Brown that Liza was better. He asked him to take a letter to the post office when he went for the mail. There was something Liza needed from the Sears catalog. A week later Elijah brought a package back from the post office addressed to Liza Banks, in care of the Croft farm. There were more letters that went out, and more packages came in reply. Elijah did not ask, and Kenneth did not offer, but they turned out to be art supplies.

Along with an art course in two volumes came rolls of canvas that Kenneth cut, stretched, and framed out for her. Oil paintings for sale began to appear on their front porch. At first they were scenes of the tidewater marshes, with geese flying very high overhead as if they had nothing at all to do with the earth, or mossy trees overhanging the river at nightfall, or deep oak forests with errant shafts of sunlight striking through them. In time, Liza's paintings lost any recognizable referent. The paintings she put out on the front porch presented abstract shapes in skewed perspectives, utilizing every color on the palette in a violent harmony of clashing hues.

As there were only the four families living on the property, the only paying customer to Liza's porch gallery was Mrs. Croft, who came by in her work clothes every morning, driving the Percheron horse and wagon on her way to the chicken coops. If Liza was out front in her painting smock, Mrs. Croft pulled over and came up on the porch to talk while she looked over Liza's latest work. She asked Liza questions, and every few days she bought a painting to put in the wagon and take home with her egg basket. Elijah knew of it and expected that at least Kenneth's money troubles with Sears were over.

The Banks house was next to Earling Cooper's house, so Ginny Cooper, who stayed home with her new baby, saw everything that went on at Liza and Kenneth's. She told Viola, and Viola told Elijah that since the boys were killed, it was a sorry sight to see Annabelle and little Emma out waiting for the school wagon in their dirty dresses. It looked like they only had one dress apiece, awfully frayed at the hems and sleeves.

Ginny told Viola that she watched Annabelle wipe smudges off her little sister's cheeks every day before the school wagon came, with her spit and a rag she kept as a lady's handkerchief tucked up her sleeve, and how she tied Emma's hair with frayed ribbons. Ginny said she could see girl underpants hanging up over the kitchen sink every night drying because the windows at the Banks had no curtains to speak of anymore. Having talked to Miss Berrigan, the school teacher, Ginny said Annabelle must have known the other children made fun of them because they smelled bad.

At this point in the story, the first time he heard it, Elijah noted that Ginny Cooper's boys would be the first ones to hold their noses and laugh behind somebody's back, and Viola had to agree with him. Then Elijah asked why Annabelle and little Emma smelled bad.

Viola said, "Why, because there's no soap in that house, Elijah."

CHAPTER THREE

Elijah made sure the sticky brake lever of the Model T was off and the motor sounded right when he advanced the spark and gave the Ford a little gas. Then he steered it out of the shed and around to the front of his house. He left his boots on the porch and went in, pulling off his flannel shirt and canvas trousers. Viola and Delphina were almost done with breakfast.

"Won't be a moment," he said.

"Tub's already filled," said Viola.

When Elijah was shaved and cleaned up, he got back into his work clothes and boots and found Viola and Delphina already in the Model T. Viola was in the front seat, smiling and cheery as always to go riding in an automobile. Delphina was in the darkness of the back seat, but Elijah knew she was probably sitting with her legs crossed and arms folded, looking annoyed.

He knew better than to say anything. Delphina did not like conversation on the way to work. She liked everyone to be quiet and respectful of her dissatisfactions.

Viola knew that, too, but could not suppress little bounces of delight as they went over the holes in the farm road. It was only a mile through the farm to the chateau, but she always got as much as she could out of the trip, even though she had to keep the window closed because it blew air in Delphina's face. When they got there, Elijah swung the car around the big gravel expanse in front of the chateau, careful not to make work for the boy who came every day on a bicycle from town to rake it smooth. Around back, by the kitchen door, he left off Viola and Delphina with their bags slung over their shoulders and their uniforms on hangers, and he started on the next leg of his morning duties, the ride to the post office.

Back through the farm, past the barns, pens, sheds, and silos, the road got better, with pastureland on both sides. Then it passed between the long row of tall pine trees he had helped plant as seedlings when he was a boy, and finally to the brick pillars that marked the end of the property. One pillar had a brass plaque facing the county road with "Tidewater Farm" at the top and "Registered Holsteins" on the line below it. The other pillar had a similar brass plaque with just the name "Croft" on it. Elijah turned right onto the macadam of the county road and continued the six miles of smooth driving into Cecilton.

He pulled up to the old Victorian mansion that housed the post office on the first floor and shut down the Ford. There was no sense looking in the little box in the wall, as usual, and when he came through the inner doors, Mr. Toddy, the elderly postmaster, was waiting for him with a pile that covered half his counter. Elijah undid the strap lock on the mail satchel and looked over the pile, whispering "God almighty" to himself. It was easy to understand why Captain Croft spent so much time in his study. There were newspapers from different parts of the world in different languages and letters from everywhere between New York, San Francisco, and London, England. Lilly said the newspapers all looked read and gone over when she picked them up outside the study every evening and took them to the incinerator.

"Good thing they give me a suitcase for this, Mr. Toddy," he said, handing the outgoing mail over to the postmaster and packing up the incoming. "Anything for Brown, Banks, Cooper, Eldridge?"

"No, just Croft mail today, Elijah."

"Well, don't smell no coffee goin' here, so I'll be on my way."

"Sorry, but I had a lot to do this morning."

"I expect you up early too," Elijah said with a laugh, hefting the heavy satchel off the counter.

Then he was out the door, off the porch, and sitting in the driver's seat of the brand-new Ford with the US mail on the seat beside him. Elijah liked driving. Ever since Captain Croft taught him on the Rolls Royce Silver Ghost and gave him use of the new Ford car, sitting in a wagon behind a horse only made him impatient. Scenery was well and good, but there was nothing like an automobile to get from one place to another and nothing he liked better than flying down the county road at thirty miles an hour. From what he could tell about Captain Croft, it might only be a matter of time before one of the sheds on the farm would have an airplane in it. That would be something. He had heard the captain say they were cheap to buy since the war was over.

When Elijah slowed down to turn in at the pillars, a bit of the exuberance of driving wore off as he slowed down for the rest of the way at five miles an hour. The road through the tall pine trees and pastures was good, but it was getting bad through the farm, especially on the curve with the pigsty on one side and the bull pen on the other. He drove by his house, the Coopers', Eldridges' and Banks', then woods again, the retirement meadow, and more cow pastures, to the fork in the road. One side went down the hill to the river, to the boathouse and docks. The other side ran the last hundred yards in nice gray gravel to the chateau.

Mr. Thompson once showed him a picture of the house in France that Captain Croft wanted his house to take after. He had it built exactly like the picture. Elijah remembered walking through the old Danforth place with the captain and Mr. Thompson when they first came to see it. At that time, Mr. Thompson was introduced to him as Captain Croft's manservant. That was before he got to be in charge of the house.

In getting rid of the Danforth mansion, the Crofts did away with every feature of the plantation houses Elijah had grown up with. No majestic columns, no balconies, no long porches with railings, nothing to spend all summer and fall painting. The chateau was three stories of stone and granite with a castle turret on each side topped in spires, all roofed in slate. Tall windows on the upper floors, long windows across the first floor living and dining rooms. On the back corners of the chateau, facing the river, were rounded extensions of the first floor behind the turrets. One was Captain Croft's study. The other one was Mrs. Croft's greenhouse.

Across fifty feet of the front of the chateau were steps that went from the gravel of the circle up to a great stone terrace and the main entrance. Elijah had seen over thirty or forty people on that terrace before and after the dinners they'd had in the first years, when Mrs. Croft's mother was alive. Mr. Thompson, in his white collar and black frock coat, trotted down the steps to open carriage doors for ladies in gowns and gentlemen in top hats. There was an inside staff of twenty in those days. He could not remember all their names now. Most of the help were foreigners back then.

Men from France and Italy and all over the country had come to build the chateau. For three years, Cecilton and Galena got rich from putting up and feeding the people brought in. After they left, Elijah thought the townspeople generally felt it was good to get back to what they had before, but everybody had stories about the foreigners, and the ones from up north, and the strange food they brought in. Things like cod fish cakes, soda bread, mutton chops, and what they called brown bread that came in cans and wasn't at all like what anyone would call brown bread. It made Elijah almost disbelieve where he was in the world when he saw it all at once in front of him. Calling it a house might give people the wrong idea, which was why, he supposed, everybody called it the chateau. It looked like a castle in France had jumped right out of a picture book and set itself down in the swampy part of Maryland, US of A.

Viola saw him coming and got out the pans for his bacon and eggs and the biscuits and gravy he liked. When Elijah came in, he kissed Viola and looked over to see if Delphina caught him patting her mother's bottom, being as she disapproved of all physical contact these days. But she was in the servants' dining hall off the pantry with a book, as he had expected, and only the long skirts of her uniform showed around the corner.

"Give me some time," he said to Viola. "Lots of mail to set out today."

There was a changing room off the kitchen. He set the mail satchel down and went in and shut the door.

"I don't want to hear it," Viola called. She laughed to herself, looking down at the stove.

"What's that?" he said through the door.

"You know what I mean. Complaining."

"Well then, that mean you ready for it," he called, "and I be loath to disappoint you."

"Now Elijah, you tell me—what's loath mean?"

"Oh, you wouldn't know. That's an old word. People don't use it no more. You might say they's loath to use it. There you go."

Presently he came out in a starched white shirt. It had a stand-up collar with the tips folded over a striped tie, and he was pulling the shirt cuffs out of a short black cut-away jacket. Viola waved her hand to blow off the heavy scent of cologne.

"That cover up the cows," he said. "Thanks for shining the shoes," he added, holding a foot up to the sunlight coming through the big kitchen windows.

"Don't thank me. That was Cassie. Oh, what were you going to tell me last night?"

"Later," he said. "After breakfast when we talkin' in peace."

He picked up the mail satchel and walked through the pantry, leaned into the servants' dining room where Delphina sat reading on the bench, and kissed the top of her head.

"That's too much cologne, Daddy." She didn't even look up.

He paused to look through the little window of the door to the dining room to see if anybody was down yet, and seeing no one, went through. On the sideboard he opened up the mail satchel, spread out the contents and began separating the correspondence addressed to Mr. Andrew Croft from the ones for Mrs. Alice Croft. Any piece addressed to both, or any in question, Elijah put in her pile. Then all the newspapers went back in the satchel.

The captain's mail went beside the gold finger bowl of the place setting to the left of Mrs. Croft's. At Mrs. Croft's finger bowl, at the head of the table, Elijah squared up what Mrs. Croft preferred to call "the post." Before he left the room he turned to make sure everything looked right. He couldn't help wondering why Cassie and Lilly had to launder and iron the tablecloth every night.

Proceeding out to the hallway with the satchel, Elijah very quietly made his way through the foyer, through the large sitting room, with its walls hung with tapestries, the grand piano and array of easy chairs at all angles, and sofas with side tables. Then he went through the adjoining trophy room with the framed photographs of Captain Croft and his two boys on polo ponies, holding up their mallets. Fine horses they were, still in the stables along with a few more, including Mrs. Croft's favorite, the Percheron, Diligence, looked after by Rodney the groom. The two boys looked like fine young gentlemen smiling proudly in the picture. So did Captain Croft. But Elijah had heard that none of them cared much for the game and only played to keep up appearances.

The floor changed from polished wood to black-and-white marble in the trophy room. Mr. Thompson was in the bar with his inventory board in one hand and ink pen in the other. His back was turned, and Elijah wanted to slip by him, but he knew he couldn't do that. He stopped and said, "Good morning, Mr. Thompson."

Mr. Thompson came to the door and said, "Good morning, Mr. Brown."

Mr. Thompson looked him over. They were dressed identically except for a little red, white, and blue bar, like some kind of campaign ribbon, that Mr. Thompson had over the breast pocket of his jacket. Nobody knew what that was, but he had come with the Crofts from Boston, and he spoke with an accent different from any English Elijah had ever heard. The first time Elijah saw him, he was astonished to see a black man as black as Mr. Thompson. If ever he had an idea of an African king, Mr. Thompson was it. He was furthered in this opinion after hearing from Viola and Delphina and the other girls who came in from Cecilton to wait on the formal dinners. They said that Mr. Thompson could stand at those parties, by the door to the pantry, at perfect attention for three hours or more while the eating and talking was going on, looking straight ahead and not being observed to move a muscle.

On the other hand, he made himself a legend one night at one of those dinners when a shriek came from the kitchen. As Viola told the story, a black snake about six feet long and thick as her wrist had gotten in the back shed off the kitchen. Mr. Thompson was through the dining room door in an instant and squared off with the snake. Viola said he crouched down low with his eyes on the snake and his arms spread out wide. He wiggled the fingers of his left hand, and when the snake turned his head, the right hand dropped down as fast as a hawk pins a squirrel and grabbed that big snake by the neck. For all that six feet of snake lashed around, Mr. Thompson had him good. Then he walked it out the door and down the hill to the river to let it go in the reeds, came up, washed his hands, and went right back to his post standing at attention at the dinner. Viola said she never thought Mr. Thompson could bend his knees that much, since he was always standing up so straight.

Elijah said he wished he had been there to see it. He liked watching a man with a skill, although he noted to Viola that he had taken care of his share of black snakes himself with the expertise he had acquired from many years of practice with a big flat shovel.

Mr. Thompson smiled and gave him a nod that he was properly attired to enter the captain's study with the mail satchel. Elijah pushed back the high, carved oak doors of the library, which he thought was the best part of the house, and entered a world gone back a hundred years. Behind the glass of fine cabinetry, leather-bound books were shelved as high as he could reach. The fireplace, framed in delft tiles, was tall enough for a man to stand inside among its iron brackets for kettles, and there was a column on each side of black veined marble. Opposed to it, a window of old leaded glass looked out on the side frontage of the chateau. A brass chandelier hung from the domed ceiling. There was a high-backed couch and long table central to the room and leather easy chairs. Elijah made his way to another high oak door on the other side of the room. He knocked, just on the chance that the captain might be at his desk or at the telephone table, and went in.

He placed the business and government correspondence on the desk. Then he laid out the newspapers on a long oak table with an inlaid leather top and arranged them with their mastheads showing, the American ones on top, then the English ones, then the French, and under them the ones with strange writing on strange kinds of paper. He double-checked the empty satchel, locked it up, and got back to the kitchen, wondering as he went if there was ever anyone who had to do so much work and running around before he got down to breakfast.

Delphina was still reading in the servants' dining hall, and Viola brought the breakfast plates over to the table as he came through the swinging door. Seeing that Elijah was about to sit down, Viola told him he'd better go change his clothes first, for all the trouble they were to keep nice.

"And you better button up those sleeves, Delphina," she said. "The captain should be down soon."

Delphina's eyes never left her reading, but her fingers went nimbly up from the cuff, giving each button a quick twist all the way up to the elbow on each arm as Elijah and Viola looked at each other in amazement.

"You sure is fast, girl," Elijah said. Then he went from a laugh to a grumble as he nudged passed Viola on his way to the changing room, pulling off his jacket, collar, and tie as he went.

"Don't you grumble at me," Viola said. "You do this every day. And hang them up nice on the hangers like I showed you."

Elijah came back to the pantry pulling himself into his tattered gray-and-white flannel shirt and brown canvas pants with a bootlace for a belt. Delphina looked up from her book and then turned her head away.

"Well, I can complain a bit, can't I?" he said.

"Elijah, turn around when you're pulling up your pants, you hear me?"

"Oh, Jesus, Vi."

"And don't talk like that!"

Elijah sat down beside Viola on the bench of the booth and put his arms up on the table, corralling the two big plates.

"Delphina, get me some coffee, will ya?"

"You could have gotten it yourself," said Delphina, putting her book to the side and getting up.

"Well, I only got two hands—and I needed 'em both for pullin' up my pants," he replied, turning to follow her with a big smile. "And besides, I don't know which coffee is black folks' coffee, and it look like you only got one pot on the stove." He thought that was funny too, but he knew she wouldn't.

"Both the same," said Delphina in a flat, indifferent tone from the kitchen.

Viola leaned into Elijah and said, "I wish you wouldn't sass her so much, Elijah."

"That just love," he said. "She know that."

"Well, instead of sassing her you could just say it once in a while."

"She wouldn't believe it. More believable with me sassing her," said Elijah. "We understand one 'nother. That's why I don't take offence when she disregards me. It jus' how she give love back these days, how she 'spress herself, you know." He sat back in the booth with a smile as Delphina put a mug of coffee in front of him and slid in across from her mother. Elijah started in on the bacon and eggs and biscuits and gravy, going from one plate to the other. Delphina went back to her book.

Viola liked the reassurance she got from watching her husband eat. As rough and coarse as he was, he had excellent table manners. That came from being raised by his grandmother. It seemed to her that the best any woman could do was to find a man brought up by his grandmother. Maybe it was too extreme to come out and say, but it struck her often enough as true, watching the manners that went around at Sunday evening church picnics.

She thought Elijah looked good for being sixty. His cheekbones stood out, and he had a strong jaw and all his teeth. Fine-looking teeth. Teeth anyone would envy. They were lined up straight and regular and were very white, so he took pride in his smile and kept smiling through his days, at least from what she saw of him in the kitchen. In livery, with the short cutaway black jacket, he looked as straight and trim as a much younger man. Only when he walked was it apparent that his stature did not have the dignity of bearing possessed by Mr. Thompson, but was due to stiff joints, back troubles, and bad knees—the ordinary afflictions she knew to be common to any farmer who lived past forty.

Elijah slowed down over his plates and sat back with his coffee mug. He and Viola smiled at each other. Delphina kept to her book. A fair part of his day was already over after the first milking. Viola was waiting for her day to start, but they always arrived at this satisfying resting place every morning, with their only child between them.

It felt to Viola that they were in a safe place, that they were old, steady, and true, and that Delphina was young, innocent, and well looked after. Reflecting on it, she sometimes felt also that there was little she cared to wish for herself anymore. It would only be tempting fate.

She would never have another child. Though she was almost ten years younger than Elijah, in her mind, there was no difference between them. She was round all over, droopy in the bosom, wide at the hips, and the last pomade she had used on her hair had turned it completely white. Her sister, Veroqua, said she'd be happier with it as time went by, and it was turning out to be true now that she had begun to think of Delphina giving her grandchildren. Looking forward to that time, she kept it brushed back and pinned in a bun as her own grandmother had worn her hair.

She had lost a tooth for each of the four boys she had lost before they were a year old. That was the only tragedy of her life, four times over, which made Delphina all the more her greatest happiness, and at the same time, the reason for her only apprehensions. Delphina was high color, which Viola attributed to her use of the pomade just before giving birth, and beautiful of face, with the cheekbones and straight teeth of her father. She was as tall as he was now and stood up straight in a proud and graceful way that came to her naturally. It was such a shame that she had become petulant and moody.

"Well," said Elijah, pushing back from the table with his coffee, "I know you don't want to hear it, but I still don't know why I got to get into the livery for that short run through the white part of the house when nobody there to see me—well, 'cept Mr. Thompson. Nobody's 'splained that to me adequate. An' shavin' every day. That what I mind most, 'specially in the wintertime. When I was strictly outside with Danforth, what did I do, Viola? I shaved Sunday morning for church, just like everybody else, remember?"

"I don't know why you don't want to look nice," said Viola, frowning.

"Most ladies think I do," he said, leaning over to kiss her.

"I don't know what ladies you're talking about, Elijah, unless you mean the ones out grazing on four legs, but speaking for the two-legged ladies—not with that stubble coming in white, we don't. It's all right to look unkempt when you're young, but when you're the age you are, it just looks unkempt. You're going to be father of the bride one of these days. I don't want you going into town in those ratty work clothes neither. You're going to scare off the better people."

"Don't think there any chance a' that, Viola," he said, "'cause nowhere else to go for a gal as pretty as Delphina. Even the white girls in town turn their heads when she go by."

"Just stop it, Daddy." Delphina slid out of the booth and went to peep through the little window in the door. "Oh, the captain's down," she said. "Lower your voices. I don't want to hear you talking back here. Or go back to the kitchen."

Delphina went to fill up the carafe from the coffee pot, stopped in the pantry to look at herself in the mirror and set her cap just right, and then shouldered out the swinging door to the dining room.

Viola turned to Elijah. She had put on her white chef hat, and the band bent her ears over. She had to keep pushing up the front so Elijah wouldn't laugh.

"I don't want you provoking Delphina and making her discontented. This is a good situation for her here. The Crofts are good people. Remember them cabins we used to live in with the Danforths? And the last one—you remember the last Colonel Danforth from when he beat your aunt Ida so bad? Now we got a real house, Elijah, and the Crofts brought in the electric for us. We got the water tower and the septic, and he pays everybody decent. And they let Delphina take any book she wants out of the library. Not like how it was."

"Well, nothin' ever like it used to was, Viola. It jus' that some house rules make sense and some don't."

"Well, Delphina don't know what it was like with the Danforths, so I don't want you talking bad of the Crofts in front of her. You can see it makes her discontented with her place in the house."

Elijah narrowed his eyes at his wife. "That ain't what makin' her discontented."

"Well, we disagree on that," said Viola. "No need to talk about it here."

"All right. But I don't see why I can't complain a little here and there. That's a freedom everybody got in America, electric and septic or not. It just a curiosity to me. I wish I knew which one a' them is 'sponsible for the rules. Sometimes I think it him; then sometimes I think it her—"

"I believe it's her."

"Well, that's funny. I was jus' thinkin' it was him. Who knows? They both got it in 'em for makin' rules and then doin' the opposite. Now, for all Mrs. Croft look like a lady, she work at the farm like she know what she doin'. An' jus' incidental, I seen her collect eggs at the coop—she got a soft hand under a hen, Viola. Not a one stir off the nest. 'Markable how she do that. Anyway, out here in the country, I don't see why anybody got to keep up high notions all the time. I mean, 'specially me. Puttin' on livery just to go in white people rooms for five minutes when nobody lookin'. And callin' everybody who live here colonel. I can't speak for old Danforth, but don't it seem funny to you that the war betwicks the states got fought entire by colonels? On the south side anyways. Not a private to be had in the whole 'federate army. Maybe they'd a' done better in the war if they had some privates workin' for 'em."

Viola thought that was very funny and bowed her head with mirth as Delphina came back through the swing door with a disapproving look.

"What's so funny?"

"Just talking about colonels. Your daddy thinks he knows why the South lost the war between the states. You couldn't hear us out there, could you?"

"No, Mama. Mrs. Croft not down yet. Captain Croft just sitting there like nobody asked him to dance. Just staring out that big window." Then she covered her mouth and tittered.

"I can tell you," Elijah went on, "Captain Croft ain't no real colonel anyways. We give him that title just automatic since he took over. And it was him that demoted hisself from colonel down to captain. Remember that, Viola? Well, if he ever been in a army, I doubt he got high up to where you don't get shot at. That's what I think. That's what I wanted to tell you before I got sidetracked."

"It's out of respect, Elijah," said Viola, as she suddenly thought of a good reason for all the changing of clothes they did. "For the fine things in this house. All those old pictures on the walls and the ones of Mrs. Croft's people—they go way back. And those brass pots with jewels on them that the captain brought back from far off places. City people pay money to go look at things like that, and we got it here for nothing. Sometimes I just walk around the house in wonderment."

"Well, that bring up another thing," said Elijah. "How come none a' his people hangin' on them walls? You know what I think? I think he born common. And how come they so good to the coloreds 'round here? That ain't like rich white people a'tall. And another thing. Cassie from upstairs tell me—"

"What business you have talking to Cassie?"

"She stop by the shed sometimes."

"How long has that been going on?"

"Nothin' going on at all, Vi. Now you want to hear or not?"

"I probably already know," said Viola, "I just have the decency not to talk about private things."

"Well, we'll see then if you know this. Cassie said they have they own rooms up there, but every morning, she say one bed's not been slept in. And they both old like us. Ain't that funny?"

"They're not old like us, Elijah. He might be fifty, but I know she's not," said Viola, but she had to cover her smile. "Well, I'll admit I didn't know that, but that's private, and Cassie got no right to spread it around to you."

"Maybe you too much up in the clouds with wonderment wandrin' aroun' this house to inquisitate," said Elijah, "but there's mighty less wonderment where I am, out with the corn and soybeans, so I might put two and two together better than you, and my 'pinion is that Captain Croft come up workin' for his bread."

Viola just shrugged her shoulders. "Well, what if he did?"

"Well, why would he hide it?"

"It's nobody's business. That's why."

"Then let me tell you this—"

Delphina looked up from her book.

Viola frowned at Elijah. "Never mind, Delphina," she said. "You better check the glass for Mrs. Croft."

Delphina got up and looked. "She's down," she said. Delphina went to the kitchen to get the coffee, then out again through the swinging door.

Elijah bent closer over the table and Viola leaned in.

"Yesterday, with that storm comin'—"

Viola started chuckling.

"Well, I wasn't gonna say it, but that right, the Big Train. You just check me sometime. Weather always goes summer to fall in one swoop. Like a big train come through. Well, anyway, the captain come out to help get the hay in. I tell him last spring when he got them ten acres from Johnson that it might be too much for four men, but he went ahead anyway. So with the rain comin' he come out to help us get the hay in, and you know how awful hot it was yesterday before the weather change. So he had off his shirt like us—and the Johnson boy there to see it too. The captain got scars and welts all over, and I ain't no expert but I'd say that man got bullet holes showin' on him. You can see where the skin grew 'round 'em some places. And he got this slash across his middle like it made with a big knife. And that not jus' my 'spective. Lamont, Earling, and Kenneth see it too, and you know a man like Kenneth seen bullet holes in people. Captain strong too. We go hard all day till after dark, and he right with us the whole time, workin' like a cart horse. You can't see for all the clothes he got on all the time in the house, but he built like Kenneth. An' mos' tellin' of all, he know how to work in a team. You know what I'm sayin'? That man know how to work, Viola. You'd think he laid iron for the railroad at one time."

Elijah sat back and let Viola consider what he had just said. Then he moved the coffee cups over and leaned forward again.

"Look here," he said. He pulled up his sleeves and put a forearm up on the table and flexed the muscles as hard as he could. "That what his arm look like. Somethin' like that."

Satisfied that he had provided irrefutable proof of Captain Croft's arm muscles, Elijah took his arm back and rolled down his sleeve.

Delphina came back through the swinging door with a frown on her face.

"You two have to go back in the kitchen. You're too loud, Daddy. You made Mrs. Croft turn around."

"Did she say anything?" said Viola.

"No, she just looked. You couldn't hear any words, but you could tell people were talking in here. Now go on back to the kitchen if you want to talk. I'll let you know when Mrs. Croft takes off her glasses, Mama."

"Well, just keep checking at the window, Delphina."

As they got up to go, Delphina sat down in the servants' dining hall and went back to her book. Elijah and Viola went back in the kitchen, where Viola busied about and got her butter and pans ready. Elijah pulled up a stool and set it against the back counter, out of the way.

"Keep checking the window, Delphina. You got your nose in that book too much," Viola called in a whisper.

"I am. I am."

"You got time, Vi," said Elijah. "They got plenty to read today. Big letter from Autie and lots of invites. But what I was sayin', what caught my eye most was—well, it look like the captain had a rope burn. A real bad rope burn."

Viola looked over the dishes, silver, and glassware for spots. That was Delphina's job, but she didn't want her back in the kitchen. "I don't know what you're talking about," she said, not really paying much attention.

"I mean to say," Elijah went on in a low voice, "he had a rope burn. On the side a' his neck. I seen what that look like from when I live in Raleigh—"

"I know what you're going to say," Viola said, cutting him off sharply, "and I don't want to hear it. I told you before I don't want to hear about such things. It doesn't happen around here."

"Well, as a matter a' fact, it do. Even in this day and age."

Viola stood for a moment looking out of the window over the sink, as if all the old agonies of slave times had just come down on her shoulders. Then she turned to her husband, and keeping her distance, spoke low between her teeth.

"Well, I can face facts as good as you, Elijah Brown. Don't think I don't know what goes on. You don't have to tell that to nobody. Now you listen to me. All we got—all anybody got—is the little space right around us. I don't know by what good graces the Crofts came to be here, but they made us a safe place. If it's nothing like the big world, that don't bother me. Can you blame me for not wanting Delphina going out there? You should feel that way too, but no, you go all over creation in that automobile like a big man and get big ideas that everybody's equal and the same, but they only treat you right because you're Captain Croft's man. Just don't go too far away from here as where nobody's heard of the family."

"I'm sorry, Vi. I'm sorry." Elijah got up to put his arms around her, but she pushed him away.

"I got to get ready to get busy now," she said. "You just sit on the stool and think of something else to talk about if you want to stay in my kitchen." Then she turned to Delphina out in the servants' dining hall.

"I just checked, Mama. They're still reading."

Elijah sat back down on the stool, thinking. He didn't want to leave the subject because that's what everybody did. After fifteen years, there was very little anyone knew about Captain Croft. As for Mrs. Croft, there were the pictures on the dining room wall and no doubt in any mind that her face went back to when rich women got painted in hats and dresses nobody alive could remember seeing anyone wear.

"You all right now, Viola?"

"It passed," she said.

"That's good." When Elijah thought it was safe to go on, he said, "All I'm sayin' is, the captain not raised idle. And he look like he been in some right smart fights. That's all."

"Well," said Viola, "whatever he was then, he's a gentleman now, and he lives up to the name. You ever hear him raise his voice?" She paused, hoping it would be the last word on the topic, but knowing her husband, knew it wouldn't. "No, I thought not."

"Well, you right about that, Viola. I seldom seen a man more collected," Elijah admitted. "Remember how red in the face old Danforth got when any little thing go wrong? And how he'd shake his fist so hard it got his whole body shakin'—like the fist was shakin' the body?

"Well, after we got most the hay up with the storm comin' in, I said to Captain Croft, well, sir, hay's cut an' layin' there on them Johnson acres. Still time to get some in the barn if we get crackin'. But he look up at the sky and say it ain't worth nobody's life with all that lightnin' aroun' and told us to go on home. He say we just buy hay this winter if we have to and maybe plant a cash crop on the Johnson acres next year. He shrug his shoulders and say that just the cost of doin' business. That just like he said it."

Viola handed him a jar of strawberry preserves.

"Can you get that open for me?"

He strained a little, but he got it and gave it back.

"I wish either of his two boys 'herited half a' his muscles an 'durance. When I used to have 'em for the summer, that Master Rory wasn't even worth half a boy. Every time I go lookin' for him, I find out he's taken that old rowboat across the river after that pretty Eklund girl—the older one, I mean. Master Autie was good when he betook hisself to work, but overall jus' lazy. That boy jus' didn't care much for work. He said it too hot. I used to tell him, well, that 'cause it summer. Then he run off to the army behind their backs, and the war been over a year now. Like the man says, how ya gonna keep 'em down on the farm? I wonder what he's sayin' in all them letters he write. He never comin' home, Viola. I can tell you that. He know his daddy only put him to work. Master Rory too slick for that too. That why he stay out West playin' 'round."

"Well, I miss having them boys here," said Viola. "That Rory was a lot of fun. He was always in here when I baked."

"That 'cause he had eyes for Delphina. Don't think he didn't. I'm glad he in California or out West wherever. I knowed he wasn't stickin' around here long. I was watchin' Delphina too."

"Oh, she's a good girl. She wouldn't get mixed up with no white boy, let alone Rory Croft."

"For all you years, you don't know much 'bout men, Viola. How they get around girls so easy. You never see Master Rory for the charmer he is, right under you nose. Ever since he a boy."

"Like you, you mean. Takes one to know one."

"Don't get contrary, Vi. Master Rory got everybody fooled, always has, even his own mama. Not his daddy maybe, but everybody else."

Delphina came back through the door.

"Shouldn't you be getting to work, Daddy?"

"Well, I had some time. Too wet in the fields, so we be in the shed today. I got to read the book that come with the new Allis tractor. The boys and me gonna put our heads together over it. We probably end up needin' somebody smart, so don't you go nowhere I can't find ya, Delphina."

He kissed Delphina on the cheek and lifted Viola off her feet when he kissed her. Then he took his old hat off the peg as he stepped out the back door of the kitchen.

Viola had Delphina on her mind all day, thinking, as she cleaned up in the kitchen and helped Cassie and Lilly with the housework, how pretty Delphina was and the dangers that came with it, and how wrong she was about Master Rory if Elijah was right. As for Captain Croft, it was impossible not to think of him fully dressed in a white shirt with steam-ironed creases and starched collar, tie in a perfect knot, cufflinks, vest buttoned, and jacket brushed. It was no surprise to her that he had the good sense to come in out of the rain.

CHAPTER FOUR

Sunshine poured through the windows of the dining room. With the curtains fully drawn back, full sunlight reached the table at that time of morning in September, casting rainbows through the glassware and shining off the silver. It fell also on Andrew Croft's fingertips. They were placed politely on the edge of the white tablecloth with a large blue plate between them. Starched white shirt cuffs covered most of his hands, and the cuffs were overlaid by the sleeves of his herringbone tweed jacket. The color in the weave matched the gray and brown of his hair, close around the ears, long enough on top to need occasional pushing back from his brown eyes. He was waiting for Alice, and out of old habit, his attitude of waiting assumed the aspect of a lookout. With arms at his sides, he was leaning slightly forward with the weight of his upper body on his fingertips, looking through the window as intently as if he were judging the distance to the terrace outside and getting ready to take a leap for it.

On the terrace were potted palm trees rising almost twenty feet in the air. They would soon be retreating to winter quarters in a tall, heated shed. It took a team of men and horses to move each one in its cement pot down the steps and around the house. He could see the steps down from the terrace to the gravel that fronted the chateau. When Alice's mother was alive and living with them, he had gotten used to receiving company on that terrace, looking down at Rodney holding the reigns of fine-looking horses while Mr. Thompson hurried down the steps to open carriage doors for ladies and gentlemen of society, all the way from Boston. They went through a lot of money at the beginning, keeping up appearances. That was the cost of doing business anywhere. In the country, it was like putting out duck decoys on a pond. But hunting days were over. He had everything he could want. Maybe not quite up to everything for Alice, but he liked to think she had back at least as much as what she had lost.

He remembered when he and Alice had been perfectly happy in a one-room walk-up in Boston. They could have lived in a closet back then. That would take some doing now. There was no going back. Equally true, he supposed, no going back from that other thing, age, that was carving the hieroglyphics of time into their faces and bodies. But he wasn't worried about that. They had been together a long time. When they undressed in the bedroom, they had to laugh sometimes.

Alice was a handsome woman and always would be, even in the rough dungarees and overalls she wore to the farm or the everyday dresses she wore shopping in town like any other lady going about her business. It was only when taking the train that Alice appeared in full dress, in that exquisite tailoring of high lace collar, shoulder gussets, ankle hemline, and trim bodice. What she liked best were magnificent hats with feathers and sweeping brims. But whatever she wore, his gaze went immediately to her face, to the aristocratic nose, the blue eyes, and the high forehead. Her hair, always up, was still black, with wisps of white at the temples. She was going to be fifty next year.

Andrew did not know precisely how old he was. He guessed fifty-five, partly because he had kept track since the time he thought he was ten, and partly because no one hearing his age, as he kept the count, expressed surprise. But maybe he had to give some credit to the clothes.

Alice had taken charge of his wardrobe from the beginning of his rise in the business world. The right appearance was second nature to her. Fifteen years ago, when he met Peter Eklund, he hit upon the first idea of his own, the look of the college professor. Emulating the old gentleman across the river thinned out the hangers in Andrew's closets down to four tweed suits, but Alice approved and seemed content that she had made a passable country gentleman out of him.

Without turning his head from the window, Andrew could see every frontal approach to the house. He valued a good vantage point, and his attention was usually fixed at the greatest distance, to the fork a hundred yards up. He could just see some of the road that continued to the farm, and if he moved his head to the left no more than five degrees, he could see a bit of the road that ran off to the left along a grassy hill and down to the river. On the other side, five degrees off mark zero, there were deep woods that went back to thirty-foot dirt cliffs over the same river. There was a path that went down to the sawmill, but from where he sat, Andrew could not see exactly where it opened up. He and Alice often walked it down through the woods to the cliffs in the afternoons when they had their work done for the day.

Delphina came through the swinging door from the pantry and paused with the coffee carafe in one hand and tea towel draped over her other wrist.

"Good morning, Mr. Croft," she said. "Would you like your coffee, sir?"

"Yes, thank you, Miss Brown," he said, turning his gaze from the window.

Delphina returned his smile with a curtsy and poured his coffee from the right, as Mr. Thompson had taught her.

"It's a lovely day, sir," she said.

"Perfectly grand," he replied.

"Will that be all, sir?"

"Yes, Miss Brown. Mrs. Croft should be down presently. But you'll know that, won't you?"

"Yes, sir. I check at the window."

"Very good. Very good."

They smiled to each other, and Delphina retired to the pantry. Andrew turned back to the window. For a moment he might have been taken for a man trying to find his place in a book he had just put down. But once he found it, he resumed the tilt of his forward-leaning stare out the window. As if he suddenly remembered something he soon would be reminded to do, he ran the right hand once through the hair on the right side of his head, smoothing it back from where it went up in front and arched over. Then the left hand smoothed back the hair to the left side of the center part. With finishing touches completed, both hands rested their fingertips again on the edge of the table.

Alice would be down soon, casually attired in one of the loose housedresses from which she had removed the collar because it irritated her neck. The only constriction she could abide at breakfast was a loose belt slung at some indeterminate middle point, somewhere around her hips. She believed the reason women of the last generation were known to faint so frequently was due to the corsets and straps they were forced into. Just recently she had said it was none too soon that fashions were changing.

Her opinions were always strongly held, and it was not surprising to him when Alice became a suffragette. In the last few years, until the recent passage of the Nineteenth Amendment, it seemed whenever there was a rally, he had to go to New York or Washington to get her out of jail. She was away for a month on one occasion. He had offered no explanation of her absence, other than to say that the lady of the house had decided to stay on in New York to see the sights, but he knew it was rumored that her attendance at a suffragette march had ended with her incarceration. When Alice returned home, she made her commitment to women's rights and sojourn in prison a topic of lively after-dinner conversation. So rumor was soon shown the door by its more respectable cousin, common knowledge. Jail it was. Alice Croft became a celebrity felon. As far as Andrew knew, there was never a whisper from anyone who had made Alice's acquaintance that he was unable to control his wife.

They had just returned from the apartment they kept in New York City, where Alice had gone to nurse a friend through the influenza. As Lois recovered, and the infection continued to plague the city, Alice felt compelled to volunteer her nursing skills at the hospital nearby. For his part, Andrew went to work in the tenement houses of the poor and immigrant districts, not to care for the sick, but to carry bodies of the dead down narrow steps and load them on carts in the street. Neither contracted the disease, but after four weeks, they decided it was best not to push their luck any further.

It was good to be home again. Andrew turned from the window to appreciate the familiar surroundings of the indoors the two of them had created. On the wall behind Alice's chair in the dining room was a painting of the harbor of Marseilles in an ornate gold frame. At the other end of the long table, where Andrew presided at dinner, was a pastoral painting of a Flemish shepherd bringing his sheep home at evening, mounted above a sideboard. In the morning, he preferred to sit closer to Alice, and Delphina never forgot to set his breakfast place on her left, where he still had the full view of the window.

Behind him hung portraits of the grand family from which Alice had descended. One of them, a portrait of her great-great-grandmother showed best the prominent nose that had come down through the ages to the face that sat with him at breakfast. He was reminded every morning before Alice came down, glancing backward at the portrait before he took his chair, that the exquisite nose, in its fourth incarnation, had saved the life of the one who now possessed it, on the fateful day when they had met on the other side of the world. Never had it ceased to draw his eye, as it had from the start. It was the centerpiece of her face, as if the other features—the blue eyes, the high forehead, and the proud mouth of old Boston aristocracy—had hosted a get-together, to which they had invited the nose as guest of honor.

Alice was suddenly behind him with a hand on his shoulder to prevent him from rising. "Good morning, dear. No need to get up."

He rose in his chair anyway, as far as the knees, and they sat down together, turning to smile to each other for a moment, as if the night had given them a new secret to keep.

"Is Delphina coming out?" Alice asked. "I'd like my coffee. And I want to talk to you before we look at the post, dear. A situation has come up."

Andrew nodded in the direction of the pantry door. "Any moment, I think."

"She's probably reading," said Alice.

Just then Delphina came through the door. "Good morning, Mrs. Croft."

"Good morning, Delphina."

Delphina poured her coffee, added a little to Andrew's, and retreated through the door.

"We must do something about the Banks, dear," said Alice. She inclined to him even though they were close together at the corner of the table because she had a clipped, firm way of talking that she knew carried. "Liza simply cannot manage. The two little girls are dreadfully neglected. I don't think Annabelle could sew on a button to save her life. And, of course, Kenneth isn't any help."

"Well, I don't know what you can do about it. You've only encouraged Mrs. Banks's preoccupation with her paintings."

"I buy them because they're good, Andrew."

"I'll take your word, my dear. I can't say abstract art is quite to my taste."

"You don't have to take my word, dear. Andre Goddard has already sold three of the four I sent to his studio, and I see I have something from him in today's post. I know you understand money very well, Andrew, and when I tell you what they fetched, you'll understand that the art community thinks Liza Banks is well deserving of encouragement." She paused, waiting for him to give her an inquiring look, and then continued. "Fifty dollars, Andrew! The next ones went for seventy and eighty. He wired the money to my account in Chestertown last week. I don't know what I should do with it."

Andrew gave a thoughtful look to the window. His eyes went over the three Chinese pieces that stood along the window sill. A rearing horse, a dragon, and an incense burner, each a foot and a half high in enameled bronze. Ming dynasty, Hongzhi or Zhengde reign, 15th or 16th century. The pieces were already stolen when he ran off with them. He had carried them on his back over a mountain. Did that make him an opportunist? A profiteer? Or was it patron of the arts and collector? That was before Alice. And before knowing anything about art or the other ambiguities that came with the acquisition of culture, learning, and refinement.

"Well, you give it to Mrs. Banks," he said.

"I want it to go for the girls' education," said Alice.

"That would not seem to be your decision, my dear. The money should go to Kenneth and Liza. They should be the ones to decide its use."

"Certainly not in cash, dear," said Alice. "Liza might waste it on the Sears catalogue."

"I thought you said she gave up everything for painting."

"It would be a temptation she's emotionally unequipped to deal with, dear. Don't you see that? She suffered a terrible blow last year, and she hasn't recovered. It shows so painfully in her art. And I haven't any idea what goes through Kenneth's mind because he never says two words when I'm at the farm."

"He doesn't say two words to anyone, darling."

"But the facts of the matter are very plain to me. They've lost their three boys, who would normally be counted on for support in their old age. Liza's art is not only the method by which she is healing her wounds, but it's the only chance the two girls have for an education—as long as it isn't dwiddled away."

Alice bent close to Andrew, and her look beckoned him to lean close into her. In a very low, moderated voice, she said, "I know you are sensitive to exploitation of the worker, Andrew. I am also. You know that. But I think it would be a mistake to let them know about the money. I can hold it for them, and when the girls get a little older and show some promise, I'll make them aware of what it can do for them. It might be a rather large amount by then if the paintings continue to do so well. And perhaps Liza will be in better possession of her wits by then."

Andrew drew back and Alice drew back. They took sips of their coffee. After due consideration, Andrew said, "I'll tell you what you should do, darling. Open an account in their name at the bank in Chestertown and give them the bankbook. It won't be easy for them to get to Chestertown, so they'll leave it alone. Every quarter you take the bankbook back to have it updated with interest and deposits. Then you hand it back, show them how the account is growing, and say how nice it must be to know your girls will be provided for. What do you think of that?"

"I think that would be quite satisfactory," said Alice, almost taken aback. "I'm surprised at how quickly it came to you, dear, but not by the good sense of it."

"Shall we get to the mail then?"

"Just one more thing, dear. I'm worried about the girls in their present state. Annabelle is eleven now and Emma is nine. They need a woman they can count on in the house. Someone who can teach them skills women should have—no, I wasn't thinking of me."

Andrew considered again, and Alice joined him in looking out the window. Her attention was caught by a very small bird flitting between the fronds of the palm trees on the terrace.

"How about Delphina?" Andrew said. "She knows everything about running a house, and she lives one door away. See if she wouldn't mind going on detached service. We can send her back in the car after helping Viola in the kitchen, and she can spend the rest of her workday putting the Banks house in order. Cassie or Lilly can help Viola at dinner. Meanwhile, Delphina can teach the girls housekeeping and cooking when they come home from school. What do you think of that?"

"Very good. Thank you, dear," said Alice decisively. "I don't think I give you enough credit for your grasp of domestic affairs."

"It's nothing but logistics," he said.

"Well, we still have the post to look through, and Viola's been waiting."

Alice pulled her glasses case out of a deep pocket of her dress and put them on. Andrew did the same with his from the breast pocket of his tweed jacket. Then they started in on their stack of correspondence, cutting open envelopes as Delphina slipped in and out to refill their coffee cups.

"Albertsons' this Friday," said Alice. "Dinner for Judith's mother. I suppose we should go. This one is out of the blue. Remember the Westfields? Wedding coming up. It must be their eldest. Sarah, I think. You wouldn't want to go to Cleveland in December, would you?"

"Not especially," said Andrew.

"We have a month to let them know. What are you looking at?"

"Yacht club," said Andrew. "We haven't been for a while. We can't make another excuse, or they'll throw us out."

"Very well. I can wear my blue-and-white dress—unless you want to go in the boat."

"We'll see what the weather's like."

"Garden club. Oh, never mind. Ladies only. Not for you. Then we have the Barnetts' on the 19th, just Julia and Dan."

"What about the ne'er-do-well?" said Andrew.

"He went back to the Argentine. I thought I told you that."

"Well, the boy's got gumption."

"I don't know how you can call it that, Andrew," said Alice, putting down the envelope and looking up. "It's just foolishness to me. He's going to get himself killed. I don't know why Dan and Julia put up with it."

"He's a young man, Alice. He's adventuring. No different from your own boys."

"I understand adventuring perfectly, dear," said Alice stiffening. "You know I do. But it's entirely different. Rory went to California, a perfectly civilized place, seeking business opportunities, and Autie is fighting for his country—at least he was while the war was on. I don't understand what he's doing now, but it's certainly not adventuring."

"Then I withdraw my assertion," said Andrew. "I only meant to say that there's always the chance the ne'er-do-well might make something of himself in the Argentine."

Then, reflecting with a smile, he added, "It happens, you know."

"Andrew. Really." Alice looked at him over the rim of her glasses, expecting him to understand, without wasting another word, how inconceivably ridiculous it was to suppose that anyone, and most emphatically not the ne'er-do-well, could be remotely similar to himself.

"Well, what's Autie got to say? I see we've got one from him."

Alice turned to the letter with French postage and read aloud the news from Paris. She thumbed over the first of the thin pages, fell silent, then brightened up and exclaimed, "Oh, Andrew. He's coming home. At last."

Andrew sat back smiling in his chair and removed his glasses. "Oh, that's grand. That's grand."

Then Alice continued reading aloud the details concerning arrangements for passage across the Atlantic, fell silent again, and her face clouded over.

"He's bringing the girl."

"Well, that's grand too. Which one?"

"Oh, for heaven's sake, Andrew, the Belgian one."

Alice read the rest of the letter silently and said, "Oh dear—" Her eyeglasses slipped off her nose and dropped to the end of the light chain around her neck.

"What is it?"

"He's married her."

"Well," said Andrew, slowing to choose his words, "that's even better, Alice. Yes, that's very good. Marriage might be just the thing for him. He was completely at loose ends when he left."

"But what about Princeton? He hasn't taken his degree, and now he's tied himself down."

"He'll get around to it in due time."

Alice replaced her glasses and looked down at the letter again. "They're getting the papers together—it might take a month—she—Margaux—wants very much to come to America—speaks English like an express train." Alice stopped abruptly and looked up at Andrew with a face unable to resolve itself into an expression. "There's a child involved."

"Well, as night follows day," Andrew said calmly.

"Andrew!" returned Alice sharply. "It's ridiculous for him to be raising a child. Perfectly ridiculous."

"I'm sorry, my dear, but there's nothing to do but accept it."

Alice bent over the letter again. "The child is hers from a previous marriage. Husband killed—that's much better."

When she came to the last lines, Alice took off her glasses and let them fall on the chain. "Oh, honestly, that's the limit." She looked up at Andrew. "He wants me to say something to Laura Eklund for him."

Andrew raised his eyebrows. "I'd stay out of that one," he said. "I didn't know Laura Eklund had any interest."

"Oh, Andrew, how you could have missed that?"

"I thought she was after Rory."

"Well, of course she was. How could she help it? Rory's so good-looking. Not so good-looking as you were at that age, of course."

"Hardly," interjected Andrew. "But thanks for believing I once was."

"There's still no comparison, dear. But we were talking about Laura. Don't you remember how she positively lived for the boys coming home on school holidays? But the poor thing. I don't think she made an impression on either one. A potted plant would have aroused more interest." Alice suddenly stopped herself. "I'm sorry," she said. "That was most unkind. I shouldn't have put it that way."

"No, I didn't think you meant to imply that Laura Eklund could be compared to a potted plant," said Andrew.

"Of course not, dear. Where was I? Oh yes. Then Rory went off to California, so she must have given up on him by now."

Alice took a sip of her coffee. Andrew took a sip of his and waited. There was more coming. Alice seemed to be working out a new set of calculations that might solve a problem that had just been erased from the blackboard. He gave her an encouraging look.

"It might have worked out with Autie if he hadn't gone into the army so impulsively. You really should have stepped in, Andrew. I know you could have gotten him out of it."

"Maybe, but it was the first independent decision of his life, Alice. I couldn't undermine it, even for Laura Eklund's sake."

"No, for the sake of your son's future happiness. Not to mention, of course, that he could have been killed over there like the Banks boys. Laura Eklund was obviously in love with him by that time. I think she would have been a very good wife for him."

"I'm afraid it went by me, my dear," said Andrew.

Alice could not help a look of exasperation.

"I have no doubt that very little escapes you, Andrew," she said, returning her cup to its saucer. "Sometimes I think you simply feign ignorance as a stratagem to some end beyond my comprehension. If that isn't the case, then it amazes me the things you don't notice."

"Well, I noticed she was over here more than she was at the Eklunds."

"You know I had to get her out of that house, dear. Her grandmother was stifling her. It's a pity—I know her father missed her about the house when she came to live here—but Peter Eklund was no match for his mother."

"Not after his wife died, in any case," said Andrew, taking up the part of the conversation he was more familiar with, picturing in his mind the bent and ailing scholar he watched raise the flag across the river every morning.

"Yes," said Alice. "That was so unfortunate for everyone. She was so frail, but she certainly kept the grandmother at bay, didn't she? What a little tiger she was."

"She was," said Andrew. "She certainly was. And all the more admirable for her frailty. But you made a fine woman out of Laura for her."

"I did the best I could, dear, but the grandmother had already done so much harm to the poor girl's psyche. I suppose I should be happy that she could go back and be such a good companion to her father now that he needs her, but I miss her so dearly."

"I know you do, darling. Well, you've got this situation now. Autie didn't make any promises to her, did he?"

"None that I know of. Both of the boys were mad for the other one—"

"I'm sorry?"

"The older sister Charlotte. Honestly, Andrew."

"Oh, that's right."

"Do you see how much you miss, shutting yourself in your little office all day with the newspapers, dear?"

"I seem to have spared myself a lot of trouble. But back to the immediate concern. What does he want you to say to Laura Eklund?"

Alice was distracted by a pair of orioles in the palm fronds outside. "I'm sorry, Andrew. We don't see orioles very often anymore. What were you saying? Oh, yes. He wants me to break the news. But he doesn't say where he stands with her, and all I know from Laura is they've been corresponding since he went to France. I've lost track since the grandmother died and Laura went back to take over—I can't for the life of me pronounce the Swedish name they gave the place."

"Flodhöjder," said Andrew.

"Thank you, dear. Honestly, I don't know how she's coping with all the staff they have over there for just two people."

"Well, if you really feel you must take this on, you have Laura over for tea and sound her out. Maybe Autie's been writing to her about the Belgian girl all along, and she won't be surprised by the news. If she was counting on Autie, you'll be there to comfort her, and now you have some time to prepare for that eventuality."

"I hope you'll give it some thought too, dear," said Alice.

Delphina had been slipping in and out with the coffee, and Alice knew the kitchen was getting impatient, so she nodded to Andrew her intention to speed up through the mail. She knew she had some thinking to do, knowing Laura looked up to her and that Autie's marriage would be a shock to her as well. She would have to break the news to Laura delicately, and she would have to frame her disposition toward it in a fashion that Laura might find best to adopt as her own.

It was such a shame. It would have been an ideal marriage. In the back of her mind, she might have been expecting Laura to be right for her second son all along. Autie could have come home from the war, finished his degree at Princeton, and married Laura Eklund. Andrew could have taken him into the business. Everyone would have landed in an agreeable place.

Alice wondered what unknown quantity she was going to be stuck with. She found herself hoping the Belgian girl wasn't common. She did not mention that concern to Andrew. He was a great champion of one classless American democracy—so was she, all in favor of it. The aristocratic notions and trappings were just a carryover from her early childhood, those ingrained biases of social class that persist at the deepest core. She had done some reading in the new science, psychology, and if what she had read was true, people never got over their early life. It could be covered over, but the base strata was firmly down there, revealing its presence at times with a little steam coming up through the rocks.

Alice looked sideways at her husband over the rim of her glasses while he was reading. He looked every bit a gentleman of the landed gentry, but she still saw him as the true believer, the genuine article. Of everything he had learned to conceal in his life, what seemed to cause him the most discomfort was having servants in the house. After fifteen years, she still noticed the apologetic look on his face when he dealt with them, as if he were not at all convinced he required their servitude, that he was in any way deserving of it, or that he was superior to them in anything but good fortune. He had put a foot on every step of the ladder rising from the humblest of origins. And when he got to the top, he pulled the ladder up after him, leaving no trace of his ascent. She marveled at how easily he had assumed the behaviors, modes of dress, manners of speaking, and rules of conduct that governed each rung of the ladder, and he deserved a lot of credit for it. He had learned every lesson the climb had to offer and met every demand it made of him, and he had done it all for her. For that, she had not stopped loving him for almost thirty years, even when she thought she loved someone else. Whether the Belgian girl was common or not did not matter. She knew at least one who had started from there.

Alice took the glasses from around her neck, folded them at her side, and glanced at the window in the pantry door. She stayed Andrew's hand on his last unopened letters, motioning him to put them aside and said, "It's time for breakfast, dear."

Andrew smiled, placed his fingertips on the edge of the table at his sides, and took a 180-degree sweep of the view through the window before him. The stone terrace, the gray gravel, the long driveway, and the woods. What a good view it was, any time of the year, open for almost one hundred yards in every direction. From old habit, he could not help thinking that the dining table was ideal for a machine gun emplacement.

There were more than a few occasions in the past when he could have used one, but they hadn't been invented yet. At least nothing like they had now. He would have to favor the German MG08 he had been reading about. You could leave one of those on the dining room table with a three-man crew and not have anything to worry about.

CHAPTER FIVE

After breakfast, Alice went upstairs to change into the shirt and overalls she wore in the greenhouse and to the farm. She would be off on her usual rounds when Rodney brought Diligence and the wagon from the stables.

Andrew went down the hallway from the dining room to a back door where there was a dark metal chest, and he pulled out an American flag that was folded in an isosceles triangle. He came out to the rear of the house, facing the river, where the flagpole stood almost as high as the house. He took the rope off the cleat and snapped the hooks into the grommets of the flag and raised it slowly into the wind. Then he hitched the rope to the cleat and waited for Peter Eklund across the river at Flodhöjder.

From where he stood, the hill went down in a wide grassy slope to a marshy pond, where it leveled off. The field around the pond was so numerous with geese that he could only pick out individuals around the periphery of the hundreds just stirring from their overnight stay. Every evening in the fall and winter, large numbers of them bedded down for the night in the fields there and honked one another to sleep long after dark. Beyond the field lay a stretch of tidal marshland and then the river, a quarter mile wide at that point. Overhead, long Vs of geese were already on the move. There was always room for more geese. It was a safe haven for them. No one had hunted on the estate since the Danforth days.

The river turned in and disappeared to the left behind wooded cliffs, but looking far downstream to the right, Andrew could see the bridge at Galena emerging from the morning mist. He glanced at his watch. Peter Eklund would be out if he was able today. The Eklund house, a large Georgian, stood directly across the river on a hill of its own, like the Croft chateau.

Before long, Andrew could make out a limping, struggling figure against the white of the house. A large American flag presently unfurled into the breeze as it rose up the Eklund flagpole. The Swedish flag followed it up. Andrew stood at attention beside his flagpole and saluted the Eklund flags. It was a very clear morning high over the mist of the river, and Andrew could see Peter Eklund without difficulty, bent but also at attention as he saluted the Croft flag. Andrew waved once, was acknowledged, and then turned back to the house.

Andrew smiled for the affection he had for old Peter Eklund. There was no strength to admire in him, no force of will, no visible manifestation of qualities usually esteemed in men. They had long talks in the study at Flodhöjder after his wife died. The breadth of his intellect was like light on a spectrum, extending off both ends into regions outside the range of ordinary perception. At times, in the silence that came over them in their talks, nothing seemed to hold Peter Eklund to the earth but a desire to orient himself, as if he were a visitor from another planet, overwhelmed by the wonders he saw in every direction. If Andrew could have helped being what he was, he would have wanted to be a Peter Eklund. That was why he had taken to heart everything he saw of the man.

Andrew retired to the oak study. He closed the high door behind him and pulled from his jacket pocket the last of the breakfast correspondence as he sat down at his desk. Before anything else, he had to take care of Mr. Hinkley. He had already opened the letter while Alice was talking, and it had only taken a glance to assure him of its contents. So he cleared the desk, pushing everything loose up to the ship's clock and a small leather stand-up frame that held a tarnished silver dollar. From a side drawer he drew out the heavy wood-and-metal-bound check folder. He wrote out a check to the bearer in the amount of one hundred dollars and cut it from the book, leaving the stub with only the date and the letter H. Flipping through the stubs out of curiosity, he counted thirteen H stubs across the last year. Roughly one every month. Not to be arrogant about money, but small potatoes.

Andrew folded back the cover and returned the checkbook to the drawer, then sat thinking, with his elbows on the desk and hands clasped in front of him. He had addressed the envelopes of the last two months to general delivery, Ithaca, New York. So Mr. Hinkley was home. Maybe out of the army also.

The first letter had come from an investigative division of general headquarters at Chaumont, where officers suspected of cowardice or incompetence were processed after being removed from their commands. Mr. Hinkley had advised in his letter that Captain Armstrong "Autie" Croft was under investigation. The writing was done all in capital letters, the way government clerks penned their correspondence. It was only news from a friend, as Mr. Hinkley put it, but Andrew knew what would follow, and a month later, the first request for money arrived.

Exactly what did Mr. Hinkley have on his son? If charges had been filed, he would have been notified of a court martial. No news was good news. It meant none of the officers or men under his command had come forward against him. Without a legal proceeding, the only thing Hinkley held over Autie's head was public embarrassment. Going to the newspapers. Something like that.

Andrew had no animosity toward Mr. Hinkley, aside from the disdain he felt for blackmailers. Even so, he found himself considering the Mannlicher 8mm. He had not had it out since South Africa. He should look it over. It was never very reliable in '02, and it was not likely to have improved with age. It could stand an outing. He could take Mr. Hinkley out to the woods and give him the good Smith & Wesson. An old-fashioned duel. It was only decent to give the man a chance. He and Mr. Thompson could bury him in the woods.

He stopped himself right there. It was no way to be thinking. He could probably find out easily enough what had happened and where Autie stood, but if the boy didn't want people at home to know, it meant he considered it his own business, and he would deal with it alone. That was a good sign. After all the time Autie had spent floundering in boyhood, it would be a significant step toward manhood and learning the importance of a reputation. Upon this reflection, Andrew addressed the envelope and slipped the check inside. Suddenly he didn't mind putting Mr. Hinkley on the payroll at all.

Andrew took up the leather frame and let the silver dollar fall into the palm of his hand. He sat with his head bowed thoughtfully, as he remembered it first passing into his hands from Jenny Jones, back in Boston, a lifetime ago.

He did not know it at the time, but he knew it now as contract labor—or what Mr. Seward called "getting your start in life." Andrew still remembered his name. He was a kind man, and maybe he really believed the orphan and foundling home was giving them a start in life, marching them to work at the mill every day. He did not remember the food or the schooling they received, or how he came to be there. As far as he knew, he had always lived at the home and had always worked at the mill.

The girls were housed on the second floor and trooped down the stairs behind the matron after the boys had roll call. Then they marched in two lines to the mill. That he remembered well—the dull misery of working. When he was small, he walked endlessly around the machines, tying broken threads together. It was cold and dark in winter. Hot and dark in summer. Dirty windows. No air. Machines drumming in his ears. All day long, all day.

Then he was moved to the warehouse to load wagons. When he was ten years old, he decided this was not the start in life he wanted. He hatched a plot with another orphan from the house named Jenny Jones. They seized the opportunity one day when the mill caught fire. She had been sent to the warehouse for something before the alarm was raised, and they escaped together into an alley. Most of the children died in the fire, so they were assumed dead and never searched for. He and Jenny Jones took up life together in the back alleys and obscure streets of Boston.

He remembered the shelter he built for them out of scraps of boards and tarpaper at the end of a blind alley, and Jenny Jones singing to him at night when they lay awake on a discarded loading pallet. At first, they scrounged through garbage cans behind taverns and hotels for food. In the better parts of town, he picked up cigar butts. Back where they lived, he could sell ten for a penny. He found out the spines of a broken umbrella were worth a nickel to a clockmaker. Holding horses for gentlemen outside the gambling dens was worth a dime. Within a year he was hawking newspapers and patent medicines. He loaded wagons, shoveled coal and snow.

On the streets where he made his living, dead horses might not be picked up for three or four days. Dead people not much faster. Dead rats, dead dogs, and dead cats were left where they lay and became food for the raccoons that lived in the sewer drains and for the occasional scrawny fox. What a world of the dead they were trying to stay alive in. He was short but strong and became a nasty fighter protecting Jenny Jones. If a boy came near Jenny Jones, he knocked him down, no matter how big he was or how many there were of them.

Jenny Jones was three or four years older. She went to work in the laundry at the hospital. With the money, they bought food and fuel for a little tin stove he made.

They fought over Jenny's silver dollar. She had it from her mother before she died. In their most desperate times, he wanted to spend it. She said it was for their old age. Once he tried to grab it from her. He easily could have forced her hand open, but she looked at him so coldly that it immediately stopped him from trying. He never asked her for it again, and they lived together peacefully after that for four years on the streets.

She gave it to him willingly one day. First, she wanted to see him tighten his fist around it. Then she told him to keep it for his old age. He should have known right then, by how bad she looked and how weak her voice was, but he didn't want to face it. She was sick with what was going around on the streets. Nobody with it lasted long. She died of coughing that night. For a few hours he lay beside her, expecting her to wake up and be all right. But she didn't wake up, and in the early morning he carried her body to the steps of a church where they went for free soup. He tucked her shawls around her, knowing it would be cold on the stone steps. He pinned a pencil note on the shawl that wrapped her face. In letters she had taught him to make, it said, "This is Jenny Jones." Then he ran away before anyone saw him.

He went back to the house in the alley, intending to burn it down. Jenny Jones would not have wanted him to do that, saying it would be disrespectful, so he tidied it up as she had done every day and left it for someone else to live there. Before she died, she told him she would be with him always, no matter where he went, so there was no reason to stay in the misery of the streets where he was.

Down at the docks of North End, he told his age as fourteen and signed as galley help on a four-masted steam barque and went to sea for four years. When he looked old enough to say he was eighteen, he joined the Marine Corps in Corpus Christi, Texas. They sent him to Marine Barracks in

Washington, DC, where he was trained as a marksman, and in that capacity he fought with the 5th Marines in China, Japan, Korea, Mexico, Uruguay, Haiti, Samoa, Panama, the Philippines, and Cuba.

They were dirty little operations, not wars, but he learned a trade, instigating insurgencies and shoring up or bringing down little governments. After six years, he decided to go into business for himself. He left the Marines and went to work for the French against the warlords in Senegal. In Dakar he rescued a man, Shahid Mashute, from slave traders. With two years of Senegal under his belt and a manservant, Shahid, he returned to Boston with some money to rest on for a while. He followed events in the newspapers, looking for trouble spots in the world, and at the right times, he placed advertisements for his services in the better papers. As luck would have it, one of those dollar-a-week ads in the *Boston Globe* got him Alice.

CHAPTER SIX

The Croft chateau could be seen by anyone crossing the bridge between Galena and Cecilton. In a horse and wagon there was time for a good view of the house in the distance, prominent on a hill that came down gradually to the western bank of the Sassafras River that flowed into Chesapeake Bay. In an automobile, glimpses of the house passed quickly between girders of the bridge, and one was more likely to be looking down to negotiate the irregular patchwork of oak and iron in the platform that could catch a wheel and wrench it off. But automobiles were here to stay, everyone said, so they weren't building any more bridges like the Galena Bridge. Jacob reminded Laura Eklund of this every time they crossed. She waited to hear it again, fearing that this time she might be exasperated enough to say something. But she knew she never would.

Jacob Brown, at the wheel of the Hispano-Suiza—in his chauffeur livery of blue suit, black boots, and cap—was driving Laura Eklund to tea with Alice Croft. The top was off, and Laura sat on the plush leather rear seat, feeling like queen of the winds, holding down the flouncing of her best white visiting dress. In her lap she kept a hand on the lovely straw hat with a blue band and red ribbons that Autie had sent her from Paris. He wrote that it was very fashionable there, and she thought it went well with the dress. But it would not stay on her head in the wind. Now she would have to fix her hair and reset the hat without a mirror, which was quite annoying, just for the sake of being polite and letting Jacob drive without the top.

"Oh bother," Laura said to herself under her breath. One of her hair combs lost its grip on the chignon that had taken her so long to pin up, and she caught it just in time.

She took out the remaining two combs and held them tightly in her other hand, letting her brown hair play out into the wind. She didn't want to look like mad Ophelia, but there was nothing to be done about it now. Mother could help her put it up again—or make a suggestion, which was a possibility not to be discounted.

Last week the topic was bobbing hair and getting rid of the stays and corsets. Fashions were changing, she said. But Laura knew better than that. Mother did whatever she wanted, at least on the farm and in her own house. Mr. Croft was different. Nothing about his wardrobe or his habits ever changed. Even now, when Laura considered herself old enough to have a better perspective on her years living with them, it was hard to tell what those two were doing together, besides so obviously being the be-all and end-all to each other. It was something Laura attributed to the mysteries of the bedroom, with which she was unfamiliar. Her thoughts touched briefly on her own bedroom at Flodhöjder, which in childhood had served mostly as a hiding place for tears—silly girlish tears perhaps, but heartfelt in the simplicity of loneliness. That part of her life had now long passed. On the horizon were still some clouds of uncertainty, but they seemed to be dispersing. Autie must be coming home. There was something in Mother's voice over the telephone.

In the corner of his mirror, Jacob caught sight of Miss Laura's flying hair and quickly took his eyes away. It was an encouraging sight, as the general opinion held that she had gotten too starchy of late. The last thing anyone at Flodhöjder wanted, now that the grandmother was gone, was another like her in the house. He figured that as long as Miss Laura was under the wing of Alice Croft, there was nothing to worry about in her becoming the new mistress of the house. He didn't want to think about her no-good brother, Karl, taking over, because that would surely send him across the river to work for his younger brother, Elijah. He wasn't sure if it would work out so well. Their paths had diverged early in life. Elijah had come up in the world, and he had gone down. Nothing to be ashamed of, but he had his pride.

The smells of the Sassafras they had left behind moments before rejoined them as they came down the other side of the bridge. It was as if they had been up in the air high enough to clear the palate and breathe young air that had not yet taken on the character of its mother, the same stewpot of river pungencies they had just left in Galena. Again, Jacob and Laura drew in the pervading scents of river shoreline, brown water, the wet brown sand, marsh grass and reeds, cattails, crabs, moss-covered dock pilings, and other indistinguishable smells of rot and decay well-known to all who had grown up in the tidewater of Maryland. Both knew from experience how the smell of this air could be summoned as easily as any other memory of home.

Laura did not wish the pleasant ride to be disturbed, but it was important to be polite, so she leaned forward with a white-gloved hand on the back of the front seat.

"I'm sorry, Jacob. Were you saying something?" She feared it would be the business about the bridge.

"I was just saying," said Jacob over his shoulder, "in my opinion, the Suiza is a better automobile than the Crofts' Silver Ghost."

"I wouldn't know," Laura said, trying not to be short. She sat back in her seat with the hat in her lap and looked sideways out the window as if an indelicate subject had been raised in mixed company.

"Well, there are opinions going around about that—which is the better car, I mean," said Jacob.

"One would suppose," said Laura.

"Not to say either way it would get back to Mr. Croft or to your father—just opinions, that's all. Everyone has a right to opinions, don't they?"

Jacob inclined his ear with a turn of head over his shoulder, indicating that he would be receptive to hearing an opinion from the back seat.

"I'm sorry, Jacob, but I do not have opinions about automobiles," she said.

Laura thought that should be sufficient. Just to be sure, she turned her face fully sideways and threw a look of rapt attention as far as she could to the most distant dock, as if she had cast a fishing line out to a good spot and needed to keep her eyes on it.

It was so difficult managing a house. Jacob seemed to be taking more liberty speaking his mind since the passing of Grandmother. And he was not alone. It was as if the household staff felt entitled to heave a great sigh of relief. She had to put a stop to it. Now that she was, in effect, mistress of Flodhöjder, Laura felt obligated to uphold at least a few of Grandmother's standards. There was no one else to do it. Even if Father's scientific pursuits did not command all his time and attention, he certainly had no interest in domestic management. Karl and Charlotte were both married and gone. It was up to her to manage the staff. It was absurd. How could only two people, Father and she, need so many servants to look after them? No, it wasn't that at all. It was the house itself that required a butler, maids, cooks, and footmen. She knew she had to stop thinking it a trivial matter to manage a great house. Flodhöjder and the Croft chateau looked directly at each other across the Sassafras, each on a promontory of high ground. Until their shared destiny was revealed, she had to be responsible for keeping up her side of the river.

As for the Croft side, so much depended on how Autie came home. The war had been over for almost a year, and most of the men were already back. Any day, possibly today, she expected to hear that he had been released from his duties in France. It was important to plan a strategy for what she needed to do. He might come home from Paris as ebullient and confident as his last letters and ask her to marry him right away. Or he might come home burdened with wartime experiences and anxieties about his future that he had hidden from her. She would have to assure him that he need have no doubts about her fidelity to the pledge she had made the morning he left for the army.

Indeed, Laura thought, there had never been a doubt in her mind, from her earliest silly, hopeless infatuation with Rory, that Alice Croft would become her mother-in-law one day. As it happened, in that cruel turn of childbearing that can take away one life as it delivers into the world another, which, she had been told, had been the circumstances of her birth, she already considered Alice her mother. Barely recoverable in memory now, she had been carried off to the Croft chateau, almost literally over the shoulder of Alice Croft, when she was eight or ten—she didn't remember. At the time, she came to the idea, while reasoning out the workings of death and afterlife with her young mind, that in Alice Croft, the mother she had never known had come back to her, as fierce a protector as her natural mother was reputed to have been.

How well she remembered Alice Croft talking to Grandmother on the telephone after one particularly long stay at the chateau, insisting that

Laura had become quite indispensable and must be held over longer. Those were her words, quite indispensable. After that, the complete takeover was implemented.

There were the long afternoons she liked, when Mr. Croft retired to his study and Mother worked at her desk, leaving her to roam the house alone. She crept into Rory's room or Autie's to sit on their beds and look at their boy things, their jackknives, school pennants, rough clothing, arrowheads, and other findings of woods and river. Or she went to the spacious living room, to the shelves of photograph albums Mother kept, and sat on the big couch with them across her lap, looking for every picture there was of the boys.

How transparent she must have been. Surely Mother noticed photographs missing from the albums, and had Mother gone back to the letters from Philips Exeter Academy that she read aloud at breakfast, she would have discovered "Love, Rory" had been torn off the bottom of more than one. When a school holiday was coming, she studied hard with her tutors and riding instructor in order to present herself as a suitable companion for whichever boy wanted her. But, of course, when the boys were home, all she could do was hide from them. Mother must have known. It was all too funny now, looking back on those innocent and powerful passions of her girlhood, now that she was a full-grown young woman on her way to tea.

How difficult it had been at first. Mother took her to Chestertown only a day or two after she first came to the Crofts. For most of the forty-minute drive they sat in the back seat of the Silver Ghost, holding hands. Mother explained the convenience of ready-to-wear and what they needed to buy. How earnestly Mother had tried to communicate her own excitement to a young girl whose face must have seemed indelibly imprinted with confusion.

Her face was still a matter of concern, and no doubt always would be, Laura thought to herself with a sigh. There was no question that Charlotte had inherited every desirable Swedish feature that could be collected onto one face. There were simply not enough good looks to go around after Karl and Charlotte, only the leftovers. At the bottom of that grab bag was a sizable nose that turned up, ending in a square block at the end, with the narrowest slits for nostrils. Her mouth followed the direction of her nose; eyes and brow went along with the general upward slant of every expression she tried out in the mirror. They all seemed variations of looking always in doubt, lost, or in the extreme, anticipating a blow to the head. Grandmother had called her the ugly duckling. Mother said she was pretty, but too many times to be believed. When she was nineteen, Mother commissioned the portrait. She said it was a face that needed to be interpreted, and she had found just the artist to do it, for all the world to see. Unfortunately, not much of the world went through the grand hall at Flodhöjder to see the only acceptable interpretation.

They came home from Chestertown with dresses, shoes, hats, and accessories for young girls. So many shopping trips as the years went by. Corsets, corset covers, chemises, hip pads, petticoats, bodices and sleeves, skirts, and tailored jackets, as well as house dresses, afternoon dresses, walking dresses, and visiting dresses. Not to mention shoes, in boxes stacked to the ceiling. Everything a young woman needed. Mother called Lilly to help manage the clothes and assist in dressing. Laura remembered afternoons in her bedroom after the shopping trips, Mother and Lilly buzzing around her with armfuls of dresses and undergarments. At some point, Mother would always say, "We're all women here." Then it was, "No dear, that goes in back. First the short one, then the long one. Shoes before the corset, dear. The side with hooks goes in front, laces in back. Lilly, hand me the other one. Stand up straight, dear. This goes over your head."

The sleek Suiza passed the Granary restaurant and the general store and filling station of the little settlement at the base of the bridge. Jacob raised a hand and smiled to every Negro on the street, touching the visor of his cap with two fingers to every white man, and removing the hat for every white woman. Around the outlying houses, where most of the colored people lived, there were a few old-timers on their porches, women hanging laundry, and children playing in the road. Jacob waved, and everybody smiled.

Then he turned onto the county road. He liked driving and took some pride in a fine automobile that turned heads. It might not be for long. Peter Eklund's health seemed to be in decline. Everyone knew that. It had brought Miss Laura back to Flodhöjder. He heard that Karl was not far away, living in Baltimore, waiting in the wings. He was known to be reckless. Jacob thought he must have debts and might be living on credit, borrowing on his future inheritance. If it came to a fight, Jacob didn't have much confidence that Miss Charlotte and Miss Laura would be able to defend their interests against their brother, weasel that he was. The prospect of Karl becoming master of the estate had created some stirrings in the farm families of Flodhöjder. Jacob knew of some making plans to leave. He was going to wait and see. Miss Laura seemed like she had more backbone to her since living with the Crofts, and there was no question that Mrs. Croft would stand with Miss Laura in any fight, even if it meant going to jail. Jacob had to laugh to himself, trying to imagine Alice Croft in prison stripes, if the stories he had heard about her were true.

Hadn't he seen every ripple on the pond? He thought he had. But gathered at the water's edge now was the next generation of Eklunds, with stones in their hands ready to throw—flat skipping stones that would glance off the surface, little round pebbles that could be thrown high for a plip in the middle, and big, heavy wave-makers. It worried him at seventy-two—having attained the age mostly in the service of the Eklund family, beginning with the Old Swede himself—that a big splash might be coming.

It was good while it lasted, sent to be young Peter Eklund's valet at the university in Hamburg. He had the time of his life in Germany for ten years. When news of the Old Swede's death reached them, they sailed for home. The trouble was where to put him, as he had not lifted anything in ten years heavier than Master Peter's books, which rendered him unsuitable for field and fen. Consequently, he had served as kitchen help and chauffeured Peter to Chestertown every weekday to a professorship in philosophy at the college there. Between waiting for classes and faculty affairs to conclude, he became go-between in a romance between the new professor and a student.

The young lady picked up the ball and took it from there. She came to dinner at Flodhöjder, endured Peter's mother, and married him. Baby Karl arrived the next year, with Charlotte following the year after. There ensued four years of ill health for the wife, rumored to be bouts of malaria. She died two days after giving birth to her namesake, Laura, and the house was left with the tough old widow, grandmother to three young Eklunds, back in charge.

Laura loved the tidewater, but she felt ready to go wherever Autie wanted to go. He had written from France about finishing his studies at Princeton. She could imagine living in a little house in Princeton for a year or two. She could keep house while he went to classes. They would have their first child there. Or they could go back to Paris. He wrote so well of the city since he had been placed in an administrative position there. The cafés and artists and museums sounded so enchanting. She couldn't think what he would do there, out of the army, but she was willing to follow him. Maybe she could join him in Paris. There still might be months or even a year of work for him to do with the army before they let him come home. How pleasing it would be to have their first child born in Paris.

Autie's first letter came from St. Nazaire, where he had gotten off the boat in November of 1917. She knew from Mother that Mr. Croft had used his connections to get him into officer school and then to have him assigned to lead Negro troops. Autie was mad over that in his letters because it meant he would be behind the front, unloading ships, building roads, and transporting supplies. It frustrated his men terribly, he wrote, after eight months of it. Then they were called up. Only a few letters came from March until October, and they terrified her. Each one was written as if it were his last. He was wounded but made a full recovery. The war was over, and he had been awarded the Croix de Guerre and Distinguished Service Medal. They had him in an office now, and he wrote that he talked to generals every day.

The Hispano-Suiza sailed through recently harvested fields of corn on both sides of the country road. There was nothing left but stubble and turned earth, and the landscape easily brought to mind Autie's description of no-man's land in France. He said when they first came up to the line, they were eight hundred yards from the German trenches. She wondered how far that was. When he was home they could walk out eight hundred yards together in a meadow. It would be good for him to talk about it with his wife. In the distance, the woods were slipping into fall colors.

Laura thought she was completely over Rory. He had only been interested in Charlotte after all. She was foolish to think she ever had a chance with him because he was so good-looking and could have any girl he wanted. But she remembered how her hopes flew up one night when Rory kissed her. It was after her sixteenth birthday dinner. He was nineteen then. He caught her alone on the stairs, and his hands explored her body without inhibition as he kissed her. Then he let her go. He smiled and his eyes had a smirk in them when he said, "Just trying you on for size." He went down the stairs, and she heard him join in with the laughing in the foyer as the guests took their leave. She went up to bed and lay awake all night, not knowing what to think.

She brought it up with Mother one day, as an abstract, hypothetical situation between any boy and girl. Laura remembered a blush rising to her cheeks when Mother looked at her.

"That," Mother said, "should be taken as an insult. A man with any shred of decency waits for the consent of a woman. Otherwise, it shows a lack of respect—and don't think for a moment that men do not understand that. They do."

It was funny how it went. She remembered asking in her complete innocence, "What if—what if he doesn't ask? How can one grant consent if there isn't a verbal or written request?"

"Well, that's simple enough. He will come close and ask you with his eyes."

"Mummy—"

"And you will answer with yours," Mother said, firmly narrowing her eyes into a frown.

"I don't understand."

"You will when the time comes," Mother said. "You're too young to be kissing boys now anyway. But soon you will be, so here—this is what the boy's question will look like—"

Mother made a silly face. "And then, if you want to be kissed, you'll look back at him like this." Mother made another silly face. "But if you don't want to be kissed by this particular individual, you turn your face to one side and make sure you put on an expression like this. That means—well, it means—throw the baggage out!"

Mother laughed, and Laura said it too. "Throw the baggage out!" Then they said it again in unison.

They got very silly sometimes, just the two of them. She still remembered the silly faces Mother made and remembered how hard she foolishly tried to commit them to memory.

It had been almost two years since she had last seen Autie. Laura wondered what he would think of her now. She was very thin two years ago. Now she was more womanly, but she thought her figure would still be pleasing to look at and might be encouraging to a man wishing to father a number of children. Her husband would be the only man to see her naked. By then it would be too late for him to back out. It would be worse to find out you had married someone with a bad temperament, but Autie already knew she was mild. There was nothing else to worry about but him finding out about the other thing. It was her own fault. She had been so desperate to join the Secret Society of the Coven. It would have been such a feather in her cap at the college.

How could girls be so mean to other girls? She made her way back to the school, walking naked through the dark New England woods, drunk with something they made her drink, not really understanding what had been done to her, bare feet bruised by stones, stumbling over roots, afraid of the dark, in tears.

Mother came up on the train and was in Rhode Island in a matter of hours after the telephone call. She said she would send someone to bring back her belongings, and they took the next train to New York without speaking to anyone at the school. Mother said Mr. Croft would take care of the school later. At the station in New York, Mother called for a cab and told her they were going to stay a few days.

It was an apartment in Greenwich Village that Mother kept for her suffrage meetings, art dealings, and getting away from the country. Lois, a young artist in her thirties, stayed there to keep the place lived in and the cockroaches down. She and Mother seemed to be great friends, despite an impression that Lois seemed to have gone a few steps out of the sphere that they might once have shared.

Lois dressed like a man in trousers, shirt, and tie, but somehow it looked natural for her. She cut her hair like a man. She had gone to Vassar and had come out a socialist and advocate of free love, nudism, and goddess worship, and she was lots of fun. She wrote free verse poetry with indecent words and knew everybody. The story Laura heard later was that somebody fingered Lois for a Red, and she was going to be deported to Russia, but Alice went to the lawyer who had managed her suffragette troubles and got her pulled off the ship just in time. It was a close shave. Mother called ahead of their arrival from Rhode Island, and Lois had a nice dinner prepared for them and had made up the other bedroom.

Mother and Lois heard the whole story of the Coven affair after dinner by candlelight. Mother and Lois smoked cigarettes, and she had some, too. The next morning, Mother took her to a woman physician in Manhattan. The diagnosis was in medical terminology she had never heard before. Mother explained it to her in the cab on the way back to the apartment. Mother said it didn't matter. She said it was ridiculous nonsense.

"It doesn't matter to women any longer—independent women, I mean. I took care of it myself when I was your age—just to get it out of the way. I got tired of thinking about it. And you know what? I never missed it. And neither will the wonderful man you'll marry someday."

Then Mother held both her hands in hers. "You'll find someone nice, dear. I know you will."

They bustled about the city for the next few days, shopping for new clothes, sitting in cafés where they openly smoked long, delicious cigarettes, and frequenting soirees that Lois said were attended by the artists and literati of New York. Every night they ate by candlelight in the apartment, the three together in low intimate conversation, or at round tables in exotic, quaint, or grand restaurants in company with interesting people. Mother and Lois got her talking with writers about their writing, painters about their painting, and musicians about their composing. Mother and Lois told her at the apartment every night in their candlelight sessions that this one or that one was positively in love with her. They had so much fun the night Lois slipped them into the Arensberg circle on West Sixty-Seventh. They were the only partygoers not world renown and were quickly ejected.

"Well, phooey on them," Lois said with one eyebrow raised. "Goes to show you, Laura dear, you really don't want a poet. They may not always be rude, but they're always somewhere else, even when they're standing right there looking at you."

"You don't want an artist, either, my love," Mother added, "They never get over being famous males."

Laura remembered saying, "I know what you're trying to do, Mother."

And she remembered Mother replying, "Just getting your sights up, dear." How they all smiled at one another in the candlelight.

Then the portrait. They met Mr. DeCamp down from his school in Boston and Mr. Curren at the Goddard gallery. Mr. DeCamp suggested a young man named Karensky for the job. Mr. Curren knew him from summers at the Cragsmoor colony and knew where he kept a studio in New York.

"Well," Mother said, "I don't want something that's a little face and all dress—I think you know who I mean."

"Oh, I wouldn't worry about that," said Mr. Curren. "Karensky likes an interesting face. Wouldn't you say so, Joseph?"

Laura remembered sitting on a little stool in the middle of them, like a frog on a lily pad.

Mr. DeCamp agreed. "Yes, interesting faces. He does conventional beauty perfectly well, but I noticed he really has no patience for the conventionally beautiful. You would wonder why he bothers with portrait at all until you've seen what he does with—well, the unconventional."

At this, Mr. Curran put his hand up to her cheek, almost touching it, and said, "Yes—a face like this—an interesting face. You'll be surprised, Mrs. Croft. He'll see things in a face like this. And the remarkable thing about it—well, it's nothing that he does to the face—and don't mention this to him—he doesn't want for ego, you know—nothing is added or taken away from what is there. He's technically perfect. But suddenly you see the face differently. He was the big sensation last year at Cragsmoor."

"He enjoyed being a sensation in Boston as well," said Mr. DeCamp, in a tone that she knew was skeptical. "But it's a fault worth overlooking."

"And something else, Mrs. Croft," cautioned Mr. Curran.

"I think I know what you're going to say, Charles," Mr. DeCamp affirmed.

"You should know," continued Mr. Curran. "He's a seducer, Alice. Don't leave your daughter alone with him."

"Oh my," said Mother. "That's just the thing, isn't it, dear? A sensational seducer to paint your portrait!"

She remembered an off-hand, shrugging of the shoulders look on Mr. Joseph DeCamp and Mr. Charles Courtney Curran. She was thoroughly embarrassed by the whole affair. And yet she never felt so well-protected and cared for than she did during those days with Mother and Lois in New York.

They stayed another week for the portrait. Laura remembered little of Karensky but his fierce eyes, his stringy black hair and beard, and sitting perfectly still for long stretches as those terrible eyes darted back and forth from her face to the canvas. If ever she imagined being seduced by an artist, the idea was completely dispelled by the experience of being in the presence of a working one. What she saw of the artist and writer life during her stay in New York showed her that she had absolutely no interest in a life without order and discipline. It was strange to her that she should feel that way because the order and discipline that her grandmother had imposed at Flodhöjder had been so abhorrent to her. She became aware that after three years at school in Rhode Island, she was grown up and thinking of marriage, pleased by her natural instincts for what she wanted in a man.

On the first day of the sittings, Laura was just able to catch a whisper that Mother made to Mr. Karensky as she passed behind him setting up his charcoal and drawing pads. She heard Mother say, "Give her some confidence." They almost lost Mr. Karensky right there. He immediately stood off. Mother met his look with a look of her own that seemed to take its authority from the very large hat she had worn to the studio that morning. There followed a completely nonverbal exchange between Mother and Mr. Karensky in which it seemed to her that the conventional beauty that Mother had at her command was cracking a whip at the sensational seducer in Mr. Karensky. Still without words, a compromise was reached in which Mr. Karensky took up the tools of his trade again, and Mother sat quietly with her hands folded in her lap on Laura's side of the easel.

The portrait turned out just as Mr. Curran had foreseen. As Mother told her later, it was as if Karensky had divined in the Eklund face the native beauties of the Scandinavian, painted them in, then contemptuously painted them out, threw on a background, wiped it off in a fury, brooded over the canvas, attacked it, caressed it, worried it, struck it with paint, smoothed it with hand and rag, and in so doing finally brought the image to the surface. Every detail of the upward slant of her eyes was there, the furrowed brow, the look of doubt, the upturn of her nose, the mouth pulling downward at the cheeks, just as it was in life. But whatever it was in life, in art it was now transformed into a face uplifted in prayer. And there was no mistaking a suggestion of St. Joan in the portrait, the warrior maid in the hour of supplication before battle, with a promise of God's beneficence in the light enveloping her face and shoulders.

Laura was transfixed. She felt as if a question she had been asking all her life had finally been answered. What was she? Suddenly she knew, and suddenly she felt the presence of something larger than self-confidence in the room.

On the train home, they sat with the wrapped, unframed portrait between them. It was to be framed by Mother's man in Chestertown and would hang at the Eklunds'.

"I want your grandmother looking at it when we visit for tea," Mother said.

"She called me the ugly duckling once."

It was the first time she had ever told anyone.

"Well, we'll show her, won't we dear," Mother said.

Jacob slowed down to turn in at the brick pillars that marked the Croft estate, and they started up the mile and a half of road through the farm to the house. The air was sweet with mown hay and cow manure. When they came to the turn at the bull pen, the bull stamped in his yard and snorted at the noise of the automobile. The double reinforced boards of the fence attested to his renown as the Cecil County blue ribbon champion four years in a row.

"I heard it took six men to get him through the chute to the wagon and over to the fair last month," said Jacob. "Even with that ring in his nose. You'll remember, Miss Laura, Lamont Eldridge got crushed up against the side of the chute."

"That's what I understand," Laura replied.

"I think he's fine now. But he doesn't have a good opinion of the bull. Or of Elijah's judgment with the cattle prod—there they are now."

Coming toward them was a new tractor with Elijah at the wheel. Lamont was sitting on one of the big fenders, his oldest boy on the other. Earling Cooper and Kenneth Banks with another boy between them were standing behind on the bar. Everyone on the tractor waved and shouted hello as Elijah steered it over to the side to let them pass. Jacob shouted, "Out for a Sunday drive?" as they went by.

Laura smiled demurely. She wished she had her hair up and hat in place for the farm hands, but it was too late for that now. She knew she would have to get better at anticipating what might happen unexpectedly. According to Mother, husbands depended upon their wives to warn them of flaws in their plans, schemes, and ideas and to alert them to social missteps. As far as she could tell, Mother never had reason to put into practice such skills. But where would she ever find a man like Mr. Croft? Well, naturally, Autie. And maybe she could catch that apple before it rolled any farther from the tree.

Around the next bend, the rail fence on either side of the road left off and the gravel began, marking the beginning of the estate proper. Laura closed her eyes, waited for the feel of the last curve, and opened them to the full view of the chateau. It really was grand to see it all at once. Jacob wheeled in a large circle before the house and came to a stop at the foot of the steps to the terrace. Jacob got out without any haste and held the door for Laura. She immediately regretted stepping out. She hadn't thought to put on her hat and tuck her hair under it, and there was Mr. Thompson in his black suit at the main entrance, commanding the heights of the terrace and the palm trees.

He came briskly down to escort her up the steps. There was a bow on his part and verbal formalities between them. Laura was very careful to lift her dress with one hand and hold her hair combs and hat in the other as she took the first step. She was ready to admit the need for a handbag. The next time she went to New York with Mother they could shop for a nice handbag, not too big. She would not want to give anyone the idea that she needed a big one.

Alice was sitting in the large, spacious living room and rose from an armchair when Laura entered. Laura held out her hair combs.

"I thought you could help me with these, Mother," she said.

Alice took both her hands and said, "Oh no, dear, put those away. It's a good look for you, fresh and airy. You've been riding in the open again."

"Jacob likes the top down," said Laura.

"Well, he knows the air is good for you, dear. You look so nice, Laura. You put me to shame. But everyone can take me as I am now. I've decided to modernize."

Alice held Laura off at arm's length to give her a good view of the modern look for a mature woman—the print dress and red silk scarf around her neck that went almost to the floor. A loose black strap of a belt slung from her hips.

"I don't need any help dressing now. It's marvelously liberating. No more corsets for me. I think you could wear something like this. Well, you could wear anything, and you certainly don't need any help with your bust any longer."

Laura felt a blush rising and turned away to choose a chair. She knew Mother noticed that she had gotten heavy, but there would never be anything but a complimentary word from her. People noticed, there was no doubt about that, but they were too polite to say anything. There was no one to blame but herself.

Alice took an armchair across from her and sat back with an arm over the side in an attitude of having thrown off a great burden. She picked up a little bell and gave it a discreet tinkling with a practiced, barely noticeable action of her wrist.

"It's foolish to spend any more time than necessary on my wardrobe. That's the watchword of the new age we're in. But maybe I look at too many magazines. They still want to sell clothes, of course. But there are so many other things going on in the world to worry about. Now then. I want to ask about your father. It's only been a week, but we worry, you know. Andrew says he still puts up the flag."

"Yes," said Laura, "he still gets up for that, and most meals. Dr. Rushmore comes by almost every day, and we've had a change in diet. It turns out father has gout, on top of everything else."

"Oh, the poor dear."

"So the wine had to go, and the seafood. Dr. Rushmore left a list with Cordelia."

Delphina came in with the tea tray and pastries. When she left the room, Laura turned again to Alice and said, "A very curious thing though, Mother. I read to him at night, and he falls into kind of a half sleep, and then he speaks in Swedish. He'll go on speaking, quite clearly and precisely, without any hesitation. Then he'll arrive at a syntax that can only be the words of a question, stops, and then he'll repeat it. A moment later, he'll open his eyes and smile at me—that shows he knows me, I suppose—and he'll say in English, 'It's a perfectly legitimate question.' Then he shuts his eyes and goes back to sleep."

"That's very strange, isn't it?" said Alice, with a furrow across her brow.

"Oh, Father is just as mystified by it. He said he spoke nothing but Swedish for the first five years of his life but remembers nothing of it now. And he cannot account for the question either. I couldn't for the life of me write down the Swedish, so I don't know if anything can be done."

"Short of finding a Swede to come to the house one night," said Alice.

"It would be the one night he doesn't do it."

They both laughed and took up their teacups.

"I love your hat, Laura. Did we get that?"

"No, Autie sent it from Paris. He said it's the most fashionable of ladies' hats over there." She noticed a momentary look on Alice's face, as if she had been distracted by a noise in another room, but it quickly vanished. "I'll only wear it when I can get Jacob to drive with the top on the automobile."

They poured themselves a little more tea and talked about Laura taking over at Flodhöjder. They discussed the unlikelihood of Charlotte returning because she was happy with her husband and two young children in St. Louis, and they speculated about how probable it was that Karl would come back into the picture when there was a change. Laura said she knew nothing of his circumstances, only that he lived in Baltimore. They went into less distressing topics, concerning books they had agreed to read together, and from there, Alice suggested that it would be nice to talk in the greenhouse.

Laura followed her through the house to the large, wonderfully steamy place of flowers and bright green leaves. It was there that they talked most privately. Alice had explained to Laura the mysteries of their sex and what she had learned about men, always making it sound as if it had come from textbooks, or as secondhand knowledge from older women. Laura had always found greenhouse talk embarrassing, but at least Alice was matter-of-fact about it and always carefully differentiated biological facts from anecdotal information.

Alice put on her smock and put another over Laura's head. She had just put a miniature trowel in Laura's hand when she stopped. She took a deep breath and said, "Laura dear, I've heard from Autie."

Laura put a hand up to her throat. It was an involuntary reaction from the war, when she had expected every bit of news to bring word of the killed or missing in action.

Seeing this, Alice quickly said, "He's coming home." Before Laura's hopes could fly up, she followed it directly by saying, "He's married someone."

It was terrible to see Laura's face. In an instant Alice understood what had gone on all these months in Laura's mind over Autie. She embraced Laura right away, not knowing what else to do, and not sure what to say. She had always had the right words and a suggestion for what could be done, whatever it was that upset her dear girl. This time, the only thing she could think to say was that it was not the end of the world, but of course it was, so she just held her until something better came to mind.

"Would you like to go to New York together for a week or two?" she asked. She continued to hold Laura and waited until she was able to compose her voice.

"I can't leave Father," she said.

"No, of course not."

"What will I do, Mummy?"

Alice was at a loss. "We'll see. We'll see," she said.

"I should be getting back. Dinner is always at six," Laura said, but she continued to hold tightly to Alice. Alice could feel her tremble.

"Oh, Mummy."

Alice held her tightly. She knew that as close as Laura had ever come to tears, she had never cried. She stubbornly endured everything that happened to her. It was her way of subverting every pain, to set her face in that hurt look of determination and fight back tears, as if every injury were her own fault, and there was no comfort of which she was deserving.

"I'll tell you what to do, dearest," said Alice. "You go home to dinner then and look at your portrait. You'll see there is great strength in that face. It's still you, Laura darling. The painter—what's his name—he saw the strength that was in you then and always will be."

"Oh, he was just crazy, Mummy."

"Karensky, that's it. He didn't like me very much, did he? Yes, he was nutty as a fruitcake, but he painted what he saw—the greatness of spirit in you."

Still holding Laura in her arms, Alice felt some of the tension let go. If there was the tiniest ember of hope down there in the ashes of the poor girl's heart, she wanted to blow on it delicately. She drew back and looked at Laura with the gentlest of smiles.

"You've been brave all your life, my darling, and waited for happiness to come along. As much as things have changed, women still find themselves waiting. But everything will come to you. That is the trust women have always put in waiting. Even independent women."

Laura turned her gaze down at the first sense of being physically apart from Alice. She looked at the smock and the little trowel in her hand as if there were a monumental task before her and she had been given the smallest of tools to do it. She held up the little trowel with a questioning face. Alice took it out of her hand and pulled the smock over her head. She stood back and ran her hands through Laura's hair, spreading it out over her shoulders.

"You'll come tomorrow if you can, won't you? We can talk then and make some plans."

"I will, Mummy," said Laura. "I'll come tomorrow."

Laura got through dinner sweetly with her father. He had received another letter from Mr. Einstein and read it aloud at the table. Then they talked about curved space and time bending back on itself until the hour was late. He planned to spend many days in his study replying to Mr. Einstein. They had spoken together once or twice in Vienna, so Laura noticed a tone of familiarity in their letters when she read them over. She was very grateful that her father had an intelligent friend.

While she was reading to him at his bedside that night, his eyes closed and he slipped into Swedish. He asked his legitimate question again and fell asleep without an answer. Laura prayed that God would be kind when taking him.

She wandered around the house. Everything her eyes fell upon in the dark belonged to her grandmother. Her real home had been with the Crofts. What would she do now that Autie was married and coming home?

Lying in bed, she remembered she had left the hat Autie sent her in the living room at the chateau. She wanted it back more than anything in the world, to crush it against her breast and cry, but after staring into the dark a long time with tearless eyes, she fell asleep wanting nothing more than to leave it lost and never see it again.

CHAPTER SEVEN

By the time Captain Armstrong "Autie" Croft finally reached the front in France, he thought for all the trouble it took getting there, he might as well have walked down the gangplank at Saint Nazaire, stayed for dinner, and caught the next boat home. But that was before it got hot, before he faced death and saw for himself everything he had ever wanted to hear or read about war. When he was on the boat going home two years later, it was not a troopship but a luxury liner. He held a little boy in one arm at the rail of the upper deck, and as he looked out at the ocean, with his other arm around the slim waist of the prettiest girl, he thought the war was the luckiest break he'd ever had. It was just as well that nothing had gone the way it was supposed to.

Most of the other officers in the regiment were young college men from the north who had volunteered to lead colored troops, looking to get the chance to fight, as he did. The one exception was a captain named Reynolds from Alabama, who made a joke the first time the officers got together in a ward room on the ship. After the briefing, when they were milling around in the tight quarters below decks getting to know each other, watching the coffee slosh in the mugs from the rolling and pitching of the ship, he described his qualifications to lead colored troops by saying, "I never owned one myself, but—" He left the sentence unfinished and looked around smiling. The lieutenants laughed, but the captains turned away as if they hadn't caught it.

Reynolds picked up the ball, assuring the others they were in the wrong place to see the front. He said with colored troops, they would be in support positions. That meant working well behind the lines in supply and ordnance and doing hard labor for the engineers. It brought the mood down, but he was a well-intentioned, cheery sort of fellow, and he speculated that it also meant they would have a roof over their heads every night and probably get into whatever towns they were near for some fun.

It didn't look good to Autie right from the start, but there was no denying that he was on his way to the war. Whatever else happened, when he got back home, he could say he had been with the army in France. He hoped that he would also be able to say that he knew what life in the trenches was like, and that he had combat experience fighting for his country. He could only hope it would come true, and that the war didn't turn out to be the waste of time that Reynolds predicted.

After eight months of doing everything Reynolds had foreseen, they were finally needed up front. It was July, and all hell had broken loose. The regiment was called up on an hour's notice, which sent everyone flying around the wooden barracks they had built, gathering up what they needed and sorting out what was too late to send home. Orders were overcoat and full pack. Barracks bags and souvenirs had to stay behind. A last look through the doors fell on turned-over chairs, playing cards discarded on the floor, scattered magazines, books, and bottles of cologne left for French scavengers. Rumor spread fast among the men that they would get a chance to fight, and they were in high spirits.

First, they marched in formation to a railway depot a few miles away. There they camped out along the tracks, and sometime during the night a steam engine with a line of open boxcars pulled in. Each of the cars was marked "Hommes 40 Chevaux 8." They piled in forty to a car and rode mostly standing up until dawn. Trucks were waiting at the last railhead. For the next two days, they were part of a short convoy going west that kept pulling over to let longer convoys by, heading east. As the men in Autie's truck looked over to the men in the trucks going the other way, word spread that nothing about to happen concerned them.

Autie heard one of his men say, "Them's fightin' men—goin' the other way. They just sendin' us to build more roads somewheres else." Because the idea came from a truck with a captain, it became the new version of the story when the company fell out for rest stops and talked among themselves. It was hard to ignore the simple fact that if they were headed to the front, they would have been issued helmets, rifles, and ammunition. It was dispiriting, but at least they were on the move.

One more day on the road brought them to some torn up country with little farmhouses here and there all blasted to pieces. They could hear artillery going at it in the distance. Where the trucks dropped them, at an intersection of two roads, the landscape was nothing but flat earth from horizon to horizon. Autie didn't think it was possible to have nothing break up so large an expanse of land, but there was not a tree, fence, house, or sign of life left standing as far as the eye could see, nothing but ground ploughed up by artillery, with broken bits of human civilization sticking up out of the mud here and there. For all he could tell, it could have been yesterday's work or land fought over three years ago. He had no idea where they were, except that it was the part of France subject to bombardment.

After waiting at the crossroad a few hours, trucks came up the other road. Over that bleak expanse of earth, Autie and the men could see the convoy from more than a mile off. They were French camions, coming from the rear. When they pulled over and supply officers got out with ledgers under their arms, the first sergeant shouted, "Great day in the mornin'," and the men fell in as fast as they did for a chow line. Autie and the first sergeant rushed to take positions. On orders from the French commanding officer, they got the men formed up to file past the trucks by company.

Every face lit up as they were issued French gas masks, French helmets, and French rifles and bayonets, with cartridge boxes of a hundred rounds each. It was two hours before every man was equipped, and the company commanders were kept busy maintaining order.

The men had never drilled with arms before because their destination in France had never been the trenches or the parade ground. Assuming command, the supervising French officers stood on the hoods of the trucks to instruct in the proper handling of the rifles. Then each company fired a volley on command. It made a pretty big noise, and Autie figured that was part of the lesson. Not many of the men flinched. Formed up for the first time properly outfitted, they looked like a real regiment of soldiers to him, and he saw pride and confidence on every face.

Toward evening, another truck brought a detachment of pioneers to act as guides. They were French colonials, Africans, who jumped off the trucks and greeted the American black men like long lost brothers. The regiment slung arms, bent forward, and set out overland behind them.

The lead companies shoved off and soon stretched out a mile ahead. Autie's company brought up the rear of the column, but it was not long before his men took up a chant that must have started with the Africans up front and worked its way back. It sounded to Autie like "ah-huh," repeated in a rhythm that was followed by a slap on the chest and a shake of the rifle in one hand. Officers up ahead let it go, so Autie let it go when it got down to his men. They weren't in formation anyway. They were just on the march across rough terrain, moving around shell craters and trying to keep to high ground above the mud, each man following the man in front of him. The chant unnerved him a little. The men in his outfit were just colored boys like the ones at home, but he could see the chant brought out the African warrior in them. His first sergeant informed him that it was intended to instill fear in the heart of the enemy. He would bet dollars to donuts the colonials found the American Negroes somewhat out of practice.

Anything to pass the time. Nothing was more dreary than long marches. Whenever he thought an hour had gone by, he looked at his watch and saw only ten or fifteen minutes had passed. There was nothing to look at but the ground and the boots of the man in front of him. He watched the whistle dangling from a chain around his neck. It was his over-the-top whistle. Each of the officers was issued one when they rendezvoused with the French trucks. He wanted to try it out, but that was like pulling a fire alarm, so he left it alone. As they marched along and the hours passed, he watched the shiny metal whistle swing from the chain and bounce off his brown wool overcoat.

They kept marching through the night, falling out for breaks every two hours. No talking, no lights, no smoking. Autie's company fell behind because it was responsible for collecting stragglers. They got a wagon for that but no horse, so they had to pull it themselves. Autie put it under the command of a sergeant he knew to have a sharp eye for fakers.

Whenever Autie looked up, the lead companies ahead could be seen standing out like silhouettes on the horizon. All through the night, the black earth and lighter sky met so clearly in a line interrupted by no other sign of life than the moving column. In the early hours of dawn, he was surprised to find how wrong he had judged distance in that strange landscape.

His company came in two hours behind the rest of the regiment, when he thought he was right behind them.

They took up residence in a zig-zag line of abandoned French trenches. They learned that the French were in position on either side of them, and they would be acting under French tactical command. It was looking better that they might get their chance, so they got out their American flags. They put one up, but it was shot at, so they rolled it up again and waited. The German trenches were about eight hundred yards in front of them; Autie spent most of his time looking at them through his binoculars.

When they first moved into the trenches, Autie's biggest concern was adapting to living in the elements. Since the regiment's arrival in France, wherever they were sent to build roads or load trucks, they had lived in hastily built barracks or billeted in abandoned stables or warehouses. From here on they were going to live outside in the weather. Summer would be over before long, then autumn would bring cold, rain, and snow.

With the aid of his field glasses, Autie made out two parallels of wire on the German side. In his daily reports, he noted places that he thought could be machine gun emplacements. The prospect of launching an assault against what he saw through his glasses soon eclipsed his worries about the weather. Once in a while, he spotted a helmet pop up on the other side, which immediately drew fire from his lines. It made him jump but let him know his boys were paying attention, and once in a while they gave him reason to believe they were getting better with the French rifles. Inevitably, everyone settled into the anxious and boring routine of waiting for something to happen.

It was too far forward for a field kitchen, but American rations started coming up to them every day. After their eight months behind the lines on British biscuits, cheese, and tea, the men were glad to see canned tomatoes, salmon, beans, coffee, cigarettes, and once in a while, real bread.

In a bad rain, the dugouts they slept in flooded out almost as fast as the trenches. At least the heat of the summer was over, and there was always the chance the war would be over before winter. The prevailing opinion was that the Germans were pretty done up. Everybody knew there were already a million Americans in France moving up to send them packing. The everyday question was, how long were they going to be sleeping in the same wet clothes, eating field rations, and keeping their heads down?

Nothing was likely to change very soon as far as Autie could see. He put in his time walking the company's sector of the line, patting the men on their backs, observing the opposing trenches through his field glasses, and writing daily reports in the dugout. Every night before he lay out on his wooden pallet of a bunk, he went out to climb the ladder. With his eyes just over the top of the trench, he scanned the horizon strung with barbed wire and listened to heavy guns roll in a barrage far off. So pervasive was the sound of distant artillery and so omnipresent the smell of this vast expanse of turned earth that the essential character of the front line was easy to take in. More subtle but just as overpowering were the confined smell of wet woolen overcoats and a peculiar clanking of equipment that made each man sound like a peddler's wagon on a bumpy road, attesting to what was belted around his middle, carried on his shoulder, or strapped to some part of him. Letting it all sink in as he looked over the edge of the trench toward the German lines every night, Autie said to himself, with no difference of opinion from his five senses, "I'm really here. I'm really here."

A month went by, and just as Autie was beginning to wish they hadn't left the playing cards behind, they were told to get ready to move again. No trucks this time. Big doings were afoot. The front was in motion. Orders flew. How fast could they move out? How fast could they march, and how much ground could they cover in the next ten or twelve hours? They were given two days' rations and told to strip down to essentials for a forced march. It was afternoon when they set out. They got to a good road just before dark and marched all night through ruins of villages. It was a clear night. They could see flashes from distant guns, high in the sky like the northern lights, but the relentless constancy of barrage made it impossible to judge how far away it was by counting seconds between sight and sound. It could only mean they were part of the storm.

At five o'clock in the morning by Autie's watch, a messenger came down the column with orders to stop and deploy in a strip of woods. Cries of "Fall out" went from company to company. One after another, white rockets went up when each company was in place. Autie spread his men out in their sector of the woods and sent one up. In front of them lay a meadow with a rise on the other side that showed against the lightening sky. The men kept on their bellies between the dark tree trunks and rummaged for their rations and canteens, expecting not to be there long. Orders came to advance from the tree line at 0530, cross the meadow, and take the ridge beyond. Then came the order to fix bayonets. Autie shouted over his shoulder and heard it picked up by each man amid a great rattling of latches locking steel to steel.

These were the first set of orders that didn't make sense. The men weren't ready. They had marched all night and hadn't eaten much in twelve hours. There weren't any trenches for protection. Beyond the trees was all open ground. The only way to get to the Germans on the ridge was to go straight at them. Even the woods where they were now wouldn't give cover once daylight came. The tree line would be a conspicuous artillery marker, and then they'd really get a pounding.

German whiz-bangs started going over their heads and exploding behind them. He had to think. There wasn't any wire that he could make out through his binoculars, but the meadow might be mined, and snipers would be on the ridge. They might make it to the trees on the other side of the meadow, but then they'd be in range of machine guns on the ridge. How were they supposed to get up that hill? They didn't have a chance. It was 0520 by his watch. He should have the whistle in his hand. He felt around for it, but it wasn't there. Maybe the orders were a mistake. Maybe they would be rescinded just in time. Somebody started the African chant, and it spread through the ranks, working the men up for a charge. A few range-finders came down in front of them, sending dirt up in the air and shrapnel flying everywhere. Cries went up.

Then whistles started blowing. Autie fumbled for his whistle again, but he still couldn't find it. He struggled to undo the big buttons of his overcoat, looking for it as a groundswell of men getting to their feet all around him pulled him up like an eruption of the earth, carrying him involuntarily forward. He faltered and turned against the tide and found himself in the path of a juggernaut of rifles and brown greatcoats that knocked him down, fell over him cursing and went over him like a wave.

He heard a twice-repeated shout in his ear, "Are you hit, sir?"

Autie shouted back, "I can't find my whistle. I had it right here."

"It's around your back, sir."

Autie pulled the chain around and there it was. It didn't make any sense blowing it now, but he gripped it tight in his hand. The man who stopped for him had gone on. Autie got up, drew his pistol, and started out across the meadow. His men were all ahead of him. A second line was already forming up behind. Suddenly the ground was exploding on every side. He lit out running for the trees and got across the meadow. It was light now, and he could see that what they had perceived in the dark as woods was nothing but a windbreak row of single trees down the middle of a much larger field. That was a big surprise.

He could see nothing but bodies strewn about on the other half of the meadow and men flattened against the hillside beyond, wounded or pinned down by machine gun fire that seemed to come from all sides. He started across the meadow, fixing his eyes on the hill and moving toward it as if he were in a dream he couldn't get out of, watching himself walking, then running. Suddenly a sharp impact spun him around. He staggered backward into a shell crater, pulling the trigger on the revolver as he went down. The bullet tore off the top of his boot, and the force of the fall left him wedged in at the bottom of the hole.

Then everything stopped. He found himself on his back with both feet in the air, looking up at the sky. The helmet was around the back of his head, propping his face out of the water at the bottom of the crater. He cleared the mud out of his eyes with one hand, but that was all he could do. The other arm was pinned under him.

It was peaceful and quiet down in the hole. No poison gas. Through the wall of earth packing him in on all sides, he could feel the artillery, both the recoil of firing and the impact of shells. He didn't know soil was such a good conductor. Between the artillery rounds was something else, boots. He could feel the boots of the second wave coming. A moment later the men flew over him, blocking the light like starlings crossing the sun over a cornfield.

How long he lay in the hole looking up, he didn't know. Losing an arm was something he had to think about. He could bleed to death, too, before it was safe to come out. Suddenly the thought came to him that if the bombardment started again, a shell might hit nearby and bury him alive, and the dread of that happening seized him. He didn't want to die with his face pushed into the earth and the weight of the ground crushing his lungs. He had to get out. With no rational thought behind it, his arms and legs lashed out wildly until the heel of one boot caught a root jutting through the earthen wall. He pulled himself up by one leg enough to free his stuck arm. Then he pushed off the bottom, bent and squirmed, and made it to a higher part of the crater, feet first. Getting to hands and knees wasn't hard from there, and even upright, he was still in the safety of the bomb crater.

He couldn't feel his right arm and had to look to confirm that it was still there. The right hand was white and bloodless, but it still gripped the pistol. He looked over the edge of the hole. All he had to do was get out and run like hell. Not ahead to the ridge. No use going that way. The other way. He crawled out of the hole. No bullets. The coast was clear. He stood up, put his head down and made a run for it. He never ran so fast in his life, even with staying low, watching his feet, dodging shell craters, and jumping over bodies in his way.

Not much was left of the trees they had started from. It looked like half the company never made it more than a few yards from the starting point. He couldn't look at them. If anybody was alive, it probably wouldn't be for long. At least no one was screaming. The only thing to do now was to get to an aid station. He couldn't tell if it was blood down his sleeve or mud. He could be bleeding to death and not know it. The sound of gunfire was far off, and there was no one in the woods. None of the men were coming back, but neither were the Germans coming down to take the position.

Going back to the road, he saw a relief column double-timing up. They deployed into the woods, moved past him without any acknowledgment, and formed up for attack on the edge of the meadow, just as Autie's company had done. There was an ambulance in back of the column, but when Autie got to it, the driver said he couldn't go to the rear with just one man.

The driver looked him over and said, "You don't look wounded to me, bud, but if ya are, you're walkin' anyhow."

So Autie walked down the road. The driver told him he'd find an aid station only a few miles down because everything was moving up. He thought he'd better check to see if he was losing blood. He took off his overcoat and saw no blood and felt around his shoulder, but there was nothing.

At the aid station he didn't want to make a fuss, but he thought it would be pretty quick and simple to put his arm in a respectable sling and send him back to a hospital before the wounded started coming in from what he had just witnessed. They were kind enough to oblige him, but he had to wait by the ambulance until it had enough men to take back. There were only white boys in the truck who did not seem to feel like talking. Autie did not consider himself much of a talker, but he had gotten used to being around men who talked a lot. His men, the ones who weren't dead now, would be talking up a storm through their bandages about the good luck that had brought them to be lying down in comfort in a truck, riding back to Paris or London or Montgomery, Alabama, with a medal or two and combat pay.

The field hospital was in the open ruins of a church in a town a few miles behind the lines. They found him a new uniform and new boots and kept him for a few days. The doctor said he didn't need an X-ray machine to tell nothing was wrong with the shoulder.

A few days later he was back with his company. He was surprised to hear he still had a company and more surprised to find out they had taken the fortifications on the ridge and gone on a quarter mile more to take the second line of German trenches. Reynolds filled him in. He came down the line one day, counting heads. Autie had just gotten back and was getting familiar with the German trenches they had taken over. The first thing Reynolds said was, "What do you think of the new digs, Rosco?"

Autie recognized the voice right away. When he turned around and shook hands with Reynolds, he was afraid he could not disguise the shock. The smile was still there, but it seemed he had to work hard at it. There were some teeth missing from the smile and dark circles around his eyes, and a brow that seemed still under the helmet after he pushed it back.

"The Huns vacated rather abruptly," he said, with his old jocularity. "They left us some pretty good wine, though, and tins of sausage, crackers, that sort of thing. But aren't these trenches nice? Much better than ours. The boys have decided we aren't going to dig trenches anymore—we're going to take them. Nice to see you, Croft. We feared you went missing."

"No, not quite. I was hit," said Autie. "Nice to see you too, Reynolds. I got hit in the shoulder, but they fixed me up. I didn't want to miss anything out here. Smoke? I picked these up at the hospital."

"Oh, those look like good ones. Sure."

They lit up on the same match. Autie felt a little better about Reynolds, watching the twitching in his face calm down a bit after a few draws.

"Well, you'll get your chance to charge to glory with this bunch, Croft. Haven't heard any plans to pull us out, and there's been some heavy guns moving up behind us, so I think we're going to take another bite out of their pants any day now. In the meantime, we sit through a barrage every day, go across at night, cut a few throats, nab a few prisoners. The Huns are afraid of us now, you know."

A few days after Autie's return to the company, a staff car came up as close as it could to the line without getting stuck in the mud. A captain and a corporal stepped out and slogged over to inquire the whereabouts of the company commander. Autie stepped forward and was requested to pack his belongings and report promptly to the major in the car. While gathering his gear in the dugout, from what he caught going on outside, it sounded like the captain and the corporal were staying behind to conduct some kind of interrogation of the men.

It didn't look good. He thought he should take the earliest opportunity to report the good conduct of his company in the recent action. When Autie got in the back seat of the car, the major said they were going to Chaumont to take care of some paperwork but stopped him from asking any other questions. He said the performance of the colored regiment would be evaluated at a higher level and advised Autie to attach his comments to the official report. Then they drove in silence for several hours over rough roads.

Autie was put up that night in a pleasant little cottage not far from the castle with some other officers who didn't know why they were there either. They were from outfits all over France, and each had seen front line duty. In the morning at breakfast, a clerk came in and requisitioned their service revolvers. That put a quiet over the table. They were picked up by a truck at 0830 and taken a mile or two to a complex of one-story wood frame buildings he would have taken for barracks, but they turned out to be offices. Inside, the floor was busy. Typists and secretaries were working away at their desks while staff officers flitted from desk to desk, picking up papers and reports like honeybees collecting pollen.

Autie was sent from room to room along one of the hive-like sections. In the first, he was examined by a doctor who looked into his eyes with a very strong light, tested his hearing, and went over his shoulder with his hands. The doctor passed him on to another room, where he found a major waiting for him with a stenographer. The interview began with informal questions regarding the regiment. He said they were looking into the viability of using Negro units in frontline positions. While the stenographer addressed himself to his steno pad, the major asked him a few questions concerning the conduct of the men in support operations prior to their deployment to the line. Then he got down to business.

"In the action of September 15, Captain Croft, did you comply with the order to advance?"

"Yes, sir."

"Did the men follow you?"

"As far as I know, sir." Expecting that it might be an unsatisfactory answer, Autie hastily added, "I was only aware of my immediate surroundings. Then I was wounded and temporarily incapacitated."

The major jotted down a note. "Can you tell me where you were when you were incapacitated?"

"In the field before the slope to the ridge, sir."

"Then you never got to the fortifications on the ridge."

"No, sir."

The major looked down at the papers on his desk with a doubtful expression.

"Our physician was unable to confirm this wound to the shoulder. As to being incapacitated, as you attest—exactly what do you mean by that?"

"I was unable to move, sir, for a duration of perhaps fifteen minutes. When I regained mobility, I was disoriented."

The major seemed to think this over. Then he looked for a paper in the file, and having found it, leaned forward with his elbows on the desk and began to read from it. "The attack was launched at 0530," he said. "Your company in unison with the other three companies of the battalion crossed approximately one kilometer of field under heavy fire and reached the base of the slope in strength at 0604. The assault on the ridge commenced from there at 0642. The battalion attained the ridge by 0730. The fortifications were secured and occupied by 0742. Without orders, the battalion pursued the enemy one-half kilometer to the enemy's second trench line, secured it and were ordered to halt any farther advance at 0859.

"That's a fast fight across a considerable distance, Captain Croft," he said, returning the slip of paper to the file. He paused long enough to take another paper from the file. "Now we have a report of you meeting a relief column on the road at 0551 in the vicinity of your company's position before the attack. You arrived on foot at aid station M107 at 0900. We know that to be nearly eight kilometers distance from your starting point. I would say you made good time for having sustained an incapacitating wound."

"Am I giving testimony in an investigation, sir?"

The major did not answer immediately but folded his hands over the papers on the desk and looked sideways to the stenographer.

"Can you offer a better explanation than disoriented, Captain Croft?" he asked, turning back to Autie.

"I am not sure what you mean, major."

"I'll take that for your answer."

The major gathered the papers in front of him, drafted a few sentences of his own on a separate sheet, and ended with a scribble that must have been his signature.

Autie spoke up as forcibly as he could. "I would like to add a statement to your report, sir. I request permission to return to my command."

"That will be included in the report," the major said, but he only returned the papers to the file and closed it. The stenographer folded his note pad.

That was the end of the first interview. An hour later, Autie was escorted by military police to another room, where he was questioned by a full colonel. Autie stuck to his story, that he had been temporarily incapacitated and disoriented by a blow to his shoulder, and he could not account for being seen on the road by the relief company while the fight for the ridge was going on.

Then he sat in a waiting area for an hour. Another MP conducted him to an office in a connecting building where a corporal sat at a desk.

The corporal bade him sit down. He told Autie he was being reassigned and that the paperwork would be finished in a moment.

"It should be in the report that I requested a return to my battalion," Autie said.

"That's not possible, sir," said the corporal without looking up.

"I'm going back up, aren't I? Any frontline assignment would do."

"That's not possible, sir."

"I would like to see my file, corporal."

The corporal stopped typing and looked up at him with the perfectly expressionless face of a true clerk. "That's not possible, sir," he said.

"Why not?"

"One reason or another," he said. He looked at the clock on the wall and resumed typing.

"I have a right to know the contents of my file," said Autie.

The corporal finished typing and glanced up at him again. "No, sir," he said. He pulled a sheet of paper from his typewriter, folded it, and put it in an envelope that he drew from a side drawer of the desk. "Take this to the secretary outside the door and wait for him to make travel arrangements to your new assignment. Departures are usually within the hour."

"I request a meeting with a senior officer," said Autie decisively, declining the envelope held out to him over the desk.

"It would be denied," said the corporal.

"On what grounds?"

"One reason or another." The corporal left the envelope on Autie's side of the desk and put another sheet of paper in the typewriter as if he was moving on to another case.

Autie saw it was useless talking to an insubordinate corporal who must have been led to believe that he had no need to recognize rank. There was nothing he could do. They weren't going to give him another chance in the front lines. But it seemed they weren't going to take the matter any further either. It had occurred to him that a mistake in the field and a snap judgment in an office could have put him in front of a firing squad. The war was almost over anyway. He hadn't done anything wrong. He never panicked, except for a moment in the bomb crater, but anyone would have. It didn't make sense to go forward when he thought the assault had failed. It was just bad luck that it succeeded. There was nothing to be ashamed of. They never prepared him. The officers in white units were sent all over France for combat training before they were sent up. He knew that. If it was anybody's fault, it was Dad's for getting him hooked up with the colored troops. He picked up the envelope and walked out to the secretary.

The consolation was Paris. In his letters home, Autie made it sound better than it was. He said he was recovering slowly from a concussion and a rifle butt blow to his shoulder and was out of the fighting for the time being. He was in an office now, part of Services of Supply, the S.O.S. He couldn't say he liked office work, but the doctors wanted him to be tip-top before they sent him back to the front. The army put him up in a room in town but might be moving him anytime, so only letters addressed to the Poste Restante in Paris would be sure to get to him. They (the army) gave him a liberal allowance for meals, so he ate in the cafés. You wouldn't know it for a war capital, he wrote, for all the merrymaking that goes on at night, so it's safe to say Paris and Autie Croft are out of danger for now.

It was all true except the part about going back to the front. He didn't know how he was going to manage that.

Autie only wore his uniform to work the first day. Headquarters for the S.O.S was in Tours. The office in Paris was a technical center where the director advised civilian clothes as a measure to prevent confusion about lines of authority. As far as Autie knew, a corporal was in charge of the group he was assigned to, and none of the other ten in the office had the bearing or look of an officer. They were proficient at their work, however. After a week of training, he was dropped into the unit and expected to hit the ground running.

His job was to track the comings and goings of a three-inch, nickel-plated bolt used in the repair of truck chassis. The bolts were manufactured in Cleveland, Ohio, and shipped in boxes of five hundred. Autie was responsible for their whereabouts once they docked in France. From the docks they went to storage depots, then to regulation centers, then to the motor transport corps, and finally to division quartermasters. Notifications arrived every day of shipments sent or received by the different departments. With each notice in hand, he left his desk to walk down a quiet, dark corridor to the file office to get the file on the numbered batch he was working on. Returning to his desk in the corner of a very large room with little high windows through which could be seen only the gray sky of autumn, he had to match his batch to the dates of it moving from one place to another and attach the requisition forms submitted for each distribution. If the numbers matched the dates and requisition forms, he was supposed to type up a report and then return the file to the file office.

The typewriting machine was utterly confounding to him. He could not make it work right. He got letters when he wanted numbers, and to make capitals, he had to hold down one key while he thumped down on another one, and if he hit one button in particular—he could never remember which one it was—it sent the carriage flying over to one side or another. Each report on each batch took him many tries and lots of paper, and that was in the rare case when all the paperwork matched with a batch.

The others in the office tried to help, but he began to notice that whenever he looked up from his desk, the heads at the other desks went down. As the group supervisor explained to him, they all had their own work to do, and they could not continue diverting themselves to assist him. Pointing out that he was the stainless steel hex nut man as well as the supervisor, the stout little man went back to matching his own batches.

Autie was not dismayed at all that he floundered. There was no reason for the army to think an obscure office was the right place for him. It was punishment for one little mistake on the battlefield that anyone could have made. No one from major on up knew what it was like out there. He didn't have to prove anything to men like that, and he sure wasn't going to give them the satisfaction of seeing their wrong decisions turn out right and make them look good because he made a big effort to succeed at a trivial job.

The next time numbers of a batch did not match or make sense, he put the unfinished file in his desk drawer. Then he took another notice down to the file office and tried that one. When he was unable to complete work on the new one, that file went in the drawer also. By the time he was called to the director's office a month after beginning the job, almost all the incomplete files on his bolts were in the drawers of his desk, or hidden under it, or stacked behind the manuals on the shelf.

The director was a uniformed army colonel. Sitting beside Autie was the stainless steel hex nut man, the unit supervisor, who, Autie had just learned as they entered the director's office, was nothing more than a corporal. Autie explained that he had not submitted any reports yet but was working on them. He told his side of the story, that he had not been adequately trained and that his typewriting machine did not work properly. Permission to answer these charges was then given to the unit supervisor.

"He can't track his batches, sir," the supervisor said. "He can't match them, sir, with the result that he can't track them."

"Have you worked with him, corporal?"

"Yes, sir. We all have, sir. Everyone in the unit."

"Can the situation be rectified?"

"No, sir. He can't track his batches."

"Is there anything else, corporal?"

"Yes, sir. There is nothing wrong with his typewriting machine, sir."

The supervisor was sent back to his unit, and Autie was asked if he had any personal belongings at his desk. Replying in the negative, he was escorted out of the building and told he would receive new orders, delivered by messenger to his living quarters within a month. Until then he was ordered to report in person to AEF headquarters, Paris, every morning at 0800 to check in.

It was a low point. Autie wrote to his parents to say that office work was not for him, and he had requested a transfer. He said he had received assurances that it would be forthcoming. If he was reassigned out of Paris, he would send his new address along as soon as he had one.

He knew he should write something to Laura. She was probably still living at the chateau. But he had to think about it. She was too plain for him really. He had to have a pretty girl. It only made sense. He wouldn't be happy with a girl who wasn't pretty, so what would be the point of getting involved with someone he wouldn't be happy with? Something might turn up. He shouldn't forget that. There were so many pretty girls in Paris. He had to be careful about what he wrote to Laura because he wasn't going to get killed over here now. He could be held to something he wrote in a letter.

It was a good thing the war came along when it did. Laura was nice to have around when he came back from Princeton and lay about all summer. The parents wouldn't have let him alone about his future if she hadn't been there. But he didn't like the idea of getting into a rut. He wanted to have an exciting life. If he was going to get stuck with one girl, he didn't want to have to look at her and wonder if she was pretty or not.

Autie sat day after day in his room waiting for new orders. He checked in at AEF every morning. From what he heard there, men were being rushed to the front again. It sounded like the last great offensive of the Western Front was underway. He pleaded at the reception desk but never got a foot in the right door. He accosted senior officers outside the building once and was ordered off the steps.

It was clear that the army had no use for him, but he stuck it out, reporting every day in the vain hope the Germans would break through and try to get their hands on Paris. He sat in cafés and read newspapers, then went back to his room, where he usually remained until dinnertime. He ate in the cafés and stayed late, drinking.

A little mistake had taken him out of the war. Of all the rotten luck. That's all it was, bad luck. And now it looked like the war was almost over. As the days and nights went by, it began to erode every inspiration he had for living. Food he didn't feel like eating, drinking he got tired of. Whores, better than the ones at Fort Riley, were everywhere, but there was nobody he wanted to take upstairs. He could walk around the city all night looking. The little mistake was bleeding him to death.

If he could get back to the front, it would be different. Now that he knew what it was like, he'd have a decent chance to come home a hero. Or die trying. Posthumous fame wouldn't be bad. He was willing to put in the extra effort either way.

On November 11, 1918, the war ended. He wrote it down in the pocket diary his mother had sent him. It was the first entry he had made in it.

"So much for the war," he said out loud as he tossed the book over to the bed in disgust.

Maybe the rules would change about resigning his commission because the war was over. Or Dad could write some letters and get him out. It wasn't outsmarting either the army or the bad luck by much, but it was a thought encouraging enough to take him out to the street where all the celebrating was going on, and he got drunk like everybody else. He would blow his brains out if he had to stay in the army without a war. Maybe that was why they took away his service revolver. He couldn't see how anything could have been different. It started out fine. Then everything went wrong. The story of his life.

CHAPTER EIGHT

Phillips Exeter Academy was hard enough. Rory was two years ahead of him there, and for a while Autie rode the coattails of his older brother, renowned hero of the Plimpton Playing Fields. It was said after every losing match against archrival Andover that all Rory Croft needed was a team. He excelled academically as well as in sports, and Harvard waited with open arms. But sunny California was the only thing on his mind after four years of New Hampshire. When Rory departed for Stanford, it left Exeter with a two-year losing streak to Andover that the younger Croft could do nothing about. Autie's academic performance was equally disappointing.

Then Princeton. More of the boys were top flight like Rory. It was nothing like the mix of fellows Autie had gotten used to at Exeter. He came home from college at the end of freshman year with a notice. He said he'd try harder, just to get the parents off his back. He was going to work on the farm that summer, but most of the time he just kicked around, roaming the woods, swimming in the river, and lying in the sun on the dock. There was nothing to do.

Thank God Laura Eklund came back from Rhode Island and moved into her room at the chateau. Autie never knew why she was even there, when she had that big place across the river, but it was better than being alone with Mom and Dad. She looked more grown up. It would have been easy to miss if she weren't the only girl around. He thought Rhode Island must have done her some good. At least she was getting some shape to her that wasn't all what came with the dresses.

It was a big improvement talking to a girl for a change. She sounded pretty smart, but that didn't bother him because it was so easy to get her flustered. They stayed up late in the library and talked. He could toss out anything he wanted and sound like he believed it, just to get her worked up. Nothing got her going as much as the topic of war. When the archduke got shot and the war in Europe started, things livened up at dinnertime. He said he wouldn't mind going over to France or England and enlisting.

"Don't be ridiculous, Autie," Mom said. "You're going back to Princeton in the fall."

He knew she would say that, but this time it wasn't about his idea to hike the Appalachian Trail from Maine to Georgia, sail around the world, or go out to California to live with Rory. Something big had finally come along. War. There was precious little she could do about that.

"It's not ridiculous at all, Mom. If we get into the war, I'd join the army anyway, as my patriotic duty. Even if I was at Princeton." He looked down the table at Dad when he said it.

Laura followed him to the library after dinner. He took the place he usually did, lounging at one end of the enormous sofa. Laura sat at the other end and brought one of the pillows to her lap and put her arms around it. She looked at him intently.

"I don't know why anyone would want to go to war, Autie," she said.

"Because it's exciting."

"I don't understand why that would be exciting."

"You wouldn't."

Laura looked down at the pillow, and her face had that expression of injury, as if she was personally responsible for the world's history of armed conflict.

"But war is killing people, Autie. How can that be exciting?"

"Well, because they're trying to kill *you*. That's why."

"But don't you see that it isn't a situation you should try to put yourself in, though? I just don't understand," she said, shaking her head.

"Well, I have to say again, you wouldn't."

After a long pause in which she seemed to be getting a grip on her emotions, she said, "Do you think your father would understand that?"

"Dad? Forget it. The old man's been in business all his life. He doesn't know anything about the real world. He hasn't had any experiences. And if I stay around here much longer, I'll end up just like him. Who cares about making money? I want to have experiences in life, not sit at a desk all day."

"I think you should go back to Princeton, Autie."

"Well, they'll probably make me. Then I'm back at a desk, and the war will be over before I get there."

"I'm sorry you don't have a very high opinion of your father," Laura said quietly, looking down at the pillow in her lap. "I think he's very smart."

"Well, sure, he's smart, but there's nothing manly about pushing a pencil around all day. There's nothing exciting left since they got to the South Pole. It's about time a war came along. Watch how fast everybody joins up."

"But don't you think," she said earnestly, "that a man can be manly without fighting in a war? I think your father is very manly. He's just very sweet and considerate too. I find those very manly traits."

"I don't know what you're talking about."

"I mean, why can't a man be sweet and considerate and manly in your sense of the word at the same time?"

"You're talking apples and oranges now."

"I'm sorry, Autie. I didn't mean to upset you."

"I'm not upset. It's just that your arguments don't make sense."

Even when she had a point, she never stood up for it. There were plenty of chances to look her over because her eyes were usually lowered during so many conversations like that. He couldn't decide if she was pretty or not. She was thin as a rail, and even on hot days she wore a lot of clothes. Rory said he kissed her once. He said he felt her up too, just to see if she had everything, and he said Laura Eklund was regulation female. They had a good laugh over that. Rory knew what he was talking about because he had girls out West.

Rory finished his third year at Stanford and came home for a week that summer. He did nothing but talk about California and trying to make up his mind between law school and business. It was irritating to see how worked up Laura got over him. Every night at dinner she came down looking different. One night she had her hair pinned up, one night it was over her shoulders. Then it was a little red on her lips, powder on her cheeks, and something she did to her eyelashes. The smell of perfume hung over her like a cloud. One night she came downstairs in a dress like the one in a picture of Mrs. Stuyvesant Fish summering in Newport that everybody had just seen in the papers. Rory didn't pay much attention to her. He was used to girls getting made up for him. Once in a while he might glance her way. If Autie was looking down at his dinner plate and missed it, he could tell it had happened because of the blush that had just appeared on Laura's face.

It burned him up a little because Rory wasn't the one who talked to her in the library half the night and listened to her on the dock go on and on about her philosophy and math classes at Rhode Island.

The last straw was the night before Rory left to go back to California. The five of them had coffee in the library after dinner. Laura said she was tired out from the day on the river and excused herself early. As she passed Rory, Autie saw her hand follow the seam on the leather of Rory's chair up to his shoulder, alight upon it briefly with her fingertips, then return to her side as she exited the room. Rory went up to bed a little after that. Autie stayed up with the parents another hour before he turned in for the night.

Just out of sheer curiosity, he crept up to the third floor and listened outside Laura's door. There wasn't a sound, so he went down to the second floor to go to his room and pulled up short at Rory's door. There were sounds. He could tell there were two people in there. He stayed outside the door listening. The sounds were coming from the bed. He didn't want to get caught, so he went to his own room and fumed about it half the night.

In the morning, he made some coffee for himself before Viola and Delphina got in, and then took the car up to Baltimore with the newspaper clipping address of the recruitment center. He was the first one in the door, and he enlisted in the United States Army. He signed all the papers and got home in time to take Rory to the train station.

Laura was nowhere to be seen as Mom and Dad saw them off. The train was delayed, so he and Rory sat on the bench with Rory's suitcase between them, smoking cigarettes and drinking coffee.

Rory said, "Just to let you know, old man, if you're ever hard up, Cassie will do it for you. I had to give her ten dollars, but I have to say she was worth it."

"What?"

"I had her in the room last night."

"Jesus, Rory."

"I just thought I'd let you know—in case you're ever hard up. Or come out to California. I'll show you around."

Autie needed a moment to take it in. He didn't want to bring it up, but he said, "I walked by your room and heard something. I thought maybe it was Laura."

Rory laughed. "Laura? Not in a million years. She's a cold fish."

"I thought you said you got her going once."

"That's true to the type, Aut," he said. "They always back out. That girl's a textbook case. You can tell. That's why I didn't bother."

On the drive home by himself, Autie cooled off about Laura, but it was something else remembering he had just joined the army. Morning seemed a long time ago. He didn't like to commit himself to anything, even if it meant excitement and seeing the world, but now he had gone and done it. Dad could probably get him out of it, but suddenly he didn't care about Laura Eklund or Princeton or working on the farm all summer.

He'd go. It was a week before he had to report to the induction center in Baltimore. He decided to tell the parents two days before he had to leave, too late for Dad to do anything. Going back to Princeton or staying on the farm after Laura went back to Rhode Island seemed more and more dismal to contemplate now that there was an idea in his head of a war he could get into. The ticket was in his hand and nothing was holding him back.

The next few days he made himself scarce. Then Laura caught him coming up the grassy slope from the river one day. She must have been looking through one of the upstairs windows and spotted him. When she met him at the flagpole, she was breathless.

"I was wondering where you've been," she said. She turned at his side and followed him toward the house.

Without looking at her, he said, "I took the canoe out."

"You went without me?"

"I had some thinking to do," he said.

Autie kept walking and Laura sped up to get in front of him. She blocked him at the door with her back to it and her face turned up to his.

He pulled back. He had never been so close to her before. Then, whatever it was, the moment was gone. She looked down at her feet, and he stepped back from her.

"I want you to talk to me," she said. "What's wrong?"

"Nothing's wrong."

"Something's bothering you. I can tell." Then she added, "It started the day you took Rory to the station."

"Nothing's wrong."

"Did Rory say something about me?"

"For Pete's sake, no."

"I thought we were friends," she said.

"Sure, we're friends."

"Friends are honest with each other."

He let her continue blocking his way, but he didn't know what to say.

After waiting a few moments without a reply, Laura said, "You'll visit me at school, won't you?"

"Rhode Island is pretty far away."

"Not from Princeton," she said. "You can take the train."

"I don't know if I'm going back. That's what I've been thinking about."

"Oh, Autie," she said. "We can talk about it."

"I know what you'll say. Just like Mom and Dad."

"But they're right. You can't give up Princeton. It's your future."

"Well, the future all depends," he said. "I've been thinking of enlisting in the army."

Tears came instantly to her eyes. "If there's going to be a war, I mean, if we get pulled into it, they'll be drafting men. You won't have to go right away."

"I don't want to miss out," he said. "It could be over before draftees get there."

"Well, if you aren't going to think about yourself, you should think about your parents, Autie. And me. What if you're killed?"

"I'm not going to get killed."

"You don't know that."

"I have to make my own decisions. I'm tired of everybody telling me what to do," he said.

"Autie, anyone who loves you would not want you joining the army." Then she looked down again and very softly added, "Please don't."

There was no getting around it.

"I already did," he said.

Laura instantly turned around and went in the house. He heard her running up the stairs to her room.

As far as he knew, Laura did not come down from her room all afternoon. He went through the house, dodged into the living room to grab some cigarettes out of Dad's box and a few matches, and headed for the woods. He followed the path down to the sawmill, then through the deep leaves to the ridge over the sandbar. It was too wet to sit down out there, so he climbed back up and found a spot with a pine needle floor and good view of the river.

He remembered Dad and Rory and him. They looked for arrowheads in the sand of the riverbank. He was too young to know what they were doing, but he picked up stones like they did and looked at them the way they did. Some they put in their pockets, some they threw in the river or dropped in the sand. It was a mystery. He went to school for other mysteries. Tutors came to the house. He never had to figure out anything on his own. Maybe that was what had taken all the adventure out of life.

It didn't matter about Laura. In two days he was going away for how long he didn't know. She had been part of the background for—he stopped to count on his fingers. Five years it must have been. He didn't know why she started living in their house. It was obvious she liked Rory, but she must know by now that she didn't have a chance with him. She just wanted somebody to notice her. It was all the talking they did that got her romantic. He had never talked to her before this summer. But neither did Rory, and she was romantic over him. Anyway, it looked like nobody was going over Niagara Falls in a barrel in the next two days before he had to leave. He finished the last cigarette he had taken along—maybe he was just thinking about Laura because she was a girl. It could have been any girl.

He couldn't stand the thought of going through dinner that night with Laura sitting across from him looking cross-eyed. Better to get it over with. The news stopped Mom cold for a minute. Then she put her napkin down.

"Autie," she said, "that's perfectly ridiculous—Andrew?"

Dad did not exactly line up with her. He said they had to respect his decision. He said from his reading of the newspapers, America was not going to get in the war.

"That gives you a chance to get the best out of a military experience," he said. "Princeton will mean more to you after that."

The last part he knew was for Mom. Laura ended up with the same expression on her face that Mom had. They were probably banking on what Dad could do in the next two days to get him out of it. He said there was no need to talk about it now. Autie tried to look determined on going. The rest of dinner was about a letter from Rory that morning about a girl he met on the train to California.

Autie didn't want to make a special occasion of his last two days. He went to the farm to say goodbye to Elijah and the boys to get it out of the way. He was back on terms with Laura, so after Dad disappeared into his study and Mom went off to nose around the farm, they went down to the river and took the canoe out. Autie called up to the house from the telephone in the boathouse to have Delphina bring some sandwiches and bottles of Coca-Cola down the hill for them. Later they swam halfway across the river and back and lay on the dock sunning. They talked about deep matters of philosophy from the books Laura was reading for school, and when they'd had enough of that, they dove off the dock and swam again. Then they lay down and sunned on the warm boards. As the geese flew over in their long formations, Laura tried to count them because geese mated for life and she said she liked to see the Vs make an even number.

Autie couldn't help thinking a life like this wouldn't be so bad. Maybe he could get in and out like Dad said. If he didn't like the army, Dad could make some telephone calls for him before the summer was over. It would be warm enough to swim into early October.

Laura was pretty layered up in wool for swimming, but when it was wet, he could see she was regulation female all right, like Rory said, but now he was thinking ahead. He was counting on picking up some experience in the army. There were always women around army camps. That was half the fun of going to war.

Mom came down in her robe at four thirty in the morning to cook breakfast for them. Dad was taking him to the train. They sat on the benches in the servants' little dining alcove. Mom kept a thoughtful silence and looked at Dad again and again as if she had just thought of something else to remind him to say in the car.

"Autie," she said, "I don't think Laura is coming down. When you've finished breakfast, you should go up and say goodbye to her. She'll never forgive me if I let her oversleep."

Autie took a last sip of coffee and slid out of the booth. He went through the swinging door to the dining room. It was so quiet in the house. All of a sudden, he just wanted to go upstairs to his room, go back to bed, and forget he had enlisted in the army. In the afternoon he and Laura could walk down the hill to the river with their towels and a picnic. It looked like it was going to be a nice day.

Autie knocked softly on the door, and Laura said, "Come in." She had a clear voice without any trace of sleep in it. She was sitting in a chair in the dark by the window. He wondered how long she had been there. He wasn't going to stall around awkwardly, so he went over and sat on the edge of the bed, across from the chair.

"I have to get going," he said.

"I know," she said. She got up and came to sit on the bed beside him. After a long silence, she took his hand. They had never held hands before. He didn't think he had ever sat on her bed.

"I had fun these last two days," she said.

"I did too."

"I hope you'll remember it."

"I will," he said.

"I didn't want to come downstairs because I thought I might cry."

"I hope you're not going to cry now."

"Oh no. Mummy and I will cry when you drive off."

"Mom doesn't cry."

"She might this time," said Laura.

It was no use telling her that not everyone who goes to war gets killed or that America wasn't even in the war. She had a mental block about that. To her, just joining the army made him a goner.

"Well, I better go," he said.

"No, just a little longer. I want to tell you something."

"I can't miss the train."

"I would have done something last night," she said. She faltered a bit, then started over with more resolve in her voice. "I would have done something for you last night. If you had asked."

"What?" he said.

"I'll tell you when you come visit me in Rhode Island," she said.

"I'll remind you," he said as he escaped the grip she had on his hand and stood up to go.

"You won't have to," she said.

Laura stood up too, and walked behind him to the door. He knew she wouldn't follow him downstairs, so goodbye would be at the door, and he turned around for it. This time, when she raised her eyes to his, he kissed her. It felt too quickly done for a big experience in life, so he put his arms around her and kissed her again, staying longer on her lips. She put her arms around him and pressed against him, and then it was her kissing him. He had not imagined kissing a girl would feel so physical, so much like putting a mouth on a mouth, but there it was, he had kissed a girl. He double-timed down the stairs. It was his first kiss. Her second. He wondered if she might lie to him someday and tell him it was her first kiss, too.

In the car to the station he was seized with a panicky feeling that the kiss might be construed as engagement. That's what it usually meant when the girl was old enough, and eighteen was. In the light off the dashboard, Dad noticed the sweat breaking out on his face and asked if he was feeling all right. He said it was just from running down three flights of stairs. It wouldn't be the most honorable thing to do, but he could just deny he ever kissed her. She couldn't prove it. He'd have to wait and see. The first letter from Mom would tell the tale. He'd just have to sweat it out till then. The only thought tamping down the panic in his head was that she never said, "I'll wait for you." He could swear on a stack of Bibles she never said it. The idea that she might not want him for a husband never entered his mind.

CHAPTER NINE

There was not much to remember about basic training at Camp Klauder near Buffalo, New York, except several hundred men in their underwear, standing in line for haircuts, vaccinations, and uniforms, then trying to sleep on rough wooden bunks with thin mattresses. The next day and every one after were spent cleaning the barracks and drilling. The last weeks were memorable for long marches in full pack, for which the drill instructors seemed to prefer inclement weather. Next came advanced infantry training at Camp Lee, Virginia, another school of hard knocks, where he decided the only way to live well in the army was to get some bars on his shoulders. Looking out the window of the train taking him across country to officer training camp at Fort Riley, Kansas, Autie knew he probably had Dad to thank. He didn't think he did very well on the test.

At Fort Riley, he finally got the chance to go into a real town. Brothels were everywhere. The first time he got a twenty-four-hour pass, he went with a bunch of buddies also new to the territory. Just outside the gates of the base, they got a cab, and once they were all piled in and the driver asked where they wanted to go, Autie took the lead and asked him in the most discreet way for conveyance of the party to a whorehouse.

"Do you want the white whorehouse or the colored whorehouse?" he asked.

Autie looked around and there seemed general agreement that the white whorehouse would be their choice. "The white whorehouse, please," he said.

The driver took them no more than a turn or two around the block and charged them an astonishing amount of money, which he explained was mostly for the information. The middle-aged lady who came to the door in a thin gown that hardly covered anything, especially with the light coming from the room behind her, said, "You boys look pretty young to me. Where'd you dig up the smart uniforms?" There was a hard but bemused look on her face.

"We're in the officer school at the camp," Autie said. "We'll be lieutenants in a few weeks."

"Then let's see your passes," she said.

They eagerly pulled out their passes and gained admittance. Once inside, they picked out girls who suited them and went upstairs to the rooms.

That such places existed in the world was fantastic to Autie. All you needed was money. In the next few weeks, he discovered an appetite within him constrained only by the hours granted on the passes as he went shopping for women in the best whorehouses in town. Getting to know what was under the clothes guided him in making his selections represent a broad range of body types. It was rare that he allowed his personal preference for thin girls with dark hair to interfere with a disinterested, scientific approach to information gathering. In a high-minded way, he respected every girl as different from the others. He took each one as a unique individual, and he had as many as he could. At the time, there was nothing untoward about the pairing of those two thoughts in his head.

Something worth learning had finally opened its books to him: the body of the human female. It fascinated him in every variation of touch, sight, smell, and sound. His hands followed the hollows and curves as if he were an explorer charting the coasts of unknown lands and their dark primeval interiors. He was amazed also by the agility of women, the range of motion in legs and arms, free of clothing, that he never would have guessed for all the layers of material in which they appeared in public. New to him as well was passionate breathing never heard in polite drawing rooms and convulsions of pleasure never brought up in the tomes of literature. He learned what excited women, their capacity for pleasure, and the importance of timing. As ardently as any Princeton scholar, he put his growing knowledge to repeated and intense application.

A few of the boys got syphilis and dropped out, but he was lucky. His chums gave him the nickname "whoremaster." His reputation got around, and he was called in to talk to a colonel. Moral character was the topic, and a message to the troops from general headquarters was read aloud to him: "A soldier who contracts venereal disease not only suffers permanent injury but renders himself inefficient as a soldier and becomes an encumbrance to the Army of the United States of America."

He had heard it before, but this time he had to sign for receipt of the warning. Autie expressed regret, and they let him off, but for the last week of officer training he was restricted to base and his whoring days in Kansas were over.

Completing three months at Fort Riley, Autie was commissioned a second lieutenant and sent a hop and a skip across the prairie to Fort Leavenworth. When he found he had been enrolled there in the Sherman School of Application for Cavalry and Infantry, he suspected his father had something to do with the assignment. He didn't mind school so much because America wasn't in the war yet, and Kansas City was close enough for some fun once in a while. At Christmas, he wrangled a decent leave and went home to Maryland, but a blizzard held him up, and all he ended up with was a few desultory days with Dad alone in the big chateau. Mom brought Laura home from Rhode Island for the holidays the day after he had to get back on the train to Kansas.

He wrote to Laura every few weeks during that year and a half at Leavenworth. Getting into the habit of it, he discovered he liked writing to her more than he wanted to go through the much greater trouble of seeing her and dealing with conversation. In a letter, he could put down his thoughts as they came to him without her interruptions or having to listen to one of her long stories.

Something was brewing in Mexico. In March of 1916 there was a dustup along the border, and Autie thought he was going to get his chance to do some fighting. As luck would have it, Laura had just written about coming out to Kansas to see him, and he had to write back to say he was being deployed.

It turned out to be no fun living in tents in the desert. The men of the 10th Cavalry from Fort Riley were the ones chasing Mexicans. Autie and his contingent of forty men kept the home fires burning. At least he was in charge. There was nothing to do in their little outpost but manage supplies, do the cooking, care for the horses, and burn the trash. He read every newspaper that came his way. Every story of the European war taunted him. Now he was counting on his position in the army because he thought it was just a matter of time, but sometimes he almost gave up hope. When he started to add up the time and think he might have been ending his last year at Princeton, it left him down in the dumps.

Early in the new year, the newspapers got up in a fury over Germany resuming unrestricted submarine warfare, and in February they reported on the intercepted Zimmermann telegram, which proposed an alliance between Germany and Mexico. The public was hot. Autie was glad when he was brought back from Mexico and ordered to Georgia, a little closer to the action, where he was to assist in the building of a camp north of Atlanta big enough to train thousands of men. It looked like America was finally getting into the war. Another month went by. They said President Wilson was ready to go to Congress for a declaration of war, and on April 2, he did. On April 4, 1917, the Senate passed the resolution.

The army was rushing men over to France as fast as possible, but Autie got two days leave at the last minute and made it home. He only got the two days because there was a logjam of troop trains to the East Coast. First, he was supposed to leave from New York. That got changed to Hoboken. Then Newport News. The last change of embarkation gave him the two days.

Mom had just left to take Laura up to Rhode Island. Whenever they were away for a few days, or at the apartment in New York, Dad let the staff off, so it was just the two of them. It couldn't have been a drearier two days. There was nothing much to talk about, so Autie was glad that Dad wanted to hear about the army. The only change was on the last night, when they sat with coffee in the living room.

Dad set his coffee cup down and leaned forward.

"I want you to remember something," he said. After a pause in which he seemed to debate raising the topic, he said, "I can get you out of it."

"No, Dad," Autie said right away. "I want to go. I've been waiting almost three years for a chance."

"I know that, son, but just remember. There might be a time."

"I'll be all right, Dad," said Autie. "I'm pretty used to the army now. And I'll be careful."

Dad sat back and said, "Well, tell me what they taught you about being careful."

He listened carefully, looking down at the rug, nodding as if he were marking off a checklist of his own, as Autie described the lessons of not making yourself a silhouette against the horizon, not to bunch up, staying low, and everything else he could think of. Dad gave him a few tips and ended up talking about guns.

"You'll only get a sidearm," he said. "Look for something better. You'll probably see rifles lying around. It's worth your while to get familiar with what the men are using. If I'm not mistaken, that will be either the Enfield or the '03 Springfield. You can't go wrong with an Enfield. If you pick up one of the Springfields, though, be careful not to pull the trigger on a partially closed bolt or the striker will slow the pin enough to not fire the primer."

Autie wasn't sure what he was hearing.

"I don't remember where I read about that," his father said, looking down as he reached for the silver cigarette box.

After they turned in on the last night, Autie quietly stole up to the third floor to Laura's room. She and Mom must have bought a whole new wardrobe, because it looked like everything he ever saw on her was still there. He turned on the little light beside the bed and listened for any sound in the house. It was just curiosity. He couldn't help looking through the drawers of the dresser. In one of the top drawers were stockings, very precisely rolled.

In the other were the rolls of the same kind in rows and stacks, but they didn't look like stockings, so he held one up and let it unroll. It was underpants—or whatever they called them. It looked like Laura Eklund had about forty sets of underpants. Because they were here and not in Rhode Island, Autie conjectured that Laura Eklund might now be possessed of forty spares.

It was not a gentlemanly thing he was doing, so he made himself close the drawer and only glanced into the water closet. At the door of the little sitting room off the bedroom, he imagined her writing letters to him at the desk. It was easy to imagine her reading his letters in bed. The dresses in the armoire were all ones he had seen on her. He wondered what she was wearing at college. He hadn't heard from her in a while and hadn't seen her in more than two years. She must have gotten over thinking he was going to get killed—just when it really could happen.

He lay awake a long time that night, taking in the sights and sounds through the open window in the place where most of his life so far had been lived. The moon was high in the treetops. He could hear geese navigating the night overhead. The smell of deep woods and river were in the air stirring the curtains. This was the peaceful country he was leaving.

Ten days across the stormy Atlantic, rife with lurking submarines, lay the continent of Europe, blighted by a well-reported hellish underworld that had risen to the surface of the earth. Untested, he went. Victorious he would return. It was only in the remote reaches of his mind, where thoughts strayed off the path or passed through like wandering gypsies, that he briefly wondered before he fell to sleep if this pilgrimage held anything else for him but fame and glory.

CHAPTER TEN

Autie had it with life in one room. Christmas came, and the new year, 1919, brought snow and cold weather. It was Paris, the war was over, and things in town were back to what Paris was known for. But not knowing what the army was going to do with him made him too miserable to partake. They kept him on ice longer than he expected, and he made up his mind to write to Dad and clear out. He could be home by spring. He could take the summer off to decide about going back to Princeton or something else. He could already hear Mom saying, "Make yourself useful." He thought he could endure that easier than this purgatory.

He had a good excuse this time. He had been to war. That was worth at least taking the summer off when he got home. If nothing turned up in the meantime, he'd look in on Laura. He wasn't sure why she had been on his mind off and on all this time. Almost two years had gone by since he had arrived in France. Counting the two before that in Kansas, it had been almost five years since he'd seen her. Maybe they could get together, but he'd have to see what she looked like first. In his letters home, he said he was still in the Services of Supply office.

On his way to report to AEF one morning, he stopped at a street vendor, thinking to pick up something to take home to Laura. He bought a hat with ribbons for her. He had seen them around on nice-looking women. There was no one else at the stand just then, and the vendor looked at him in the way they had of getting at the customer's weak spot. He said he had something the captain might like to bring home and produced two jewelry boxes from under the counter of his cart. Reverently, he opened them. In the red box, pinned to a black satin pillow was a Croix de Guerre. In the black box, pinned to a black satin pillow was an American Distinguished Service Medal. They looked genuine. Autie bargained him down because they didn't come with citations, even though he would have only gotten rid of them, because they would have had names.

When he got back to the room, he tucked them away and found a letter had been slipped under the door from the army. He had already decided to let Dad get him out, but he knew it would be better to end his military career on a high note, so he read the letter with an open mind. It turned out that the new assignment was more than he could have hoped for.

A new hospital had come into existence in the old American Students' Club, and he was appointed liaison officer. It sounded like a new position, and there was no mention of between whom he would liaison. There wasn't even a date specified for reporting. Perfect for someone they didn't know what to do with. Inquiring about the new hospital with a cabbie on the street, he learned it was in the Latin Quarter, so he was close enough to walk. That night, with his prospects looking up, Autie left his shoes outside the room for the first time.

The next day he put on his uniform and newly shined shoes and walked around to the hospital to get the lay of the land before he reported. He spent the morning ambling around the floors with the officious air of one who had business in the place, looking straight into the faces of the nurses and doctors who passed him in the corridors. It was great fun. He discovered generals, colonels, and majors on the top floor, captains and lieutenants on the next, and enlisted men below that. The ground floor was administration and kitchen, which he didn't look into. It was just a scouting mission.

It was a great surprise when Autie was making his way along the beds, chatting with the fellows of the third floor, to hear someone call out from the row on the other side.

"Well, I'll be a dirty bird—Rosco!"

Autie knew Reynolds's voice immediately and turned around. He couldn't tell which one was Reynolds for all the bandaging, until a hand went up from one of the beds. He went over and pulled up a chair.

"What are you doing here, Reynolds?"

"Just trying to stay above ground, old man. But what about you? One day you were there. Next day you were gone."

"They said they needed me back here."

Reynolds seemed fatigued by the effort of trying to talk the way he always had, and Autie patted his arm to let him know he didn't have to make the effort.

"They put me in an office in Paris."

"Oh," said Reynolds, "an office in Paris. Well, you're never going to get killed that way, Croft. You should have rejected it right away. I know a glorious death was what you were after. Now it's all over, and you missed your chance. Hard luck, old man."

"Well, Reynolds, what happened to you?"

"One of those whiz-bangs got me. Took a piece out of my head—that's what all the wrapping is. You can feel the dent. Put your hand up there."

He took one of Autie's hands and held it to the bandaged side of his head.

"Go ahead. I can't feel a thing up there, but they told me not to press in too much."

There was indeed a depression over Reynolds's right ear, about three inches in diameter. Autie just touched around it to be polite and took his hand away as soon as he could.

"They said they can put a metal plate in there," said Reynolds. "Then I can put a magnet in my helmet and forget about the chin strap. Nobody's said when, so I think they want to see if I'll live before they go to all the trouble. That's still up in the air right now because the whiz-bang also left one of those little shrapnel bits in my heart, believe it or not. But the old ticker keeps going."

"Well, I'll be coming through every day to see about you, Reynolds," Autie said, looking at his watch and standing up to move on. "I'm on the job. I'm your new liaison officer."

"I didn't know we had one," said Reynolds.

"Anything I can bring you?"

"Not right now, but there's one thing you can do since you've got some pull around here. I've been listening to the talk that goes around, and it sounds like some of the men from the outfit are here. Make sure you go see them, will you?"

"Sure thing."

"We were in the line for a hundred and thirty days straight when I got it, and I think they stayed in to the end. See about them, Croft. They're fine men. They did a good job, everything they were supposed to do."

"I'll go find out what's going on. See you tomorrow sometime."

Autie thought he'd make a rule of taking an hour for lunch every day. He bundled up for the January cold and walked around a little, chose a café, and got a table in a corner warmed by the heat coming out of the kitchen. Every time a waiter went in or out, the door swung wide enough to see a pretty girl with a rolling pin working on a pastry board. She was the prettiest girl he had ever seen. He decided to come back every day and try to get the same table. The day walking around the hospital, having a new job, and discovering the prettiest girl in the world sent his hopes flying. The weight of his idleness left him. There was an open sky above. He felt himself rising to it like a great meadow of grass and flowers springing up, weeds and all.

In the afternoon he went looking for the men of his old regiment, and he soon found them in the basement. Only the brick pillars holding up the building interrupted his view from the stairs. For a moment he thought the Western Front had been recreated in the bowels of this hospital for a museum tableau. No beds were to be seen on this half acre of men lying on the dirt floor in rows, some on blankets, some almost stripped of their clothing. There must have been two or three hundred of them. Two lone women in Red Cross smocks and caps were distributing cups of water from jugs they carried, stepping over one man to get to the next. No doctors in sight. No nurses. He was so startled by what he saw that he had to sit down on the step. He let himself be overwhelmed by the stench of blood and sweat and urine and feces and the sounds of pain and buzzing of flies.

These were some of the men he had never taken the trouble to know. But for sure they knew him, as they knew all the white officers. According to Reynolds, they did their duty as soldiers and went beyond. None had spoken against him. His career could have ended in front of a firing squad if they had. Headquarters was always looking to make an example out of somebody. It wasn't the majors and colonels who let him go. It was the pass granted him by the wretches in this cellar. It came over him slowly, with regret and shame, the error he had made in his estimation of these men. His tendency to seek the respect of the wrong people was a different matter, but it was that too.

The life he now enjoyed was in their debt. He had to do something for them, and he made himself sit on the step and take in all the misery of the place until he had an idea that might do the job. When he stood up an hour later, it was with a determination within that he had never felt before and a redemptive appreciation for the three months he had sweated in the office of the SOS.

The next morning Autie walked right by the corporal at the reception desk of the hospital director's office and went through the door. He caught the colonel eating breakfast at a table by the window. Without a salute, presenting orders, or offering his hand, he said, "Armstrong Croft, liaison, GHQ Chaumont."

The colonel got to his feet and took his jacket off the back of the chair.

"You needn't get up," said Autie. "I don't want to interrupt what you were doing."

Once the colonel had his jacket buttoned, he assumed a more confident stance. "MacNeil," he said. "Colonel MacNeil."

"My pleasure, MacNeil." Autie placed the satchel he carried on the colonel's desk. "I'm here to look at your operation."

"I wasn't notified," said Colonel McNeil.

"That is our standard operating procedure."

"May I see your orders, captain?"

"I'm afraid that's not possible, sir. But, of course, I'll see what I can do for you. I realize you have a lot at stake here. Most of the time, inefficiencies and noncompliance simply go unnoticed. Nobody's fault. I understand you are Medical Reserve Corps, not regular army. They might make allowances for that."

Autie stood with his arms behind his back, looking around the room as if he were there to exterminate insects. "I'll need an office and access to hospital records," he said. "We like to talk to the staff and inspect the building and grounds as well. Usually nothing to worry about. We're only interested in reportable infractions."

"I'd like very much to review your findings," the colonel ventured.

"Oh, that's quite impossible, sir," Autie returned. "Once I affix a date and time to a sheet of paper, it falls under the restrictions of document control. No way around it."

Autie and the colonel remained standing throughout the short interview. Autie left the office within a few minutes with assurance from Colonel McNeil that he and the staff would cooperate with the inquiry in every way possible. It was almost too easy. If the fellows at the SOS had been there, Autie was sure they would have made him an honorary corporal.

The first task the next morning was getting through the maze of desks that lay on the first floor in an area that matched the dimensions of the basement below. It spread out before him through the window of his new office. Word must have been sent around because all the heads at the desks went down when he stood at the door.

"Who's got the Negroes?" he said, raising his voice just a little in the quiet that swept over the floor.

A hand shot up right away from the back, and Autie took the most direct path he could see through the maze of desks. Arriving there, after looking side to side at a great many corporals assiduously applying themselves to their work, he quietly leaned over the one who had raised his hand.

"You're in charge of the Negroes?" he asked.

"Yes, sir."

"Well, you've got to get rid of them."

"I don't think I can, sir."

"We want them out of here," Autie said. "They came from a French sector, so send them back to the French."

"I don't have orders, sir."

"Here," said Autie, handing him a script order he made up the night before and signed himself. "Send them over to St. Mary's. I don't want to find any Negroes in the basement tomorrow morning. You're not going to have any trouble matching your batches, are you?"

In the afternoon he had a few drinks with the wounded generals and colonels on the top floor and watched out the window as a fleet of motor ambulances pulled up to the docks at the rear of the hospital. He went down and rode in the first one to St. Mary's and was happy to find he didn't have to go out on a limb again. The French were more than willing to care for the brave and gallant men from Harlem who helped save Paris in the last months and fought so long in the line for France. He watched as doctors, nurses, and nuns spread out through the triage areas and went to work like angels.

Autie visited the ward every week and got to know some of the men well. Often he wished he could do it all over again from the time he got to France, knowing what he knew now. But then he would know who would lose their legs, who would never see again, who would have a foot or an arm taken off, and who would not be going home. He wanted to stay away from sobering thoughts, now that life was picking up for him.

Autie never saw Reynolds again after the first day. He came up to tell him what he did with the men and found the bed occupied by another wounded man. He didn't want to ask what became of Reynolds, and in the weeks that followed, as he got to know which men weren't doing well, he decided that not asking was the best policy. He could see that the war was never going to be over for some men, and he didn't want to be one of them. He was grateful that his own experience had been brief enough to consider unreal if he didn't think too much about it. Not being altogether sure his one day at the war really happened gave him a measure of immunity to the aftereffects, he supposed. That was the best way to get the most out of the experience if he was going to think back on it.

Over the next months, the job at the American hospital quietly mended the rips in the tattered flag of his will to live. In the morning he walked the administration floor unnerving everyone with his clipboard and notes, then through the kitchen and housekeeping just to look around, smiling more because they weren't the people he wanted to unnerve. In the afternoon he walked the wards, keeping company with the wounded, those abed and those ambulatory about the halls in wheelchairs and other devices. It made him feel good when they looked happy to see him come through the door. Raising spirits got to be the best part of the job. After a while, he couldn't help noticing it had the effect of raising his own spirits in the process. Naturally, those poor fellows made him grateful for getting through the war in one piece, but even if the army had a medal for good deeds, he wouldn't take it, selfish motives notwithstanding. There was nothing he had to prove in a place like this.

The day ended with drinks on the fourth floor with the wounded brass, who needed cheering up as much as the men on the floors below. Being everybody's friend wore him out a little, so he dined alone and turned in before ten every night, usually happy enough with the day not to feel too lonely. It was Paris. Dad was sending him plenty of money to live on, and he saw the girl of his dreams every day at lunch.

The pastry girl at the café was a Belgian refugee named Margaux du Pret. She worked mornings at a bakery and afternoons at the café. She was nineteen. Her husband was killed in the first days of the war. She got to Holland while there was a chance to get across the border and had a baby there. She'd been in Paris almost a year. The boy was four years old and played in the back pantry of the kitchen while she worked.

Not all of it made sense. She was married at fifteen? The proprietor of the café, the cook with the big mustache, took another cigarette from Autie, wiped his hands on the dirty apron hanging over his belly, and shrugged his shoulders.

"Give me a light too," he said. "I don't know. She says the boy is three, but I'd judge him to be four. That would make her knocked up at thirteen, am I right? That's young even for the Flemings. Knowing the Boche, you can put two and two together and guess how it happened. I don't know why we didn't let them take Paris when they wanted it. It would have saved everybody a lot of trouble. Like in '71. The Prussians took Paris, gloated over it, and gave it back. I was just a little sprout. My mother fought beside my father on the barricades. We had to kill the animals in the zoo for food, but when we gave up, the Boche just turned around and went home. What's the sense in putting everybody through a war?"

Autie nodded and waited for him to get back on track.

"But she's a pretty little sprig all right, isn't she? Personally, I prefer women with a little more meat on their bones—you've seen my wife—but to each his own, right? She lives up top here. Gets off at four o'clock, takes the brat around the corner for dinner at Josephine's at five—you know they have rats there, don't you?"

Autie fished in his pocket for more hundred-franc notes and gave them to the cook and glanced at the doors to the kitchen.

"Nothing to worry about," said the cook. "When she leaves at four, she never comes back to the kitchen. What else do you want to know, monsieur?"

"Anything you know."

"Well, she speaks English. I heard her once, with a man out front. But she's standoffish. Doesn't talk, doesn't smile. Carts the brat around like a sack of potatoes. But I think she's smart. And there's a good one you should know."

He paused and indicated that he needed a little more money for the good one, so Autie anted up.

"This might be important to you," he said. "She'll have nothing to do with men. And she wants to go to America. Also, she tells stories. Her papers say she's French, but we know she's Belgian. You wouldn't know the difference, but we can tell."

He put both his big hands to his chest and laughed. "She's good with pastry. Not so much with people, so I don't worry about losing her to the competition."

Autie left the kitchen and went through the tables with their chairs turned up and out to the lights and sounds of Paris in the dead of a winter night. He had dropped almost a thousand francs, and he'd have to go looking for cigarettes, but his heart raced with the excitement of the advantage he had attained.

Every day at lunch he caught sight of her through the door to the kitchen, working at the pastry table. All he could see of her was a stern expression of fine features on a smooth white face, short black hair, and thin strong arms with delicate hands, bearing down on the handles of a rolling pin, flinging flour or slapping dough on the wood. Since his first glimpse of her, no other woman in Paris, in the cafés, or passing on the street, caught his eye. She was the girl he had to have. He wanted to see her lift her head and watch the hair fall away from her forehead. He wanted to see her turn her head this way and that way and be close enough to her prettiness to dwell on it and hear the sound of her voice. It wasn't going to be easy to meet her. It had to be the right approach. He didn't want to tip her off and not get another chance. It might not be wise to let her see him at the café where she worked, but changing tables was all he could do about his need to see her every day.

He went over to Josephine's café a few times, a little after five o'clock, to scout. He stood outside smoking a cigarette where he could see most of the floor through the window. She always sat at the same table with the child in her lap. The other chairs at the table filled up with people she never looked at or spoke to except in the smallest interactions. It was going to be tough to engage her. It didn't appear that she mixed well with other people, like an insoluble powder that returns to the bottom of the glass after each stirring. As far as he could tell, she and the boy lived on pancakes.

After a few nights missing a chance to get a seat with her, he had the bright idea to get there an hour early, grab the table and hold down two other chairs with his hat, coat, and scarf. On the night he put his new scheme into action, the place was crowded, and he knew the plan to hold the chairs wouldn't work for very long. He was getting ready to buy off the waiters when suddenly Margaux du Pret, in a brown military overcoat too big for her, holding the child bundled in shawls, stood in the doorway. He was surprised to see how tall she was and how straight she stood when she wasn't working. As fast as the winter air blew in the café door behind her, she was at the table, claiming a chair, just ahead of a young domestic servant girl in cap and tunic and a tradesman of some kind.

Autie struck up a conversation with the tradesman in passable French and brought the servant girl into it with a trivial compliment. Then he successfully involved Margaux to the extent of having the child passed over the table to his own lap, having begged the pleasure of holding a child after a year of hard fighting at the front, away from the endearments of domestic life. There wasn't a word out of her in the transfer, except to say the boy's name was Robbie.

The servant girl stayed for coffee and little fruit tarts. Autie picked up the check for her and placed the little boy in the empty chair, remarking on what a grown-up little man he was. Then he turned to the tradesman with a lively story. Margaux continued eating her pancakes, looking up only to see that Robbie was eating his.

When the check came for the tradesman's dinner, Autie reached for it. One more stranger got in before the dinner crowd thinned out, but he only stayed for a coffee and a pudding. Autie took care of his check too. Then it was just the two of them and Robbie. Margaux followed her pancakes with an order of blood sausage, fried potatoes, vegetable greens, and the same for Robbie. Autie ordered a lobster and oyster platter with everything. She still had not said a word to him, but it looked like throwing money around did the trick. Naturally it would. She didn't have any.

While he played marching silverware with the boy, Autie snuck looks at her. She could easily be nineteen—if that—and would have looked a trifle young to be the governess of the boy in the chair beside her, let alone be the mother. Her black hair was straight and parted down the middle. It fell long in the front, framing her face down to the jaw line, but when she turned her head, he could see the back was short, just cupped over the back of her head and clipped like a man at the neck. Her brown eyes were anchored in the clearest whites he had ever seen. Her nose was prominent but lean, and her lips were full, parting over very white teeth as she brought the last of her pancakes up to them.

And now she was looking at him. Their dinners came, and Autie helped the boy get started. Without looking up, he ventured, "Mademoiselle—"

"I speak English," she said.

"Oh, very good," Autie replied, without turning too much in her direction. "I didn't do so well with French at Princeton."

With the connection established and the boy doing well enough on his own, Autie took up his napkin and silver and bent over his platter.

"Then the war came along," he continued, in the most casual manner as he began working on the lobster. "I joined up before America got in. It came at the right time, really. I was in a fix trying to decide between law school and business. That wasn't the only thing, of course. I've always had an affinity for France. Before the war, I'd come over just to walk around the city. I've been doing some writing, you see—not back then, I mean since the war. A year and a half in the front lines gives you plenty to think about. You must have read about it—not like being there, you know, living through it day after day. That's what I want to communicate, how it really was. I was wounded, but

I'm pretty good now, almost right as rain. Pretty big battle. Didn't think I'd get through. Just luck, I guess. Are you following me? I might be going too fast. Sorry about that, wasn't thinking. It's been so long since I talked to a civilian. I hope I can get over that after so long in the trenches. I'm assigned to Paris now as a liaison officer, so I'll be—"

"What's Princeton?" she asked, looking at him for the first time since he started talking.

"University. Princeton University. It's an Ivy League school. That means it's top flight."

"What part of the country is that in?"

"New Jersey."

"Is that near New York City?"

"Not far. Two hours by train. I'm not sure. My parents keep an apartment there to get away from the country, but I never stay there when I go up. I like the hotels in New York—grand as any I've seen in Europe."

"I thought you were in the trenches."

"Before the war, I mean," he said.

"I want to go to New York City," she said, as if she was alone, talking to herself.

"You'd love it," he said, trying to make it sound as if all she had to do was say the word.

Autie insisted on taking the check and asked her availability for company the following night, same time, same place. To this, she assented once he had introduced himself. When she stood up and took the child in her arms, Autie thought she was just the prettiest thing in the drab wrappings of her clothes—the starched white chemise, the black skirt down to her ankles and the brown overcoat that looked like a French army discard. She looked carefully at him once and went off through a light snow, declining his offer of escort.

After that, there was little need for his informant, the chef, but Autie kept him on retainer anyway. In the meantime, he had dinner with Margaux and Robbie every night at Josephine's until he gave her some money for clothes and moved them to a better restaurant. She looked terrific in new clothes, but Autie attributed the good taste of what she wore to the shop ladies. It was clear that Margaux put no stock in fashion.

"It is a waste of money, these clothes," she said one night when he started asking questions. "Even if they are made well. I understand you have to put them on to come here, but that is a waste of money, too. The expensive places you take me."

"I thought you liked it."

"Why would I turn it down?" She reached for a roll. "You're paying the chef to spy on me, aren't you? The one where I work, I mean. You don't have to make a face. I know about it. How much are you paying him?"

"Five hundred francs."

"For what?"

"For a time," said Autie. "Each time he tells me something."

"Don't waste your money anymore. What has he told you? No, never mind, I don't want to hear his made-up stories."

She went on eating and moving dishes in front of Robbie. It seemed immaterial to her that he had gone behind her back, only that it was a needless expense.

"My father is a baker. We lived in Belgium before the war. My husband, Stefan, was killed when the Germans came. That's all there is to know. I close the door on it."

The only thing she wanted to talk about was America. They walked around the city in the evenings as winter gave way to spring. Robbie rode on Autie's back. It was no trouble winning over the boy, but he had no way of telling about Margaux. If she smiled at all, it was to something going through her head, and she scarcely looked at him. They said good night at the bottom of the stairs up to her door every night, and he never made a move to hold her or kiss her. That did not seem to leave her wondering. Increasingly, he felt that there was very little she wondered about. But sometimes, when she looked at him while they drank coffee and smoked cigarettes in a café, while Robbie drifted off to sleep in his lap, Autie had the feeling her eyes were following cards dealt around a table and she was trying to make out her stake in the game.

One night in midsummer when they were walking along one part of a high cement quay above the Seine, she slipped her arm through his for the first time. They came to a place shadowed by trees where one of the lamps was out. She stopped and turned to him, and they kissed. He was pretty sure she would fall in love with him when she got to know him. She was only nineteen. He didn't know what he wanted at that age either. Anybody could see she was beautiful.

CHAPTER ELEVEN

BELGIUM, JULY 1914

Monsieur DeSmet's clever son-in-law got his hands on a small steamship boiler out of a sunken canal barge. He drove a team of draft horses down the road to Antwerp, got the thing on a sled and had it back in Brasschaet by morning. It sat for a few months behind DeSmet's bakery before he got around to it, but when he did, DeSmet had an outdoor baking oven such as the world had never seen, almost big enough for a man to stand up inside, with vents, flues, and working gauges. Inside the corrugated furnace, baffles kept the outside temperature of the iron hardly warm to the touch, and he added an airflow duct that made it almost smokeless and suppressed the burning of fuel, which for DeSmet had always been rhododendron wood.

In the north of Belgium, where it rained a little almost every day in spring and summer and remained cloudy and cool, the rhododendrons grew as high as trees. They banked the roadsides, divided the fields, and thickened the woods everywhere with their dense branches and fat, sticky leaves. The cut wood cured fast and burned slow and hot, as good as coal, but it was everywhere free for the taking. With the new oven, DeSmet started baking bread for the residents of Cappellen, Merxem, Schooten, and Ekeren. He found he could use the pressure adjustments of the oven to alter the action of the yeast, and he created a texture and taste that made his bread unique and popular. It became a real moneymaking business when he sent a wagon down to Antwerp, and Monsieur DeSmet was on his way to prosperity. At that point, the clever son-in-law took Zurie, DeSmet's older daughter, off to America and excelled as a shipyard ironworker there.

DeSmet made the most of his flourishing business. He added a few tables and chairs out front and started up a little café to get all he could out of the town. Brasschaet was a small village of cobblestone streets and brick houses with thatched roofs and red-and-white painted doors and shutters. At one end of town was a stone Catholic church built eighty years before, and a more recent annex that served as the children's school. At the other end was the gate to an old estate property taken over for taxes and sold to those who farmed the adjacent land. The high gates always stood open since the estate owner moved away and an old lady named Pier lived on a pension in the gatekeeper's house beside it. A few men worked up the road in Cappellen, but most everyone else worked on the farms, at the flour mill, or in the little shops of the village.

Madame DeSmet and her younger daughter, Margaux, tended the shop of the bakery and the café tables. By afternoon, the work in the bakery was done, and Mr. DeSmet sat out with the old men who gathered to drink coffee, smoke, and while away the time with nothing new to talk about until the war started in August of 1914. When he came out to sit with them on the day the Germans crossed the border, he had the newspaper from Cappellen in his hand.

Madame DeSmet, in the room behind the shop, inclined her ear and heard him say, "We've been spared the indignity. The pigs are going for Brussels." Then she turned back to Margaux with her scissors raised.

"No Ma'ma," Margaux said. "I don't want the bangs anymore. I want a part in the middle, and the back cut short. All that in the back can go." She pulled the towel around her neck tight.

"I don't know why you want to look like a boy," said Madame DeSmet. "You don't even have your figure yet, and now people are going to look at you and wonder what you are."

"I don't care. I'm tired of my hair making me look like a child."

"You're thirteen, darling—all right, fourteen, by a month. That's still thirteen. But don't be surprised if people treat you like a strange boy."

"Why should I worry about that?"

Madame DeSmet sighed and went around the back. It had been so easy to cut it straight across at the neck. She didn't welcome the difficulty of what to do about the underneath. It was very thick and dark, with a little curling.

"And don't just hack away at it, Ma'ma. Cut a little and step back and look."

"Well, if you want it short like a boy, there's nothing to keep even."

"The sides, Ma'ma. They have to be even. And I want them short too. And don't do too much on one side before you look at the other side."

Madame DeSmet sighed and ran her long fingers through her daughter's hair with an adoring and regretful sadness. "It's such a shame to take this off, darling. It's so lovely," she said.

"Ma'ma—do you want me to go to Pier?"

"No, no. I'll do it. I couldn't bear to see her sweep it up off the floor and put it in the dustbin. I'll save it in a box."

The haircut turned out good enough, and at first Margaux was pleased. She had been reading the newspapers; her idea was to dress as a boy and go into the army like her brothers. That night she stole into their rooms and tried on some of the clothes in the drawers. In the mirror, she saw that she could never pass for a boy. It had nothing to do with her hair. She had a girl's shape of face and eyes, delicate chin and jaw, and a girl's lips. There was nothing to be done about the girl body either. Her frame was slight and her arms and hands, though very strong, betrayed no visible musculature despite the hours in the bakery with the rolling pin. Margaux saw very plainly that she could sooner pass for a lady who did no work than a farm boy leaving plow and shovel to take up arms for Belgium.

So Margaux bitterly gave up the idea of soldiering and went along with a commitment to another year with the Jesuits at Our Lady. They took a few girls every term but mostly the sons of wealthy farmers. Because of the new oven, Monsieur DeSmet was rich enough, and by temperament ostentatious enough, to send her to the school. Margaux loved classes and lectures, but school made her days very long. She went to school from ten to four after work at the bakery, which began at four o'clock in the morning. It would be three or four more years before she would take exams for the university, but the Jesuits seemed to be impressed with her grasp of mathematics and the sciences. Philosophy was difficult for her because she saw everything in black and white, having no patience for wasteful thinking that was of no practical use, pointless, futile, or moot. The Jesuit fathers might have suspected religion to be at the top of that list, but they told Monsieur DeSmet he should start putting away his money for the university at Louvain.

Margaux had a boyfriend, Guizot, who got off at four o'clock from the mill, where he stitched flour bags on a machine and filled them. He was going into his father's grocery business when the time came, and Madam DeSmet thought it would be a good match for Margaux, until her husband got rich in the bakery and talked her out of thinking so small. Guizot waited every day outside Our Lady for Margaux to get out of school and walked her home. There were duties she had with the oven, so he followed her out to the shed. After she closed the wooden doors, she let him kiss her. Two times was the limit. The first one was plain. For the second, he was allowed to put his arms around her. If he pressed his body up against her, she pushed him away and said, "That's all, Guizot."

By October the King and the remnants of the Belgian Army, after their heroic stand on the Yser, held only the northwest corner of the country. The rest of Belgium fell to the Germans and became an occupied country.

"We're in for it now," said Monsieur DeSmet to his table of old men outside the bakery. "We should have let them through."

"No no, DeSmet," said one. "Of course we had to fight."

"Maybe so, but now the pig bastards are going to punish us. They're in Antwerp now. And they'll be up here too, doing what they did down south. They're going to take your horses, Albert. You can count on that. And there's nowhere to hide anything that's worth a centime to people in the countryside. How are you going to hide the grain harvest from these thieving swine?"

"Well, that's just it, DeSmet. We can always grow more. We should be glad we're not in the city. They're not going to have any food there this winter."

"No, it's just the opposite," said Monsieur DeSmet. "The Germans can't let a whole city of people starve. It would look bad on them. No one cares about us out here."

Within the week, the first Germans appeared in Brasschaet. A motorcar with an officer and a couple of enlisted men came bumping down the cobblestone street. They nailed handbill proclamations in French, Flemish, and German on every other house stating that removal of any notice would be punishable by imprisonment of everyone in the household. There were going to be assessments and requisitions. The village was too small to have a mayor, so there was no one to make an official complaint.

When the Germans started over toward DeSmet's café, the old men cleared out fast, and Madame DeSmet sent Margaux to the oven shed and told her to stay there. Between a little French and a little German, Monsieur DeSmet fawned over the men in field gray at his tables and got no money for his best wares. They stayed, eating up everything in the shop, drinking all the coffee and smoking their pipes, until a column of twenty or more wagons came into the village. The officer and men got back in the car to lead them around. In a few hours the wagons were full of flour from the mill, with a string of cattle behind each wagon, hogs, geese, chickens, and anything from the shops that appealed to them. DeSmet saw Albert's horses on their way out of town, and later found out that Albert and some other farmers he knew had been shot dead. He had heard an occasional rifle shot outside of town and had already guessed the worst.

The next Germans, who came to Brasschaet a week later, knew nothing of the first party. They were young conscripts and old men, twelve of them, dropped off in the middle of the village by a motor truck. The highest rank among them was a sergeant, who formed them up in a line, got them to attention, and made a little inspection walk around them. They had rifles and full packs and bayonets hanging from their belts. But despite the military equipage, they were all either too fat or too spindly to pose a real threat and made such ungainly soldiers that no one was scared into their houses. The grocer came out of his shop to look at them. Then the supply store man. Then the shoemaker and the tavern keeper, and then Monsieur DeSmet. They all came over to find out what was going on. While the sergeant talked with them in Flemish, the soldiers relaxed on their rifles and smiled around at everyone.

This was the garrison for Brasschaet. The sergeant explained that they were sent to guard the mill warehouse against black-market profiteers and the franc-tireurs. The men were to be posted on shifts twenty-four hours a day, beginning immediately, and they were to continue for the remainder of the harvest. At least until then they would be quartered in the village, meals included. Before the little crowd that had gathered around him could say anything about it, the sergeant began assigning his men to houses along the street.

"You—there. You—there. You—there," he ordered.

The men fell out right away, and those citizens who had their house pointed at hurried in tow behind their man. Considering the first group that came through, DeSmet thought this bunch wasn't so bad. If they could get through the war with these old men and boys, they could count themselves lucky. He caught up to the young man heading for the bakery and introduced himself. The boy said he was Lance Corporal Stefan Deutche from Grafhaven in southern Germany, and that he was sorry for all this. He spoke perfect Flemish.

"Not at all," said Monsieur DeSmet. "Not at all. We're happy to have you. I mean, I know you would have wanted to stay in your own country doing what you were doing and not get yanked out to a different country."

"I was at university," said the young man.

"Well then, we're glad to host a man with an education."

"Everyone was enlisting—"

"I know," said DeSmet as they got to the café tables and the door of the bakery. "Of course, you're patriotic—as any good man would be. Alles fur

Deutschland, eh? Ha Ha." Coming to the door and holding it open for him, he said, "Louise, this is Corporal Deutche."

The corporal removed his hat and gave a little bow to Madam DeSmet, who was standing behind the glass display counter.

"The corporal will be quartered with us for the time being. We can put him in Ernesto's room. Doesn't he remind you of Ernesto?"

Seeing that Madame DeSmet looked confused by the word quartered, the corporal proposed that he leave them alone for Monsieur DeSmet to explain what he had heard from the sergeant, while he made an inspection of the premises, which he was obliged to do. He suggested they might like to wait outside at the café tables.

The corporal went upstairs first and looked into each of the four little bedrooms under the eves of the thatched roof. Then he toured the drawing room and went through the kitchen. The oven was stone cold, strange for a bakery. He went around back and guessed that the working oven was in the shed. There was a girl and boy in there kissing, and he quickly said, "Oh, I'm sorry. Excuse me," and closed the door.

When he came out to the café, he said the oven was a work of art.

"My son-in-law made it," said Monsieur DeSmet. "He's in America now, building ships. The oven, as you can see, has great capacity. It can feed a lot of people, and that's why I have to be sure to get enough flour. Here, sit down. You see I bake for a lot of people, not just this little village. My bread is counted on in the towns around here and in Antwerp too. They depend on it, you see."

"I'm sure they'll make allowance for you, Monsieur DeSmet."

The girl was at the door. "What's going on, Papa?" she said.

"Oh," said Monsieur DeSmet, "this is my youngest, Margaux. Corporal Deutche will be staying with us for a while. They're quartering a garrison with us to guard the mill."

"Please call me Stefan," said Corporal Deutche.

"That's good. Then you must call us Emile and Louise."

Margaux sat down with them across from the corporal. She was sorry he caught her with Guizot. He had very light blue eyes and blond hair clipped close at the sides, with a wave on top. The fine bones of the cheek and jaw line stood out as he talked or took a bite of cake. Margaux glanced rapidly up and down at Stefan Deutche. All of a sudden, Guizot looked like an oafish brute. She made up her mind not to have anything more to do with Guizot.

Presently, a slip of paper was delivered to Stefan by one of the little boys of the village.

"It's my orders," Stefan said, giving it a quick look. Then he paused to read, and said, "That's good. Regular day shift. 10 a.m. to 6 p.m. Four men on each shift, round the clock. But I have to start right now."

"Then you'll be back for dinner?" said Madam DeSmet.

"If the next shift comes in on time," he laughed. Then he became apologetic and said, "I'm so sorry to impose upon you like this."

"Think nothing of it," said Monsieur DeSmet. "We're going to enjoy having such a nice young man here."

Guizot was standing across the street when Margaux got out of her Jesuit class the next day. He came over to walk her home, but she turned the other way, and he had to catch up with her.

"Where are you going?"

"Nowhere," she said.

"All right, I'll go too."

"No, I don't want you along."

"Why not?"

"Just because," she said.

"Give me your books."

"I don't want you to carry them."

"What's wrong with you?"

"Nothing," she said. "I just changed my mind. I don't want to walk home with you anymore."

"Why?"

"Just because." She kept walking, holding her books tightly so he wouldn't try to grab them away.

He stopped and let her go on. He shouted after her, "You're a stupid girl. You know that?"

That finished it with Guizot.

Margaux came to the mill. She pretended she had a pebble in her boot and sat down on a bench across from the big wooden warehouse. She took a very long time to undo the laces, and finally Stefan came around the corner in his forage cap, with his rifle over his shoulder. She pretended she didn't see him, so he came over.

"Got something in your shoe?"

"Yes," she said.

She stretched out her leg and let him take the little boot off her foot. He turned it over and tapped it against the butt of his rifle.

"Nothing there," he said. "Maybe it's a callus. Let me see your foot."

Margaux withdrew her foot right away and put it back into the boot. "That would be indecent," she said.

"It's all right. I'm almost a doctor," he said. "In two more years anyway. I was in medical study at university. I've already done anatomy and seen dissections on cadavers. Won't you let me take a look?"

"What's a cadaver?" she asked.

"That's a dead person. You open them up and you can tell how they died."

If anything, that made Margaux less likely to give him her foot. She noticed the other three Germans had stopped marching around and were looking at them from the warehouse door, joking around.

"No, everyone is looking at us," she said.

"All right then. Suit yourself."

Stefan went down on one knee and took up the laces of her boot. That was just as bad as putting the foot in his hands. She looked around to see if anyone but the three Germans saw it, and then Stefan was standing up again, looking down at her.

"What are you studying?" he asked.

Margaux put a hand on her books and said, "Mathematics, chemistry, Latin, philosophy, and this term I'm taking English. I want to go to America."

"So do I," he said, with a smile brightening his face. "We can speak English together." Then he went on in very good English, at least as it sounded to her. All she caught was that he had to go.

"I don't know enough yet," she said. "You said you have to go?"

"The sergeant comes around every so often."

Before he left to go back to marching around the warehouse, he said very sincerely, "I hope I didn't embarrass you."

"It was only your friends," she said.

"No, I mean in the shed."

"Oh that," she said. "It's over with him."

In the next few weeks, the chestnuts were coming down, and Stefan went out to the woods after dinner with Margaux while there was still enough light to collect them. They talked all the while, tossing chestnuts into large shoulder-strap baskets over their shoulders. Stefan said when the war was over he wanted to complete his medical training and emigrate to America. He had an older brother who had gone to New York City to become an artist who said it was fantastic and exciting there. One evening, a thunderstorm came up, and they ran to an old lean-to woodshed. They were very wet when they got to it and out of breath from the run, but all at once they were kissing. It was nothing like kissing Guizot.

It was worrisome to Madame DeSmet how many evenings the two went out to the woods for chestnuts, and how few they brought back. Something was going on, but Monsieur DeSmet saw the advantage in it.

"Let it go, Louise," he said when they talked quietly in the bedroom. "But don't let her get ideas. With the rationing, we're going to need that pig bastard's help."

"I don't see that he can do anything for us," she said. "He's only a corporal."

"A corporal who guards the warehouse."

"I don't know what you mean by that."

"Well, he can take a little flour out once in a while."

"Oh, Emile. That's dangerous."

"No one would miss a bag or two, Louise," he said. "It's every man for himself now. Just keep her on a string. Don't let anything go too far."

In the lean-to, Margaux and Stefan sat together with their legs hanging over the edge and talked. Since they kissed and held each other, Margaux felt free to ask him medical questions that had begun to come into her mind. He addressed them easily from his medical studies. The explanations sounded crazy to Margaux sometimes, but he said they were true.

When the ruse of the chestnuts played out, they just went for walks in the evening with consent of the parents and without the shoulder-strap baskets. They always ended up in the lean-to. Sometimes they used up all the time they had, lying on their backs with their legs up in the air, just talking.

"You must be pleased with yourself, to know everything," she said.

"Nobody can know everything," he said, smiling.

There was a squirrel on a tree stump off the lean-to, sitting up on his hind legs.

"He hasn't moved since we lay down," she said. "How can he do that?"

"I don't know. Particulars of anatomy."

"Does he recognize us? Does he think like all other squirrels?"

"Don't ask me," said Stefan. "I don't know anything about squirrels. See what I mean? You can't know everything."

"Then what's the point of knowing anything?"

"Well, you satisfy your own curiosity," he said.

"What if you want to know everything?"

"Then you're going to be disappointed."

"Don't laugh at me," she said.

"I only meant you're going to be learning all your life."

"That would be a good way to live."

She put both hands to his face. Her eyes looked into his, and she wanted to jump off a cliff holding hands with him. She understood wanting to be one with another person forever and have there be no other people in the world but the two of them. She felt herself beginning to understand philosophy and decided to love him until the end of time. She kissed him and lay down again.

"At school last term, they had two days for the boys only," she said. "No girls were allowed. That's why I ask so many questions."

It was getting colder in the evenings, and she had smuggled a blanket out of the house for the lean-to. She put it over them, and they huddled together under it.

"I bet it was about girls," she said. "They don't have that for girls about boys. Why don't they want girls to know anything?"

"I don't know," said Stefan.

"Do you know about girls?"

"All about them," he said confidently.

"Then tell me. About boys, too."

"What do you want to know?"

"Just tell me everything," she said. "I don't want any fairy stories either."

Stefan explained how everything worked to Margaux the next night, using the proper names. He explained all about the cycle she had recently started. That cleared up another mystery.

"Zurie told me, but she had it all wrong. So did Ma'ma. She said to come to her right away when it started. It's so stupid, Stefan. No one explained it right."

"It's not their fault," he said. "It might never have been properly explained to them either."

"You shouldn't have to go to university to know simple things like that," said Margaux angrily. "That's just stupid."

She lay on her back looking up at the bare rafters and roof above.

"I want us to do that," she said.

"It's not advisable until you're married, Margaux."

"That's stupid," she said. "Having to get married to do a perfectly natural thing that lovers do. And anyway, who would I want to marry but you?"

"You don't want to have a baby at fourteen."

"I would be fifteen if we did it now."

"No, that's too young."

"We can do it when I'm not fertile. Wouldn't that work?"

"Theoretically."

"I'll tell you when," she said. "I'll count days, and you can check my arithmetic."

A few weeks went by. On the night she chose, Stefan still said they really shouldn't. Margaux went to the back of the lean-to and started taking off her clothes anyway. She stood up naked in front of him and said, "Well?" Then he came over and they did it.

When it was over, she was angry because it hurt so much.

"I'm not going to America with you," she said bitterly. She tried to push him away, but he held her tightly.

"It's like that the first time," he said.

"No, Stefan. It shouldn't be," she said, without losing any of her anger, but suddenly thinking of it as a failed experiment. "We must have done it wrong."

"No, it was correctly done," he said. "You're really too young to be doing it."

Now she was just angry at herself.

"Then we'll do it again," she said. "Tomorrow night. Then it won't be the first time."

Margaux made him yield to her insistence on eliminating the first variable before she would concede the other. She said then she could wait until she was older to make it a regular thing they would do. The next night was better, and Margaux agreed to marry him and go to America. Whenever her mind slipped into the tedium of the bakery and school, she reminded herself that she had a lover, and it made her feel very happy.

Monsieur DeSmet was very solicitous toward Stefan that fall when the rationing of flour got severe. Every month the German sapper trucks came through the village, took their allotment from the warehouse, and then went through every house and shop in the village taking anything they wanted. There wasn't a chicken or hog left for miles around.

"You can get shot if you protest," said Monsieur DeSmet at the dinner table one night. "Listen, Stefan. Is there any way you can get a fifty-pound bag out of the warehouse for us?"

"Oh, Emile. They measure it out in ounces now."

"I wouldn't ask. You know I wouldn't ask, but people around here are starting to have a bad time of it. Winter is around the corner, and some people have nothing put up. You know I'll give the bread away. It's not like the black market. We won't make money on it. You're guarding it against the black market, so it wouldn't technically be a dereliction of duty."

Stefan was polite, but he had to laugh. "I don't think an attorney would be allowed to make a case like that, Emile. The only question would be, do we shoot him before breakfast or after lunch?"

Papa laughed too. "I know, I know. But maybe you can figure out a way without taking a big chance. Just think about it. I know you don't want anyone starving to death around here." Then he laughed and held up one of Margaux's slender arms and said, "Look how thin she's getting."

Margaux could have died of shame on seeing her father work on Stefan that way. He put her on a hook like a worm and dangled her in front of Stefan. Whenever she took him to task for it in the bakery, where they worked alone in silence most mornings, he insisted it was perfectly innocent. At times she felt as much in a corner as Stefan because there was no one she could talk to about having a German lover. That would have to wait for the end of the war or if they could run away to America.

It got worse with the Germans that winter. When the trucks came up from Antwerp again, they took all the food away, leaving only the supplies from the commune that could be accounted for with ration cards. There were rumors that the Germans were going to deport men to Germany as forced labor, and several young men in the village went into hiding. In February, the DeSmets heard that Guizot had been shot and killed trying for the Dutch border.

Stefan came up with a plan. He said on his inspection through the warehouse he could move a bag off the pile to a back room by a little window he could leave unlocked. He thought he could wrestle it through from the outside when he walked the back of the building. Then he could roll it into the dry creek bed and cover it with brush. At night, he and Monsieur DeSmet could walk the bag down the creek bed to where the ravine came out behind the bakery. They carried out the plan one night and got away with it. At the table late that night they were like a couple of conspirators. Margaux and her mother were deeply frightened. It worked so well it seemed easy to do again.

"We won't get caught," said Monsieur DeSmet. "It's too good a plan." Then he leaned over the table to shake Stefan's hand and pat him on the back.

Margaux's fears were only assuaged by imagining the good feelings she witnessed would be repeated when Stefan asked for her hand in marriage. Stefan said he was going to talk to her father if new orders came for him to leave Brasschaet. Then the plan was to desert the army and get to America. He said he had someone in Antwerp who had connections with the American food relief. They had safe conduct through the lines and might be able to sneak them through to Holland.

There were some tense moments, but Stefan got another bag of flour out for Monsieur DeSmet during the winter. No change of orders came before early spring, when farm operations would bear watching again, so it looked like life could go on as it was with the same garrison.

Then Margaux got in trouble. Stefan said it was time to activate the plan to run away to America. Margaux tried to hide her situation, but something caught her mother's eye one day when they were hanging the wash. She came over and put a hand on Margaux's stomach. Her face turned deathly pale.

"I know what it is, Ma'ma," she said. "Stefan is going to talk to Papa. We're going to get married in America. He has a way to do it. Don't say anything. Stefan is going to talk to Papa. Do you hear me?" She shook her mother by the shoulders and said it again.

Her mother turned her face up to her as if coming out of a trance and nodded her head.

That night after dinner Margaux took her mother out walking, leaving Stefan to talk to Papa. They walked around the cobblestone streets for over an hour. Her mother kept asking if it was enough time, as her feet were getting sore. When they got home there was no one in the dining room. The dishes were all there, and the coffee cups at Papa and Stefan's places were half full. But nothing looked like it had been kicked over in a rage, so that was a relief. Ma'ma slumped onto the couch in the sitting room and took off her shoes. Margaux didn't want to call out. She went looking around through the dark kitchen and bakery and out the back door. There was a light in the shed. As she opened the door, her father was in front of the oven and going for something on the floor. She cried out when she recognized Stefan's forage cap. Papa stood up and tossed it in the oven and closed the door fast. Margaux shouted, "Papa, no! That's Stefan's hat," and rushed to the door. The oven was going full blast and there was no hope for the hat, but then she saw the white bones of human fingers and a skull blackening in the flames. She collapsed to the floor.

"What have you done? What have you done?" She tried to stand up. "What have you done to my lover?"

Her father yanked her to her feet.

"Your what? You don't have a lover. You don't know what that means. You think I'd let you go off with a Boche?"

Margaux banged her head against the cast iron of the oven as she cried and fell to the floor. Ma'ma came in and rushed to her.

"Ask Papa what he's done," she cried. "Ask him, ask him."

"One less Boche," said Monsieur DeSmet to his wife.

CHAPTER TWELVE

Late that night, Monsieur DeSmet took Stefan's helmet, rifle, and ammunition belt out to the woods and threw them in the deepest part of the canal. He came back and waited in the shed for the oven to cool so he could crush up the bones. In the morning he went over to the grocery and told the sergeant that he discovered Stefan missing. He said he had heard him talking about deserting to the French, but he didn't think much about it at the time.

Margaux cried in her bed for two days. She was horror-struck by what her father had done. She would never be able to look at him again. Her mother sat by her. It was a situation she was unable to fathom, but she stayed with Margaux and would not look at her husband. On the second night, Margaux and her mother crept down the stairs, took a little money from the till in the bakery and walked eight kilometers to Cappellen in the dark. They sat on the doorstep of Madame DeSmet's sister and her family until morning.

They were going to stay there, but after a night, Margaux cleared her head enough to realize she had put her mother in an impossible situation. She wrote her a note that said she forgave her father, but could never go back to him. She urged her to return to Brasschaet because he needed her. Margaux thought that would show her mother that she was old enough to understand marriage.

Then she got out of the house after everyone had gone to sleep. They might look for her going to Antwerp, so she swung east and headed south toward Brussels. She didn't know how she was going to do it, but she was going to get to America. That was the only thought she permitted herself as she walked the dark road bordered with the tall rhododendrons that burned so hot when they were cut down and dried.

It was easy enough to find work in Brussels with so many men gone. She told a friendly looking baker what she could do and showed him how easily she worked with dough. His pleasant little wife came in and pulled him aside for a little talk. Then he hired her. They put her up in a little room in the house. She told them the whole story of where she came from, except for the baby, but the wife had already guessed.

Margaux stayed in Brussels for the next three years. She had the baby with the baker's wife and a midwife attending. She didn't know what to think of the baby. One part of her loved the boy because he was Stefan's. Another part of her hated him for ruining their plan. It was not his fault, but he was the reason Stefan was dead. She named him Robbie and had to nurse him for a long time because there wasn't much food around that a baby could eat. The Germans patrolled everywhere in the city and were always shooting people for no reason. The baker was easygoing with the Germans and gave the regular bunch free coffee and cakes. But he always raised his elbow to them when they turned around. Then he looked over his shoulder at Margaux and made her laugh.

The baker knew a printer who was licensed to print ration and identity cards. In his spare time, he forged documents of all kinds. As he put it, under the occupation, every patriotic Belgian became a criminal. Even parish priests smuggled, stole from the occupiers, and passed messages. They were all in the same boat. The forger made Margaux a set of papers that showed her to be Margaux du Pret, widow of Stefan du Pret and mother of Robert du Pret, all of French nationality.

When the war finally ended and she could take her next step toward America, Margaux said goodbye to the baker and his wife with tears in her eyes. Their kindness to her made it hard to leave, but what could she say of human kindness? It was like the bits of grass that grow between stones in the city. Maybe there was a little of it everywhere, just because grass was.

Margaux made her way to Paris with Robbie. She had a little money, but it was costly to raise a child. He began to look like Stefan, and that was hard to bear. Sometimes she thought wanting to go to America with Stefan was part of the past she should forget, but it was the only part of her that wanted to live, to keep Stefan alive within her. After Robbie was born, it entered her mind to find Stefan's brother in New York City and give the boy to him. Then she would be free to follow Stefan into death. Whenever she found a safe place with food and was able to rest and think, her thoughts argued back and forth between living and dying. At times, the aspect of one seemed as narrow to her as the other.

It took a month to get herself and Robbie to Paris, and it used up most of the money she had saved. She took a job at a bakery. When she got established there and in a room near it, she went out looking for more work and found a café that needed a pastry chef in the afternoon. The sign out front said a room over the shop went with the job. She convinced the owner that she could pick up French pastry in no time and would work at half scale until she did. That got her the job and the free room.

The baker was full of questions every day, and she didn't like it. This time she didn't want to tell her story to anyone. She wanted to be unknown. It put her in a corner sometimes. When he asked too many questions, she felt she had the right to lie. Soon she got the feeling that the baker wasn't asking just for his own curiosity. When the door to the kitchen swung open to the café, she began to notice the same American soldier at the same table every day having lunch. Margaux thought it must be him asking the baker about her. Then the American turned up at Josephine's at five o'clock, sitting at the table she liked, and she knew it was no coincidence.

He wasn't bad-looking, but he was an idiot. He threw money around and made a big show of himself. Stefan wasn't like that. She took the American's money for dinner the first night because everybody at the table was doing it. She took advantage and got good food. He said his family held properties. He said something that showed he knew she was Belgian—his only mistake, but she pretended not to notice. It would take time to tell if this was too good to be true. He made a date for dinner again.

The dinners went on through the winter and into spring. He talked too much. He went on about silly things, always trying to impress her with money. The money did not seem to have an end to it; they went to better restaurants and cafés, and it never ran out. He gave her more money than she could possibly spend for clothes. He had no idea what anything cost. He was always showing off what a good father he would make for Robbie. She didn't mind when the boy left her side and ran to him when he came to the door. It relieved her of both of them for a while.

Months had gone by without him making the advances she would have expected from a man. After so much time courting her favor, it only lowered her respect for him that he had not made a pass. The best that could be thought was that he might have bigger ideas in mind. But he didn't look smart enough to be following a plan.

To exonerate her conscience, in the event that this campaign of his came to a proposal of marriage, Margaux resolved never to be dishonest with him. She wanted to be able to say she never gave him incorrect expectations or an incomplete view of her character. But nothing she said put him off the track. One night, lying in bed with Robbie asleep beside her, she made up her mind. All she needed to know about this Armstrong Croft was right there in front of her. He might be hiding the tip of his true nature, but the iceberg was plain to see. He was a showoff and a phony. He said he had been to the war, but there was no sign that he had ever experienced an event in his life that had had any effect on his adolescent frame of mind. The world still looked like a child's playground to him. All he had learned was it took money to keep the carousel going around. If she married him, she would stand outside the fence and watch him go up and down on the painted horses.

She knew a husband like Autie Croft would do whatever she wanted. It was only deciding to be with a man again after Stefan that she deliberated. She was nineteen years old. How could she live another fifty or sixty years without a man? There was no man who had attracted her since Stefan. There was no possibility of happiness again after Stefan. But if she wasn't going to follow Stefan yet, at least for the sake of the child, she had to live, didn't she? And didn't a woman need a man to live? One man was as good as another as far as that went.

The next night after dinner, Margaux made Robbie walk by himself all the way back to the café to tire him out. They left Robbie in the room, and they went to the river. She let him kiss her without a disturbance of conscience. If it was entrapment, it was him, caught in his own trap.

CHAPTER THIRTEEN

In a matter of a few days, Margaux left her two jobs and the room and moved into a bridal suite at the Hotel Majestic, considered to be the best in Paris. A nurse provided by the hotel kept Robbie occupied while they went to town hall for the license and then for a civil ceremony. Autie wore his uniform and Margaux a simple white dress. They came back to the hotel for dinner.

It looked like this was the first time for her husband. He was nervous and distracted all through the meal. They finally got to coffee. It was no use. He was so preoccupied all he could do was smoke one cigarette after another and look all over the restaurant, and she got fed up with it. She had him call for the check, and they went up to the room. The nurse was staying over for the night with Robbie.

"You have to go out and get a skin," she said, pushing him away when he put his arms around her.

"It's late," he said. "I don't think there's anything open."

"I don't want a baby. Maybe the hotel has them. Go down and ask at the desk."

He put his jacket back on and went out. Margaux did not have long to wait. When he returned, she got undressed and turned down the covers of the bed. Then she drew the curtains, pausing to look out the window at the lights of Paris many floors below, not thinking of anything in particular. Stefan was so different from this man.

He was out of his clothes when she turned around, sitting on the side of the bed trying to get the skin on right. He had no experience. He was fumbling all over. She knelt at his feet and helped him with it, but the minute she had her hands on him he lost control of himself. She stood up, got into bed, and reached for the light on the nightstand.

"Good night," she said. "There's no shame. We'll do it tomorrow." She moved far over to one side of the bed to sleep. She didn't think he would bother her. He could hold her to the promises she had made that morning in town hall, and the living part of her would go along. But the part of her that was promised to death could not, as far as the dead were able to make promises back to the living. She had been trying to tell him all along, in so many words.

She should have thrown herself into the oven that night. Why didn't she think of it? But Papa would have stopped her and never let her out of his sight after that. Her husband was so far from knowing about her. The day would come when he would get far enough to think he had made a mistake marrying her, and that would be all he would ever understand about it.

The next morning they had breakfast in the hotel restaurant without looking at each other. Autie had to take care of a few things at the hospital and then go across town to the travel office to finalize arrangements for their wedding trip to the Alps. He wanted to have Robbie along on the trip, but Margaux told him it would be inconvenient, so Robbie would be staying in the hotel with the nurse. Margaux lay down to rest while Autie was gone, and the nurse took Robbie out for a walk.

Autie came back to their suite at seven o'clock with brochures, tickets, and vouchers. Looking them over, Margaux began to see that there was a world beyond how far she could walk with a baby and a bundle, and her husband had money to go there. From the way he talked about these places, it was clear he had no other resource but money to deal with the boredom and idleness at the core of him. On the table before her were glossy brochures with painted photographs of mountains in snow and villages in verdant valleys, exquisite wooden lodges, bright fireplaces, and good-looking blond people in heavy sweaters skiing and drinking hot beverages.

But Margaux could tell he would not be himself until he felt better about the night before, so she kissed him and started undoing the buttons of his uniform. It made all the difference and got him back to the way he was before. Then they went downstairs for a late dinner. He was very excited about the trip and talked a lot. He left a stupidly large tip for the waiter. That night she let him sleep with an arm and a leg over her. She wondered how much more there was to the man than this. He was nothing like Stefan. She had to wonder what it would do to her to be with this man a long time without learning anything.

The Alps were beautiful. They went to Italy next. Then England, Ireland, and Scotland. To account for the first months of their marriage, they could have drawn little pictures of themselves into the brochure photographs of mountains, beaches, cathedrals, and dinners overlooking famous rivers. When Margaux asked about his job at the hospital, he always said they didn't need him right now, so she didn't ask anymore. They went to Norway and Greece. He always wanted intercourse with her, and she went along with it. He was unimaginative in lovemaking, so it never took very long. All he had to do was look at her face and he was finished. She finally said, "Then don't look at my face." He laughed. She almost found it funny too, but she did not want to change for a man like him or sacrifice the one happiness she ever had to the silliness of the life they were leading.

Robbie stayed in the Hotel Majestic with the hotel nurse while they were gone. When they got back, Autie hired a German refugee to be his governess, a young woman named Gretchen. They signed a year's lease on a master suite with servant quarters for one, a spacious living room, a little kitchen, and a study. It was ridiculously expensive but it suited Margaux. Autie would have preferred a house, but Margaux didn't want to cook or housekeep. It was only going to be a year before they left for America anyway. Robbie started at a French school and went in a cab every day with Gretchen. He spoke French with Margaux, German with Gretchen, and English with Autie. He had very blond hair and blue eyes and was turning out to be a solid little boy. Gretchen was dressing Robbie in his little school uniform when Margaux came in one day. "He looks very German, doesn't he?" Gretchen said with delight.

It was the first time it occurred to Margaux that someday Robbie would be twenty years old and look like Stefan when she had known him alive. She would be thirty-five then. It made her aware of a changing age difference, established upon Stefan's death, that would continue to increase until the day she died. When she was eighty, Stefan would still be twenty. The books she bought said the same value added to both sides of an inequality will preserve the inequality. Did that also mathematically prove that a wrong could never be set right? The marriage was new, and they were going to America. Those were the unknown variables. Stefan remained the only constant. That was fitting. He could have explained it so easily. Confusion was hard to bear.

By the spring of 1920, the State Department had finally approved Margaux's citizenship and issued her a passport. It seemed there was a big business in war brides that year. They were ready to leave for America. Autie would still have two more years in the army, but he told Margaux his father had arranged a transfer to the States. It came with an indeterminate leave before reassignment to active duty. He was informed that could mean up to four months while the army decided what to do with him. The hospital had cleared out, and the last returning regiment had paraded through New York several months earlier. Mention of the war had fallen out of the US newspapers.

It was an easy crossing from Le Havre. Autie and Robbie roamed the decks of the giant liner RMS *Olympic* in pleasant weather all the way to New York. There was a wealthy land baron cowboy on board who taught Autie and Robbie how to lasso, and the three became great friends. Gretchen, relieved of duty by the attention Autie gave the boy, played shuffleboard with a pack of single ladies. Margaux sat in a deck chair reading mathematics books she had brought along. At night she went up to the top forward deck to look at the stars and smell the ocean. Autie caught her one night leaning against the railing with a young university man. They were smoking and speaking in French with their heads together over the rail.

Margaux had never seen jealousy before in her husband. It obviously came from his inflated egotism, which she had no desire to bow down to. He didn't raise a storm with her. It was the kind of jealousy that sulked and went off by itself, wanting to be sought, but it would get no help from her. She let his sulking jealousy come back and knock at the door when it was ready to be forthright.

"Why would I want another man?" she said.

She told him she was only interested in other men intellectually, and because she was married, there was nothing for him to be concerned about. She said she was only interested in one man otherwise, and felt that was a very true thing to say.

What was she going to do on an estate in the country? What was the family like? Did they want her to work on the farm? Did they want her for the kitchen? She never wanted to see a kitchen again, let alone cook for this man. They must have servants and a cook if there was so much money. How would she learn to order servants around? Realizing there could be no answers until she was there, Margaux put the questions aside. She turned her face into the wind and watched the waves of the Atlantic Ocean part so briefly for the ship and come back together as if they had swallowed it up.

She found out from talking to an ensign from the chart room that they had just crossed the position last reported by the *Titanic* eight years ago but a day. She had sense enough not to raise the topic at dinner, but she imagined her dining companions with lifejackets over their gowns and dinner jackets. She stayed out late on the deck that night. The ocean looked so cold. It had no personal interest in how people died. It let their bodies sink to a floor built up by the shells, bones, and spines of ancient creatures. No one could see to the bottom any more than one could see the last destination of rising smoke.

A man named Flo Ziegfeld sat beside Margaux at the captain's table on the last night of the voyage. He was about her husband's age, and well dressed. His face was rounded everywhere that Stefan's face had been sharp and angular, so she did not find him pleasing to look at. There was nothing interesting to her about the entertainment business. She had never heard of him or his famous Follies, and that seemed sufficiently enchanting to distract him from the others at the table. Her husband made conversation with a middle-aged English lady across from him, but Margaux could tell he was listening in. There was a keen look of pride on his face when Mr. Ziegfeld devoted his attention to her. The engaging smile and the inquiring eyes never dropped their pretense of innocence, but Margaux sensed the predator that lay underneath. Before dinner broke up, Ziegfeld had put a hand on her knee under the tablecloth. She brushed it off and turned away from him. She didn't care if it looked like she had slammed a door in his face. How absurd it was that her husband had been so affronted by the innocent university boy, and yet delighted in Mr. Ziegfeld's bad behavior.

The *Olympic* was going for a record crossing. It didn't beat the Mauretania in '07, but the attempt to break the record got the ship into New York harbor almost a full day early. Autie wanted to take a train down to Baltimore, freshen up at a hotel, hire a car, and get to the estate just after dinner. Taking them by surprise was going to be a lot of fun, he said. Gretchen was so tired out that she balked at the rush and wanted to spend the night and come down the next day. It was an inconvenience to be without her services for the night but it was acceptable to Margaux when Autie assured her that she would never be without help with Robbie on the estate.

At the hotel in Baltimore, Autie got a haircut and had his uniform pressed while Margaux had a long hot bath and Robbie napped on the bed. A little dinner was sent for, and then they set out at six o'clock in a very nice car with a colored man driving. The excitement her husband showed as they got into farm country began to make Margaux uneasy. Now he had a medal pinned on the left breast of his uniform and another one on a ribbon around his neck, as if he were going on stage. He knew his audience, but she didn't.

Evening fell. Robbie was asleep between them, and Autie bent forward toward the driver.

"Slow down now, it's coming up on the left. Two brick pillars. That's the drive. There it is."

The driver turned in at the brick pillars, and they drove along between the tall pine trees and came to the farm. Autie pointed out all the barns and buildings in the dark, and showed her the four tenant houses with a few lights on inside. As they came to a curve in the road, he had Margaux cover her eyes. It was only for a moment, and when he told her to take her hands away, the chateau was right in front of them, dead ahead, all lit up. His eyes went from the house to her face, and he shone with pride, as if the sight of the towers and massive front was a vindication of every story he had told.

A butler or footman must have seen the headlights and was standing very straight on the terrace at the main entrance. He was at the bottom of the steps in time to open the doors as the car pulled up. Even among the Moors in Paris, Margaux had never seen a man so black. He spoke in very precise English.

"We weren't expecting you and Mrs. Croft until tomorrow, sir," he said in a deep, accented voice.

"Nice to see you, Thompson," Autie said. "Ship got in early. We'll just go on up. I want to surprise them."

"Mr. and Mrs. Croft are in the living room, sir. With guests."

Autie looked back at Margaux, who was waking Robbie out of a slumber and trying to get him on his feet. "Perfect timing," he said. "Come on."

He bounded up the steps to the terrace, leaving her to trail behind with Mr. Thompson, who introduced himself to Margaux and set an appropriate pace on the steps for a sleepy little boy and a young lady needing to compose herself.

Everyone was standing when Margaux, holding the hand of the sleepy little boy, appeared in the doorway of the living room. Her eyes shot around the room. The tall woman just pulling away from embracing Autie must be the mother. The older man beside him in the tweed suit must be the father. The husky young woman with her arms at her sides, standing in front of her chair with a stunned look on her face, must be the adopted sister. There was a very handsome man coming forward offering his hand. That must be the brother. Another man held back beside the adopted sister.

The mother came toward her with her arms stretched out. She was a tall, large woman in a loose casual dress with high forehead, black hair, blue eyes, and an elegant nose.

"My dear Margaux," the mother said, embracing her as she spoke at her ear. She said how much they had looked forward to meeting her and how sure she was that they were going to be great friends. Margaux felt the tension and fret in her give way to tears she didn't understand, but she held them inside. She didn't know where they came from. The mother drew back but kept hold of her hands.

"Let me look at you. Oh dear, you're such a pretty thing," she said with delight. "I'll expect you to call me Ma'ma, and the boy can call me Grandma'ma or Bonnemama—we'll see what comes naturally. What's your little man's name?"

"Robbie."

The mother took a handkerchief out of her pocket and dabbed it to Margaux's eyes. "I know you must be tired from the trip, dear," she said tenderly. "We won't keep you long before bed, but first you must stand for introductions. Everyone has been so eager to meet you."

Margaux had guessed everyone right. The only one she didn't know, the man standing beside Laura Eklund, was her brother, Karl. The father took her hand and spoke to her softly, saying little but so gently and reassuringly that she loved him as instantly as she loved her mother-in-law. It was easy to see that he worshiped his wife and easy to see that her strength must come from him. Rory was as handsome a man as she had ever seen, but he wore it on his sleeve, and it made his beauty distasteful to her. Laura, the adopted sister, looked like she had been hit over the head and had no idea what to do until she saw Robbie. Then she went to him and got down on her knees to embrace him. In a moment, she had him in her arms, with her dress displayed around her on the floor as if a portrait of mother and child was in progress. She was very flushed and fussed over the boy, doing everything she could not to look at Autie. She must be in love with him. Nothing else would have that effect. Everyone but her took a turn greeting him before they went back to couches and chairs.

It was after eight o'clock. Delphina and Viola had already gone home. Mr. Thompson saw to a new round of coffee and sherry. Alice offered to cook something up. Autie looked at Margaux and declined for both of them, but Alice thought Robbie looked like he hadn't had enough dinner. Laura said she wanted to cook up something for him and rose faster than Alice.

"Let me take Robbie then," said Alice, hoisting him into her lap and engaging him with a hug and questions to which he answered "five," "on the boat," and "in a car" in perfect English.

Rory offered Margaux a cigarette, and Autie went after Laura to see if he could help in the kitchen.

Laura was having trouble tying the apron in back when Autie came through the kitchen door.

"I'm just in time," he said.

"Oh, thank you, Autie. I could have gotten it. I guess you can see I've put on a few pounds—but it's only temporary. I've just been so busy I haven't paid much attention to myself."

"You haven't changed a bit," he said.

"You must need glasses then," she said with a laugh.

When she turned around, they were as close together as they had been on the morning he left for the army.

"Look at your medals," she exclaimed as she stepped back. "What's that one?"

"The Croix de Guerre. That's from France, of course."

"And what's that?"

"Distinguished Service Medal. That's American."

"What are those?"

"Oh, those are campaign ribbons. You get those just for showing up. That's my infantry badge, division patch, and captain's bars. The one for getting wounded hasn't caught up to me yet."

"Did you get your excitement and life experience then?" she asked very quietly.

"Oh, I got plenty of that."

Laura lowered her face. "Your wife is very pretty," she said.

"She is, isn't she? She's been a terrific good sport about everything. Meeting all the family at once is a little much after a long trip. Most of her family was killed in the war, I think. I don't really know. She doesn't talk about them."

"I'm so sorry to hear that," Laura said, with tears coming to her eyes. She backed against the counter and looked down. "Your mother and father were surprised to hear you got married. I was, too."

"It was a little sudden, I know," Autie said. They were not looking at each other. "I know you might have been thinking—"

"Oh, no, it's all right," Laura said quickly.

"You just looked upset when you saw me. You didn't come over."

"My father died, Autie. You didn't know that."

"Oh, I'm sorry."

"Well, I don't want to keep your little man waiting," Laura said briskly. "What does he like to eat?"

"Pork chops."

"I know we have those. Let me look around."

Laura went into the icebox while Autie looked around the kitchen. Nothing had changed. He looked into the servants' dining room and remembered his last breakfast there with Mom and Dad. For a moment he wished he could start all over from there, knowing what he knew now. But that was strange. He usually thought that way when things did not turn out well. He had come home in one piece and he had brought back a girl who turned heads. It was the war part. He could live without being a hero, but if he had to do it over, he'd probably get killed. No point in thinking any further than that.

"Does he like carrots?"

"No, but he likes peas. And he likes fried potatoes, but he won't eat them without mayonnaise."

"Well, that's all easy. You better put on an apron. I don't want you to get anything on your uniform."

She got a clean one out of the pantry and tied it in back for him. Then they went to work, side by side over the stove and cutting board.

"Rory's been wonderful," said Laura. "He came back from California when my father died. It was so sweet of him. He said he was worried about me. He's actually been a great comfort. Karl's taken over the house. It's been so horrible. I don't know about his wife, Camille, yet, so I shouldn't say anything, but they came down from Baltimore and moved in the moment he heard Father died, and he's been so disagreeable that your mother made me come back here to live until all the business with the will is settled. He was over here tonight because Mummy wanted to be blunt with him or punch him in the nose if all else failed." She laughed and turned over the pork chop with a fork. "I think she was just about to bonk him over the head when you came in."

"Well, I know Mom and Dad will back you up."

"And Charlotte's on my side too. She has her own lawyer, but I guess we just won't know anything until the lawyers get together. Here. I'll do the peas and you do the potatoes."

"How long has Rory been home?"

"A week. He came right away. He's been so nice. He isn't the way he was—you know how he was. He's been very sweet. We've walked in the woods a little, and he took me out on the boat—we just sit and talk."

Then she rallied with a boldness Autie had never seen in her or thought her capable of and looked up with something in her face trying to be confident.

"Well, you know. It gets my hopes up," she said lightly. "That would be something, wouldn't it? What a tight little bunch the four of us would make," she said with another of those discreet laughs that seemed intended as a course correction to her words.

Autie could not imagine where all the cheerfulness suddenly came from, but he could see that Laura Eklund's mind had matured into something that might be working a little differently from the one she started with.

"I love your little Robbie, and I know I'll like your wife," she said. "Can you find a tray? Let's get this out there before Rory thinks I don't know my way around a kitchen. Oh, wait. I want to give Robbie one of Viola's strawberry tarts and a glass of milk."

On Laura's insistence, Robbie slept in her room that night. Alice and Andrew brought down Autie's childhood bed from the attic and set it up in Laura's little sitting room. Margaux and Autie went to his old room to have their privacy.

Autie went to sleep right away. As tired as she was, Margaux had too much to think about to fall asleep. Her husband must have been happy with how the surprise arrival went. He got to wear his medals for his family and showed off his young wife. The brother had the same look in his eye as Ziegfeld on the boat. She wasn't sure what to make of the adopted sister, but she knew she must be in love with her husband. He only mentioned her once or twice when they were in Paris because he got letters from her. Maybe they had been lovers like she and Stefan. Then it would be terrible to have him marry someone else.

The mother and she might turn out to be great friends, just as she said. When the adopted sister lured Autie off to the kitchen, the mother and she had talked, and there was no falseness in her warmth. The father was good, too. She could tell that from how he looked at his wife. When she married Autie Croft, she had expected the family to be like him. Then she would run away and go to New York City and find Stefan's brother. Anonymity in Paris had suited her. She didn't like being the center of attention or being part of a family. The Crofts would leave her alone for a little while, and nothing would be expected of her. It was a comforting thought. But the life of the house and the goodness of the mother and father would draw her in, and the thought of it, when she only wanted to be dead with Stefan, tore her between gratitude and resentment.

Alice slept in Andrew's bedroom that night. She knew he preferred that. He always said he felt out of place in her bedroom, with all the little pillows, half-finished embroidery projects, and pins lying about. They lay side by side in the dark listening to the geese, the ones going over, and the ones on the ground still awake and honking.

"Well, what do you think?" Alice asked him.

"I'd say you're as good as ever," he said, patting her thigh.

She gave a little snort. "You know what I mean."

"Oh, she's lovely."

"Isn't she, though. I hope she really is nineteen. I would have taken her for sixteen."

"Well, she's young all right," said Andrew.

"I'd like to say the child isn't hers, but he looks just like her, doesn't he?"

"Yes, I don't think there's any doubt about her being the mother."

"Well, she seems to be very bright, don't you think?"

"Oh, yes."

"You aren't falling asleep are you?"

"Oh, no. Just thinking."

"You don't have any reservations about her, do you?"

"No, just wondering if Autie isn't in a little over his head."

"Oh, Andrew. You don't think she's a schemer, do you?"

"No, nothing like that," Andrew said quickly.

"Well then, what?"

"Maybe the best way to say it is, if Autie had come home with, say, a Laura Eklund, we'd have a better idea of what he's dealing with."

"Well, that's just because Laura Eklund is a known quantity. We don't know this girl yet."

"Yes, that's exactly my point, darling. I'm not sure if this particular girl will ever be a known quantity."

"I don't believe that at all, dear. I don't know why you would say such a thing."

"I don't know either," said Andrew. "Just a sense that she may not be inclined to say much about herself or her past. I hope you won't take it personally."

Alice sat up and turned to him, even though it was so dark her eyes were of no use to her at all.

"I would not be offended in the least if she wanted privacy, Andrew. I would certainly expect it from any young couple starting a family. It's just so unfortunate what people might think. I suppose she was raped by the Germans. That would be the logical thing to deduce, unless she was particularly loving toward the boy, but she wasn't very good with the child, was she?"

"No, not especially."

"Autie certainly was. Honestly, I was a bit surprised. But really, neither of the boys—did you see the impression she made on Rory?"

"Oh yes."

"I hope he doesn't push it too far. He shows absolutely no sense whatsoever when it comes to attractive women. Now he's shown Laura so much attention that she's got her hopes up. If he loses interest in her and buzzes around Margaux the way he did tonight, it will absolutely crush her. She's already been so disappointed in life, and now her brother is going to try to cheat her out of her house. Karl's no good, Andrew. I don't suppose I have to tell you that."

After a long silence, Andrew said, "No, he's nothing like his father."

"I know, Andrew. You've lost a good friend, and I feel as sorry for you as much as I do for Laura."

Alice put her head on Andrew's chest. She knew he would stroke her forehead.

"I don't want to go to sleep thinking about it," she said. "Thank you for stroking my head. Aren't you glad we knew about each other right away? I'm sorry I made you give up adventuring. But I had to."

"No, it was time I did something else in life," he said.

"But I lived with the business for a while, didn't I?"

"I know you did, my dear."

"I just couldn't bear the thought any longer that you might be killed. I couldn't go on living without you, Andrew. I didn't want to be a widow a second time at twenty-four, and I couldn't have had another man after you, you know. I would have blown my brains out."

"Aren't you overlooking your second husband?"

"Oh, yes, what was his name again?"

Andrew laughed. She was glad of that and lay down again beside him.

"Well," she said, "if you popped off now, dear, I would join clubs or maybe become an activist again. There's always a good cause somewhere. Maybe I'd have a man every once in a while just for lovemaking—but I wouldn't want to be disappointed with that. Then I really would blow my brains out. Could you move your arm a little?"

Andrew laughed, and Alice settled on his chest just under the shoulder. She ran her free hand over his chest and abdomen, lightly over the scars, tracing with a finger the one he got for her.

"This one would have killed me, wouldn't it?" she said.

"Probably."

"You would have been sorry, wouldn't you? We were already in love at the time. What would you have done if I'd been killed?"

Andrew continued stroking her head while he thought. "Well, for one thing, I would have been out the ten thousand dollars your father gave me for bringing you back alive—that would have put a significant damper on my drinking and whoring, but—"

Alice pinched him. She could feel him quietly smiling in the dark. She moved her hand as far as it would reach down his legs and up to his private parts—as far as such parts might still be regarded as private when she was thoroughly familiar with them.

"I was so hopelessly in love with you," she said. "You never appreciated it. You always fought me."

"Just because I fought you doesn't mean I didn't appreciate you."

"I'm glad that's all done with. I never stopped loving you, even when we fought."

"I never stopped loving you either."

Alice felt him drifting away and she wanted to drift away with him. "I love you, Andrew," she whispered.

"And I love you, my dearest Alice."

"We're hopeless cases," Alice said. She sighed very deeply. "Oh, when are we ever going to get old, Andrew?"

CHAPTER FOURTEEN

Andrew came down to breakfast the morning after Autie came home and was surprised to see what Alice had done. She must have slipped out of bed during the night and gotten Laura to help her. Two or three leaves had been taken out of the table to shorten it up. He looked underneath and saw that the massive oak base supporting the top had been recentered, and all looked sound. It must have been quite a job, but they were two strong women. A fresh tablecloth had been thrown over the top and set with seven places close together. Completing the picture was a new centerpiece, Alice and Laura's spring creation from the greenhouse, lilies of the valley in black soil, with daffodils arching over. They were the only names he knew among the pinks, purples, reds, and greens also represented.

His eye was caught by a sheet of white paper on the plate at the end of the table. In Alice's handwriting was written "Andrew," and Elijah had put his morning mail to one side of the plate. It gave him a presentiment that his breakfast-time peace was over. He would no longer sit by Alice at breakfast. Not until everyone cleared out and it was just the two of them again. And Laura Eklund.

Delphina was not surprised to see what had taken place overnight and the first gentleman of the family relocated to the head of the table. On the way home the night before, a Baltimore city taxicab had gone by them on the farm road, heading toward the chateau. Elijah and Viola thought it was Master Autie in the back seat with a woman. Viola wanted to turn around, but Elijah said, "Nope, you done a full day's work, Viola. You goin' home now. If anybody hungry, they fend for themselves. They 'preciate you more tomorrow for it."

As Delphina poured Captain Croft's coffee, steps were heard on the stairs, and a moment later Mrs. Croft came into the dining room looking ever so pleased.

"Good morning, Delphina," she said, kissing Andrew on the cheek. "Yes, I'll take my coffee now."

She sat at the other end of the table and took her napkin from the ring without moving her gaze from Andrew. "You look very patriarchal down there, dear—but not too far away. Laura and I fiddled with the table last night. I think it should work out very nicely for seven." She put on her glasses and gestured to her husband that he might do the same. "I'd like to get the post out of the way before anyone comes down. I wouldn't want Margaux to think we're rude. Push back your hair, dear."

There was another letter from the blackmailer that Andrew slipped into his side pocket. The rest he could pick at while Alice went through hers.

"Here's one of Autie's from the boat," she said. "Well, he beat the mail from New York. It was such a nice surprise seeing them last night. I don't think it was too awkward, do you?"

"No, not at all."

"Except for poor Laura," Alice said in a lowered tone. "Well, there was really nothing to be done to prevent that. Oh, dear. Here's one from Goddard." Alice paused to read. "He wants everything Liza Banks can send him. What are we going to do if a newspaper reporter finds her here—the new sensation of abstract art living on a farm?" She looked up. "Andrew?"

"I'm sorry, dear," he said. "I was just listening to upstairs. It must be Robbie running around. I don't think there's anything to worry about. I'm sure Goddard is keeping Liza Banks his big secret."

"We'll have to talk about it later, dear. Someone's on the stairs."

Rory appeared in the entryway to the dining room and came over to kiss his mother good morning before he took the place on her right in the full sunlight of the window.

"How intimate we are," he said, looking down the shortened table to his father. "Nice flowers there, Mom. Pop, I want to talk to you after breakfast."

"First, we're going to the river to show Margaux the Belgian cottage," said Alice.

"Oh, that's right. Mind if I come too? I want to see her face."

"No, I think it should be just your father and me."

Alice looked critically at her son. "Before they come down, I'd like you to roll down your sleeves, Rory. And button your collar. You needn't appear at breakfast looking so loosely put together."

"I thought we're casual at breakfast. You didn't mind yesterday."

"Yesterday morning you weren't putting on a show for your brother's wife. Honestly, Rory."

Rory did as she asked without making it into more than it was. "She's a pretty girl, Mom. Just a natural reaction." Then he smiled down to his father.

"I'm with your mother," said Andrew, as if he had been called upon to arbitrate a moral question. When it did not come seeking wisdom, he considered it undeserving of acknowledgment.

Laura came down next, sweeping in cheerfully in her best white dress with well-brushed hair swirling around her shoulders. She went first to kiss Andrew on the cheek, then to kiss Alice, nodded smiling to Rory, and took her usual seat on Alice's left.

"Aren't you pleased with the table?" said Alice.

"Oh yes, Mother."

"I wish you had gotten me up," said Andrew to Alice.

"We didn't need you, dear."

"Are we going to show them the cottage today?"

"I think it best if Father and I take them alone. I don't want the poor girl to feel on the spot in front of everyone. I really have no idea what she'll think. I don't want her to feel we're tying them down—but Autie never mentioned any plans of his own. Well, they can live here as long as they like."

"Well, maybe Rory and I can do something together while you're at the river," Laura said, looking hopefully at Rory.

"Got to talk to Pop first."

"Well, it won't take long to show the cottage," said Alice. "But here they come. Don't say anything."

Autie came in first, followed by the little boy and Margaux.

"Good morning, all," said Autie. He went to his mother and kissed her cheek. Robbie and Margaux followed his lead. "Where are we sitting?"

"Margaux, why don't you sit by Father?" said Alice. "Robbie can sit on his other side, and Autie, you'll go by Laura."

"Margaux, dear," said Alice, "would you like tea or coffee first, or shall we proceed with breakfast? I don't know what you're accustomed to. We're just having our regular breakfast, but you can let me know what you'd like for the future. And we can do anything you want for your young man."

Margaux said she was agreeable to following custom, and Alice caught Delphina's eye in the window of the door to the pantry.

Alice was very pleased to see Andrew show Robbie how to manage the serving dishes Delphina presented at his side, and how tenderly he bent over to whisper instructions to him. In the past she had thought her husband remote when Rory and Autie were little. Perhaps they did not remember. There were certainly worse things she hoped they would not remember. Now her Andrew was exhibiting the makings of a fine Bonpapa.

"Did you sleep well, dear?"

"Yes," said Margaux. "But it's so quiet here, madame. The only sound is the geese. You keep so many of them."

"Oh, they're not ours," said Rory. "They're wild. They stop here for the night or for a little holiday. They migrate from north to south, and we're right in the middle."

He said it in a gentle, benign tone that Alice had never heard him use in correcting an innocent mistake. It was only because of the pretty face. There was no denying that Margaux was simply lovely. She was in the plainest dress she could possibly have picked out for herself, and the freshness of youth shown round about without affectation, pretense, or awareness of itself. Alice had to remind herself that Margaux was old enough to be a wife and mother. Her natural leaning was to take Margaux under her wing as she had Laura, and she also had to remind herself that Robbie, the rosiest and sweetest little boy she had ever seen, was the child of that girl and not her own.

"Laura," said Alice, turning to her, "why don't you and Rory go riding today? While you're at it, you can let Elijah know I'd like him to look around for a pony for Robbie. Do you ride, Margaux?"

"No, madame."

"I'd love to go riding," said Laura, brightening up. "Will you take me, Rory?"

"Sure, I guess we could—after a chat with Pop."

"Well, first we have a little walk to take down the hill," said Alice. "Andrew?"

Andrew looked up from helping Robbie chase his scrambled eggs around the plate and said, "We have a little surprise for you, Margaux—and Autie. And you too, Robbie."

"Well, let's get practical then," said Alice. "Father and I, Autie, Margaux, and Robbie will go down to the river while Laura and Rory wait here. Rory, while you're waiting, you can help Laura in the greenhouse. Yes, why don't you do that. When we get back, Rory can talk to Father, and then you two can go riding. The rest of us will just figure out the rest of the day for ourselves." She looked at her watch. "It's only nine o'clock. Plenty of time."

Alice looked down the table at everyone. She put a hand over Laura's right hand, and the other over Rory's left. "I couldn't be happier to have you all here," she said.

Andrew took Robbie along with him to raise the flag and to do honors across the river to the house at Flodhöjder. He showed Robbie how to stand at attention and salute. He told him he would have to do that if he wanted to be an army man like his father someday. Andrew lifted Robbie up to his shoulders and pointed to distant parts of the river. "Look at all the geese, Robbie. Have you ever seen so many?"

"No, Bonpapa. Can we go see them?"

"Well, yes, we're going down to the river when your Bonnemama and your mommy come out, but we don't want to scare the geese, so we'll have to be very quiet."

Autie and Margaux came out before Alice, and Andrew started them going down through the woods along the side of the slope. Autie would have noticed the roof of the cottage if they had walked down the grass and spoiled the surprise. Just enough showed to tell that a house of some kind had been built where there had only been trees when he was last at home. Alice came out dressed in her rough farm clothes and joined them on the path.

"It's much more pleasant walking down through the woods," she said. She took Margaux's arm and walked beside her. "See how high above the river we are?"

The end of the path brought them out face to face with the cottage. Andrew and Alice stood back with Robbie and let Autie and Margaux go up closer. Autie turned around. Then Margaux turned around, and they both had the same look on their faces that Alice guessed was knowing that it was built for them, and not being sure if the other one wanted it or not.

"How did you do it, Dad?" said Autie.

"He went to the library in Baltimore and found some pictures," said Alice. "Then he had the architect who did the chateau draw up plans. We had to guess about the inside though. I hope it's right. It still smells like wet paint in there, but that will go away."

"It was a mild winter, so they got it up in time," said Andrew. "The hardest part was finding men who knew how to thatch a roof."

To Autie it looked like the perfect replica of the cottages he had seen in Belgium, built very solidly in brick, with red-and-white shutters and doors, and thick thatching on the roof. But on this one there was the windowed garret of a third floor, under its own thatched roof, which made it much larger than any he had seen in Belgium. The finishing touch was a pole mounted above the garret, displaying the black, yellow, and red bars of the Belgian flag.

"If you two want to make use of it, it's yours," said Andrew. "You aren't held to anything if your plans are different."

"Thank you, madame, monsieur," said Margaux, lowering her eyes.

Alice embraced her and said, "I don't want to hear you call me 'madam' again, dear. Do you want to see the inside?"

"Not now," said Margaux. "The others are waiting."

"It's a fine house, Dad," said Autie.

"We hope you'll be happy here, if you want it."

"Well," said Alice, "You can move in whenever you like. Let's go back and see what Rory wants with you, Father."

She took Margaux's arm, Autie hoisted Robbie to his shoulders, and they walked up the grassy hill to the flagpole.

Alice said to Margaux, "Of course we'll get you a motor. Do you know how to drive? Well, Autie can teach you. And we'll go up to the attic to see if there's any furniture you like—and certainly you may have anything from the house. And you'll need a housekeeper—and a cook. I think it will be such fun, don't you think?"

While they were at the cottage, Gretchen, the governess, arrived. Elijah brought her from the station in the Silver Ghost. They found her in the kitchen, talking over tea with Viola. Margaux handed over Robbie to Gretchen and went up to the room to lie down. Autie and Elijah stepped outside to smoke, and Alice went to the greenhouse to snatch Rory away from Laura and send him to Andrew's study.

Rory closed the door behind him and drew a chair up to the desk where his father had settled himself. He turned the chair around with one hand and sat on it backward with his arms across the back. "I got into some trouble in California, Pop," he said.

"What kind of trouble?"

"Oh, nothing legal. Just some debts. You know I didn't want to ask you to stake me out there, so I borrowed a little to get along. There were some good opportunities, but I couldn't decide which one to go with."

"What about your position at the bank?" Andrew said, putting his elbows up on the desk but keeping his hands folded together at his chin.

"Well, that was just a job, and the banking business is a terrific bore, Pop. You know how it is. It's just a dreary business, so I left it. But as I said, I ran up some bills."

"How much?"

"About twenty thousand."

"Twenty thousand."

"Maybe a little more."

"Rory," said his father very quietly. "Do you have any plans?"

"Well, I thought I could lay low around here for a while."

"I mean plans to alter the financial situation you're in."

"I don't know. To be honest with you, Pop—I know you want me to be perfectly honest with you—I was thinking that Laura might come into some money. I know she's always had the idea we might get together, so I was thinking I would wait and see what happens with that bastard Karl and his lawyers. There's a chance Laura and Charlotte can make an end-run around Karl and come out on top," he said, laughing. "I mean, it would only be fair to split everything three ways. There'd be enough there to get me square. I've looked into the business and found out old Pete Eklund did pretty well. He was worth a few mil. Even if Laura only gets one, it would be worth it."

"Marrying her, you mean."

"Yeah."

"Then what?"

Rory laughed. "Then I wouldn't have to do anything."

Andrew stood up and turned his back to his son.

"I'm just being honest with you, Pop," Rory said in a contrite tone that to Andrew had no honesty in it.

He stood before the window for a few minutes looking out. It had been peaceful in the house for a long time. It was not just a little bit of the outside the two boys had brought in with them, it was the great outdoors. Through the window he could take in one side of the front of the chateau. Elijah was on the gravel at the foot of the terrace, touching up the Silver Ghost with a leather chamois. Little Robbie was playing at the steering wheel with Gretchen beside him. Earling and Lamont had brought up the chestnut and the roan from the stables. Autie was catching at the bridles and helping Laura into the stirrups on the chestnut. She was decked out in her full English riding habit. She looked fairly authentic in the short red jacket, tan jodhpurs, and black boots. He noticed she had forgone the helmet in favor of letting her hair go in the breeze. It was a worthy go at the attentions of a suitor wholly unworthy of her. Alice was at Autie's side, looking up, talking to Laura astride her mount. Now she had two to call daughters, and it looked like she could not have been happier.

Andrew turned around and came back to his desk, where he remained standing.

"Rory," he said. "You and I are going to speak in plain terms. First, I'll take care of your debts."

"Thanks, Pop. I knew I could count on you."

"And I will back you in any business you want to get into so long at it meets the standards I go by. But I want you to understand something. If you ever repeat to your mother what you have just said to me or let the substance of it be known to her in any other way—or if you ever make a proposal of marriage to Laura Eklund, or if you encourage Laura Eklund with an expectation of marriage—or if you ever hurt Laura Eklund, I will disown you. That means you will be left out of my will."

"Sure, Pop," Rory said, seeming not in the least taken aback.

"Do you fully understand that I can effect that by legal means to make it irrevocable even if I am survived by your mother?"

"Yes, I do."

"And you agree to the conditions?"

"Fair enough."

"Then go riding now. Laura's waiting for you. You can bring me your debts tomorrow morning. One more thing. I'm going to send you to England in a few days with a message for a business associate of mine. You may be there for a while. Would you mind doing that for me?"

"Sure, Pop. Wouldn't mind that at all. Sounds like a nice little trip. And about the other stuff you said—I understand. I don't take it personally."

It could have ended with exacting a solemn promise from Rory or a gentleman's handshake between them, but Andrew felt either one would require more character than he could expect to find in his son. He dismissed Rory with a nod. Then he sat down at his desk and looked at the door.

He felt he had just witnessed a good example of a man without a sensible woman in his life. What had once been flaws in Rory had become traits of character. Why hadn't he seen it? While he wasn't looking, little pebbles must have skittered down the mountain. When his back was turned, down must have come a few larger rocks. How a woman could prevent an avalanche was beyond him to say, but he was sure the right one for Rory would keep the mountain where it belonged, if anything of it was left.

Most of the afternoon, as he tried to review his business correspondence, his thoughts went back to his two boys. One was, as far as he could determine, a completely amoral opportunist. The other had been suspected of cowardice under fire, with two hundred men under his command. He had first-hand experience of the first, but only unconfirmed reports of the second. The medals Autie brought home, saying he had lost the citations, only seemed to support the accusation and add fraud to cowardice. Maybe there was still a chance to right whatever had gone wrong with both of them, but it depended on others now. His hope for Rory lay with his friend Montagu Norman in England. His hope for Autie lay in this young girl who was now his wife. How could he have gone wrong with both boys? Two out of two.

"I thought dinner went very well," said Alice that night as she started undressing for bed. "Let's stay in my room for a change."

"All right. Why not," said Andrew. He threw his jacket over a chair and began to undress.

"You should hang that up, Andrew. Can you do these buttons for me—you only need to do the top three," she said turning around. "I hope the girls get along. Margaux doesn't seem too interested in that, do you think?"

"Well, Laura's mild. Margaux shouldn't find her too hard to get along with."

"Oh, don't be fooled," said Alice. "Laura does have passions, Andrew. She hides them, but they're there. Didn't she look nice tonight? All flushed from riding. They were out a long time, weren't they? Maybe something will develop with Rory after all. I know she's pinning her hopes on him again."

Andrew came over from hanging his jacket in the closet. Alice was bending over to get her underwear over the heel of her foot, so he came up behind her and put his arms around her middle.

"You always come over when I'm naked," she said. "Is that the only way to get your attention? I should try undressing at one of those parties where you just drop me and go off with your cronies—no, stop playing with me, Andrew. I want to talk to you."

Alice got away from him and went for her nightgown on the chair beside the bed. It was inside out and in knots, as she always left it in the morning. The uncountable times he had been with her came to mind, and how energetically she went at it when they threw off the covers. All the poise, all the dignity fell away like a dress dropped to the floor when she wanted to enjoy herself in bed. No one would believe it. But no one was ever going to see it either.

He watched Alice turn her back to the light coming from the closet, still fiddling with the nightgown. She swept her hair behind one ear with two fingers and did the other side with the same quick turn around the ear, but both sides came back over her shoulders and separated over her breasts. In the dark there were no traces of the gray he knew to be at the temples, and it looked as black as it was when she was twenty. Her belly protruded a little, and just under it, an excess of skin folded over the shadow below. Her body had drifted into middle age, but his attraction to it had drifted right along. For him, the allure of all women still began and ended with Alice.

Getting into bed, Alice said they weren't going to do anything tonight. She had some questions for him. Andrew made his way to the bed in the dark, got in beside Alice, and pulled up the covers.

"I think Rory will have a good time in England," she said. "How long do you expect him to be there?"

"Difficult to say."

"What do you mean? A day or two, or a week?"

"Well, he might find an opportunity over there."

"But I thought he was just on an errand, Andrew."

Andrew knew it was going to be difficult to evade the questions from here on. It was only a moment before he noticed a change in the atmosphere. Alice sat up abruptly.

"What have you done, Andrew?"

"I'm sending him to Montagu Norman. Rory told me his prospects in California are limited right now, so I thought Montagu would be the right man to talk to. That's all."

"Then, realistically, how long will he be gone? Be honest with me, Andrew."

"A year or so."

"How could you do that to Laura?"

"I was thinking of the boy's future."

"You don't have to worry about Rory. He always lands on his feet. The only thing he needs is a good wife. It took so long to get Laura where she is now. I know she's up to handling Rory."

"Well, a year more with you will only make Laura better at that, and a year will make Rory less of a handful."

"I honestly cannot believe your thoughtlessness, Andrew. Don't you know how critical timing is to women? Laura is twenty-four. She should be married now. I already had both boys when I was that age. I know she wants children, and you can see she's built for it—far better than I was—and Autie was such a disappointment to her. This will utterly ruin her happiness. I don't know how you could have done such a thing."

"Alice," he said, not knowing quite where he was going, "I might have mistaken the situation, but if Rory and Autie were more or less interchangeable until Autie brought a wife home with him, then you might as well get Laura started on looking elsewhere. There are plenty of other men in the world. As for Rory, he can find a wife any time. He's got all the time in the world to do that. But he's running out of time to establish himself in a worthwhile occupation. It's too late for the professions, and he's never shown an interest in anything that difficult. So it's got to be business, and it's now or never."

"Oh, Andrew, he can always get into something," said Alice. "But you're ignoring the happiness of two people, not just one. He could make Laura a perfectly good husband. Oh, this makes me furious, Andrew." Alice lay down again and turned on her side away from him. "I think what you're really trying to do is get everyone out of the house. Anything that upsets your precious peace and quiet has to go. You haven't had a high opinion of Rory in recent years. I know that. Maybe you resent that he didn't want to come into your business, and maybe you think he looked down his nose at it. Well, apparently he did well for himself in California without your help. So it shows he has some ability that you never saw—or looked for in him. I just don't understand why you're so dead set against both your own son and Laura's happiness." She stopped there and pulled the covers up to her neck like raising a drawbridge.

"I thought you had some feeling for Laura," she added.

"I care very much about Laura."

Several moments of silence went by. Andrew decided to be forthright.

"I think Rory would be the wrong man for her."

Alice turned over to face him.

"Then you *are* sending him away intentionally," she said.

"Yes," he said. "I think it's best for both of them."

After another long silence, Alice turned away from him, then turned back.

"Why do you think so?" she asked.

"Will you listen with an open mind?"

"Yes."

"All right then. From our talk this afternoon, I think he has to do more than land on his feet this time. He needs direction, and he has to learn things he should have learned by now. I have the highest regard for Laura, but I don't think she's up to seeing a man through the adjustments Rory is going to have to make. So I believe Montagu can do more for him than Laura."

"Well, that's fine for Rory," said Alice. "You're a better judge of that, but I suppose you know, if he's over there for any amount of time, he'll find an English girl."

"Probably, yes."

"Then I should get busy looking for someone for Laura."

"Parents don't arrange marriages anymore, Alice."

"I mean keep my eyes open."

"Well, there's nothing wrong with that, but you never know. She may find someone on her own."

"I could argue the point, dear," said Alice wearily. "I suppose anything can happen. Lois says young women these days are free to approach any man they like. But you've worn me out now. Let's go to sleep."

"Will you go along with me then?"

Alice put her head down on his chest, the way she usually slept, and said yes, she'd go along with him for now.

In his old room at the end of the hallway, Autie was getting ready for bed. Margaux sat in the window seat with the window open.

"What are those? Not the geese, I mean."

"Tree frogs. They come out pretty early in the spring. They're all over."

"I can smell the river from here. And the woods."

Autie got under the covers.

"Turn the light off, please," she said. "I want to sit in the dark."

"Down at the cottage you'll be able to hear the water lapping up on the shore and the docks and the boat. When it warms up, we can go swimming if you want, even at night."

There seemed to be a lot of silence in the room despite the tree frogs croaking and the geese honking.

"I thought we were going to live here," said Margaux. "I like it very much here."

"Don't you want our own place?"

"It's a beautiful cottage," she said. "But Belgium is behind me. I don't know why I mention it. We'll live in the cottage. Your parents meant well. Your mother is expecting me to have children with you, isn't she?"

Margaux got up from the window seat and took off her clothes. She stood naked in the starlight as if she were expecting to be taken up in a beam of light. "I've never seen so many stars," she said. "Why is that?"

"There aren't any city lights," he said.

"Oh, naturally."

She got into bed, and Autie moved to her side.

"You don't have to use the skins anymore," she said.

Margaux turned her face away from her husband and lay flat on her back with her hands over her little breasts. She let him do what he wanted to do. This was what she had gotten into when she agreed to marry him. Why hadn't she thought beforehand that this might happen? She thought marriage would be just a piece of paper that could be torn up. It was an impossible situation. She felt Stefan watching her.

"Did you send this man to me, Stefan?" she demanded of him. "Is this your doing?"

Stefan did not answer her. He smiled over his shoulder and walked back to the lean-to woodshed.

"Tell me, Stefan."

Still he did not answer.

"What do you want me to do, Stefan?"

Stefan sat in the lean-to with his legs dangling over the side, and his silence was surrounded by the quiet woods and the fire of sunset.

CHAPTER FIFTEEN

"Will it be worth writing letters?" Laura asked timidly.

"I don't know," said Rory. "Pop wants me to talk to this big wig at the Bank of England. I don't know what it's about. There's a letter he wants me to take over. I guess I can steam it open. I can do that on the boat tomorrow."

"I don't think you ought to do that, Rory."

"Nobody will know the difference. It's not fair sending me into the lion's den without knowing what I'm up against."

"Letters are private, Rory."

"I shouldn't have told you. Forget about it."

Laura put her head down. They were sitting on the dock. She watched the tide pulling at the moss on the wood pilings under them.

"How long will you be gone?"

"I said I didn't know. Jesus."

"I'm sorry," she said. "I didn't mean to upset you."

"Let's get back to the house. I could use a drink before dinner."

They got to their feet and walked up the flagstones from the dock to the clearing and the Belgian cottage. Laura wished she was Margaux. She would have been so happy to have her own house. She would have fallen into Mummy's arms crying with happiness. Margaux was just cold and ungrateful. She could have at least tried to look happy. Now they were expected to be sisters. Could two girls be more unlike?

How did she let herself get fat? Margaux was so thin. She had no figure at all. What could Autie have possibly seen in her? It was her face. She knew Autie. She knew him better than Margaux. She was too young for Autie. She was too young to have a child. It must have been illicit relations—the man who did it couldn't have been her husband. Didn't women like that drown themselves? She would start having children all over the place just because she was scheming enough to see how much Mother wanted them. Children would be her hold on Autie too.

Laura was sharply arrested by these unpleasant thoughts. She should never have allowed them to go so far. It was unfair to think terrible things of a girl who was so obviously out of place. It was only because she had waited so many years for Autie. If he had not gone to the war, they would have gotten married and she would have had two children by now. Time was going by so quickly, and she had never been with a man. What was she going to do if it didn't happen soon? She would never have children.

There was no one to blame but herself and wanting to be in love with the man she married. There was nothing wrong with that. But all the good things she wanted and all the good things she tried to believe in were only hurting her. She could not help being what she was, and now she was such an old-fashioned throwback. Everyone just wanted to have fun since the war ended. She had read in the papers that everyone was drinking illegally and having fun and making love to anyone without so much as a howdy-do.

She followed Rory up the slope toward the flagpole at the top of the hill, watching the back of his boots go through the high grass, watching the back of his trousers. All right, she decided. She could be like everybody else.

She decided to give herself to Rory that night. Sneak downstairs and slip into his bed. He had women before, she was pretty sure of that, so he would know what to do. She tried to remember where she was in her cycle. It didn't matter. Mother would make sure Rory did the right thing. They could be very happy.

"Is there anything special you want to do tonight?" she asked.

"Well, after dinner I'm going over to your place."

"Oh, Rory, no."

"I have to talk to Karl about something. Nobody's suing anybody yet, right?"

"Does Mummy know?"

"She has nothing to do with it. Karl and I were friends once, you know. Maybe I can get an inside track on what's going on. It might save all you Eklunds a lot of money taking each other to court if you had an intermediary like me."

"Maybe you should ask your father."

"What does he know?"

"But it's your last night at home, Rory. I thought you came back from California for me."

"Sure," said Rory. "I won't be long."

With Rory leaving for England, Alice thought it would be nice to take a photograph while everyone was still at home. Before dinner, when the light was gentle, she called Delphina out of the kitchen and marched everybody out to the terrace in front of the chateau. They arranged themselves around one of the potted palm trees while Alice and Delphina went down the steps and walked off to sight the camera. It proved to be too long a walk across the gravel and onto the drive to get the towers into the picture, so Alice came back toward the house and planted Delphina at the foot of the steps looking up. She showed her how to hold the camera and look down into the viewfinder.

"Don't cut our heads off, dear," she said, as she returned to the terrace. Once everyone was in place, she told Delphina to be sure everyone was in the picture and had her call out "one, two, three," before she snapped. Then Alice went down the steps again to show Delphina how to turn the film for the next picture.

Alice had Delphina take a number of pictures to be sure they'd have a good one. Then Rory said, "How about one with just the family?" And he started separating them out.

"You go over here, Pop. And Mom, let's put you a little in front of him. Come on, Autie. You come in over here beside me. Delphina, you can come up a couple steps. That should get us all in."

He was so quick and acted with such an authority, like a moving picture director, that Alice did not think to object.

The photograph that Rory asked her to send to him in London turned out very nice of mother, father, and the two brothers, close together, standing in front of the main entrance to the chateau. Everyone was good-looking and smiling. The only fault Alice could see in the photograph was that the camera had caught her eyes looking to one side, where Margaux stood off with Laura, holding little Robbie in her arms. It was a good photograph for a man who wanted to go off to England with no attachments, she thought. What a pity that Rory could be like that.

After dinner, Rory slipped a bottle of bourbon out of the bar and snuck it out to the garage. He was looking forward to drinking on the boat and drinking in England because it looked like Prohibition was going to be taken seriously. What a stupid idea that was. The United States was going to get real dreary, he thought, and he was glad he was getting out for a while.

Laura waited at the window of her third-floor room. Ten o'clock came, and she began to look for headlights coming down the long drive in front of the house. She was in her best nightgown. It only came to mid-thigh. The only thing she had underneath was a brassier to lift up her breasts, which she had perfumed and powdered. She tried not to think that one little thing or another would make a difference in him loving her or not. Beside her on the windowsill was a stick of dry cinnamon she was going to put in her mouth to make her breath fresh when she saw the headlights.

Eleven o'clock came and went, and then twelve. She put her arms on the windowsill and laid her head down. She would still be able to hear the car with her eyes closed. The next thing she knew, there was a soft knock at the door. She woke up to gray morning light coming in the window and Rory standing over her.

"Pop and me are taking off now," he said. "Mom sent me up to say goodbye."

Laura struggled with the stiffness in her body from falling asleep at the window, but suddenly realized everything was showing and jumped to get up and cover herself. The effort made her pass wind loudly, and Rory had to laugh.

"You don't have to come down," he said. "Really, we're out the door."

Laura stood up but couldn't look at him.

"You're all right now, aren't you? I mean about your dad. I hope me being around helped see you through. You'll have Mom here anyway, so you'll be fine. I've got to get going. I'll bring you something from London."

He kissed the top of her head and took off out the door and down the stairs.

Laura lay down on her bed and drew her knees up. She heard two toots of the horn and the crush of gravel beneath tires below her window as the car left. She kept blinking her eyes, but tears would not come from them. Feeling as hopeless and wretched as she had ever felt in her life, she tried to look into her soul for the tears she wanted to cry, but there she found only a house broken into, and things missing.

CHAPTER SIXTEEN

Laura Eklund could not look at her brother as she entered the large drawing room at Flodhöjder. A conference table had been set up, and Karl's lawyers from New York stood on one side, three in a row. Laura took a chair at the table beside her sister, Charlotte, and her lawyer. Andrew Croft sat between Laura and the Croft attorney. Karl's three lawyers extended their hands and smiled pleasantly. Karl and his young wife, Camille, were together at the farthest end of the table.

Charlotte patted Laura's arm and smiled, turning her head away from Karl to avoid any misinterpretation of warm feelings toward him. Laura did not have the aversion to Karl that Charlotte had; she just could not look at him in the midst of the trouble he was causing.

After a glance at Charlotte's lawyer, the Croft lawyer opened the meeting.

"Mrs. Charlotte Eklund Kellogg's attorney and I have conferred on our independent findings, sirs, and feel strongly that there is sufficient reason to negotiate a realistic settlement in this matter."

"Do you contest the will?" asked one of Karl's counsels.

The Croft attorney looked over his eyeglasses at the interruption. "Not at this time, sir. We would like, however, for your client to consider the terms of the will in the light of our discoveries." He looked down the table to Charlotte's attorney and said, "Please correct me if I miss anything." Then he took a folder of papers from his satchel, spread them out and began. "The South American equities that Peter Eklund has bequeathed to his two daughters, Charlotte Kellogg, née Eklund, and Laura Eklund, are to all practical purposes, worthless. Under the terms of their original purchase, they may be used as collateral, but they cannot be sold, transferred except by death, traded, or in any way cashiered by a non-resident of the country in which they were purchased. This means that in order for my client or Mrs. Kellogg to realize a gain—their inheritance—it would be necessary for them to apply for residency in six South American countries." He removed his glasses, looked for assent from Charlotte's man, and returned his gaze to the three attorneys on the other side of the table.

"Have these equities retained their cost value?" asked Karl's lead attorney. The question was also addressed to his colleagues, who produced papers from the folders in front of them and went looking for the appropriate pages to reference.

"Yes," said one of his colleagues. "The stocks that Mrs. Kellogg and Miss Eklund have been directed to divide between them have a current value in excess of 2.5 million United States dollars, which is substantially above their combined cost of 1.9 million."

"Thank you. You see then, that leaving the equities to the two daughters and leaving the estate to our client represents, as close as can be determined—in the vagaries of the market—an equal distribution of Peter Eklund's assets."

"Then may I infer that you would agree," said the Croft lawyer, "that it was Peter Eklund's intention that the assets be equally divided between his three children?"

"Yes."

"But you see plainly that they are not."

"On face value, they are, sir. This is a simple will, gentlemen," said the lead attorney, looking at everyone around the room. "I suggest that if Mrs. Kellogg or Miss Eklund feel the need to dispute their inheritance, that they take it up with the South American nations in which they now hold equities."

Charlotte's man then spoke up, after a nod between him and the Croft attorney.

"At this impasse, perhaps we will be permitted a direct appeal to Mr. Karl Eklund. Sir," he said, addressing Karl, "you grew up in this household, as did your two sisters, and were well-acquainted with your father's generous disposition toward all three of his children. Legal disputes can damage the lifelong good feelings that should exist among members of a family. To forestall such an unfortunate deterioration of gentle sentiments, we would beg you to consider not the alteration of your father's will, but an extension of his intentions toward his daughters—your own sisters. There are many means by which this imbalance can be addressed. If you have a willingness to explore such avenues, it would mean a great deal to your sisters and to the furtherance of agreeable family ties."

"The Eklund daughters are granted life tenancy at Flodhöjder," Karl's attorney said, standing to dispute. "That should be noted. Our client is receptive of such arrangements in the warmest spirit of filial duty, sir, but he might justifiably look upon any circumvention of the will as disloyalty to his father."

With that, he turned toward Karl, whose approval showed only in the corners of his mouth. A recess of two hours was agreed upon. The Croft and Kellogg attorneys came back across the river in their cars, following Andrew, Laura, and Charlotte in the Silver Ghost with Elijah Brown at the wheel. At luncheon, Autie and Margaux fell in with Alice at one end of the table while a question-and-answer session went on at Andrew's end with the lawyers, Laura, and Charlotte.

It seemed nothing could be done without great legal expense or reliance on Karl's sense of fair play. Karl's legal costs, as owner of the estate, would be covered by the cash account maintained for the running of the farm, so it was advised by the two attorneys that Charlotte and Laura abandon hopes of legal redress.

Under the circumstances, Laura decided not to go back for the afternoon at Flodhöjder. Instead, with no less anxiety than she would have experienced across the river facing Karl and his attorneys, she talked with Alice in the greenhouse about Rory. There was only one letter from London after he had been gone for two weeks. It was addressed to his father, and he had declined reading it aloud at breakfast.

"I don't know what he says in it, dear," said Alice, "other than he's very excited about the banking business all of a sudden. I think Father knew that would happen if he talked with Mr. Norman. He's quite a character. Very flamboyant." Alice raised her head impersonating a haughty look, with a gesture of tossing a wild scarf around her neck. "He's like that. I'm sure he made an impression on Rory."

"Well," said Laura, with her head down to a tray of geraniums, "how long do you think he's going to stay?"

"Oh, I don't know, dear."

"Do you think he'd like me to come to London?"

"Well, he's been excited about business before, but Father thinks this is different. And Mr. Norman is watching him. So maybe we should just wait and see."

"Everything is wait and see," said Laura. "Oh, Mummy."

"I know you're discouraged." Alice took Laura's hands when she turned to her. "Laura, I know you have feelings for Rory. Maybe it will all work out. Father thinks Rory needs motivation. He doesn't think he's found himself yet. We've disagreed about that, but I think both you and I know Rory can be better than he is, or better than he's been, anyway—and you deserve the best that any man can make of himself."

"Mummy—I don't want to sound so desperate, but I want to get married and have children before it's too late."

"Well," said Alice, bucking up, "that's positively the worst way to turn up on Rory's doorstep in London. It may be the lot of women to keep their feelings under wraps, but sometimes there's good reason for it. Why don't we shake off these country fetters and go to New York for a few days? It will do you a lot of good."

"I know Margaux would like that."

"No, no. Margaux needs time to settle in. I mean just us."

Charlotte came back from Flodhöjder fit to be tied. The afternoon session was very brief and the last word on the topic. She spent the night in a bad humor, and Laura went to the station with her the next morning to see her off on the train to St. Louis.

"I'm so sorry I've been miserable to be around, Laura," she said on the platform. "I just hate him so much, and there's nothing we can do about it. Oh, it makes me livid."

Laura looked down and said, "I don't think I could hate anyone."

"Oh, Laura, you've always been such a doormat," said her sister. "I'm sorry," she added endearingly. "Just once I'd like to see you get up and bite back. I know you won't, but if you ever think of a way to get back at that snake in the grass, just let me know, and I'll do it for both of us."

Laura was glad to see her laugh, and they parted smiling as the porter jumped down from the train to place the footstool in front of the steps. She left the station and waved for Elijah, standing by the Silver Ghost. She could not hate her brother as Charlotte did, but she could not live under his rule at Flodhöjder.

In the afternoon, Elijah took Laura across the river in the car, with Lamont and Earling following in the farm truck. The two men brought out the desk, the dresser, and a few boxes and suitcases from Laura's room and loaded them onto the bed of the truck while Elijah talked to his older brother, Jacob, at the car. The last thing to leave the house was the Karensky portrait. Laura wrapped it in a blanket so that Lamont and Earling would not see what it was. They would probably just laugh.

Laura took a last walk around the house she had grown up in, thinking it would be the last time she ever set foot in it. Never leaving her side was Karl's wife, Camille, a sharp-eyed young girl outfitted in the latest fashion, a straight, shapeless dress down to the ankles. When she followed Laura into the attic and down to the basement to see for the last time the hiding places of her childhood, Laura caught on that the wife's assignment was to be sure she removed nothing of value. Karl never showed his face.

Two months went by before Margaux asked Autie one night, "Who gets the chateau? Rory or you? Which one?"

"Oh, I don't know," Autie said.

"You should find out. You wouldn't want your brother to throw you out."

"We'll have the cottage anyway," he said.

He lay down and nestled into the pillow. Margaux remained sitting up.

"Would you be satisfied with that?" she asked, looking straight out the open window. "Do we have a deed to this place?"

"I don't think there is a deed. It's just a house on the estate."

"Then we don't have the cottage," she said.

"Well, I'll talk to Dad," said Autie.

"Tell me when you do that."

Margaux turned out the light and lay down beside him. He knew she would not be saying any more on the subject. It was a simple matter to her, and she had made her thoughts known.

So many nights were like that. Autie knew everyone must have judged his wife as shy and reserved. In the dining room every night, and later in the living room and library, where the family and occasional guests talked for hours after dinner, she hardly said a word. But when they went up to bed, a Margaux closer to the truth came out. Her mind was quick to perceive patterns of behavior and the motives behind them. Mom had always wanted a daughter. Peace in the family meant more to Dad than anything else. Rory used people and was a danger to everyone around him. Laura Eklund only moved of her own volition to take advantage of those who indulged her.

It took only a few cocktail gatherings or dinners for Margaux to come to conclusions about people, and Autie waited for her late-night pronouncements on visitors to the chateau. The Stevensons were social climbers. The Owens needed other people around to arbitrate their marital disputes. Lois from New York was a good woman whose eccentricities were not a put-on for show. Montagu Norman could learn something from her. He should stick to money. His political ambitions were going to get him into trouble. And he had an annoying habit of flicking the ash of his cigar on Alice's potted calla lily in the front hallway. She was generally right about anyone who provoked an opinion out of her.

All too often, in her black-and-white assessments of people, it came down to a final judgment of worthy or unworthy, and there was no appeal. Once she had arrived at a verdict, she never changed her mind. But no one would ever know because she never voiced an opinion in public or expressed personal feelings toward an individual.

As far as his own case, he thought the jury was still out because she talked to him about everyone else but not about him. In Paris, she had asked him questions on every imaginable topic and was frequently displeased with the inadequacy of his answers. She didn't bother asking him questions anymore. She found books in the library, or she went to Dad in his study or to Viola in the kitchen. He couldn't let it bother him anymore. If they could do something for her that he couldn't, so much the better. He needed all the help he could get. Getting jealous of Dad and Viola would make no more sense than resenting the books she picked up at the bookstalls of Paris. It was a wonder that he didn't catch on then how smart she was. Getting around him was as easy as turning a street corner for her, in a language that was not even her native tongue.

Margaux was asleep on her side, turned away. Autie took his hand off her shoulder and lay on his back thinking. He didn't know what to make of her. While he had not quite added her up before he proposed to her, he was becoming aware that she had done a close calculation of him before she had accepted. Well, he had his pretty girl all right. Maybe she loved him by now, maybe she didn't. He couldn't tell. She called all the shots. Asserting himself over her wouldn't fix anything, even if he could.

All the questions were on his side and all the answers were on hers. That must be the way she wanted it. If she felt that letting herself be understood would be the end of her, what chance did they have?

Standing before that impenetrable wall, and deciding to give up on it for now, he fell back into the comfortable nostalgia of when he had been a mystery to Laura Eklund. It was the only way he could get to sleep some nights.

A few mornings later, there was a letter waiting at Autie's place setting when he came down to breakfast. In the months he had been at home and out of uniform, he had almost forgotten about the army. Alice and Andrew had seen it by his plate and waited for the opening to put an expression other than apprehension on his face.

"They're sending me back to Fort Riley." Autie looked at his father dejectedly. "Dad?"

"What's the assignment?" said his father.

"Training officer candidates."

"That isn't so bad. You're married, so they'll give you a house."

"But it's Kansas."

"I thought you liked it when you were there," said Alice.

"That was five years ago. I wouldn't like it now."

"Can't you do something, Andrew?"

"I'll look into it, dear," he said.

"Kansas is out west, Margaux," said Alice, patting her arm.

"When do you have to go, Autie?" Laura asked.

Autie looked back at the letter. "The twenty-first."

"That's the end of next week," said Laura, looking at Andrew with the same imploring expression that had been sent to his end of the table from Autie and Alice.

Andrew quickly spoke up. "That means you'll have to be on the train by—let's see, probably by Monday. So that gives you three days here. I'll see if there's anything I can do, but I wouldn't count on it. The people I knew may not be where they were last time, and the army probably operates differently in peacetime. There might be more red tape to get through."

"Well then," said Alice briskly, "Father will see what can be done, Autie. You have three days to get ready in case you have to go, and the rest of us can just put it out of our minds for now." She looked at Margaux and Laura and said, "We'll try to have a good time together while we can, won't we? I want to take Robbie to the farm today. I'll take him in the cart, and Laura, maybe you and Margaux would like to come along riding—oh, and Gretchen too. Does Gretchen ride, Margaux?"

"I wouldn't know."

"Well, you really must learn anyway, Margaux. Laura can teach you. We'll drop you at the stables. You can put Margaux and Gretchen on the western saddles, Laura. That's what you'll get in Kansas, dear. But show her the sidesaddle. I learned on the one you'll see hanging up in the corner—you won't be able to guess how to sit on it—or how we stayed on the horse, Margaux," she said, laughing. "But that's the only way ladies rode back in those days. Now we have high heels. What are men going to devise for us next? Some sort of arrangement where we sleep upside-down like bats?"

Autie put the letter aside. Alice took off her glasses, and Delphina came through the door with her serving dishes.

On the way up the stairs to change after breakfast, Alice whispered to Laura that perhaps they'd better postpone their trip to New York until they knew if Autie was going to Kansas.

"We'll keep Robbie here with us if they go, naturally," she said. "We could bring him along to New York, or would you rather not?"

Observing that the question put Laura in a dilemma, and knowing what must be the answer, Alice quickly whispered, "No, let's keep that for ourselves."

"Margaux," Alice said, turning as Margaux caught up to them on the landing, "the other day in the village, I picked up a pair of dungarees for you—those are men's trousers. I wear them at the farm, and riding, and I think you'll find them much more convenient than a dress. Cassie must have put them in your room by now."

"I thought they were for my husband," Margaux replied.

"Oh gracious, dear. If I were that bad at guessing a woman's dress size, I shouldn't dare go shopping alone. But you will try them on, won't you?"

"Yes, Mother."

Alice took both their arms and looked adoringly from one to the other. "We'll meet downstairs in a few minutes," she said. "But give me a little longer. I'll have Cassie let Mr. Thompson know we'll need the Percheron hitched and your horses bridled and saddled."

Alice was so pleased with the expedition to the farm. Robbie could scarcely keep from jumping up and down in the wagon when he saw the cows. Then the powerful bull pacing his yard, then the pigs foraging for black walnuts in the pigsty. In the chicken coop, Alice had him stretch one of his little hands through the doors to the nests and carefully pull out the eggs. Everything delighted him. He kept remarking on every new animal he saw with, "Oh, Bonnemama, look!"

The dungarees fit the young mother, who stood ably in the stirrups on the gray gelding as if she had been born to the saddle. How she looked the beautiful adolescent, Alice thought, with her short black hair and narrow hips. How responsive she was to every movement of the horse. Bringing up the rear was Laura in her full riding habit—tan jodhpurs, English boots, red jacket, and black velvet riding helmet, looking so staid and solidly mounted that Alice thought she could easily pass for Margaux's mother. It was such a shame for Laura that if Autie had to bring home a wife, it had to be such a stunning, lithe creature.

Autie waited for his father to raise the flag and send a salute across the river to Flodhöjder. Then he followed him through the library and into the study.

Andrew sat behind his desk, and Autie took a chair across the room without moving it closer. Andrew removed his jacket as if he were about to get down to business but then leaned forward with his elbows on the edge and concentrated an attentive silence on his son.

"Are you going to get me out of Kansas, Dad?" said Autie.

Andrew was not long in his reply. "I don't know that I can."

"I've had enough of the army, Dad."

"You only have two more years, boy. That shouldn't be hard to do. I might be able to influence a change after you've been in Kansas a respectable amount of time."

"Aw, Dad." Autie leaned over with his elbows on his knees and hung his head.

"You wouldn't want anything to blight your military record, Autie."

"Well, I don't know why they couldn't show a little leniency. I served in the trenches. You don't know what that was like, Dad. It was kill or be killed. You couldn't stand up straight or a sniper would get you. I was wounded. Doesn't that count for anything?"

Andrew was glad Autie never brought up the Croix de Guerre and the Distinguished Service Medal. He had only worn them the first night and never mentioned them afterward. As far as Andrew knew, the case against his son might still be open. Lacking a formal court martial and acquittal, it might mean they were still investigating him. In any case, they would be watching him closely in Kansas.

"A lot of officers have left the army," he said. "They need men of your experience to train the next generation of officers. You should try to see it as an opportunity—and a trust. They're trusting you to prepare men to go through what you went through."

"Well, can you understand that I don't want to be on a firing range again? Or maneuvers, or marching through mud, or God knows, being anywhere near artillery?"

"I can understand that."

"I don't want to be disrespectful, Dad, but I don't think you can. You sit here in your office all day, reading newspapers. I guess that's what you did all through the war. And you think you know all about it from the papers."

"Going to Kansas isn't going to war, Autie."

Autie stood up. "You're not going to do anything for me, are you."

"No," said Andrew. "But I want you to know it isn't because of the reasons you're attaching to it."

"Then what is it?"

Andrew waited until his son stopped and turned fully around to face him at the door. "It's because I think you're the right man for the job they have for you. And I want you to see that you can do it well."

The last words Autie had for his father in the matter sounded strange as they came out. "Thank you, Dad," he said. "I guess I better go pack my bags." He came over and reached across the desk to shake his father's hand.

Autie and Margaux left for Kansas a few days later. On the way home from seeing them off at the train station, Alice remained unusually quiet in the back seat, with Robbie between her and Andrew. She knew there must be a reason he had not lifted a finger to get Autie's assignment changed, but after her talk with him about sending Rory to England, she didn't want to hear it. She could not doubt her husband's wisdom, for he had always been able to take a long view when she could only see the immediacy of a situation. But she felt herself responsible for the conditions of the present more than he did. Rory was going to stay in London. Laura did not know that yet. He probably had a girl by now. From one day to the next, Robbie was without his parents—not so much missing the mother perhaps, but Autie was a perfectly wonderful father, and now he was off on an unnecessary escapade. Explanations were going to come due. Andrew could sequester himself in the little fortress of his study all day, read the papers, walk with her down to the river, and make public appearances at meals. He stayed undercover most of the time. She was the one out in the open.

CHAPTER SEVENTEEN

On the train to Fort Riley, Margaux watched the eastern woodlands thin out as they journeyed west. One morning as they passed through to the dining car for breakfast, Margaux saw that the trees had been replaced by grasslands while they had slept. Then it was sand and dirt and the terrible heat of July in the Midwest. Autie did not remember it being so oppressively hot.

Once at Fort Riley, they were assigned a little one-story frame house on the army base. It was exactly the same as the other houses for married instructors, set down on a short street lined with young trees offering only the smallest patches of shade and a perch for cicadas that droned incessantly in oscillating waves.

Autie had to report right away, so the car waited outside the house while he installed Margaux and their bags and took a quick and discouraging look around inside. Then he was off to report.

It was hot as blazes, so Margaux opened all the windows and turned on the two table fans. While it cooled off inside, she sat outside on the steps. There was a young woman sitting on the steps next door, but Margaux pretended she had not seen her and lit a cigarette. As she smoked, she stared straight ahead to the wire fence around the base to the flat fields beyond it. She never would have come here with Stefan. They would have lived in the East, where it was nice. In her eagerness to come to America, Margaux felt she had overshot the mark and landed in the very middle of the country—a very unpleasant place. Then she went inside and walked around the house.

It was furnished very economically, with the same chairs, tables, bed, and icebox that Margaux thought must be identical to the ones in the other houses. It had a bedroom with a closet, a kitchen, a living room, and a tiny bathroom. The coal stove in the living room must do for the whole house in wintertime. It was very clean, and there were starched linens in the closet, so she made the bed first. There was nothing in the icebox, but it was clean and there was ice in it. What was she going to do for dinner? Everything in the beginning was going to be up to her husband. But whatever being here could turn out to be would never be what she wanted. She faced the fact when she first saw the house. It wasn't the house, really. It was expecting to be the cook, housekeeper, and washerwoman. With Stefan, chores would have been ways to show him how much she loved him. With her husband, it would be going around in circles for nothing. She wanted to be with Alice and Andrew. One was lively, the other was wise and quiet. Her husband was neither, and now he and the house would demand all of her attention.

A little after five o'clock, her husband came home. He was in tremendous spirits.

"Come on," he said at the door. "We're going out to dinner at the officers' mess."

On the way over, he told her the car was theirs and that training was going to be like a regular job, eight in the morning till five, with the weekends off. He explained that first they would be training him for a week in the courses he would teach: Military Protocols, Fundamentals of Leadership, and Infantry Battle Drill. Then he would be signed off in time to instruct a new class coming in. Ten weeks with them included eighteen-day maneuvers and war games at the end, where he would act solely as observer. After the class was commissioned, he would get a month off before the next class came in.

Margaux was glad to see him relieved of the dread he had exhibited all the way across the country on the train. He had no ability to rise above disappointment or reversals, so it was better for both of them if he was happy. She asked if there was a library on the base or in the town, and he said he could find out. And he said she could have the car all day. All the married instructors lived on the same street, so he could catch rides.

At the officers' mess, Margaux was introduced to four or five other officers and their wives. The names came too fast, and she didn't remember any of them. One was the girl she saw sitting out on the steps. They were all very nice and very talkative. But people in groups never talk about anything important, and Margaux wished she were sitting in her father-in-law's study, listening to a quiet, thoughtful man choosing his words, or walking with Alice in the woods when the adopted sister was somewhere else and the boy was with his nurse.

She overheard one of the other officers say to her husband when they were leaving the club, "Your wife—God almighty, Croft." It did not help her like Kansas any better. Birds of a feather.

Autie was far happier at Fort Riley as an instructor than he had been almost five years before as an officer candidate. When he drove Margaux through town, he kept his eyes straight as they passed the brothels he had frequented so often and was glad no one was around who had known him back then. Remembering that he was still in the army and would be reassigned had dragged him down since he got back to the States, but he realized his father was right. It was a new start, and he had a chance to end his military career with a better feeling about the whole thing.

He hadn't thought of it as a career before. The army was just a way to get to the war. That didn't turn out so well, considering all he expected a war to do for him, but he didn't want to sell it short, either. As wars go, it was a doozy. After the first week of instructing, he saw how lucky he was. Every officer candidate in his classroom was a young man who had missed his chance and might never have another. He was one up on them.

Two months after they arrived in Kansas, Margaux told Autie she was going to have a baby.

"I want to go back home," she said.

"When the time comes, maybe I can get some weeks off."

"No, I mean now."

They were in the kitchen. She took a cigarette from the pack in front of her. He took one too while she stood up to empty the ashtray.

"There's plenty of time," he said.

"That doesn't matter. I can't stand it here," she said, coming back to the table. "It's too hot, and the bugs in the trees are driving me mad with that noise they make."

"Well, all right. If that's the way you want it."

"I'll go tomorrow."

"Fine," he said.

He felt as if he were watching a biblical devastation spread over the ground they had covered in the last year.

"Do you mean Maryland?"

"Where else would I go?" she said.

"Is it just because of the baby?"

"No."

"I don't understand, Margaux."

She gave a dismissive toss of her head and looked at him with an expression hardly above indifference. "I'm sorry," she said. "I thought you did."

He knew he shouldn't go any further, but there was a compulsion rising within him to ask what was wrong with so much between them.

"I know it's hard for you to get over the war and what happened to you," he said.

"That's what everybody in your family thinks. Well, it's true. There are other things."

"What things?"

"I don't tell the other things," she said.

"You can tell me."

"I don't tell them."

It wouldn't do any good to keep asking. He looked around the kitchen. He had gone about as far as he could. He was trying to be like Dad, and she could tell he was not close enough to the mark.

"You're making me be cruel to you," she finally said. "I don't want that. I'll stay your wife and have the baby. But I have to get out of here."

"All right," he said. "You can go home."

CHAPTER EIGHTEEN

Dr. Rushmore came to the chateau on the morning of May 18, 1921, very pleased that his prediction of the day was going to prove accurate. Margaux had the baby just before midnight with encouragement from the doctor, who seemed to be looking at his watch more than necessary. It was a boy. Viola had predicted that. Lacking a medical degree, the denizen of the kitchen had relied for her pronouncement on her intuition and the divining sensitivity of her hands on the belly of her friend. Although Viola's fifty percent odds of guessing the gender were better than those against Dr. Rushmore predicting the day, Margaux would have put more stock in Viola anyway. She had gravitated to the kitchen during her pregnancy and often sat on a stool in the afternoon, watching Viola prepare dinner. She liked Delphina, and Elijah always made a fuss over her when he passed through.

Margaux was exhausted and depressed for weeks after the delivery and said she didn't care what the baby was called, so Alice named him Edward, after her own father. A cable was sent immediately to Autie in Kansas. He came home every few months. Margaux and her mother-in-law became close after Laura Eklund moved out. She talked to her father-in-law in his study and came to respect him more and more for his knowledge and his mind. When she finished nursing, she gave the baby over to Gretchen. She was grateful for the time Alice doted on Robbie and the baby. It gave her a chance to be by herself a little every day, to sit on the dock, and to watch the tides of the river. She passed the Belgian cottage on her way and could not avoid the pretty front of it when she came back up the flagstones. It sat empty. Maybe she would live there when her husband returned from Kansas in two years, but not now alone.

Autie got used to the seasons in Kansas and devoted himself to training the young officer candidates. It was nice to be regarded by them as a veteran of the Great War, and he rarely missed an opportunity to begin a class with, "Here's how we did it in France."

He drove by the brothels every day without the slightest inclination to go in. He wrote husbandly letters to Margaux, but she seldom replied. He wrote brotherly letters to Laura Eklund at her new address and received frequent and lengthy letters back from her about her new job as postmistress of Cecilton.

She said it was a job with little pay, but she wanted to be independent. It took up all her time, she said, because after she closed the post office, she went around in her car ("Yes!" she wrote, "I bought a Ford car with my own money, and Elijah taught me how to drive it!") and delivered letters to shut-ins and people she knew who could not get into the post office during regular hours. She used the words "keeping busy" many times in every letter, as well as her expectation that she would be losing weight and getting her old figure back "very soon."

There were long, tedious sections of the correspondence. In one letter, Laura recounted an incident in great detail about finding that the key ring for her Ford automobile had managed to hook through a loop of stitching at the bottom of her bag. She said she had to turn the bag inside-out and put on her glasses to bring the thread around to the closure of the key ring and get it through the barest slip of opening between the metal bands of the ring. Even a wizard at threading needles would have had trouble doing that intentionally, she said. The point to the story was her thought that the loose key ring flopping about in her bag—finding the only possible way to get itself through the smallest loop of thread by itself—well, what could more perfectly illustrate the working of chance? This singular event was written up cheerfully, but Autie sensed an undertone in the telling that suggested that the former mistress of Flodhöjder, now postmistress of Cecilton, had come to ambivalent feelings about the workings of chance.

PART TWO

CHAPTER NINETEEN

PEKING, CHINA MAY 1890

It took almost two weeks for Andrew Croft and Shahid Mashute to get from the harbor of Shanghai to Peking, making use of a patchwork of rail systems built by the French, Germans, and British. Walking made up the difference, and they finally arrived in the capital not far off their projection of when they should have been passing through it on their way home.

With their western suits packed away since setting out from Shanghai, and dressed in the padded jackets and trousers of the rural Chinese from whom they provisioned themselves, they walked through the market streets of Peking, each with a hard suitcase in hand and a rucksack on the back. Going west toward the Tartar Wall took them through one market after another, where they pushed through throngs of slippered feet, silk tunics, and cotton jackets, at eye level with rice hats, guan caps, and the black hair universal to the Han people. Not so many with the queue down the back as last time, Andrew noticed. The Qing must be losing their grip. That could only mean trouble. Chicken and pork were cooking over charcoal fires everywhere, and the air in the streets was as full of smoke as it was with rapid language in high pitches. Here and there they stopped to put coins into the hands of squatting merchants for cured and dried sustenance for the next leg of their journey into the countryside.

The American consulate was against the Tartar Wall, so they followed it east and were soon standing before a loose collection of Western architecture that marked the Peking Legation Quarter. All they needed to do then was look for an American flag. But first they stopped at a barbershop where they saw Caucasians through the windows, sitting in plush chairs with white aprons tucked into their collars.

There they had a bath and changed into their Western clothing. When their turns came, they sat down in red leather barber chairs that bore the metal plates of manufacturers in Chicago. Andrew, in a stiff white collar and serge suit had his hair clipped close on the sides in military fashion. Even tilted back in the chair for a shave, he kept his eyes on the front door and one hand hanging down touching the suitcase by the chair. Shahid, the tall black man, had his head shaved and smiled at the job from every angle the mirrors in the shop would allow.

They presented their papers inside the consulate, and inquiring about the marine detail assigned to the post, they were referred to the guardroom. Following directions took them down back stairs and through a short corridor. Two US Marine sentries came out of a door and went by, looking them over as they passed.

"Must be the place," said Andrew, catching the door.

Inside was a wooden desk with a sergeant behind it. He looked up with a menacing expression at the two civilians standing in front of him. It was a face as rough and cunning as any sergeant's face the Marines had in their arsenal, and Andrew remembered this particular one.

"I'm Andy Croft," said Andrew. "We served together in Haiti and Panama. You're Daly, aren't you?"

"You don't look familiar, but that's right, Daly. What's he doin' here?"

"We work together," said Andrew.

Before Daly could raise an objection to a black man in his guardroom, Shahid extended his hand, and Andrew stepped aside.

"Shahid Mashute," he said, "Sergeant, third battalion, Kenya Regiment, Royal African Rifles."

There was an uncertain moment on Sergeant Daly's part.

"Sergeant to sergeant," said Shahid, with his hand still forward.

Daly put his head up in a soldierly way to the tall, powerfully built man before him, and stood up. "Soldier to soldier," Daly said, and the two shook hands. Then he came around the side of the desk and sat on the corner. "What can I do for you, Croft?"

"I want to know if anybody here can help us out. We're on a job."

"Private bodyguards?"

"No. Passing through. Paid to get some people out of China. Maybe you can tell us something we should know about the territory."

"In business for yourself, then?"

"A few years."

"Well, I heard there's money in it all right," said Daly. "Stow your gear over there and let's have a drink."

"No time for that. We're already behind, and I got another job lined up someplace else."

"I'll take a drink with you, sir," Shahid interposed.

"All right. Just one," said Andrew.

The three withdrew to a table in the corner, where all signs indicated it was where the guard ate, drank, and played cards. A bottle of scotch and three glasses came out.

"Got this off the Brits down the street." Daly poured a round and sat back. "Well, all right then. Where do you want to go?"

Shahid nodded his appreciation of a good whiskey after taking a sip, and took the lead. "North from here, maybe two hundred miles or so."

"Oh. Well, I wouldn't know anything about that far out, except I heard there's been some trouble up there. There's always bandits, but now they got religious people worked up about foreigners. They've killed some missionaries, I've heard."

"That's what the job is," said Andrew, reasserting himself.

"Bringing in missionaries?"

"Five. Well, four and a nurse."

The sergeant refilled his glass and lit a cigar. He motioned the bottle toward Andrew and Shahid, but Andrew declined.

"I also heard some government troops are in with them, and they got good weapons, so you can run into more than dirt farmers. I'd get in and out of there as fast as you can. Just you two?"

"Just us," said Andrew. "But we got some good weapons too." He tapped a toe against the suitcase under the table between his feet.

"Better have some chink clothes in them bags," said Daly with a smile. "You look like two country gents going out to shoot grouse."

Shahid laughed, but Andrew didn't see the humor.

"We picked up the local stuff," he said. "It's packed."

The three of them looked over the map Andrew spread out on the table, and Sergeant Daly showed them where they could probably get a boat to take them up one of the rivers to the village where he thought the mission might be. If they could do that, he said, it would avoid any long treks across open land. He didn't know what the ground was like, but he thought the river must have good cover along it in summer. Depending on the current, they might be able to get upriver in a week or two and back downriver to the capital in a few days.

That night, Andrew and Shahid shook hands with Sergeant Daly. They didn't want any trouble at the gate, so they scaled over the Tartar Wall in their brown linen trousers and quilted peasant jackets padded with goose down. It was shoving off into the unknown with carbines slung over their shoulders, revolvers around their waists, and plenty of ammunition in their rucksacks. They were only two against whatever was out there, but at the same time, Andrew was glad he wasn't still in the Marine Corps and obligated to lay down his life for the American consulate at fourteen dollars a month.

In the dark, they skirted Chinese soldiers gathered around cooking fires and by morning had gotten well beyond the city and outlying districts. In the countryside between the mountains, men were out in the fields. Andrew figured they would be able to handle any group of hostile peasants up to maybe a hundred or so, but a confrontation like that did not seem likely. Neither did seeing government troops this far out of the capital, where the warlords held sway. They walked along dusty little roads with their carbines over their shoulders and took them in hand when they went through villages. Where the villagers hid or shied away from them, they kept going; where the people stayed out, eyeing them with curiosity, they bought hot rice cakes and roasted chicken, paying in jiao or fen to avoid word getting around that they carried bigger money. At night, they hid themselves well and never lit fires.

They wanted to avoid the bigger rivers coming down through the TaiHang Mountains. In a few days they came to a river that looked good. It was bustling with commerce as if nothing unusual was going on. Their presence did not seem to concern anyone, and they were able to engage a sampan and a boatman named Ku to take them upriver. Ku appeared to be middle-aged, but that was hard to tell with Chinese. He was tall and muscular and said he'd been a boatman all his life. Andrew looked the boat over with a mind for it accommodating five more passengers. It was shallow draft, pine, twenty feet long, and had a small shelter toward the bow. The shelter had black canvas stretched over curved bamboo supports. To his surprise, the boat was outfitted with oarlocks amidships, which he knew might come in handy. Two oars, a sculling oar, and pole should be all they would need.

Arranging passage to the mission and back was transacted with hand signals, gestures, and a little English. The map had to come out. The boatman confirmed the approximate position of the Christian mission and communicated that he had taken supplies up there during the winter. But as Andrew and Shahid were given to understand, a drought had lowered the water level and the current was slower. The trip upriver might be faster, but coming back with the current might take just as long. With the additional weight of five people on the way back, it would be slower still. Ku wanted to avoid the bigger river going through the gorges because he said there was nowhere to land and too many pirates. To Andrew, it was only concerning because there was a job waiting on the other side of the world that he was anxious to get to, and he didn't want this trip to take longer than it was worth.

Andrew and Shahid stowed their carbines and packs on the floor of the boat and sat over them like the old men they had seen in the villages sitting over their wares. The current was weak at the broadest part of the river where they started from, but they seemed to be making good time with Ku on the long sculling oar. Watching other boats laboriously poling along the shoreline in the same direction gave them a better idea of their own speed, and it wasn't long before Andrew and Shahid decided to take shifts at the oars. The larger boats had two or more men on each side, running the decks up and down with their long poles, but oars soon proved to be better.

Andrew would have preferred to stay out in the river overnight, but the boatman let him know they would be in greater danger of pirates, so they pulled into shore when darkness crept up. Ku cooked a little rice every night, to which they added their dry provisions. They found the boatman could make some good meals in the one pan he used for everything. Later, while Ku slept tightly rolled up in a light blanket by the fire, Andrew and Shahid reconnoitered a perimeter through the woods and began turns on four-hour watches through the night.

A week on the river went by uneventfully. There were no pirates and no sign of any trouble on the shore. The villages they passed looked peaceful. The traffic thinned out as they went north until they were the only boat on the river. Everything was very quiet and peaceful. Shahid finally brought up something that Andrew had begun to worry about.

"What if they don't want to leave?"

"Don't know. I been thinking about that."

"You can show them the letter from the church in Boston. Let me see how they phrased it."

Andrew fished around in his pack and brought out the letter. Shahid helped him with some of the big words. Then Andrew put it away, and they sat back in the bottom of the boat looking at the scenery, which was getting tiresome. With so much of the river sided with high rock cliffs and no cover for snipers, it was beginning to look all the same.

"The letter might not do any good," said Andrew. "It only says they're concerned. It doesn't order them back."

"Can't very well force them."

"Well," said Andrew, "we can do without the two thousand from the church, but I'm not going to give up the ten from the family. So we've got to bring home at least the nurse, whatever it takes."

"Perhaps no more than your talent for diplomacy," Shahid ventured.

"Then you do the talking, damn you." Andrew knocked his fist against the side of the boat. "I didn't count on a boat ride. Nothing to laugh about. We should have been halfway back to the States by now and on our way to Algeria."

Shahid respectfully suppressed his laughter and went under the shelter to look for a book in his pack. Finding one to suit the long afternoon, he came out to sit in the sun. He offered a choice of several titles to Andrew, who declined, saying he was not fond of reading and had never found any reason to do it.

In the afternoon of the fourteenth day, the boatman let them know they would be at the mission before long. A thin line of smoke was just then rising over the trees up ahead. Ku's scant eyebrows showed an apprehension of bad tidings, which he indicated by making the sign of the cross and pointing toward the smoke. Andrew gestured the question of how long until they got there, and Ku made motions with his fingers as hands on a clock face going around once for an hour. The boatman poled as far out into the river as the length of the pole would allow and put his weight on the sculling oar. Andrew and Shahid armed themselves, got lower in the boat, and watched the shoreline.

There was a dock and a path leading up to the mission. Andrew gave gestures to the boatman to wait for them there, making sure he understood to come back after dark in case he had to push off to escape an attack. Andrew took a gold coin out of his bag to show what was in it for him. Then he and Shahid shouldered their packs, tucked revolvers into their belts, and checked their carbines. They started up the path, and when they were able to determine an absence of voices or disturbance ahead, they quickened their pace.

The shanties of the Christian village were burnt to the ground. Bodies lay in the dirt road to the mission. What looked to have been a school was falling into a bed of coals and ashes with patches of live fire. Across a small clearing, the uprights of the mission house and church were collapsing into a pile where smoke was still rising. The only buildings not burned down were the outhouse and the pig shed, but the outhouse was knocked over, so Andrew took for granted there wasn't anybody in that, and there was no sign of pigs anywhere.

The missionary looked like he had been speared right off the front porch. There were two ladies in white dresses lying beside him at the foot of the steps. Andrew saw both his two thousand from the church and ten thousand from the Sheffields going up in smoke. But turning the two ladies over to see their faces, he thought maybe he was still in business. Neither looked like the photograph he had in his pack.

While Shahid was checking behind the ruins of the mission, Andrew turned his gaze back to the village and realized that what he first took for a fence was actually a line of staked human heads. Even at a distance he could see they were all Chinese, so it was no use getting close. It looked like the fanatics had it in for the converts more than the missionaries. He had seen plenty of heads on stakes in Senegal and the Philippines. It didn't bother him much, but he wouldn't work for such people.

Andrew poked his head into the pig shed from around the edge of the doorframe. He looked into the four dark corners first. The long iron trough up on a bed of rocks in the middle looked like a good place to hide. With the Colt revolver in his hand, he entered the doorway and reflexively pulled his foot back from his first step into the mud. He didn't think anyone could be in the trough, but he had to get dirty to find out. Just then, Shahid came up, slinging his carbine over his shoulder.

"Found the young man, sir," he said. "Dead. That leaves one."

"Try along the path. See if she tried to get to the river. She could be hiding in the bushes."

Andrew proceeded into the pig shed. This might be the last hope. Maybe they'd give him five thousand for the body. It was worth a try. He looked carefully at the mud and manure and cautiously paused a few moments to let his eyes get used to the dark before he approached the trough. Around the corner of the rock pile, he spotted something white. He stopped in his tracks and looked at it until his eyes adjusted enough to recognize it unmistakably as a nose.

"Alice Sheffield? Alice Sheffield?"

Nothing moved, so he slogged through the mud to the trough. He bent over and put his hands into the deep muck where he judged the arms of the body might be, and immediately there was a terrific thrashing of arms and legs as the body surged up like a volcanic eruption. He fell backward into the mud, and suddenly there was a boot on his chest pushing him down. Before his head went under, he shouted, "American! American!"

The boot came off none too soon, and Andrew struggled to his feet. The pistol was still in his hand, but the carbine had come off his shoulder and was somewhere in the mud.

"Oh, bloody hell! What's the matter with you? I called your name two times."

"I'm sorry," she said. "I had mud in my ears. I couldn't hear you."

"Are you Alice Sheffield?"

"Yes," she said.

"Well, that's good. I was sent here to find you. I'm Andy Croft. I had a carbine. I got to get it out of the mud."

She helped him search the area around the trough. They were both up to their elbows in mud, and it was falling in wet clumps from their hair and faces.

"Are you from the marines?"

"No ma'am. Private contractor."

"You mean a mercenary?"

"Whatever you want to call it, ma'am."

"It's miss," she said, curtly, "not ma'am. I was here in the pigsty when they came to the mission." She said it as if she needed to explain why she had bothered to put on rubber knee boots just to lie down and cover herself with mud and pig manure. "Do you know where the others are? There was the pastor, Dr. Neary, two ladies, and a young man."

"Sorry. They're dead." Andrew found his carbine and pulled it out. It would have to come completely apart. "We got to get out of here."

"Are you sure they're dead?" she asked.

"One man, two women. Off the porch. Young man dead around back."

"All right then. We'd better go."

He was surprised she was so cool about it. He was expecting a demand to dig them graves.

"The river is the only way out," she said.

"That's where we're going."

They met Shahid coming up from the dock. He started laughing when he saw them.

"Miss Sheffield, this is my man, Shahid Mashute."

"I won't offer my hand, Mr. Mashute," she said, looking down at the mud on her hands and her dress. "But it is a pleasure to meet you."

When they got to the dock, Alice insisted on a bath in the river before she rode in the boat.

"No time for that," said Andrew. "They might come back."

"I am not going to sit in a boat muddy like this, sir. You could stand a washup yourself."

There was enough of her face showing through the mud to tell it would be futile to argue with her. He dove in right away just to demonstrate how much time a quick rinse should take. He even came up and went under a few times. Then he climbed up the rocks and sat dripping in the sampan, watching her as she stood waist deep in the water, putting on as good a show of a woman bathing as could be done wearing clothes. She began with her face and spent several rinses on her hair and then attended to her white blouse and her navy blue skirt with her back turned. Then she swam out for a final rinse beyond the muck and weeds she had stirred up from the bottom. When she finally climbed out of the water and onto the flat rocks, the blouse clung to her, and Shahid bolted out of the boat to put his jacket around her shoulders.

"Thank you, sir," she said, politely. "Now we'd best go."

Shahid sat in the bow, and Alice sat facing Andrew amidships in the sun outside the covering of the shelter. Andrew passed a gold coin back to Ku. After what he had seen of the missionary post, he knew what a risk he had taken leaving the boatman alone and what a risk Ku had taken in waiting.

They made slow progress poling along with the limp current, as far from the shore as they could. Shahid and Andrew helped at the oars, and they kept going all day without rest just to get out of the area. Alice asked what she could do, and Andrew told her the best thing would be for her to concentrate on looking for any sign of people in the brush along the river.

"Give me a gun," she said.

Andrew had the carbine, his .38 Navy Colt, the Army .44, and the Nagant revolver spread out on the floor of the boat. The rucksack had gone into the mud too, but the oilcloth lining had kept the two spare handguns dry. Just to be sure, he checked the loading gate of the Nagant before he handed it to her.

"It's got a heavy trigger pull," he said, "but it's a good one. Here's what the bullets look like. See how they're different? I'll show you how it works."

She moved in closer to him with a bright, eager face. She still smelled of the pigsty, but she was a pretty girl, much prettier in person. The photograph he had been given in Boston was a portrait to the shoulders of a girl with her hair up, wearing a high lace collar, and a dress with puffy shoulders. Decked out, he would say. Not much like the real thing sitting in the bottom of the boat in front of him, with her legs apart and skirt tucked under while they finished up with firearm instruction. He was glad to have her in the bag, but he could tell Alice Sheffield was going to be a handful.

There was a haughty look to her face that held consistent between the photograph and the real thing, but the picture did not clearly convey the blue eyes or how dark her hair was, now that it was down over her shoulders against a white blouse. He wouldn't have guessed her to be tall from the photograph, but he thought she might have an inch on him. She was a big girl. Not heavy, just big. The parents had said she was twenty. The nose was elegant, and she must have known his eyes were on it when they talked. But she seemed to not care that he looked at her nose or that his eyes moved to her blouse whenever she looked away for a moment. She kept Shahid's jacket over her shoulders while she pulled the blouse out of her skirt to let the pleating dry.

"Sunlight dries better than air," he said.

"Thank you for the advice, Mr. Croft," she replied.

She stopped waving her blouse to the air and leaned back to stretch it out in the sun, pulling taut the loose play in the cloth with her fingers. Nothing underneath showed, but Mr. Croft looked long enough at her front to make the point that she was in his world and not he in hers. She was going to have to do what he said. Between him and the black man, she would not have taken Mr. Croft for the brains of the outfit. But it appeared, by some twist of fate, that he was in charge. It was going to be a long trip down the river.

Andrew watched Alice closely as they went back to cleaning the carbine, how she threaded a dry rag around each piece with care and handed it back to him. Her hands were large but slender, with long, lean fingers. It had been a long time since he had seen hands he liked looking at. Every lady of fashion he had passed on city streets in America, England, and Europe seemed to take enormous pride in her pudgy little hands with short, stubby fingers that came to points. At last, in Alice Sheffield, were hands worthy of a word he seldom found a use for: beautiful. It fit just as well to everything he could see of her. He smiled to himself. He liked her looks, simple as that.

CHAPTER TWENTY

Through the long days on the river, Alice Sheffield trailed a hand through the water and watched the woods passing by as she sang softly to herself. Andrew was content to listen to the melody without catching many words, but Shahid called from the bow that he'd like to hear her sing in full voice, just not so fortissimo as to carry over the water to lurking enemies. The lady seemed pleased to be asked and sang a ballad directly to him, over Andrew's head. Shahid applauded when she finished and asked for another song. After that, the two harmonized on a piece they both knew. Then, upon the insistence of the lady, they became the audience for Ku with his Chinese boatman songs. Alice finally turned back to Andrew.

"Do you sing, Mr. Croft?" she asked.

"No," he said sullenly. He didn't know what to say, but he didn't want her giving her attention back to Shahid or the boatman when he was the one who had saved her, the only one who seemed concerned about the rest of the trip and, more recently arbitrated in his mind, the only one in the boat or this part of the world, for that matter, who would lay down his life for her.

"A girl used to sing to me once," he said.

"Oh, tell me about her," said Alice.

"She died."

"I'm sorry. Do you mind me singing then?"

"No. I like it."

"What did she sing to you?"

"I don't know. Songs."

"Won't you tell me about her then? Perhaps I can guess the songs she sang for you."

"They were old songs. It was years ago that she died."

"That's all the more reason you must tell me about her," said Alice.

"I don't know why you think that's a reason."

Andrew looked over his firearms and shuffled his pack around.

"Why, to keep her memory a happy one," Alice said brightly. She pictured herself in her playroom at home when she wore white stockings and little strapped shoes, sitting in one of her pretty dresses with her toys around her, officiating at doll tea parties, listening to her mother playing Chopin with variations on the piano downstairs while she took her naps, servants bustling quietly about, and Nurse telling her to get down from the windowsill when she was at play.

She smiled at Andrew in the most encouraging way. He was so businesslike and concentrated, but when the girl came up, Alice realized that she was at fault for having thought there wasn't much to him. She had failed to see the situation as he saw it. When he pulled her out of the mud in the pigsty, she had considered herself rescued. To him, she understood now, there were dangers yet ahead. That was probably the reason he was so serious. There was a long way to go before he would consider his mission fully accomplished, perhaps all the way to Boston. Until then, she could probably expect Mr. Croft to be on guard and humorless. Yet he was a young man, and there was a girl in his past, one who sang for him and died. He had no idea how romantic that was in literature and song, being as coarse and uneducated as he appeared to be, but Alice began to wonder what was tender and sweet within him, around that one soft spot, the girl who sang to him and died in real life.

"Won't you tell me about her?" she asked again, more sympathetically.

He still hesitated. "All right," he finally said.

He told her about Jenny Jones. He told her about the foundling home and their escape from the mill. He described in detail how he built the house of sticks and tar paper in the alley, and the hard life of his first memories. She didn't know the street, she said, but she and her father drove through Boston on Sunday afternoons and might have gone by the alley as they stopped to buy newspapers from the ragamuffin boys on the street. Andrew pulled a silver dollar from a leather bag tied to his leg and showed it to her as he related the death of Jenny Jones and how he left her body on the steps of the church. It was the same church Alice and her family attended and the same church that paid him to find her in China.

Alice was moved by the story, but Andrew expressed no feelings as he told it. Nonetheless, Alice saw that even without a mother in his life, Mr. Croft had known a feminine love, and it had exerted its power to soften, break down, and dissolve the hard mineral deposits of the masculine when it was recalled. She broke the long silence that followed his conclusion by saying that he must be something like her father—under the exterior dissimilarities.

"Anyone would think him austere and a hard man," she said, "but he has a tender heart." She thought Mr. Croft might be regretting that he had told too personal a story or was expecting her to add to the comparison of her father to himself. So she stopped and waited for him. What he said next was truly astonishing.

"He had side-whiskers, didn't he?"

"Why yes—he still does."

"And you had a little dog, a pug or terrier, something like that."

"Yes, that was Alfonse."

"You rode in a blue bonnet, didn't you?"

"I did have a blue bonnet—yes, I remember it now—for riding in the carriage. But I don't remember you—or seeing a girl selling newspapers."

"She stayed back of me. But you looked right at us sometimes."

"That surprises me very much, Mr. Croft, that you remember so many details from so long ago."

"I'd remember a man who gave me a dime for a penny newspaper," Andrew said. Then he stretched his arms across to the sides of the boat and leaned back with a reflective look. "And Jenny Jones liked that bonnet for sure. But she never had any grand notion of becoming a lady. She was down-to-earth. Back then I thought it would automatic make her a lady just to put a fine bonnet like that on her head."

"That isn't such a far-fetched notion at all, Mr. Croft. The bonnet often makes the lady," said Alice. "But did you give any thought to yourself?"

"Not when it come to Jenny Jones. No, I didn't. Never did."

"I mean, did you stop to consider that if you had the means to provide Jenny Jones with a lady's bonnet, and by magic it made her a lady, your generosity would immediately render you unsuitable as a companion for her?"

"I don't take your meaning," said Andrew.

"No, of course you wouldn't."

"Then say it plainly."

"All right then," said Alice. "Plainly said, a lady would never be seen in the company of a man who was not a gentleman."

"Oh. I knew that. I saw it on the street."

"Then have you ever wished to become a gentleman?"

"Not since I wasn't born to it."

"But you don't have to be born to it, Mr. Croft. Ambitious men often find it advantageous to improve themselves."

"Fine for them."

Alice did not find his attitude at all exasperating. His face remained open and receptive. She could tell he was enjoying the attention. "Becoming a gentleman could do so much for you, Mr. Croft. But you don't see that."

"Not in my business, no."

"You would not have to change your vocation, sir," said Alice.

"Then what good would it do me to be a gentleman, even if I could?"

"That might hold for most men in your profession, Mr. Croft," said Alice. "But certainly not for you." She paused and looked him over.

"You are a practical man, are you not?" she finally asked, seeing that her last remark failed to draw him out.

Andrew nodded.

"And do practical men not value useful information?"

"They do," he said, nodding again.

"Then let me put it this way. In the process of becoming a gentleman, one acquires a good deal of useful information. I will simply pose a simple question to you. Would you enjoy throwing a bomb any the less for having learned a way to throw it farther?"

Alice gave him time to understand what she had said. Andrew stretched his legs out straight, then crossed them again and looked over the gunnels of the boat.

"No," he said, still thinking it over. "I have never thrown a bomb for the fun of it, but when I have needed to throw a bomb, I admit that it would have been good to know how to throw it farther. So I take your point. But I don't know of any gentlemen among them I know of, who looks like he ever threw a bomb in his life. So maybe you should spare yourself worry about persons in this boat who's not up to the idea you have in your head to make gentlemen of."

"You may put me off all you like, Mr. Croft," said Alice, completely undeterred. "But there is one other point to be made before I leave you to your own devices, and this one I care especially about—for your sake only, I assure you. Becoming a gentleman will make you equal to any occasion. What could be more useful than that?"

"I can't see it," said Andrew.

"You would," said Alice, with a sudden zeal in her eyes and a tremor of excitement in her voice that were difficult to check as she went on. "If you would allow me to instruct you in what I know about gentlemanly conduct, I am sure you would see its value. It's the very least I can do to repay you for my rescue."

"I'll get my fee."

"I know you will, sir, but I think becoming a gentleman will, in the end, be worth more to you. Then you will remember me and, I hope, think of me as you think of Jenny Jones."

At first he laughed. But then he looked to the river, showing with a furrowed brow that he was thinking over what Alice had proposed. When he turned back to her, the lines had smoothed away and his smile was gentle and tolerant.

"If it'll pass the time for you."

"You are humoring me, Mr. Croft," Alice said.

"No, I mean what I say. Go ahead. Do the best you can."

"I am most encouraged by your open mind, Mr. Croft," said Alice, both relieved and impressed by his sincerity. "I trust you have made a decision you will not take lightly and, in that spirit, I will accept you provisionally as a gentleman for the duration of this trip. Perhaps we can get going right away."

Turning to the bow, where Shahid was lying with one hand behind his head and the other holding down the fluttering pages of a leather-bound book, Alice asked what titles he had in his bag and if he would be kind enough to lend one or two. Shahid sprang to his feet, went to his bag and proudly brought out a fine little collection, mostly small travel editions but handsomely bound. From them, Alice selected Francis Peabody's well-known volume *On English Manners* to begin the lessons. Alice leafed through it and was delighted to have a proper textbook. She looked at Andrew and whispered, "You can read, can't you?" She was glad to see he did not deem it necessary to whisper back.

"They taught us a bit at the foundling home," he said. "Jenny Jones taught me more from the newspapers."

"Then I'll complete her work, and by the time we're back in Boston, you'll be well on your way to becoming well-read." Turning to petition Shahid's assistance, she added, "With the help of Mr. Mashute's library, of course. What do you think of that, Mr. Croft?"

A clever reply would have come swiftly from one of the well-dressed young Beau Brummells of Boston society, but nothing clever or erudite looked to be forthcoming from Mr. Croft just yet. She let him pause to think because she knew he was actually thinking. Unlike what might issue from the lips of the dandies of Boston, Alice expected there to be sincerity in whatever he came up with. She thought she could count on an honest and unequivocal answer to any question she might ask.

Without any sacrifice of dignity, Andrew finally looked up from his thoughts. He gave her a little nod of his head and smiled. Alice looked into his clear brown eyes with the sun-streaked brown hair blowing across them in the river's breeze and was aware of something between them that had not been there a moment before. When she turned discreetly to ascertain whether or not the black man under the rice hat in the bow had been following all this, Mr. Mashute gazed nonchalantly to the shore going slowly by them and back to his reading, as if he had been expecting this to happen from the beginning and had resigned himself to look elsewhere for entertainment once it did.

CHAPTER TWENTY-ONE

One day between lessons, Andrew cut strips of green bamboo and tied them together with as much of his bootlaces as he could afford to give up to the project. Alice didn't know what he was making until he sized it to the Nagant revolver. The result was a serviceable holster. Then he made a belt for it from loose straps he cut from the interior of his pack.

"You'll still have to keep the bullets in your pocket," he said as he watched her hook the belt around her hips.

"Pretty good guess on my girth, Mr. Croft," she said. "But I don't think my pockets are good for much. Look at me." She turned out the two pockets of her navy blue skirt and showed him how the cloth was getting thin. "You're going to have to lend me your shirt soon. And I am sure it won't be long before Mr. Mashute will be offering me his trousers."

"You may have to bargain for the shirt," he said, with one of the private smiles that were beginning to pass between them more often as the slow days went by.

"Just like that, you've undone a whole day of lessons, Mr. Croft," she said, snapping her book shut.

They pulled to the shore whenever necessary to relieve themselves, and they beached the sampan every night to camp. While Andrew and Shahid armed themselves to patrol the woods, Alice and Ku cooked rice and a ration of what remained of their provisions over a small fire. They sat cross-legged while they ate, Shahid and Andrew with their carbines across their knees, and Alice with the holstered Nagant in her lap. When twilight came, they doused the fire and sat listening to the woods. The boatman showed them how to roll themselves into their blankets as the Chinese did, and they had some good laughs perfecting the technique. Then Shahid and Andrew split up the watch, and Alice and Ku went to sleep for the night.

For Alice's amusement one day, Andrew demonstrated his skill at escaping from bonds. Shahid tied his hands behind his back, with Alice looking on as the knots were made. Before a count of fifty seconds could be called, Andrew thrust his arms in the air free of the ropes. Alice tied his hands with double knots, but he got out of them just as fast. After watching this repeated several times, the boatman asked for a try and stepped down from his perch at the stern. Using gestures, Andrew made him understand that he needed to see how the Chinese bound the wrists, and he watched closely while Ku tied Shahid's hands and untied them. Then, as Ku tied his hands behind his back, Andrew asked Alice and Shahid to make sure the knots were done the same way. When Ku was satisfied with his work, Andrew asked Alice and Shahid, "Are you sure he tied me the way he tied Shahid?"

"Yes," said Shahid.

"I think so," said Alice.

"Are you sure, Miss Sheffield? Suppose my life depended upon it?"

"Well, all right then," said Alice carelessly. "If Mr. Mashute thinks so, I do too."

"Then start the count," said Andrew.

He stood up, took a step, and dove headfirst over the side of the sampan, leaving nothing but bubbles rising to the surface of the brown water. Shahid had begun the count. He sat up with a start but kept counting. Alice's hand was at her mouth in surprise, but she recovered quickly and dove over the side, came up, and swam to the spot where she thought Andrew went under. Shahid got there a moment later, and they both took deep breaths and went down in search.

The current was sluggish, and the muddy bottom was only a little over their heads, but they dove down and came up, dove down again and could not find him. The boatman tried to keep the sampan in place against the drift, and shouted and pointed with his pole to air bubbles rising to the surface around Alice and Shahid. Two minutes had already gone by.

Suddenly Ku waved his arms in the air and yelled in Chinese. Andrew was climbing into the boat on the other side with his hands free, gasping for breath but looking very pleased.

Alice would not speak to him for the rest of the day. He denied that it was a foolish thing to do, due to the water being so shallow that he could have kept bouncing off the bottom until they pulled him out. He said Shahid should have known that.

After more than a week of poling along the riverside, Andrew and Shahid were disappointed to spot a distinctive tree limb sticking out of the water with a slew of turtles stacked along it. They could not say exactly, but they agreed it was roughly at the halfway point on the trip upriver. There was nothing to do but just keep going with the oars and the pole and watch the days go by.

When Shahid finished his turn at the pole, he sat in the bow to read or to write in Arabic in a leather-bound book of blank paper he carried in his pack. When the boatman went off duty, he sat in the stern with his eyes shut and arms folded over his chest for a nap, and when Andrew turned over pole and oars to sit across from Alice, they went on with the lessons. Sometimes they broke off to tell stories of their lives. Wherever she could, Alice gave him historical background to references they came across in Shahid's books, and sometimes they talked heatedly, differing in earnestly held opinions, with Shahid happily coming in on one side or the other. When Shahid took her side, as most often he did, Alice gave her appreciation by addressing him as "The Right Honorable Gentleman of the Bow," which was received with great amusement.

Alice soon found Mr. Croft true to his word to be a student without resistance to learning. For a young man of twenty-six, and for being the rawest of raw material, a military man from hardscrabble beginnings, he seemed to have the makings of a good academic student. Of course, she knew he was motivated by virtue of the attraction of the male to the female, but it was baffling how fast he progressed notwithstanding. The more they talked, the more his vocabulary expanded and the more complex his sentences became. As the days went by, Alice noticed more precision in his ability to bring thoughts into words, and he seemed to achieve this, as well as the eradication of the low Boston accent, with the facility of a child picking up the intricacies of language from a parent. Alice began to feel she was imparting to him something he would value as much as a rifle or revolver. He would not be able to shoot his way out of a dispute with the grocer or throw a bomb at a surly coachman. She meant to introduce him to the world of men bearing words rather than arms.

On the tenth day, when they were out of food and talking over the risk of trekking inland to a village for supplies, they noticed a column of smoke coming up the river behind them. They immediately swung into shore and came in under the overhanging vegetation. They got low in the boat and peeked out over the sides.

A shallow-draft steam paddleboat under a British flag came chugging very slowly around a bend. Ku seemed astonished to see a vessel of that size on the river. They stood up quickly and pushed out of the brush with the oars, waving and shouting. Someone on the boat must have identified Alice as a Caucasian woman in Western clothing, because the starboard deck of the steamer was suddenly lined with red jackets and khaki pith helmets. Ku skillfully shot them across the current with the sculling oar, and Shahid caught a line thrown from the steamer. Pulling themselves up to the low hull of the boat, they were assisted aboard, and in short order the steamer was back up to steam with the sampan in tow.

Alice was quickly covered with blankets by three ladies in white dresses and large straw hats and ushered below deck. Ku went to talk to a pair of coolies on the bow taking string and weight soundings, and Andrew and Shahid were welcomed by the commanding officer. He introduced himself as Lieutenant Griswold of the British Royal Marines, in charge of a sergeant and a squad of twelve. They were on their way back to the capital with missionaries they had rescued from the mountains.

It was a mystery to Griswold how he had gotten to this point. According to his map, he had started out on the Yonging, a good wide river, and somehow gotten off on a branch. After Ku had a look at the depth of the buckets on the paddlewheel and the draft of the steamer, he gave signs to the lieutenant that the water level was sufficient down to the landing he pointed out on the map. Despite these assurances, Andrew could not fail to notice that nothing seemed to brighten Lieutenant Griswold's face so much as the sight of Alice.

It was tight quarters, but the boat had all the comforts of home, including a bucket-shower, a water closet for the men, one for the ladies, and a staffed galley. The two rescued pastors bunked under a lean-to on the aft deck with the four Chinese crewmen while the ladies shared the largest room below, which also served as a dining area for the rescued. Along with the marines, Andrew and Shahid roughed it on deck with their packs and bedrolls. The lieutenant said they were low on coal but expected to be at the landing in another day or two. Then they would march with a show of force through the countryside and fight their way into Peking if they had to.

Andrew thought it hardly seemed necessary to do that. He was glad to have gotten this far without having to kill anyone. Furthermore, it seemed to him that any man who proposed to shoot his way through China should probably take a second look at his ammunition stores. Respectfully, Andrew withheld comment.

After a shower and change of clothes, Alice and Andrew were invited to dine with the lieutenant and the ship's captain that evening. They understood the invitation to include Shahid, and when they found out he had been sent to eat on deck with the coolies, Andrew confronted the lieutenant in the narrow passage outside the captain's quarters.

"See here, lieutenant," he spoke up. "I entreat you, sir, that Mr. Mashute must be included with our party in capacity of his being an officer in the Royal African Rifles."

"Oh, I'm sorry," said the lieutenant. "It isn't customary to receive colonials below decks."

"With your permission, sir," Andrew continued, "may I submit, sir, that Mr. Mashute is a gentleman, equal to any occasion, and on that basis alone, it is imperative that he be under summons to the table at once, without prevarication that might be regarded as an omission or refraction on the part of another gentleman such as yourself."

Alice was very proud of her champion. While his statement was wordy and imperfectly ordered, it was delivered convincingly. The lieutenant was taller and cut a better figure in his red uniform than the young man standing before him wearing a loose jacket and baggy trousers borrowed from the missionaries. But Andrew Croft not only stood his ground resolutely, he held it with perfect composure.

"Well, then. All right. I see. Very well," said Lieutenant Griswold.

As the lieutenant called a crewman to the cabin door to fetch Shahid, Andrew added, "It might be wise to forego an apology to Mr. Mashute, lieutenant. He has an uncommon understanding of the Chinese art of saving face, in which calling attention to offenses is discouraged."

That was even better. Alice stood by with a face calculated to show neutrality, but as the lieutenant turned toward the door to instruct the crewman, she smiled on the side of her face to Andrew and gave his sleeve a quick yank. He was going to have to face her parents in the near future when he brought her home, and she knew she could only play an auxiliary role in that part of the mission. There was no doubt he would get his fee from her father, but if he could speak up as he had with Lieutenant Griswold, and conduct himself as a gentleman, she had no doubt Mr. Croft could walk away with both the money and the girl, if indeed that was Mr. Croft's intention. She was not altogether sure of that as yet.

It was only one more day before the steamer entered the busy waters of commerce along the river, and another day before it arrived at the landing. Andrew and Shahid spent most of the last hours on the afterdeck, looking over their firearms and trying to talk to a coolie who spoke a little English. They drew maps of the uncertain march from the landing to the capital, and the coolie was able to estimate the location of villages where they would be able to obtain provisions without encountering bandits or hostile government troops and where their presence would not endanger the inhabitants.

On the last day, Andrew tried to keep his eyes off the upper foredeck to avoid Alice conversing with the lieutenant. He could hear nothing of their conversation over the engine and the turning of the paddlewheel at his ear, but every time her face broke into laughter or her dress blew across the lieutenant's fresh black trousers, the sight of it dug into him sorely.

Alice admitted to herself that she was flirting with the lieutenant. He was handsome and well-bred, and expressed his interest in her with erudition and wit. If it made Andrew Croft miserable, let it be part of his lessons. He had to see what he would be up against in society. To be honest with herself, the flirtation was nothing more than the fight of the bird in the net. Perhaps she had betrayed too much of her heart already in the way she looked at Andrew and sometimes touched his hand during their lessons. How could he not have guessed that she was in love with him?

Alice was very aware of her youth at that moment, and of being in her best years, but she was uncomfortably aware also that she had never had a serious suitor. Since her debut in Boston society two years before, men had been attracted to her, and until now she hadn't cared that she had scared them off with her strong opinions and by speaking her thoughts frankly. With every crane and egret that flew across the river, she turned her head, pretending to be following its flight while her eyes skirted to the lower deck under the pretext of bird watching, catching Andrew's eyes dropping swiftly back to his firearms and ammunition belts.

She had read French novels, Russian novels, and British novels. It was from long literary immersion that she knew what men and women did to each other, and now at twenty, with girlhood over and spinsterhood looming, she wanted some of that done to her.

At dinner that night, it came out that Shahid and the lieutenant were both former Oxford men, reading in the classics. Thus went the conversation for the rest of the evening, with Alice in rapt and sparkling attention as the discussions drew from the bookshelves of two bright minds and filled the little boat cabin with intelligent discourse. The coffee was gone and the last drop of sherry sipped as evening darkened into night and the table broke up.

"Miss Sheffield," the lieutenant said, "would you like to take some air?"

"Certainly," she replied.

Andrew made sure to follow directly on their heels as they left the cabin. At the stairs to the upper foredeck, he interposed himself between Alice and the lieutenant.

"A moment, if you please," he said, looking sharply at the lieutenant. He put his hand on the elbow of the lady and steered her up the stairway. In the absence of further comment from Andrew, the lieutenant excused himself reluctantly, as if the situation required excusal more appropriately required of the other party, and stood back as Andrew followed Alice up the stairs.

In a moment the two were standing silently together at the rail of the upper deck, turned away from each other and looking at the light of the moon on the water. After some time with nothing coming from Andrew, Alice took the pins out of her hair and let the breeze take it as she shook her head.

"You didn't have a word to say to me all day, Mr. Croft, and then you top it off with rude words to our host. Now you have me all to yourself, and you stand there like a post."

"You were with Griswold all day," he grumbled.

"Well, you could have come up the steps and said something like 'Would you mind terribly if I joined you?' or 'I'd like your opinion on something that just occurred to me.' Then you make something up. That's how you do it. How was I to know you even noticed that I was monopolized by Mr. Griswold? I know you aren't shy."

Andrew considered this. They both leaned forward over the railing on their elbows and looked into the distance above the river without speaking. Their shoulders touched but they did not move apart. When Alice turned to him for an answer, he gave her a nod of acknowledgment.

"So it was a lesson."

"Precisely. Books will only take us so far, Mr. Croft, but nothing is fully learned until you are able to apply it to real-life situations. I am sorry if it was a harsh demonstration."

Again, he gave a nod. "No need to say anything more about it," he said, smiling reflectively. "My error. Won't happen again."

Alice was very pleased. With her responding smile, she tried to communicate the confidence she felt that the two of them could continue to work together.

"You must stop calling yourself Andy," she said.

"What's wrong with Andy?"

"Andrew will be so much better as we improve you. Like a magical, transforming blue bonnet."

She let herself be silly and put an imaginary bonnet on his head and took her time tying the ribbons under his chin. He was tolerant of it, thank goodness. Then she left to go below and keep company with the ladies in their little bunkroom around a card table.

During the game, Alice endured the terrible distraction of wondering how long she would be able to maintain propriety. It was only a matter of time before she would have to say something to Andrew Croft. Her heart and nervous system were more than ready for her first kiss and to fall in love for the first time, but of course it was a two-way street, and he had taken no steps. There had been few signs on his part of a similar desire, aside from the jealousy he had just dismissed as a self-inflicted wound. Could it be that bringing the man up to gentlemanly conduct had extinguished the passions that had come with the original? Was there an antidote? Should his reading list be expanded?

Andrew walked around the deck and had a smoke with the marines on duty while they kept watch for river pirates. He asked where they had served, and their stories were similar to his own. He suspected it was a life he might be leaving behind, depending on Alice, if she was just amusing herself with him, and if not, how it went in Boston. Sitting on the deck at night—passing through hostile territory in the company of fighting men, smoking, listening, and watching—he felt a difficult kind of nostalgia come over him for the many places he had been in the last six years, most of them not far removed in spirit from this one.

A premonition also came to him that if he stayed with Alice, he might be able to get away with one more expedition before she made him give it up. It would have to be a job for a lot of money because he wouldn't know what to do next.

The next morning, they finally docked at the landing they had left almost a month before and prepared for the overland march. Andrew dismissed Ku the boatman with enough gold coins to make him happy for a very long time. The sergeant formed up his twelve marines, placing Alice and the three ladies of the rescued mission, all in white blouses and blue skirts, in the middle. They were such fine examples of chaste Anglo-American womanhood that, glancing over to them, Andrew was sorry to recall the two left dead in the dirt at the mission. The three rescued ladies were gathered around Alice, admiring her revolver, which she held out for them as she might show off an engagement ring. The lieutenant came over to Andrew and Shahid, who were shouldering their carbines and strapping on their holsters and ammunition belts.

"You'll take the rear," he said.

"No," said Andrew. "We're better at scouting ahead."

"I have men for that."

"Save them for the column."

The lieutenant paused, then spoke in a tone that had perceived insubordination in Andrew's reproof.

"Mr. Croft, Mr. Mashute. You must consider yourselves under my command back to the capital," he said.

Andrew and Shahid looked at each other and reached a consensus without speaking.

"It would be decent of you to include Miss Sheffield in your party, sir," said Andrew.

The lieutenant gave a courteous nod of his head, as if he were accepting an official resignation, and Andrew and Shahid withdrew to a grassy hill above the soft sand of the shore. The lieutenant went to say a few words to Alice, and she looked around in a brief state of panic before she saw that Andrew and Shahid had not disappeared into the woods. Lieutenant Griswold talked privately aside to Alice for a moment before she left the group to approach Andrew and Shahid. It looked like she was coming over to reason with Andrew, but she sat down beside him and brought the handgun and holster around to lie in her lap. She waved pleasantly at the ladies and marines and gave an appreciative salute to the lieutenant.

"You can't make me go with them," she said out of the corner of her mouth.

There was still time to send her back, so Andrew insisted she go, but she said the matter was settled.

"The lieutenant told me what transpired between you," she said, "and I feel it would be negligent on my part if I left without completing your lessons. So I choose to remain with your party."

"I was perfectly civil to the lieutenant."

"I think we should read Jane Austen."

"Haven't I read enough?"

"Something must be done about that pride of yours, sir."

Andrew turned his face from Lieutenant Griswold's view while Alice continued waving encouragement to the British contingent as it filed onto the road south toward Peking.

The plan was to make the trip through the country easier by slipping ahead of the British, so they brought up the rear until the opportunity of a shortcut presented itself. Alice kept up well, and they were soon past the column by several miles.

They marched along the road for a few days through undisturbed fields and villages without encountering any reason to conceal themselves. A larger village was coming up, and they decided to go into it and try to buy some supplies. An older man in the robe and cap of a scholar came out to meet them when they entered a market in the middle of the village, and they found out that disturbances in the countryside had calmed down from there to Peking. They took to the straight roads after that and made it to the capital two days later.

First thing upon arrival, Andrew went around to the British legation and showed them on his map the approximate whereabouts of their rescue column and advised them to send a detachment out to meet them. At his own expense, he engaged a carriage for the missionary ladies. He could have done without Lieutenant Griswold, but it was the least he could do to show gentlemanly appreciation for the help.

A few nights in the American consulate was all it took to restore all three with hot baths, new clothes, and fine dinners as they found the Western enclave in Peking awash in such amenities. Andrew sent a cable to the Sheffields in Boston to tell them that their daughter was safe in his custody and would be home as quickly as transportation services could be arranged. Alice sent him back to the telegraph office to send another, saying there were no other survivors of the missionary outpost. She knew her father would inform the church with sensitivity.

CHAPTER TWENTY-TWO

The newspapers in Peking said American ships were in Shanghai, loading for San Francisco. The railroad was running, so Andrew arranged berths, and they made the short trip to the station by rickshaw with their bags packed for the States.

It was crowded in the station with travelers getting on and off the platforms, and faces of all nationalities swept by as they pushed through the current of humanity. But between the heads and hats, Andrew noticed one man approaching with a different look on his face. He was not making his way in and around people, he was in a direct line for Alice, slipping through a break in the crowd with his hand gripping the handle of a butterfly sword partially hidden by his jacket. Andrew shoved Alice away and made a grab for the assailant's hand, but not fast enough. He parried the thrust but the short blade slashed across his stomach as it deflected. The man fell backward from Andrew's forward momentum, and there were screams as a wide circle formed around the two men. Alice and Shahid came up in time to see Andrew with his foot on the assailant's sword and his revolver aimed at the man's head.

Andrew paused to study the eyes fixed on the end of the barrel. Was he after her purse? Was it because Alice was the only Western woman on the platform? Did he know she was a nurse with the missionaries? Was there a heresy in wearing the feathers of sacred birds on the band of her hat? What difference did it make?

It must have been a hundred times he had seen that face. What was going through that mind? Was the moment before the bullet enough time to understand what was about to happen? Did he know his life was over? Was it flashing before his eyes right now? Is there a difference between death and the last experience of life? As if he were holding these questions over himself, he began to feel weak and sick to his stomach, but he steadied his hand. He motioned with the gun for the man to run away.

Shahid caught Andrew as he fell.

The razor edge of the short sword had gone through Andrew's jacket and shirt and every layer of the skin of his abdomen, from side to side, as fine as a scalpel. The internal organs and intestines were spilling out. Shahid and Alice held them in the body cavity with their hands as best they could until the police came and wrapped him all the way around with bandaging. The last thing Andrew heard was Alice insisting he be taken to a Western hospital.

Andrew lay on the ground outside Methodist Episcopal Hospital for a night before they had room for him. Alice stayed by him, giving him water and applying pressure to the wound to stop the bleeding. Shahid went to the markets and came back with a stone mortar and pestle and bags of dried herbs. Over a small charcoal burner he brought along, he cooked some of the ground mixtures and rubbed them through the bandage. The powders he stirred into the water Alice administered by spoon.

Andrew developed a roaring fever, and on the second night, when he was finally brought into the hospital, Alice thought he was going to die. But the fever broke in a few days, and the infection magically disappeared. The doctor who sewed him up said the strength of Andrew's constitution was too much for the infection. Without any English, the Chinese doctor described Andrew's constitution eating up the infection in a pantomime of eating rice very fast with chopsticks from a bowl held to his lips. After several days of letting tears streak freely down her cheeks, Alice found a great relief in laughing.

Another telegram was sent to Boston saying they would be delayed in leaving China due to an injury to Mr. Croft. During the next two weeks, as his condition improved, Andrew was moved from one ward to another in Methodist Episcopal and finally back to rooms in the consulate, where Alice took over from the nurses and scarcely left his side. As fine a nurse as Alice proved to be, Andrew drew the line at sponge baths and assistance in the water closet. Nursing the rural poor of China had been her reason for going to China with the missionaries, and it was all he could do to keep her from poking at the wound and changing his bandages every day.

Once the idea of rushing off to another job was out of the question, Andrew accepted his incapacitation and Alice began to notice the changes brought about by his education in the sampan. They read to each other books borrowed from the consulate library and discussed them. One thought never failed to generate another as waves on the ocean rise to the wind. As he expressed them in better-turned sentences, it was apparent to Alice that Andrew's mind had escaped the safe harbors of imitation and rote memory and was sailing the seas under its own power.

Sometimes they paused over a passage of George Eliot or Marcus Aurelius to think and allow the quiet of thought to pass over them like clouds crossing the sun. Alice felt quite at peace at those times. And when she talked about her life, she felt no one had ever listened as closely as he did, and no one had ever tried to understand so much of her.

Everything had turned out for the best, Alice thought. She had always avoided glib sayings, but circumstances brought this one to mind. They would never have had so much time alone if he had not been wounded. On the other hand, she had to concede that it would not be easy to believe everything turned out for the best if Andrew had died in the train station.

They touched upon the idea one day while discussing the related concept of the end justifying the means.

"However you look at means and ends," Andrew said, with the sheet tucked up to his chin against the draft, "it only holds water if you are sure you are speaking from the standpoint of the end. But suppose what you consider to be the end right now, in due process of time, becomes but a step to a different end?"

After that, there was no question of declaring herself to him or saying that she understood the hardships of China to have been means to the end of bringing them together. When he seized upon a different viewpoint, perhaps he was thinking of a girl he was going back to in the States. Or a lady who had been beyond his reach until now. That made Alice Sheffield, his teacher, only a means to that more distant end.

It was the only talk they had that did not bring them closer, and Alice left him alone that evening with supper on a tray. She came back later to read to him after awakening to the insight that perhaps Andrew thought of her as above his sights. If he had only been with fast women, what could she do about that? She knew nothing of fast women—their ways of getting men, their affectations and tricks. The idea of observing fast women had never suggested itself to her. Perhaps it was telling of their skills that Alice could not recall ever spotting a fast woman, let alone catching one in the act.

When money began to run low, Alice only mentioned once that her parents could wire them whatever was needed, but Andrew said he did not want to confuse his fee and expenses with advances. He let her try to reason with him, but he remained adamant about making his own way. He promptly had some of his own wired from Boston.

In the meantime, Andrew read the newspapers and pondered his life, how it had changed, and what he could do to keep his future from falling into the hands of anyone other than Alice. To stay occupied, and not without an eye to taking up a less dangerous occupation, he came up with a business venture. Currency exchange. He explained to Alice how they could make money changing currency for foreign travelers, business people, and Chinese workers paid in European script.

He proved to have a quick head for numbers and spent much of his recovery time figuring with a pencil and paper until his bed was covered with notes and newspaper clippings of exchange rates. He asked Alice not to disturb the piles when she tucked him in at night. Across a week's time, in the mornings or afternoons, he sent Shahid and Alice to the banks. With calculated amounts to exchange, they brought back a good sampling of the currencies circulating in Peking, which became the starting inventory.

The newspapers listed the rates every day of each national and local currency against the others. When Andrew was ready to launch his business, he sent Shahid out on the heels of the first edition of the newspapers with francs, pounds, dollars, deutsche marks, and yuan—with explicit instructions. Dressed in a splendid new suit, Shahid moved around the legation quarter of the city throughout the morning hours before the regular exchange dealers opened.

They made a little on every transaction, and Alice was pleased beyond measure to see the profits. She praised Andrew's business acumen to the skies and foresaw a brilliant future for him in finance. He took it all in stride. He didn't want to tell her it was nothing like the money he was used to, and the only thing his alleged acumen guided him to was the apparent truth that fifty dollars was considered a lot of money only to poor people and the very rich.

By the time Andrew was fit to travel, a new track went to Shanghai with only a few interruptions. It was a narrow-gauge that spliced into the sections constructed by the French, the kind Andrew had guarded or blown up in his career, depending on whom he was working for. The locomotive and passenger cars were modern enough to get them to Shanghai in four days in a level of comfort that was a far cry from their trip the other direction in May.

Shanghai was cosmopolitan and busy with international businessmen. They agreed it was altogether more pleasant than Peking and would be a good place to set up a permanent currency business. Shahid reported from the harbor that it would be a week before any ship was leaving for the States, so they put up in a hotel on a main thoroughfare. Shahid went out exploring business opportunities every day while Alice and Andrew rested and took short walks.

The voyage across the Pacific was very long but peaceful all the way. Andrew walked the decks with Alice at his side, stepping with spirit in the mornings, but allowing her to support him on her arm when he tired in the afternoons. Believing Andrew might have some anxiety about meeting her parents as a gentleman, not as a mercenary, and that returning her might result in something more than a business affair, Alice used the time on the boat to begin telling him more about her family and to refine her lesson plans.

Andrew read effortlessly now, without hesitation or working his way through long words syllable by syllable. There was a small library on the boat, and having discovered it, he was seldom without a book in one hand and a notebook in the other. It was very strange to him that everyone did not take notes while reading. Alice could only say that taking notes as one reads was certainly permissible, but not the practice. That prompted her to think of the many instances in the beginning of his education when her only answer to a confounding question was to say, "It's just the practice, Mr. Croft."

Coincident with telling stories of her family, Alice began to realize how little she had questioned her own upbringing and the societal rules she had readily accepted all her life. From there she questioned her own growing misgivings about returning home with the soldier of fortune her parents had employed to rescue her. It might be immediately evident to them that the man she intended to marry could never be brought up to her station in life. For as much as she knew about Andrew Croft that she thought no one else had ever known or found out, had she missed anything obvious to others? There was no way to tell.

In a business suit, winged collar, and black wool felt homburg that added a few years to his appearance, Andrew crossed the United States in the role of some unspecified government official, accompanied by his secretary. Although it was only one of many ways to explain Alice as an unmarried woman traveling with a man, it began to dawn on Andrew that he was entering a period of life in which his success in ventures would depend on how many people he could deceive. At the moment, it came down to small practical matters of everyday life. Without wedding rings, they could not look at each other as they had freely done in China. In the dining car, they could not share a glass, and he had to remind himself to keep the cuffs over his rough hands and his hands below the table or resting with just fingertips on the edge.

Shahid took his usual job as a Pullman porter when they traveled by train. It took a fair amount of money to get him on the crew on short notice, twice as much as a first-class ticket would have been, but Andrew didn't mind. He told Alice it was just the cost of doing business. Shahid said baggage handling, shining shoes, and making up beds was a welcome change from hiking terrain and getting shot at, and he had fun in the company of the porters he had come to know through the years of traveling this way.

On the first night of the train from San Francisco to Boston, Alice realized she was running out of time to flush out Mr. Croft. With no plan other than to be herself, she walked bravely down the corridor to Andrew's compartment in the sleeping car with a coat over her nightgown. She knocked softly and found the door unlocked and laughed when she opened it. It was just like her room, where the bed came down from the wall and filled up the little room entirely, so that the door was the only way to get in or out of bed.

"Would you mind if I joined you?" she whispered.

"Perhaps you'd like an opinion on something that just occurred to you."

He was being clever, but she could allow him that. He never would have expected her to visit his sleeping quarters. Alice put a knee up on the mattress and climbed in, pulling the door behind her.

"You have a wonderful memory for the lessons, Mr. Croft, but you are advanced enough now to use words of your own."

"I have none suitable to the occasion."

"I thought you would be equal to every occasion by now."

"This one would have required prepared remarks."

"Then I should ask, would you like me to visit in your cabin for a little while?"

"You mean my berth, of course."

"Yes."

"Please do."

Alice lay down with her head on his chest with the sheet and blanket between them and found it very comfortable. He raised the window shade, and the darkness of the little room allowed a good view of flat countryside going by under moonlight. The clattering of the train and the rocking motion would have put Alice to sleep in a moment if she had been in her own room alone. But she had stepped out of all boundaries coming to his cabin, and she had come there with a specific intention. As she waited for her courage to rise, her heart beat faster, she felt flushed and fought the urge to tinkle. She was on the brink of doing something she had never done before.

"I came to kiss you, Mr. Croft," she said boldly.

"I've never heard a tremor in your voice before."

He said it as if the only surprise was the tremor.

"Well, did you hear what I said?"

When Andrew made no immediate reply, Alice sat up suddenly. "If you are not up to it, Mr. Croft, I won't trouble you any longer."

Alice felt his hand on her head, lowering it back to lie on his chest. Then he stroked her hair and restored the peace.

"That's very comforting," she whispered. "I like you stroking my head. Just like that."

When she was feeling ready and brave, she got up on her elbows again, facing him. Andrew was looking sideways out the window. She wanted to ask what he was thinking, but she had done enough of that. No more words. The next time he turned his face back to her, she put her lips against his. Then she said good night very softly, drew the coat around her neck, and backed out of the little door.

Andrew and Alice went to the day coach every morning to watch the West and Midwest go by and had their meals in the dining car. When the locomotive took on coal and water in the smaller towns of the Great Plains, they left the train with the other passengers to stroll around the towns and buy books and newspapers.

"I'll never get used to seeing signs like that," Alice said, back on the train after another of those towns. "Whites only, no Negroes here, no Negroes there. It's really appalling, Andrew. I can't imagine how those people live here."

There was one more as the train pulled away from the dusty station, a painted board sign with an arrow indicating the separate waiting area for coloreds. When it was quickly replaced by a horizon of wheat, they sat back into the deep upholstery of the day car.

"It's just the practice," said Andrew.

"Well, it's very upsetting, Andrew."

"You find it mostly in the South. There isn't as much up north."

"Did anyone ever bother Mr. Mashute in Boston?"

"No, I wouldn't think so. He's too intimidating."

"But what about the other Negroes?" said Alice. "What about the ones who don't look so dangerous?"

"I guess they lay low."

Alice found it very disturbing. She made up her mind to do something about those hurtful signs. Someone had to point out how mean-spirited and unkind they were. She resolved to bring the issue to her father's attention. He was just the kind of man to do something about it. She had often read in the Boston newspapers that Mr. Sheffield, head of the largest privately owned bank in Massachusetts, had backstairs influence in the government. He would put a stop to it.

Once she had thought through the details of how her father could end racial bigotry in the United States of America, she explained it to Andrew in the most instructive way. She thought it was time she included in his lessons how influence worked at the highest levels.

Andrew listened carefully over breakfast as her face animated with passion. Her thoughts were admirable. He could not say anything against her ideas, and there was no question he would stand by her in whatever she set out to do. But he was beginning to see that she was young and innocent of the world. She had to find out on her own, and there was plenty of time for that; if the idealism in Alice Sheffield persevered through disillusionment, he was sure it would always find new holes to dig.

The next night, when Alice came to Andrew's room, she took off her coat and lay beside him under the covers in her nightgown. He was in a long nightshirt, so the only naked parts of them that touched were their feet. They lay on their sides to kiss, and then lay on their backs. Alice felt as comfortable and settled as if they were already married and had been for a long time. It did not bother her that such would be the only justifiable circumstances for what they were doing. The rules were out the window.

"Have you ever had sexual intercourse?" she asked.

Alice looked out the window and relaxed to let the motion of the train calm her. Andrew usually took some time to answer a personal question, but she thought this was an easy one.

"Yes," he said.

Alice abruptly threw off the covers, fiddled with her coat until she found the front, and thrust her arms into the sleeves. Without a word, she slid the door open to the little lamps of the corridor and removed herself from the sleeping compartment of one gentleman she'd suddenly had quite enough of.

The next morning, Andrew had breakfast alone in the dining car. When he went to look for Alice, he found her talking to a Negro lady in the last car before the caboose. She agreed to come back with him, and as they walked single file through the second-class cars, she spoke in hushed tones at his ear.

"It's positively inhuman, Andrew," she said. They had just opened the door to the next car and were standing outside with the railroad ties rushing under them, the wind coming at them with the thunderous noise of the wheels. They stepped from one moving metal plate to the next to cross to the next car.

Andrew opened the door to the next car, and Alice closed it behind her as fast as she could. They went through all the cars to the head of the train that way, to the annoyance of passengers sitting closest to the doors. Breakfast hours were over, but Andrew had them make up something for Alice, the same bacon, eggs, and muffin she had every morning.

She was passionate about the neglect she had seen regarding the Negro people, but she kept her voice low in front of the colored waiters who were sweeping the carpet and changing the table linens for the first luncheon. By the time they poured their last coffee, the storm had passed, leaving only one small cloud in the sky, the intercourse topic.

"I'm glad I found out now," she said. "It was foolish of me to think a young man with an attractive countenance and bearing who has traveled the world would not have had scores of women."

"I thought you wanted an honest answer. And it never amounted to scores."

"Just for the record, Andrew," she said, "and take it as part of your lessons. There is only one appropriate answer to such an intimate question posed by a woman. She will want to believe it is an act without precedent."

"Well, it will still be that if it should take place."

"You know what I mean."

"Alice," he said very seriously, following some moments of thought, "where you are taking me, I'm going to have to be untruthful to everyone I meet. You may be the only one I won't have to lie to about myself. If I can be honest with you, I won't mind being dishonest with the rest."

"Andrew," she said quietly, "I don't think I'm wrong in wanting to take you to my family, and I fervently believe you are ready for a life with wider horizons and greater challenges."

"Well, we'll see if I pass muster with your parents before we get to the greater challenges."

"Oh, Andrew dear, I know they'll love you. You can tell all your stories as adventures, and everything will fit in very reasonably that way without being untruthful."

His skeptical expression made her laugh. Then he smiled, and they spent a few moments looking into each other's eyes. Alice had her elbows on the small table and chin propped up on her hands.

"So, mister adventurer," said Alice, "why didn't you marry this girl after you had besmirched her reputation?"

"I'm afraid her reputation was beyond my powers of further besmirchment," said Andrew.

"Well then, why did you have anything to do with such a woman?"

Andrew thought and replied, "I heard about her."

That night Alice came to his room and got under the covers with him again. Before she went any further with her marital notions, she wanted to see how it would feel to hold a man without the impediment of clothing. Not that a disappointing experience would change her decision, but she expected a good one would strengthen her confidence in the rightness of it, aware that she might have to assert herself in its defense when they reached Boston. She slipped out of her nightgown and put it on top of the covers, and Andrew followed suit out of his nightshirt. She was interested in only a limited, carefully controlled sensory experience and did not permit the roaming of his hands. She made it clear by blocking one as it advanced up the inside of her thigh. Without words, Andrew relocated his errant hand to her shoulder and lay still.

"I don't want you to be startled," she said. "Oh, nothing about me in particular. But since you've had other girls—"

"One," he said.

"One is a hundred. So perhaps you already know and would not be shocked to find out that girls have hair covering their—what's the word for it, do you know?"

"Only a crude one," he said.

"A man like Lieutenant Griswold, who has assuredly been to museums and gotten his idea of the female form from its portrayal in the white marble of Greek statuary—well, he would definitely be put off. The men in statuary always have discreet curls, but the women have only bare mounds. I doubt Lieutenant Griswold would be able to bear the demolishment of his illusions."

"I don't think Lieutenant Griswold would be deterred in the slightest," said Andrew.

"Well, putting that aside, can't you see the glaring omission of presenting the human female as lacking a distinct physical characteristic of the species?"

"I don't think I've ever heard it discussed," said Andrew. "Even in rough company."

"Well, I only brought it up because I know you'll be comparing me to these other girls you've had."

"You mean one."

"And another thing, Andrew. How would you feel if it were the other way around? What if I had had the experience of sexual intercourse and you had not? Isn't it just as natural for a woman to desire physical congress as a man? Oh, I know the way things are, but why is it that way? Too much is expected of women and not enough of men, if you ask me. And for that matter, why is any one gender in charge anyway?"

She lay her head back on his chest. After the lights of a little station flashed by, it was again as dark outside the window as it was within, and Alice felt she had once again let intellectual fancies interfere with experiencing life at its hot center. Why did she do that? When her bare skin first touched his naked body and she opened her thighs to clutch one of his legs between them, the riot of her nervous system flashed high alarm and wildfire. But when she opened her mouth, what came out? Pubis. That's the word she was looking for. How did Lieutenant Griswold get into it? And women ruling the world. What was the matter with her? It was so frustrating to open the gate for her physical yearnings, only to have them run up the chute to her mind and jump into thoughts. Was that all her intellect amounted to, a cowardly subversion of sexual urges?

"It would be all right with me if it were the other way around," Andrew said.

"What are you talking about?"

"What you just said."

"Don't pay any attention to me," said Alice. "I don't want to talk anymore."

Their bodies had warmed to each other, and they cradled together. She had to think a minute more before she moved. What was sticking out against her leg? Oh, that. The thing under the fig leaf. It must get that way for intercourse. Does it only happen in the dark? How could her heart stand the beating it was doing now? Was she breathing? Mother should have told her. Enough for one night.

"You know you have me, don't you?" she whispered to Andrew. Then she kissed him, untangled her legs from his, and gathered nightgown and robe. With a last touch on his hand, she slipped out the door, felt the carpet of the quiet corridor under her bare feet, and stole away from the bed of her great revelations.

Good enough for the last word on the topic for now. She was satisfied that Andrew must know she had done more with him than she ever would have done with anyone in Boston, and the rest would wait until they were married. It didn't bother her that marriage had not come up. It was her own fault for talking too much, but she had done it. She had lain naked with a man and knew what might have happened next if she had been a fast girl.

Trying to quiet herself and fall asleep that night, Alice could not keep out of her mind other practical matters more pressing as the train sped them eastward. It was her childhood home she was returning to, and again she would sleep in the bedroom she knew from her earliest years. Mother might come in and sit on the bed to talk as they had so often. Nothing had to change just because she was old enough to have a man.

On the last night before the train got to New York, Alice lay with him under the covers again and decided to ask.

"Why haven't you asked me to marry you, Andrew?"

He had to think a little while.

"Well, you seemed to have your mind made up without it," he said. "If I had asked you at any time other than the moment you came out of the mud in the pigsty, it might have left the impression that wanting to marry you might ever have been in question."

At length, Alice said, "That was very well said, Andrew." Then she lay on her side and looked at his profile, set off by its reflection in the window. "Tell me what you first liked about me."

"Everything," he said.

"No, specifically."

"Then I would have to say, the first part of you I saw."

"My nose."

"The rest was not a disappointment."

"Well, you may have the whole package if you like. Would you like to marry me, Mr. Croft?"

"Yes, I think I would like to try it."

"Then it's settled," she said. "We don't have to talk about women ruling the world anymore."

In New York's Grand Central Station, they met up with Shahid and boarded an express to Boston and arrived in the late afternoon. It was all too sudden for Alice to go directly to the house after so long getting to the end of the journey, so she decided it would be better for them to rest for the night at a hotel. It was exciting for her to be back in Boston, and she was eager to present Andrew to her parents. Then she wanted to show Andrew the house, where she had gone to school as a girl, and the sidewalks and sites familiar to her. But she needed a night to compose herself first.

It was not a friend from college she was bringing to the house. It was a man, and as much as she was bringing home one of those, she was bringing herself as a changed person. She was still their daughter, but now, as she knew at least her mother would perceive, she was more powerfully bound by another tie. It crossed her mind to get married at Boston town hall the next morning and announce it at the door as she flew into her mother's arms. Ideas like that came up and fell back all through dinner at the hotel restaurant. She was fearful that her homecoming would somehow be seen by her parents as a betrayal of all that had gone into her upbringing. Andrew stroked her head until she fell asleep that night, and for the first time they woke up together in the morning.

CHAPTER TWENTY-THREE

Andrew came back from dinner at the Sheffields' brownstone with a check for ten thousand dollars. He met Shahid downstairs in the restaurant and had a few strong drinks. He told Shahid what had happened.

"At least we got paid," said Shahid.

"He offered me two thousand more to make myself scarce, but I turned it down."

They both lit cigars and sipped whiskey.

"What are we going to do now?" Shahid asked.

"I'm going to wait for a while. It depends on Alice. I don't think anything they say is going to change her mind."

"Then let's get the old rooms back."

"Well, maybe you'd better do that. I have to stay here. It's the only place she knows to find me."

They stayed until the place closed. Andrew only had one more drink. He didn't want to be impaired if Alice turned up that night. She might be upset or exuberant, and he'd have to know what to do, now that he was supposed to be equal to all occasions.

A week went by. Shahid leased two rooms in the same boarding house they had lived in before China. He moved into one and roamed the old haunts, looking up his friends. Andrew remained in the hotel, passing every day and night at the window, looking out for Alice. No message came. A fine carriage went by one day, a little too good for the neighborhood. It had a nice-looking horse, so it caught his attention. He saw it was Alice under a large feathered hat, in nice clothes, and the lady beside her must have been the mother, under another large hat. Alice didn't look up. They turned at the corner and went out of view. From then on, Andrew kept his field glasses on the windowsill and waited like a sniper.

He reminded himself that impetuosity was spark to the tinder of every mistake he had ever made. Without knowing how it had happened, patience had been forged from those fires as iron in a furnace. Even so, it took everything he had to resist going back to the Sheffields'. All he needed was a few minutes alone with her. He could refrain from doing injury to her father, but no one else would eject him from the house without a fight before he had the chance to speak to her. They would see the restraint and gentlemanly forbearance he had shown leaving it the first time.

Patience prevailed, even after sighting Alice in the carriage. But as he waited by the window every day and lay awake wondering every night why Alice had not looked up, he discovered there was another way to look at it. She must have known he would be in the window. He decided that if she had looked up, it would have been a renunciation, a last look at a life she had been persuaded to abandon. Because she did not look up, it must mean they were still in league with each other, and driving by in the carriage was her sign to him. He was sure of it. Every voice inside that rose up to say he didn't need her, that there were other women in the world—to those, he had only to remember her sitting in the sampan with the Nagant in her lap, or smiling over her shoulder at him, and all doubt went out of the patience of his waiting.

Alice came to the door late one night. He knew it could be no one else as he unlocked it.

"I've run away," she said.

She dropped her bag in the hall, and he took her in his arms.

"I'm sorry it's been so long. I tried to talk to them. I finally gave up. I knew you would wait for me."

He brought her in and turned up the gas on the little lamp on the wall.

"Do you have anything to drink? I walked all the way. I didn't want Father asking around the cabs. I left a note for Mother. I said I would be with you, so she'll know I'm safe. I want to get married tomorrow, Andrew. We can go to town hall."

She sat down on the bed, and Andrew reached for the canteen he kept on the windowsill. Alice took off her broad-rimmed feathered hat and set it down carefully beside her. It had been almost two weeks since he had seen her. She looked more womanly, poised, dignified. Maybe it was the dress with the collar and high shoulder gussets and lace flounces, but he felt he hardly knew her.

"Wait a minute," she said.

Alice let her hair down and started unbuttoning and unhooking herself out of the intricacies of dress and stockings. Stopping at the shoulder-length petticoat, she threw herself backward on the bed with her arms stretched over the sides and gave a great sigh of relief.

"I nearly died of the heat in these things every day," she said. Then she moved up to the pillow and propped up her head. "Can we get married tomorrow?"

Andrew joined her on the bed and lay on his side, looking at her, remembering everything he would have reminded her of if he had forced his way into the Sheffield house. "I believe there's paperwork," he said.

"You aren't backing out, are you?"

"No, I mean it, Alice. There's paperwork. Before we go to town hall, though, are you sure you want to do it like that?"

"I'll save the big wedding for next time," she said, laughing. "Oh, I love you so much."

First thing in the morning, Andrew sent a note around to Shahid in the rooming house asking him to meet them at the town hall at ten o'clock to be their witness. Then they had a nice breakfast in the hotel restaurant and went back to the room to dress. Andrew helped Alice back into all the pieces she had arrived in the night before because she said one was no good without the others. Andrew put on the suit he wore to meet her parents and felt a good deal better for the substitution of this occasion for the last. They caught a hackney to town hall and spotted Shahid standing by the big doors, holding the hand of a little girl.

"This is your flower girl, Dora," he said.

Alice bent over without a moment's hesitation and took Dora in her arms while Shahid held her basket.

"And oh, what beautiful flowers. This makes the day, my darling. Thank you for coming to help us, Dora."

"Dora lives at the house," said Shahid. "She always wanted to be a flower girl."

Indeed, the girl looked like being a flower girl was her dream come true, and her presence seemed to be just what was wanting. Procuring the license took a little time, but before the morning was out, Alice and Andrew stood before a judge in a hallway outside the city courtroom with Dora between them, repeated the vows of marriage to each other, and kissed. They used rings Shahid thought to pick up at a jeweler's on the way to town hall. He had excellent taste. Alice knew he would.

Turning from the judge, Alice bent over and whispered to Dora. "Now you'll walk ahead of us and hand out flowers to the people in the hallway," she said.

As they were crossing the stone plaza in front of town hall toward the cabs, Alice announced, "We're going to the Parker House for a wedding dinner." Then she whispered to Andrew, "Do you have any money?"

"Just for the cab," he said. "I didn't think we were going anywhere."

Shahid didn't have much on him either.

"I have plenty of money," she said.

They had a very good time at the Parker House and finished up with large servings of its famous Boston cream pie put together as a wedding cake. Alice and Andrew went back to the hotel for a last night before they took up residence in the rooming house. Shahid took Dora home in a cab and had their driver go through the nice parts of the city to see the lights on the way. Alice gave the girl many kisses as she got into the carriage, and Andrew put a silver dollar into her hand. It was a day they thought Dora would never forget.

It was the last of summer, and still light after the heat of the day was over. Andrew helped Alice undress, and she went down the hall to bathe while Andrew drew the shades and tidied up the room. When she came through the door in her robe, the little signs of fatigue that had begun to show in her face at the Parker House were replaced by a keen, bright look with an edge to it that suggested an eagerness to get to bed.

"The bath was very refreshing," she said. "I know you'll find it equally so."

He had not planned on it, but he went down to the men's bathing room and made short work of a bath. Alice had turned down the covers and was lying on top with the robe drawn about her and her dark hair spread over the pillow, as if she were reproducing for his return to the room a pose she had seen on the wall at an art exhibition. He turned away to undress in the early evening light coming through the shades and threw his shirt and trousers over a chair.

She was afraid her expression gave away a sudden apprehension as Andrew turned around naked.

"We don't have to—" he began.

"Oh no, we have to do it today," she said. "We did all the paperwork."

Alice told Andrew afterward, as she lay in his arms with her head on his chest, that the experience had quite taken her breath away. She felt invigorated by her first completed intimacy with a man and wanted to get up and walk around the city. But she was equally contented to remain where she was. She told Andrew about a young woman in an early English novel whose husband found her sleeping in a closet known to be inhabited by spiders—just to avoid the bedroom.

"I don't remember, but I think the husband was an unpleasant character in the book. Just the same, would you not feel terribly hurt if you were her husband?"

"Naturally. But maybe she just didn't like—you know."

"Sexual intercourse?"

"Let's say lovemaking."

"That's what it's called, Andrew. I know you and your soldier friends have vulgar terms for it, but you should put them aside."

"Well, nobody calls it anything anyway. I've never seen it referred to in all the books I've read so far."

"I know. That's very unfortunate," said Alice. "But you should know, writers are not permitted to use even the proper medical words or go into the subject at all. I think it may be because the readers of novels are largely women, and you know—I've never thought of it before, but I think it might have been purposeful on the author's part, to indirectly associate spiders with intercourse—that's the impression the book would leave with any woman."

Alice got up on her elbow, very excited to follow the idea. "Don't you see, Andrew, how misled we've been? If you tell women in so many words that intercourse is worse than spiders, they aren't going to want to have it." She paused a moment and then reflected, "How frightened men must be of promiscuity in women. Don't you think?"

"I've never worried about it," said Andrew.

"Well, what would you say if I said I wanted a night with Lieutenant Griswold, just to make love with him?"

"Probably the same thing you would say if I said I wanted a night with the serving girl in the restaurant—the one with the freckles."

"Oh, she's sweet, isn't she? But no, Andrew, I'm only making a point. The difference is I would ask you if you were in love with the serving girl. You wouldn't think to ask me if I was in love with Lieutenant Griswold." She lay down with her head on his chest again. "Men and women just think differently, I suppose. If you accept that as a premise, you couldn't say one gender was smarter than the other, could you?" She was very glad to see her husband considered the idea thoughtfully and did not dismiss it as perfect nonsense.

While they lay together quietly and the light faded in the room, Alice thought of her parents and wondered what Andrew was going to do now that he was a married man with a wife and would be responsible for the child she expected to have in nine months. That would be April or May. She started to cry for no reason. Andrew put his arms around her and stroked her head without saying anything.

"Will we be all right?" she said after he wiped the tears away.

The answer came in the gentleness of the arms around her. There was such strength in them. She knew he was ready to take on any task and capable of any work that needed to be done to make everything all right.

"We'll be fine," he said. "I've been thinking. I have some ideas."

"Don't tell me now," she said.

"Well then, let's get dressed in something comfortable and go downstairs for some coffee and pancakes. Then we'll come back and go to sleep."

What an excellent suggestion it was. Alice brightened up with that and felt better already. She asked him if he would be in a frame of mind to try it again that night by the light of a candle. He replied that at the risk of encouraging promiscuity in his wife, he would be pleased to go looking for a candle and place himself at her disposal.

Alice was inclined to believe that night, as she fell asleep against her husband, that ninety-nine percent of marital accord lay in satisfactory sexual intercourse. She was also sure that her mind needed no help from the energies down below to go off on tangents. Andrew was tender, gentle, and loving, and she could be fearless. What a relief.

Andrew and Alice had breakfast and checked out of the hotel in the morning. First, they moved their bags into the rooming house, unpacked, and got settled—then they decided to walk around the city. Nothing Andrew remembered of his youth was left standing. Even the alley where he had built the house for Jenny Jones was gone. The new streets in the area went in different directions, and he couldn't tell where the alley might have been. Back at the church where he had left Jenny Jones, they looked up and down the rows of headstones in the churchyard for her name. Alice thought there must be a potter's field somewhere in the city, but Andrew preferred they spend the rest of the day looking for Alice's memorable places. Since she had only been away two years, everything she had known was still there.

The next morning, Andrew and Shahid took a train to New York on business, expecting it to take two days. Alice sat at the writing desk, looking around the room and out the window. The furniture was a little worn, but it was very clean, and the rugs showed around their edges a very fine wood floor underneath. She thought it must have been a very beautiful town house before the neighborhood slipped. She could tell also by the molding around the high ceiling and the lovely flora-design wallpaper with rich but faded colors. They would have passed for the decor of a fine house in an earlier time.

When she knew what she wanted to say, Alice began a letter to her mother. Another try and another finally led her to conclude that her mother might be more receptive if she did not bombard her with how happy she was. The letter she posted to the box on the corner that afternoon was a simple invitation to tea tomorrow at 4 p.m. at The Crystal Tea Room nearby. She had signed it "Mrs. Alice Croft." Then she went back to the room and wondered what she was going to wear.

"Mrs. Croft," said Mrs. Sheffield as a greeting, walking briskly up to Alice on the sidewalk.

"Yes, Mother."

"Well, that's done with then. Let's go in."

Alice and her mother went in the glass doors of the Crystal Tea Room and were shown to a table by a window. Alice had thought it best to get into the corset and the rest of the business she had worn to town hall. Her mother was in one of her customary walking dresses with the voluminous skirt needed to accommodate her giant stride, a white blouse, and short jacket. The brim of her hat swept up in front and plunged in back, leaving her face in the curl of the wave. She was a large, youthful woman, just as Alice foresaw herself becoming in the future. Sitting closely together at the little table, they might have been taken for sisters but a few years apart.

"We'll have tea, and then I want to see where you are living," said Mrs. Sheffield.

"Very well, Mother. But I won't have any criticism," said Alice.

"Then you shall not have it. You see I have come to talk to you, and that is what I shall be doing. Your safety, not your comfort, concerns me most."

Tea and little biscuits were set before them. They spooned their sugar, stirred, and took sips and nibbles.

"Are you expecting a child, Mrs. Croft?"

"Mother, please."

"Alice," said Mrs. Sheffield, softening her tone.

"Not out of the respectable period of time commenced by marriage," said Alice.

"Then you are legally married?"

"Yes, Mother. We were married at town hall on Monday."

"Well then. The matter is settled."

"Thank you, Mother."

They spoke no more on the topic. They drank their tea and repaired the damage with conversation on little incidents of the two years Alice had been away. It was such a lady's place, the Crystal Tea Room, warm, polite, and comfortable. While they talked so pleasantly and kept an ear to the conversations of ladies at other tables, it struck Alice that it was a world she was leaving. She had run away from home. Whatever the future held with the kind of man she had married, it might be the last time she would be at tea with ladies. It was difficult to imagine attending performances of the orchestra with Andrew or receiving company as the mistress of a grand house. Who knows what else she had given up so blithely?

When they left the Crystal Tea Room, Alice took her mother's arm as they walked through the busy streets to the rooming house.

"I was very much like you at one time," her mother said.

Nothing more followed, but Alice was grateful to hear it said. What exactly Mother remembered from being young was impossible to say, but Alice had overheard stories from the servants. There were also whispers of how Father had won her. Now that she was discovering what she herself was capable of doing for a lover, what would be hard to believe about Mother?

At the rooming house, Alice kissed Dora on the landing as she was trudging up the stairs to the fourth floor. "This is my mother," she said.

Dora gave a little curtsy and looked from one to the other as if she were seeing double. Mrs. Sheffield bent over to take her hand.

"She was my flower girl," said Alice as Dora scrambled up the next flight. Alice unlocked the door to the room.

Mrs. Sheffield stood in the doorway and looked around, trying not to take note of the bed. "This is very pleasant," she said. "You know, you can purchase a screen."

"Andrew likes to be able to see the door at night."

"Oh, yes, of course."

"He's very protective of me, Mother."

There might have been a world of things her mother wanted to say, but Alice trusted the truce between them and let her mother roam about the room, looking something like an animal well accustomed to captivity but suddenly put in a new cage.

"When you need more room, darling, we can help you."

"We'll see, Mother. Andrew is in New York investigating business possibilities right now. He is very independent of mind and wants us to make our own way in the world."

"I understand that very well, my dear, but there are limits, and if you are already starting a family, he must be prepared to consider assistance if you are in need of it."

"Well, it's all up in the air now, Mother. He'll be home tomorrow. He's full of ideas. When we were delayed in China, he supported us in the currency exchange business and did quite well with it, so I'm hoping he'll go into it here."

Mrs. Sheffield took a chair, and Alice drew another one up beside her.

"I'm sorry it didn't come up at dinner. I know Father and Andrew would find a lot in common. I was thinking that if Andrew did well on his own, father might offer him a position in the bank."

"I would not expect that, dear. At least for the present. I'm afraid bad impressions have a lasting effect on your father."

Alice looked down to think as she smoothed the pleats of her skirt over her legs.

"Does he know you're here?"

"No, dear. It was too soon to approach him. I will tell him I know where you are, and that you are safe—and properly married—but I cannot be an emissary between you. All I can do is visit from time to time when he isn't looking. I would not like him to think I've run away too, you know."

Despite the circumstances, Alice and her mother had a little laugh together. At that moment they both looked up to a soft knock at the door just before it opened.

"I'm home," Andrew called, thrusting his bag ahead of him through the passage. "We finished up early and caught the train—Mrs. Sheffield."

"Mr. Croft."

"Oh, Andrew, I'm so glad you're home."

Alice ran to kiss him on the cheek as he put down his bag. The warm lilt in his voice as he first appeared in the door abruptly vanished on his sighting of Mrs. Sheffield and was replaced with a stiff formality that Alice could feel taking over the movements of his body like a rigor mortis. He kissed Alice back as if he were punching tickets on a trolley and moved toward Mrs. Sheffield, who remained seated but put forth her hand.

"Welcome to our home," he said, removing his hat and taking her hand. "I regret leaving Alice to receive you alone."

"We've had a very nice time, Mr. Croft."

"Everything is fine with Mother," said Alice.

"That's very good of you, Mrs. Sheffield. I would have preferred to speak to you and Mr. Sheffield together the other evening, but as you know, we had business to conduct, and immediately after, I was escorted to the servants' door. But I asked for Alice's hand before I left, as duty called upon me to do. I don't know if your husband told you that."

"It is no surprise to me that he did not. Please sit down, Mr. Croft. I knew something was between you when you first arrived. I won't make apologies for Mr. Sheffield though. There was no indication of a romantic connection in your correspondence. You had plenty of time to alert us. I'm very sorry that you did not.

"Alice," she said, turning to her daughter as she resumed the chair beside her, "You should have intimated in your wire from Peking or the hotel in California, or anywhere along the trip home. It would have given your father time to adjust his temperament to a new state of affairs."

Turning back to Andrew, she said, "Alice may have told you, Mr. Croft, that I also married beneath my station. I am familiar with the adjustments one or the other must make. Once Mr. Sheffield has taken a position on a matter, it is not his habit to alter it, even in view of changing circumstances and reasonable argument. I have had to work around that on many occasions."

"If there is any fault to the way we presented ourselves, Mrs. Sheffield, it would be mine," said Andrew.

"Just so," said Mrs. Sheffield.

"But I would like to say, with due respect to the mother of my wife, that as much as it is an honor to stand as the representative of those beneath you, you should know, and should communicate in any way you can to Mr. Sheffield, that I intend to come up in the world. Pursuant to that, I have received an offer of employment and will leave with my man for the South African Republic next week."

Alice was stunned.

"Did you know about this Alice?"

"No, Mother. We'll discuss it tonight. We discuss everything together." Turning to Andrew, she added, "That is how we reach decisions."

"I should hope so," said Mrs. Sheffield. "I understand that South Africa is an unstable region of the world, Mr. Croft."

"You knew that to be within the purview of my occupation, madam, when you and Mr. Sheffield engaged my services to go to China."

"Well then, I will leave you to your discussion," concluded Mrs. Sheffield as she rose to leave, looking with compassion at Alice.

Andrew spoke up quickly. "Alice will be supported while I'm away by regular advances against the balance of my fee."

"I'm sure she will find that a comfort in your absence, young man," said Mrs. Sheffield, extending to Andrew her hand at the door.

Alice followed her mother down the stairs and assisted her into the carriage while Andrew waited upstairs on the landing.

"Don't let yourself be turned on his finger, darling," were Mrs. Sheffield's parting words through the window.

Alice burst into the room. Andrew was looking out the window to be sure the carriage was taking the mother-in-law away.

"You can stop being so formal now, Andrew," she said. "You can let down your guard, whatever it is, and stop being an ass. Mother accepts the marriage, can't you see that?"

"You went behind my back."

"You went behind mine. What is this proposal?"

"Guarding gold shipments. Just routine."

"If it's routine, why do they have to bring a man from America to Africa?"

"They don't trust the people they have. I can make a lot of money. Our future is going to depend on that."

"Our future is going to depend on you being alive, Andrew. Have you lost your mind? You're married now. I thought you were intelligent enough to understand that you would have to do something civilized for a living when we got married."

"If you don't like what I am," he said, going toward his bag on the bed, "maybe I don't have to unpack."

Alice sat down and tears came to her eyes, but her anger pushed them back. When he turned around, she looked at him straight in the eyes.

"Damn you," she said. "God damn you."

Andrew clenched his fists and looked around the room. Alice kept a little porcelain dog on the nightstand that she had brought from home the night she ran away. He picked it up and was about to throw it through the open window when Alice was suddenly in front of him.

He lowered his arm. He could have broken the legs off the little thing with a squeeze of his hand, but Alice had the same look that he had seen on the face of Jenny Jones when he tried to take away her silver dollar.

"I won't have a violent man, Andrew," she said quietly. "You can leave if that is what you want to be."

Andrew sat down on the bed. He put the little dog back on the nightstand and looked out the window. Alice came over and stood to the side of it. There was a little breeze coming through, lifting the light curtains. She would have to wash them. After he left and again before he came home.

"Will this be the last time you leave me?" she asked quietly.

"Yes."

"Will you promise me that?"

"Yes."

"Then you'll promise to come home and cleave to your wife forevermore?"

"Yes. I promise."

They lay down on the bed and turned to each other.

"How long will you be away?"

"Three months. They wanted me for a year, but I said I could only give them three months. They're going to pay the same as for the year."

"I can live three months. Mother will want me to come home, but I'll stay here and wait for you. I'm sure I'll be having a child, Andrew, and I want you here for that."

"I'll be back by then. When my three months is over, I'll come home, no matter what they want to give me to stay."

Alice sat up. With the back of her hand, she wiped away the last of the tears on her face. "Then let's get practical," she said. "When do you leave?"

"As soon as the advance money is wired to the bank. I gave them the number for First National. The one down the street. It will be under both our names so you can draw on it. Shahid is on his own pay, so what's in the bank will be all yours. It's a committee that hired us, so we'll see if the money really comes in. If it does, it will probably come through next week or so."

"Well, let's go get some dinner," she said.

They walked a little way around their neighborhood and chose a place they had not tried before. They had some beers with dinner, and Andrew carved their initials in the tabletop in almost the last space left smooth by lovers of past times.

Just before Christmas, Shahid Mashute returned alone from South Africa. He changed his name to Charles Thompson and took a job as kitchen help in a hotel. Within an hour of his arrival in Boston, he went to tell Alice that Andrew had been captured and hanged by the British. He had witnessed it himself.

When the money from South Africa stopped coming to the bank and was gone, Alice went home to her parents' house. She had a baby there in the spring. She was still wearing black at the christening. She named her son Rory for no other reason than she wanted a name with no connection to the past.

Then she cried every night for a year.

CHAPTER TWENTY-FOUR

SPRING 1892

Procter Darlington stood on the sidewalk before the Sheffields' tall brownstone on Myrtle Street, Boston, looking up to the polished black door with all the confidence of one who came highly recommended. Twenty-six years of age, descendant of the venerable Darlingtons of Massachusetts Bay Colony, Phillips Academy '84, Harvard '88, and now a junior in the House of Morgan. He stood at six feet in a tailored suit, with a fine athletic body built on the playing fields. Short auburn hair parted in the middle and slicked to the sides, wearing wire spectacles that framed the excellent blue of his eyes.

The Daimler motor carriage parked on the street behind him attested to a streak of recklessness in him not yet brought to heel by financial constraints or marital impediments. Marriage had been frequently suggested as a remedy to his sometimes immoderate behavior. Words of parental remonstrance had gone through his head again as shutting off the motor emitted an embarrassing loud bang! from under the seat, followed by a puff of black smoke. Along the avenue, startled carthorses shook in their traces, saddle horses standing at hitching posts tugged at loose reins and clattered off down the street. There were faces in the windows, but Procter only glanced up with a winning collegiate smile and took the steps up to the door in quick, effortless bounds. It was too late to go home, change clothes, and ride back in a cab, so he would stick with the Daimler. It showed he was a man with a vision of the future, unperturbed by its occasional inconveniences.

He had come to dinner on the invitation of Edward Sheffield, the result of an introduction he had schemed during a Sunday breakfast at the Atwater Hotel. The regular get-together, attended by the business beau monde of Boston, was his own discovery, and to Procter, in his professional capacity as an agent for Morgan, the introduction to Mr. Sheffield represented a breakthrough in a year's research into the old man and his bank. Privately, the compiling of a dossier on Mr. Sheffield and his business had allowed him the pleasure of including newspaper clippings from the society pages, in which photographs of the daughter, Mrs. Alice Croft, proved numerous. Feigning complete ignorance of the daughter until she was brought up by Sheffield, Procter was quick to catch on to the old gentleman's interest in having him to the house for dinner; old Edward Sheffield meant to slip a Morgan man into the family.

Procter yanked the doorbell chain again, harder this time. Bad bell or old butler, he thought.

At first it was just an amusing speculation, but as Procter felt himself becoming the odd duck among his associates at Morgan, and as he felt more uncomfortable in his childhood home on the weekends with his parents in Boston, he knew he had come to a point where appearances were beginning to generate unpleasant inferences. It was time to consider a marriage of convenience.

He kept a woman in New York, but she was an artist and freethinker and not a suitable candidate. She would have laughed at the idea of marrying into society anyway. He met her in a café in Greenwich Village. When he saw how she was living, he set her up in an apartment in the village and stayed over with her three or four nights during the week. She turned the second bedroom into an art studio, painted and sculpted most of the day, and cooked for him in the evening. All he had to do was give her a ring before he left the office, and by the time he got there, dinner was ready. Available any time, of course, was all the recreation a young man could want in the bedroom.

Lois was avant-garde in lifestyle as well as in art. More than a few times he had walked in to find mattresses thrown on the floor of the drawing room, candles lit on every shelf, and a crowd of new acquaintances as strewn about the room as their discarded clothing. Lois encouraged him to view his initial objection to joining the party as the self-enforcement of an outmoded morality, instilled in him by the debunked authorities of church and state designed to obstruct his path toward self-discovery and opposed to the fulfillment of mankind in its natural state. She was well educated, recently out of Vassar College, and knew how to make her points compelling.

Lois was sympathetic to his situation, and they discussed it by candlelight, drinking gin and smoking cigarettes. "I see the dilemma," she said the other night. "You don't want to get booted out of JP for being a queer bird, but you don't want to get tied down. The girl is the easy part. You've already picked her out of the herd. Don't look at me like that. You know what I'm talking about. The one in the newspaper clippings. You're in love with her."

"Spare me."

"No, I can tell. Don't think you can't change your spots, Procter. Maybe you have it in you to be a decent bourgeois. Love works in mysterious ways. The only question will be how open-minded she is. Just send her down here. I'll find out for you. You can't lead her into a marriage blind. If something comes up out of the blue later on, you're going to be sorry. I'll be able to tell how amenable she'll be to all those little things about you."

"What little things?"

"Now listen to me, Procter. Two heads are better than one. And this one has your best interests at heart. She'll have to know about me anyway, won't she?"

Lois stood up and came around to him. She put her arms around his neck. Her breasts slipped out of the kimono, and the pink tips of them swung over his eyes as he looked up at her.

"Let's go to bed now. I shaved myself with your razor," she teased merrily, glancing downward for a moment, then back to his eyes. "Just for something different. I thought you might like it that way. Feel how smooth I am."

After another forceful tug on the Sheffield's doorbell chain, a maid in a dusting cap called down from a window above to say that the doorbell pull chain no longer worked and advised him to use the brass knocker in front of his nose. Not trusting the maid to take it upon herself in her lowly station to alert the household, Procter gave the knocker two sharp raps, and resigned himself to begin waiting anew.

During the week between receiving the invitation and standing in front of the Sheffield door, Procter had found more photographs of Mrs. Croft to clip from the newspapers. He couldn't tell exactly how tall she was until she was pictured receiving an award from the Children's Aid Society standing with David Rolstover. Procter knew him from Sunday gatherings at the Atwater. The top of her head was about level with Rolstover's eyebrows, so that would put Mrs. Croft at roughly five foot eight or nine. Tall for a woman—unless it was the shoes.

At times during the four-hour train ride from New York to Boston on Friday nights, Procter shook himself awake from staring blankly out the window. Coming down to earth, he realized his imagination was running away with very little to go on. But getting together with Alice Sheffield began to feel as sensible a solution to his situation as supply finding demand. He was fairly certain of the intentions of the father from Sundays at the Atwater, so the only doubt remaining was the daughter's unknown disposition on marrying again.

She certainly was a peach, at least in the newspapers, with her arms embracing a rescued child, handing a check to the director of a foundling home, or speaking at a dinner to raise money on behalf of children injured in the mills. Always smiling. Did that mean she was content with remaining a widow doing good works? That would be a waste; he had looked her up in public records and found her to be only twenty-two. As near as he could tell from the newspaper photographs, her hair was black and her eyes were light, probably blue. One portrait in three quarters view showed a regal nose that he had missed in the other photographs. She seemed to like large hats. He could do without that.

Business, he knew, would not come up that evening. It was well-known that Morgan men never talked. Related, but altogether a different matter, Procter could guess at his host's opinion on the rumor that Morgan would underwrite the proposed U.S. Steel merger. From delving into Sheffield's finances, he knew that he was a large holder in American Steel & Wire, and if the merger went through, the consolidation would cash him out. Thereafter, he would have to buy shares in the new company at market prices if he wanted to stay in steel. He wouldn't be happy about that. Neither were they likely to discuss the future of Mr. Sheffield's bank, the largest privately held bank in Massachusetts. Morgan could eat it up with no more trouble than one takes to moisten a finger on the tongue to pick up a breadcrumb. That had to be an unsettling prospect and touchy subject for the soft-spoken gentleman with the quaint side-whiskers.

Procter was finally received by an elderly butler, who escorted him very slowly to the library. Walking through, he could see the layout of the house was similar to his parents' brownstone a few streets over, just a little more old-fashioned in its furnishings and artwork on the walls. The library was dark with heavy drapes, sturdy furniture, and tables crowded with picture frames under lamps with very large silk shades.

Mr. Sheffield turned from the fireplace and advanced to shake his hand. He was dressed in an out-of-style suit that Mrs. Sheffield would probably have preferred discarded. Because of the side-whiskers and stuffy surroundings, Procter felt as if he had been transported back to mid-century.

"Glad you could make it, my boy," said Mr. Sheffield. "I'd like you to meet my wife."

The lady of the house rose from a heavily upholstered wingback chair placed sideways to the fireplace and extended her hand. Mrs. Sheffield was a tall, well-dressed woman, possessed of a stately bearing. Standing side by side, she and her husband seemed to represent a perfect joining of business class and aristocracy, but Procter felt his skills were sufficient to play up to either one.

"A pleasure I have long anticipated," said Procter. As he bowed slightly, his eye caught the entrance of the daughter through the tall oak doors.

"And my daughter, Mrs. Croft," said Mr. Sheffield.

"Delighted to meet you, Mrs. Croft."

"I heard your motor carriage, Mr. Darlington," said Alice curtly, as she extended her hand. "From the back of the house."

"I'm afraid it can be noisy," he said behind his most winning smile while pressing her hand slightly and releasing.

In conversation over sherry, Mr. Sheffield brought up the family history Procter had related to him at the Atwater, looking to his daughter at every turn to make sure she was taking it in; the Mayflower landing, the American Revolution, and every other notable event in which his ancestors had taken a prominent role. She sat across from him and occasionally reached to a low table where they had set their glasses. She was apparently no longer in mourning, dressed in a pleated gray skirt and white blouse. The side panels of a matching gray jacket dropped away to reveal a handsome bust when she sat up straight again with glass in hand. She wore her hair in the same style as her mother and every other woman in public these days, the soft pompadour of the Gibson Girl as depicted in magazine illustrations.

Alice certainly was fetching all right. If there was anything to be gained in foretelling the lasting quality of her beauty, the question was simply thrown back at him by a glance toward Mrs. Sheffield. The two might have been taken for twin sisters if they had not been in the same room sitting side by side, where age had left only the most fleeting of imprints on the elder. The nose was decidedly the dominant feature to both faces as he looked from one to the other. Its long history became apparent to him when the maid announced dinner at the door and they made their way through a portrait gallery of Mrs. Sheffield's ancestral predecessors in the hallway to the dining room.

Procter was placed on the right of Mrs. Sheffield, with Alice across from him and Mr. Sheffield at the far end of the table. Procter asked Alice, as he held her chair, to speak of her year in China and of her charities at home, subjects he was careful to choose as having been touched on previously by her father. Alice complied dispassionately at first, through a tasty chowder and oyster crackers, relating a chronology of both experiences without any mention of her deceased husband. But when she came to her advocacy for child labor laws during the rack of lamb, she became flushed and passionate. Mrs. Sheffield rushed in to save the dessert conversation, taking advantage of her daughter pausing to draw a breath.

"You always flit from this to that, Alice dear," she said, dismissing the subject in one swoop and turning to Procter, placing a hand over his on the table.

"Now, where were we with your family, Mr. Darlington? It's positively engrossing. So different from what we are usually treated to at table," she added, with a benevolent look thrown to her daughter.

With mild protest, Procter agreed to finish up his tale, but first he invited Mrs. Croft to tell him about her crossing of the Pacific, reasonably confident that the voyage would not have been made memorable by the discovery of a social injustice of some kind onboard.

After dinner, they adjourned to a second-floor drawing room that displayed a woman's light and airy touch, throwing the library below into relief as the male underworld of the house. Procter brought his family history up to the current time, ending with news just received that his request for a two-week holiday in August had been approved by the firm. He was going to Canada for two weeks, to the family island in Georgian Bay.

"I haven't been up there since I joined the firm," he said. "That will be four years. It's quite a remarkable place. No electric, no gas. No telephone. No modern conveniences of any kind. We live in tents, like the Indians," he said.

"Roughing it, eh?"

"That's right, Mr. Sheffield. We live like the Indians. The parents built a cabin for themselves, but the rest of us are in tents—my five older brothers, their wives, and my two sisters and their husbands, lots of young nephews and nieces—positively everyone comes up. There must be forty or fifty of us by now."

The numbers seemed to give Mr. Sheffield pause until Procter caught on that he should explain that the behavior of his family in the wilds was nothing like socialism, and what might have been perceived as a commune was nothing of the sort and about to change anyway.

"Last summer my brothers and sisters began staking out parts of the island," he said. "Now that we're so many families, I don't know if anything is going to be left for me. That's what happens to the last unmarried one, I suppose." He laughed. "I might end up sitting in a little tent on a rocky point nobody claimed."

It was not exactly the last thought he wanted to leave with the Sheffields. He had spoken without thinking. The careless statement of his availability as a single gentleman, that he might be interested in marrying their daughter, and that they would live in a tent like Indians on a remote island might have been dropped too unexpectedly. He felt he had made a thoughtless move on the chessboard and taken his hand off the piece too quickly. There would not be any signs tonight. The parents would have to talk. Then one of them would talk to Alice. Then he would have to wait to see if there would be another invitation to dinner.

Just when Alice expected Mr. Darlington to say he really must go, her mother turned to the entrance of the drawing room and said, "What is it, Nurse? Oh yes. But first, do come in and show Mr. Darlington the baby."

It was clearly her mother's doing, this staged walk-through, to determine what Mr. Darlington might think of taking on another man's child before too much was invested in the scheme.

The nurse stepped down to the polished wood floor of the drawing room, carefully holding what appeared to be an armload of blankets, and approached Mr. Darlington. Mother rose and came over to fish through the covers for Rory's pink face and pulled out a chubby little grasping hand at the same time.

"This is little Rory, Mr. Darlington," she said.

Mr. Darlington appeared surprised but gamely took the tiny hand between his thumb and first finger, giving it a little gentleman's shake. Clearly he was delighted with the boy or made a good show of it. Alice had had about enough of her mother for one night.

She stood up and summoned Nurse to her side. "Please excuse us," she said, making it evident that she, Nurse, and the bundle of blankets were leaving the room. At the entrance to the hall, she turned and said, "It was a pleasure to make your acquaintance, Mr. Darlington. I am a nursing mother, you see, and my presence is required for that purpose in the nursery. I gather from your surprise, sir, that knowledge of my having borne a child was withheld from you before you accepted the invitation for this evening."

She paused long enough before leaving the room to see that her last remarks left Father in wordless disbelief and Mother putting a hand wearily up to her forehead.

The next morning at breakfast, before Father came down, Alice looked at her mother straight and said, "Father intends Mr. Darlington for me, doesn't he?"

"Can I have my coffee first, dear?"

Alice poured them each a cup and set the pot down.

"He comes from a very nice family, Alice."

"I wouldn't be marrying the family, Mother. Or living with them in a tent like an Indian."

"No, of course not. But marriage is so much more than just the two of you. You don't know that yet."

"I know what's important in marriage, Mother," said Alice. "You might remember I was married once before. I am familiar with sexual intercourse."

Her mother's reaction included coloring in the face as she rose in her chair. "I *wish* you wouldn't speak like that, Alice."

Alice reached out and took her mother's hand. "But that's what it comes down to, doesn't it? All the fuss that goes on around the simple act of mating, getting the male and female together in a suitable pairing."

"Oh heavens, Alice! No, it comes down to many other things—compatibility, consideration, respect—many other things," insisted her mother. "What happens in private does not matter half so much. If you think it does, you are going to find yourself with too much time on your hands when you get to be my age."

"Well," said Alice, conceding the argument, "there's nothing really to quibble about. He's a good-looking man, and I find him physically arousing. I would not mind having sexual intercourse with him. Not in the slightest. You can tell Father I will consider Mr. Darlington."

The admission of her daughter's willingness to marry, so easily procured, was a great relief to her mother, notwithstanding the way it was expressed.

"That will make your father very happy, dear," her mother quietly returned. "But please, darling. Never speak like that in front of your father—in consideration of his heart, you know."

There were more dinners at the Sheffields' and one or two at the Darlingtons' that seemed to confirm everyone's conviction that the uniting of the two families would be agreeable to both. Subsequent to that, Mr. Darlington asked permission of the Sheffields to visit their daughter, to talk with her alone, and to take her on rides in his Daimler motor carriage.

With the courtship officially underway, Alice sat on the floor of her room one night before the fireplace and burned her letters from Andrew. It was a pity to watch those queer smudgy little postage stamps from the Transvaal curl and catch flame.

She had to stop crying every night. A good mother should not be doing that with an impressionable child around. The past would never come back. She had to accept that. She had to stop talking to Andrew every day in her head, stop seeing him every time she raised her eyes, stop listening for the sound of his voice. She had to forget the dream she had of them last night. There was nothing she could do but put a stop to all that remembering.

The courtship of Alice and Procter was conducted on weekends, utilizing only parts of those two days, taking into account Alice going off every four hours to nurse the baby. Procter came back to Boston late every Friday night and was back on the train to New York Sunday evening. Saturday was their only possibility of a full day together because Sunday incorporated dinner at her family or his. Still, matters went along as they were supposed to. The young couple began to address each other by their first names, and Alice took his arm when walking. The only time Alice did not feel the eyes of two families on her were the occasions when she went to New York with Nurse and little Rory to visit Procter during the workweek.

Because Alice was on her honor not to visit his lodgings, Procter put them up in a hotel close by and met her there after work. Following dinner, they strolled about town or took a cab to the theater.

Alice was surprised to find that Procter was a patron of the arts, which she discovered one night when they stopped in at a very nice little apartment in Greenwich Village, just off Washington Square, where she was introduced to an artist known simply as Lois. Several of her fellow painters and sculptors were there, lounging on the couch and stuffed chairs and reclining on the floor. She learned also that Procter kept the apartment at his own expense for those in the art world striving to make their names. Everyone was very nice, and Alice hoped she was not too much the lady in the gathering, as she had come to New York so properly corseted and laced up, with one of her large hats that was too complicated to remove. Lois was particularly warm toward her, and Alice found her refreshingly free-spirited. She was glad Procter had so many stimulating friendships in the art world to ruffle his businessman feathers a little.

When they left the apartment that night, Lois embraced her warmly and exclaimed, "Oh, you're perfect."

The first time Procter lifted her onto the padded red leather seat of the motor carriage, Alice exclaimed, "Oh dear—no horse! How strange. It's going to go without a horse. Oh, how very odd. It makes us so conspicuous without a horse in front. Don't you feel like we're sitting on the edge of a cliff?"

She laughed and leaned against Procter on the seat. Several months had gone by since the first dinner, and Alice felt comfortable touching him and getting used to the feel of him around her. It was refreshing that this new man of hers was so unencumbered by cares and responsibilities. On the weekends, Procter Darlington was free to be himself, footloose and fancy-free, and Alice was beginning to notice the liberating effect it had on her.

"Oh, Procter, let me steer," she said.

"Well, all right. We'll just switch places."

With the raising of her long skirt above her knees and a parting of her legs that would have shocked her mother, Alice simply went over him to get into the driver seat. Then she patted everything back in place and listened carefully as he explained the little wheel with a handle, the levers, and the bars coming up through the floor.

"You'd better take off your hat, Alice. And you'll be wearing these," he said, holding up a pair of leather goggles.

"Oh dear, what about my hair?"

"Well—let it down. I'll braid it for you."

Without a word, she took the pins out of her hair, shook it out and turned herself around. Procter gathered it into thick strands and began a tie that showed he was aware of everything that went into a comfortable braid for a woman. It was so pleasant to be in close company with a man again after more than a year. She closed her eyes and let herself enjoy the scent and aura of the male around her as she felt him touching lightly against her back. When all was said and done, she knew she was ready to have a man again, and this one was quite something in every department. If he made an offer, she was going to accept it, and if she happened not to be in the mood when he asked, well, she would make herself say yes anyway, on the strength of coming to the same decision so many times in the last few weeks. It could not be far off. There were signs that he was getting close, especially in the liberties he took touching her shoulders or the small of her back.

After her braid was completed, Procter turned her around to face front. He adjusted the strap to the goggles and put them over her head, looked her over and said, "Ready to go?" Then he turned on the motor, and off they went.

Alice felt perfectly in control with one hand on the steering handle and one on the break lever, and Procter looked very pleased with her quick mastery of driving. In a little while, going at twelve miles per hour, faster than Alice had ever gone in the open air with the road right under her feet, they were into the countryside. She took the Daimler up to top speed and weaved the vehicle from one side of the road to the other to test the handling. How free she felt! How exhilarating it was!

The next weekend, early Saturday morning, they set out in the Daimler with a picnic basket. It was early summer, and the countryside was all fields of corn, wheat, and colorful wildflowers. The gentle breeze in the air was quickly replaced by the stiff wind generated by their speed of fourteen miles per hour.

"Where do you want to go?" she shouted.

"Anywhere. Remember that little bridge last week? Let's go there. Good place for a picnic."

"I hope nobody else is there with the same idea."

"I don't think anyone will have the same idea I have," he said, not shouting, but leaning close with his lips at her ear. "I have a question for you."

It seemed forever to get to the bridge, and it seemed an inordinate amount of time taken in choosing a suitable place by the stream, and so long to throw down a blanket, and pull out the picnic basket. All the plates of pheasant and chilled asparagus had to come out, along with little pots of butter and condiments, covered bowls of salad, wrapped pears and apples, cakes under cloth, silverware, dishes, bottles of milk, tea, and coffee. And then he was hungry and wanted to eat. Mostly he was laughing and bringing up stupid little things and smiling his winning smile. It was quite maddening. When they had finished all the courses of the luncheon, Procter took off his jacket and rolled it up.

"Now for a little nap," he said. He gently pushed the picnic basket and dishes to the edge of the blanket. "Now lay back on this."

Alice lay her head down on his rolled-up jacket and folded her hands over her middle. "I have to get back to nurse the baby," she said.

"Just for a little while." Procter took off his glasses and lay down with his arms behind his head.

"What was your question?" she asked, in a very straightforward way.

"Well, it's like this, Alice. You'll marry me, won't you?" He rose up on one elbow facing her. "I mean, we have a lot of fun together, don't we? I've already asked your father."

"When was that?" It was hard to keep annoyance out of her tone.

"Last Sunday at the Atwater. He said it was all right with your mother too."

She wanted to say there was more to marriage than having fun but turned her head to him and stated very seriously, "I have to go home and feed my baby, Procter."

He had not asked her the right way. Alice got to her feet without his assistance. Together they put the dishes back in the picnic basket without speaking. He shook out the blanket and folded it. Alice stayed by the stream while Procter went to put the blanket and basket in the Daimler. She watched a leaf fall into the water and slip into the current. It would play on the water to the Mystic or Charles River, and then to the sea. Nothing came back the other way. How could anyone believe in suffering loss and finding new happiness? She felt tears coming to her eyes over some impossible squaring of Procter and Andrew that could not be helped, the brazen presence of one and the pull of the other, the strange reversal when, for a short time, life could demand the forfeiture of all things death.

Procter came back and stood beside her quietly for a moment, as he might add his presence to mourners at a gravesite. Then he turned her and held her in his arms. Against his shoulder, Alice cried for the last time over Andrew. When she was finished, she pulled back to wipe her eyes and nose with Procter's handkerchief.

"Will you marry me, Alice?" he asked.

With her head against Procter's shoulder, Alice listened to the birds, the rustling of the leaves above, and gurgling of water over rocks in the stream. As she pressed herself against him, she put everything else out of her mind but the necessity of moving forward, and said yes.

CHAPTER TWENTY-FIVE

The engagement had the same restrictions as the courtship, differing only in the urgency of getting a wedding together before Procter's two-week holiday in August. The wedding trip would be taken in Canada if all went to schedule.

With little less than a month to spare, Mrs. Darlington and Mrs. Sheffield teamed up to put on the show. Though Mrs. Darlington was a good fifteen years older than Alice's mother, both believed no challenge was too great when sufficient energy and money could be brought to bear. Established practice favored energy over money in both families, and Mrs. Darlington proved more than able to uphold her particular reading of Darwin that explained how, through many generations of Darlingtons, by means of natural selection, strong and tireless women had emerged whose dominion over all things domestic was undisputed. Husbands were obliged to step back as plans went forward.

Messengers were sent to enlist young ladies of societal charities, who knew Alice, to be her bridesmaids. On Procter's side, no such improvising was required, for the continental railroads enabled Mrs. Darlington to bring in reinforcements from all points of the compass in the form of her five other sons and two daughters, accompanied by their wives, husbands, and squads of grandchildren. To all this, Procter and Alice were aware only of the inconvenience of long fittings for Alice's wedding dress. Behind the scenes, the two mothers took charge of dressing the groomsmen and bridesmaids, securing the church, contracting for a reception hall, and arranging for the orchestra, food, flowers, transportation, hotels, photographers, and incidentals of all kinds up to the triumphant day of the spectacle.

Alice Croft and Procter Darlington were married at the Anglican Church of Boston. It was the same church that had engaged Andrew to bring her home from China only a little more than two years before. She lowered her face to the hail of rice thrown by the better half of Boston, and she lifted the billowing skirts of her splendid wedding dress to descend the marble steps upon which Andrew had left the body of Jenny Jones in rags, so many more years before. Departing the reception early, the newlyweds, with little Rory in the arms of his nurse, rushed to catch an afternoon train to Toronto. Alice thought it best to sit up all night with the baby.

"Nurse can have my berth," she told Procter. "And I want you to go to bed too. You go on now, Miss Lantz. I'll mind the baby tonight. You'll need your rest for the island. It's in the first sleeping car, berth number twenty-two—an upper. Mind the ladder."

After Nurse went off, making her way through the car catching the back of each seat as she passed it, Alice smiled to Procter. Miss Lantz was a lady's maid who had come from Switzerland to attend Alice's mother in the early years of her marriage. She had served as Alice's nurse and governess and stayed on as a companion for her mother. All Alice had ever heard of her past was that her fiancé had died. Now she was approaching middle age. Her hair was going white, but she was lean and lively and very pleased to have a baby to look after again.

"She's not very steady on her legs, is she?" Alice said to Procter. "I'd better take care of the baby while we're on the train." Then she leaned to kiss her new husband and whispered in his ear. "We can have sexual intercourse when we reach the hotel in Toronto."

It was amusing to see Procter's eyes pop out when she said it. She hoped having sexual intercourse with this man was not going to be like conversing about it with her mother. He must be experienced. He was too good-looking not to have done it with somebody. But it would be nice, too, if he was new to it. She could show him the ropes.

"There isn't any reason to rush, and I'd like to freshen up," she said. "I hope you don't mind me being outspoken, Procter. I wish you would say something. You've done nothing since we got on the train but sit and smile at me. It makes you look silly."

Procter sat back with his arms crossed behind his head and smiled. "It's just working out so well," he said.

"What were you expecting?"

"I don't know," he said with his winning smile. "Maybe when you've thought about something for a long time, you think it will take a commensurate amount of time to get it crossed off the list. And then suddenly—it's done." Seeing her eyebrows narrow, he quickly added, "I mean the wedding."

"Well, I hope you'll get used to me being forthright," she said.

She leaned over her sleeping child and kissed Procter. "Now you go off to bed too. I'll see you in the morning. What time do we get to Toronto?"

"Ten."

"So we'll have time for breakfast. I know I'll be starving. Good night, Mr. Darlington."

"Good night, Mrs. Darlington."

The lights dimmed in the car, and Alice sat dozing with the infant in her lap. She put up the window shade to watch the dark countryside go by, remembering crossing the country with Andrew. She nursed Rory when he woke up fussing, and it put him back to sleep. There were signs that he was going to look like Andrew. In a way, she had brought Andrew back into the world. She couldn't really believe he was not with her. Then she could not believe he had ever existed. But he had, and she was holding their child, a new life. A new life had been offered to her as well, and she resolved to let this bright, enthusiastic young man draw her into it.

The first night at the hotel in Toronto met Alice's expectations and matched her experience with Andrew. On the second night of their stay in the city, she quickly came to understand that sexual intercourse would be different with a different man. Alice had to conclude that Procter's observance of modesty on the first night was only to feel out her disposition on intimate activity. How unlucky it would have been for him to discover she was averse to the wild range of lovemaking that he felt safe to unleash upon her on nights two and three.

While they kissed on the second night in bed, the tip of his tongue slipped between her lips. It was a surprise, but she kept kissing, and before long their tongues were playing together, which she found pleasantly arousing. On the third night, he went from her lips, kissing down her throat, between her breasts to her belly, kept going down, and then went burrowing under the covers. "Just close your eyes and let yourself drift where you will," he whispered.

The dream Alice had the next morning just before waking up beside her man was of a city train station. The Andrew Local had just pulled in. Gentlemen and ladies stepped down from the cars amid a billowing release of steam from under the great wheels of the locomotive. Everyone was smiling after a perfectly lovely trip. Without warning, the Darlington Express roared through on the next platform—no brakes, straight through the station, throwing high into the air little old ladies, bird cages, hats, umbrellas, and portmanteaus. It did not stop for a mile down the tracks. It didn't even stop. It just exploded. Engine and cars, all at once. Bang!

Alice woke up suddenly. She was not strewn in wreckage but in bed with sheets so rumpled that it was impossible to tell the top from the bottom. She was lying in the morning light beside her man. His body was stretched out before her as he slept. It was almost without hair, except for light curls crowning the pubis. His form might have been sculpted by an Athenian of the Golden Age, so smooth it was, so modeled. His balls were very tight and pink. To think she had them in her mouth in the last hours of the night brought the heat of a blush surging to her face, though no eyes were upon her. His penis arched over them, astonishingly long and athletically lean like the physique of a pole-vaulter caught in a photograph at the moment of curving over the high bar. On her own initiative she had quite swallowed that up too. How lustful she was last night! How agreeable he was! How refreshed she felt in the morning!

As satisfied as she had been with Andrew's lovemaking, she was now aware of a state she had never achieved with him. It was the act of reaching the peak of a mountain and throwing her arms into the air that made the satisfaction of the climb so much the smaller accomplishment. It had nothing to do with Andrew's male parts lacking a certain fun-loving quality possessed by those of Procter, or that his chest was hairy, or that his hands were coarse. It was nothing she could put her finger on. Perhaps loving so seriously had been as much an inhibition as inexperience on both their parts. She only wished that she had known then, with Andrew, what she was now discovering with Procter.

She admired Andrew for what he had been and would always think of him as worldly. But that was the world of men, guns, and war. Most pleasing to her about him had been his willingness to strive for the higher planes of life and to learn from her. Now she had a husband who was already where she would have wanted Andrew to be, not due to her example and teaching, but instilled by many years of education in the finest schools and preordained by his breeding.

Procter woke up smiling, and she laughed. She was happy to know more about herself than she had known yesterday, and she was glad she and her husband were likeminded in this business regarding matters of the flesh. So far, that ninety-nine percent of marital accord she had hypothesized was holding true.

They smiled at each other all day, and all day waited for another night.

Procter was very amused by little Rory, even at two o'clock in the morning. He sat up with Alice, and she was grateful for his company, but it was sometimes annoying when he could not resist tickling the little thing.

"Don't do that," she said. "He'll suck air. If you're going to keep tickling him, you can stay up and burp him for the next hour and let me get some sleep."

"I don't think you're managing him well, Alice. Now look, just now. When he bites like that you should smack him."

"Procter, I am not going to smack my baby while he's feeding. What a ridiculous thing to suggest."

"All right, but you're just going to make him spoiled, fat, and greedy."

"Well," she said, "when you can produce milk and feed a baby with those useless little buttons on your chest, you may reserve the right to smack any baby who is so unwise as to avail itself of your services. Until then, I must ask the audience member to refrain from offering advice specific to a gender not his own."

"All right. Fair enough," he said. "But I'll have a say in the next one."

"Oh, Procter," she said with genuine dismay, "I want you to feel Rory is yours too."

"I do," he said immediately. "The attorney sent over the adoption papers. They're in my place in New York. All we need is your signature."

"Oh, Procter. You must have read my mind. I wasn't sure how to bring it up. I didn't know how you would feel about taking on a responsibility that wasn't really yours."

"I'm taking on you, aren't I?" he said with another of his most winning smiles. "And haven't I changed his diapers once or twice? We should be related if I'm going to be doing that, don't you think?"

"Well, maybe when he's officially yours, you won't be so quick to want him smacked. He already knows you from sticking him with the diaper pins."

Poking fun was her only defense against that smile, the blue eyes, and the finest attributes of masculinity hiding beneath his smart, stylish suits. She had to wonder at her luck. Even before Procter showed up, she had begun to feel the need to move from the wasteful and numbing stasis of grief. And if she had to live, why not have a new life? Procter must have known she didn't love him. That's why he made everything so easy for her. A man like Procter, wanting only fun out of life, would never ask love or honesty from anyone, and perhaps only a man like Procter could coax her into believing that a meaningful life could come of it. How long would it tug at her heart that it had to be someone other than Andrew?

From Toronto, they took the train to Parry Sound, the last town of any size, and they took rooms for the night. In the morning, while Alice slept with the baby, Miss Lantz and Procter went off to do some shopping, and they came back with a baggage cart piled high. Included in the purchases was a selection of men's dungaree trousers. Before the last leg of the journey, Alice and Miss Lantz disappeared into their rooms and reappeared in the dungarees, feeling better attired for life on a Canadian island.

The railroad trestle at Pointe Au Baril Station was on a cliff above the harbor, and it was late in the day before they finally stood on the dock with all the baggage. Procter looked at the boats tied up and decided to ask around at the little grocery store. Mr. Higgman, the grocer, came out from behind his butcher's block to greet him. Same mustache, same fantastically bushy eyebrows, same striped shirt and tie, and possibly the same bloodied white apron in which Procter had last seen him. Heartily shaking Procter's hand, he said, "Glad to see you. Glad to see you, young man. Married, I hear."

"Yes, there she is," said Procter, pointing out the front window, where parts of Alice could be seen between numerous red-lettered signs advertising special prices.

Wanting to curry favor with the wives as always, Mr. Higgman said, "Bring her in. I'll get together some samples for her."

"We don't really have time, Mr. Higgman. I'd like to hire a boat to get us out to the island before dark."

"No need for that, my boy. Your brother left a motor launch at the dock for you."

"I'm surprised anybody made it up before us," said Procter, decidedly puzzled.

"Oh no, a batch of them—I don't always remember who's who—were up here last month. A few barges went out with lumber and some men from the Pointe. Some building going on out there?"

"I knew it," said Procter sourly. "They must have divvied up the island without me, damn it all. Well, that's not your problem. What's the launch look like?"

"About twenty foot, high in the prow, with an open wooden cabin, painted gray, named "Ark" across the stern. I think it's a Richardson boat. Your brother said you'd know how to run it. You remember the channels, don't you, or do you want Hector?"

"He still around? I'll remember the channels all right, but I could use a hand loading the boat."

Hector was a tough little Ojibwa who seemed to have been around since Procter's childhood days. He did work for everyone during the summer and trapped during the winter. Two dollars US were well worth the help with the loading, but Procter didn't hire him as a guide. He figured that even with the slow part through the inland channels, they'd get out to the open water, where he would recognize the island before it got too dark.

With Hector's help and Miss Lantz assisting, they got the Ark loaded. The two men lifted the box of the engine cover and looked everything over.

"Well, can you beat that?" exclaimed Procter to Alice, sitting up on the dock. "It's a Daimler."

Hector didn't know what the two of them were laughing about, so he just went on to point out a few things and helped them cast off. He waved in the gathering twilight as they chugged out toward the buoys marking the entrance to the harbor.

Procter did not remember as much as he thought he would, but he followed the buoys through the little islands and finally got to open water. Miles ahead he could see the beam from the lighthouse standing at the last tip of the archipelago where the channel opened up into the Georgian Bay of Lake Huron. Now all he had to do was steer toward it for about another hour and then start looking for the break in the darkening line of islands to starboard. When he thought the time had come, he sent Miss Lantz out from under the roof.

"It'll be to starboard—that's the right side, Miss Lantz. Look for a channel opening up. Sing out if you spot it."

Some time went by without a sighting, and Procter decided they needed to be closer to the shoreline and steered in. He didn't want to let up on the throttle because he didn't want to be out on the water all night. But they were getting in close, and he didn't want to get lost in the islands either. Suddenly there was a scraping sound under the heavy stern, and he knew they had passed over a reef. His relief was short-lived because the next scraping sound came from the bow, went along the keel and stopped at the stern. The Ark was grounded. The engine stalled out with a cough.

"Oh, hell's bells," he said.

"What's happened, Procter?" said Alice.

"We're on a reef."

"Oh dear. Well, what do we do about it?"

"That depends."

Procter shut off the battery to the engine. Then he moved aside some of the light baggage to get at the bilge plate. Down on his hands and knees, he peered under the floorboards and felt around the bottom. Satisfied that the Ark wasn't taking water, he put everything back together and stood up. To Alice and Miss Lantz's questioning faces, he said, "Well, we aren't sinking. Nothing to worry about."

"The situation is intolerable, madam," said Miss Lantz under her breath to Alice, sitting close beside her on the bench just under the cover of the roof.

"You're quite right, Miss Lantz," said Procter. "Quite right."

Then he turned again to thoughtfully consider the pile of baggage in the rear of the boat.

"We'll look for the liquor," he said with a laugh.

Alice was nursing the baby to keep him quiet, so she couldn't get up.

"Procter, come over here please. Bend down to me." Into his ear she whispered, "Nurse has to go to the loo. So do I. I don't mind going over the side, but not Miss Lantz. We've got to do something."

"I'm afraid we're here for the night."

"That won't do, Procter. Here, you take Rory. Put your finger in his mouth—but wash your hands first."

Procter knew she'd find out soon enough for herself that they were stuck, so he washed his hands over the side and came back to take the baby.

There was an oar and a boathook mounted on the roof of the boat. Alice got the boathook down and began taking soundings along the sides of the Ark with it. Then she shimmied out on the bow on her stomach with one hand working the pole, looking hard to judge the readings in the dark.

"I think I have it," she said, coming back under the roof. "We move the baggage up here and swing the back of the boat—"

"The stern," said Procter.

"All right, the stern—that way. Starboard?"

"Starboard. Very good."

"We have more depth on that side. Then we use the weight up front, and Procter, you push off with the pole on the other side to pivot the stern off, then we move the baggage back and that will raise the bow."

Within a few minutes they were off the reef and chugging slowly along the shore of the islands again with Alice lying over the bow watching for reefs, ready with the boathook in hand to push away from anything dangerous. How much easier everything is, she thought, wearing men's trousers.

Alice was the first to spot a light. She shouted back to Procter, and he steered for it. They pulled in at a dock, and while Procter was tying up, Alice clambered up the rocks to a set of wooden steps toward the lights of a cabin. A moment later she called down to the dock, "Miss Lantz, give the baby to Mr. Darlington and hurry up here." She started down the steps swinging a kerosene lantern, met Miss Lantz on the trail, and led the way around the cabin to the outhouse.

Much relieved, the two ladies waited for Procter and the baby at the top of the steps with the middle-aged couple who owned the cabin.

"One of the Darlington boys, you say," inquired the gentleman.

"Yes," said Alice. "Procter, the youngest. We're just married, so I suppose I'm a Darlington as well."

"Big family," commented the lady of the cabin, returning with a blanket just then to put around shivering Miss Lantz.

"The Darlingtons always put up strong teams at the islander regatta. We missed them this year."

"Oh, I'm sorry," said Alice. "Everyone was at the wedding. They'll be up late this year."

The lady, Mrs. Bogartus, laughed very heartily and said there was nothing to be sorry about, as it gave the other summer islanders a chance to bring home some blue ribbons for a change.

Mrs. Bogartus made up a nice little dinner for them, and they sat warm and comfortably around the fireplace. Then they retired for the night on cots in back rooms recently added, which were as yet bare and smelled pleasantly of the pine flooring and walls. In the morning, after a delightful breakfast, they set out once again to find their own island. Procter said he knew exactly where they were the moment he stepped out the cabin door around dawn.

It was easy to explain why he had missed the inlet, and he laid it out for Alice in detail. He wanted to make sure he put to rest any idea she might have that he did not know what he was doing. He also never liked taking the blame for something that wasn't his fault. For that matter, he didn't particularly like taking responsibility for anyone other than himself, and if he could push that off on someone else, so much the better.

Alice sat in the stern, perched in a nest she had made in the baggage, her back against the warm wood of the engine compartment. It was very chilly over the water, but she wanted to be out where she could see the trees and rocks as they went slowly by. She pulled her hair close around her and tucked it into her jacket against the wind. Nurse and the baby were under the roof, quite bundled up. Miss Lantz had her eyes closed and a stern expression on her face, as if she were escaping the chill through Buddhist meditation. When Procter looked back at Alice from the steering wheel, she shouted over the force of the wind and racket of the engine, "It's so beautiful!"

Only a half an hour from the Bogartus camp, Procter turned in from the open. In front of them now was Darlington Island, the length of it in full view. As they got closer, Alice came up to stand beside her husband at the helm. He pointed through the window to a flat expanse of rock ahead that was just above the water line. It had letters painted in white, and presently, she could make out the name "Darlington."

"And look up on the hill. I helped carve that totem pole when I was a kid."

Procter slowed down when they got about ten yards offshore, steered the Ark to the left, and after a few minutes traversing the front of the island, swung around the end. Not long after, they came to a dock. As they passed it, Procter pointed up to a Swiss chalet on the hill above and several tent platforms partially hidden in the pine trees and rocks.

"That's the parents' place. We'll camp out there, but I want to circle the island first. I don't think anybody's here yet, and I want to see where they're building."

Down to almost idle speed, Procter took the craft through some very shallow channels and back around to the open front of the island. It was a big mystery to him where a couple of barges of lumber could have gone. Giving up on that, they returned to the parents' chalet and tied up at the dock. Alice followed Procter up the trail to the house. It was a nice little place, and Alice was very glad to have finally gotten there. They found the doors locked however, and stained wood shutters were on the windows.

"Wait a minute," said Procter. "What's that?"

Against the porch railing, a wooden arrow had been tied with red lettering that spelled out the word "Cove." Procter knew what it meant and shouted down to Miss Lantz that he and Alice would be back in a few minutes. They set off on a trail around the chalet, which led to a wooden bridge over a channel. Crossing it, Procter said it was actually an inlet that partially divided the island. The cove was farther up where the inlet opened into a protected bay with a little sandy beach. When they got there, they were amazed to see another Swiss chalet, just like the parents'. Across the steps was a weather-beaten canvas sign with "Happy Wedding / From All of Us" on it. The lettering was surrounded by painted flowers.

"I've got the cove," Procter said, turning to Alice with a startled look on his face. "This is the best spot on the island. They gave it to me. And a house. I can't believe it. Everyone wanted this part. We were going to draw lots."

The door was locked, but hanging from the handle was a corked bottle on a ribbon. Alice could just get a finger in the neck and started drawing out pages to hand to Procter.

"This is Marjorie's work," he said. "Listen to this."

He read to Alice a cute, funny poem titled "The Key is under the Mat," a puzzle that held clues in its lines. When he finished reading, he left Alice sitting on the porch and went off through the woods. It took him over half an hour by Alice's pendant watch, but he came around the chalet laughing, with the poem and the key in one hand and a big woven Welcome mat in the other.

"The clues took me all over the place."

"Where was the mat?" Alice asked.

"At the back door!"

Alice looked around the inside of the chalet while Procter went to bring the boat around with Miss Lantz and the baby. He judged there to be enough draft in the inlet because the barges made it in, and there was a newly built dock just down from the house.

Procter's brothers and sisters gave them a week to themselves on the island. Procter hauled everything up from the boat the first day while Alice and Miss Lantz unpacked and set up the kitchen. Miss Lantz conjectured that the sisters must have had help from their cooks at home because the kitchen was well furnished with every kind of pot, pan, and utensil that could be needed in a kitchen. Seeing that the pantry was stocked to her satisfaction also, Miss Lantz began teaching Alice a few things about cooking.

The week was spent walking the paths across the island, swimming in the cold, clear water, and sitting on the porch of the chalet in the warm sunshine. According to family custom, as Procter explained to Alice, bathing was done in the morning, women skinny-dipping on one side of the island, men on the other. Alice said she would be willing to go along with that, but for the time being, before the others arrived, she would prefer to bathe with him. While Alice had the baby, Miss Lantz took her bath in a quiet, secluded spot of her own. From what was hung out on a discreetly placed laundry line among the trees, Alice deduced that Miss Lantz at her bath was not going native.

The Darlingtons senior remained in Boston a little longer to allow the next two generations to establish themselves in their tents and open up the chalet for them. Alice and Procter happened to walk around to the front of the island one day, not knowing when the others were coming but thinking it must be soon, when they spotted a flotilla of ten boats turning in toward them from a mile out in the open water. Alice beheld them with amazement. After being alone with her little family on the island and finding kinship of spirit with its rocks and trees, she almost did not recognize the vessels for what they were, and she was due for the surprise of her life when they came near enough to see people on them. As if she were the first Indian to see the first European, or a modern-day Robinson Crusoe, the sighting made her fearful, for she was desirous of neither confrontation with conquerors nor rescue by well-meaning intruders. She had been so happy without more people in her life than she needed.

When they got closer, Alice saw that each of the ten boats was towing in its wake a line of canoes and rowboats. Procter was so excited that Alice had to run to catch up with him. To reduce her anxiety, she kept reminding herself that she had already met all of them at the wedding. But when the first of them came ashore on the other side of the island in front of the parents' chalet, they looked so different in flannel shirts, striped sailing outfits, mackinaws, rough frontier jackets, and boots of all description. The men had red or blue bandanas draped from their back pockets. The women employed them as headscarves or tied them pirate fashion. Everyone was laughing and glad to be there.

Only one boat could be docked at a time, so the one with the ice blocks and perishable food supplies came in for unloading first while the others anchored off. The young boys Alice knew to be from ten to fifteen shed down to their shorts and dove off the motor launches. She watched them scramble into the canoes and rowboats like monkeys to untie the towlines and paddle them in and swim back for others. When the boat with the tents came up to dock, the men wrestled the canvas rolls up to the platforms around the chalet. With everybody helping, it became a barn raising of heavy canvas over ridgepoles that was great fun.

The last week before Procter had to report back to work was as enjoyable for Alice as the first. She found that she liked everyone she was marooned with and was sure everyone liked her. There were three young governesses along, six teenage girls, and with the five wives and the two sisters, including Alice, it made seventeen women bathing together in the morning. Alice thought they must have made quite a sight getting out of their bathrobes and into the water, shivering, laughing, tossing the bar of soap to one another, swimming naked and free. All around was the wilderness, a thousand islands, and an open horizon of blue water to the west.

In the afternoons the women lay out on the dock and the warm rocks, sunning and talking while the men fiddled around with the boats or went fishing. Alice was the only nursing mother, so she slipped away every few hours. But there were several other young mothers, and she got some very good advice about infant formulas that she politely listened to before politely dismissing.

With the other governesses around, Miss Lantz took the opportunity every day to leave Rory in their care and go out for her solitary nature walks across the island. On these occasions, she wore her dungaree trousers and a Swiss mountaineering hat with a bright feather that must have come from her homeland. Slung around her neck was a small pair of binoculars. The young governesses had their own tent in which they had riotous fun at night, so Miss Lantz was grateful for the privacy of her own room in the chalet.

Alice surprised herself with tears as they left the island on their last day. She stood in the stern of the Ark with Rory in her arms and watched the wake of the boat spread out toward the rocks and trees and the last sight of the chalet. She felt the island was now a part of her life as much as her husband and child. There was nothing she wanted more than more years of summers there. Everything had gone so well that she did not think of Andrew again until the island was out of sight.

CHAPTER TWENTY-SIX

Alice was glad that her parents and the Darlingtons did not give them one of those dreary brownstones. They found a bright little Tudor within walking distance of their two houses. The two mothers walked her through it, and she loved it right away. At the same time, her father and Mr. Darlington were having a serious talk with Procter in the Darlington study. The two fathers and the young husband agreed that five hundred dollars a month from the Sheffields and a matching amount from the Darlingtons would suit the needs of the young couple in their first year of marriage. At the conclusion, hands were shaken among the men in the study as embraces were politely exchanged between the women around the block at the Tudor house. Then the Darlingtons were off on the train to Canada, where they expected to put an end to everyone's fun. Procter went back to New York for his first workweek after the wedding trip. Alice, Rory, and Nurse returned for the night to the Sheffields.

Furnishings were to begin arriving the next day, and Alice was so excited to see what the two mothers had picked out for her that she hardly slept that night. By the time Procter came back on the train Friday night, the last empty box had been taken away, and the last workman had departed. He said the house looked as comfortable to come home to as if he had lived there all his life. Alice was beaming as she showed him through the rooms and introduced him to the staff. Then they had sherry and little crackers in the library as they waited to be called to the dining room.

Miss Lantz had agreed to assume charge of the household. Because the house was too small for servant quarters, the cook, her helper, the butler, and the maid were day help. Miss Lantz had a room attached to the nursery. Alice liked it that way. It gave her the flexibility to decide on short notice to lock the place up, give the help a few days off, and spirit herself, Nurse, and the baby down to New York to spend a few days with Procter during the week.

They took a better apartment there with a bedroom for Miss Lantz. By day, Procter went off to work, and after a leisurely breakfast, the two ladies and Rory walked for exercise and shopped or took cabs to museums and galleries. Sometimes it made Alice wonder why she had so easily capitulated when they had just gotten back from Canada and her mother said, "Well, of course you're going to live in Boston."

Out to a restaurant one night, a dress-up occasion for them without Miss Lantz and the baby, Alice brought up something she had heard from her mother.

"Father would really like you to come work with him in the bank, Procter."

She just dropped it into a silence while Procter was looking over the décor, but he did not even consider the proposal.

"Oh, I couldn't give up Morgan."

"He thinks it would be a chance you don't have where you are now."

"What's that?"

"Why, to be the boss of course. When father retires, the bank would be all yours."

"He isn't going to approach me, is he?"

"I don't think he'd do that unless there was an indication that you have an interest," said Alice.

"I really don't."

"I think he's counting on it, Procter. Wouldn't you like to be your own boss?"

"Have you been talking to him?"

"No, of course not. I never talk to him, really. I talk to Mother, though, and you know, things go back and forth through channels."

Their dinners came out, and they placed their napkins and picked up their knives and forks.

"I thought you liked New York," he said.

"Oh, I do, Procter."

"So do I. Then I think we're agreed we don't want to put ourselves down too firmly in Boston. But nix on the bank job idea. Put that through the back channel—but not sounding like I don't have what it takes. I know you can make it sound good. Just let me know before anything goes out over the wires."

"I will, Procter."

"I don't know why everyone in business wants to be in charge. I see J.P. and the partners every day, and it doesn't look like any fun at all."

"Well, then, I don't know what we're going to do," said Alice.

Procter sat back and brought his napkin to the corners of his mouth. "We don't have to do anything, Alice. If he approaches me, I tell him I have to think about it. No, I'll tell him I have to ask my wife."

"Then you blame it on me."

"No, no, Alice. Not blame. It's simply a matter of liability. We shift liability from here to there. It's a well-known practice. We do it all the time."

As Procter said it, he made an amusing movement of his two outstretched hands, from one side of his place setting to the other, and Alice had to laugh.

"Come on," he said, looking at his watch. "We've got a little time. Let's go see what's doing at Lois's."

That was a very welcome suggestion to Alice, so they took a cab over to the village. There were a lot of people there, some sitting on the stairs smoking as they walked up, some lingering over the railing on the landing, and some crowding at the door as they pushed their way in. Lois quickly spotted them and came over brimming with smiles. She was in a long, flowing gown and had her head wrapped in a bright red turban.

"Oh, look at you," she said, standing back after she had embraced them both. "You're brown as berries."

"Just got back from the island a few weeks ago," said Procter.

"I want to hear all about it, but I have to find Dominick. Go get some drinks, won't you? There's some liquor in there somewhere. Don't worry, Alice, lots of other girls in eveningwear. Gladys had a show at the Bancroft Gallery."

With that, Lois went skipping down the stairs, and Procter and Alice made their way inside. There were young gentlemen stretched out on the carpet, using the fireplace as an ashtray, ladies draped over the arms of the two sofas, and others wrapped in close conversation on their way from one room to another. A great deal of laughter was coming from the kitchen and what sounded like the reciting of poetry from the bedroom. Alice and Procter knew a few of the guests, and they spread out through the cliques.

It was such fun for Alice and so stimulating to hear so much talk of art, literature, music, politics, and everything else under the sun. Feeling she did not really have a place in such erudite circles, she kept to the fringes, but that enabled her to get away from one when she heard interesting ideas coming from another. When eleven o'clock came, she reluctantly went to find Procter, and within a few minutes they were back at the apartment, walking up the stairs to the sound of an angry baby.

Rory was twenty months old. He had crawled at six months, walked by ten, had his teeth by eleven, and was talking by thirteen. His rudimentary abilities, however, had frustrated him terribly at eighteen months; things he grasped slipped out of his hands, he tripped and fell, he ran heedless of obstacles in his way, and he was unable to express his demands in the right words or intelligibly. Two more months brought him out of that stage, but he seemed to be arrested in the development of his relationship to food. Miss Lantz had been trying purees since he was four months, but he would have nothing to do with food. Milk was all he wanted, period. His little mind seemed to have forged a fixed and unalterable connection between his mother and sustenance.

Alice tried stewed this and stewed that, and her mother tried shredded this and shredded that to no avail. Even Procter tried, but Rory pursed his lips together very tightly when a spoon appeared at his face. If any stewed vegetables or beef sauce got in, he spat it out and kept spitting as if ridding himself of a deadly poison. Then he cried piteously. There was nothing to do after these frequently messy efforts but to put him back to the breast, where he would linger a long time before his eyes closed. Mrs. Darlington observed all this with reserve. She had a remedy, but her terms involved a transfer of authority that Alice was unwilling to grant.

The only advice from the medical profession was to keep trying purees with different foods. One young doctor suggested putting her breast milk into a bottle and using one of the new rubber nipples. That proved to be as offensive to the child as stewed vegetables. Nothing remained but the hope Rory would grow out of his fixation.

Procter's idea of hiring a wet nurse was simply out of the question for Alice. At least she could give him to Miss Lantz and put the problem out of her thoughts for a few hours. It wasn't so hard in Boston, where she spent most of her time in the house, but on her visits to New York, she wanted to get out of the apartment. Lois had included her in a widening circle of interesting friendships that far surpassed the small circle she had in Boston, which was presided over by her mother and Mrs. Darlington.

In the company of her new friends, Alice wanted to excel in the world of art. She wanted to paint and sculpt, write poetry and plays, play a musical instrument, dance in the ballet. Every introduction at Lois's little salon excited a new yearning in her that wanted to burst into art.

So many fascinating talks. So many revelations of soul came out over that table and across the sofas in Lois's salon. It might have been just talk for the way everyone drank and went on, but Alice came to know that those same people who left the apartment—staggering down the stairs and drawing the collars of their coats about their necks against the weather—walked home to cold attics and cellars and went to work. Far into the night they toiled with their art, seeking to bring forth a new understanding of modern man. Lois assured her of that with many stories of those who struggled and sacrificed to pursue their work. It was hard to forget her story of a dear friend who died at night in a snowstorm for the sake of painting the perfect leaf on a wall. Whenever she told the story to new visitors to the salon, everyone was in tears.

Alice made her own efforts, but they were constantly frustrated. Dancing was out because she was heavy on her feet and had too much up top. Every one of the dancers Alice met at the salon had started as a skinny, little six- or seven-year-old, and as women had somehow avoided the acquisition of all that gave shape to the natural human female. And when she watched a quintet from Harlem improvise at the salon and saw how fast the fingers moved, she despaired of any musical aspiration.

It was very encouraging when Lois told her that amateurs could write poetry, pen novels, and paint pictures without training or experience. Exploring each of these in turn, the most successful were painting sessions with Lois in her studio. Alice applied paint with wild abandon, but after the cathartic release she experienced, it was often impossible the next day to recognize her soul in what she had transferred of it to canvas.

"I'm nothing," she said to Lois one day, utterly at a loss.

"No, you just feel that way," said Lois. Then she laughed. "I heard you talking to Marshall DeWitt in the kitchen the other night. What a ponderous topic. I wasn't sure where your train of thought was going, but it was thoroughly engrossing."

"Oh, it was just silly talk," said Alice.

"But I'm sure Marshall went home thinking about it, and one of those pithy phrases of yours is sure to turn up in his next book. You can count on that, dear. That's why I like to see you and Procter show up. I know somebody is going to go home with new ideas. Not so much from Procter—he's strictly one-dimensional, or he tries to be, but he hasn't the depth to pretend he's shallow. But you, Alice. You don't have to be an artist. I mean, it's nice that you've given it a try, so you understand the work that goes into art, but I'm sure you've realized something you didn't know before. If you want to really do anything significant in the arts—and I mean significant by your own standards—you must give your life to it. For some that means only a small interruption in the way they already live, but for others it demands the sacrifice of—well, of everything. You aren't made for that, Alice. You're a conventional woman. Nothing wrong with that. You're built to face life, not abstract it into art. You're source material for these people."

When she finished, Lois looked at her with a face so sincere and honest that it dispelled any doubts Alice had toward her decision to give up trying to become an artist.

"Does that make you feel any better?" said Lois.

"I suppose I feel a little less like an imposter," said Alice.

Lois was the same age, but from the first time they had talked, Alice felt more like the younger sister to this well-grounded woman who lived by herself and had gathered around her such bright minds and talents.

Lois smiled and patted her hand. "Well, my darling Alice, I hope you know I only want to encourage you to be yourself—and every wonderful conventional or unconventional thing your self wants to be."

The kindness of the words and the quirky smile on Lois's face brought a tear to Alice's eyes. They had another cup of tea and laughed over one thing and another until time was up and Alice had to get the milk wagon across town to a baby who would someday be old enough to look at his watch and scowl when she came through the door.

CHAPTER TWENTY-SEVEN

Procter stayed at J.P. Morgan, and Alice, Rory, and Miss Lantz went down to New York every other week from Tuesday to Thursday to keep him company. Alice gave enough hints to her mother and Mrs. Darlington about moving to New York that the parents were happy enough to have them in Boston as much as they were. While Procter was at work, Alice and Miss Lantz spelled each other with the baby. He was quick on his feet now and had to be watched whenever he wasn't sleeping. Making good use of her free time, Miss Lantz went to museums or sat in the parks.

In New York, Alice began taking people to lunch. It came to her one day as a very bright idea. She could drop in on any of her friends from the salon and always find them easy to pull away from their work for an hour or two—which was all the time she had anyway. Lois was always the favorite, but she also had a good time with Jim Rider, a Yale man from Iowa, who was actually writing a novel in a garret, and Marcia Malcheveski, a freelance writer on social issues. There were a few others, and it seemed every time she and Procter went to Lois's place, she met someone else she could look up for lunch.

At five o'clock every day they were in New York, Miss Lantz had dinner in a restaurant down the block where she was developing some acquaintances. Alice suspected there might be a gentleman involved because she always returned in the best of spirits. When Procter got home at seven, they either stayed in with Alice's experimental cooking or went out, and then they left it up to how they felt about going out again after Alice took care of feeding Rory. Frequently they ended up at Lois's for a salon night.

One night they arrived late, not expecting to find many people, but a lot of the regulars were there, lying about on the carpet talking philosophy. Alice and Procter got drinks in the kitchen and came to join Lois at the table where she was playing solitaire and talking to Gerri, a poet with frizzy red hair and lithe body whom Alice had found enchanting.

A tall Russian ballet dancer with high cheekbones and a striking physique, who had just started showing up and was a lot of fun, came out of the kitchen with apples in both his hands and one in his teeth. He said something, but no one could tell what it was. Because he remained standing in front of everybody and kept saying the same thing as if he were popping out the doors of a cuckoo clock, everyone turned from their private talks and looked at him, guessing at what he was trying to say. When no one got it and everyone was laughing, he said loudly and distinctly, with the apple still in his mouth, "Does anybody want to dim the lights?"

There was a groan from some of the ladies, but the general consensus was yes, and all got to their feet. Some cleared the drawing room of chairs and moved the sofas back while others went into the bedroom.

"Not my table," said Lois. "Just put me over in the corner."

Two of the men immediately came over to relocate Lois and her table. Once there and straightening the rows of her solitaire game, Lois looked around the room, and finding Alice, called out to her, "Alice, come here and sit with me."

Alice crossed the floor from the fireplace, where she had been talking to a very interesting young architect named Harry French, and sat down across from Lois, who was just then lighting a candle to put between them.

"I thought I should prepare you, darling," she said. "They're going to take their clothes off. It's nothing to be alarmed about."

A vivacious little art school blonde named Eloise came over and sat down with them. She put her arm around Lois and said, "You don't mind, do you?"

"Not as long as you put the bed back together with hospital corners," said Lois, in an off-hand manner.

"That's a promise," Eloise said firmly. Then she looked at Lois as if she were dealing with her grandmother and said, "Just tell us when you want everyone to leave."

"Oh, I will," said Lois, laughing. "No one keeps me up past my bedtime."

"You'll be coming, won't you, Alice?" Eloise asked, with excitement rising in her eyes.

"We're not sure," Lois interjected.

Eloise already had her blouse off and was standing up to get out of her skirt. At the sight of underwear, Alice had to lower her eyes, but in a moment Eloise was gone, the gas lights were off, and the dark was softened by candles coming out all over the room.

"I didn't know this went on," said Alice.

"Just once in a while. It's not for everyone, of course."

"Does Procter?"

"He has in the past. Not since you married, but you two haven't been here on one of these nights either. It's always spontaneous. You never know when someone will kick it off. I guess there's a sense of when the right people are here. So there you are, Alice. It means they've accepted you."

"That's very nice, Lois, but I don't think I'll be taking my clothes off."

"You don't have to do anything you don't want to do, dear," said Lois, putting her hand on Alice's.

"Do you?"

"Sometimes. Depends on the mood, depends on the crowd."

Alice had her back to the room, but she could hear the sounds of men breathing vigorously and women purring.

"Can you see Procter anywhere?"

Lois looked around Alice and squinted her eyes. "I think so," she said. "Oh yes, there he is."

"Who is he with?"

"John, the poet from Queens."

"John?"

"He's keen for the men, you know," said Lois.

Alice leaned toward Lois with her mouth open. Something had begun to dawn upon her about Procter, but it wasn't a keenness for men.

"You didn't know that? Oh, it's just for the novelty," she said quickly. "Everyone gets mixed up with everyone else at one time or another. It's just what you feel like doing at the moment."

Alice recovered herself enough to press Lois on the subject, and she was honest in her replies to Alice's questions.

"It seems my husband has a double life," said Alice.

"Alice, dear. It's really a very natural thing. I don't think he's any less interested in you. It's just another side to the complexity of any human being."

"Then tell me, Lois, do you make love to women?"

"Sure, sometimes." she said.

"Oh," said Alice, turning to look around at the room for the first time.

Her eyes had just come from the candle on the table, and when they adjusted to the lower illumination of the room, she saw moving white naked bodies everywhere, in every contortion, with hardly anything showing of the mattresses or carpet. Procter was just climbing over the back of some woman, it might have been the Arizona girl with the short hair and long legs, toward another man, she couldn't tell who it was.

Harry French, the young architect, must have been waiting for her to turn around from her conversation with Lois, for as soon as she did, he got up and came toward the table. When he got to her side, he stood with a hand outstretched as if he had crossed the room to ask her to dance. Alice put her hand on his bare stomach to detain him a moment while she turned back to Lois.

"Lois, do you think I should?"

"If you feel adventurous. Procter's in the pool. But you can do anything you want, Alice. You don't have to do anything either. I'll sit with you."

"But I don't want to spoil your fun."

"I have fun either way. If you go, I'll go. If you stay, I'll stay, and we'll have a nice talk."

Alice turned back to Harry French, still with her hand up to his stomach, with her fingers curved so that only the tips were actually touching his skin. He was certainly a very handsome man naked, and she could see that her reticence had only elevated his ardor—perhaps by an inch or two.

"Lois?"

"If you want to try it, let yourself try it. That's my motto," said Lois.

"All right," said Alice decisively. "I'll do it."

Alice had already decided to go ahead when the mattresses were flopped on the floor, and she had guessed what was about to take place. It seemed to be a lucky solution to a dilemma she saw coming with Procter. The vacillating with Lois was just the time she gave to the possibility of an intervention coming down from heaven to render all this unnecessary, at least a sign. But there was nothing but silence from above; and down here, the only perceptible pointing arrow was Harry's penis, which perhaps only attested to humanity's unfortunate inclination to get into mischief.

Alice stood up from the table and started getting out of her dress. She only wore light dresses now, without the constricting undergarments. Only the slip and corselet and short panties, which she was soon folding and laying neatly on her chair. Harry French took her hand and led her onto the mattress. The cushions had come off the two sofas and had been placed on the floor, and for a moment there was a space open on the mattresses as people went for the plush cushions. Harry was down on the mattress, and Alice was still stepping over bodies toward him when there was the tink, tink, tink of a spoon against a wine glass. When Lois had everyone's attention, she announced, "Ladies and gentlemen. Just a word, everyone, please. About Alice—no hands on baby's dinner."

Alice was glad Lois said something, because she needed every drop of milk, but standing naked when everyone stopped to look up at her was somewhat embarrassing. She got down on the mattress with Harry and was soon engaged with him. It surprised her how easy it was to get down to business with a man she had just met, without flirtation, falling in love, meeting the family, courtship, and wedding ceremony—not to mention spending weeks in a sampan—before getting around to what males and females want to do with each other. And how strange to think that everyone knows how to do it without ever going to school.

Right beside them, Eloise was on her haunches, sitting on someone with long, muscular legs—it must have been the Russian dancer. She leaned over inviting Alice to kiss her. Then Harry French was suddenly gone and Gerri with the frizzy red hair pulled her into an embrace and drew her down to the mattress on top of her. After the kiss with Eloise and a little exploration with the hands to show she was open-minded, Alice had enough of women. By the time the night was over, Alice had learned a new, nonverbal language of bodily movements that got her around the floor as successfully as any fashionable hostess might use her wits to circulate through a social gathering, making sure to have a few words with everyone attending.

On the way home that night in the cab, Alice felt it important to be as bright and talkative as she always was after a night with their friends at the salon. She knew Procter was putting on the same show, but he had more to be happy about than she did. The secret was out. That must have concerned him, but it was all right with her. Their eyes had met on the mattress several times as he engaged with almost every man at the party. He could have easily had any of the women, but his heart's desire was for the men.

She leaned against his arm and put her head on his shoulder. "Don't you get jealous seeing me with other men?"

"I don't get jealous," he said. "I'm happy to see you enjoying yourself."

Alice believed that was true. From the very beginning, he had always taken pleasure in seeing her happy—from learning to drive the motor carriage to eating ice cream in the park, to watching her look closely at the brush strokes on an old master painting in the Boston Museum, to finding new pieces in a gallery.

"I hope you enjoyed yourself too," she said.

"I always do."

Alice wanted to show him that knowledge of his secret made no difference to her. But when she brought it up at home while she was nursing Rory late that night, he was evasive. He gave her his winning smile.

"You know how it is," he said. "Anything goes. No rules. Just doing what comes naturally. I'm glad you got in the swing of it, Alice."

"Well, I'm just curious, Procter. I wonder if you're attracted to the same things in a man that a woman finds attractive."

"Oh, Jesus, let's get off it."

"No, I really want to know."

"Just mixing it up once in a while. No big deal."

"Procter—"

"I better get to bed," he said, standing up.

Alice sat alone with Rory in her arms. She didn't mind the time spent nursing. Sometimes she needed to think. In her wildest dreams, she could not have guessed that Procter had this secret. Neither could she scarcely believe that she had just had sexual relations with a room full of people, some of whom she had never met.

She could accept what Procter was. In daily life he had made no effort to hide his vanity, recklessness, and childish unwillingness to do anything that wasn't fun. Now he had let another eccentricity slip out. But it was clear there would be no discussion of it. As casual and freethinking as he portrayed himself, the door was closed on this one, and nothing seemed to Alice more securely locked as the door to what Procter would not admit to himself.

As for herself, Alice had her own reasons for remaining at the salon when it went into after hours. Procter had been making love to her almost every night they were together for almost a year, and there had yet to be any sign of a baby on the way. No one in either family was so indelicate as to mention it, but every day that went by without news from her body left Alice feeling more and more like she was sitting at the window looking down the street, waiting for the postman.

She was expected to deliver the next Darlington. The missing baby was on her mind, as strongly factored into her reasoning as her desire to have another child was felt in her heart. Marrying Procter was unquestionably the right thing to do. They got along well and had fun together. It was best for Rory. A year was long enough to think of marrying Procter as a decision she had made. It had become a commitment, and whatever came, she would stick with it. What worried her was the part of Procter that thrived on distraction, novelty, and whim. The bond between them sometimes seemed as tenuous as a gentleman's agreement. She needed a Darlington child to tie the marriage down, and she would go get one. When Harry French asked her to dance, it had flashed through her mind that the solution to her problem was quite literally at hand.

The next Darlington had to come from someone other than Procter. She would have to choose a man to sire her Darlington child, and the salon was a genetic pool that might give her the results she wanted. She could get herself with child, and with a little luck and planning, no eye would see whence came the seed thereof. She was the only one who would know.

The male she selected had to be tall. He had to have blue eyes and brown hair—straight, not curly, and a fair complexion. He had to be built like Procter and have the bone structure of his face and the shape of his head. It would not do for the next Darlington not to feature the Darlingtons in physical traits as much as possible to the inquiring eye. It was her own preference that the males she chose were also quick-witted and intelligent, but in some of the Darlingtons she had met, those qualities appeared to be recessive and not required for the lineage, so Alice was not going to be picky on that score.

Harry French fit the bill fairly well. She finished the first night of sex parties with him and let him stay with her until there were indications that he had given her what she needed. In the bathroom, there were dribbles before she tinkled, and she was newly encouraged out of the despondency she had begun to feel toward the prospect of her husband fathering her next child.

For the next few months, Alice waited for salon nights and checked the charts she kept secretly of her body rhythms. During periods when she wasn't fertile, she let other men make their attempts, just to show she was a good sport like the other girls, but got up immediately afterward to douche because she didn't want to take chances with the cleverness of sperms. Now she understood the bidet and the array of douches Lois kept on a shelf beside it. But when she was at highest fertility, she only allowed certain men to mate with her and would push the others off or get away from them; or, as females of the species had always done in primeval glades when subdued by superior strength, snarl menacingly over her shoulder until the brute got off and took his disagreeable genetics elsewhere.

There were a few others besides Harry who were right for the job. Jack Bittenger was good, Alex Davenport had everything, and Jim Rider the garret novelist had just enough of the traits she was looking for, provided they all came through. At least one of them could be found at Lois's on a sex party night. Sometimes all of them were there, and Alice really had to budget her time to fit everyone in. They were always gentlemen and tried to restrain their pleasure while they were with her, but she could always induce them to stay long enough to leave her with dribbles in the bidet and a hope that she had just conceived the next Darlington.

It was a little nerve-wracking, keeping to schedules. It was always on her mind, as much as the trouble she was having with Rory. She could stretch the feeding intervals for four hours at the most, but then he would find her and cling to her legs until she took him up. Or he would sit in his crib screaming "Mommy." If there wasn't enough milk to put him to sleep, he sucked hard and bit or pummeled her breasts with his little hands. Sometimes she wanted to smack him, but she just could not bring herself to do it.

Rory was a dear little boy otherwise, and Procter played with him, changed his diapers when Miss Lantz wasn't around, and put the thermometer in his bottom when he was cross, sweaty, and agitated. Almost every day, Procter had a new toy for him or was down on the floor showing him a different way to build towers with his blocks. It gave her a little more time to herself, but she began to feel very lonely and hopeless when Procter did not sit up with her at night while she had feedings. It exasperated him that the boy was so demanding of her time and always got his way. She asked Procter to help her think of a way to wean the child, but his only suggestions were harsh, and they got nowhere when they tried to discuss it. She knew it had grown to be more than an inconvenience, but how could she deny her child the sustenance and comfort that nature had provided for him?

Procter looked on sometimes with the resentment of eyeing a rival who had outplayed him. "This business makes it effectively impossible to get away," Procter said, with his arms folded across his chest and his eyes narrowing.

Alice never allowed him to raise his voice while the boy was nursing. Respecting this restriction, he just watched, shook his head, and murmured, "No, no, no" under his breath.

"He's never known anything but indulgence," he said.

"I know, Procter. I know. At this point, it doesn't matter. I just need help finding an answer to it. I know you can think of something better than what always comes first to your mind."

"Because it's the right thing to do. All you have to do is smack him once or twice when he climbs up, put him in the high chair, and have a bowl of sweet potato mush ready. He'll get the point. But you don't want to do that."

"I will not hit a child, Procter." What could be done about an impasse when both stood on a valid principle?

"Well, if you won't even try, I won't bother you anymore about it. I have to get to bed. I'm going to need my sleep. Something's kicking up on the Street."

"Oh, something's always kicking up on the street," she said bitterly.

"It's different this time."

"What's so different?"

"You'll have to ask your father about that, not me," he said.

He didn't fail to kiss her before he left, but he did leave and go to bed. For a little while, Alice was drawn away from her troubles with Rory when she saw her husband so uncharacteristically distraught. The last weeks of greeting him tired and worried at the door of the Tudor house or at the apartment in New York were taking a toll. She was afraid for him. He wasn't built for adversity like Andrew. Procter's shoulders threw off burdens like a reflex. "Too much trouble" was always on the tip of his tongue. Morgan was the first hard thing she had seen him stick to.

It was the first hint of a financial stress that she at first took to concern only their household. Procter would not discuss it with her or reply to her questions. He had always talked freely to her of their expenditures and their savings, so she could only assume that the trouble had to be in the firm, and that perhaps his job was in jeopardy if the great J.P. Morgan was going belly up. Not long after the first signs of worry appeared in Procter, Alice noticed something similar depressing her father's good nature. Not much was in the newspapers. The price of wheat was down. One of the railroads was in trouble. Something to do with Argentina was upsetting the financial people. At least she was relieved that whatever it was, it was going to happen to everybody, not just the Darlingtons and Sheffields.

Alice lifted Rory out of his crib and set him down on the floor. He tottered around for a moment but came up to her knees as soon as she sat in the rocking chair, and she let him climb up. His face was very cross and impatient. She patted his diaper and found it dry. These days he was showing a crafty intelligence by taking as much time as he could. She wasn't getting any sleep. She was exhausted, depressed, and getting irrational. Sometimes she thought she had an evil baby who was going to drive her insane.

The moon made its full arc in the window of the baby's room. Through the nights, when Alice came in to get Rory up, she usually found him standing against the bars of the crib about to begin fussing. She sat in the rocking chair with him and watched the moon as it passed from one pane of glass to another. It took two hours to cross from one frame to the next. When dawn came, the moon would still be there, and a few hours later, with the full morning sky around it, the silvery wafer in its phase would look out of place, as if the darkness in which it flourished had forgotten to take it along. Another hour would bring its disappearance, and for that it stood waiting like the condemned.

CHAPTER TWENTY-EIGHT

Within six months of her first after-hours salon night, Alice knew for sure she was pregnant with the baby that would make her unquestionably a Darlington. Keeping count of the nights the mattresses went down, Alice knew that she and Procter had attended five sex parties. She also knew that on many of those five nights, as she had recorded in a notebook kept secret in her underwear drawer, she had received genetic material from at least one of her chosen males, on one occasion or another, and from two newcomers who matched the requirements. But a sense of propriety had kept her from recording the names, so it could have been anybody from the first three months. It could even have been Procter, for he had not neglected her during the same time period.

When she knew she was pregnant, the sex parties were over for her. And so was any physical interest she had in the men she had used to secure her position with Procter and his family. When she told Procter he was going to be a father, the elation she saw in his face and the hope for the future she felt between them assured her that what she had done was right. Her marriage was secure, and her children would grow up with every advantage such a family as the Darlingtons could provide. It would now be her life's purpose to make a home life for Procter and the children. Two children were enough. As much as she wanted more, she had come to her moral limits in acquiring the Darlington addition. Procter believed he was the father of the child, and that was as far as she needed to go.

Alice began to turn the Tudor house into a proper home during her pregnancy. After the life they had been living, she meant to have peace and quiet and to have it in one place. Her mother and Procter's mother believed their campaign to keep the new family in Boston was finally showing results, and they redoubled their efforts by supervising renovations to the interior of the house while winter was upon New England. Miss Lantz was training Rory to the toilet and reported that he was doing well with it. He ran around the house, falling down and hitting his head no more than was expected, according to Mrs. Darlington, who had seen eight children through the stage. At every outbreak of wailing, Miss Lantz flew in like an angel from wherever she was to pick him up and quiet him down. He talked in a stream of words that were getting closer to intelligible and fun to decipher.

It should have been a carefree time of life, but Alice was aware of the aggregate of strains that had come along with it. Procter's persistent state of anxiety was always on her mind. The new baby was making its presence felt, and the noise of the workmen in the house began to grate on her nerves.

One morning when Miss Lantz was out at the shops and the workmen had not come yet, Alice was sitting in her chair in the bedroom, exhausted from another night up with Rory. She heard him in his playroom and looked over at the little clock on the bedstead. Any moment he would be coming to find her. Seized by a sudden assertion of her own will, she got up and went to the closet. She got in and sat down on the floor, closing the louvers just as she heard Rory in the hallway. Then she heard him in the room. He called "Mommy?" and was quiet for a moment, listening. She reached up, feeling for the two handles, found them and held them, her head between her knees, breathing as quietly as she could. Rory pulled at the handles from the outside. She held tight. She heard him go out of the room and down the steps to the first floor. She opened the louvers enough to listen to him go in and out of every room. When she heard him coming back up the steps, she closed the doors again and held them shut. Rory tugged at the handles.

"Mommy? Mommy?"

Alice realized it wasn't going to work. He must have been able to smell her or hear her breathing. He pulled on the door handles again, but she held them tightly. She couldn't let him find her there hiding. He would not trust her anymore if he caught her deceiving him. So she waited. He tried the door one last time and whimpered. Then he went to look for her in the other bedrooms, and she heard him calling, "Mommy? Mommy?"

Quickly, she left the closet and got under the covers of the bed.

"Rory," she called, as if she had been there all the time in a deep sleep and had just awakened. "Rory, where are you, sweetheart?"

Rory ran in overjoyed and climbed on the bed, repeating "Mommy, Mommy," without stopping until he was on top of her. She had to turn on her side because he was too heavy to lie on her stomach. She consolingly caressed the little boy against her. How could she have done that to her child? What was she going to do with another one? She was running out of time to think of something.

Alice slept whenever she could, but it was so little that sleep, at its own wits end, took leave of the dark hours and came looking for her by day. There were times in broad daylight when she was overcome by a stupor in which she had the most complex delusions and disturbing dreams that escaped memory an instant later, leaving her skittish and fearful. She was aware of herself going to pieces when Procter left her on Sunday afternoons. Rory had her all to himself then. Another baby was coming. He might be worse. What had she brought upon herself? It was her fault, using Procter to restore her to living and men at the salon to get her pregnant. What was she doing? She did not want any babies anymore. She didn't want the one she had. If only he would disappear and the one inside her die before it came out. It was only a moment's thought, but she'd had worse.

CHAPTER TWENTY-NINE

The excitement of welcoming 1894 faded quickly. The new year began to look like the decomposing corpse of 1893. In the Tudor house, Alice frequently had tea with Miss Lantz, her mother, and Mrs. Darlington. They talked about their needlework, plans for the house, and concerns of women. Only rarely did they bring up Mr. Sheffield, Mr. Darlington, or Procter, away at the war between the armies of the Sheffield bank, J.P. Morgan, and The Street on one side and the barbarian hoards of insolvency on the other. They were aware of railroads going into receivership, overseas investments collapsing, and the national treasury running out of gold. There were troubling headlines in the newspapers, and they had seen with their own eyes nervous men and women in lines outside of the banks. One or two had already failed in Boston. Mr. Sheffield's bank seemed to be holding, but Alice's mother began to wear the face of one surrounded by rising water.

Alice no longer took the train down to New York during the week. If Rory were any other child, she could have left him with Miss Lantz and gone off for a few days without a worry in her head, but she was rapidly losing the desire to make the trip as the pregnancy advanced and as Rory's behavior circumscribed her movements.

It was a snowy winter, and sometimes Procter was not able to get home. In February, she did not see him at all. They talked on the telephone every night. He was sounding more chipper. From the newspapers, she learned that Morgan was not going down like the rest. In fact, the old man was going to let the government borrow some of his gold reserves. Of course, she got nothing out of Procter, but the anxiety in his voice during the fall had been replaced by a cheery optimism. Increasingly, she had the distinct impression that every bad story in the newspapers was good news for J.P. Morgan.

All Procter could tell her was that he had been promoted and moved to the second floor, where he shared an office with another prospective partner. Before that, he had been in a line of desks downstairs by the front door with the other juniors. She had never heard about the previous arrangement and had never doubted that his position merited an office, so it did not come as a surprise to her that he was advancing in the firm.

Procter began to drop hints about looking for a bigger apartment in New York. On one of the weeks when he didn't come home, he sounded on the telephone as if he was ready to make a move, and she had to pin him down on the topic. First she brought up how distraught her father was and that she thought the bank might be in perilous straits. She asked if there was anything he could do. He reminded her that he was under professional constraints of confidentiality. The silence in the wires following those words confirmed her conviction that she had gone as far as she could for her father.

"Put Procter Darlington back on the line, will you please?" she said.

He laughed and said he wished she'd come down. "I thought you liked New York," he said.

"I do, Procter, but this is really our home. You haven't seen the new dining room. Your mother and my mother have put so much work into it. I won't let them do anything in the bedroom until we talk about it."

"Well, I don't really care that much. I can live anywhere."

"Then why do you think we need a better apartment down there?"

"It's just a little small for having people over."

"Who are you having over?"

"Nobody special. I wouldn't have to have anybody over if you were here. It gets damn lonely, you know."

She would rather hear that the loneliness he felt could wait with the candle in the window until he was with her, but she knew how outgoing he was and how much he needed to have people around. It reminded her that he still thought of himself in an outmoded way, as if he weren't married.

"Have you been to see Lois?" she asked.

"A few times."

"Talk nights or you-know?"

"A few talks, a few you-knows. Everybody asks about you, darling. It's not the same without you."

"I wouldn't think anyone would notice me missing in the dark."

She heard Procter laugh.

"You're quite the sensation with everybody down here. You're the cat's meow with Harry French, you know, and that fellow Bittenger, the city councilman, is always asking after you. Oh, and Jim Rider is getting his novel published. He wanted me to tell you. Everyone wants to know when you're coming down."

"That might be a while," she said.

"I thought if we lived down here, we could settle down. You know, have a routine. Not like the routine we'd have in Boston with, you know, my family, your family. That's no fun. You liked those evenings out, didn't you? I mean, all the interesting talk and nobody gets too serious."

Alice changed hands holding the receiver.

"I thought we were going to settle down here, Procter," she said quietly.

"We don't have to get into that now."

"Will you come home this weekend?"

"I think I'd better stay here. I've got a lot of work to do, and I can't take any of it on the train. It would only be time lost, and we're getting pretty busy."

"All right," she said. "I'd better go. Good night, Procter."

Five minutes later he called back. He never let her down when she was feeling blue. He never left her dangling. He always called back to make sure they ended on a good note.

"You know I love you, darling," he said.

"I love you too, Procter. I just want us to be together."

"I do too, sweetheart. When all this financial mess is sorted out, we'll have plenty of time. We can live anywhere we want. I'll talk to you tomorrow night."

He sent her to bed with love and kisses. The telephone was so wonderful for that.

After the last snow melted off and the ground dried, work started on the exterior of the house. The mothers had decided that the Tudor house needed more Tudor. The big windows were being replaced with many little ones of leaded glass, a second-story overhang was built on with the addition of aged beams sticking out here and there to give it more of the Old English look.

Rory started eating from one day to the next without any explanation that he cared to give. Alice was inclined to accept the hypothesis offered by Mrs. Darlington, who proposed that it was only when the child had developed sufficient motor skills to feed himself that he became interested in sitting at a table with a fork, spoon, plates, and cups. She recommended that it be followed up immediately with instruction in table manners, but Alice and Miss Lantz agreed that imposing rules might induce a relapse. At night he still wanted to be put to sleep at the breast, but that was no more trouble than the frightful mess Rory made at the table.

The baby arrived in April. The birth went easily, and as the hammering and sawing went on outside, a new Darlington was ushered into the world. In attendance were the Sheffield and Darlington mothers and a midwife. Alice rested with the clean-wiped, swaddled baby on her stomach and heard Miss Lantz downstairs on the telephone.

"Mrs. Darlington and baby boy are doing well, Mr. Darlington. Everything went very well. Congratulations. Eight pounds, four ounces. Mrs. Darlington is still asleep. Yes, I'll tell her."

Under the chloroform, Alice had a dream that Procter had come up from New York. He had taken Rory back with him on the train. He had a talk with him. He said, "Now see here, young fellow. No more milk for you. You're going to have to be a man and eat steak and potatoes." He took him to Delmonico's. He ordered steak and potatoes and beer. "And no more fiddling with these messy diapers. You go down there and pee in the urinal," he said, pointing down a long dark hallway. "We're going to get you squared away this week. Baby days are over."

She knew Procter could do it. Now that he was a family man, he would see the wisdom of leaving Morgan and working for Father in the bank, and he would make the Tudor house their home. She would have a girl Darlington next time. Everything would be all right now. A baby was crying. It must be the one that just came out of her. She would take a look in the morning.

CHAPTER THIRTY

Procter was able to get up to Boston a week later to see the baby. They talked on the telephone, and Alice had agreed to name him Armstrong after Procter's grandfather and to call him Autie, as the grandfather had been by his business associates. Because it made the child that much more a Darlington, it suited Alice as a fine name for the boy. She was so glad to see Procter, and she ran to the door to meet him late Friday night, scarcely able to stay in the entryway and hold back her joy while he paid the cab fare. Then he danced up the steps, dropped his bag, and picked her up off her feet in a strong embrace.

"You look very nice," he said.

"I have dinner in the oven," she said, bringing her voice down to a whisper in the hallway. "Rory's in bed, and Miss Lantz has the baby. I have to feed him in a little while, but he can wait. He doesn't fuss at all. He's been perfectly wonderful. Let's get to dinner while we have a chance to be alone."

Alice wanted to make it romantic. She wanted everything to be perfect for him so he would always want to come home, but while she was going through drawers in the dining room looking for the nicer candles, Procter turned on the harsh gas lights in the kitchen and was lifting lids over the stove.

"Let's just eat in the kitchen," he said.

"Well, all right. But Procter, please don't eat out of the pot. I'll get you a plate. Go sit down at the table. I'll bring everything over."

"That four hours on the train just takes the stuffing out of me."

"It only seems that way because you haven't been up here in so long, dear," she said, looking in the oven. "Cornish hens. You'll like these. I made them myself."

"They're kind of small."

"These aren't. Look." She brought the baking pan over to the table to show him. "I won't be able to finish mine, so there will be plenty for you." Then she stopped and smiled at having him there all to herself. "I'm so glad to have a husband again," she sighed. "I made you biscuits too. And cookies for dessert."

Miss Lantz brought little Autie into the living room after dinner. He woke up with wide, staring eyes when introduced to his father, contentedly nursed for only a few minutes, and obligingly fell back to sleep. Miss Lantz took him from Alice, and on her way to the nursery asked, "Are you ready for the boy, Madam?"

"Yes, thank you, Nurse," she said. Then she turned to Procter. "You haven't seen him in so long. I hope he remembers you."

Rory appeared in the doorway, dressed in his pajamas, and steered immediately toward Procter, who lifted him up to his lap.

"Well, I'm not sure," said Procter, looking at Rory, "but I caught 'Daddy' and 'train.' What's 'ooh-ork'?"

"New York," said Alice. "He has a good vocabulary if you take every sound that comes out as a word, which they really are."

"You're going to be a fast talker, aren't you."

"I talk on telfrom," said Rory. "Anmum talk to me."

"Oh, she does?" He started bouncing the boy on his knee.

"Oh, Procter, don't do that. We want him to go back to sleep."

Procter stood up with Rory in his arms. "Well, I know what you're here for, little fellow," he said to Rory, putting his nose to Rory's and bringing him over to Alice. "I better get to bed. It's after eleven."

Alice let him go without showing her disappointment. She knew he was tired from his week and the four hours on the train. She put Rory to bed and came back to the kitchen. The dishes were in the sink, and there were the pots and pans to wash. It would be inconsiderate to leave them for the cook and her helper, but looking at the plates in the sink brought tears to her eyes. She didn't know why. It was just hard to do anything. She thought she would have her energy back after the baby came, but it felt like she didn't have any at all now. She sat at the kitchen table with her head down and cried into the dirty napkins. Time to feed the baby. First, she did the dishes and pots and pans. Twice during the night, she got up to feed Autie. She felt like a horse about to drop in its traces.

Alice was getting accustomed to the banging and sawing, but during breakfast she could see that it was an annoyance to Procter. Halfway through his eggs and toast, he got up and went outside. She could see him through the window, standing on the lawn with his hands in his pockets, looking up. When he came inside and sat down again, he was no less agitated.

"I didn't want to tell you last night, Alice," he said, "but I've got to go back this morning. I've got a meeting at four."

"But it's Saturday, Procter."

"There's nothing I can do about it. I thought I'd be all right if I caught a train by eleven."

"That doesn't give you much time. You should have told me last night."

"I didn't want to make you feel rushed."

"Oh, Procter."

"But I can get away next weekend. I'm pretty sure."

The next two weekends, Procter had Saturday meetings again and could not make it up to Boston. Alice told him how pretty it was in the yard now. The mothers had been planting bushes and flowers everywhere. When she said how much she was looking forward to the island in August, she thought to mention that he should make sure to put in for vacation days. His voice lacked enthusiasm, but he said he would take care of it. He didn't call for the next several days. Procter had never missed a night, so she telephoned the apartment, but there was no answer. Another day went by. She heard the telephone ring the next day, but it was in the morning, so she let the butler pick it up. A moment later he came to the door of the living room and announced that Mr. Darlington was on the line. Alice was so relieved to hear his voice.

"Oh, Procter, where are you?" She could hear other voices in the background, and Procter was laughing.

"I'm in Maine," he said.

"Maine?"

"Yes, Bucksport, Maine, to be exact."

"What are you doing there?"

"What? I didn't hear you. Just a minute."

When he got back on, it was quieter behind his voice, and she asked again.

"It was a spur-of-the-moment thing. I was out with a bunch of the fellows, and someone said he had a cabin in the woods, and next thing you know we were on the night train to Bangor. It looks like camp up here, but without the islands and open water. It's more woodsy, and they have these little gnats—swarms of them. They get in your eyes. Alice? Are you there?"

"I'm here," she said.

"There are people waiting for the telephone. I'm using the one in the general store. Nothing else up here, so I've got to get off. I'll call you when I get back to New York."

"Procter, wait. If you're coming back through Boston—" She stopped because she heard the line disconnect.

Rory had seen the baby. Between Alice, Miss Lantz, and the mothers, the two had been kept apart, but Alice knew that couldn't go on for long. When she nursed the baby, Rory knew perfectly well what was going on and wailed at the door of the nursery. When his turn came at bedtime, he vented his anger by pushing her face away and screaming, "It's mine. It's mine." Little Autie took so little milk and was so passive that it was easier to let it go on as it was than fight it. She didn't know what could be done. It was beginning to look like a hopeless situation. The same could be said of trying so hard with Procter, coping with a difficult child, not getting any sleep, and going crazy. In that order.

Procter came up a few weeks later. He was able to plan for a week in Boston because, as he explained on the telephone, where he was in the firm was entirely different from his years as a junior. On the first night at home, she told him she was perfectly all right for making love, but he said he was tired from the trip up and needed to catch up on his sleep. It was good enough for Alice to lie beside him for a little while, knowing she had him for a week, but she didn't sleep any better for it because little Autie needed his night feedings.

During the day, they took Rory along on rides in her father's carriage. Procter held him up to give the horse a carrot before they set out. Then he held Rory in his lap as they drove past the harbor to see the sailing ships and the steamers. Rory looked like such a happy little boy that it made her think all would turn out well when Procter finally moved up to Boston and they all lived together in the Tudor house.

Alice was glad to have found out from her father that his bank had weathered the storm. Because she had gotten the story directly from her father, she wasn't sure if it was public knowledge that Morgan had come to the rescue. On a walk to the park one afternoon, she put her arm through Procter's and said, "Thank you for helping my father, Procter. I've been meaning to mention it, but there wasn't a good time."

"I can't talk about it," he said.

"You don't have to," she said happily. "I know everything. J.P. himself telephoned Father. They talked for two hours, and the next day the check came. Father was so impressed because it was signed Procter Darlington. That's you, isn't it? Of course it is. How could there be another Procter Darlington?"

"Let's hear what else you know," he said, disguising his pride in himself for the sake of Morgan confidentiality.

"All right. Father said he and J.P. worked together for Anthony Drexel for twenty years. They were great chums. Why didn't you ever mention that? No, I know why. Father never said anything about it either, even to Mother, because he saw how private J.P. became as he got on in the world. What I really think is, J.P. doesn't want to admit that he ever worked for anyone. That's it, isn't it?"

Alice suddenly stopped in her tracks and looked at Procter with grave concern. "Morgan isn't going to lose his million in Father's bank, is he?"

"No, no. Don't worry. J.P. looks into the banks he helps. It wasn't purely sentimental. That's all I can say about it."

After that, Procter was fun to be around again, the way he was at the beginning. It was so encouraging to see him free of the worry and cares he had been bringing home when it was just weekends. Whatever the attractions New York held, he could not fail to notice, as she did, that he was content here. He was still fun, curious about everything, a little erratic and excitable, but smoothing out to preferring his spirits not to rise or fall too many degrees off room temperature. She was sure that would tell the tale when he returned to New York, to the lonely apartment without her and the children.

In the evenings that week, they dined out at restaurants and went to the theater or the symphony. Alice could stretch out the time away from home to four hours, but then they came home to the baby apologetically expressing his mild discomfiture by waving his arms and wiggling his little hands. Meanwhile, the boy was locked in his room banging his toys around. One night while she was nursing the baby, Rory got out and ran into the bedroom. Before Procter could intercept him, he was up on Alice pushing and punching the baby, shouting, "It's mine. It's mine." His finger went in the baby's eye, and the little thing burst into a fearful crying, waving his arms helplessly to fend off the attacker. Miss Lantz rushed in. Procter pulled Rory off and dragged him screaming by the collar of his pajamas and locked him in his room. Then Procter ran to the street to call a cab, and Alice and Miss Lantz bundled up the baby.

They spent the night and most of the next day in the hospital. Autie had to be put under to stitch up a rip in his eyelid. Luckily there was a specialist surgeon who was able to rush over from another hospital. He hesitated to operate on a baby, but Procter talked to him privately, and he agreed to try it. After several hours he came out to the waiting room to say he had repaired the damage, but he had to sew the eye shut for six weeks while it healed. Then they waited for Autie to be examined for a broken nose. They weren't sure, so they taped the bridge and said to leave it on for two weeks.

It was very difficult to get the poor little thing to nurse after that. When Alice finally got him to try it again, she looked down at the bruises on his face and felt so sorry for him. To keep him from hearing threatening sounds, she had to press him gently into herself and put a hand over his exposed ear when Rory started fussing in his room. He would stop nursing if he heard his older brother's voice and would begin to tremble with his one eye open very wide.

If it had not been for Procter, Alice thought she would have gone over the edge. He was calm through everything. The worst he ever said was, "When does anyone get any sleep around here?" But then he smiled, and she found she could smile back, as if they were in the same boat. It seemed to be slowly turning out that they could work together and have a good life, and it gave Alice new heart for getting through the rough patches.

The last work on the outside of the house did not seem to bother Procter until it reached a noise level that crossed the line. But even then, to amuse her, he began to review the production outside as if he were an opera critic.

"Oh, that was a nice one," he exclaimed one morning at the breakfast table, after a large board, apparently tossed from the roof, hit a pile of lumber on the ground. "Something below F_2, if I'm not mistaken. Well, you take your chances throwing boards, don't you? So much of the sound quality depends on what's in the pile below. In this case, some empty paint cans might have added a whimsical note to the auditory impact of wood on wood."

It made her laugh and feel good because he was being clever just for her. His tone was gentle and accepting of the situation, but she knew he really was annoyed.

"They must go to the store," he continued, "or wherever they go, and say, 'See here, Mr. Tool Vendor, are you sure this is the loudest hammer you have? This saw does not disturb the neighborhood enough. Can you order a noisier one for me?'"

"Oh, that's very funny, Procter," said Alice.

It was encouraging to see him rise above the situation and not just get up and leave. It was sign of maturity. With a household and two young boys to bring up, it would be nice to be able to count on him.

"We don't want any complaints to get back to the mothers. The impresarios on the roof would only take it out on us."

"They've been such dears, Procter. I mean our mothers, of course. They really have."

"Not to the boys outside. I heard them this morning, right under the window. You were asleep. It must have been my mother they were talking about."

"I was afraid of her, too, at the beginning," said Alice. "Do you remember?"

"I kept telling you there was nothing to be afraid of."

"This is my favorite time of day," she said, suddenly quickening so as not to lose any of it. "Let's take our coffee in the living room. I've only got an hour before I have to feed the baby."

Procter went for the coffee pot on the stove and followed Alice out to the living room. He angled a heavy upholstered chair to face the one Alice sat in and pulled a side table between them for their cups.

"It will be so nice to be with your mother in camp this year," said Alice. "Does she wear trousers up there like your sisters?"

"Oh sure. She was the first one. I don't know any woman up there who hasn't been put in dungarees by her."

"She'd never get my mother in a pair of those. Not in a million years."

"Oh, I bet she could," said Procter.

They both laughed and stirred their coffee.

"Are you sure you can go in August, Procter?"

"Quite sure."

"I don't understand how you can do that. And don't tell me you can't say anything about it. I'll call Mrs. Morgan and ask her."

"Oh, that would be rich. No, you see, where I am in the firm, you're allowed as much time off as you need. By that I mean, specifically, as much time as you need to take care of something. Vacations and holidays can't be mentioned. But you can go away any time you like—to take care of something. Do you get the idea?"

"Well, that's marvelous, Procter. Then you can take care of me and stay here," she said lightly.

"I thought a week would do it. Well, I still think so. I don't know."

"To do what?"

"Well, I've been trying to decide something," he said, becoming more serious.

That sounded ominous—not like the gathering of a storm, but like the more subtle feeling in the air of one coming later.

"What are you trying to decide, Procter?" she asked as calmly as she could.

"Well, you know. We've been together a long time."

"Two years."

"I've been thinking. You know, maybe we could use some time off. You know, go our separate ways for a while. You're pretty busy with the kids, since there are two of them now. You've always been so independent, and it's such a long trip up here for me."

Alice suddenly felt as if she were caving in. The house was falling down. He didn't want her anymore. "Is there someone else?" she asked after a long silence, looking away from him.

"No, nothing to get serious about. That's why I had to take some time off. You know, to decide what I want to do."

"Is it a woman?"

"There's one I like," he said, brightening up.

"Was she with you in Maine?"

"She's great with the fellows. It was actually her idea to go. Everybody likes her."

"So you met her at Lois's?"

"Sure. There's no better place to meet people. You know that yourself. She's one of the gals from NYU. Sometimes we really get into it over issues of the day, that kind of thing. It sounds funny, but we argue all the time. Just one of those things, you know."

Alice brought a hand up from her lap to stop him from saying any more. She felt like closing her eyes and waving her hands around her head like little Autie fending off attack.

"How are you going to decide what you want to decide?" she asked, in a state that seemed so far from where she was.

"Well, I thought I'd start by coming up here to see if I want to stay. You know, to see if I can do things the way you want to do things. Or if I'd rather do things the way I want and stay in New York."

"Procter." Alice started, but stopped.

He respectfully waited for her while he moved the cups and sugar bowl casually around the tray as if he were playing a game.

"Procter," she said, "you aren't in one of Lois's salon nights. You're in a marriage."

"I know. That's what's making it so hard to decide. We've in kind of deep, aren't we? I mean, with the house and the two kids."

"I thought we were managing."

"Well, no need to let it get us down," he said with a smile. "The jury's still out."

What could she say to that? What words were there to ever make a difference to the indifferent? A jury was to arbitrate the case. In two days he would be going back to New York. If she could last one more month as a Darlington, she could get him away to Canada. She could fix it there. She could fix what was wrong with Rory. Then she could move to New York and begin to fix herself.

"Well, I better get to bed," said Procter. "Let's see if we can have some fun tomorrow. I think we could both use a bit of that, don't you?"

Alice let him go up to bed. She walked quietly into the nursery.

She took Autie out of his crib and sat down in the chair with him. She called Miss Lantz from her room.

"Miss Lantz, I'd like you to take pains to be sure Rory is quiet for the next two days. Mr. Darlington will be going back to New York on Sunday, and I wish him to have absolute peace and quiet tomorrow and the next. He's under some pressure, and it's very important for him to relax while he's here."

"Very well, madam. I'll do my best."

"I'm sure we all will, Nurse. Thank you."

Alice finished with Autie in the nursery and tiptoed down to Rory's room. It was late by the time she got him tucked in, but the day was finally over. She thought the boys would sleep through the night, so she went to Miss Lantz's room to let her know she would not be needed until morning.

At last she slipped into bed at three o'clock. The child stratagem may have failed, but there might be hope for their old way. She tried to arouse Procter. He woke up to say he was a little tired but maybe, so she tried to get him interested, but he fell back to sleep and she gave up. She still had two days.

They had fun together without the children on Friday and Saturday. Procter went a little wild buying toys for Rory and Autie and seemed to have a good idea of what was right for the ages of the boys. They took carriages around the city streets and walked arm in arm through the parks. The weather was wonderful, and they had a nice time together, perhaps the best time she had ever had with him. It helped her spirits rise to hear no more of the decision he was trying to make. Alice could not avoid getting to bed late and took what comfort there was in lying beside him. It was no use trying for more at that hour.

On Sunday morning they begged off the afternoon with the families and had a quiet breakfast alone. They did not say very much due to his impending departure, but they smiled at each other enough that Alice put all her heart into what she felt was still between them. They kissed goodbye at the door when the cab came to take him to the station. It was in her interest to want him as confused as possible on the train to New York, and push off his decision, but there was some evidence in his eyes at the door that made her feel a judgment in her favor had already been reached.

Alice waited for his call that night, and it came at the usual time. The sound of his voice cheered her right away and dispelled any doubts she had. He had a good chance to think on the train, he said, and didn't they have a time of it these last few days?

"I have your son in my lap right now," she said.

"How's the eye doing?"

"Still sewn shut, but the swelling's gone down."

"I'll send him a get well card."

"I think he'd rather see you, dear."

"I'll wait till he has two good eyes."

"That will be six weeks," she said. "He can't wait that long. He longs to see you, Procter. He yearns to be held in your arms again. You know, I think he's positively nuts about you."

After a short silence, Procter said, "I don't think I'll be coming up, Alice."

In a voice she could barely manage, Alice said, "What are you saying, Procter?"

"Well, I see it like this," he said. "We've already gone in different directions for a while, don't you think? I mean you have your friends up there, and I have my friends down here."

"I don't have friends up here, Procter," she said in another small voice.

"Well, you don't get out enough. You used to be more—I don't want to say more fun because we really did have some fun this week, but the house and the kids and all that—I want to help you out, but it's gotten to be—well, too much trouble, you know? I guess that's the point."

There was no sense to it. She was willing to live with Procter however he wanted. Didn't he know that? There was no reason for him to kick over the table. Tears came to her eyes.

"I'll get around to a lawyer when I have a chance. Is that all right with you? I'll make sure everything is down the middle."

"All right, Procter. I have to go. Good night."

She felt like a hammered scrap of metal falling off an anvil. She took the receiver from her ear and held it to her forehead. She wanted to express herself in the silence she made before she hung it up. She thought Autie must have sensed the hurt done to her because he stopped nursing and stared at her with his one eye blinking. He looked as pitiable as she felt, and she added his bruises and hurt eye to her own wounds.

Procter wouldn't let it end like that. He would call back. He would not consider it a successful call until she agreed with him. He relied so much on others coming around to his point of view. But there was an equal chance that he would change his mind. She hung up the telephone and started waiting. Five minutes passed and the telephone rang.

"Yes?" she said into the mouthpiece.

In the next moment, Alice fainted. She slouched forward over the chair and crashed to the floor with the baby in her arms under her full weight. Miss Lantz heard the fall and rushed from the other room. She pulled the baby out from under Alice. He was still breathing. Thinking quickly, she picked up the receiver dangling from the table, put it to her ear, and spoke into the other side of it.

"Hello! Hello!"

She heard the voice on the other end say her name.

"Yes, this is Miss Lantz. Who is calling? Oh, yes, Mrs. Croft has spoken of you, Mr. Croft. Yes, I would say Mrs. Croft would like to see you. Are you in town? Do you know the address? Then I would come quickly, sir. Mrs. Croft needs you to come as soon as possible with an ambulance. Yes. Thank you, sir. Goodbye."

Alice was insensible to all entreaties from Miss Lantz. Beside her, the baby lay wrecked on the floor. He had drawn his arms and legs up to his body, but one arm was broken and hanging to the side. The little bare chest went up and down rapidly. His one eye was open wide with fear, his mouth was tightly shut, and he made no sound lest his brother, the demon of this terrible place, should notice his presence and trouble himself to come finish the job.

PART THREE

CHAPTER THIRTY-ONE

After the night Alice and the baby were taken to the hospital, Mrs. Sheffield and Mrs. Darlington convened a predawn meeting in the heavily draped parlor of the Darlington's brownstone. It had been a long night, and the two were not restrained in supporting themselves with numerous refreshers of coffee. The Darlingtons had left for the hospital immediately after a telephone call from Miss Lantz, while Mr. and Mrs. Sheffield arrived later, learning of the mishap after returning home from a benefit for one of their daughter's charities. This left Mrs. Darlington as the one in the know, a position that was in her nature to believe the normal state of affairs, whatever the circumstances or composition of the company.

"It's quite serious for the baby, you know," said Mrs. Darlington, looking over the round wire frames of her spectacles. "He was sent right away to special care and placed on a breathing apparatus. They fear he has broken bones and crushed organs. No one was allowed into the room to see him. I daresay the next news we receive of little Armstrong may not be favorable." She brought a handkerchief to the corner of one eye. "What a pity."

Mrs. Sheffield brought a handkerchief to her eyes as well. "He was a delicate child from the beginning."

"Well!" pronounced Mrs. Darlington firmly, tucking her handkerchief up her sleeve. "They're doing all that can be done. As for the mother, the diagnosis was nervous exhaustion. Any woman with children could have told them that."

"Undoubtedly," said Mrs. Sheffield, also dismissing the services of her handkerchief. "I brought it up with her on numerous occasions. Unfortunately, Alice disregards opinions not conforming to her own."

"Well, heavens, what on earth did she think it was?"

"I don't think she had any notion of her condition at all."

"Precisely my view," said Mrs. Darlington in return. Finding it a good opportunity to ring for the maid, she applied herself to a little glass bell on the table. They put their hands in their laps and raised their eyes to the window, from which dawn was beginning to spread its warm, yellow, rosy light across the high ceiling.

"Well, she just did not see it then," Mrs. Darlington resumed after the maid had left another pot of coffee and a fresh plate of croissants, turned down the gaslights, and departed. "Nervous exhaustion is very common after having a child—just another of the many inconveniences to which the tender sex is susceptible. I put up with nervous exhaustion myself—no fewer than eight times. I quickly found it best to nip it in the bud. That's right, nip it in the bud. Whenever I felt the symptoms coming on, I put myself on a strict regimen of brandy and little chocolates four times daily or as needed. I advised Alice to do the same when we had lunch a month ago, but of course, she couldn't be bothered."

"I'm afraid that is very much like my daughter," said Mrs. Sheffield, "still the headstrong girl she always was."

From the wrapped chocolates Mrs. Darlington was known to keep in the pockets of her dresses and the decanters of brandy about the downstairs of the Darlington house, Mrs. Sheffield surmised that her friend did not, even at a distance of nearly thirty years since the birth of her last child, feel far enough removed from the hazards of nervous exhaustion to discontinue the treatment.

"New mothers lack training these days," continued Mrs. Darlington, who could not help a note of pique in her voice.

"Alice was always so sure of herself," Mrs. Sheffield rejoined in her own defense. "There was nothing I could tell her that she did not purport to know before I brought it up."

"Oh, I did not mean to suggest that you were negligent toward your daughter in any possible way, Elizabeth," said Mrs. Darlington, reaching out to touch her friend's hand. "I know you have assiduously addressed yourself to this business with the older child. Well! That would have resolved itself soon enough, and she would have shaken off nervous exhaustion in time—she's a strong young woman—as long as no further stresses were introduced."

"I'm sure," said Mrs. Sheffield, "but now we have further stresses. This young man—"

"Indeed," said Mrs. Darlington. "I overheard him tell the nurse that he had forced a rider from his horse in the street in order to conduct the baby to the hospital with all speed. He left word, should she regain consciousness in his absence, that he would be back directly after returning the gentleman's horse.

To me that is all very strange. I don't know how Alice would be acquainted with such a character. But she must be—for the familiar way in which he spoke of her. And after all, he had the baby in his possession. He was definitely an acquaintance, not a random Good Samaritan, Lord bless us."

Mrs. Sheffield was satisfied that Mrs. Darlington had related to her everything she had been able to find out at the hospital. Now she found herself in the position of knowing more than her friend knew: the identity of the mysterious young man. When she and Mr. Sheffield had been admitted to Alice's darkened room at the hospital, he was sitting at the bedside. He rose immediately, acknowledged her with a glance, and left the room without a word or offering his hand to Mr. Sheffield. Mr. Croft was undeniably alive and had returned from South Africa.

"I don't know what is keeping Procter," said Mrs. Darlington. "I telephoned him last night. He said he would be here as soon as he had a chance to get away. I telephoned again earlier this morning, but he wasn't in. He's dreadfully serious about his work, you know, so either he was detained at the office, or he's on the train right now. We'll soon see, I suppose."

Mrs. Sheffield decided to keep her in the dark about Mr. Croft. It was difficult for her to withhold anything from Mrs. Darlington because they were such good friends, but if quick action on the part of Procter could get rid of Mr. Croft and restore order, there was no need to upset her. Procter, acting fully within his rights, could see Mr. Croft escorted out of the room, by policemen if necessary, and Alice would awaken with the more desirable husband at her bedside.

"Well!" said Mrs. Darlington. "We're not going to let the situation deteriorate any further, are we?"

"Certainly not," said Mrs. Sheffield.

"You'll take Miss Lantz back with you, of course, and the baby when he is released from the hospital. The little boy will come here. What do you think, Mrs. Sheffield?"

It sounded logical enough to Mrs. Sheffield. She had every confidence that Mrs. Darlington had the ability to take charge of Rory. The only reservation she had was the same point upon which the proposal had her approval. Rory seemed to be afraid of that particular grandmother. When she stopped to think about it, Mrs. Sheffield could not recall ever witnessing a smile on Mrs. Darlington's face in the presence of a child. But perhaps that was precisely what was needed.

"I fear that such a division of labor would leave me with very little to do and quite a lot for you, Constance."

"I have raised six boys, Elizabeth," said Mrs. Darlington. You needn't fear that Master Rory will bring me to nervous exhaustion. It will be a welcome challenge. There hasn't been a young boy in this house since—well, since I've worn a bonnet!"

They mutually repressed a titter of laughter and agreed on the plan.

CHAPTER THIRTY-TWO

Andrew held Alice's hand while the nurse was in and out of the room. When they were alone, he leaned over to her and stroked her head, but Alice was in a deep sleep and unresponsive. Hours passed. Two nurses came in, one to lift her up and the other to get her to swallow a dose of what they told him was laudanum. In the morning he was turned out of the room to allow the nurses to get Alice to the water closet, change the sheets, tidy her up, and put her back to sleep again. The doctor said he wanted her to sleep for forty-eight hours.

As far as Andrew knew, the sole cause of her collapse was his telephone call. He had considered the advice of Mr. Thompson. But he wanted to see for himself, or hear for himself over the telephone, Alice's first reaction to his return home in order to best determine her true sentiments. He had gone directly to the boarding house when he got to Boston and found Shahid living there under his new name, Charles Thompson. He was immediately informed that he had fathered a boy, now three years of age, and that Alice had married again. Mr. Thompson also told him that it was a marriage of equally distinguished families and said he had recently read a newspaper announcement that Alice had borne a child to her new husband.

These were reasons enough to leave Boston without making his presence known. He would never try to take her from a man she had chosen to marry. But he had to see her. That's what made him pick up the telephone with a trembling hand and his heart in his throat. He had to ask if she wanted to see him. Even if her answer was no, he could watch the house, wait for a glimpse of her, or follow her when she went into town. He could probably get close to her without detection on the street. Then he could leave her to the new life she had chosen and look for a tolerable one for himself, although he could envision no happiness in what lay before him without Alice. But he had failed to imagine a wider range of possibility, and here he was, sitting at her bedside. Just the same, the outcome left him even up with the capricious working of chance, still without an answer to the question whether Alice would want to see him or not.

She might have been dead for as still as she lay. In the dim light of the corridor coming over the transom, her face was as he remembered it, but impassive and without spirit, as the dead always look. Sometimes her brows knit together, and her eyelids tightened in the disturbance of dream. Then the line dividing her lips contracted to resemble a map drawn of a crooked river. It must have been the laudanum. He had been on it in China, recovering from the work of the knife across his middle.

He loved her as he always had, but he knew that neither loving her in the past nor loving her now invested him with any claim on her affections. Apart from that, possession was nine-tenths of the law. What kind of man was Procter Darlington? It was four hours to New York. The trains were always running. He should have been at the hospital by now. Andrew kept an eye on the door. Coming from South Africa would have made a better excuse for Procter Darlington.

For the first time in months, Alice felt calm in the quiet around her. Frets and cares were gone. All she had to do was lie still and float in the air. When she had slept long enough, she lay awake with her eyes closed, and it was the same as sleeping.

Andrew was there. Why? Oh well. Nothing to get excited about. He was in the dream she was dreaming. Weren't there some babies? What happened to the babies? There were too many. They went away. Didn't Procter know all he had to do was close his eyes and he would not be bothered by them? Now he was gone too. Oh well. Let's do something different today, Alice. Let's go through our drawers. Let's open every drawer and look inside. Did you know poor people put their babies in drawers for the night? Maybe that's where babies come from. All those men at the salon. Some husbands would not have wanted her doing that. How lucky she was to have Procter. He could change his mind and come back. He was always changing his mind. Andrew changed his mind out of being dead. If she died and came back to life, she would not bother anyone. People have enough problems without the dead coming back. Oh! Oh! Coming down, coming down. Big field with mud puddles. No! No! Help! Help! Nurse. Drink this, dear. Going back up. Wave goodbye. Go away, Andrew. He's not. Oh well.

Alice woke up when the sunlight edged around to the south side of the hospital and brightened her window. Andrew was sitting in a straight-backed chair beside the bed, but he had fallen asleep. His head hung down over his chest, and his hair had fallen over his eyes. To all appearances, he was the man she had married. It might be the same suit he was wearing when she saw him off to South Africa. No, it was too new. How could she have forgotten what he was wearing the last time she saw him?

"Andrew," she said.

He woke up and looked at her. He smiled, but she could not smile back. "Push your hair back. It's falling over your eyes."

He smoothed his hair back and came over to sit on the edge of the bed. "You look so uncomfortable. Lie down on the bed."

She moved to the other side as he lay down and turned away from him so it would not look bad if Procter walked in. They were married after all and had shared a bed before. Which one was she talking about? How could she be married to two men? How simple it would be if it was all a dream and she woke up in the boarding house with Andrew. She would not tell him the dream. It would be her secret. She could run into Procter Darlington on the street. He would go over to see Lois and tell her that a woman he had never met had come up to him and said, "I had a dream about you."

The nurse came in and found them both asleep. Another frowning nurse followed behind, and they promptly returned Andrew to the chair. Then they made him leave the room while they attended to Alice. She licked the bottom of the cup of medicine brought to her lips and went back to sleep as Andrew sat down beside her again in the chair.

The next morning, the nurses sat her up and brushed her hair. They did not bring the cup of the medicine she had found so agreeable. She was told that a doctor was coming to visit her. She waited with her hands folded in her lap. Andrew crossed his arms across his chest and also looked down in silence. It was so awkward not talking to him when he was right there. It was like looking at an artifact from an ancient civilization in a museum. And she was the lump under a light on the other side of the room. She had loved him once. It would be much easier if he went back to being dead in South Africa and buried too far away to bring flowers.

There was a knock at the door. The nurse stood to the side as a trim little gentleman in a business suit entered the room.

"Good morning, Mrs. Darlington. My name is Dr. Epstein. I'm glad to see you looking well."

"I am not, sir," said Alice. Turning to Andrew, she said, "I believe Dr. Epstein would like to speak to me alone, if you please."

Andrew and the doctor shook hands in parting as Andrew left the room. The door closed. The doctor took Andrew's chair and sat down.

"What seems to be the trouble?"

"I am overwrought," said Alice.

"You are taking the medicine, are you not?"

"Not this morning, sir."

"Well, the nurse will put you back on it. I'll tell her when I leave. That will ease your anxieties."

"Thank you, sir."

"As I think you have been informed, Mrs. Darlington, I am here to examine your mental condition." He opened the last button of his jacket and sat back in the chair, crossing one leg over the other.

"I was not so informed," said Alice.

"Well, I don't suppose it matters," he said with a reassuring smile. "I am told by your physician that there is nothing physically wrong with you, Mrs. Darlington, but because of the injury done to the baby, they would like an evaluation from me before releasing you from the hospital."

Alice was startled. "What injury done to the baby?" she said. "Where is he?"

"He's here in the hospital. He is in good hands, and they tell me he is recovering. Do you remember how his injuries where sustained?"

"No," she said.

"Apparently you fell on him. You have no memory of that?"

"No, sir."

"It seems you lost consciousness and fell while holding him."

"I only remember the telephone," she said. "I received a telephone call."

The memory of hearing Andrew's voice suddenly returned with the stark difference between the dreaming in her head and the reality of where she stood. She was not about to lose her children for not speaking up.

"I received a telephone call from my first husband," she said, "whom I believed dead. I had remarried during the years he was gone. My second husband had just told me—also over the telephone— that he intended to leave me. It was then that I received the call from my first husband, Mr. Croft, who is outside the door just now. That is the simplest way to explain the nervous agitation I was experiencing when I fainted."

Doctor Epstein rose and rebuttoned the last button on his jacket. "Well, I see no reason to probe any further into the situation." His face lost the interest it had shown upon entering the room and took on a twist of impatience to get on to more challenging work. "You are not in need of mental services, Mrs. Darlington," he said. "I have no reservations in authorizing the return of the child to your custody. Therefore, I will recommend that you be released whenever you desire to return home. However, you may wish to rest a day or two first. Good day, Mrs. Darlington."

After shaking hands with the doctor in the doorway, Andrew came in, reset his chair to its place of vigil, and sat down. He waited for her to speak, but she looked out the window for a few minutes.

"Are you staying in the rooming house where Mr. Thompson resides?" she asked.

"No. I'm in the hotel. The one we were in when we got married. The same room."

"Can you remain there?"

"If that's what you want."

"Thank you, Andrew," she said. "As you see, I am in a rather fragile state at the moment. There are many things I have to think about before I'm able to talk to you. I would like to be alone now. Will you come back tomorrow?"

"Yes, certainly."

Andrew got up and leaned over to kiss her. Alice had to turn her head away. She didn't want to refuse him, but how could she pretend nothing had happened since they had been together? It was plain that he wanted her. It seemed Procter didn't. What would she do if Procter changed his mind? He was always doing that. The path of least resistance was his mind's main thoroughfare.

He came with a family and a life that suited her and was good for the boys. She never had a married life with Andrew, just a week in a hotel. She would have to take Procter. No, on trust that Andrew was the same man she had loved, she would give up the Tudor house, the island in Canada, the ease of wealth, and start over at rock bottom with him. It was hopeless. She didn't know what she was trying to evaluate. Whatever began in her thoughts as a gain ended up feeling more like a loss.

Confusion was new to her. Decisions had always been reached before conflicting impulses could dissuade her from the first course of action that seemed reasonable. That was the way she had married Procter. That was the way she had tried to forget Andrew.

Advantage Andrew. Death had drawn the beginning and the end around him. The dead are unchanging, the living imperfect. He had come back, but was the Andrew now living the one she had kept alive in her heart? And what if he had returned only to say goodbye?

After Andrew left, Alice had the nurse bring her clothes. Dressed and feeling more herself, she asked the nurse to take her to see her baby. They took the stairs to an upper floor where the sickly babies were kept. Alice stood on the other side of a glass window, watching a nurse with Autie in her lap giving him a bottle. He had bandaging around his head and around his chest. One arm was braced straight out in a splint with bandaging around it. His sewn-up eye was still sewn shut, his open one was closed. He must be feeling safe. Even now, he must be forgetting what had happened. Can anyone remember being three months old?

Alice was admitted to the room and offered a chair beside the nurse feeding the baby. The minute she sat down, the good eye opened on little Autie, and the good arm went up in the air reaching toward her. How good it was that he knew her and wasn't afraid of her. She wanted to feed him herself, but the nurse said he was to be strictly on a bottle, at least until he was up to the weight he should be, but she allowed Alice to hold him. The nurse convinced her it was best for the baby, and the nurse from Alice's floor reinforced the point as it applied to Alice's need for complete rest. The pediatric nurse told her she would stop lactating in about two weeks and advised icepacks on her breasts if they hurt.

The young nurse was unmarried and had no children of her own, but she was a wealth of information. Alice felt it sobering, how much she had not known about being a mother, even after two babies. She had placed too much trust in her natural instincts. At least it was correctable with the little pamphlet the nurse gave her. How she went wrong with Procter would take more than a pamphlet.

That night, Alice needed the laudanum to get to sleep after it entered her mind that she had to talk to Procter. In the morning, her parents came to see her. Andrew had also just arrived. He deferred to the Sheffields and left, saying he would be back in a few hours. Mother said Rory was doing fine with his other grandmother. Father knew what was going on now. He said he had conferred with his lawyer. The first marriage did not necessarily take precedence over the second, he said. Either Procter Darlington or Andrew Croft could make a case, and it was largely up to her to choose between them. They presumed she would want Procter. Even on the laudanum, Alice could not tell her parents that Procter did not want her anymore.

In the afternoon, the Darlingtons came to visit. Andrew left the room again, but not before introducing himself as Mr. Croft. Evidently neither Darlington made the connection. Mrs. Darlington was so gruff and dear. Alice deeply wished that she were going to Canada with her this year, with her new Darlington baby and a clear title to her husband, Procter Darlington. But she would not be a Darlington for long, and the Darlington baby was under repairs. Procter must not have told them he did not want her. He always put off taking care of unpleasant duties.

Andrew came back to her bedside that evening. Alice could not help her reluctance to talk. She sent him away when her dinner came. The hospital was no longer a restful place. That night she needed the laudanum to sleep. Before leaving the hospital, she would get the prescription. The dosage suited her. It would be nice to have Miss Lantz with her and to have the baby back. Andrew could visit. They could go see Rory at the Darlington's, but she would leave him there for now, for the sake of the baby. And she would leave Andrew at the hotel for now, for the sake of her peace of mind.

Andrew got her out of the hospital the next morning and took her home in a carriage to the Tudor house. She let him look around, and then she sent him back to the hotel. Miss Lantz was glad to see her. There was a letter from New York waiting for her. It was from a legal firm. Procter had filed for an annulment of the marriage. It gave her thirty days to contest the action.

Alice sent Miss Lantz out to the apothecary for laudanum. Then she sat down and let herself cry. She called Lois on the telephone. Lois was forthright and honest. She said she had heard from Procter about her first husband coming back, but not about the baby in the hospital.

"I think you've had enough of Procter," Lois said. "I don't know why you still want him."

"I don't know either."

"It's not that he's a louse. He really isn't. And he isn't a cad either. Both of those are pretty easy to spot. So don't feel like you had the wool pulled over your eyes. He does it to everybody. He's charming, he really is. You just fell into the gravitational field of a giant gaseous planet with no center—are you still there, Alice?"

"Yes, I am, Lois. I'm sorry. I'm just thinking."

"Sometimes that's the problem. You can't let yourself think too much about a situation you had so little control over."

"No, I let too much go by without thinking."

"Tell you what, Alice. The baby's going to be in the hospital for a while, and the older one is with grande dame Darlington, isn't he? Why don't you come down to New York? You could use a change of scenery. And bring your man along. I'd like to meet him."

"I couldn't do that."

"Why not? It would be good for you."

"I don't feel natural with him. Nothing I say in front of him sounds like myself. It's so awkward."

"Then you need an intermediary, Alice. That's what I mean. He must feel the same way. I could mediate between you. The awkwardness is going to be there until you get back into practice with him. A disinterested third party can help you do that."

"I know he wouldn't like it."

"He'd do it for you, wouldn't he? I mean, sit down and talk to you with me there."

"Yes."

"And you'd do it for him, wouldn't you?"

Alice could not answer right away. It brought her back to doubting if she knew Andrew anymore. He might not be anything like her memory of him. She felt the ground going out from under her again.

"Alice. Can you hear me?"

"Yes, I'm sorry. I'm here."

"You have to forget about Procter. He threw you over. You can't think he's better than he is, and you have to allow yourself a low opinion of him. Now, you can go on alone with your two kids—which would be tough—or you go on with the first man in your life. You're lucky. You have a chance to start all over again. You loved him before, didn't you?"

"Of course I did," said Alice. After another long pause, she added, "I'm tired. I don't know if I want a man in my life at all."

"We can talk about that, too. So what do you think?"

"All right, Lois. I'll bring it up with Andrew."

After she hung up the telephone, Alice was surprised by how much better she felt. Talking to Lois was the right thing to do. Making herself get up and go to New York was the hard part, but lethargy was killing her, and if she could just do it, just get on the train and go talk to Lois, it would be good for her. She knew she could count on Andrew to do anything she asked of him, but she wondered how it was possible to feel so wretched and powerless when everything was in her hands.

Miss Lantz came back from the apothecary and brought her a tray with a glass and a new bottle of laudanum. She carefully poured out a little bit. Getting the right dosage would take some experimentation. It was two o'clock. If she was feeling all right, she would call Procter at six and try to catch him at the apartment before he went anywhere. She lay down on the couch and closed her eyes. The laudanum began to make her feel her life was not really so difficult and she didn't need laudanum anymore, which was just where she wanted the drug to get her.

At six, Procter picked up the telephone as if he had been expecting a call.

"It's me, Procter," she said.

"Alice. Glad to hear from you."

"I received the notice. The one from the lawyer."

"Oh good. I heard you took a fall, and I was thinking maybe it should have been sent to the hospital."

"No, I'm home now. So I'm calling to ask if that's what you really want."

"I think it's better than the other way, don't you?"

"What other way?"

"Oh, you know—divorce."

Alice did not know why she thought the other way would have been something else.

"Annulment means it never should have happened, doesn't it?" she said. "As if getting married was a mistake. Is that what you think?"

"Oh no, Alice. Furthest thing from my mind. I wouldn't have missed it for the world. It just ran its course, you know? When I found out from

Dad that your old beau showed up—well, I thought it was convenient for everybody, wouldn't you say?"

"No. Not for anyone. Maybe for you."

"Just give it a little time. You'll pick up where you left off with the fellow. Well, I have to get going. Dinner reservations."

"Procter," she said, wanting to stop him from hanging up, wishing almost desperately to keep him longer and listen to a voice that had no worry or concern. It was the old carefree Procter, the man she first knew. How did he do that? It only meant he had extricated himself.

"Can't talk now, Alice. Maybe we can have lunch sometime."

"Why? I know you don't want me anymore."

"It's not that."

"Then what is it?"

"I thought we went through this already," he said without any impatience.

Alice tried to keep her mind on what she meant to get to. She did not want to call him again. Did it matter why he didn't want her?

"Do you want your son?"

"He's pretty banged up, isn't he?"

"He'll be all right," she said.

"No, you can have him. What would I do with a little kid? You can have the house, too. Nothing has to get complicated."

"All right, Procter. Then I suppose this will be goodbye."

"Be seeing you," he said.

They hung up. Alice wondered where he got that expression. She had never heard him say it before. She took another dose of the laudanum. A little more this time because she needed to forget Procter Darlington as much as she needed to sleep. How could everything fall apart so fast? The last day they spent together, walking in the park, had been so happy, maybe the best day they'd ever had. She never would have thought it would be their last.

The evening passed without leaving any memory of it in Alice's mind. Miss Lantz told her the next morning at breakfast that she had had a light dinner and retired early.

Andrew came in a carriage at ten o'clock. Alice took her laudanum at nine to prepare herself to talk to him. They had to talk, Lois or no Lois. Andrew joined her over coffee in the little drawing room of the Tudor house. Miss

Lantz brought him a tray from the kitchen and set it down on the table beside the leather armchair. Alice thought Andrew might have an ally in Miss Lantz. She caught signals between them as she left the room. Andrew removed himself from the couch and took the leather chair opposite, better for talking, he said.

"Did you sleep well?" he asked.

"Yes."

"Do you feel better?"

"Somewhat."

Another new suit. A new one every day, each more stiff and unlike the man in it than the one the day before. Someone must have advised him on the fashion. He wouldn't have any idea. Alice wished she could tell him he was not expected to fill the place that had just been vacated by a man who dressed well. His hair was still brown but lighter on top from being in the sun. He must have had his thirtieth birthday in prison or hiding in a hole in the ground somewhere. Maybe it was the suit making him strange. In her memory he wore the coat and trousers he wore in China. She had to turn to the window when tears came to her eyes, remembering him on the river a long time ago.

"I thought you were hanged," she said when she was ready to talk.

Andrew had been looking down at his shoes, and at the first sound of her voice he looked up at her as if startled to find there was someone else in the room.

"Well, yes, I was," he said.

"How did you get out of it?"

"I was pardoned," he said. Then he added reflectively, "It would have been nice if the pardon had come before the hanging." He opened his collar and tilted his head to show a long red mark across the side of his neck.

"I don't understand you."

"You have to know how the British are with their paperwork. I owe my life to a fast runner and the crafty fellow who sent him. I'll tell you about Montagu Norman sometime."

Alice shook her head. It was too much. He had to understand that. The doctors wanted her to rest. She could not listen to long stories. It was unbearable trying.

"I'd like to go to the hospital now to see the baby," she said.

While Alice was in the nursery giving little Autie his milk bottle, Andrew spoke to a nurse. She went to fetch the charge nurse, who came out from behind the glass windows of an office with papers in a clip. Answering his inquiries, the nurse told him the baby had suffered a broken arm, a skull fracture, cracked ribs, a broken collarbone, and multiple contusions. If the child were not as young as he was, she said, the ribs would not have been so elastic, and he might have broken all of them, resulting in piercing of the internal organs. Then nothing could have been done.

"Are you master of the household, sir?" she asked.

"Not at present," he replied without hesitation.

"What is the precise meaning of that, sir? If you please."

"Briefly, nurse, it means I may be assuming responsibility of the household in the near future."

"Are you Mr. Darlington?"

"No ma'am. Mr. Croft."

"Are you the father of the child?"

"No ma'am. I presume Mr. Darlington to be the father of the child."

"Then what is your relationship to Mrs. Darlington, if I may?"

"I am her first husband. I am taking the place of her second husband."

"That is not the way it usually works," said the nurse.

When Andrew let his statement stand without correcting it to comply with conventions of sequence, the nurse drew a line through the name heading her paperwork and poised her hand to write.

"First name, Mr. Croft?"

"Andrew."

"I'll need your signature on this, sir," she said, handing her clip of papers to the new owner of the damaged baby.

Alice did not ask what he had learned of the child's condition. From what Andrew could see of the child on the other side of the glass, he thought the baby looked better than the list of injuries would suggest, so he withheld from Alice all he had heard from the nurse.

Andrew dropped Alice at the Tudor house for lunch and a rest, and said he would return in the evening to convey her to the Darlingtons' for dinner. As he went off in the carriage, he thought it was high time for time to start its healing of all wounds.

CHAPTER THIRTY-THREE

In front of the tall Darlington brownstone, Andrew sat with the Sheffields' coachman while Alice was at dinner. The man had been with the family many years, before Mr. Sheffield married into it. Andrew had come up to the carriage box to have a smoke and got him talking. The only thing Andrew knew directly of Mr. Sheffield was the anger he had displayed at their one dinner together, and the dismissive way he signed the check in his office before having him escorted out of the house. If Mrs. Sheffield was truthful when she said her husband had come from a lower station in life, he hid it well. The coachman confirmed, with a little coaxing, the lower station in life from which Mr. Sheffield was reputed to have had his beginnings.

"Mrs. Sheffield was maiden name of Wellsley at the time, you understand," he said, taking a light for his cigar from Andrew. "Thank you, sir. A 'singuished old family, you understand. So when Sheffield come along, it stirred up trouble because he was just a military man and no higher than that. But Miss Elizabeth had set her mind on him, and that was all there was to it. They was to run off west where he was going to fight Indians, but old Wellsley got wind of it and locked her up.

"I was footman at the time. I got it from the housemaid there was nothing old Wellsley could do with her on account of his wife passing, who was only one had say over the girl. Miss Elizabeth was headstrong on marryin' no one but Sheffield, notwithstanding he come from across the tracks, hero or no hero, Sheffield being fresh back from the war, you understand. He made good in the Union army and come back a captain, and they was going to make him a major to go west.

"Considering his place in the army, he did the honorable thing, you see, so he come to call on old Wellsley. They had it out at first—I could hear it downstairs and outside. It went on a while. Oh my, it went on. Sheffield come in his uniform with his sword and sidearm. I knew old Wellsley kept a brace of pistols, and it might have come to that. But then it got quiet in the house, and the maid got called in to bring Wellsley's whiskey, and after a while she got called back to fetch whiskey for Sheffield. They talked and come to an agreement like gentlemen.

"For his part, Sheffield got the girl all right. But he had to give up the army and make his living at Wellsley's bank, where he'd be kept an eye on. And from what I heard, he had to pledge never to leave Boston unless it be by himself alone. Well, you give and take in a bargain, don't you?" the coachman said, summing up. "I never was an adventuring man—but neither was I ever a rich man up in society and head of a bank, so I can't say who got the best of who."

"As you say, it's give and take," said Andrew.

"Well, I hear where you've got dealings of your own to do, sir. I wish you luck with Mr. Sheffield. Those that remember might tell you he came to be just like his father-in-law since he got along in years."

Andrew relieved the driver up top and sent him to the inside of the carriage to catch a little sleep on the upholstered seats. It was a fine autumn night with the barest sliver of a moon to think by. The Sheffields had a handsome carriage horse who looked like he could sleep standing up as well as the next. You didn't need patience if you could do that.

Now he knew more than he knew before. Alice had only spoken of her father as the gentle and indulgent man he had been to her. When they were on the river in China, she said her father never talked about his past. Maybe that was part of the deal he made with her grandfather.

If he had come to dinner at the Sheffields' that first time, knowing the way her father had won the hand of her mother, he could have come with a plan. He might never have left Boston. He might have been working at the bank and have four years experience by now. He never would have lost Alice. How foolish it was to take a chance like that, going to South Africa, but he didn't know what he wanted most out of life back then. He was too young, and the world seemed big enough to give whatever he could think to want of it. Alice had come into his life fast and maybe a few years too soon. He wasn't thinking right as a young man, no better than any other young man, he supposed. But even in prison, with nothing to do but take stock and figure out where he went wrong, he wasn't thinking right. Even up to an hour ago.

He had expected to find Alice living with her parents, waiting for him. How much of what he had learned about people had he put out of his head to make that mistake? Captivity had removed him almost four years from his last free decision and narrowed the dimensions of his life down to a few square feet. In the same time, the dimensions of Alice's life had expanded to include another man, two children, and two families. That was a whole life to which he was irrelevant and extraneous. But Procter Darlington had not shown his face. He was either overconfident or careless. If they had separated, who was the one who walked out?

All Andrew knew for sure was that he had come back at the right time. That was fortuitous. A month earlier, he might have been politely received, invited to view the fortifications of established relationships, and sent on his way. Now everybody—the Sheffields, the Darlingtons, Alice, and the two boys—was off balance. It looked like he was the only one on his feet.

CHAPTER THIRTY-FOUR

Inside the Darlington brownstone, Rory was up immediately from his seat to welcome his mother as she was shown to the drawing room. Mrs. Darlington also rose and came to embrace her, saying sharply to Rory, "Feet on the floor, young man."

Alice released the boy quickly, as if the command had been issued to her, and she moved to embrace her mother-in-law warmly.

"He's much too big to be picked up," said Mrs. Darlington firmly. "Mr. Darlington has a business affair this evening, so it will be only the two of us and the young gentleman dining."

They sat down in the drawing room first and had sherry. Rory sat at a little table that had been set up for him, where he sipped juice out of a cup and very carefully picked up little finger toasts and put them into his mouth one by one.

"Chew with your mouth closed, young man," said Mrs. Darlington.

"Yes, Grandmother."

Rory was dressed in a perfect little suit of matching jacket and trousers and wore a collared shirt with a precisely knotted tie.

"We're doing quite well, as you can see," said Mrs. Darlington. "I took charge of him myself. He has learned a great deal. Haven't you, young man?"

"Yes, Grandmother."

"Oh my," said Alice.

"I think we have made great progress." At this, Mrs. Darlington looked over at Rory again with expectation in her sharp eyes.

"Yes, Grandmother," he said.

"I believe—well, it has been my experience—that children with older brothers and sisters develop language skills faster than those who don't, so we've had to work very hard on that. I have devoted extra attention to vocabulary, constructing sentences, and better enunciation. Singing has been a helpful aid to his concentration in these areas. Rory, won't you please sing our song about springtime for your mother."

"Yes, Grandmother," he said, climbing off his chair and standing before his mother with his hands at his sides.

Mrs. Darlington began to hum a tune and cued Rory with a point of her finger. All by himself he sang a little song:

"There's music in the branches high,
the thrasher sings in woods nearby,
the apple trees are blossoming,
all the elms are dressed in green.

There's color on the ground below,
the buttercups in pastures grow."

There he stopped and looked at his grandmother for direction.

"That is as far as we've gotten," said Mrs. Darlington. "You may take your seat, young man."

In her great surprise over her son's mannerly deportment as well as the impromptu performance, Alice applauded as heartily as the frailty of her condition allowed. He had faltered on a few of the words but slurred through them intelligibly enough.

"We will improve, won't we?" said Mrs. Darlington.

"Yes, Grandmother."

"And how will we do that?"

"By practicing every day, Grandmother."

"Precisely," said Mrs. Darlington, showing great satisfaction with her protégé.

In the dining room, the footman asked Master Rory if he cared for a little of this and a little of that. When Rory said, "Yes, please," he forked or spooned the request onto the little boy's plate. Once his adult dinner plate had a full complement of servings, Rory passed it in both hands to Mrs. Darlington. His attention was quite fixed upon her.

"Grandmother cuts his meat for him," said Mrs. Darlington. "But he is perfectly capable of doing the rest with his fork and spoon. Now, Alice," she added briskly, "as I am sure there are several practical topics on both our minds that would be unwise to discuss in the presence of *le petit garçon*, I suggest we speak for now of this beautiful weather we are having. Hasn't it been lovely?"

"Yes, Mother, quite lovely."

"It must be refreshing to be up and about again, dear. Are you feeling better now?"

"Yes, Mother, much better."

"And are you taking fresh air?"

"When I am able, yes. I tire quickly though."

"You must carry chocolates with you, my dear. I'll give you some of mine. They are very good with brandy, you know."

After a dessert of cherry tarts with ice cream, Mrs. Darlington asked Rory if he would like to be excused.

"Yes, Grandmother," he said.

"And how do we do that?"

Very slowly, carefully enunciating each word, he said, "May I please be excused?"

"You may, Rory. You may go to the playroom and play with your toys, or ask Nurse to read a story to you. And how do we do that?"

"Kindly read me a story, Nurse."

"Very good, young man. You may go. Walk please. No running indoors."

Alice watched the little boy climb down from his adult chair and leave the dining room.

"Mother, I am very much indebted to you."

"He's been quite manageable, Alice. On the first day, I confess I was obliged to smack him. Regrettably, it is the only way we can be induced to learn in certain phases of the early years."

"I fear that may be so," said Alice. The laudanum was wearing off, and it was leaving her fatigued and drowsy. The coffee cup seemed almost too heavy to lift.

"Mr. Darlington and I will be taking the boy with us next week to Canada. It will do him good to be with other children and learn his way about. I'm sure he'll manage with the little cousins his age and take instruction from the older ones; there's a great deal of roughhousing that goes on, you know, but he needs that. He has to learn to swim and play on the rocks. That should give you most of September to rest and do what you can with the new baby, my dear. I know you'll put the time to good use."

"I'm very grateful for your help, Mother. I'm sorry this has interrupted your summer."

"You needn't worry about that, dear. I've no doubt the young people have not missed our company one bit. And Mr. Darlington is not so keen on life in the wilds as he once was, so immediately after camp we will be taking the train directly from Toronto to Florida. So many of the family visit during the winter that it's as good as camp, only dressier, naturally. Rory will be coming along, of course. Are you quite all right, dear?"

"Yes, Mother. I'm just a little weak."

Mrs. Darlington left her chair and settled beside Alice on the settee, almost enveloping her with an arm around her shoulders with all the lace and fabric of her voluminous dress following in support. She patted Alice's hand in her lap. "Oh, don't worry, my dear. We always come up around Christmas or January. Mr. Darlington has his business affairs to look after. And you know Rory will be in good hands. It's time he had a governess and a tutor. I'll look into it right away when we get to the house. Then, when you're quite settled in your little Tudor house again and little Armstrong is doing well, you can have him back. Now doesn't that sound like the right thing?"

"Of course, Mother," Alice managed to say. She had seen photographs of the Darlington house in Naples, a magnificent white stucco of Mediterranean design, roofed in terra-cotta, with columns and balconies and surrounded by fountains, well-kept lawns, and palm trees. Of course it was the right thing. How could she fight it?

Mrs. Darlington brought Alice around with a hand to her cheek and a gentle voice so different from her usual brusque way of speaking even the kindest sentiments. "I'm so sorry about Procter," she said. "I spoke with him over the telephone. We had words. He is not up to responsibilities, you know. It quite baffles me. He was brought up better than that, and I am very much ashamed of his behavior."

Tears came to Alice, and she drew a handkerchief from her sleeve.

"I know you are taking it hard, my dear," said Mrs. Darlington.

"How could I not, Mother? I don't understand how he could leave me."

"It is entirely independent of you, Alice. You must understand that. Procter—Well!—I don't know what it is myself. He is good-looking and speaks well. Perhaps that is all he amounts to. I hope not. I'm sure I do not know the reason Mr. Morgan has retained him this long. Maybe they smack him at the office. I don't know."

When the gaslight was turned up over the front entrance and the door opened, Andrew alerted the coachman and jumped down from the box. Mrs. Darlington stood by Alice at the door and waited until Andrew and the coachman came up the steps to escort her. Mrs. Darlington embraced Alice and told her she would write from the island and include greetings from Rory. Alice was feeling very weak on the steps and had to be supported all the way down to the pavement, where Andrew lifted her into the carriage.

Alice just wanted to get home and take her laudanum. Andrew said something to her. It seemed to come from far away.

"I can't talk tonight," she said to him. "I'm very tired."

She was aware of his arm around her. She closed her eyes and listened to the wheels of the carriage and the clatter of horseshoes on the cobblestones. The next thing she knew, a light went on, and she found herself on the couch in the drawing room of the Tudor house. Andrew and Miss Lantz were talking softly in the hallway. Andrew came around the couch. He kissed her forehead. Then he was gone.

Alice woke up. A blanket had been put over her. She called for Miss Lantz.

"Nurse," she said, "I'll see myself to bed in a little while. I have some notes to write first, so you may retire for the night. I'll need my medicine before you go, if you would be so kind."

"Certainly, madam."

Alice felt her strength returning with the thought of relief on the way. She had distracted herself for six hours. At last, Miss Lantz appeared with the laudanum bottle and a small glass on a little tray.

"Thank you, Nurse. Good night."

"Good night, madam."

Alice decided not to take the laudanum until she had finished her writing. If she could do that, it would make eight hours since her last dose. Maybe she could do better, but it would only set the next goal at too long to repeat tomorrow. There were a few sheets of nice paper and a pen at the writing desk. She had to look through the drawers for an ink bottle, but the search only took a few minutes and only too soon was she putting down "My dear Procter" in her best hand. It was a very complicated letter to write, and she stopped after writing down the salutation.

Alice waited for the words to come. It did not matter if they never did, as far as Procter was concerned. He was not waiting for them. She got up and went to the couch and poured her dosage. Six and a half hours was good enough. She would do better tomorrow. It went so easily down her throat. She licked the inside of the glass. There was only one more dose left in the bottle, and she decided to make sure she had enough to get her through the letter and to sleep after that. She turned the bottle upside down on her tongue when it was empty, tapping the bottom as long as she could feel drops coming off the inside. Then she lay down to think and covered her eyes from the lights in the room. She tried to keep her mind on the letter, but she needed to rest before she got going on it. Then she forgot to whom she intended to write. Andrew or Procter? Oh well. She would get to it later. Then she was dreaming again, gliding weightlessly down a pleasant corridor to a library. Dreams were on the shelves, and she could choose any one she wanted. She chose to dream about the island in Canada. She could go there and watch herself last summer when she was a Darlington. It was so beautiful, and everyone was so nice.

Alice opened her eyes because she was lying in a cold, wet place that was not the warm rocks of Canada. It was the couch, and it was wet under her, so she closed her eyes again to get away. Then she was lifted into the air. Then she was in her room. Miss Lantz was busy all around her.

Morning came. Alice sat up in bed. Andrew woke up in a chair beside the bed on hearing her.

"How long have I been asleep?" she asked.

"About a day and a half."

"Have you been here all along?"

"Miss Lantz called to have me come over and help get you to bed. The doctor was coming, so I stayed."

"Why did the doctor come?"

"Miss Lantz thought you might have taken too much medicine."

"What did he say?"

"He just looked at the medicine bottle and said you would sleep it off. He suggested we talk about it when you're feeling better—"

"I need it right now," Alice interjected. "For my nerves."

"I understand that."

"Then we don't have to say anything more about it."

"All right," he said, rising from the chair. "I'll leave you alone. You'll want to go to the hospital later, won't you?"

"Yes, it would be nice if you could take me."

Alice was glad he did not come to kiss her but left quietly. She did not know why they weren't getting anywhere, but they weren't, and if there was any hope for it, it seemed fast dying.

CHAPTER THIRTY-FIVE

Andrew came every morning for coffee that week and returned later in the day to take her to the hospital to see the baby. Autie was getting better, and Alice was aware that even while she held her baby, her thoughts were shifting from him to the untenable situation with Andrew. She could not go on living with this strain between them, but there was nothing about him recent enough in her memory to connect to the man who sat for hours with her, read to her, and kept watching her for signs. He seemed such a stranger that she wondered how they ever could have known each other on intimate terms. And it seemed impossible now to expect that simply putting two people side by side would suddenly join them together like two balls of mercury rolling on a plate.

Alice stuck to a regular dosage after the bad night. It let just enough reality through the cracks to keep her from thinking that Procter had changed his mind and Andrew was keeping him away. She still tended to come to her senses and lose them again as indistinctly as night and day share a permeable divide. Sometimes a life alone seemed the right thing for her, to give her children away and let the rest of her life play out where she could do no harm, spinning in a little circle like a top, living on the spin of the last twist of the fingers until she stopped and fell over.

But she knew in her heart of hearts that she was not meant for that. Everything she had done since Andrew was within her rights, understandable, excusable, forgivable, or at least acceptable by precedent of human history. It was perfectly natural to reach for another man when the last one let go of her. But why Procter Darlington? Had she ever loved him, or had she only taken his arm to dance? It made discordant music go around in her head to think of him when she only wanted to feel the ground under her feet.

What was she looking for in Procter when she married him? Andrew had been dead a year. She was coming out of her grief and nearly at full strength when she met Procter. She was raising Rory. She was active in charities in the city and known for getting things done. She did not have friends, only acquaintances and colleagues in good works, and she remembered once saying to her distraught mother, "Once you have a social life, you spend money and don't get any work done." Andrew would have understood that better than Mother. Occasionally she did miss social calls and having someone to talk to, but keeping busy and accomplishments came first. Vulnerability could not have had a better disguise.

Then Procter burst upon the scene, and how easily she had slipped into a life she would have envisioned for her and Andrew. Mistaking Procter for Andrew was her mistake. Procter was a hollow man, vain and self-absorbed. What did that say of her desperation to hold onto him? It was hard to face up to what Procter was. It was hard to explain what she had become. Maybe it was just the way married people begin to look like each other.

One night, a month after her hospitalization, Alice sat in bed about to take her medicine. She poured the right amount into the glass and waited. There was a sound she was listening for. A night bird. The bedroom windows were open. The bird had been calling every night. She understood suddenly that he was not singing to himself just to make the night pretty, and she was afraid he would go away. Alice carefully poured the laudanum back into the bottle. She went to the window and dropped the bottle to the grass below.

She did not want to dream anymore. She wanted to be herself again. In the next hours, she lay wide awake, more awake than she had ever needed to be in the daylight. The beating of her heart was sluggish. Every muscle in her body ached as if she had been cutting wood all day. She had to remember to breathe. Then her heart raced and sweat poured out of her body everywhere, drenching the sheets. Nowhere could she put down a thought without it flying away like a scrap of paper. It was a supreme task of her willpower to resist running downstairs to the grass below the window. She had not heard the glass bottle break. Time went so slowly. She looked at the clock on the bedside table. The hands did not seem to be moving in the right direction.

By five o'clock that morning, Alice began to feel her courage rising. In the last hour, groping her way through the caverns of a vacant mind, the part of her that had languished in the dark stood up and struck a match, and in that burst of light, she could see the stones she had stumbled over, the wrong turns she had followed, the blind alley she had named after herself. Hardest to bear was the painting her imagination had done to cover the walls. The self she had lost held the light above her head like the lady in New York harbor with the torch, and in its far-reaching beams, Alice could see the way out.

It was a struggle, but Alice pulled herself out of bed and washed her face with cold water in the bathroom. She put her hair up and dressed in a light summer dress. Leaving a note for Miss Lantz, she went down the stairs and stepped out into the street. It was fully light by then, but the sun had not yet shown itself. After walking a few blocks into town, a hackney came to her signal, and a few minutes later she was standing outside the hotel where she and Andrew had first lived together. The clerk told her Mr. Croft's room was number 432. Fourth floor.

"But you can't go up there," he said.

"Why not? If you please."

"House rules."

"Do you think I am a prostitute, sir?" she said indignantly.

"No, ma'am."

"Then why am I not allowed to his room?"

When the clerk offered no reply, Alice defiantly showed him Procter's gold wedding band on her left hand and said, "I happen to be Mrs. Croft."

It might not have taken the display of the ring, for Alice had just come from her victory over dreaming and insensibility, and her face showed no reluctance to engage another opponent. The clerk struck his colors without a fight.

"The stairs are on the other side of the lobby, Mrs. Croft. That way."

"Thank you. Good day, sir."

Alice knocked softy at the door, and she heard sounds of getting out of bed and fumbling with clothes. Presently, Andrew came to the door.

"Alice," he said.

"May I lie down with you, Andrew?"

Consenting with a nod of his head to the interior of the room, he let her in and closed the door behind. He shed his robe and trousers on the way to the bed and threw them on a chair. Her dress, shoes, and underthings were as quickly put by, and they lay down together with only the light sheet over them. She lay with her head on his chest and put one arm and one leg over him as she had when they were married.

"I don't want to do anything, Andrew," she said. "I don't want to talk. I just want to have physical contact with you."

She was ready to put a hand to his lips, but he did not try to say anything.

Procter and the other men she had been with at the salon parties had the feel of bread dough, soft and perfumed bread dough. Andrew smelled like sweat and earth. She felt for the scars she remembered and found them. As one body warms another, she recognized the man she had first married on the evidence of her senses. She lay on him for a long time before speaking again, fearful that even one wrong word might throw them into misunderstandings.

"Thank you for coming back to me," she said against his ear.

"Thank you for coming back to me," he whispered back to hers.

They went out for breakfast. Alice wanted to put her arm through his and walk for a great distance, to feel the matching of their stride. So they set out across the park in front of the hotel and went by several restaurants and cafés they had frequented in the past. She began to tire after only a block, but she wanted to complete her reacquaintance with Andrew by getting used to him in those dreadful new suits. At the corner, Andrew pointed to a sign hanging out a few yards down.

"Let's go there," he said.

At the door, Alice said it looked a little rough for her taste, but Andrew assured her she would like it.

"We've been here before," he said. "You liked it then. Remember, we were trying to save money, and you liked it because they put a lot on your plate."

"No, that was somewhere else."

"You'll see," he said.

The best tables by the windows were taken, but Andrew seemed happy to see one available in the back corner and hurried over to take it. Alice stood doubtfully in the doorway. She waved him back, and he came, but only to take her hand, put an arm around her, and lead her back to the corner. It was one of those thick wooden tables that had been heavily carved with initials and stained by innumerable sloshing pitchers and mugs.

"You thought they had the best fried clams," said Andrew.

"I don't remember that at all, Andrew."

"Well, we'll come back for dinner sometime. Let's see how they do with breakfast."

They ordered platters of eggs, sausage, and bacon, and Alice found their hot cranberry muffins especially good with lots of butter. It felt like their first breakfast together when they got married, and they talked very little while they ate. Alice remembered how confident she was then about the new life they were starting.

The plates were cleared, and they sat over their coffee.

"I didn't feel right with you until now, Andrew. I know you didn't feel right with me either, did you?"

"I thought it would only take a day or two to get used to each other."

"I'm sorry it was so complicated. I still have to think, Andrew. You had more time to think about getting together again than I did. I thought you were dead."

"No, you're right. I never thought you were dead."

"I wanted to kill myself, Andrew. That's how bad I felt when I heard you were dead."

"I'm sorry," he said. "I thought I had gotten word to you. I wrote letters, but they must have been held."

"It would have ended up like Romeo and Juliet when you came back. If you came home and found I had killed myself over you."

"Yes," he said. "That would have been bad luck."

Alice looked down at her plate and felt tears rising. She didn't feel like laughing anything off. Maybe it was too soon for her to be all right. It was senseless to be talking like this, but she wanted him to understand how hard living without him was, not just the rationale of her marriage to Procter.

"I'm sorry," he said. "I shouldn't have made light of it."

"I had to live for Rory, Andrew. That was the only reason I had for living. It's the only reason I got married again. I hope you can understand that."

"You didn't do anything wrong."

"But do you think you can live with it?"

"I was alive and you didn't know it. If I keep that in mind, I don't think anything will bother me."

"Thank you, Andrew.

"Well, so long as everyone's alive, can we start by saying no harm done?"

Andrew smiled in a gentle, tentative way that only invited her to put the past in storage and look forward with him.

"Understatement of the year," she said, smiling again after so long.

"All right then. When am I going to meet him?" Andrew asked. "I mean Rory."

"He's gone to Canada with the Darlingtons. It's lovely up there, Andrew. I want a place like that for us. Well, maybe someday. They'll be back in September." She didn't know how to tell him it might be a few more months before he would get to meet his son or that she was too fragile right now to stand up to Mrs. Darlington. He had already seen too much of her weakness. "I know you'll like Rory. He was a little terror for a while, but Mrs. Darlington has done wonders. You would have been able to handle him, but I couldn't, even with Miss Lantz. And we were on our own most of the time. I'll tell you everything sometime, but not now. And I want you to tell me what you've been through."

"There's one thing I do want to ask you."

"Not now. Please, Andrew."

"Just one thing. It doesn't need a long answer. Just a yes or no."

"I don't know if I can. What is it?"

"Darlington isn't going to show up, is he?"

"No, not now."

"Oh," said Andrew. "Do you want him back?"

"How could I?" she said.

Andrew seemed to accept that without asking anything else, and for a few moments, he moved his coffee cup around on the table as if he were looking for something.

"Then we're together?" he asked, looking up with a smile.

"Yes. Together. I want to get married to you again—at the city hall, the way we did before, and start over. Don't you think that's how we should do it?"

"I think it would be fine that way."

"But not right now. I gave up taking the medicine they gave me. Just last night. So I don't feel very well. But I had to stop taking it sometime. That's when I had the idea to come over here."

Andrew did not laugh, but she knew he found that amusing.

"One bad habit for another," he said.

"I like this one better," Alice said, reaching across the table to touch his hand.

They drank their coffee, and Alice took a few puffs off his cigarette. No one would notice a woman smoking in a place like this, she thought. It was dark, but there was a comfortable feel to it.

"I still don't think we've been here before," she said.

"Look down."

"Where?"

"On the table. Move your cup over."

Alice moved her coffee cup and looked around the table. "Oh dear," she said.

The names Alice and Andrew had been carved inside of something that looked roughly heart-shaped.

"I lost the knife in South Africa."

"Well, we'll get you a new one, and you can carve our hearts out all over Boston."

Andrew packed his belongings back at the hotel. He checked out, called for a carriage, and that afternoon he put down a portmanteau and a valise in the master bedroom of the Tudor house.

CHAPTER THIRTY-SIX

Little Autie was in the hospital for over a month. The eyelid surgeon came to reopen his eye six weeks after the repair he had done, and Alice was holding him when he woke up from the anesthesia. There suddenly seemed to be twice the trepidation and wonderment in his two eyes than he had had with one. What a poor little thing he was, even without the bandages around his chest and the splint on his broken arm. The discoloration of bruises had not yet faded from his face, and he looked worse than he had in the white gauze wrap. But Andrew seemed to take to him right away, perhaps seeing in him something of his own uncertain beginnings.

Autie was kept on the bottle, and when he came home from the hospital, Miss Lantz successfully introduced him to mashed potatoes. Very soon afterward, he was mostly finished with the bottle and willing to eat anything brought to his mouth by a spoon. It was such a relief to Alice that her second child seemed to have the makings of a regular baby, and it made her desirous of trusting to luck with another. She wanted a girl this time and began to yearn deeply for a daughter to bring up.

Before that, Alice wanted to be married again, and Andrew had to settle himself into an occupation. She knew that was very much on his mind from their first days together in the Tudor house. He spent long hours reading the Boston newspapers and the *New York Herald*, and more hours writing letters. There was no question in her mind that he had given up any ideas of going off on his old way of making a living, even when he walked into town to talk to Mr. Thompson every week.

When Andrew saw the monthly checks that arrived from the Darlingtons and Sheffields, Alice explained they were a parental endowment that had supported her marriage to Procter. Seeing no need to explain an idea that would not seem unreasonable to her, Andrew calmly said, "Well, we can't go on with that. When the Darlingtons come back from their travels, you'll return their check. I'll take the other one back. I have business with your father."

"I don't mind doing that, Andrew. Not at all. I anticipated how you would feel about taking money. But what kind of business do you have with my father?" she asked.

"I'm going to offer him my services."

"I don't know what you mean."

"Ask him for a job in the bank."

They were having coffee after breakfast, sitting at their little table in the kitchen before the bow window. Alice looked out at the trees. The leaves were turning. How sure of themselves the leaves of the big elm were until the planet tilted. What a surprise it must be to turn brown and die. And then the other surprise of getting green and growing again.

"Is that what you want to do?"

"I've been thinking about it since I got back," he said. "I think your father might see it as an opportunity to accept me without losing face. Before we get married again, I want to see if he can bring himself to hire me. It's what I should have done the first time."

"You wouldn't have been happy in the bank back then," said Alice.

"Everything's different now."

"I still want to see you happy, Andrew."

"I'll be happy. Don't worry about that." It was not a statement to be made in a brooding manner, so he smiled. "I told you about Montagu—Mr. Norman—who had a hand in extricating me from the trouble I got into in South Africa. In the course of, well, negotiating with him, I learned there's plenty of adventure in the banking world. We're in something of a partnership."

"Oh, Andrew," Alice said. "I don't want you taking any more risks or going anywhere."

"It's not like that, Alice. I'm a silent partner. It's a business that runs without me." She had to know a little bit, and he thought he could frame it out in a fairly simple way by saying it honestly.

"In South Africa, I made off with some of the gold I was watching."

"I don't think I want to hear this, Andrew."

"No, I shouldn't have phrased it like that. I diverted it to the men I worked with."

"It's still stealing, isn't it?"

"Well, see if you think so. Those men didn't have anything, and I started wondering what's the difference between the Dutch and English? They were fighting over who had the right to take whatever they could steal from the Africans, and they had been doing it for years. I worked out a plan to give a little back to everybody in the labor camps. Then I started thinking, well, Alice and I have to live too, and I had already gotten a lot of shipments through hostile territory, more than they would have had without me. So I took a 2 percent handling fee."

"Andrew, please. I don't want to hear any more."

"Almost done. Do you want to have a cigarette?"

"Will I need one?"

"No, really. I'm almost done. Remember, it had a happy ending."

"Well, you go ahead. I might take a few puffs. Just don't make it a long story. You can tell me everything when I'm better."

"All right," he said, lighting a cigarette. "But you'll have to know this part of it. Montagu, well, he's connected with the Bank of England. He was doing calculations of his own back in England on how much gold the treasury should have gotten out of there. He found out about me and thought I might have something to do with the shortfall he turned up. So he came down to talk to me in prison, and we made a deal. I knew where the gold was, and he knew how to get it into circulation. Neither of us could make use of it without the other one."

"Oh, Andrew. It doesn't make me happy to hear this."

"But I'm not directly involved now. I sent Shahid—Mr. Thompson—down to South Africa the other day to manage a transfer. I just want you to know what we have to work with."

"Would you mind if I turned a blind eye to it? I think I'll have to."

"I might have to go to London once in a while, and I'd want you to come with me. Or Mr. Norman might come here. I think your father would be interested in meeting him. In the meantime, I want to be working, and banking is what I need to know."

"As long as you know what you're doing, Andrew," said Alice doubtfully. She put her hand on his arm. "I want to leave the business affairs to you. But it would make me very happy if Father came to city hall with us. I know he thinks I only make decisions and take actions that displease him. If you can make up with him, maybe he'll understand why I love you and why I ran away from home to be with you the first time. He has to see it's something that will last, doesn't he?"

CHAPTER THIRTY-SEVEN

Alice Croft and Andrew Croft swore their vows to each other a week later before a judge in the Boston City Hall on the morning of December 15, 1894. In attendance were Mr. and Mrs. Sheffield, with Miss Louise Lantz as maid of honor. The little girl, Dora, from their first wedding, had died of diphtheria the year before, and the tears in Alice's eyes were partially for her. She turned to face Andrew. He put a ring on her finger, and she put a ring on his, and they took each other again for better or for worse.

There was to be no wedding trip for a reason they frankly admitted to each other and to anyone who asked. Neither felt inclined to disturb the peace of where they were by straying too far from it. The weekend was good enough, and on Monday Andrew was to take his new position at the Sheffield Bank of Massachusetts. The reception was held at the Sheffields', with the only addition to the party appearing in the person of Master

Armstrong, bundled in the arms of Miss Lantz, who bore him about the main drawing room as she would a tray of hors d'oeuvres.

Mrs. Sheffield whispered to her daughter. "Can you afford her, darling?"

"Oh yes, Mother," said Alice. "It would be a false economy to do without her. She is going to teach me cooking and will be of use in many other ways in teaching me how to keep house."

"Oh dear. I would certainly be of no help to you with that," said Mrs. Sheffield.

"The servants had to go, Mother."

"Oh, Alice, won't you let us give you a staff?"

"We don't need one. We'll do quite well, I'm sure. Andrew will be happy to come home to dinners prepared by his wife. While he is away at work, I will do housekeeping and laundry and learn cooking from Miss Lantz. We'll live as ordinary people do, and when Rory comes home with the Darlingtons, Andrew will see that his son behaves himself. Isn't little Autie adorable, Mother?"

"I must change him, madam," said Miss Lantz, stopping on her way to the stairs. "Then we should be going if you would like to maintain his napping schedule."

"Very well, Nurse," said Alice.

The men were outside smoking cigars on the wide veranda, but the glass doors were open. Alice looked over her shoulder and whispered to her mother what her plans were for the evening.

"Alice, I think you say those things just to upset me."

"No, Mother, I want to be close to you. You've been such a dear big sister to me. Really Mother, I should rightly call you Elizabeth. Nurse was the one who raised me."

"That's just how it was done in those days," said Mrs. Sheffield.

"Well, I wanted you to know that I'll probably be conceiving a child tonight. I'm very excited. I want a girl this time, and I'm going to name her Elizabeth after you. I know, Andrew's been living in the house, and we've been sleeping in the same bed, but we haven't done anything. We wanted to wait until we were married again. Keep your fingers crossed for me tonight, Mother. I'm so glad Father came to the wedding. I think they'll get along famously, don't you?"

"We'll have to see, Alice," said her mother. "I would not get your hopes too high. Your father does not have the best opinion of your young man.

He's certainly more presentable now, but your father liked the other one better, frankly."

The men came in from smoking on the terrace. Andrew and Mr. Sheffield entered the room mutually expressionless, and each looked more than ready to mix the company of the other with the women at hand. Miss Lantz came downstairs with little Autie bundled up for the carriage. Hands were shaken all around, and the Croft family departed.

Back in the cozy warmth of the Tudor house, Alice and Miss Lantz put together a light dinner for the three of them while Andrew read the newspaper. Not a sound came from the nursery until they had finished their coffee. Then Miss Lantz urged them to take some air before bed and went to bring little Autie in the dining room for his rice and broth.

Alice was glad for the suggestion. The chilly air relieved the dulling effects of the champagne she had after the wedding. She wanted to briskly walk it off and be rid of all encumbrances for the night ahead. They sat down on a park bench, and Alice pointed to a life-size bronze statue of a goat nearby.

"I used to sit on the goat," she said. "All the children did. If we come in the daytime, you'll see how the bronze on the back has been worn down from generations of children. Rory sat on the goat too. I don't suppose you ever did."

"I never got to this side of town."

"No, of course not," she said, with a mix of small and large sympathies in her voice. "You know, Andrew, I devoted much of my time to charity work around the city while you were away. I worked with groups concerned with orphans and child labor—that was because of you, of course. I had to leave when I had so much trouble with Rory, but I'd like to get back to it. I think the effort made a difference in the lives of the people we helped."

"I'd be happy to see you do anything you like."

"Do you really mean that?"

"Of course I mean it."

"Then I can be free to do what I want?"

"You're always free to do what you want."

"But I want to have children too, Andrew."

"Well then, have children."

"We might have to move to a bigger house. But I like the Tudor. Now that you're there, it's a very sweet house."

They moved closer together on the bench. It was getting dark, and the lamplighters were abroad in the park with their long poles and kerosene rags. One by one the lamps lit up like fireflies, and the light spread under the trees and across the dead grass.

"I was thinking," said Andrew. "Do you want to stay in Boston?"

"I hadn't thought about it," she said.

"Well, I was thinking I would like to have a farm. Someday, I mean. I'm committed to your father now, but after a respectable amount of time, when we're on a sound footing, I thought we might like to move out to the country."

"I'd like that, Andrew."

"I know you went to that place in England for farming."

"Agricultural science," Alice corrected. "Briarwick College. You should have seen me in my beekeeping suit. Oh, Andrew, I think it's a wonderful idea. I remember quite a lot of animal husbandry as well, and I still have all my notes. The college maintained a working farm, and they had us girls do positively everything. It was a wonderful experience. I don't know why I never thought of you as a farmer—well, now it would be a gentleman farmer. I just thought of guns when I thought of you. Come to think of it, I haven't seen any."

"I put them away."

"But you still have them?"

"You don't just throw away firearms."

"I still have the Nagant you gave me in the boat," she said with nostalgic affection. "The holster you made fell apart, but I kept the pieces. But I don't want to talk about guns. I want to go to bed with you. And tomorrow we'll have to look over your clothes for work on Monday."

Alice felt a little self-conscious when they were undressing. It was the first night since Andrew had moved into the house that she had let him see her without her nightgown. "I think you'll notice I'm not twenty and virginal anymore, Andrew. I've had two babies. My body is different. It's not what you had before. I hope you don't miss it."

"How could I want any more than what I have now?"

"That's a sweet thought, Andrew," she said.

He was in bed under the covers. She hurried from the chill of the room to warm herself against him. She lay her head on his chest to calm herself for a moment and then encouraged him. There were no fireworks, but she felt deeply contented afterward. Conceiving a daughter would make it a memorable night, Alice thought as she fell asleep in Andrew's arms, but contentment was just fine. Contentment was worth all the excitement in the world. Excitement had no staying power.

CHAPTER THIRTY-EIGHT

Andrew walked to work on Monday morning, dressed in a plain brown suit, carrying his lunch in a paper sack. He tried not to imagine his old self looking down at his new self. It had finally come to this great banality of life—going to work. At the bank he reported, as Mr. Sheffield had directed him, to the office of Mr. Blakely, who referred him back down the stairs to the main floor where he was to introduce himself to Mr. Penne. A stool was procured for him upon reaching that milestone, and he spent the day sitting on it, watching a young man by the name of Mr. Metter conduct business at his little window.

Every action Mr. Metter executed was accompanied by an explanation given over his shoulder, which carefully omitted the names of customers and sums deposited or withdrawn. When he had time to come away from his window, Mr. Metter showed Andrew how to enter figures in the daily ledger books and how to use the addition and subtraction machine.

At twelve o'clock, Mr. Metter closed his window and went for lunch at a restaurant. Andrew went across the street to a little park with his paper sack and sat alone. Alice had made him a bacon and cheese sandwich. The roll was rather hard and yeasty, but it was her first try at baking. There was an apple and a baked potato and two little chocolates for dessert. He was as happy with his lunch as he was with Alice.

At three o'clock, the doors of the bank closed. On the first floor, the tellers counted their drawers and reconciled the day's business in their account books. Up on the second floor, junior and senior officials came out of their offices. They stood like naval officers on the bridge of a ship at the railing that went around the immense building, looking down at the tellers below. They were seen to chat with one another, sometimes lifting a hand to colleagues on the other side of the cathedral-like space created by the high, domed ceiling.

Four enormous chandeliers hung at the level of the second floor. It was a magnificent edifice of granite, limestone, and marble. The country was not yet out of its financial difficulties of the last few years, but it did not seem to Andrew that Mr. Sheffield had anything to worry about. Still, a run on the bank was a run on the bank, no matter how big the bank was.

At four-thirty, the tellers delivered their ledgers to the second floor for examination and brought their cash drawers to the vault downstairs. Then they sat in their teller booths until five. During the interim half hour, as Mr. Metter explained, they had to wait for Mr. Penne's telephone to ring. If it rang before five o'clock, it meant that one of the tellers was summoned upstairs for an error in his figures. If they heard the telephone ring promptly at five, Mr. Penne would come to the door of his office and signal the release of the tellers. On Andrew's first day, no one was sent for, and he left through a side door with the others at five o'clock.

By five-twenty, he was at the front door of the Tudor house, with Alice very surprised to see him. She sent him upstairs to change his clothes, calling up after him to look in on the baby.

Miss Lantz and Alice were in the kitchen working on dinner when Andrew came down, and Alice sat him down at the kitchen table out of her way and brought him a bottle of Yuengling beer.

"He's playing in his crib," said Andrew, pouring his beer. "He's still not sure who I am."

"He's that way with everyone," said Alice. "He's just a timid baby."

"No, I think the trouble is, he knows people are dangerous."

"Well then, we'll keep him safe, and he'll forget what happened to him. Nobody remembers anything from that age. Now, why don't you tell us about your first day."

"Nothing much to it," said Andrew. "You stand at your window, you hand money out, you take money in. Then you have lunch. When you come back, you do more of the same. At three o'clock you count your drawer, punch your ledger amounts into the Burroughs machine that adds and subtracts. All you have to do is pull the handle to get your totals. It's very amazing to see. Then you carry your books upstairs and wait for the officers to check your figuring. Oh, and you take your drawer down to the vault. That's something to see, Alice. You'd have to be pretty sharp to figure how to break into one of those. So then you wait in your window. If the officers find the accounts balance, you get to go home."

"Then do you think you'll be home at this time every day?"

"I don't see why not."

"Oh, that's wonderful, Andrew. It will be so good to have a regular life, don't you think? I just wish you had let Father start you higher up. You are his son-in-law after all. Everyone knows that."

"Then I probably wouldn't be home at five twenty. I didn't see any of the officers leaving with us."

"Oh," said Alice. "That's right. I never saw Father when I was growing up. We'll just leave it as it is for now. When we get tired of regularity, we'll move you up the ladder."

Andrew laughed. "Well, it's not exactly for you to decide. But I hope you don't like regularity so much that I'm stuck behind the little window for the rest of my life."

"Well, I'd be a sorry daughter of a bank president to let that happen," she said. "You have too much potential, Andrew. Dinner is served."

One night in bed, Andrew was surprised when Alice slipped her tongue into his mouth while they were kissing. She had never done that before. It had never been done to him, and it had never occurred to him to do it to her. She put her head under the covers and began kissing down his chest to his stomach. He pulled her up when he discerned what her next move was going to be. They went on to complete their lovemaking in the usual, orderly way, but afterward, he lay awake a long time. He knew she was also awake. In the years he had been away, she seemed to have compiled a list of skills a lover should not be without, which apparently did not include those he had demonstrated.

The impression he had gotten from both Alice and Miss Lantz was that Procter Darlington had spent little time in the Tudor house. When he came to live there, Andrew had found the closets barren and drawers empty. All evidence of the other husband and the last sweepings of Alice's marriage to him had been taken out to the dustbin. History was being rewritten, and now he had a hand in the matter. The child in the nursery would grow up believing he was a true Croft like his brother.

But the thoughts that coursed through Andrew's mind on the strongest current while he lay awake had to do with the other man who had slept with his wife in the same bed. Nothing could have brought Procter Darlington more vividly into existence than the new activities of the bedroom. But he resolved that the first words about it would have to come from her. A few nights later they did.

"Andrew? Are you awake?"

"Yes. What is it?"

"I want to tell you something."

"Now?"

"It has to do with being in bed. So yes, now."

"All right."

"I want to give you some information."

"That sounds very formal."

"Well, it's science, so it can be taken impersonally. That's how I would want you to take it."

Usually when they talked in bed, she was on her side, up on one elbow, excited by the topic and looking at him. Tonight she lay on her back talking to the ceiling. It wasn't completely dark in the room. He had the feeling she wanted to say what she had to say in a confessional box, talking sideways and looking straight ahead.

"Well, go ahead."

"Very well," she said. "I want you to enjoy being with me."

"I do."

"Well, I think you could enjoy it more. And I know you would want me to enjoy being with you."

"Don't you?"

"Well, naturally, I do," she said. "But if there were ways for both of us to enjoy it even more, wouldn't you want to explore them?"

Andrew cautiously assented. It sounded something like her argument about throwing bombs when they were on the river in China.

"Well, along those lines, I want you to know something about me. Well, it's really something about the female sex. Not many people know about it because it isn't taught in medical schools. I have a friend—a woman friend," she quickly added, "named Lois. I mentioned her before. Well, she knows everything about women. Her cousin is a woman doctor who has a clinic for women in the city. New York, I mean, not here. She's made a study—and she talks to other women doctors too—and she says we're really quite different from men."

"I think everyone is aware of that, Alice."

"I mean, in how women experience lovemaking, Andrew. Anatomically. Lois's cousin says we have—this is difficult to talk about. I'll show you." She took one of his hands and brought it under the covers. "Do you feel that? It's actually a little organ. We're brought up not to touch ourselves, so many women don't even know it's there. Lois told me the only thing it does, the only reason for it, as far as the doctors know, is to give pleasure. That's why so little is known about it—because men don't want women to find out they can get pleasure out of lovemaking as men do. Lois's cousin said she has Arab women come to her clinic, and they told her the Arabs know what it does, and they cut it off their women when they're girls. Can you imagine that?"

Andrew still had his hand there. In his adventuring years in different parts of the world, he had seen some barbaric things, but this unusual little fact of domestic life made him shudder.

"It's awful, isn't it?" Alice said.

"Yes, it is."

"At least it's not a practice here."

"Well, is that the information?"

"Not everything. Lois says what happens to women when the little thing is excited is called an orgasm. It's similar to what you have. I'm sorry. I don't want to embarrass you."

"You got all this from your friend?"

"Yes, from Lois. She lives in New York."

"So, the things you want me to do will bring you to this state?"

"I'm telling you this because I know you would want to please me, Andrew."

"All right."

"So you won't mind me showing you things to do?"

"No, we can do it the way you want."

"Thank you, Andrew," Alice said, rising on one elbow and turning to look at him for the first time. There was some moonlight coming through the blinds, and he could see she was happy to get this off her chest.

"I wish you'd told me sooner," he said.

"I've been trying to hint at it for the last few weeks. I thought you would catch on."

There passed a few moments of silence, which to Alice seemed a throwback to the early days when he had to think so much before speaking.

"I didn't want you to think you had to do things for me," he said. "I didn't want you to demean yourself."

"How could it be demeaning, Andrew? It's just between us."

"No," he said, "I think sometimes intimacies can be perpetuated in a demeaning way."

"But I mean us," she said earnestly. "We would never use our privacy unlovingly. We can just agree that nothing between us in bed is demeaning. We'll be free to become completely intimate. And it will be fun too, don't you think?"

Andrew was smiling with bemusement as he leaned to kiss her.

"What's so funny?"

"Just listening to you is half the fun of being in bed."

"Well, I wish it wasn't. That's why I'm telling you all this." Then, without further delay or another word, she began to put theory into practice.

CHAPTER THIRTY-NINE

Rory came home from Florida the last week of January, accompanied by a great deal of baggage. Alice arrived at the Darlington brownstone in time to watch a wagon being loaded with four trunks. A few small suitcases were placed in the passenger compartment of the carriage before the Darlingtons' postilion climbed up to wait with the coachman, and a footman stood ready to jump aboard to assist in delivering the prodigal, his luggage, and his mother to the freshly painted second-floor bedroom of the Tudor house.

Rory was tanned very brown from the months in Florida. He was happy to meet his mother again but seemed doubtful as to the leadership qualities of his new custodian, for her first act of taking command was not inspection or drill, but to pick him up in her arms and apply kisses liberally to his face. Alice had seized the opportunity when Mrs. Darlington stepped outside to see that the trunks were not roughly handled, and she put him down quickly before the mother-in-law returned. Rory was dressed in a little suit that was almost a perfect replica of one that Andrew wore to the bank, complete with winged collar. He stood up very straight, with his hands at his sides, and he spoke in complete sentences. It was difficult to take him for a normal four-year-old.

"When we get home, I am going to introduce you to your father, Rory," said Alice, when they were seated in the carriage. "You've never met him before. That is because he was away. Just like you were away in Florida."

"Was Father in Florida?"

"No, he was in Africa. For a very long time. He wants to meet you very much."

"Very well, Mother."

"And your brother wishes to meet you. Do you remember him?"

"No," said Rory.

"He was just a little baby when you left with Grandmother."

When Alice lifted Rory down from the carriage in front of the Tudor house and took his hand to lead him up the walk, he balked and stood looking at the house.

"What's the matter, dear?" Alice asked, going down on one knee, ready to be close if it proved to be homesickness for Mrs. Darlington.

"It's so small."

"Oh. I thought you liked our house, Rory. Remember when you lived here?"

"I do not wish to live here, Mother. It's too small."

"Why don't we try it and see, dear. It's very cozy inside. I think you'll like it very much. Come on, Rory. Your father wants to meet you. He's waited so long. I've told him so much about you."

Reluctantly, Rory followed Alice up to the house. Andrew met them at the door, throwing it wide, out of all character for his frugality in winter, and ushering them inside with a show of blustery welcome.

"Kindly sir," said Rory, removing his woolen hat and holding it out to Andrew. "My father, if you please."

Alice was unbuttoning his coat and realized right away what was going on in the boy's mind. "Rory dear, this is your father, not the butler."

"Where is the butler?"

"We don't have a butler, dear."

"We don't need one," said Andrew, picking up the little boy. "We can open the door any time we like." Sensing the indignation of the child, Andrew set him down right away and restored order by offering his hand. "I am very pleased to meet you, Rory."

Rory addressed him as Pop. Alice thought that was something to ask Mrs. Darlington about. At least he seemed perfectly at ease with Andrew.

They got out of the foyer and into the drawing room, leaving to Miss Lantz the supervision of Mrs. Darlington's men. Unfortunately, little Autie had a perfect memory of his older half brother. His eyes grew wide with terror when Rory was brought to the side of his playpen while he was playing quietly with his soft animal toys. He did not make a sound, nor did he move, as Rory put his arm through the bars to shake his trembling little hand.

"Let's go unpack your clothes, Rory," said Alice, wishing to remove Rory before any hostilities broke out. "I am eager to see what grandmamma bought for you."

That night, Alice fell into bed exhausted but glad to have Rory settled in his little room across the hall. She had left the door open and lay awake, half expecting to catch a whimper or the sound of crying into a pillow, but all was quiet.

"I don't know, Andrew," she said. "He seems a little emotionally flat, don't you think?"

"Oh, he'll loosen up. You saw what happened when he found out I wasn't as significant a personage as the butler. He's just gotten used to a different way of life, and he'll get used to this one faster than you think."

"I'm so sorry he was with the Darlingtons so long. I shouldn't have let it happen."

"Mrs. Darlington is a formidable woman."

"Oh, she is, Andrew, but very dear. I don't want you to have the wrong idea of her, and she did such a good job making Rory into a manageable little boy. I had such a time with him."

"Well, now we'll see what we can do to keep him right."

"I just don't want him to upset the household."

"I know. Don't worry. We need to get some sleep now. I have a feeling we're going to have a lot of explaining to do."

That proved to be true. In the days that followed Rory's return to the Tudor house, he asked, "Where are the servants?" He asked to be led around on his pony. He wished to have a picnic luncheon brought down to the beach cabana. He thought someone should be taken to task for his bed sheets not being crisply ironed. He asked Alice to have the houseboy bring a cream cheese and jelly sandwich to him by the warm bubbling pool. Alice and Andrew exchanged looks at each question posed and every request or demand made by the child. Then one of them would sit with him and explain why things were the way they were. Fortunately, Rory never insisted or fussed but seemed to accept whatever he was told, so long as it came from a duly constituted authority. Alice made him cream cheese and jelly sandwiches that he found quite satisfactory.

It turned out the boys got on tolerably well, and everyone ate at the table together, with Autie safely perched in his highchair. At times, Rory would stare at his mother across the table as if he was dimly groping for a memory—or had a memory land in his lap and was not sure what to do with it. But he was easily distracted. He might not be the most warm and personable little boy, but the last thing Alice wanted to see was a retrogression to the boy he had been six months ago.

Even Miss Lantz found little Rory well-behaved. The only lapse occurred a day after Alice spent an entire afternoon with Autie. The next day Rory took one of Autie's favorite toys and buried it in the backyard along the sunny garden wall. Andrew sent him to bed without dinner that night, but he had Miss Lantz take him a plate later. Reasoning together over it, Alice and Andrew thought such a sequence of actions would establish in the boy's mind a humane addendum to the rules of crime and punishment he brought with him from Mrs. Darlington.

CHAPTER FORTY

Andrew had worked at the bank six months when he was called away from his daily ledger to the teller window one morning by a well-dressed young gentleman about his own age.

"I've been out of town for a while, and I'd like you to check my accounts," he said. "There should be four of them."

"Very good, sir," said Andrew. "Has there been any recent activity in any of them?"

"No, not for several months."

"Then I'll require the ledgers from the second floor, sir, if you will permit me the time needed to procure them from the document room."

"Take all the time you need."

"Thank you, sir. May I beg the privilege of your name, sir?"

"Procter Darlington."

Andrew looked up from his notepad as if he were doing nothing more than verifying a name to a face in accordance with bank policy and nodded. "I'll be a few minutes, Mr. Darlington," he said.

As he walked up the marble stairs on the side of the building, Andrew thought there were a hundred better ways to meet his wife's former husband. But this was as good as any other because he didn't care what impression he made. It was just another of those cruel sports like bear baiting or public hangings that made him question the character of those who practiced them and of those who went to watch. Procter knew who he was. There was no doubt in his mind.

Returning to the teller window, Andrew looked up the accounts. There was in excess of ten thousand dollars in one, over three hundred thousand in another, and half a million in each of the other two. He wrote the account numbers down on his notepad, with the amounts opposite, and gave Procter the page.

"Thanks very much," said Procter, turning sideways to look at the figures in the better light through the great windows on the sides of the cavernous building.

"Will that be all, Mr. Darlington?"

"Oh, yes," he said, as if recalling another trifling matter, "I came here also to make the acquaintance of Mr. Croft."

"I am Mr. Croft, sir."

"Oh yes, I knew you were. May I make your acquaintance, sir?"

"Yes, you may, sir."

"Then, how do you do, Mr. Croft?" Procter said, extending his hand through the gate of the teller window.

Andrew had to shake hands with Procter from the lower position of the teller stool, raising his hand to the level of his chin.

"I heard you were employed here—through the grapevine, you know. I had to come take a look at you. Idle curiosity. Are you doing well here at the bank?"

"Well enough, I think, sir."

"I never cared for it. I mean, banking on this scale. I'm with Morgan in New York. You probably knew that."

"Yes, sir."

"Alice might have told you a bit about me."

When Andrew had nothing to say, Procter looked at his watch.

"Must be going. I thought while I'm in town I'd swing around to the house and drop in on old Alice. Maybe take her to lunch. You don't mind, do you? Just for old times. We had a lot of fun together. It's nice while it lasts, isn't it? Nice meeting you."

Procter put out his hand again and smiled confidently. Andrew did not bother to watch him go through the doors. He closed his window and gathered the account books to return to the document room. Mr. Sheffield was standing at the railing of the second floor. He beckoned Andrew into his office when he returned from the document room. There was no need to sit down in the fine, red leather armchairs. The conversation was short.

"If that man comes in again, you do not have to wait on him, Mr. Croft. Pass him to another teller."

"It's no trouble, sir," said Andrew.

"I'll leave it to you, then."

"Thank you, sir. I should be getting downstairs."

"Will we be seeing you at Sunday dinner?"

"I believe so. Mrs. Sheffield has been in touch with Alice."

Mr. Sheffield followed Andrew to the stairs. In a voice below the range of the upper floor's astonishing ability to throw echoes like a valley of mountains, he said, "You're worth ten of that man, Mr. Croft."

The sidewalks home were too well traveled. Even if Andrew had gotten a good look at Darlington's shoes, it would have been impossible to track him on stone until he got to the front walk of the house. That might have been just as hard to do. The milkman came up the walk. So did the ice man, the mail carrier, salesmen, and others. But his old instincts were up. He wasn't going to mention Darlington's visit to the bank. It might be upsetting to Alice. He would only touch on the subject if Alice said he had come to see her. But he could not expect her to do that, knowing it might be disturbing to him to find out her former husband had come calling. Finding out on his own if Procter Darlington had crossed his threshold shouldn't be too difficult; he looked like a careless man.

Alice met him at the door, looking well and happy but rushed.

"Dinner will be a little late, dear," she said. "Miss Lantz was out with the boys all afternoon, and I lost track of the time. Why don't you have a drink?"

"No, I think I'll go up and lie down for a few minutes first," he said.

"All right. I'll call you when we're ready. Could you check on Autie?"

Andrew went up, looked in on the baby, who lay on his back in the crib, waving his little arms at a mobile of animal cutouts dangling over his head.

He entered the bedroom slowly, looking around as he came through the doorway, and walked in a zigzag search pattern to the bed. He lay down and looked a little more around the furnishings of the room with his hands behind his head. There were no broken twigs or bark missing off trees, but he was fairly sure Procter Darlington had been in the room.

Miss Lantz got back from a walk to the grocer and helped Alice put dinner on the table. She always ate with them since putting Autie on his own schedule, but being out for the afternoon had upset the timetable. Before Miss Lantz came downstairs would have been a good time to mention the visitor from another marriage, but Alice only talked about a suffrage meeting that was coming up. She felt it was important for her to go to it. Not having a vote was bothering her more every year, she said.

In the bedroom that night was the last chance for Alice to say something if she had spent the afternoon with Darlington. To bring it up at breakfast, as if she had forgotten to mention she had run out of postage stamps, would have sounded absurdly suspicious. They talked before they went to sleep. The suffrage meeting. The trouble Mrs. Cook was having with her dahlias. How close they were getting to a new century. Not a word about an ex-husband.

CHAPTER FORTY-ONE

Several months later, Alice had to tell Andrew she was pregnant. She could not put it off any longer. She still thought he might put a coincidental two and two together and come up with the wrong answer. It was a Saturday morning, and they were having coffee in the little drawing room that got the full sun. Miss Lantz was out pushing the baby around the block in the stroller with Rory in tow.

Andrew did not react to the news as she had hoped.

"Where are you going, Andrew?"

"Out for a walk. I have to think about things. More responsibilities now. I'll have to move up in the bank."

Alice got up and grabbed his sleeve before he got to the door. "That's not what it is. Tell me, Andrew."

"Nothing more than that."

"No, something's on your mind."

"How far are you along?" he asked.

"I don't know. The usual. When you first know."

"When is that?"

She had to be honest. He could figure it out anyway after the baby came. "About two or three months. Don't go out that door, Andrew."

"What do you want me to do?"

"I want you to sit down and tell me what you're thinking."

"All right," he said, going to the brown leather armchair where he sat every evening.

Alice sat on the couch. "What are you thinking?"

"Procter Darlington came to the bank about that same time. He said he was going to stop by to see you."

"Nothing happened, Andrew," she said.

"Then he did come here?"

"Yes. I didn't want to tell you. I thought you would get upset. To be perfectly honest, I thought you might kill him."

"That's ridiculous. Why would I kill him?"

"I thought you might argue. That's not so hard to imagine."

"How long was he here?"

"About an hour. I sent him away."

"Was he upstairs?"

"He still had the key to the house. I was taking a nap, and he got up the stairs before I heard him. Nothing happened. I was dressed."

"You always said he could talk his way around anybody. Coincidentally, now you're going to have a baby."

"That's insulting, Andrew."

"I didn't mean it as an insult. But you can't blame me for thinking. All the new tricks you learned in the bedroom and how much you like them—"

"Andrew, stop. You're using our privacy against me. I thought we promised not to do that."

Andrew flung himself back in the chair in exasperation. Alice was close to tears but angry enough to hold him there and have it out.

"I don't know why I have to tell you things you ought to know. You and I were together for scarcely a year—and only intimate for a few months at the end of that year. I was with Procter Darlington two, almost three years. Twice the time I was with you. I don't like to think about it any more than you do, but I was his wife for two years—with all that that entails. I thought you had accepted that, but I see you haven't. I do not want to violate his privacy, but I will if it will allay your mistrust. The baby is yours, Andrew. You should know something about my previous husband. He is impotent. That means he is unable to impregnate a woman. He also prefers men to women. I think you know what that means. The marriage was a sham."

Andrew looked down at the floor, and Alice became fearful of his next question.

"Then where did Autie come from?" he asked, without looking at her.

"I found another man," she said.

"Oh. Where is he now?"

"I don't know."

"Do you still love him?"

"I never did. I only wanted a child, Andrew."

"Everything we're doing—did you learn that from him?"

"Yes. And Lois."

"Does he know you had a child by him?"

"No."

"Are you ever going to see him again?"

"No."

Andrew took a deep breath and sat up straighter. "Is that everything?"

"Yes," she said.

If she was ever to confess to the sex parties at the salon, it would be now. But she had strained him enough. She had been cornered into adding a man he had not known about to the list. He would never stay with her if he knew how many men she had learned from. She took one of his cigarettes, and they smoked together silently and drank their coffee.

"May I go out for a walk now?"

"I want to know what you're thinking, Andrew."

Andrew sat back in the chair.

"To tell the truth, I don't know," he said. "It sounds like all I had to do was disappear for a while."

Alice saw something in his face change. Whatever happened now was going to be her fault. She should have let him go out and walk around the neighborhood. He knew everything he had to know, he just needed time to think. He would remember saying he could put her past behind him. She had pushed him too far. He was getting ready to force the silver dollar out of Jenny Jones's hand and about to throw the china dog out the window.

"What am I supposed to do?" he said, "just put it out of my head? It might clear your conscience to tell me what you did while I was gone, but you're throwing a lot on the pile I have to live with."

"We have to be honest with each other."

"Well, you're the only one who's got confessions to make."

"Don't shout at me, Andrew."

"I'm not shouting. I should have turned around when I heard you were married. I guess it's not too late to do that."

"God damn you."

Alice got up with a start and went to the window and turned the crank to open it with all the frustrated energy she could apply to it.

"You seem to think that believing you were dead was something I did behind your back. I never expected to see you again. I know you would have liked it better if I had stayed a widow, but I was twenty-two, Andrew, with a child I was responsible for. I had to try something. Procter was a mistake. I only wanted a man again because I thought it would be like having you. But it wasn't." In a softer voice but still looking out the window, she went on. "If you're going to leave me, Andrew, just leave. Don't drag it out. If you want me and want to be married to me again, I don't want to hear you talk about leaving me every time we have a fight. I couldn't live with you that way. If you decide to stay with me, you'll have to understand that."

He was silent, and she turned around to say what might be her last words to him.

"I've only loved one man, Andrew, and you are the only man I want. I hope you'll add that to whatever else you need to think about." Tears began to come to her eyes. "I'll explain it to my father. You can go right now."

Miss Lantz was at the door just then, struggling to get the wheels of the stroller over the doorstep. Rory darted by her and ran up the stairs to his room.

"It's lovely out, monsieur, madam," she called. "You should go out for a walk."

"Maybe we should," said Andrew, looking up.

Alice quickly wiped her eyes and came over to put out the cigarette in the ashtray.

"You'll need a wrap, madam," said Miss Lantz.

In the foyer, little Autie watched the giants milling around him from his seat in the stroller. His head was turning from side to side, and his eyes were wide with complete fascination, as if there was nothing that could subdue his wonderment.

Alice got her wrap from the coat closet and draped it over her shoulders. Then she put her arm through Andrew's as they stepped outside. They walked toward town silently, first passing the other Tudor houses on the street with their old sycamores, then the larger Victorians with their old oaks. Then the shops and people, and couples with stories like theirs.

Andrew felt lucky to have Alice again, but she was asking him to accept the other life she'd had with two other men. He was expected to accept it and put it aside. For years he had yearned to be where he was now. The bedroom was not what he had missed most about her. He missed walking with her, talking with her, and what they were doing now, and he had lived to come home and have it. If he could accept everything Alice had told him, and live without it coming between them, he thought it would make him as mature as he would ever be called upon to be.

Alice and Andrew walked in step with their eyes straight ahead, silently, smiling at the people they passed. The last words that needed to be said about infidelity, betrayal, suspicion, love, and loyalty fell behind them as they walked, like breadcrumbs left to mark a path the birds would erase.

CHAPTER FORTY-TWO

Alice was six months pregnant when she thought it would be nice, before she was laid up, to run down to New York with Andrew and introduce him to Lois. They spoke often on the telephone, and Alice frequently brought up Lois's most intriguing ideas with Andrew in conversation. Andrew was reluctant to go, but he was willing to do anything for her since settling into the house. They stayed in the wonderful Chelsea Hotel for the weekend and went over to Lois's on Saturday night.

There were a few of the regulars she remembered, including Jim Rider, the garret novelist. He was getting famous now and lived in a grand house on Long Island, but he kept the garret in the city for his writing. Procter happened to be there with a comely young society girl. Andrew and Alice spoke cordially with them before sitting down with Lois, who was playing solitaire at her table. Lois had assured her over the telephone that the mattresses would not be brought out that night, but she whispered to Alice and Andrew at the table that she had no idea Procter would show up.

They had a nice talk together about art and politics. Lois and Andrew seemed to hit it off well enough. Lois suggested a little museum of firearms in the city that Andrew might look in on the next day, and it pleased Andrew very much that Lois was perceptive about his areas of interest.

"I thought it went off very well," Alice said on the train home late on Sunday. "Even with you-know-who turning up. I'm glad you saw no pressing need to kill him, Andrew."

"It never crossed my mind."

"Maybe you're just out of the habit, dear. That girl is too young for him, though, don't you think?"

"I'm not worried about Procter's girlfriend right now," said Andrew, smiling.

"I know you're anxious about tomorrow," Alice said, "but you shouldn't be. You've done so well at the bank. Mother said you're the best man Father has. She told me he said that."

"Well, that's nice to hear, but there are other people I have to deal with. The head of the department has a reputation."

Andrew smiled and put his arm around her, trying to appear relaxed, but she knew he was wondering how it would go on Monday. He was going into training for the commercial loan department. In preparation for it, he had been putting in extra time in the evenings at the Boston Public Library, reading everything he could on finance. It was a little more than she could keep up with.

While Andrew was immersing himself in banking, Alice became preoccupied with preparations for the new baby coming. Miss Lantz was admirable in her management of the two boys, and there was little Alice had to do for them. But she tired easily as her body nurtured the small growing thing inside her, diverting its energy and resources to the building of a baby, creating the protective layers around it, and provisioning her body with fat stores. Everything about life in the Tudor house seemed to be both up in the air and steady on course at the same time.

She was never so content as when she sat with Andrew and Miss Lantz in the drawing room after the boys had been put to bed. Through the winter, Andrew kept a fire in the fireplace every evening. He read history at his leisure, sipping at his coffee, Miss Lantz read Greek tragedies in French, sipping at her brandy, and Alice made baby clothes, forgetting her whiskey on the table and her cigarette in the ashtray until she looked up to hear Andrew read aloud an interesting tidbit of history.

Mrs. Darlington had picked up where Mrs. Sheffield's knowledge of needlework left off. After a few months of instruction under the elderly but energetic woman, which Alice thought must have been something like Rory's first experience with his Darlington grandmother, she felt confident enough to do her own work. She set out with enthusiasm to design her own patterns, cut fabric, and sew on her own, both manually and at the featherweight Singer machine Andrew brought home one day. For the time being, she only needed baby wear. Sleepers were easy to make, but she would need a lot of them in case of leaky diapers. A dress for the christening was important. Next on the list were booties, caps for bedtime, and caps for out of doors. Then lacy little dresses. They would suffice for either a boy or a girl for at least the first year. Alice was so sure it would be a girl this time that she made little pink butterfly appliqués to go on the caps.

Andrew did not want to intrude upon the pleasant domesticity of their evenings with talk of work, but Alice urged the news out of him not long after his big move to the commercial loan department had taken place. She saw the opportunity when he lay down his book. Replying to her questions, he told her he was quite happy up on the second floor in an office of his own.

"I've got your father considering a proposal of mine," he said.

"I'm sure it must be a good one."

"Well, he said he'd think it over," Andrew said, smiling. "It would mean a change in the status quo of commercial loan making, so I don't know if he'll go for it. It might make him look grabby to his pals at the other banks."

"Well, tell me what it is, Andrew," said Alice, finishing off another butterfly appliqué and laying it aside.

"What we usually do in commercial loans is wait for someone to come in asking for one. Then the majority of our time is spent reviewing the balance sheets of the company, hearing what the plan is, why they need the money, how much, and so forth. Then we make a decision. Sometimes, particularly when interest rates go up, or during a downturn in the general economy like the one we just came through, there isn't much demand for loans."

"Is this going to get complicated, dear?"

"No, no. That's the beauty of it. Very simple. I proposed that someone—me—goes out and talks to the businesspeople around here. That can be local or as far out as we want to extend our reach. Then, for want of a better description, I sell loans."

"Sell loans?"

"Yes, sell loans. Before that, I look into a retail or wholesale business we might be interested in and try to find out how creditworthy it is. If it passes, I go around to the establishment in a very casual sort of manner and suggest ways they could develop. Then I outline the terms of the loan it would require."

"What did he say?"

"He said soliciting was not done in the loan department. I knew he wouldn't like it at first, but I think he'll see the sense of it when his wheels start turning. I told him I could keep it low-key, get to know the men first, then casually bring up ideas like expanding their storefronts or putting up a warehouse and buying in bulk—things they were probably thinking about anyway—and now they know a banker willing to help them do it. They don't have to know we've already preapproved them for the loan."

"I think it's a wonderful idea, Andrew," Alice said, heartened by the application of his mental powers to a job he could so easily have found lacking in challenges. "You should get a promotion just for thinking of it."

"I just had one."

"I'm so pleased, Andrew. I think Father's going to finally see you as worthy of being his son-in-law."

"Well, worthy of the bank, anyway," said Andrew, getting up to put another log on the fire.

CHAPTER FORTY-THREE

Alice had a baby daughter in the spring, the same day Rory inexplicably kicked the heads off all the tulips in the garden. She mused as she nursed little Elizabeth, while sitting up in bed and looking out the window at a bad year for tulips, that one event would never come to mind without remembering the other. But her happiness that day could not be troubled, and she decided the tulips were not worth mentioning.

Rory was brought into the room. With Andrew, Miss Lantz, and his two grandmothers in solemn attendance, he was properly introduced to the baby with ceremony and was duly sworn to preserve and protect his little sister. Then Andrew and Miss Lantz conducted him to the playroom, where he was presented with a large flat box of tin soldiers. He took command of his little army immediately, deploying his men in siege operations around the playpen, where little Autie sat among his soft, furry toy animals, watching in quiet amazement as his brother laid plans to starve him out of his fortifications.

Alice was so in love with baby Elizabeth. How miraculous it was for a new life to come out of nonexistence and so bravely enter this world of chance and probability. They, chance and probability, had already held her from conception, and gender was the first work of those two hands. A baby girl had come to life, had taken breath, and would grow to womanhood under her care.

Her sons, Rory and Autie, would join the world of men. How they fared in that world depended upon qualities and elements of character that were largely unknown to her, but Elizabeth would always be part of the world she understood. She could only instruct the boys as far as their conduct toward girls. But even there, they would learn more by the example of their father, and Alice was sure there could be no more perfect a man for providing that than her dear Andrew.

He came in to be with her after Mrs. Sheffield and the midwife left. He removed his jacket, his tie, and his collar, and he lay down on the bed beside her, propped on one elbow to look at the baby.

"Don't put your face too close to her yet, Andrew," said Alice. "This is her first day of breathing air, and I don't want her breathing in your bank germs."

"Well, your father will be bringing plenty of those tomorrow. He called to say congratulations on the telephone just now. He knew you couldn't get up. And you got a telegram from Jim Rider. Which one is he?"

"The novelist. The one with the house on Long Island. How did he know?"

"I called Lois this morning. She sent congratulations and said she'll call you in a day or two when you aren't groggy."

"I'm not groggy. I only had a little of the chloroform at the end. I knew it would cost extra money."

"Damn it, Alice. You don't have to worry about money. I should have been here."

"Oh, that's very funny," Alice said, laughing. "Men aren't allowed in. Under no circumstances. That's one rule that will never change."

"Not quite true, dear. Queen Victoria has her ministers attend every childbirth."

"Oh heavens. That can't be."

"It's true. It goes back centuries. They were worried about a Catholic baby getting switched-off into the line or something like that. Can't remember where I read that."

"Oh my," said Alice. "Victoria is so private and formal. Cabinet ministers in the bed chamber. I can't imagine the indignity. But never mind about her then. Under normal American circumstances, men are not welcome in the delivery room."

"I want you to have the chloroform the next time."

"I don't think I'll need it," Alice said, feeling the pride she could take in herself. "I'm getting to be an old hand at this, aren't I? I want to have more, Andrew. At least three or four more. It will be so interesting to see what they'll look like and what they'll want to do in life. And we'll be able to help them. Even if it's not to our liking. Oh—look at her hand, Andrew. Look how tiny her fingers are. She's going to be a real escape artist."

Elizabeth had gotten one arm out of the blanket she was wrapped in, and the hand at the side of her face was opening and closing for something to grip. Her eyes were closed. She was red and blotchy, and strands of thin, black hair were wetted down on her head.

"We don't know about her eyes yet. My blue or your brown. Or maybe hazel. That's blue and brown, isn't it?"

"Don't ask me."

"Anyway, she's both of us. Rory is too, but you weren't with me then, and I was trying to forget you. When Rory came, I knew I never would be able to forget you because there you were, in my arms. He looked so much like you. I was so miserable that year, Andrew."

"Well, you don't have to think about that now," Andrew said. When he agreed never to talk about leaving her, he should have made her agree never to bring up the one time he had. "It had nothing to do with how this one came into the world. You aren't miserable now, are you?"

"No, of course not. I'm very happy. Gloriously happy."

Alice lay down facing Andrew with the baby between them for a few minutes. For as short a time as it was, it had a strong effect on her, and she wanted Andrew to feel it also, as a time of communion. Until now, he had never been part of a family, something she had always taken for granted in her own life. Later that day, she thought of a way to put in place what she thought was needed. The old green couch in Andrew's office, which they called the den, wasn't doing anything, and she thought of a way to give it a new life in the household as the gathering place for story time.

Every night thereafter, as soon as Elizabeth had gained the relative hardihood of a few weeks of age, the family gathered on the old green couch in the den for story time before bed. Miss Lantz delivered the two boys in their pajamas and then went downstairs to play the piano for an hour. Andrew sank into the middle of the old couch with Rory and Autie on one side and Alice with baby Elizabeth cradled in her arms on the other. First it was fairy tales, then longer works like *Ivanhoe*, read as a nightly serial that riveted Rory's attention and kept him from getting rambunctious. Autie kept his eyes open but yawned every time Elizabeth yawned. Alice watched Andrew with his glasses on, reading in a voice that followed the contours of the descriptive passages and jumped into the dialogues of different characters in lifelike falsetto, baritone, or bass. He was very good at it, she thought.

When story time was over, Andrew took the boys to their bedroom down the hall. They slept in two little beds with a night table between them. Rory had drawn a line down the middle of the table. It was to designate the border of whose half was whose. Andrew listened to them say their prayers as he looked down on the little dark head and the little blond head bowed over clasped hands. Then his eyes went up to the blue-and-white wallpaper of sailboats.

Now I lay me down to sleep
I pray the Lord my soul to keep.
His love stay with me through the night
And wake me with the morning light.

"God bless" was followed by a list of individuals beginning with Mommy and Daddy. After that, Andrew tucked them in and said good night. They liked the door left open a little to admit a shaft of light from the hall, so he put it that way and stood a moment to be sure there were no calls for adjustment. Every night, standing outside that door, he pondered, without the necessity of remembering, all it had taken and what he had come through to be here.

CHAPTER FORTY-FOUR

Alice began to notice the settling of the household into its male and female spheres and the influence Andrew was beginning to exert on the boys. Around six o'clock every evening, Rory sat on a little stool Miss Lantz had put out for him at the curtained window of the front drawing room. There he watched for Andrew and was always the first to meet his father at the door. As tired as Andrew might be or how badly in need of his beer and fried potato crisps, he always got out of his jacket, collar, and tie, willing to play at least one game with the boy. Then they went up together to get little Autie out of his playpen and bring him downstairs. It was Andrew's idea to get the boys playing together, and Alice was encouraged to see the resourcefulness of her husband when trouble erupted over Autie's duck.

The little yellow duck was Autie's favorite stuffed animal. He took it everywhere as he toddled around the house, and it soon became an object that Rory found amusing to knock out of Autie's hands. He did it so fast that his little brother, upon recovering his duck, sat staring intently at it in his hands, as if it had misbehaved and jumped away of its own free will. Rory would laugh and do it again when Autie had relaxed his attention.

Alice and Miss Lantz were usually in the kitchen during playtime. Alice would always come to the door to find out what was so funny, arriving too late to see it. When Andrew explained Rory's game to her one night, she did not find it funny at all.

"You have to do something about it, Andrew," she said.

"I already have," he said. "I was getting to that. You have a tendency to hear a little bit of something and jump in before I'm finished."

"That's because I usually know what you're going to say."

"I don't see how you can."

"All right. Then you pulled Rory aside and talked to him. What did you say? I won't interrupt you again."

"Well, no, I didn't do that. In fact, that's exactly what I didn't do. So you see what I mean?"

"You've made your point, dear," said Alice, without it sounding like the concession it was supposed to be. "Then tell me what you did."

"First, I got the duck and gave it back to boy number two. All the while, I praised boy number one for his speed and cunning. Then I told boy number one that it had gone on long enough to prove that his part in the duck taking flight was so well concealed by his sleight of hand, that boy number two would never figure out the trick on his own, and that it was only good sportsmanship to show boy number two how he did it.

"So boy number one explained to boy number two how devilishly clever was the gaze to the ceiling that never failed to distract boy number two. Going through his motions at half speed, he showed boy number two how to seize the moment when the hapless victim looked up to the ceiling to see what the perpetrator was looking at—and just at that moment, the duck is batted out of his hands.

"It worked out very well. Then we set it up for Autie to try on Rory—with an understanding that Rory would let him win."

"Well, that was very smart of you, Andrew," said Alice. "But I hope you didn't just make a trickster out of Autie. He's such a timid little thing and shouldn't be encouraged to take after Rory."

"No, I think the worst I did was take a little wonder out of his duck."

In the following months, Alice watched her husband assume admirably the role of father in his first experience of family life. As he tried to learn what made the two boys tick, as he phrased it, and the differences between them, the military paraphernalia around the house began to disappear. The bayonets he used as letter openers, the defused hand grenades he had on his desk as paperweights, and the Gurkha knife that came in handy in the garden all found a new home in the basement, along with the live ammunition and firearms he stored under the green couch in his den.

One night before story time, Rory was standing up on the green couch looking at Andrew's framed photograph of his Marine Corps battalion, a remarkable picture five feet long and a foot high. There were hundreds of men in the picture standing in rows. In white letters in one bottom corner were the words "First Battalion, Fifth Marines, Camp Davis, Virginia, March 1882."

Alice picked up Autie and said, "Let's see if we can find Daddy in the picture."

By story hour the next night, after Andrew had sequestered himself in the den all Saturday afternoon, Alice came in to find the picture had been turned around on the wall. Cut-out pictures from *Collier's* magazine had been pasted on the reverse side, which was now facing out. The Fifth Marines had been driven from the field by an assembly of workmen at their occupations, ladies at tea, gentlemen on horseback, wintry fireside gatherings, dogs, children, and attractive young homemakers admiring freshly baked cakes and pies.

"What's this, dear?" said Alice.

"Rearranging my den, darling," he replied. "I wanted a more contemporary look."

"No really, Andrew."

"Well, I was thinking about the boys last night, about their future."

He sat down on the green couch, and Alice curled up beside him.

"I think they're going to have a wonderful future, don't you?" she said.

"They could. They certainly could. That's why I don't want them following in my footsteps."

"No one's pushing them, dear."

"No, but the military has a natural attraction for boys. I worry about Rory. Autie's not the type, but I thought I should play it down."

"Well, it wouldn't be my first choice for either of them," said Alice. "But it might be too late. Don't think Rory hasn't gotten into every corner of the house. He was playing with one of your field caps the other day in the attic. I put it back in the trunk. I didn't know you had so much left over."

"I'll hide the stuff better. I can build a closet up there, or down in the cellar, at least for the firearms, and I'd better put a lock on it."

Alice could say nothing in opposition to that except to remind him that it was his former occupation that had brought them together. But she was glad he could look squarely at his old life and want better for the boys.

"What did you want to be when you were young?" she asked, suddenly thinking of a question she had never asked.

"I don't remember ever wanting to be anything," he said slowly, with consideration, trying to pull up the memory of any stray thought he might have had on the topic. "The mill was all I knew. Then the years on the streets, going to sea, the marines. The only ambition behind it was making a living."

"Well, I think you turned out very well," said Alice. "Father says you're the youngest officer the bank has ever had."

Andrew laughed. "Don't forget, I'm only guessing at my age. I might be a lot older than thirty-two. I sure as hell couldn't be younger."

Then he went down to the basement to put a bit more coal into the furnace before Miss Lantz brought the boys and the baby in for story time.

CHAPTER FORTY-FIVE

The bassinet was moved into the master bedroom to make the nightly nursing easier. Alice slept very well during the intervals. Right from the beginning she refused Andrew's company beside her in the chair and insisted he get his sleep. She knew it disturbed him enough when she got up and came back to bed every few hours, for he was a light sleeper. She worried that his old instincts kept him alert, especially with a baby in the room.

They were pleased to see Elizabeth's rapid development and how strong and healthy she was at a month, then two months, then three. In the heat of the summer, Alice found Elizabeth was able to get out of her sleeper and cap when she was left alone in the bassinet. They would be found bunched up with the baby blanket in a corner. It was tricky, but Alice and Miss Lantz figured out how to keep the diaper pins at the back where Elizabeth couldn't get at them. She liked to roll around, double up with her legs in the air, and put her toes in her mouth. She looked like she thoroughly enjoyed being a baby. How different little Autie had been at that age after the eye incident and the near-fatal crushing. How timidly he had looked at the world from under the blanket in his bassinet, as if he were wondering what perils each new day would bring.

That summer Rory got the measles. For a few days there was reason to be worried about him, but he came through fine. With Autie running around the house playing with Rory's toys, it was difficult to keep the sick boy confined to his room. The household was quarantined for almost a month. A sign sent over by the board of health was posted in the window by the front door with the words in bold print "Under Quarantine, Measles." Miss Lantz had groceries delivered to the house and was on the telephone every day, making similar arrangements for other necessities. Andrew stayed at home for a week when it was at its worst and sat by Rory's bedside, reading stories to him and seeing to his comfort. Before he came to bed at night, he put the clothes he had worn that day down the laundry chute and bathed.

One night toward the end of Rory's illness, when there was a feeling of great relief in the house to have had the quarantine lifted, Andrew was just getting back to sleep after Alice had been up with the baby. The steaming of the radiators made a soft background hiss and clanking, but he detected another sound. With sleep drifting in, his ability to distinguish it was hampered for a minute, but suddenly he knew what it was and threw off the covers.

"Alice, the lamp," he shouted, shaking her awake with one hand.

Alice sat up and fumbled for the matches on the bedside table as Andrew bolted across the room.

"Not the candle, the lamp. Hurry."

Alice jumped out of bed and groped for the hanging chains, pulled the wrong one first, then got a hand on the other. She struck a match and put it to the base. The mantle caught, and a white-hot light filled the room. Alice rubbed her eyes.

"What's going on, Andrew?"

"The baby."

He rushed back to the bed with Elizabeth in his arms. "I can't see anything."

Alice pulled again on the dangling chain. "That's as bright as it gets," she said.

Andrew had a finger in the baby's mouth. "I can't get it. Something's in her throat. Your hands are smaller, you try."

Alice tried. She couldn't feel anything.

"Go in deeper."

"I don't want her to choke."

"Keep trying."

Andrew grabbed his shirt from the back of the chair, threw it on, and got into his trousers and shoes.

"I'm taking her to the hospital. Get the operator on the telephone and tell her to call the ambulance. Tell them I'll be running down Calder to Lippencott. They can intercept."

He ran down the stairs with Elizabeth wrapped in a blanket There wasn't a soul to be seen on the streets. The sidewalk was slippery with dew. He didn't want to risk a fall and had to slow down. The best hope was the ambulance. After he had run a few blocks, he heard wheels over cobblestones as a two-horse team clattered up behind him. Before it could slow down, Andrew slapped the rear of the lead horse and vaulted up to the seat beside the driver with the baby in the crook of his arm.

"Drive 'em fast," he shouted to the man with the reins.

When Alice arrived in a cab at the hospital, she was sent directly to children's emergency care. Andrew was just coming out from around a curtain. She didn't really look at his face.

"Is she in there?"

"Yes," he said.

"She's all right then, thank God. Thank God. She's all right."

Before Andrew could stop her, Alice went through the curtain. Elizabeth lay on a metal table, wrapped in the blanket from the house. Beside her head was one of the butterfly appliqués from her nightcap. Elizabeth's eyes were closed, and her face was white. Alice collapsed, striking her head on the corner of the table. Andrew, immediately behind, caught her before she fell to the floor. He called for a nurse and lowered her to a prone position.

"I need a towel," he said to the nurse who drew back the curtain. "And something to lift her feet." He pressed his handkerchief on a gash over Alice's left eye.

It was a small wound, but there was a lot of blood. Under the circumstances, the doctor put her under with chloroform on a handkerchief and stitched the wound where she lay on the floor, deeming it advisable to get her home before she woke up. On the way out, Andrew picked up the butterfly appliqué. The nurse challenged him, saying it had to be enclosed with the coroner's report, so he put it back on the table.

At home, Miss Lantz had been waiting up in her dressing gown. All the lamps on the first-floor walls were on. It was two o'clock in the morning. He told her what had happened and saw her face flinch.

"We still have the laudanum, monsieur," she said. "Would you like me to get it?"

"No, it wouldn't be good for her. I'll get her upstairs myself. You may lower the lights and retire for the night. Thank you, Miss Lantz. I'll be at home tomorrow. I don't know when we'll be up, so just look after the boys, if you would."

The air of the outside had brought Alice around, but she was weak and disoriented. Andrew had to support her up the stairs.

"She's all right, isn't she?" Alice asked in a feeble voice.

Then she raised a hand as if to remove a hat, and her fingers fell on the bandage over her eye, and she remembered.

"Oh, Andrew," she cried.

He was quick to arrest her collapse on the stairs and could easily have carried her, but he knew she could stand. From the moment Elizabeth died in his arms, before he had even gotten downstairs to the street, he thought if there could ever be a remedy for this, it would have to come from the strength Alice had within her, and he had to call upon it now.

"Alice," he said, "You have to help me get you upstairs. Just a little farther."

Alice braced herself and concentrated her attention as far as the bedroom. Then she fell on the bed crying, and Andrew had to ask again for her help. As she undid buttons and loosened ties, he kept talking softly, so she had to stop crying to hear him.

"You fainted and cut your forehead," he said. "The doctor put you under and stitched it. That's why you have the bandage. He said to keep it dry, and in a few days the stitches can come out, but he said you'll probably have a little scar. You won't mind that, will you? He said you need to sleep now, so that's what we're going to do. It's two in the morning."

Andrew got her under the sheets and pulled the covers up to her chin and held her face between his hands.

"We'll come through this, Alice," he said.

"You're coming to bed too, aren't you?"

"I have to put some coal in the furnace."

"No, stay with me, please." Then she said, "No, there's Miss Lantz and the boys. Go put coal in the furnace."

In a few minutes Andrew was back and under the covers beside her. She seemed better, but only by force of will, as if she were remembering her other breakdown and was determined not to let herself give in to despair again.

"Andrew," she said, "I don't know what I'm going to do. I killed our baby."

"You did nothing of the kind."

"I did. The appliqués came off too easily. The wings were delicate. I spent so much time on the body of the butterfly. You take a piece of cording. You split it up, fray the ends and then you wind thread around it. I didn't sew that part down because it was so hard to get the needle through. So they only had one stitch holding them on by the wings, and the fabric was so light she must have pulled it right through the thread. I think of her choking, and, oh God, I can't live with it."

Andrew held her tightly as she relapsed into waves of crying that shook her entire frame.

"No, you will. You're strong. We'll get through everything."

"I can't."

"You've gotten through bad times before."

"When? What was ever as hard as this, Andrew? Tell me. What was ever worse than this?"

"I don't know now."

"Nothing was. Not even when I thought you were dead. Because that wasn't my fault."

"This wasn't your fault either, Alice. It shouldn't have happened. A million things shouldn't happen, but they do. No one can do anything about that. We just have to go on. Everything will be all right." He didn't know what else he could say to her.

"How can everything be all right, Andrew?"

"It will. It will. You'll see. We'll talk tomorrow."

"A night won't change anything. Neither will a week or a year."

"I know, darling. I know. We have to go to sleep now."

He stroked her head and did not let go of her until hours later, when she fell asleep from the fatigue of crying. He was awake long after that. The dark of the bedroom was like the dark anywhere. His thoughts reverted to other places, a dozen other places where he lay in the dark, not in a bed, but a shallow depression under some brush or at a listening post, his chin resting on the stock of a rifle. He learned to differentiate the sounds of the night in those places, the ambient sounds from those of an enemy creeping near. Moving his finger into the trigger guard and waiting. He could hit a sound in the dark.

Nothing had ever gotten by him, but this time a butterfly had, when his job was guarding women and children. He had failed in work he was supposed to be good at. His daughter was dead because a butterfly got past his ear.

With Alice asleep, he drew up his own grief, like a bucket from a well. He hadn't known how deep a well it was, and now he wished the bucket tipped over onto the ground and the spilled water quickly gone before Alice awoke. Loving the child had come as easily as finding a place for her in their lives. But he knew it to be in the character of memory to fade; and the past, in its truest nature, might wish itself forgotten. In the first and truest pain of his life, he wept for his daughter, Elizabeth.

Recovering himself toward morning, he tried to think of a plan. If he allowed silence to fall between Alice and himself, it would end their life together. But he did not know what he could do except to go on with everyday life and try to conceal from her any doubt he had in its power to restore.

Alice must have come to the same way of thinking, for she got up when Andrew got up, and she sat with him at the little telephone table off the dining room. He made his call to the bank. Then he called the Sheffields and spoke to Mr. Sheffield as Alice preferred, wishing her father to know first. Father would know how to tell her mother. Miss Lantz was with the boys in the kitchen starting breakfast, but Alice stayed with Andrew while he called the coroner's office to ask when the body would be released. Finding that the paperwork for Elizabeth was completed, Andrew turned to Alice.

"There's no reason to put off the other call," he said.

"Do you mean the undertaker?"

"Yes. You don't have to stay. I'll call the one—I'll think of the name—"

"If it's the one we walk by, I don't want to use that one. We'd always be thinking of Elizabeth when we go by."

"We will anyway, won't we?"

"All right," she said. "Call them."

"We'll have to choose a coffin. I can do that."

"No, Andrew. We'll go together."

After breakfast, Alice went to the baby's room they had made out of the sitting room adjoining their bedroom. She put away the baby clothes she had made for Elizabeth, leaving all the drawers open until each one had something in it. She took out one of the sleepers for the burial, a pair of booties, and one of her caps, and then they walked all the way to the hospital to retrieve Elizabeth's baby blanket. On the way back, they stopped at the undertaker's to choose a coffin. Alice selected a plain one and told the director that she did not wish the child to be embalmed. Alice turned over to him the sleeper, cap, and booties and asked that the blanket be used to tuck her in.

"I don't want her to be cold," she said in a little voice with Andrew's arms around her.

As they left and started toward home, Alice wanted to go back and dress Elizabeth herself, but Andrew said she wouldn't be able to bear it, and she agreed it would be too hard for her to do.

In the afternoon, the Sheffields came to the house. Alice and her mother went upstairs to get out the mourning clothes Alice had worn the year she had lost Andrew. Her mother was already in black. She had brought along an armband for Andrew and a few trappings for Alice. Some of the hats and veils were out of fashion, but her mother said all grief is alike and timeless, and so she wore them.

Andrew stayed home for the week and endured with Alice the funeral and the gathering afterward. When Sunday night came, after the two boys were put to bed, Andrew, Alice, and Miss Lantz sat in the drawing room with their coffee, brandy, and whiskey. Alice took off her glasses and put her book aside.

"I have to get some work done around here," she said, looking around the room at nothing in particular. "You should go to work tomorrow, dear. Don't you think?"

"I suppose so," he said. "But I won't if you need me."

"I'll have you at night. You don't have to be with me every minute."

"If that's what you think is best."

"I've cried all I can cry," she said.

Alice accounted for her time with a clean house, freshly laundered clothes, and ironed sheets. It was her own rule that the family ate well, so she cooked every day under Miss Lantz's instruction and baked every other day.

Summer passed hot and sweltering. Fall, first bright and clear, became dreary. Memories of winter melted with the heaps of dirty snow along the streets, and spring came again. Alice could talk about Elizabeth, how healthy and strong she was, and how handsome a girl she was going to be. It made Andrew wary of what sometimes happened when Alice spoke of Elizabeth. The tone of reminiscence in her voice was that of a parent speaking of a living child, or even of a parent relating to a grown child an amusing story of its infancy. Then, with thoughts suddenly returning to the reality of Elizabeth's never-ending absence, Alice would stop abruptly and look down with her mouth very tightly shut.

The night that the first birthday came around, Alice said, "Elizabeth would have been one year old today."

Andrew put down his book. He went to sit beside her on the couch, and Miss Lantz took out her handkerchief. They took a sip from their glasses in remembrance, and each said her name, Elizabeth. No such observance was given to the date of her death.

CHAPTER FORTY-SIX

In the next three years, Andrew rose to be vice president of the bank, and more than ever a true son and trusted advisor to his father-in-law. He became a fixture in the childhood of the boys, playing with them and teaching them manly behaviors. He looked for aptitude in them when they started school and wasn't sure what he saw except that they were growing up as two normal boys. He brought home a collie puppy one day and built a fence around the backyard. Autie named him Bow-wow. The boys played with matches one day under the front porch of the Tudor house and set it on fire. People came running. The damage was minimal, and Rory and Autie promised never to do it again.

Every Sunday night Alice made fudge and placed the glass dish on top of the icebox to cool. Andrew sat in his chair and read the newspaper. Miss

Lantz read her Greek tragedies in French and sipped her brandy. Rory played with his toy soldiers and Autie lay down on the floor to watch Bowwow eat his dinner from an old frying pan. Every night they sat together on the green couch for story time while Miss Lantz played the piano downstairs, and by repeating daily life as each practiced it, happiness kept quiet but was not allowed to leave the house.

Alice became pregnant one more time, but lost another girl to a miscarriage in the sixth month. A prolapsed uterus necessitated a hysterectomy shortly after her thirtieth birthday. There was nothing to do but accept her fate. Her day was done. She did not want to cry for the rest of her life, and she did not want it said that she was never the same after losing her two girls. So she made her recovery a prompt one and went to work with her charities as if nothing had happened. She still had two boys to show for herself, and she still had Andrew. It became important to her to keep a sense of always moving forward, not backward.

At the New Year's Eve party at the Sheffields', Mr. Sheffield suffered a mild heart attack, followed the next day by one more severe that killed him. By then, however, he had realized the ambition of his last years by throwing himself across the line of the new century and dying on the first day of 1900.

Mrs. Sheffield was happy for him that he had lived to make his goal but felt herself now without a job. When Mrs. Darlington passed away in her sleep the following year, she found herself without her dearest friend. She kept the brownstone fully staffed but spent much of her time at the Tudor house with Alice, assisting in her charity work and care of the boys. In the evening she was escorted home by Mr. Darlington, who, in the way of nature abhorring a vacuum, at length proposed marriage. They got on well enough, but the idea of spending the summer on a Canadian island wearing dungarees brought into sharp focus for Mrs. Sheffield the absurdity of marrying late in life.

Instead, she went in with Andrew and Alice on their plan to leave Boston. Andrew had found a place along the eastern shore of Maryland, a farm with an old plantation house up for sale. The three of them, and Andrew's man, Mr. Thompson, went down on the train only once to look at it before a decision was made. Then two years passed while their re-creation of a French chateau was under construction. Rory turned eleven, Autie eight. Both were excited about the woods and the river that the grownups talked about.

Alice walked around the Tudor house on the last day. The furniture had gone to Maryland. The new chateau could store away every scrap from the Tudor in one corner of its attic, so Alice was spared the sentimental agonies of leaving anything behind. The little house echoed her shoes on the bare wood floors. At the last minute, she didn't want to go. She had been so happy in this house, for a little while with Procter, for several years with Andrew and the boys. Why trade in a known world for a near-empty one? They could stay in the Tudor house. They could paint the bedroom a different color. She had the idea to mix a little violet into the white. Why hadn't she done it? Well, she could. They could bring all the furnishings back and feel like they were starting all over again.

What suddenly frightened her was change. Opening the door to change let time loose. The end result would be losing Andrew. He would go first. There was no doubt in her mind about that. Her constitution was like her mother's, delicate and contrary at times, but shod with iron. What comfort would there be in a house hardly lived in? She wanted life in the Tudor house to go on forever as it had. She wanted to go on watching for Andrew at this window, running to him at this door, walking up the creaky stairs to bed with him forever.

Mrs. Sheffield came back for Alice, lifting the hem of her skirts as she stepped up to the front porch. It was not too disconcerting to Alice because of the kind and motherly smile on her mother's face, but dressed in the black of mourning for her husband, Mother looked a little too much like the Angel of Death.

"Come along dear," Mrs. Sheffield said, taking her daughter's arm.

The last thing was the bank, jointly owned by Andrew and Mrs. Sheffield in the will. Procter Darlington came up from New York to negotiate J.P. Morgan's offer to buy them out. Alice sat across from Procter at the Parker House where they went for dinner after the deal was made. He could have been the man in the moon for all she cared.

PART FOUR

CHAPTER FORTY-SEVEN

Laura Eklund remembered the turn of the century for one event she did not care to dwell upon. She was only six at the time and not aware of the significance of the date until later, when the first day of 1900 became forever affixed to the memory she had of learning that she was to be sent away to school. It was the only time her father stood up for her against Grandmother. He insisted she remain at Flodhöjder. How lucky she was that he decided to take charge of her education himself, for she came away from his tutorials with a lasting regard for learning and a belief in the unlimited power of human thought to penetrate the mysteries of the universe. A working intellect was the best he could give of himself; as Laura remembered her father, he seemed to be weak or uninterested in many areas of life and the ordinary affairs pertaining to them. People astute in those areas frequently took advantage or imposed upon him, and it seemed to her that anyone who ever got a fair hold on his innocent and trusting nature extorted their penny's worth from the dear man.

Remembering her father sent a warm, rippling disturbance over the pond inside Laura that she had come to prefer frozen over. She was grateful he had gone gently in his sleep and that he had not lived to see the malevolent rascal his son, Karl, had become, or to see his beloved Flodhöjder laid waste by the reprehensible behavior of its new caretaker. She would have wished herself beyond the pain of those also, if such a state could be had by the living.

Making up her mind not to dwell upon the past, there was still one more task to complete before the workday was over. And so, dutifully, Laura returned to the letter she was just finishing before the thought of the year turning led to the thought of the century turning, and back to the turning of the year that her father, so dear to her, had missed.

Eric B. Miller

United States Post Office
Cecilton, Cecil County
Maryland

Jan. 10, 1922

United States Post Office
Hanging Rock, Botetourt County
Virginia

Dear Sir or Madam,
    Please be advised that mail originating from your post office bears the postmark date 1921.
    Please see that the year on your stamp is corrected immediately to 1922.

Respectfully Yours,
Laura M. Eklund, Postmistress

After checking it over several times, Laura folded the paper in thirds and tucked it into the envelope she had addressed. Not wishing to leave anything to chance, Laura weighed the letter on her scale, and finding it under one ounce as she had expected, put on a two-cent stamp and applied the postmark of Jan. 10, 1922. Then she recorded the two cents taken from the cash drawer and the stamp taken from the stamp drawer. In her logbook she recorded tomorrow's date as the day the letter would leave the Cecilton post office. Every piece of mail sent or received passed through her hands in this way, and Laura was grateful for how busy these little routines made her days.

    It was just six o'clock. Laura went to the front door and looked out to see if anyone was rushing down the street to make it to the post office before she pulled the curtains on the windows and locked the door. Passing through the office, she looked around to see that everything was in order and then locked the interior door. She remembered to go down to the basement to throw a shovel of coal into the furnace.

    Almost every business in town was set on the ground floor of an old house with rooms above, and the post office was no exception. It had a rather grand old staircase that gave a peculiar twist to her thoughts when she climbed it at the end of the day. How many children had slid down this banister? How many fashionably dressed ladies had paused to be admired on the upper landing as they touched a gloved hand on the dark mahogany baluster? How many gentlemen suitors had gazed upward, anticipating a night on the dance floor with those ladies? And how many bodies had been carried down these steps by the undertaker? Now, the hall and staircase held a scent of moldy enclosure and frayed carpet clinging to tacks.

On the wall at the top of the stairs was Laura's portrait, done when she was eighteen, when her innocence sat new on the shelf. In the great hall at Flodhöjder, among the ancestral portraits, the portrayal of her face uplifted in prayer as Joan of Arc before battle had fit in well with the flags, ancient armor, and Swedish heraldry. Here, on the landing of the old house, the dark walls seemed the very background against which Karensky the artist had set his portrait of Laura d'Arc. And here she was, plodding up the stairs, ten years older and forty-five pounds heavier, not transcending so well at all the darkness of the background.

The second and third floors were hers. It was too much for one person, but the first postmaster had had a large family. Subsequent masters and mistresses had abided by the building's federal stipulation that the upstairs not be let out as rooms. There was only her portrait, her writing desk, and her father's chair from Flodhöjder to add to the furnishings that came with the house. Karl's wife made sure of that. From the years of her long stay at the Crofts', she took only her clothing and a few books. Alice had a telephone installed on a separate line from the post office and called her every night. Mostly for that purpose, Laura put the telephone on her reading table between the two armchairs in her sitting room.

The largest bedroom had been made into a kitchen. Laura decided on soup that night. Campbell's Beefsteak Tomato. She opened a can and poured it into the saucepan and added water. To turn it into a full meal, she cut up a stalk of celery and a carrot from the icebox and boiled them on the other burner of the little electric range, then added them to the soup. There were still six Nabisco saltine crackers left in the breadbox, and a round of Edam cheese wrapped in waxed paper, from which she sliced six pieces to go with the crackers. Dessert would be four of Viola Brown's molasses cookies. She couldn't wait to be reading in her armchair, eating the cookies, but she made herself get through the soup first.

Alice called at nine o'clock as she always did. "Did you get Viola's cookies?" she asked.

"I just had one," said Laura. "I almost wish she hadn't sent them. I'm trying to watch my weight."

"That's very admirable, dear. But you look fine to me. I don't think anyone you ask would disagree."

"Well, I'm certainly not going to go around asking strange people if they think I look heavy, Mother."

"Of course not, dear. I meant if you were to."

"I'm minding my weight for myself, not for anyone else."

"There's nothing wrong with that, dear. But they are good cookies, aren't they?"

"Oh, they're very good. I'm allowing myself one a night. They make the house smell so nice. Mr. Brown put the paper bag in with the mail, so it smelled very nice in the post office today."

"Have you chosen an assistant yet?"

"No, not yet," said Laura, not really wanting to revisit the topic.

"Don't you think you should?"

"It's not as easy as you think, Mother. I don't know who would be qualified. Well, no one really is. I just have to find someone able to learn what has to be done. But that doesn't help because no one around here went very far in school."

"That's not quite true, dear, but the reason I ask—wouldn't it be nice to go to New York and stay at the apartment for a week or so? We could do some shopping, go to the theater and one of the motion picture houses—I don't know how long we can be the last ones who haven't seen a moving picture—and you aren't going to be able to go anywhere until you have an assistant, are you?"

"I know that very well, Mother. But you have Margaux. I'm sure she'd like to go to New York."

"Oh, Laura," said Alice. "I hope Margaux isn't the reason behind all this."

"No, Mother. I had to do something with my life."

"I'm so sorry about Autie, dear. I knew you were counting on him."

"I waited two years."

"I know dear," said Alice quietly.

"Then Rory was so sweet to come back from California when my father died. I thought he was going to propose. I'm sorry. I'm just feeling sorry for myself tonight."

"Well, you have every right, Laura dear. Lightning struck twice in almost the same place. But look at how well you've bounced back."

"I think Rory and I would have had a chance."

"Rory wouldn't have been good for you, dear."

"Is that why Mr. Croft sent him to London?"

"Oh, Laura darling, I don't know. He has business affairs he doesn't explain to me. Well, he tries. I just don't listen. I'm better off not knowing." Alice gave a little laugh, but the silence on the other end of the line let her know Laura was not so quick to let go of her disappointment.

"I know how you must have felt," Alice added, sympathetically. "Really, I do."

"How could you, Mummy? You've always been with one man who was perfect for you."

"Well, let's say I can easily imagine how you must have felt and how you feel now. We'll leave it at that." Remembering what her former mother-in-law, Mrs. Darlington, would have done with such an awkward terminus in the conversation, Alice then abruptly changed the subject. "Well!" she said. "Let's get practical. As soon as you find an assistant, we'll go to New York for a week, just the two of us. Lois will be there, of course, and we'll have a lot of fun. We always do, don't we? In the meantime, how are you doing with money?"

"I'm fine, Mother."

"Now what do you mean by that?"

"Well, tomorrow I'll start my quarterly report to the board of governors and send it out as soon as it's done. If there are no discrepancies in my figures, I'll get a check in a few days."

"I thought you received a salary."

"Oh no. I get a percentage of revenues."

"You can't mean postage stamps."

"Well, yes."

"So what does that mean in money?"

"Well, if sales are under one hundred dollars, I get forty percent. If sales are over a hundred but less than four hundred, I only get 33 and a third percent."

"That doesn't sound right. It should go the other way, don't you think?"

"But the base amount is larger. Anyway, it's enough to live on. I bought my Ford automobile with my own money."

"I know you did, dear. But I wish you would allow us to help you."

"You and Mr. Croft already have. Almost all my life. Now I have to be on my own."

"Oh, Laura. You know I miss you here."

"I miss you too."

Silence on both ends followed, conducted across six miles of telephone line from the Croft chateau to the post office in Cecilton. It might have inspired her father to wonder if the speed of silence through a wire could be calculated. If silence had measurable wave lengths, just as sound.

"You know who would make a good assistant postmistress?"

"Who, Mummy?"

"Delphina Brown. She's very intelligent and quick to learn, and she reads so well. Her handwriting is perfectly elegant, you know."

"I don't know, Mother. I'm not sure the town would accept a colored girl as assistant postmistress."

"But everyone knows her. Andrew can make some telephone calls."

"Oh, it doesn't depend on anyone's approval. The postal regulations say it's entirely up to me."

"Then I see it might put you in an uncomfortable position, Laura dear, but she would make a good assistant. She'd be someone you could definitely count on, and I believe she is highly thought of in town. She's a very clever girl, you know."

"Oh, everyone knows that."

"I could spare her whenever you need her, and Liza Banks seems to be a little more on track these days. Annabelle is very capable now and so good with little Emma, who isn't so little anymore. They could do without Delphina for a week."

"Excuse me, Mummy," Laura interjected. "There's someone at the door. Just a moment. I'll be right back."

Laura got up and gently placed the receiver on the seat of the armchair. She went to the window and looked down. There was a street lamp in front of the house, and she could see a horse harnessed to a wagon tied at the hitching post and a man standing in front of the post office door. When he noticed the light in the window as Laura parted the curtains, he immediately removed his hat and looked up. Laura mouthed the words, "Closed. Come back tomorrow." He seemed not to understand and pointed at the door, making sure she saw his hat was in hand on a January night. Laura thought he would be able to hear her, so she said, "Closed, come back tomorrow" loudly behind the windowpane. Just as she said it, the man raised a finger to keep her attention while he fished around in his overcoat with the other hand. He pulled out a newspaper, opened it to the last pages and held it up, pointing to something printed there. Then he pointed to the post office door again.

"I'll be right down," Laura shouted.

First, she went back to the armchair and picked up the telephone. Alice had hung up. She would call her back after she took care of the gentleman. She looked at herself in the bedroom mirror and put a little perfume behind her ears. There was really no need to change her dress. She turned on the light over the stairs and hurried down to the post office, where she turned on all the lights at the master switch behind the interior door. When she unlocked the front door, the gentleman waited on the porch until she offered him entrance.

"Thank you, miss," he said. "I'm sorry to bother you after hours. I've come for the letters you advertised. The name is Gregory Haines."

When he came into the light, Laura could see the lower part of his face was disfigured, and it gave her a start. Her eyes went directly to his eyes, which were all right and seemed to be a safe place to look without offending him with an involuntary reaction. She hoped that her smile concealed the initial shock she'd had. Not many tidewater men had gone to the war because they were needed on the farms. She had not known about the three Banks boys until after they were killed. Autie Croft was the only one she knew who had gone to the war, and she had never heard of a Haines family in the area.

"There is some paperwork to fill out," she said. "Please step around the counter."

Laura bade him sit down opposite her at her desk. She turned on the lamp and went into a drawer to locate the file of unclaimed mail. This was the first time anyone had responded to one of the notices she had placed in the newspaper.

"I will need some form of identification, Mr. Haines," she said, "as specified in the newspaper advertisement."

Mr. Haines produced a U.S. Army identity card from an inside pocket of his coat and passed it across the desk.

"That will do very well," she said.

There was a photograph on the card, but it looked like the lower portion of the face had been scratched off. The intelligent eyes and forehead were the same, so there was no need to question it, and she saw in the obscured part of the image the same damage that stood before her in person. But there was no hint of the despair and hopelessness, or perhaps the rage, that may have gone into the scratching out. She looked up at him square and honestly and made her eyes go over the warping of the skin, the dented cheekbone, the imperfect reconstruction of his nose, and an irregularity to one side of his jaw.

"We seem to be holding four letters addressed to you, Mr. Haines. One moment, please. I'll get them for you."

Laura went to the sorting area behind the main room and looked along the open rows of pigeonholes until she found the one with four letters for Haines. They were addressed in a woman's hand to Mr. Gregory Haines, General Delivery, Cecilton, Maryland. The oldest went back a year. They were all postmarked Chicago, Illinois. Laura came back to the desk and took her chair.

"Would you be so good as to sign for receipt of them? Right here on the form. Thank you. Now then, we'll have to get you on rural delivery, Mr. Haines. May I ask where you reside, sir?"

"I wouldn't expect it to be on the route," he said. "I'm out in the marshes."

"I'll show you the map. One moment again."

Laura returned from the sorting room with a large map, framed in lightweight wood, without glass. The red lines showed the RFD routes for the Cecilton post office. She placed it on the desk, and Mr. Haines stood up to look closely at one section of the Sassafras River. Laura bent over to see where he was looking. His hands were finely shaped. No wedding ring. He smelled pleasantly of soap.

"No," he said, making a circle with his finger on the map. "I'm about in here."

"Oh, I'm sorry then," she said.

Laura looked up at the same time Mr. Haines looked up, and their eyes met. In the periphery of her vision, Laura detected something different. When she turned, she was startled to see Andrew Croft standing on the other side of the counter in a full-length black overcoat, with an expression on his face she had never seen before, directed at the back of Gregory Haines. Neither of them had heard him come through the door. That was almost inconceivable to her. The door had a bell at the top that had not tinkled, and the floorboards up to the counter always creaked underfoot, but they had not. If it was a surprise to see Mr. Croft in the post office at this hour, how he could have gotten in without making a sound was baffling.

"Mr. Croft," she exclaimed.

Andrew said nothing in reply, and his eyes did not move from the back of Mr. Haines until he turned around. The question of identity between them seemed settled for both at first glance of the other, and Laura watched Mr. Croft's face return to the pleasant range of expressions she knew.

"Alice was worried," he said. "She's out in the car."

"Oh dear. I'm so sorry. There was no need to come out."

"We weren't doing anything important," Andrew said, smiling.

Turning to Mr. Haines, Laura said, "Mr. Haines, this is Mr. Croft. Would you mind if I dashed out a moment? I won't be long."

Both gentlemen graciously assented. Laura took a shawl from the back of her chair and went out to see Alice. The car wasn't in front of the post office, where she expected to see it, but was parked at the curb a few yards down. Alice opened the door for her and moved over on the seat.

"Oh Mummy, you didn't have to come check on me," Laura said, putting her arms around Alice's neck.

"It was an adventure," said Alice.

"What's this?"

Laura's hand had fallen in Alice's lap, and her fingers touched something metal.

"Oh, be careful, dear. It's loaded."

Laura looked down and saw a glint from the street light touch on a large revolver resting in the folds of Alice's dress. She took her hand away in horror. "What are you doing with a gun, Mother?"

"Andrew gave it to me when we became engaged."

Laura didn't know what to say. It wasn't the first surprise of the night. "I just wanted to come out to say good night, Mummy. And don't worry about me so much. I have to go back in now."

"All right, dear. I'll telephone you tomorrow."

"I'll want to ask you about *that!*" Laura said as she got out of the car.

Laura hurried back into the post office. Mr. Haines was saying something to Mr. Croft but stopped and stepped back from him when she came through the door. Mr. Croft showed no sign of being put off by Mr. Haines's disfigurement. If anything, Laura would have thought the two men had met before and had more to say to each other than the usual pleasantries of first acquaintanceship.

"I'll let you finish up with Mr. Haines, Laura," said Mr. Croft. "Alice will give you a call tomorrow. Good night, my dear." Turning to Mr. Haines, he added, "And good night to you, sir."

The two shook hands. Mr. Haines smiled with one side of his mouth turning up as it should and the other side pulling against scar tissue as it tried to do the same. Laura would have leaned up to give Andrew a kiss on the cheek if they had not been in the post office and she in the role of executing the duties of postmistress. Instead, she offered her hand, and in taking hold of Andrew's noticed the pocket on one side of his coat was weighted down. Just the end of a burnished handgrip showed under the flap. For the life of her, Laura could not imagine what in the world those two were doing with guns. But he was quickly out the door, and it was back to Mr. Haines and the formality of reseating herself at her desk.

"And is there anyone in the household who might be receiving mail addressed to another name, Mr. Haines?"

"No, miss."

"Are you able to get to town during business hours?"

"I'm only in town at night, miss."

"I only ask because I'm sure you would like to know if you receive mail."

"There most likely will not be such occasions," he said.

"I mean if there were."

"Thank you, miss."

"Well, we can figure out something if it happens. It's my responsibility to see the mail coming to this office is promptly delivered."

"I'm sure it is," he said, looking to the sides of the chair as if he was about to leave and checking to see if he had everything he had come with.

"Oh, the newspaper," he said. "I can use it for the fireplace."

Laura felt a comfortable warmth toward Mr. Haines and wanted him to stay longer, but she knew he had been there long enough for a first meeting. Her mind was already certain there would be another letter coming for him and there would be another chance to talk.

"Then I'll let you be on your way, Mr. Haines," she said as she stood up.

"Thank you, miss," he said, rising from his chair.

He did not turn to leave but stood looking at her with an inquiring tilt of his head, waiting.

"Oh, your newspaper," she said.

"And the letters."

"Yes, of course. I'm so sorry."

She felt so blundering and foolish and handed over his letters. At least she didn't drop any on the floor as she passed them to his hand.

"Not at all," he said. "Thank you for your kindness in opening the door for me after hours, miss."

"Eklund," said Laura.

"Miss Eklund."

Laura followed him to the door. He turned and smiled through the window as she turned the key. The effort that went into that smile could not have been better appreciated by anyone else, she thought. She watched him through the slats of the blinds, untying his horse and getting up on the wagon. A moment after Mr. Haines left the front of the post office, the headlamps of the Croft's Pierce-Arrow lit up the street, and the shining black automobile made an about-turn, bearing its two armed and dangerous desperados back to their French chateau on the tidewater. Mother with a gun. It made her laugh out loud. What a night.

Before she went upstairs to bed, Laura placed the framed map on her desktop again. It was actually a compilation of aerial photographs made by a military airplane for the geological survey. The Cecilton postal district had been bordered with a black pen and the delivery routes depicted in red lines. She did not want to deface government property, so she used only the dot of a pencil to mark where she thought Mr. Haines had put his finger. No one would notice that on so large a map. She would be the only one who knew who lived where the dot was.

CHAPTER FORTY-EIGHT

Laura slept late the next morning and went from her nightgown directly into the dress she had on the night before. Then she hurried downstairs to get the Croft mail ready for Elijah Brown, who always came in before regular hours. The mail sack from the train depot was at the back door, and she dragged it into the sorting room and spilled it out in a big pile in the middle of the floor. She spread the pile around with one hand and picked with the other. Anything for the Croft farm went in one box—Elijah Brown,

Earling Cooper, Kenneth Banks, Lamont Eldridge. Lots of foreign newspapers today, all for the Crofts. When she had the Croft mail out of the pile and in one box, she got up off the floor and brought the box to her desk. She counted the newspapers to go as one entry in the logbook and fished out the letters and sorted again by family, recording each one.

The little bell on the front door tinkled, and the smiling face of Elijah Brown appeared as he removed the battered old hat from his bald head.

"Good morning, Mr. Brown," she said, pleasantly. "Not quite ready yet."

"Good morning, Miss Laura. I don't smell no coffee. You ain't made it yet?"

"No, I'm sorry, sir. I haven't had a chance."

"Well, that likely to be due to you got no help here," he said, looking around the place. "I thought they give you a 'sistant."

"I've been too busy to get around to finding someone, Mr. Brown," Laura said, not lifting her eyes from the letters she was flipping over as she recorded each one in the log. Of note was one to Alice from Lois in New York City. One from the Bank of England to Mr. Croft that she had to put on the scale and check against her book on foreign postage. One from the art gallery in New York to Liza Banks. Ginny Cooper's sister in Detroit finally wrote back.

"Delphina has one today," said Laura.

"Maybe the one she been waitin' for. She want to go up to the Johns Hopkins for more schoolin'. So, what we doin' for coffee this mornin'?"

Laura gave him one of her tight little laughs, careful not to make it sound too dismissive.

"Well, you sit right there and go on with you work, Miss Laura," he said.

Elijah went out the door, and in a little while, just as she was finishing up with the Croft mail, he came back with a steaming pot of coffee and set it down on the table Laura had placed in the little lobby on the other side of the counter.

"This come with compliments from Mrs. Able's place down the street."

"That was very nice of her," said Laura.

"Cream and sugar too," he said, pulling a screw-top jar out of each side pocket of his coat.

"Well, you have a cup, Mr. Brown. I've got your mail ready. Do you have your bag handy?"

"Right here," he said, lifting the Croft mail carrier onto the counter. "Not much goin' out today."

He emptied out the bag on the counter and began putting in the newspapers and letters that Laura brought over from her desk.

"Do you like drivin' your new Ford car 'round town?" he asked.

"Very much," she said. "I'm glad they geared the new models higher."

"Wouldn't know much 'bout that."

Laura took a piece of scratch paper and started drawing levers, sprockets, and gears with a pencil. "Here's how they did it."

Elijah finished his coffee and left the post office better informed about the improvements over the older model Ford he was driving, but Laura watched him shaking his head a little as he went through the door.

Maybe she had not explained gear ratios in the best way. It always made her nervous when someone bent over too close, and the presence of anyone within arm's length sent all her senses out of whack, no matter how much she tried to concentrate on what she was doing. She always worried that she might smell like the breakfast she had just cooked. Last summer, her upper floors smelled like the wooden attic. So did her hair and her clothes. It was so embarrassing. Would anyone really notice? Or was it only the plague of her self-consciousness? It made her wonder how she could ever live closely with a man in a matrimonial situation. She stopped straightening up her desk for a moment to think about Gregory Haines.

It was surprising to her that she had not noticed how close she had been to him looking over the map. Maybe she could be comfortable with someone like Gregory. He seemed comfortable with her. People could live alone in the woods because they didn't like having other people around, but Gregory did not seem to be that way. People could also live in the woods because they thought no one would want them. All it would take for a sensitive man would be a disfigurement to make him feel that no one wanted him. He would be grateful if a girl loved him. If his wound had given him a compassionate heart, he would be gentle and not bitter. What about the letters from Chicago? Were they asking him to come home? His mother would always love him no matter what. Laura suddenly remembered to tell Elijah to thank Viola for her molasses cookies. She made a note for the next day and tucked it into the blotter on her desk.

It was only seven o'clock. The rest of the mail from the depot could sit on the floor a little longer. She had almost two hours before she had to open, and she plodded her way back up the grand staircase. Breakfast was a sweet roll from the bakery, hot porridge, a Stayman apple, four pieces of bacon on buttered toast, and warmed-up fried potatoes from the night before. She did not want to smell of bacon and fried potatoes all day, so she washed her hair when she was in the bathtub. On Sunday she would have to do laundry.

At nine o'clock, Laura opened the post office for business. The logging of the mail, the sorting, and the bundling were done just in time for Jerry Conrow's appearance on the back porch. He didn't like to be kept waiting to start his route. Dr. Steeple, the veterinary surgeon who was always out at the farms where Jerry Conrow lived, had told her the post office carriage was usually parked behind his house by three o'clock in the afternoon. Mr. Conrow never came back to the post office before five, so she didn't know why he was so impatient.

He was tall and middle-aged with gray hair and a gray mustache. He always wore a brown suit and a bowler hat. If she was still recording the mail to be delivered, he would stand by her desk waiting but not saying a word. Laura knew he did it on purpose to make her nervous. After he left on his route, she always felt how much it took out of her to pretend she was not bothered by how difficult a man he was.

First, he delivered around town on foot, then he took the horse and carriage to the farms and across the bridge to Galena. There he delivered but also had the responsibility of picking up mail from the box outside the hardware store. He was also authorized to supply postage stamps to the dry goods shop that served as another mail drop on that side of the river and to sell stamps on the road as he went. It was a lot of recordkeeping. That he could perform addition and subtraction correctly was the only good thing Laura could say about Jerry Conrow.

One morning, Laura told him his accounts were a penny short on the previous day. He must have stopped at the bank in Cecilton on his way back because he brought in his returns that night in pennies just to spite her. He came into the post office pleasantly enough and put his accounting notebook on her desk with the heavy bag of pennies beside it. Laura did not know what to do but did not say anything to him. She just looked at the bag of pennies that she would have to count. If he had paused a moment before he turned around and left, he would have seen her frown.

She wondered if Delphina Brown would have better luck with Jerry Conrow, and she suddenly wanted to get away to New York with Alice in the worst way. All she needed to do was to find someone who could work the post office for a week and sack Jerry Conrow for her.

Just having him off on his rounds made Laura feel better. She fixed herself a cup of Mrs. Able's coffee with plenty of cream and sugar and took it to her desk. She didn't mind at all getting up for customers at the counter while she worked on her quarterly report. It was nice to make people feel welcome with a pleasant smile and advise them of parcel post rates, weigh their letters, or do whatever they needed. Laura was very surprised that she turned out not to be shy and introverted after all and to see that she was getting to know everyone in the postal district.

Those who never came into the post office Laura imagined by their mail. Periodicals on needlework suggested that Mrs. Hopkins might be a little old lady, needlepointing cushions for her grandchildren. Advertisements for the theater season in Baltimore brought Mr. Teledare to mind as a prosperous farmer with one set of formal wear hanging in his closet. The lightly perfumed letters to Mr. Silforth Case that came from western Maryland, beautifully addressed in a feminine hand, might be the result of a romance from last summer's well-talked-about camp meeting out there.

There were other associations between handwriting and names that formed in her mind since she had become postmistress. Stories arose naturally between the outgoing mail and mail returning. There were solicitations, applications, bills, and inquiries going back and forth between people who were only names to her. Ned Granger wanted to go to Villanova College in Philadelphia. Betty Hampton spent a lot of money on patent medicines. Charlene Berry had begun to mark her mail from Mr. Calvin Atkins "Return to Sender" in strong capitals. What did he do wrong?

Some of the correspondence defied the powers of her imagination when it should have been the easiest to conjecture. Not long into her first months as postmistress, she noticed in the outgoing Croft mail, the repetition of monthly letters addressed in Mr. Croft's hand to a Mr. Hinkley in care of general delivery, Ithaca, New York. It looked like a bank draft was inside and nothing else. Holding it up to the light was all she could do. A check. She could not make out how much money was going to Ithaca, New York, or why.

The sparse amount of mail to and from Galena on the other side of the river was a virtual accounting of the ruin going on at Flodhöjder: bank statements and billing invoices to her brother, Karl; dress and jewelry catalogs for his wife, Camille; letters to and from attorneys; numerous letters from the Wilmington Trust Bank; and reports from land surveyors. Her best guess was that Karl was selling off land to pay the bills. Laura was glad she was out of it. If she was ever tempted to open and read the correspondence she handled every day, the temptation never extended to what came and went from Flodhöjder. All interest in the life of her brother and his wife was gone from the moment she drove off the grounds for the last time.

The truck carried back to the Croft chateau only her portrait, a few bags, her father's chair, and her writing desk. Most precious were her father's astronomical binoculars, which she trusted only to herself, in her lap in the back seat of the Crofts' Silver Ghost as they followed the truck back across the river.

Father called them his field glasses, but they were nothing like any field glasses she had ever seen. They were a foot long, with outer lenses four inches in diameter, converging in two large barrels down to the eyepieces. It felt like fifteen or twenty pounds in her hands. When she was little, Father would sit on the ground on summer nights, bending forward to act as a human tripod, with the binoculars on the top of his head squashing his hat. He would orient himself toward the moon while she climbed up on his back and looked through the eyepieces, her small hands holding the barrels as tight and steady as they could.

Those hands were so disappointing to her now. They were as large as Father's but lacking grace, like peasant hands. She noticed them every time she watered the African violet in the window. Alice brought it to her one day in a red clay flowerpot from her greenhouse. She showed her how to water it, lifting up the lower leaves carefully with her last two fingers to get the watering spout under. Alice had big hands, too, but her fingers were long and slender. She said Laura should feel a delicate mist the leaves seemed to emit as they drew nourishment from the watered earth under them. But her fingers were too thick, and she never felt the misting. Taking it on faith, and wanting Alice to believe in her, she always said she could feel the mist. She admired how well Alice's hands served her watering in the greenhouse, serving tea, holding the bridle of a horse, or writing short bread-and-butter notes at her desk. They were hands as confident in themselves as Alice was with Alice.

Walking up the dark staircase to the second floor after she closed the doors of the post office in the evening was always hard because of the mood that settled upon her. All day she had been busy at the counter helping people, smiling, and feeling completely happy. There hadn't been a moment for her quarterly report, but she liked it that way because it saved work for tomorrow. It was only after she closed the post office and mounted the stairs to her rooms above that the little house of cards that work built fell down.

The bright spot was a letter from Autie at Fort Riley. She placed it on the telephone table and went into the kitchen to make Campbell's Beefsteak Tomato Soup again.

Alice called at nine o'clock. Laura had Autie's letter in her hands, looking at his penmanship and imagining him, but she broke off right away to pick up the receiver.

"Mother, what are you doing with a gun?" she asked, trying not to laugh.

"Oh, we just have them around."

"Do you know how to work it?"

"Certainly, darling."

"What?"

"Well, I wouldn't have a gun if I didn't know how to work it, would I?"

"I've never seen you with a gun before, in all the years I lived there, Mother."

"I haven't needed it lately," said Alice.

"Oh Mummy, you shouldn't have come here last night. I feel so bad about that."

"We were worried about you. You should never open the door after the post office is closed. Isn't that a rule?"

"Well, yes, but there was no reason to worry. He was a very respectable gentleman. He'd been in the war. Mr. Croft must have told you about his face."

"No, he didn't say anything. He just said he knew him. What about his face?"

"It's disfigured, I suppose you would call it. He must have been badly wounded. It's only unsettling at first. But he's very nice, and you get used to it as you would to anyone's face."

"Well, you shouldn't drop your guard, dear, no matter how nice someone seems to be. And you shouldn't open the door after hours. Will you promise me that?" She waited. "Laura?"

"All right, Mother. Unless it's Mr. Haines. He only comes into town at night. I'm sure it's because of his face."

"That's the only exception."

"Then, yes, I promise."

"Good. Now then, have you been thinking about an assistant?"

"I'm still thinking, Mummy. Even if I get someone, it would take a few weeks to train him."

"Have you settled on a man then?"

"No, but I need someone to—this is just between the two of us, Mother—I need someone to fire Mr. Conrow. He's getting to be insufferable."

"But then you'll need to find another mail carrier."

"I know."

"Can't you just put up with Mr. Conrow a little longer?"

"I suppose I can," said Laura, unable to keep discouragement out of her voice. She thought she would get better advice from a woman who knew how to handle a gun.

"But that doesn't mean the assistant won't have the same trouble with him. And what if Mr. Conrow makes him so mad he walks out? I mean if the assistant postmaster walks out—not Mr. Conrow. Mr. Conrow would never walk out. He's done every day by three o'clock and hides the post office carriage behind his house while he takes a nap until five. There'd be no one to keep the post office open until I got back if the assistant quit."

"Then I must bring up Delphina Brown again, dear," said Alice. "She can be very diplomatic. I'm sure she can polish up Mr. Conrow. And I can tell you, Laura, if he is an agitation to Delphina, he's as good as gone. Colored girl or not."

"Oh, I'd like that," Laura said.

It was as warming as Campbell's Beefsteak Tomato to hear Alice laugh, and it did send Delphina to the head of the line in her thoughts about appointing an assistant. Everyone knew she came from the Crofts. She would not be on her own as a colored girl assistant postmistress. She would have the backing of the gun-toting desperados.

"Do you think she'd want the job, Mummy?"

"Well, I'll send her over tomorrow, and you can ask her yourself."

"Oh, please don't. I have to think it over. I just don't know."

"Then take your time, dear. I'm certainly not going to push you into doing anything you aren't ready to do. I know you take your responsibilities very seriously."

That was exactly the problem. Laura realized after she got off the telephone with Alice that she was this way about every decision, and never more so than if the wrong choice would cause embarrassment. She decided to put off deciding a little longer.

Autie said in his letter that he had decided to stay in the army. He liked training new officers. He said promotions were not likely in the peacetime army, but he was content with the captaincy they gave back to him. It removed him from some lesser duties, so he had more free time. The officer corps that would run the next war was in his hands, he wrote. Laura made a note to ask him in her letter back why he thought there would be another war. The last one was supposed to be the war to end all wars. The importance of that statement was something she got from the sad testimony of Gregory Haines's face. Even a war to end all wars might not be enough consolation for him.

Reading between the lines, Laura could tell that Autie saw no hope for a happy life in his marriage to Margaux, although he never came out and said what was wrong with it. She already knew that Autie took pride in having a pretty wife, something like the pride of ownership she had in her Ford automobile. But she found it strange that he rarely mentioned Margaux or the boy, Robbie, or the new baby, Edward, as if they had been signed over to his mother and off his shoulders. He was obviously going to let the marriage lie. That was the Autie she knew.

Laura closed her eyes and rested her head in the wing of the armchair. What she saw in Autie might go just as well for herself, she thought. He was clinging to the very agent of his loneliness. The longer he held on to an unhappy marriage, the more his loneliness became complete, just as the more fervently she disallowed the idea of a man and family for herself, the more she needed to suppress the desire for it in order to go on living. Unwittingly, she and Autie had fallen into being alike. His letters were always signed "Affectionately, Autie." They were both doing well without having what they most wanted, she thought. For him, the army was the substitute. For her, it was the postmistress job and owning her own automobile.

The new Ford gave her a certain standing in the community, and its importance could not be overestimated. For the first time in her life, she was earning her own money and was part of a community as an independent woman. Even at twenty-seven and losing her figure, she could hold her head up high. The customers she had at the post office might regard the position of postmistress as an institutional preserve for the spinster or widow, but she thought she looked a step up from that type of woman, and it was a distinction she wanted to maintain.

At times she would have been glad for widowhood. It would have made her less conspicuous and easier for people to understand. It would have meant that she had once been wanted and asked for, that she had lived with a man and knew everything married women know. For herself, at least, she would have memories. As it was, how could she imagine what she did not know about marriage any more than she could imagine people from their handwriting? How wrong she had proved to be about that sometimes.

Living with disappointment had finally worn her out, but she did not want to become small and bitter. Mr. Croft had sent Rory away to England, ruining her chance with him, and the little Belgian girl had taken Autie out from under her nose when they were writing letters and as much as promised to each other. The last straw was Karl taking Flodhöjder away from her and her sister.

Laura talked to Charlotte in Saint Louis every week on the telephone and found her a good example of what bitterness could do to a person. Every conversation was brought back to how they had been swindled out of their birthright. Laura tried to explain to her the comfort she had found in *Concept and Practice in Buddhism*. How a book like that had come to sit on the shelves of the tiny Cecilton library must have been fate—or by the fiat of a merciful God—but of course that wouldn't make any sense to a real Buddhist.

CHAPTER FORTY-NINE

Laura let the rest of January go by without coming to a decision on an assistant. February brought bad weather, and one day, after his deliveries around Cecilton, Jerry Conrow came back to the post office to say he would not be crossing the bridge to Galena in the snowstorm approaching. The best Laura could do was to make him stay in the office while she took the mail to Galena herself. Even the spectacle of her in full view through the window—bundled up in heavy coat, boots, hat, scarf, and driving gloves—did not bring Mr. Conrow to the door. Neither did watching her slip on the ice putting the bags on the carriage nor the difficulty she had persuading the horse to set out in the snow.

Laura returned from Galena late that night in the driving snow. As she unhitched the horse and led him to the livery stable and trudged back to the post office through a foot of snow with a red nose and frozen fingers, Laura began to resolve her difficulty in coming to a decision about hiring an assistant. And when she found a communication from Jerry Conrow on her desk informing her that he had fulfilled his obligation to hold down the office, expressed succinctly enough by a scrap of paper tucked into the blotter with nothing on it but the words "Five o'clock," it was as if she were standing in St. Peter's Square as white smoke rose from the chimney of the Sistine Chapel. Delphina Brown would be the next assistant postmistress of Cecilton, Maryland.

Laura did her shopping and errands around town, grateful for the hour difference between the opening of local shops and the federal idea of a proper hour to begin doing business. It was so convenient living in a town, and Cecilton had grown into a bustling little place with a firehouse, newspaper, bakery, filling station, hotel, two restaurants for white people, and Mrs. Able's for the Negroes. There was talk of a Ford dealership coming next year. She had heard that Galena was bigger at one time, but the railroad changed that when it was built on the Cecilton side of the river. With that came the depot and the farmers' storage warehouse that made Cecilton grow.

The rest she knew from her own time, when the Crofts came down from New England and had their chateau built. She remembered watching through her father's binoculars from the hill at Flodhöjder as the structure rose. The Crofts brought their two little boys over to meet the family. Father had invited them despite Grandmother not being keen on new people. Laura remembered Rory and Autie as big boys even though she was the same age as Autie. But most of all, she remembered how much she wanted to have a mother when she saw Alice with them.

She wondered why Alice never had any more children. Judging from how readily she had been taken in and taken over, Laura knew Alice must have wanted a daughter very much, however much she never talked about it.

When Laura got back from shopping, Delphina was standing at the door, and her father was sitting in the driver's seat of the Crofts' Model T, leaning back with his hat down over his eyes. Delphina helped get her shopping bags upstairs.

"I hope you'll like the post office," Laura said as she put a few things in the icebox. "The work is very challenging, and it may take you some time to understand how to do it. Most people think it's just working at the counter, but it's not. You may be surprised at all that goes on behind the scenes. But you're a bright girl."

"Yes, Miss Laura," said Delphina.

"Let's go downstairs and get started. We have to hurry now before Mr. Conrow comes in. He's our carrier. He doesn't like to get a late start."

Delphina followed Laura down the old staircase and into the post office. Laura thought she would have to make allowance for Delphina dawdling or looking around the rooms of the post office, but the girl was right with her. In short order, they had the contents of the heavy mail bags from the train depot spread out on the floor in the back room and were separating out the Croft mail.

"They get most of the newspapers, but you have to check," Laura said.

Delphina was quick. In one motion she smoothed her dress and sat down on the floor with her legs under her. Laura's knees would not bear that much of a bend, and she sat on the floor with both legs straight out. With Delphina there, she had to keep pulling her dress down to cover her knees. She could not help noticing Delphina's lovely hands and her hair tied tightly back out of her way and how lithe she was. In a few minutes of working together, the mail for the Croft estate was gathered, sorted by family, and on Laura's desk ready to be logged. Elijah came in, looking ready for the warmth of the post office after half an hour dozing out in the chilly car. Delphina did not acknowledge her father and kept her head down as she recorded each piece of mail in a neat block print as Laura had demonstrated.

"We're almost ready for you, Mr. Brown," Laura said. "You can leave the outgoing mail on the counter there."

"Finished," she said, just as Laura had gone to the counter for the empty Croft mailbag.

"Let me check you," Laura said.

She was surprised, looking from each piece of mail to its entry in the book and placing it in the mailbag. Everything was right.

"Very good, Delphina."

"Atta girl," said Elijah. "She take after Viola, Miss Laura. Don't take long to see that, do it?"

"Go home now, Daddy," said Delphina. "We have work to do."

Elijah turned to Laura. "I ain't had my coffee yet, Miss Laura. You gonna let you 'sistant turn me out with no coffee?"

"There's coffee at home, Daddy. Go on out of here. We're busy."

"Well, I don't want to raise no ire 'round here. I'll go."

Laura went around the counter to hold the door for him and was glad he left that easily. Delphina was already back in the sorting room, and most of the mail remaining on the floor was sorted when Laura rejoined her.

"I have in-town here, out-of-town over there, grouped by north, south, east, west. Would you like me to log it in now, Miss Laura?"

"Why yes," Laura said.

The girl's speed was dazzling. Laura heard Mr. Conrow coming in the back door. The first thing he said was, "What's she doing here?"

Evidently the two knew each other, and introductions were not necessary.

"Delphina is in training to be assistant postmistress," said Laura.

Delphina looked up and nodded at Mr. Conrow, then returned to the logbook, flipping over the envelopes swiftly and methodically. Mr. Conrow turned away with a look of disgust and exhaled his next breath with derisive impatience.

"Finished," said Delphina.

Again, Delphina's records checked against each piece correctly. The mail was bound with string and loaded to the carriage, and a few minutes later Mr. Conrow was on his way, his earliest-ever departure. The rest of the day was waiting on customers, with Delphina first observing, then assisting, then taking full charge. There were only a few times she needed help, but she caught on quickly when Laura directed her to the manuals on the shelf behind her desk. By the end of the week, it was clear that there was nothing Delphina liked better than manuals. Laura had time enough to complete her quarterly report and had begun to think she could get out and fly away to New York with Alice sooner than she would have expected. Laura was very pleased that Delphina had opened up that possibility. It made her choice of the working life seem not so deeply carved in stone. At the same time, it made her afraid of wishing again for a different life, the one she had wanted before she drew the shroud of the post office around her.

CHAPTER FIFTY

Only a week after Delphina's first day of training, Alice met Laura on the platform of the train station in Cecilton. It was a brisk morning in March, and Alice was in a long, stylish black coat with matching scarf and cloche hat. Her hair was let down under it and came to her shoulders. Laura had a woolen knitted hat pulled down over her ears and a puffy short jacket that only came to her waist, letting her skirts blow around in the wind.

"Oh, Laura dear, we're definitely going to do some shopping this week. Is one suitcase all you're bringing?"

Elijah Brown was just then bringing up two more pieces of luggage to the platform to make a total of six for Alice.

"Half of those are empty," Alice said. "I knew we'd be going shopping. Come and kiss me, dear. You didn't walk from the post office, did you?"

"It's not far," Laura said, putting a mittened hand on Alice's shoulder and leaning up to kiss her.

"Your nose is all red. Elijah was just at the post office dropping off Delphina. He could have brought you."

"I wasn't ready yet, Mother."

"Well, I hope you're ready now. Let's get away and have a good time. I have every confidence in Delphina."

"So do I," said Laura, her only doubts being now about herself, remembering it had taken her a full two months to learn what Delphina had learned in one week.

"You must be a very good teacher, dear," said Alice. "Maybe *that's* what you were meant to do. I don't know why I never thought of it. Oh, Laura darling, it seems like ages since I've seen you."

When they were seated on the train with their coats and hats in their laps, Alice gave Laura a warm embrace and held her hand.

"Oh, I know you want to be independent, dear, but that isn't going to stop me from wanting to do everything I can for you."

"I can do everything myself. You don't have to worry about me, I'm fine."

"Well, it can't be much fun."

"I don't see anything wrong with my life, Mother."

"No, of course not. I just think of you living in that big old house alone—I want you to be happy, dear."

"But I am," Laura insisted.

"Well then, I'll let you sit in the big old house to your heart's content. But I'm still going to point out opportunities—and who knows, you might meet someone."

"I meet people every day at the post office, Mother."

"I mean someone different. Lois knows so many interesting people in New York."

Laura lowered her head and quietly asked, "Didn't Margaux want to come with us?"

"She's already been to New York," said Alice.

There was a tightening of Alice's jaw, and she turned to look out the window with her lips pressed firmly together. Turning back to Laura with her warmest smile, she said, "I'm glad it's just the two of us. I've missed you so, dear."

When they got to Penn Station in New York, they sat down for coffee and a plate of cinnamon buns. A cigarette boy went by, and Alice said, "Let's be naughty." So they bought a package of Turkish Delights and smoked as they drank hot coffee out of paper cups and looked up to the dome of the station and around at the people going by. Alice said she liked to acclimate to the pace of the city before they hit the streets. The Negro porter watching the cart with their luggage was offered a seat, and Alice engaged him with questions. For Laura, part of getting used to the city again was getting used to Alice talking to anyone who came along. She wished she could be more like Alice, so confident and free to be herself. Being around her was probably good for her. She *did* want to have fun. She *did* want to be in love again. She did not want to hide herself away anymore. But there seemed to be nothing she could do about it from a hiding place.

Lois met them at the door of the apartment, looking as trim as she did more than a year ago when Laura had last seen her. Her hair was still cut short like a man, and she wore a man's pleated khaki trousers with an open white blouse over a man's cotton undershirt that hid very little. Her loose breasts flopped around so much in the excitement of receiving visitors that it was hard for Laura to look in her direction.

"Your luggage arrived two hours ago," she said. "Really, Alice, you should have told me you were moving in. Laura, darling, you look marvelous."

Lois hugged Laura and had her out of her coat and hat in a moment.

"I put your suitcases in the studio. And I pulled out the trundle bed."

"I'll take that one," said Alice.

"No, Mother, your feet will stick out."

"I like it that way. It's like camping out."

"I'll let you two fight it out," said Lois. "Do you want some coffee and sandwiches? Come on in the kitchen. I was just going to make something. What took you so long? I was getting worried."

"We walked around a little. You know, planning out what we wanted to do," said Alice, sitting down with Laura at the kitchen table while Lois put the water on and went to the icebox. "I want to do some shopping for Laura since we're here. I think we should get our hair done, too. What do you think?"

"Long overdue," said Lois.

"I didn't know we were getting our hair done, Mother."

"You see? Lois thinks it's a good idea too, dear," Alice said, putting a gentle hand over Laura's. "And one of these days we should go over to the children's home and look in on Miss Lantz—I have to remember to stop calling her that. And then we should do some galleries. I'd like to see what's new."

"Not much," said Lois. "Well, you'll have to go see, but I can tell you, nothing tops the Armory Show in '13. New was really new back then. Remember how we walked out of there, Alice?"

"Stunning, wasn't it!" Turning to Laura, Alice added, "Andrew didn't like anything."

"But since you're trafficking in art, you should know what's the rage these days," Lois called over her shoulder from the icebox.

"Liza's paintings," said Alice, aside to Laura.

"I saw one of hers in the Gallery of Modern Art a while ago. Remember the one you showed me that looks like the world's going up in smoke? Very powerful. The gallery bought it. Unheard of for a museum to buy a painting new from a dealer, but what a picture. You wonder what's going on in that sweet lady's mind."

"Oh, Liza's perfectly all right now. Well, mostly. But she wants to stay on the farm. Her husband really wouldn't like New York, and she has the two little girls. So that's as far as we've gotten with the itinerary. Children's home, shopping, and galleries. You can come with us if you like, Lois."

"Have to beg off. Thanks. Work to do. I've kept the world waiting for my art too long."

"But we're taking up your studio."

"No trouble. I'm at the thinking part, and I can do that anywhere. Mostly at McSorley's, I admit, but the company's stimulating."

"Lois had a beer with Teddy Roosevelt there one time. Did I ever tell you that?"

"No."

"I thought I did."

"I would have remembered *that*, Mother."

"Oh, I wanted to ask you, Lois. What about the rally on Saturday? The Socialist Workers of America."

"I wouldn't go to that, Alice."

"I thought it would be good to show Laura a protest march. Remember how exciting it was when we marched for suffrage? Those were exhilarating times, don't you think? I thought we could march a little bit with the Socialists." Then turning to Laura, she said, "They always have signs to hand out for the marchers at these rallies, Laura."

Lois put some plates of cheese and cold roast beef on the table and turned back for the coffee pot and cups. "I wouldn't go, Alice. There's going to be trouble."

"But there's always the chance of that."

"No, I mean more than ever happened to us."

Lois brought a chair up beside Laura and sat down across from Alice. "It's going to be mostly men—miners, and steel workers, and such. Not ladies from uptown in white dresses marching in a procession. The men have been coming into town for the past few days, hundreds of them, and the papers have been talking about evidence of foreign influence. That means the police will be looking for a fight. People are going to get beaten up."

"They wouldn't attack women, would they?" Laura asked.

"Sure they would."

Alice looked at Laura. "Maybe someone from the rally will drop in and tell us about it, dear."

"I'm sure someone will," said Lois. "I've been getting some young hotheads from NYU on salon nights lately. They're kind of disruptive, to tell the truth. Blame it on Russia. I've been tempted to call the police myself."

"Well, maybe these two country girls can still get in a little shopping today before the stores close," said Alice, looking a little disappointed but willing to take another tack.

"I think I'd rather stay in tonight, Mother."

"Of course, dear. Then let's the three of us put together a wonderful dinner."

"Not much in the house," said Lois. "I thought you'd be going out."

"All right then. Get your baskets, Lois, and we'll go to the greengrocer, the butcher shop, and the bakery. Can we find wine and spirits around here?"

"No getting around your determination to get arrested, is there, Alice?" Lois said with a laugh.

The evening was finally over when the three women got down to the bottom of a bottle of genuine Irish whiskey. Alice paid a handsome price for it in a basement cavern on the wharf end of Houston Street, and they drank all of it. The dishes and pots and pans were left soaking in the sink while they sipped away and talked intimately by candlelight at Lois's salon table as she played solitaire. And finally to bed in the early hours of the next day.

Lois had moved her easels and canvases to the side and cleared the bed of her paints and palettes. To make room to pull out the trundle bed, her plaster sculptures were pushed back against the wall. When Alice turned on the light, Laura could not help averting her eyes from the male and female figures, which stood three and four feet high in proud, shameless nakedness. Alice paused, looked them over, then went closer, getting over the trundle bed on her hands and knees to examine their detail.

"Mother!" Laura exclaimed.

"I'm sorry dear, it's just that I recognize some of the faces," she said, laughing. "Lois is a wonderful sculptress, don't you think? And anyway, who hasn't seen a penis?"

"I don't feel very well."

"Maybe you should go to the bathroom and throw up, Laura dear. You'll feel better."

When Laura came back to the bedroom, she did feel better. She had never had more alcohol than two glasses of wine except for that terrible night in the woods at college. Alice had settled the question of the trundle bed. She was sitting in her nightgown in the middle of it, laughing as she draped her undergarments over the extravagant penises projecting from the male figures along the wall. Within easy reach were also the plaster breasts of the female figures, across which Alice had laid out her dress.

"Utilitarian art," she said. "Lois could sell a million of these."

Laura got into bed and moved to the side next to the trundle bed. Alice got up to turn off the light and started laughing when she tried to get herself under the covers.

"Are your feet sticking out, Mummy?"

Alice tried to answer but was having trouble with outbursts of laughter. Laura could not remember seeing her drink as much as she had tonight. She was a big woman, and it was surprising to see her showing the effects.

"You can come up and sleep with me, Mummy."

"No, I like roughing it. It reminds me of when I was first with Andrew."

"You never told me about that."

"It was on a camping trip. I fell in love with him at first sight. There were bears in the woods, and he was so protective of me. It was a canoe trip actually. A church canoe trip. Up a river. No, down a river. I forget what river it was. I don't remember very much now. It was so long ago. I just remember how handsome he was. That was when he gave me the pistol—in case we ran into bears. There, now you know."

Laura let the quiet of the room descend. There were questions she might have wanted to ask, but Alice had stopped talking in a way that seemed purposeful, as if she had noticed a door she had carelessly left open and wondered if the cat got out. Laura tried to think of other times they had talked and if Alice had ever told anything about herself. All she could think of was the train from Rhode Island, when Alice brought her home from college and was trying to comfort her. She had said virginity didn't count for anything, and then she had said she had nullified her virginity by herself. Laura did not want to make too much of it. Alice was happy, and she let people infer that she always had been. There was nothing to learn from the face value of that. Questioning the world was the legacy of her father. But what were the questions? Strong women never told you how they got that way.

"Mummy?" Laura said into the dark.

"Yes, dear."

"I've never seen a penis."

'Oh, I was just talking to myself. Don't think I wasn't given a jolt when the light came on. Lois's work can be, well, very frank. But don't worry, dear. When the right penis comes along, I'm sure it will make an appearance. At least you'll know what it is. One might just walk in the door while we're here. I'd be so happy for you."

"I'm not going to expect it."

"That's exactly when it happens, my darling."

"Don't you think we should go to the rally?"

"No, I think Lois is right."

It was very pleasant being in bed and talking in the dark, letting the talk go where it would. There were no facial expressions to read or the distractions of fidgeting hands. The distance between them might have been a mile or the space crossed by a whisper. Sound traveling without wires from one heart to another heart through the medium of darkness. Words thrown by one and caught by the other.

"Are you afraid of going?"

"Certainly."

"I didn't think you were afraid of anything, Mummy."

Alice laughed. "Oh, Laura."

"I mean, you've been arrested before."

"I should tell you a few things about that, Laura dear. I don't particularly mind the thought of being arrested. In fact, it was a badge of honor in those days, and I welcomed it. Some of the women were sorely treated in jail—not me, but some of the others. I probably would have welcomed that. No, I really can't say that. They were treated very badly."

There were a few moments of silence. Only a fire engine siren, downstairs, outside, moving away. The Doppler effect. Father had made funny sounds to show her how sound behaved. There was science behind everything perceptible, he had always said.

"Mummy?"

"I'm sorry, dear, I was just thinking of someone I knew from jail. I forget what I was going to say."

"About getting arrested."

"Oh yes. I wasn't afraid of that, or what might happen to me in jail, because my heart was in it. I believed in what we were marching for. And you see, we won, didn't we? Women can vote now, and the politicians have to listen to us. I don't know anything about socialists or the Workers' Party, and I don't know what will happen at the rally. But I do know that I shouldn't risk my life for anything I don't believe in, and certainly not yours, just for the sake of having an experience. And that's the other thing I wanted to suggest you think about before you do anything without thinking. That didn't sound right. I've had too much to drink. Are you still awake?"

"Of course I am."

"I shouldn't keep you up. Well, one last thing, Laura, and this I mean very seriously. You have to judge how much an experience is worth. That includes the experience of being lonely. There can be a purpose behind it, and you can give it all the time it needs, but I hope you'll know when the purpose has been served."

The silence came from Laura this time. She was not sure what an honest reply would be.

"I've been thinking about somebody, Mother."

"Who? Someone at the post office?"

"Yes, a man."

"Well, you must know everybody in Cecilton and Galena by now, and I haven't heard a peep from you about anybody, so it must be the one you scared us to death with."

"Yes, it's him."

"Do you know anything about him?"

"No. I just think he and I might be alike."

"That would be nice, wouldn't it?"

The words were getting further apart, and there was more silence in the dark than words. It made Laura think about atoms and the universe. She was glad she had thrown up. Lois knew her way around the city. She could hold her liquor. So could Alice. She could keep her thoughts coherent. Alice and Lois were such good friends. She wished. She wished what? Was darkness made of dark atoms?

"But you don't have to be alike, Laura. You can fall in love with anyone. You shouldn't limit yourself to men you think are like you. It can be very exciting to fall in love with someone you have to work out understandings with. Andrew and I aren't at all alike. But we understand each other. But anyway, I can tell you this much about your night caller at the post office— Laura?"

"Gregory Haines."

"Yes, Gregory Haines. Andrew trusts him. He didn't say why. That's all I could find out. Andrew doesn't like to talk about people behind their backs or listen to gossip. I suppose it's a good principle to stand on, but it makes it so difficult. That's why men are so obtuse. They never know what's going on."

Then Alice started laughing and they got silly again.

The next day they walked into the hairdressers down the street and got Dutch bob haircuts. Laura was quite anxious seeing twenty-four inches of her hair fall to the floor, but Alice was thoroughly enjoying it. From one barber chair to the next, Laura asked, "Are you sure Mr. Croft won't be upset?"

"Everything I do is all right with Mr. Croft," Alice replied.

"I suppose I don't have anyone to account to either," Laura said doubtfully, holding up the hand mirror.

"Then you're in the best frame of mind to try something different. That goes for clothes too. Let's get going."

They came back to the apartment that evening with tired feet and enough to fill the empty trunks Alice had brought. Lois heard the delivery men tramping up the stairs and came out to look over the railing.

"You want to stand over the stove for an hour or do you want to go out?" she called down to Alice.

"Definitely out," Alice shouted up.

Lois tipped the boys, locked up, and flew down the steps with her coat and hat in her hand. She had forsaken the trousers, and the dress that clung to her lean shape and flowed with her legs was unlike any Alice and Laura had seen in a dozen of the finest department stores that day. The colors ran away with themselves. It was an impressionist painting in mixed media.

"What an extraordinary dress," said Alice.

"Where did you get it?" said Laura.

"I made it. I cut up two old dresses I was going to throw out and got out my paint brushes. Better not touch it. Paint's still wet. Let's go to Marlo's around the corner. They've got cheap giggle water."

CHAPTER FIFTY-ONE

The next morning, they took the subway up to lower Harlem to visit the children's home. The first one was doing so well in Boston that Alice and Andrew had decided to put another one in New York. The clincher in the deal was meeting Miss Lantz's beau from the restaurant where she often ate in the days of the Procter marriage. Mr. Price was an assistant professor at NYU who had champed at the bit for a school of his own, and when he proposed marriage to Alice's childhood nurse, governess, and companion, it occasioned a fortuitous meeting of several minds. Andrew made some inquiries and saved a grand old house on 125th Street from the wrecking ball.

Mr. Price left his digs in the West Village, married Miss Lantz, and honeymooned with his bride among carpenters and carpet layers for almost a year before the school opened with its first class of sixteen orphans. Bright young student teachers from the university served as the faculty, with a few living in as dormitory masters and mistresses as the school filled to capacity by its second year.

Above the door was a bronze plaque with the words *The Croft School*. A few feet above that was a wooden plaque carved with lines from Longfellow:

The heights by great men reached and kept
were not attained by sudden flight,
but they, while their companions slept,
were toiling upward in the night.

"That was Andrew's idea," said Alice. "He thought it sounded inspirational. He fell off the ladder trying to get it up there. I'm sorry, I shouldn't laugh. He didn't hurt himself. And he was the first one to appreciate the irony."

As Alice and Laura stood in front of the house with their attention upward, it seemed as if there was not a busier establishment on the street. In every window there were children shaking out dust mops, whacking rugs, peeking out and running away. Down below, surrounding the house, was a former empty lot, plowed up into garden plots ready for spring. Children were everywhere, with no way of telling which ones belonged to the school and which inhabited the neighborhood.

"That's how Andrew wanted it to be," said Alice. "We're probably educating and feeding half the children around here, but I think he was right."

Their appearance at the front door was heralded with shrieks and shouts throughout the house. Mrs. Price opened the door with delight and ushered them in. Little girls and boys took their coats and hats and ran off with them. Alice noticed that Mrs. Price said nothing about their bobbed hair.

"We suspended school and adoption visits and declared a holiday in your honor, madam."

"Oh, you shouldn't have, Miss Lantz," said Alice. "I'm sorry—Mrs. Price."

"I hope you've come for the day, madam. And Laura, dear, you've grown into such a lovely woman. The children have a presentation and a play, and we've been working on a testimonial dinner. They'd be so disappointed if you rushed off."

"We'll do nothing of the kind, Mrs. Price," said Alice, without a hitch.

On the subway back that evening, Alice and Laura agreed it had been an exhausting day. The train rattled them back and forth in their seats and in and out of the tunnel lights, screeching horribly.

"I don't think I've ever been the object of so many little bows and curtsies," said Alice wearily.

"They were certainly very respectful," said Laura. "And what a lovable man Mr. Price is. Did you see how he let them climb all over him after dinner? He just went on talking in his armchair."

"By then I was ready to have him tuck me in for the night with the others."

They fell against each other and laughed. The train slowed down for a stop, and Alice looked out the window, checking the white lettering on the wall as it went by their car four or five times.

"Not us," she said.

The train got underway again, and Alice sat back with her eyes closed.

"Mummy?"

"Yes dear?" said Alice without turning or opening her eyes.

"Do you ever think of bringing one of the children home?"

"All the time."

"Why don't you?"

"Which one?"

"I don't know."

"Which one would you choose out of all those poor children? Which one would you try to give a wonderful life to?"

"It wouldn't have to be just one."

"All right then. Which five would you take? Which ten? Or look at it the other way. Which thirty or forty would you not take? Which ones would you leave behind? That's more to the point."

"Oh Mummy. I didn't mean to make you cry."

"I cry too easily," Alice said, wrestling with her coat to get her handkerchief out of her sleeve. "I always cry coming home from the school. I want to take all of them home. I don't trust myself to be a mother. That's what it is, I suppose. I didn't do very well with Rory and Autie. They're both—I don't know what it is. There's something else too, but I can't talk about it, dear. Maybe someday."

Then Alice really cried. Laura put her arms around her.

"You've been a good mother to me, Mummy," she said.

Alice straightened up, sniffled into her handkerchief for a moment, and put it away in her coat pocket.

"Well, I'm glad you think so, dear. The first time I saw you at the table with your grandmother, I wanted you for my daughter. And now look at you," she said, brightening, "You're a grown woman. But I want you to be happy, Laura. That's the only thing I worry about."

"I am, Mummy."

"Well!" said Alice, with Mrs. Darlington firmly in mind, "Until I'm sure of it, I'll remain on duty. We'll have a good time the rest of the week, won't we? No more tears."

CHAPTER FIFTY-TWO

The next day Alice and Laura slept late, but they made it to the Gallery of Modern Art by early afternoon. As they wandered through the rooms, Alice seemed to be looking as much at the other visitors to the gallery as she was at the Picassos and Matisses.

"Keep your eyes peeled for a nice-looking man your age without a wedding ring," she whispered to Laura. "If you spot one, give me the signal."

"Oh Mother, stop it."

"I'll faint and fall to the floor. He'll come running. Make sure you have your left hand showing."

"My hands are just awful."

"Nonsense. You have beautiful hands, dear. He has to see you aren't married. It can be love at first sight. Oh, I'm sorry, darling. I'm just being silly. I haven't the faintest idea how to meet men. It was all put together by the parents in my day. Maybe we should have done that with you."

"I wouldn't have liked that at all," Laura said with a decisive frown.

"It might not have been easy. You're one of a kind, you know."

"I know. A real doozy."

"I didn't say that, dear," said Alice, taking Laura's hand as she wheeled to follow a handsome young man into the Alberto Giacometti exhibition.

A few hours later, in the museum café over coffee, Alice sighed. "Well dear, there really wasn't anyone the right age worth a fainting performance, was there?"

"I don't care. I really don't. I just wanted to be with you this week."

"That's sweet of you to say, dear, but nothing would make me happier than to see you meet a nice man and drop me like a hot potato."

They caught a cab back to the apartment to pick up Lois, and then they went out to eat. That night, some literary people stopped by, occupied the armchairs, and stretched out on the floor to compile their essays and articles into a proof of a new literary review. Someone finally got up to open a window and let the cigarette smoke out. Alice and Laura sat with Lois at her table and talked while she played solitaire. One or two young gentlemen nosed around Laura, but she wasn't interested.

"It's not that," she said. "I'm not well-read in modern literature. I wouldn't know what to say."

"You can't worry about that, kiddo," said Lois cynically as she flipped a card. "Most of them are gasbags. The interesting ones come here to listen. They like to be around regular people and hear how they talk. Talk about anything. That's where they get ideas. I think you'd like Arnold Blessing. He's a mural painter. He did the lobby of the McNair Building a few months ago. Unattached, soft spoken, self-effacing, easy to talk to. He's the one going into the kitchen. Quick, girl. Go."

"What?"

"Go in the kitchen."

"What do I do when I get there?"

"Ask him to help you look for Vienna sausages. We don't have any. Go ahead, go."

"All right," said Laura, getting up from the table reluctantly.

Laura did not come out of the kitchen the rest of the night. When Lois went to get a last round of drinks for her and Alice, she came back and said, "They're necking."

"What's necking?"

"New nomenclature. Go look."

Alice went and stole a peek into the kitchen and scurried back to Lois.

"Oh, that's wonderful," Alice said, clasping her hands together.
"Do you want me to teach you how to play solitaire?" Lois asked.
"Oh horrors, no."
"Well, look around, Alice. We're the old guard, aren't we?"
"So what if we are? We had fun, didn't we? I don't mind getting old. As long as the mattresses don't come out. I hope you can squelch that while we're here."
"I already spread the word," said Lois.

Laura was head over heels with Arnold Blessing after that night. She kept Alice up late making plans to move to New York and applying for a job in the post office. The next day she insisted on going to see Arnold's work at the McNair Building so she would be able to discuss it with him. Then they had to go to an art supply store, and after an hour of looking around and asking questions of the clerk, Laura bought a selection of palette knives in a soft leather case to give him. There was new spirit in her for the clothes shopping they did every day, and every evening after dinner Laura disappeared into the bedroom for a long time before emerging in a new outfit to await the salon goers.

"At least she doesn't have to decide what to do with her hair," said Lois.
"It doesn't really suit her, does it?" Alice whispered.
"No, it doesn't, frankly. She's a little heavy for a Dutch bob."
"Well, we won't say anything. It'll grow out."
"And overboard on the perfume, don't you think? I sure hope Arnold shows. I know he'll be here Saturday. Saturdays are unofficially artist night."

A few of the nights passed without any company. During the days, they visited small art galleries and stopped in to see Mr. Goddard, who continued to hold exclusive rights to exhibit Liza Banks and made a business of keeping her whereabouts a mystery to the art community. One day they walked miles through Central Park because Alice wanted to see how many starlings were around. She told Laura what Lois had told her about the hundred that got transplanted thirty years ago by the crazy group that had wanted America to have every bird that appeared in Shakespeare. Satisfied by numerous sightings, they rode the Staten Island Ferry and ended up walking on the beach at Coney Island. After that it was good to get back to the warm apartment.

Alice was going to say they should go to the opera one night, but she knew Laura wouldn't want to take the chance of missing Arnold. So they sat and waited every night, talking about art, politics, and men. At midnight Lois closed up, and they went to bed, but Laura stayed awake long into the night, listening for a knock on the door.

Friday night looked promising, and Laura talked to a few young gentlemen before settling down on the floor at the feet of a middle-aged astronomer who never budged from one of the armchairs. As enthralled as Laura seemed by his conversation, Alice caught her eyes going to the door whenever it opened for a man. No Arnold.

On Saturday, their last day in New York, Lois sent them to a matinee of the moving picture *The Three Musketeers*. She had already seen it and gave them a briefing on their first motion picture the night before.

"There's nothing to the men," she said. "I don't know what all the fuss is about Douglas Fairbanks, but the women are worth watching. You look exactly like the Queen of France, Alice, and Laura, you're the spitting image of her cute seamstress. Well, you tell me. Oh, and don't forget your glasses. There's a lot of note-passing. You might like it. I just can't get over watching people talk with no sound coming out. You'd think I wouldn't miss it with the kind of people who come here. Well, see what you think. It'll take your mind off things for two hours."

At that, Lois took Laura's hand and patted it with the other before she saw them down the stairs. Alice could also tell that Laura was going through ups and downs as her mind played cruel games of building up hopes with Arnold Blessing and tearing them down the next minute. Arm in arm, they walked a few blocks to the motion picture theater and bought their tickets.

There was nothing in the early papers about the Socialist rally, but the later editions were full of eyewitness accounts, casualty reports, and commentary from city officials. They didn't want to be washing dishes if people started showing up, so they went out for a light dinner and got back to the apartment in plenty of time for Laura to fix herself up for a do-or-die night with Arnold Blessing. Lois had been unable to find out anything about Arnold's disappearance. At least she knew for sure he wasn't married and that he lived alone somewhere in the East Village.

Lois and Alice were sitting at the table where Lois played solitaire, waiting for Laura to come out of the bedroom in something chic.

"The way they were going at it in the kitchen last time, I thought for sure he'd be around," said Lois in a low voice. "If I had known he was going to drop out of sight, I could have asked around for the scoop. But I'm pretty sure he'll show up tonight. He's always here Saturday nights. I don't know who feeds him the other nights of the week, but he always comes to raid the icebox Saturday night. If he shows tonight and the romance is on, I can find out all you want to know."

"If the romance is on, I don't want to know anything. Then it's her affair, and she'll tell me whatever she wants to tell me about it. Well, if there's anything bad, maybe I should know. I don't want her to be crushed."

"I'm discreet," said Lois.

"I know you are, dear. You've been wonderful this week. It's done Laura so much good. Even if the romance fizzles, it boosted her spirits and gave her some experience with a man. I think she needed that very much." Alice saw the bedroom door open. "Oh, Laura, don't you look lovely."

Lois turned in her chair as Laura entered in a black sheath dress with cuts up the sides to mid-thigh, and a daring neckline that plunged.

"Wowee," exclaimed Lois. "Looks great on you, doll."

"Mother picked it out."

"Very flattering. Very adventurous. You know your clothes, Alice. I can't imagine what you must think of what I wear," Lois said with her half smile.

"Well, for one thing, if your feet are always going to be up on the furniture, keep wearing men's trousers," said Alice.

Around seven-thirty, a few early birds flew in, and by ten the living room and kitchen were filled up, but still no Arnold. Laura never let her face fall. Procter came with his new wife, a smartly-dressed Fifth Avenue kind of woman who looked down-to-earth. He was still with J.P. Morgan and was now a partner in the firm, but Alice only found that out later from Lois. Alice got up to meet the wife and called Laura over.

"This is my daughter, Laura. Laura, Mr. and Mrs. Darlington. Mr. Darlington is an old friend of ours from Boston."

Procter remembered Andrew's name and asked about him. They talked cordially of New York and the Eastern Shore. She needn't have worried that Procter might betray any sign to Laura that they had ever been anything more to each other than casual acquaintances. At first it was agreeable, then it became irksome. To Alice, who remembered very well the man she had married thirty years ago, this attentive listener, considerate and thoughtful in every word, was such a blaring, walking antithesis of their past and all he had put her through. She wanted him to slip up and expose himself for what he really was. How much easier seeing him again would be if he had been condemned to wear sandwich placards around his neck, spelling out in big letters his old self-centeredness and insensitivity so the world would know.

Yet it did not look entirely like an act. Alice watched him out of the corner of her eye as he and his wife circulated through the little cliques. It made something inside her hurt to see Procter in this guise. The coming apart of a marriage was to her the most devastating of failures, and the new Procter Darlington made it look like it was all her fault. She suddenly wanted to be home again, alone with Andrew. But she had to see the night out for Laura's sake. If Arnold Blessing would only walk in the door.

They were sitting with Lois at her table around midnight. Lois was teaching them solitaire. Laura's eyes suddenly shot toward the door.

"Karensky's here," Lois whispered to Alice.

"I can't turn around," said Alice. "Is Margaux with him?"

"Afraid so."

"I hoped this wouldn't happen."

"Mummy— it's Margaux!" Laura whispered.

"I know, dear. I was going to tell you."

"That's the artist who painted my portrait, isn't it?"

"Yes, I'm sorry to say. He was here when I brought Margaux up to meet Lois last month. She didn't come back with me. I guess she's been living with him."

Lois confirmed with a nod.

"Does Autie know?" said Laura.

"I don't think so."

"Shouldn't you tell him?"

"I know you're upset, Laura. I am too. I've been trying to think it through. I don't think anyone should tell Autie yet. If it blows over, he may never have to know. That's what Andrew thinks."

"You don't think that too, do you Mother? He has a right to know."

"He won't be back from Kansas for a month or so. We'll talk about it on the train. They're coming over. We can't ignore them."

Lois sat still, looking down, busy with her hands, straightening the rows of her cards.

"Mrs. Croft. Good to see you," said Karensky. He still had the intense eyes and wild black hair. He put out his hand, and Alice touched it briefly as she rose to embrace Margaux.

"And you are the daughter I painted once."

"Yes. Laura," said Alice.

Laura turned away and would not look at either of them.

"Margaux, dear, how are you?"

"Very well, Mother."

"She's the best model I've ever had. She keeps me working."

Margaux showed no trace of emotion but found Karensky's hand at her side and grasped it as she continued to look steadily at Alice. There was nothing else for anyone to say. Karensky gave a slight bow, and he and Margaux slipped into the crowd in the living room.

Lois flipped another card over. Laura continued to look up to the door every time it opened. Alice went to the kitchen to fix herself a drink and spent the better part of their last night in New York trying to think of a few words to give Margaux before she and Karensky left. When she saw them heading for the door, she got through the people in time to embrace Margaux again and whisper in her ear the only thing she could think of to say.

"We miss you, Margaux. Come home soon."

CHAPTER FIFTY-THREE

Andrew and his grandson Robbie started down the long grassy hill behind the chateau, heading to the river. Henry, the young Chesapeake Bay retriever, ran on ahead. Bow-wow, the collie, followed behind as if he had decided to come along only because he had no pressing engagements or prior commitments other than blocking doorways in the house. The forsythias were about to come out on the south side of the Belgian cottage at the base of the hill. As they got closer, Andrew could see the ivy was getting high on the brick walls.

He didn't want Alice to come home from her week with Laura in New York and hear he had the boy pulling ivy off the Belgian cottage all week. But now he had to figure out how to water down what he knew of manly activities to the physical abilities and comprehension level of a seven-year-old. He had given the staff the week off with pay. So far he and Robbie had fended for themselves tolerably well. At least he had let Alice put little Edward in the hands of Mrs. Cooper to give his nurse, Gretchen, the chance to visit her brother in Buffalo and relieve him of caring for a baby.

Well, Autie and Margaux would be the ones to decide if they wanted ivy or not. Maybe if they had moved into the cottage when they first got to Maryland, Margaux might have liked having a home of her own. Autie seemed to dearly love the boy he had taken on. He was just stuck in Fort Riley. Margaux was a different story. A little bit of the boy seemed to go a long way with her. Robbie would have liked living closer to the river. Little Edward would have been born there. It might have pulled all of them together.

He still thought building the cottage had been a good idea. If it had been here when he and Alice bought the place, he wouldn't have built the chateau. Alice would have loved a little cottage like this. She loved the Tudor house. They were about the same size. Why didn't they have the Tudor house dismantled and moved down here? Just didn't think of it. Rory and Autie might have turned out better, growing up on the river like Mark Twain.

If Margaux came home before Autie showed up from Kansas on leave, he might never have to know anything about her going off. She might want to start over, move into the cottage, and have a family life. It might work out fine if people around here knew how to keep secrets a little better.

"Well, Robbie, if you want to be an army man like your daddy," said Andrew, still looking up at the ivy on the brick chimney, "you have to have training. You can't be an army man without training."

"How long does that take, Bonpapa?"

"That depends on what kind of army man you want to be, Robbie. You can be infantry—that's what your daddy is, where you walk on the ground. Or artillery—that's cannons. Or the tank corps. Remember the pictures of tanks I showed you in the newspaper? I don't think they're going to have horses anymore. But there are also army men who do regular things, like doctors and truck drivers. Oh, and there's the Army Air Corps with the airplanes."

From the cottage, they took the flagstone path down to the river and walked out on the dock to the boathouse at the end. The motor yacht was just back from winter storage at the Galena basin. She looked good, the teak deck well cared for and the hull scraped and painted. Ready to go out in the bay. When Robbie and little Edward were old enough, it would be fun to take them down the coast to Cape Hatteras like they did with Autie and Rory when they were boys.

It was low tide, and Henry was out in the middle of the river.

"You better find a stick to throw for him, or he'll just keep swimming straight across," said Andrew.

Robbie called Henry back in and ran down the dock, jumped to the beach before he got to the end, and sank to his ankles in the brown sand. Henry met him and shook himself from head to tail, sending water flying in all directions. The boy picked up a solid piece of driftwood and threw it as hard as he could a few times until Andrew said the water was still too cold for the dog to be in and out retrieving that long.

Bow-wow finally made it down to the beach and sniffed along the waterline. While they watched from the dock, he waded out to his chest in the brown water, then slid in like a duck, hardly causing a ripple as he glided out with nothing showing but a little of his back, his head, his ears, and his long muzzle. A few yards out, he made a stately circle as if he were performing in a dog show, and returned to the beach. There he shook the water off his coat and went up on the dock to lie down in the sun, where Andrew and Robbie were sitting with their legs dangling over the river.

"I don't know what my real father was," said Robbie, sitting between Henry and Bow-wow with an arm over each wet dog.

"He was probably in the infantry," said Andrew. "Tanks weren't around in the first year of the war, and I don't think the Belgian army had airplanes. Well, you can't go wrong with the infantry, Robbie. Your dad can tell you what you need to know when he gets home from Fort Riley."

Robbie never asked when either of his parents would be home. Andrew was glad that the boy was so adaptable. Bonpapa and Bonnemama were effectively his parents for now. There was also Gretchen. And Viola and Delphina because he was always in the kitchen. Elijah took him on the tractor once in a while, and Cassie and Lilly played around with him inside while they cleaned house. It wasn't the worst way to get raised. He was quite aware of who his parents were, but it did not seem unusual for his father to be getting on the train back to Kansas or if his mother went missing.

"Were you in the army too, Bonpapa?"

"Oh, no. But I read a lot, you see. I was just reading today about something you might want to do this week while school's out. I mean, if you want to try being an army man right now."

"You have to be big."

"Not to go on maneuvers you don't."

"What's maneuvers?"

"It's when the soldiers leave barracks—that's where they live—and go out to live in the woods. We can do that if you want. We can go back to the house and get what we'll need to camp in the woods. I'll show you how army men do it."

The boy was so eager. No anxieties crossed his face. Well and good. He had every advantage in life. He never worked in a mill or scraped for a living. But still, he was a child brought into the world by war, invasion, conquest, and violence. He might figure out for himself someday who his real father was and the circumstances of his mother. There was no getting around the blue eyes, the blond hair, the prominence of cheekbone and jaw. Just the overall look of him. It was hard to miss the German.

"The first thing we need to do," said Andrew as they walked back up the long grassy hill to the chateau, "is figure out what we need to live in the woods."

"Matches to make a fire," said Robbie.

"And food," said Andrew, noting to himself that food had risen considerably in his priorities since he first went soldiering.

Maybe he had gotten a little carried away. He had not lived outside for some time. There was a reason animals had short life spans. Living outside is not easy. It would confuse the dogs. Their faces would ask what are we doing out here? We sleep inside. Only for a week. That shouldn't be too bad. They could raid the kitchen. Foraging. He had done it before, living outside for months at a time without any shelter. He never gave it a second thought. Hardship and living off the land built esprit de corps.

He wondered about the guns—if seven was too young. All it means to a boy, having a gun. Alice might get mad. But there was nobody else around to teach him how to handle a gun and shoot. He could say that. He had to get Robbie out of the henhouse. Shouldn't say that. Alice spoils him.

The Stevens .22 Long Rifle would be a good choice. They could take some cans out of the trash and set them up on the sandbar. Don't want to scare the geese. He could show him how to sneak up on geese. Camouflage. Should call Elijah Brown to tell him gunfire in the woods. Nothing to be alarmed about.

"It's called a bivouac," said Andrew. "It's a temporary camp you set up when you're out on maneuvers. You look over the ground first because there are certain things you don't want, like exposure to enemy fire, or snipers—that's men in the trees. So you want open ground on your perimeter where there's no place the enemy can use for cover."

On the bluff over the river, Robbie followed the example of his Bonpapa, sweeping leaves away with his foot for a place to put down their packs. They dug out a fire pit in the center of the bare circle of earth they had made, gathered kindling, and dragged over some long-fallen branches to chop up after dark with their hatchets. Below them was the part of the river that had eddied and built up the sandbar, forming also the marshes behind it. Henry was off in the woods. Bow-wow lay down on a patch of moss and pointed his long nose over the river, with his eyes half closed.

"Now, Robbie, this is a .22 caliber rifle," said Andrew, holding it up. They were sitting cross-legged on the ground in their ring of leaves, and the boy was so excited he could hardly sit still. "Butt, stock, barrel, sights here and there, shoulder strap. It's bolt-action, so you see how this works? This is what your bullets look like. They go in here, then you work the bolt. Opens like this, closes like this. Let's see you do it."

Andrew handed the rifle back to Robbie and gave him a bullet.

"You shouldn't have to force it. Should go in easy. Now eject it. Just tap once or twice, and it'll drop out. Good. Make sure you always know if it's loaded or not. Let's go put some cans on the sandbar. Put the strap over your shoulder."

"Where'd you get the guns, Bonpapa?" Robbie asked as they started down the slope to the sandbar with their rifles slung over their backs.

"Some people gave them to me."

"What people?"

"Well, army men, of course," said Andrew. He suddenly stopped in his tracks. "There's something very important you should always know about the weapon you're using, Robbie. You have to know the range. That's how far it shoots. Your Stevens is accurate to maybe fifty yards. Do you know how far that is?"

"No, Bonpapa."

"See that first patch of cattails down there? That's about fifty yards. My Springfield here might make eight hundred yards. That's way over there on the other side of the sandbar. But you have to be real good to shoot that far. And you have to figure on the drop of the bullet across that much distance if you want to hit anything smaller than an elephant."

"There aren't elephants around here, Bonpapa."

"That's funny. I saw one out here just the other day."

"Where?"

"On the other side of the sandbar, up on the hill where that old shed is. He was just out of range. See, I didn't have to waste a shot or give away my position because I knew the range of my rifle. But that reminds me." They were climbing back up the hill from the sandbar. "Before we start shooting, I want both dogs up there on the cliff with us. Bow-wow's up there. Where's Henry?"

Robbie called Henry in all directions, and suddenly Henry came bounding out of the marsh behind the sandbar. Andrew was quick to see the opportunity as the dog started up the hill in great leaps.

"Quick, Robbie, look. Get your rifle ready. A wild boar coming at us. Line him up in your sights. Hundred yards. Snug the butt to your shoulder. When you fire, just squeeze the trigger, don't jerk it. Don't fire till I say."

Andrew bent over to line up behind Robbie.

"Watch him. No, no, across the sights. Eighty yards. Sixty yards. He's not coming straight. He's going to dodge that rock. If you fired, then you would have missed. I'll tell you when to fire. Forty yards. Twenty. Now, boy. Fire! Bang! You got him."

A second later, Henry plowed them both over, all swamp-wet and muddy. Robbie hugged the big, brown, curly haired dog, and Andrew scratched his ears. He felt a tinge of remorse. He shouldn't have made Henry a target. Well, someday Robbie might be in Africa and have to stop a lion. A lion was something like a dog. That's what he could say. Good thing Alice didn't see that.

Maybe he shouldn't have gotten Robbie started with guns. Too late now. Killing was the only worthwhile purpose to them. No pretense about it in the Marine Corps. The targets were cutout silhouettes of men. He had kept guns out of the hands of Rory and Autie when they were growing up, and what difference did it make? It only ill-equipped Autie for a war he went to willingly, without any idea of the destructive forces involved in the enterprise. If he had ever seen what a .30-03 bullet did to a soup can, he would have gone into it better prepared. Harder to tell with Rory. If he had learned how to handle a gun, his vocabulary would have included words like danger, caution, and careful. Even without going to war, his behavior as a man might have been tempered by the fragility of life that holding a gun in the hand brings to mind. Every good emotion can follow from that in the formation of character. Well, most people anyway.

That night they made a small cooking fire, fried up some hamburger and potatoes, and toasted bread on sticks. The dogs settled down with a couple of ham bones Viola must have been saving for soup. As night closed in, they built up the fire. Andrew smoked and told a story he made up as he went along about a soldier rescuing a girl from the Indians and their adventures rafting down a river. It started to rain. They threw more wood on the fire and turned in for the night, rolled up in blankets out of the linen closet.

The rain got harder and came down in sheets. No more fire. The ground under them soaked up the rain and turned into mud. Around midnight, Andrew heard a little whimper coming from the other blanket roll. The dogs looked like two miserable heaps of shivering wet fur. He gave up on his sodden blanket and lay with his face up to the rain falling through the bare branches of the darkness above.

"I don't know about you, Private Robbie," he said, "but I think it's time to make what we call a strategic withdrawal."

The library never felt more warm and cozy. Dry clothes never so good to be in. Hot cocoa never so tasty. A fire in the fireplace and all the big armchairs, rugs, curtains, and lamps of the great indoors seemed to outdo any other human accomplishment one might mention. Henry and Bow-wow yawned and went to their beds in the kitchen. Andrew and Robbie left their cocoa mugs on the tables beside the great armchairs and went up the carpeted stairs in their slippers to quilted beds.

Andrew lay awake not long, listening to the rain. Well, there you have it. One was too old for army life, one too young. Someday Robbie would be just right. His brother Edward, too. Just in time for the next war.

Unwilling to completely abandon manly pursuits while the women were out of the way, Andrew took Robbie to the woods every day to shoot at tin cans on the sandbar. On two mornings, he got him up at four o'clock to go to the farm to milk cows. One day they heard the sawmill up and running when they turned into the woods, so they worked a few hours with Lamont and Earling, making split rail. That led to digging postholes in the fields with Kenneth Banks. Robbie had some fun riding the auger for extra weight, with Kenneth at the wheel of the new John Deere and Andrew dropping posts and tamping.

Andrew gave Robbie a sheath knife. He wore it on his belt from that time on, proud as punch. They snuck up on their bellies through the marshy wetland and got pretty close to the geese before the sentinels honked up. They rode Diligence, Alice's Percheron, to the farm one day to visit General, the old warhorse, in the meadow of retired milk cows. Andrew hoisted Robbie up sixteen hands high, and General walked the fence line in a stately way with the boy on his back. They stayed out of doors every day that week, even if it was only crabbing off the dock or looking for arrowheads along the river. When Mr. Thompson came back two days early from business in Africa, he joined Andrew and Robbie for maneuvers in the woods, and they had great fun.

Alice called late Saturday night. Miss you, she said. Coming home tomorrow. Saw Margaux with Karensky. Laura knows and might tell Autie. Told her she shouldn't. Should we do something? Tired. New York so noisy. Did you check on Edward? Want to lie in your arms. Can't wait. Don't know why I thought this would be fun. Life no fun without you. Sleep well, darling, good night, sweet dreams. We bobbed our hair. Don't be mad.

"Bonnemama says good night and said you better get to bed," said Andrew, putting the receiver down on the hook.

Andrew saw Robbie to the stairs and went into the kitchen. A week's worth of dishes to wash. Pots and pans soaking. Sink in the back room full too. All the women back tomorrow. Don't want Viola upset. Men as welcome in her kitchen as raccoons. She'd never say anything. Never without a smile. Hard early life in the Danforth days. Lived in cabins of the old slave quarters. She lost some children, like Alice. No doctors for Negroes anywhere around here. Should see to it. Put an ad in the paper and get a good Negro doctor down here. Should write that down before I forget.

In a few hours the dishes were done. Everything was washed, dried, put away. Pans oiled. Viola will think we didn't eat.

He was going to have a last smoke in the library but thought better of it. He had too many in the woods. Time to go to bed. Should get the clothes off the floor before Alice gets back. How quiet it is without her. Without her. Wouldn't have amounted to much without Alice. Might have been living in the woods. Almost funny. Margaux and Autie are going to be on her mind. She'll want to do something about it. Do what? The ball was in Margaux's court. Strange girl. Beautiful girl, no question about that. No surprise Autie jumped in with both feet. Bit off more than he could chew. Maybe it all depended on Autie now, not Margaux.

Andrew reached for the clock on the side table and pulled it over to his face, tilting it to the moonlight coming through the curtains. Twelve-thirty. A steamer should be getting to the three-mile limit any time now to rendezvous with Haines. He wished he was out on the boat. He didn't like leaving dangerous work to others, but he had too many responsibilities now. And getting old. High-quality Irish whiskey was in demand. Not that he needed the money. He could consider his participation in illegal activity a protest against the most ill-conceived law ever passed in the United States, but it was mostly for Haines he was doing it. Giving him a chance to make some money was all he could do for him. It might improve his disposition on living. Now Laura Eklund was involved. Haines wouldn't tell her anything, but of all the dumb luck. Only the most unlikely chance could have brought them together. For a shrinking violet, that girl sure gets around. Alice with bobbed hair. She said it was all the rage. He hoped all the rage would not interfere too much with ordinary normal. He reminded himself not to say, "What did you do to your hair?"

CHAPTER FIFTY-FOUR

Delphina was expecting the bag of pennies. Mr. Conrow came through the back door Thursday morning. The mail from the depot was sorted and bundled, and she had just finished the entries in the logbooks at her desk.

"Good morning, Mr. Conrow," she said without looking up.

He said nothing and placed his account book on the desk. Then the bag of pennies.

Delphina stood up on her long legs, almost as tall as Mr. Conrow, and looked down into the bag. There was no expression on her face. Her hair was pulled in a tight braid down her back, held by a silver clasp Alice Croft had given her.

"Please wait here until I return, Mr. Conrow," she said. At the door she added, in a flat, straightforward voice, "The mail is not yet authorized for release."

She returned in a few minutes with a bundle of coin wrappers in her hand.

"We are going to count yesterday's returns together, Mr. Conrow," she said, as she returned to the chair behind her desk. "Please take a seat."

"My job is delivering the mail," he said, with cold impunity.

Delphina folded her hands in front of her on the desk and looked up at his face, which was set with the vacant expression of an owl.

"Mr. Conrow," she said patiently, without her sharp brown eyes leaving his, "the postal department takes its revenues very seriously. If I count your returns myself and find the amount short, even by a penny, it will make two consecutive days the post office has failed to reconcile your accounts. That will put your position as carrier of the mail in jeopardy. I reference Accounting Practices, section three B of the *Code of Postal Regulations*. You may find it on the shelf behind me."

Mr. Conrow said nothing but made no move to sit down.

"Mr. Conrow," said Delphina very plainly. "I went to the colored school as far as the eighth grade. I may make a mistake. Do you see this rubber stamp? This one here. When I stamp the entry in the logbook on the line where I record my count of this bag of pennies, I have certified the amount written. There is no appeal after that. That is the entry the auditor will see. Your accounting may be correct, but who can say what might happen while counting this bag of pennies? One might drop onto the floor and roll unseen under the desk. So I think you can see that it would be in your best interest to count this bag together."

Mr. Conrow stood still a moment with his little gray mustache twitching. Then he sat down. Delphina cleared the desk and carefully emptied the bag of pennies. Mr. Conrow's fingers were too thick to manage the penny wrapper rolls, so they had to find a way to work together. He counted groups of ten off the desk into his hand, passed them to her, and she stacked them. When there was a line of five stacks in a row, each one equal in height to the other stacks, Delphina put the group into a fifty-cent wrapper with her long, dexterous fingers and folded the ends over neatly. They found a pace and never lost a penny off the desk.

As they counted and stacked, Delphina made an observation, almost talking to herself. "You know, Mr. Conrow, the United States Post Office Department in Washington doesn't understand how things work in a small town, how people get along with each other. That's the reason they have so many regulations. I know it gets tiresome sometimes."

A little further along, she said, "I'm glad you're helping me count. You're a smart man. We couldn't have just anyone keeping the accounts on the road as you do. We would not want to lose you. I think we're going to come out exactly right." Glancing at the amount in Mr. Conrow's account book, she said, "We should end up with twenty-two dollars and fifty-eight cents."

She smiled when they did.

"Next time you'll take my word for it," said Mr. Conrow.

Delphina finished wrapping the last group of fifty.

"You know, Mr. Conrow, The U.S. Post Office Department makes it easy for us."

"How's that?"

"They have rules. The rules are in that big black manual on the shelf there. You can think of the rules as a little box. If you work for the post office, all you have to do is stay inside the box."

CHAPTER FIFTY-FIVE

Andrew looked up from his breakfast coffee and turned when he heard Alice at the entrance to the dining room. It was so good to have her back. She was as radiant as the morning sunshine coming in the windows. It found the blue in her eyes as it did in the portraits of her ancestors on the walls and ran down the bridges of all their magnificent noses. In this setting, the bobbed hair was as abrupt as the word "stop" in a telegram.

"It'll grow back, dear," said Alice as she took her place at the head of the table, with Andrew on her left. "I feel quite badly about Laura, though. I shouldn't have goaded her into it. It really doesn't suit her."

"As you say, it will grow back."

"No, with Laura, she'll probably keep it that way. You know how she is. She gets stuck sometimes. One change a year."

"I wouldn't say that. She's made some big changes."

"Well, she's had to. Nothing turns out very well for her. I thought I was going to mold a confident, modern woman, but I think I got her too late. They're saying now that the personality is fixed by the age of five. How can that be true? I think it's just an excuse."

"Laura is just fine, Alice. You don't have to worry about her. She's a fine young woman."

"But this postmistress job. Who is she going to meet?"

"Alice, you have to accept that she might prefer living alone at this stage of her life."

"Nonsense. Excuse me, dear. I don't mean to be so emphatic. But she's a very passionate girl. She always was. Deep down she wants a man of her own and children, and she's almost twenty-nine. She knows time is running out. Oh, here's Delphina."

Delphina emerged from the kitchen with the silver coffee pot. "Good morning, Mrs. Croft."

"Good morning, Delphina."

As Delphina poured her coffee, Alice said, "I do hope everything went well at the post office last week."

"Very well," said Delphina, standing back with the coffee pot and smoothing down her apron.

"Miss Eklund expected a call any time. You had our number in New York, didn't you?"

"Oh yes, I had the number. There was no need to trouble Miss Eklund though."

"Well, that's very nice to hear, Delphina. I had every confidence in you."

"If it could be arranged, Mrs. Croft, Miss Eklund asked me if I could come in for a few hours in the afternoons. Monday through Friday."

"Certainly, my dear. I'll talk to your mother and inform Mr. Thompson after breakfast. Thank you, Delphina. That will do."

Turning to Andrew, Alice said, "Well, we have the mail to look through, Andrew. Then breakfast. Then I want to go to the farm and collect little Edward from Mrs. Cooper. I'll take Robbie if he comes down. I hope you're not going to let him wear that knife on his belt to school tomorrow."

"Why not? In a few days all the other little boys will be wearing knives on their belts. They probably have them in their pockets anyway."

"Well, I'll leave that to Miss Hampstead and the principal. You know, I think Robbie's old enough to take his meals with us at the dining table, don't you think?"

"But that means Gretchen, too. And I'll have to sit all the way up there at the end."

"No, Robbie can sit at the head of the table. He'd like that very much. Of course, I'll have to dress better," said Alice, looking down her front. "By the way dear, you handled me rather roughly last night."

"I'm sorry. I didn't mean to."

"Oh, I liked it. It reminded me of before you became a gentleman."

"The whole week reminded me of that," said Andrew with a sigh.

CHAPTER FIFTY-SIX

On Sunday afternoon, after getting off the train from New York and saying goodbye to Alice, Laura oversaw the two porters hefting her trunks of new clothes up the staircase. She had them left on the top landing. She could unpack there and have Elijah Brown take the trunks back to Alice when he came to get the mail Monday morning. Then she handed the porters the tip Alice had put in an envelope and followed them downstairs.

It was good to be home, even though it was so quiet and lonely in the house on Sundays. She unpacked the trunks and suitcases, hung up what she had hangers for in the closet, and put away the rest in the dresser. The flapper dresses she put in the dresser in the other bedroom. She couldn't imagine when she would ever wear them. The city made her a different person. She only understood that now. But it was such fun. Except for seeing Margaux, but to be honest with herself about it, she didn't like Margaux. She really had to get back to her Buddhist book. Just the thought of achieving harmony with the universe put the kibosh on remembering how good she had looked in the flapper dresses in the changing room at Bloomingdale's.

Laura had Campbell's Beefsteak Tomato with cheese and saltines for lunch and lay down on the bed. When would she ever wear those clothes? The hair bob wasn't so bad. It took care of the split ends. Her hair was always dry and lifeless. Or oily and flat. She shouldn't wash it every day.

Cleaning anything was always harsh. Some things couldn't be cleaned. She always drifted into sleep when she lay down.

Later that afternoon, Delphina Brown came to town in the Croft Model T. She seemed very sure of herself, as if it was perfectly natural for a young woman to drive an automobile, and she came to the door in a regular visiting dress, not the plain frock she usually wore. Laura didn't think anyone noticed her letting Delphina in. It wouldn't be looked upon favorably by people if they thought she was friends with Delphina, which was all the more an ironic pity for remembering how awful her white girlfriends proved to be in Rhode Island.

"I thought I should come tell you what happened while you were away, Miss Laura," she said. "Before Monday morning."

"Please come in."

For a moment, Laura didn't know if it would be proper to take Delphina upstairs and offer her tea or unlock the post office. Post office, she decided. It was a business call.

"Let's go in here," she said. Thank goodness she had the keys in her pocket. It would have been awkward making her wait downstairs.

Laura went to her desk right away and sat down. Delphina took the chair on the other side. Her hat was wide-brimmed and feathered tastefully. One of Alice's old ones. It looked very becoming on her. It would have been the most natural thing in the world to lean over, touch her hand and say, "I love your hat, Delphina." But she knew she shouldn't.

"I had a little trouble with Mr. Conrow that you should know about," said Delphina.

"He didn't quit, did he?"

"No, he didn't quit."

"Then what happened, Delphina?"

"His accounts turned up one cent short on Wednesday, just like you said might happen. So I mentioned it to him. On Thursday, he brought in his returns, twenty-two dollars and fifty-eight cents, in pennies. I made him wait while I went to the bank for coin wrappers. Then we counted it out together. He was a little late getting out, but I think the matter was settled. I don't think he'll do that again."

Laura didn't know what to say. "You better tell me what you said to him," she said. "If you can remember your exact words. Then what he said back to you. I might have to write a report, so exact words are important."

Delphina recounted word for word what she had said to Jerry Conrow. The unhesitating manner in which she did so did not allow Laura a pause in writing it down. She wanted the exact words more for her own use than for her report.

"I think you handled the situation very well," said Laura when Delphina finished.

"Thank you, Miss Laura. I know it's what you would have done. He just caught you unprepared the first time. I was ready for it. Nothing is too hard to deal with if you have time in advance to figure out what to say."

"Well, that doesn't always work," said Laura, "but I'm glad it did for you. I'll look over your logs tonight. I'm sure everything is right."

"I think so, Miss Laura. I was very careful."

"Thank you for taking over while I was away, Delphina."

"I hope I left the upstairs neat and tidy. I moved the African violet to the other window. They like the morning sun better than the afternoon sun. That's why it was dying."

CHAPTER FIFTY-SEVEN

Autie was coming home. Alice had a feeling when she saw the letter from Fort Riley, Kansas, on top of her mail at the breakfast table. She read it to Andrew before the others came down.

"We've got to get Margaux back," she said in earnest.

"That's interfering, Alice."

"I should let her know at least. That's not interfering."

"It's bringing up a subject that's none of our business," said Andrew.

"Oh, Andrew. How can this be none of our business? She left us with her two children to take care of and a husband coming home to find his wife has run off with another man."

"Margaux doesn't need someone with an opinion on her behavior, darling. The best way to do it is to call Lois. Let Lois get word to her that Autie's coming home."

"That's better," said Alice. "Now you're being helpful."

"And have Lois ask Margaux what she wants us to tell Autie if she isn't going to come home."

"All right. That's what we'll do. Thank you, Andrew. I'm glad you took an interest."

"Well, why wouldn't I?"

"Because it's none of our business," said Alice, not dismissing the gravity of the situation, but delighted to have cleverly appropriated her husband's favorite remark.

Robbie came bounding down the stairs and through the entrance hall to the dining room, saying good morning to Bonnemama and Bonpapa.

"You'd better get a move on, old man," said Andrew. "Mr. Brown is sitting in the car. Do you have your school books?"

"Out in the hall, Bonpapa."

Delphina's face appeared in the window, and a moment later she came through the swinging door with Robbie's scrambled eggs and bacon, biscuits, and hot cocoa.

"Thank you, Miss Brown," he said.

Andrew stood up and went to the head of the table and stood behind Robbie. As the boy ate his breakfast, Andrew took the school tie from around the boy's shoulders, put it around his own neck, and tied it in a double Windsor knot for him. Then he slipped it over Robbie's head and trued it up. As he bent over to get it under the collar, he whispered, "Don't let Bonnemama see your knife."

"Your father is coming home, Robbie," said Alice. "He'll be here next month."

"Oh," said Robbie.

"We think your mother might be home by then too."

"How come?"

"We don't say 'how come,' Robbie," said Alice in her best Mrs. Darlington. "We say 'why is that?'"

"Why is that?"

"Because they want to see you, dear."

Robbie said nothing to that and finished wolfing down his breakfast. With a goodbye thrown over his shoulder, he was next seen through the dining room window with his schoolbooks under an arm, getting into the back seat of the Pierce-Arrow.

Alice waved. "You wave, too, Andrew. I know he doesn't look back, but if he ever does, I want him to see both of us."

They went on with the mail and breakfast, silently thinking.

"He seemed rather indifferent, wouldn't you say?" said Alice.

"It's understandable," said Andrew, without looking up.

"They *are* his parents, I mean."

"I think he considers us his parents. Or as good, anyway. There's nothing wrong with that."

"Well, you know how I feel about it. When we had our two boys, there was never a question. At least when we lived in the Tudor house and when we first came here. I loved that house, Andrew. Maybe we should have stayed there. I don't know why we took on all this. I think it only gave the boys false notions and the wrong kind of ambitions. We had a better hold on them in the Tudor house. You weren't too unhappy at the bank all those years, were you? I know Father adored you by the end of his life. And Mother, too."

"Well, I put some effort into that one," he said. "No, I wasn't unhappy. They were pretty good years. We have to stop thinking we ruined the boys though. At a certain point, it's up to them to make something of themselves. Then the women they marry roll up their sleeves."

"It may be the other way around this time," said Alice thoughtfully. "I think Autie has settled down. His letters sound more mature, don't you think? It would only be good for Margaux."

"Maybe so. Maybe so. We'll see what happens if Margaux comes home."

"I don't think she will, Andrew. What will we do then?"

"We'll stay out of it."

"Of course, dear," said Alice. "That's settled. Oh, we have an invitation from the Lovelands. I hope you aren't going to let Sam talk you into the tugboat business."

"Well, I've been thinking about it," returned Andrew. "I might need a tugboat."

"Why would you need a tugboat, for heaven's sake?"

"That business I told you about."

"Oh, that. I don't want to hear about it," said Alice. "If you get into trouble, it's your own fault. I'm not bailing you out."

"Think of the times I bailed you out."

"That was for a good cause, dear. There's no comparison."

CHAPTER FIFTY-EIGHT

Autie Croft walked from Penn Station down to Greenwich Village. It was June, and people were out. He didn't notice any faces. They went by like telephone poles along a road in Kansas. All the same to him. He had no bag or valise. Just civilian clothes with enough pockets. One day up from Maryland, one day back.

Mom didn't want to explain anything. She sent him to Lois. He found the apartment without any trouble. He remembered the stairwell from years before. Lois let him in and brought him into the kitchen.

"I haven't seen you for a long time," she said. "What are you drinking these days?"

"Thanks, but no."

"You might as well have something, Autie. We're going to talk before you go anywhere."

"Is Margaux here?"

"She's out right now."

"When will she be back?"

"What do you want? I've got coffee." Lois leaned against the icebox with her arms folded across her chest. "Be patient. We'll get to it."

"Coffee's fine," he said.

Lois started the water on the stove and made a lot of noise with the coffee grinder for a minute.

"Your brother was here a couple of months ago from London. Business trip," she said over her shoulder. "He was only here a few days and had to get back on the next boat. Your mom came up with Laura Eklund. She's a nice girl. A little unsure of herself, but I like her a lot. I think she'll get over it."

"Mom wrote me about Rory."

"It's too bad you couldn't make it. But I understand about the army. You don't get to leave whenever you want, do you?"

Lois came over and sat down at the table across from him.

"Be a moment for the coffee," she said, taking out a cigarette.

Autie lit it for her. She crossed her legs, sat back, and looked him over.

"You're a fine-looking man, Autie. The army's built you up."

"What are you supposed to tell me, Aunt Lois?"

"Just a minute."

Lois got up and came back with two mugs of coffee.

"Margaux came up in February with your mom, Autie. She met a man. She's been living with him."

Autie bent over his coffee. He looked sideways one way, then the other way.

"Can I have a smoke?"

"Sure."

Lois watched him through the silence. He kept looking around the kitchen as if he was lost in a strange place.

"Does Mom know?" He checked himself. "Of course. Then Dad must know too."

"I'd think so."

"Why didn't Mom tell me?"

"I don't know, Autie. Maybe she thought it would be easier to hear it from me."

"Is that where she is now? With him?"

"Yes."

"Do you know where he lives?"

"Yes."

"Will you tell me?"

"If you want to know."

"Of course I want to know."

"What are you going to do?"

Autie looked up with a steady gaze for the first time. "I came here to bring her home. That's what I'm going to do. That's all. Just bring her back."

"I wish you all the luck in the world, Autie."

"Could you write down the address?"

"Sure." Lois got a pen and wrote the address on the margin of a newspaper and tore it off. "It's just a street over and a couple blocks down. I'll be here, Autie, in case you want to come back and talk."

"Thanks, Aunt Lois. I think we'll go right to the station. I want to get her home tonight. I'll have Mom call you when we get in."

Lois gave him a hug and a kiss, the way she did when he was a boy, and watched from the landing as he went down the stairs.

One street over. Two blocks down. Second floor, number twenty-three B. Autie knocked on the door. A man opened it. Burly, dark hair, dark eyes. Flannel shirt, sleeves rolled up.

"I'd like to talk to Margaux."

"Who are you?"

"Her husband."

Karensky turned his head and called to the back rooms. Margaux came out, wiping her hands on an apron. When she saw who it was, she stopped, then came on toward the door.

"What are you doing here?" she said.

Autie turned to Karensky. "I'd like to talk to her alone."

Karensky eyed him. He touched Margaux on the shoulder and dropped back inside the room to the windows.

"You should not have come here," she said. "Why are you here?"

"I want to bring you home with me."

"Why?"

"You belong there. Not here."

"Who belongs anywhere?"

"Then you may as well leave this place."

He made a point of wordlessly looking down at the apron around her.

"I want you back," he said. "Robbie and Eddie want you back. Mother and Father want you back."

"That's no reason."

"It should be reason enough for you."

Margaux looked down at her feet.

"Come home with me," he said gently.

"What if I want to die?"

"You can do that at home."

"Will you leave me alone?"

"Yes, I'll leave you alone."

"Will you understand?"

"Yes."

"You say that without knowing anything."

"I don't have to know anything. Come home with me. Sleep in your bed tonight. I'll leave you alone."

Margaux stood in the doorway with nothing but abject weariness on her face. There was no hint as to what passed through her mind as she untied the apron and let it fall to the floor. When she stepped over the threshold of the doorway, Autie took off his coat and put it over her shoulders. They walked down the stairs side by side, Autie with his arm around her. When they got to the base of the stairs, Karensky accosted them from the upper landing.

"Forgot something," he said.

What he dropped fell through the open stairwell and shattered on the floor.

"*Non!*" Margaux exclaimed with a hand over her mouth.

Autie looked up. Karensky was gone. Autie went down on his hands and knees and began picking up the pieces of what appeared to be a small china dog. He got up to open the door to let in more light. He had Margaux cup her hands, and he put his handkerchief across them. She stood holding the fragments he had gathered while he went over the floor again, finding the smallest flakes.

"I'll fix it," he said, getting to his feet.

He folded the corners of the handkerchief over and carefully put it in the pocket of his coat. A cab was waiting on the other side of the street.

In the cab, and then in the train station, Margaux held onto him. She held his hand when he bought their tickets. Waiting on the platform, she kept under his arm. He had never seen her without strength and needing him. He had wished for it so many times in the past and was surprised that his only thought now was to make her strong again, even if it was only to see her leave him.

On the train, Margaux spoke for the first time since the apartment.

"Your mother gave it to me. It's a little dog. She said it meant something to her."

Autie patted her hand. "We'll see how I do with glue and a brush. Then it will mean something to you, too."

"I don't have any clothes."

"Your clothes are at home. We're going there."

"Oh, that's right."

Margaux woke up from sleeping on Autie's shoulder. It was dark out.

"It's just Washington," he said. "About two more hours to go."

"I have to tell you something," she said. "That story. What people think. It's not true. Nothing was done to me. I had a lover. A German boy in the occupation. We were going to marry. My father murdered him. Robbie was from him, my lover. I want to die and be with him."

"You'll have to tell me about him," said Autie.

"I've told you," she said.

PART FIVE

CHAPTER FIFTY-NINE

It was late when they got in. Autie carried Margaux up to their room in the chateau and laid her down on the bed. Alice was right behind and called him over to the door.

"I put your things in the blue bedroom," she said. "You still haven't unpacked from Kansas. You should leave her alone for a little while, don't you think? She seems very fragile."

"That's what I was going to do."

Alice helped Autie out of his overcoat. "Well, I don't know how you did it, dear boy. But you did, and I'm immensely proud of you." She embraced him with tears in her eyes. "Have you had anything to eat?"

"Not since this morning. I don't know about Margaux. She slept almost all the way on the train. I think she might be sick."

"We'll have Dr. Rushmore come by in the morning. You go downstairs and talk to Dad. Get something out of the kitchen. Could you make up a tray for Margaux? There should be leftover roast beef and boiled potatoes. Just warm them up in the oven."

Alice closed the door and went to sit on the bed beside Margaux. She looked like a street waif. She was sitting upright, and her short, black hair, knotted and tangled, could only be smoothed away from her face.

"I'm so happy to see you, Margaux," Alice said, leaning to kiss her.

Margaux put her arms around her for a moment but said nothing.

"Do you want to come downstairs? You should eat something."

"No, I don't want to go downstairs."

"Of course not," said Alice. "It's quite late. Then let's get you undressed and under the covers."

Margaux let Alice help her unbutton her dress and get it over her head. She didn't have anything on underneath, so Alice pulled up the sheet and blanket as Margaux bent her knees to slide her legs underneath.

"Oh, Margaux, you're skin and bones. We'll have Dr. Rushmore in to look you over. Does anything hurt?"

"No. I'm fine. I don't need the doctor."

"All right, dear. We'll brush your hair tomorrow. Autie is putting a tray together for you."

"I want to go to the Kastelje, Ma'ma," said Margaux. "The little house."

"Oh, the cottage."

"I want to live there with my husband and my children from now on."

"I'm so pleased to hear it, dear." Alice went to the dresser for a nightgown and pulled out a light flannel one. "Do you like this one?"

"Yes, I like that one."

Autie knocked at the door and came in with a tray. Behind him was Andrew. The tray was set down on the end of the bed. Andrew smiled and presented a bottle of wine with the cork pulled, and then they went quietly out of the room.

Margaux ate the roast beef, potatoes, and green beans, nibbled on a biscuit, and finished all of the chocolate pudding, sipping wine as she went. Alice kept filling the glass.

"You should sleep very well tonight, dear."

"I have not slept since I was fifteen."

"We'll fix that. I know we can. We want you to be happy here," said Alice.

"It's impossible to be happy."

"Oh heavens. That's never impossible, Margaux, dear. There's always something inside you that wants to be happy."

"No," said Margaux. "Not when you don't want to live."

"Everyone feels that way at times," Alice said, wasting no time in reply. "But you shouldn't be thinking about things like that. You're young, Margaux. Wonderful things are ahead of you. It's hard to see that now, but I know you'll be happy one day. Then you'll want to have a long life. So we must take good care of you now."

"Is that what you tell yourself, Ma'ma?" There was no hesitation in asking the question.

"I don't know what you mean, dear."

"To be happy—you imagine wonderful things that can never happen?"

Alice took Margaux's hands in hers and looked as honestly as she could into the girl's face. "I wasn't always happy, Margaux. I was very unhappy once. When I was your age. I was like you."

"What did you do?"

"I let my husband help me. That's what I did."

Alice moved the tray and put her arms around Margaux again. She felt the girl's isolation as acutely as she felt the need of her body to be warmed and nourished. For a moment, she thought she felt it as Margaux must feel it. With all the strength her arms and heart had gained from her own times of despair, she held Margaux a few moments longer.

"I don't want to be with a man for a year," said Margaux. "Will you tell that to my husband?"

"Of course, dear."

"If I love him then."

"I'm sure he understands that. He's changed since he's been away, Margaux. I hope you'll see it too. We'll go down to the Kas—"

"Kastelje."

Alice laughed and started again. "We'll walk down to the Kastelje tomorrow and look at it if you like." Then she took both of Margaux's hands in hers again and looked into her eyes. Very sincerely she went on. "We've loved nothing more than having you living with us, Margaux, but Andrew thought you would want a house of your own. He said that before you first came to us. That's why he had the cottage built. I hope you'll let yourself be happy there."

Margaux looked back at her with a tepid smile that Alice found encouraging.

Andrew and his son sat in the living room, Andrew on the couch, Autie in a facing armchair, marking time as if they were waiting for a baby to be born upstairs. They looked at each other and around the room, glancing up to the ceiling, thinking they might hear snatches of what was going on up there.

"The upper house deliberates," Andrew said to himself.

"I don't think anyone is coming down," said Autie, leaning forward to take a cigarette out of the silver box on the table. He lit it off the lighter and took a sip from his coffee. "Sorry to keep you and Mom up so late, Dad."

"Oh, don't be. Nothing makes your mother happier than feeling useful. And she's always thought of Margaux as a daughter."

"That's why I thought I could stay in Kansas," said Autie dejectedly. "I should have left when my two years were up. I knew she wouldn't want to be out there. She didn't like Kansas. She doesn't like the military either. I'll see what Mom can find out. I think Margaux will talk to her."

"You have to talk to her too, you know."

"We did on the train. A little. But I came to a few decisions on my own. Nothing I've told her about yet, but I was thinking about the way things were these last two years, and I've got to do something different."

Autie leaned to the ashtray on the table and tapped his cigarette on the rim.

"I'm going to leave the army, Dad. I like training the men, but it's hard to see the point. There's never going to be another war like the last one. Who's going to come after us? We're the strongest country in the world. The war just built us up and left everybody else in shambles. There won't be another war for two or three generations. So what am I training these fellows for?"

"That might be a short-sighted way of looking at it, my boy. There's a buildup going on in Japan right now."

"That's clear across the Pacific. Who cares about that part of the world anyway?"

"Well, airplanes are only going to get better."

"You should see what's going on at Riley, Dad. Airplanes are ending up in the dump along with tanks and all kinds of ordnance. They're scrapping everything like it's obsolete. I got busted down to first lieutenant. It's not just me. Everybody else lost a rank too. Morale is pretty low. They only put me back up to captain because of all the vacancies. The smart ones are leaving."

"Oh, that's too bad, Autie. But before you give it up, maybe you should start by requesting a transfer to somewhere around here, like Aberdeen. You could be home every night."

"No, I want out, Dad. I don't believe in it anymore. There's no future in the peacetime army. I should be with Margaux and the boys. I don't want everything to fall apart like it did. The only trouble is, all I know is the military. I'm going to have to find something I can do."

"Well, you know we can use you on the farm."

"It's been running fine without me, hasn't it? You don't really need me, and I should be able to make my own way. Anyhow, I'm not going back to Princeton, that's for sure. I'm too old for that."

Andrew got up and went to empty the ashtray in the bar. He brought back a bottle of brandy and two glasses. By the time he had poured the brandy and resumed his position on the couch, he had finished thinking.

"Well, if you're going to quit the army, son, we want to help you get a start. We did more for Rory than we did for you."

"I didn't think Rory ever needed help from anybody."

"I won't go into it, but he ran up some debts. California didn't work out as well as he hoped. He needed some direction."

"Could have fooled me."

"I'm afraid—well, he's doing better now in England, as far as I've heard. So we'd like to help you, too. As soon as you know what you want to do."

"Thanks, Dad. It depends on Margaux. I don't know if she wants to stay here. For all I know, she might want to go back to Belgium. Then I'd have to think of something to do there."

"Well, you brought her back from New York. That was the first hurdle."

With that, they fell back into couch and chair and listened for something from upstairs again.

"I hope they're having a good talk," said Andrew.

"I just remembered something, Dad. Do you have any glue around here for china?"

"I've got some in the study. No, you stay here. I'll be right back."

While he was waiting, Autie went to his overcoat in the hallway. He fished the lump of handkerchief out of the pocket and brought it into the light of the room. He spread it out on the leather top of a side table. It looked like it was going to be a real job. At least he could tell it was a dog. He pulled his chair over. By the time his father came back with a jar of glue in his hand, Autie knew where a few of the pieces went.

"Something I have to fix," Autie said.

He worked on it while Andrew read a newspaper he had brought back with him from the study. Around one o'clock in the morning, Alice came downstairs. She looked over Autie's shoulder and gave a start, then smiled and said, "Oh, I didn't know what you were doing. Show your father."

Autie held his hands away from the little china dog, now back together and standing on his own.

"Do you remember that little fellow?" Alice asked.

"As if it were yesterday," said Andrew, putting on his reading glasses and leaning over to inspect the repair. "Glad I wasn't responsible for his little accident."

On the favorable report from Alice that Margaux had eaten all of her dinner and was now fast asleep, the three went up to bed. Autie tiptoed in and placed the china dog on its side to dry on the nightstand, and then he stood for a moment over his sleeping wife, grateful to have her back home.

He was confident that the worst was over, although he couldn't say he had any way of knowing what the worst might be if it wasn't this. He closed the door and tread softly down the hall to the blue bedroom.

He knew he might not have a wife for a while, but she was back at home, in the room down the hall. He knew about the German lover now, but that was all she would say about him. At fourteen, she could have made a schoolgirl romance into something it wasn't, but there was no getting around having a baby. It wouldn't be so hard to believe that she might have been in love with him. If she had been in love once, it meant that somewhere down there the land had once been warm and verdant before the ice age. It was going to be hard to compete with a dead lover. It should be the other way around. Alive is supposed to be better than dead. It was no use closing his eyes. He knew he was going to be awake for a while.

CHAPTER SIXTY

The next morning, Alice brought Robbie and little Edward in to see their mother. Margaux pushed the breakfast tray down to the end of the bed to take the squirming infant in her arms.

"He'll settle down," said Alice, "but don't let him pick up that spoon. He'll hit you in the face with it—not on purpose, of course. He's using all the appendages, but he doesn't know how to control them yet."

Robbie, in his school clothes, stood by the bed with his hands politely folded in front of him as one who had come to pay his respects to an invalid. He seemed very glad when Bonnemama ushered him off to Elijah Brown, who was waiting outside in the car to get him to school.

In the afternoon, Margaux and Alice walked down the hill to the Kastelje. The rooms were empty and echoing.

"It's sat for almost three years, but it looks ready to be moved into, don't you think?" said Alice.

"We have no furniture. Nothing for the kitchen. Nothing of our own."

"That's easily fixed, dear. We'll do some shopping. It's better starting out with everything new.

"I like things old."

"Of course, dear," Alice said quickly. "We'll go up to the attic of the chateau then and see what's hiding there. It's everything we brought from the old house in Boston. I couldn't bear to part with any of it. You'll like that much better."

Margaux stood at the door of one of the upstairs bedrooms and looked inside.

"This will be Robbie's room," she said. When she turned around to Alice, there was the fixed look of having made a decision on her face. "I want to raise the boys myself."

"I know, my dear. I won't interfere."

"I mean, I will let Gretchen go."

"Oh, dear. Then you really mean by yourself. Well, you needn't worry about Gretchen. I've heard from Viola that she's considering an offer of marriage made to her in Buffalo, where her brother lives. Would you like me to tell her?"

"Yes, Ma'ma."

"Good. Then that's settled," said Alice. Moving to embrace Margaux, she said, "I'm so pleased to hear you know what you want to do, dear."

"It's nothing much."

Alice took Margaux's hand as they started down the stairs. "Little things can make a big difference, Margaux."

"We'll see."

CHAPTER SIXTY-ONE

Delphina called up the stairs, "I'm ready to close up now, Miss Laura. Do you want to check the logs?"

Laura put her head around the bedroom door. She was in the middle of dressing.

"No, that's all right, Delphina. I'm sure they're correct. You can lock up."

"Thank you, Miss Laura. Then I'll be going. Good night."

"Good night, Delphina. Thank you."

Laura returned to the clothing dilemma. She was set on the boots and the riding jodhpurs, so she could lace up the boots, but she had to sit down because the boots laced up almost to the knee. Then she stood in front of the mirror and patted her tummy, wishing there was less of it. She profiled for the mirror and looked at her bust. Why couldn't it have stayed small? But then, how could body parts suddenly be out of fashion? She had to stop looking at magazines. The brassieres she bought in New York were so flimsy. Back to the Symington-Side-Lacer and white blouse. Long jacket. No, not with the riding jodhpurs. Oh, the short leather jacket Mother picked out. Just the thing.

Laura couldn't exactly say why, but she liked the white sailor cap and moved it around on the back of her head until it looked cute with her Dutch bob. It seemed to bring out the Swedish in her face. Before she left her second-floor rooms, she telephoned Alice and told her she had had a busy day and was going to bed early. They could talk tomorrow night. She thought that would cover any eventuality.

In the car, she bent over the steering wheel to look up at the sky. It would be light out until eight o'clock or so. That should give her plenty of time. On the passenger seat beside her was the letter addressed to Mr. Gregory Haines, and she glanced over to make sure it wouldn't blow out the window as she picked up speed on the Dixonville road.

When she was past the last houses of Cecilton, she started looking for a road that went east. Any one would probably do. She went by a few that did not look as if they went very far into the scrubby pines and oaks, but then she spotted a good one. Looking over her shoulder to see if anyone was watching, Laura slowed down and turned off the paved road into the woods.

At that moment, the full import of the act came to her. She had left the straight and narrow. No one knew where she was. She could disappear and never be found. Already the Ford had vanished into the wilderness. Why was she doing this? Why was she taking this chance? As her hands gripped the steering wheel tighter and her concentration was needed to negotiate the rough path and the pine branches against the windshield, Laura dismissed both her troubling doubts and the thrill of doing something wrong for the first time in her life. No, it was very simple and easily explained. It was her duty as postmistress to see the mail delivered. Right there on the other seat was the letter to Mr. Gregory Haines. Exhibit A, if evidence was needed.

The road went far back into the woods indeed, but gradually narrowed down. Brush began to scrape the sides of the car, and the hard gravel under the wheels turned into sand—first hard, compressed sand and then softer and more pliant sand. Laura tried to keep up her speed as the car began to bog down. Finally, any semblance of road ended. The Ford stalled out, and the wheels sank into the path.

When Laura got out, she could see the wheels were in up to the hubs. She didn't know what to do. Gregory had a horse. He could pull the car out. But she had to find Gregory first. The road had turned to the west, straight into the sun going down, but it was too narrow to turn around. How far back was that? A mile?

Laura took the letter off the seat, put it in the inside pocket of her jacket, and started walking through the brush with the sun at her back. That was east. Now it was a question of finding Gregory before the sun set. She tried to remember where he had circled on the map with his finger, where she had put the pencil point. On she went. There were swampy places to go around, forcing her to go north. If she could only get up high. Weren't there fire towers out here? She could only see a few yards ahead of her, and the sun was starting to go down. The river must be ahead.

The light faded very fast in the woods. She was in a swampy part again and could not get out of it. She slipped and sat down in the mud. The letter was all right. That was the point of all this; she got to her feet and went on, knee-deep in mud, then ankle deep. When she got to a higher patch of ground, she stopped and looked around in all directions. Nothing but darkness closing in, as if she were slowly going blind. She could hardly tell what was east or west anymore for all the trees.

Laura sat down on the wet, marshy ground, ready to cry. It could have been the dark woods of Rhode Island, made fresh in her memory by her current predicament, or the dark closing in around her. But the bad association of the past was easier to fend off than the rising sense of futility and despair in the present—that ten years after college, she was still single and childless.

She had been living perfectly well on her own until Gregory came along. Now she had allowed herself to build foolish and fantastic hopes. She was really out here in the woods not to deliver a letter but to get a man interested in her. In her long history of making something out of nothing, it was time to face the fact that no man had ever been interested in her, and Gregory wasn't either. If he had not come along, she would have been at home right now, making a pot of Campbell's Beefsteak Tomato soup and upholding the pretense of living perfectly well alone. That was what her life amounted to, the sum of all the soup and cheese and crackers that had gone into making her fat and unattractive.

What happened to her sailor hat? It was gone. She'd have to go back for it. It only cost fifty cents, but it was pretty, and she liked it. She didn't know how much she liked it until now. Maybe it didn't make her look young and cute at all, but that was no reason to abandon it in dirty swamp water when it belonged clean in a closet, even if she never wore it again. Tears came up to her eyes, and she began to cry, and the walls came tumbling down. She cried her heart out for all lost things left behind, herself included.

Laura took her hands away from her face when a light appeared through the trees. Suddenly terrified, she shouted out, "Stay away from me. Stay away from me. I have a gun. I'll shoot you."

The light went out. She listened. There wasn't a sound anywhere. She waited. Still not a sound. Then a rush of feet through the leaves behind her, and she turned her face into a sharp, white light. She closed her eyes against it and did not move.

"Miss Eklund. What are you doing out here?"

The light dropped, went out, and then Gregory Haines lit a match that turned into the warm glow of a kerosene lamp. "I'm sorry. I didn't mean to rush you like that. I didn't recognize the voice. Sorry about the flashlight too. What are you doing out here, Miss Eklund?"

"I came to deliver a letter to you," she said, not knowing how to make herself or her clothes presentable. "My car got stuck in the sand back there, so I started walking. Then it got dark, and I got lost."

Gregory set the lantern down and helped her to her feet.

"Let's get you back to the lodge," he said. "Pete," he called over his shoulder.

A big dog sprang out of the ring of darkness held off by the lantern and cautiously approached. He bared his teeth.

"Don't worry. That's smiling."

Laura put her hand out to his nose, and a very frightening row of upper teeth showed.

"Go on now, Pete. We're heading home," said Gregory. "You weren't far off, Miss Eklund. You would have seen the lights go on in the lodge before long."

The dark shape of a cabin soon came into view, and in no time Laura was standing inside, watching Gregory raise a fire in a very large, open fireplace.

"This is all we have for heat, and I can see you got into some water, so I'm going to get it nice and warm in here. It only takes a few minutes. Only one room."

It was the finest one room Laura had ever seen. It was a log cabin all right, but the logs had been planed, sanded, and varnished to show the grain of the wood as well as a fine tapestry might display artistry in needlework. Blackened hooks, irons, and cooking pots adorned the interior of the fireplace. As Gregory went about the cabin lighting lamps of every description, a bed joined the lighted space, then a tall armoire and dresser, oriental carpets, tables, chairs, bookcases.

"Oh, this is quite nice," said Laura.

"I hope it doesn't look too much like a single man lives here."

Gregory was at the armoire and dresser looking through his clothes while Laura was standing on the mat at the door, not seeing anywhere in front of her to step without getting mud on the carpet or the polished wood floor. He came over when he saw she didn't know what to do.

"Let's get you out of those boots first, Miss Eklund," he said, bending over and starting on the laces. "I have to go out for about an hour to finish up some business. Meanwhile, you can change into anything I've got over there. Just leave your wet clothes by the fireplace. We'll get everything straightened up when I get back. Have you had anything to eat?"

"No, I thought I'd be home by now, Mr. Haines."

"Well, I'm afraid this is going to be home for the night, Miss Eklund," he said. "Now lean over me, and I'll pull off the boots."

Laura did not know what to do but lean over his back and try not to put too much weight on him.

"I'll clean these up for you tonight," he said, standing upright with the boots in his hands. "Pete can stay here with you. Back in about an hour. Oh, there's an outhouse around the back. Just down the path. Better take a lantern if you go outside."

He went out the door. Laura stood blinking at the swiftness of all that had happened. Pete came over to her. She held out her hand. He sniffed at it and showed all his teeth. He was a coonhound. A big one. They were North Carolina dogs, she thought. She had never seen one as big as Pete.

"Good dog," she said.

He went over and lay down by the fire, which was roaring and warming up the lodge quickly. Laura went over to the armoire and dresser and started looking. The windows had heavy curtains over them. She got out of her jacket and pulled off her blouse and Symington-Side-Lacer. They were the only things half wet. The jodhpurs were soaked. So were the bloomer briefs. If Gregory was going to hang them up to dry, she couldn't be embarrassed about them. Glad she kept the label. He might recognize the name Lane Perkins and know she had good taste.

She looked around first, then dropped the jodhpurs and bloomers to her knees and stepped out. She rolled up the bloomers and tucked them into a back pocket of the jodhpurs and scurried completely naked to the fireplace, dropped her clothes in a heap and scurried back, bent over, covering herself. As quickly as she could, she got into a pair of Gregory's drawers, a pair of Gregory's blue denim trousers, and one of Gregory's flannel shirts. The sock drawer only had one pair. She shouldn't take the only one.

What would she do for an hour? In a burst of inspiration, she said to herself, "I'll show him what kind of girl I am." In the cabinets by the fireplace, she found Campbell's Beefsteak Tomato Soup. It must be his favorite. There were six cans. Dry kidney beans. Bread in the breadbox. A jar of saltines. Something that looked like cocoa mix. In a cold box outside the cabin, she found butter, milk, and cheese, and took everything she might need in one hand, the lantern in the other, tiptoeing on her bare feet back inside.

Losing only a little time figuring out the fireplace ironwork, she soon had the soup cooking in the kettle, bread sliced and ready to toast, and the beans going in another pot. She didn't want to use up too much of the cheese, but it looked so nice neatly sliced and arrayed on the plate with the saltines.

When Gregory returned, she heard the scraping of his boots on the wooden steps outside, then the lifting of the metal latch and the creak of the door opening. She wanted to look too busy to turn around.

"Smells good in here," he said.

She stood up from the soup kettle with a wooden ladle in her hand.

"Everything fit all right?" he asked, looking her over.

"A little big for me," she said.

"What about your feet?"

"I didn't want to take your last pair of socks."

"Oh, don't worry about that."

He went over to the dresser and got out the pair of socks. Holding them in one hand, he got down and fished around under the armoire.

"I think there's a pair of slippers under here. Never wear them."

Laura put her hands on his shoulders and held up one foot at a time as he put on the socks and slippers for her.

"That's better, isn't it?"

"They're very nice. Thank you, Mr. Haines. I didn't know what you like to eat, so I just cooked up what I found. I hope you don't mind."

"Oh, I don't mind anything. You're the one stranded out here. I hope you don't mind camping out for a night in the swamps."

"Well, that's exactly where I would have been if you hadn't found me, Mr. Haines. I'm very grateful to be inside your wonderful lodge. Do you think you can get my car out of the sand tomorrow?"

"That shouldn't be any trouble," he said. "I just didn't want to try it in the dark."

After dinner, they made the bed together. Gregory pulled out fresh sheets from the bottom of the armoire. Laura stood on one side, Gregory on the other. They worked in unison, from the head to the foot, pulling out the slack in the middle and tucking in the corners square and tight.

"You'll want a pillow," Gregory said, looking around at the ones on the couch.

"No, I can use this one," she said.

"All right."

Gregory put on a new pillowcase and placed the pillow at a slant against the headboard. Then he gathered up an extra blanket and a pillow off the couch and plopped them by the fireplace.

"I'll bunk over here with Pete," he said. "Would you like to sit by the fire for a little bit before bed? It's only ten thirty. We have hot cocoa, water, or a very fine single malt scotch whiskey—if you don't mind taking liberties with the law of the land."

Laura wanted to say whiskey to show that she was a sophisticated woman, but in a fraction of a second, it flashed through her mind that it might be better to show the side of womanhood that he may be looking for.

"Quite aside from the question of taking liberties with laws of the land, Mr. Haines, I think I would prefer hot cocoa."

"Two hot cocoas it is," he said, turning to his kitchen cabinets with what Laura thought was a satisfied smile that the right kind of girl had just landed in his lap.

Never was Laura more at ease talking to a man. Sunk into a very comfortable armchair, warmed by a good fire, wrapped in Gregory's clothes, she felt fully at peace. There was no question about it. At peace. Maybe for the first time in her life—if peace was desiring nothing more than what was present, if peace was the end of conflict between her disparate selves, or just the calming of the stormy seas within. There was definitely a feeling of peace within her, and she was not so carried away with excitement that she could not recognize it.

Gregory sat on the floor in front of the fire and looked like he was thinking over something she had just said. Pete came over to her. She wasn't apprehensive of the smile anymore, on dog or man, and patted the dog on the head.

"All the books you have," Laura said, gazing toward the bookshelves on every wall.

"I was a teacher before the war."

"Where did you teach, Mr. Haines?"

"I taught philosophy at the University of Chicago. Only for a year though. I was one of the first ones drafted. I would have gone in anyway."

"Don't you want to go back to it now?"

"I don't know, Miss Eklund. I've thought about it. When I finally got out of the hospital," he said, with the gesture of a hand to his face, "I didn't feel like going home. I traveled around a little. Then I got into business here."

"What kind of business are you in, Mr. Haines?"

"Import business."

"What do you import?"

Gregory looked around the room. Laura was sorry she asked but thought it was too late to retract the question as long as he seemed to be thinking over an answer.

"What you might call niche market products," he said. After a long pause he elaborated, "A little bit of this and a little bit of that, extravagances for the rich, loaves and fishes for the poor."

He laughed, and Laura laughed too.

A topic to avoid, she noted to herself.

From the bed, Laura peeked over the covers to the fireplace where Gregory was bundled up on the floor beside Pete.

"Good night, Mr. Haines."

"Good night, Miss Eklund."

He extinguished the last lamp. Then it was just the red coals in the fireplace and the sounds of the last of them dropping through the grate.

"Can I be at the post office by eight?" she asked. "Really, I should say by seven."

"I'll get you up at four," he said. "I'll take you into town on the horse and go back for the car."

"Then I'll take you home in the car," she proposed brightly.

"I'll show you a better way to get here. You won't have to walk through the swamp."

It was encouraging to think that an invitation to visit the lodge again was implicit. That was all it could mean, at least no less than that. A last remark about how quiet it was in the woods at night brought them back to conversing, and far into the night they talked philosophy across the dark between them, from one topic to the next without start or finish. Divine and natural law. Free will and determinism. Pragmatism, hedonism, stoicism. The Greeks' eight different words for *eros*! If the limitations of the human mind can conceive of the infinite, shouldn't it follow that there must be infinity plus one? And would that not be merely a restatement of the ontological argument? Laura felt it was the first time anyone had ever been interested in her ideas since her father had sought to bring them out, and Gregory's replies confirmed that he had been listening attentively and thinking deeply over what she had to say. It made her examine the logic of her reasoning, and she chose her words carefully as she brought out the intellect that her father had so lovingly fostered.

Gregory said he would give her an introductory book on philosophy to take home. Their thoughts and voices trailed off as sleep overtook them. Laura wasn't sure, but she was afraid she might have been the one to fall asleep first and bring to an end a perfect day.

It was still dark, but Laura heard the birds waking up. Inside the lodge there were muted sounds of noises made accidentally, metal spoon against cast iron, teacup knocking into teacup, kindling snapped. She kept her head under the covers. She wanted to be awakened by a touch on the shoulder and a whisper, and presently, she was.

"Miss Eklund. It's four o'clock."

Laura pulled the blanket and sheet away from her face, looked at him in the light of the lamps around the room, and smiled.

"No one's done that for a long time," Gregory said.

She hoped he meant smile at him, but there was no need to ask. He turned away to let her get up and get dressed in his clothes again, and busied himself at the fireplace. When Laura took her seat at the little table, there was a bowl of oatmeal waiting for her.

"Bacon and eggs coming up if you want them," he said. His back was turned to her, but one hand was in view, theatrically posing with an egg ready to crack on the edge of a frying pan at her signal.

"Go ahead, Mr. Haines." It felt so good to laugh and feel easy and intimate with another person.

Her clothes were hanging from stones jutting out on the sides of the fireplace—the bloomers too, almost dry. He had smoothed the wrinkles on the shirt as it dried. He must have been up very early. The letter was still in the side pocket of her jacket, and she got up to put it on the high mantelpiece.

"Your letter," she said. "I logged it as delivered yesterday. I'll have to correct that."

"Don't bother. It was in the lodge."

"But not delivered."

"I won't hold you to it," he said, smiling.

The sun was just coming up when they started out on the horse. Gregory helped her into the saddle and swung up behind her, bareback, and put his hands through her arms to hold the reins.

"I'd let you drive, Miss Eklund, but the horse is new to you. He's a good old chap, but nothing like a Ford."

"What am I supposed to hold on to?" Laura asked, looking down at the rounded pommel of the English saddle.

"Well, not my arms. I'm steering. You can hold Plutarch's mane—no, that's not good either. A pull would confuse him."

"We're already going. Tell me quick."

"Bring your arms back, grab my coat. Both sides, both sides."

Laura grabbed his coat, pulling his chest snug against her back.

"Now loosen up a little and get your balance," he said. "You've been on a horse before, haven't you?"

"Yes, but not like this."

They came out of the brush and onto a dirt road much sooner than Laura expected, and Gregory had to rein in the horse.

"This is the kind of ground Plutarch likes best. Do you want to see what he can do?"

"Sure," said Laura.

She felt Gregory's legs drawing up behind hers to give Plutarch a nudge. The horse picked up to a trot. Another nudge brought him to a canter. A moment later, she felt Gregory's knees spur the horse again, and Plutarch plunged into a gallop.

"Can you stay on?" Gregory shouted.

"Yes, it's exhilarating," Laura cried.

She raised her eyes to the canopy of leaves and branches flashing overhead. She wished she hadn't bobbed her hair, that it was long and spreading out behind her in the wind. Gregory's face was at her shoulder. Gripping tightly the flaps of his coat, Laura pulled him so close against her back that their bodies fell into the rhythm of the galloping horse. The only way to stay on was to grip with the legs and rock the hips as one rider. She had never experienced such a high state of physical arousal, and in its duration of passage through the trees and underbrush to the road, she blocked out the protests of her mind and threw to the wind every restraint of her modesty.

When they slowed to a trot and down to a walk on the paved road, Laura was glad Gregory could not see the flush that had risen to her face. She had been overcome by physical stimulation. That's what had happened, she thought. Physical stimuli had triggered the natural sensual responses of her body. It was just science. $F = uN$. The friction of her body against the saddle was directly proportional to the applied force. Amontons' law. But to do the calculation she would have to write down how much she weighed. Never mind. It was more like bodies in motion anyway, which, as far as she understood, suggested human mating. Contact with any male of the species could have initiated such a disturbance in her nervous system.

But it was *this* male, this man, Gregory Haines, who had taken her in and treated her with the greatest respect and tenderness. She could lose herself in the details all she wanted, but the larger picture presented itself with undeniable clarity. Up until this point, no passion for a man had ever contested the supremacy of her mind and the imposition of its will. That had brought her only confusion and loneliness. But after the most wonderful night of her life, a new Laura Eklund thought it was time for her mind to step aside and let her heart take a turn at the helm.

Laura was glad no one was out on the street at six o'clock in the morning. Gregory swung down and helped her out of the saddle.

"I'll be back with the car," he said. "I still have to find it."

"Thank you, Mr. Haines," she said. "For taking me in for the night. And for everything you did."

"See you later on then," he said.

Then he was back on Plutarch and down the street at a good clip, and Laura stepped inside the post office. Once she was upstairs and undressing, she realized how much she smelled of wood smoke and went to draw a hot bath. There was no time to dawdle. She would think about what had happened to her when she went to bed tonight. No other corporeal experience compared with the gallop through the woods, and she wanted to contemplate it without distraction.

In the tub, she wondered where Gregory bathed. In that bathtub behind the house? She knew he would have heated up water for her and rigged up a curtain had she asked. Half submerged, she relaxed and noticed how sore her legs, hips, and back were after the ride. It had made her feel so athletic and vigorous. How could she keep that up? Maybe he would leave the car out front and just ride off, and she would never see him again. He must know she felt something for him. It could not have escaped him that she was willing to accept him as he was. The disfigurement of his face meant nothing to her. Wasn't that love? It was up to him now.

CHAPTER SIXTY-TWO

Laura told Alice all about her adventure with Gregory Haines when she called at nine o'clock that night. She could hear the concern and disapproval in Alice's voice, and it didn't take long for it to come out.

"Oh, Laura. You should never have gone out there alone. And don't tell me it was part of your job because I know from Delphina that it isn't."

"I just wanted to do it, Mother."

"Anything could have happened out there at night. There are people out in those swamps you know."

"I was perfectly safe with Gregory. He was a perfect gentleman."

"He had you in his lair."

"It isn't a lair, Mother. It's a very nice lodge."

"I'm sure it's nothing more than a cabin."

"No, it's a hunting lodge. Gregory said a man from Philadelphia built it and used to come down to hunt geese. It's really very nice."

"Well, I'm going to talk to Andrew about this Mr. Haines."

"Please don't do that, Mother. I don't want Mr. Haines to think I've betrayed his confidence."

"Nothing will get back to Mr. Haines, dear. I just want to know if there is anything objectionable about this man. Andrew can make discreet inquiries."

"I won't listen to anything bad about him."

"That's just foolishness, Laura."

"You think you know what's good for me and what's not good for me, but I don't think you know me at all, Mother. You have your own ideas about everything, and you have your own ideas about me as well. You always wanted me to be something that I'm not. If I want to go live in the woods with Gregory, I will."

There was silence for a moment from Alice. Then she said very softly, "Do you want me to come over?"

"No, Mummy. I'm sorry. I didn't mean what I said. I know you mean well."

"Andrew does too, darling. He loves you as much as I do. I know you could never call him Father because you loved your real father so much, and he understands that, but he loves you just like I do, and we want the best for you. Please say you understand that."

"I do, Mummy. It's just that I feel so deeply that I know Gregory's soul, and nothing will change my mind about him."

"Then I want to meet him. When can we do that?"

"I don't know. It's too soon."

"You spent the night with him. How can it be too soon?"

"It wasn't like that, Mother. It was impossible for him to get me home."

"All right, dear. I'll let you manage it. But when the right opportunity comes up, I want to meet him. Oh, I forgot something. You got a letter from Arnold Blessing. I don't know why you sent it over here."

"Because it was addressed in care of you. That means it has to go to you first."

"Isn't that a little silly, darling?"

"Those are the rules."

"I thought you weren't following the rules anymore, dear."

They both laughed, and it seemed a good time to end the call.

"I'll send it with Elijah tomorrow. Read it! Lois says he's a nice boy."

"All right, Mother. I will."

"Give him a chance."

"I will. Good night, Mummy."

"Good night, my darling girl. Sleep well. Sweet dreams."

Laura put the telephone down and lurched from her chair. "Oh no," she exclaimed, running to the window.

She thought she had heard an automobile outside, but she wasn't listening for Gregory just then. Now she knew it must have been him. She looked out and saw her Ford parked in front of the post office. Losing no time, she ran down the stairs, fumbled with her keys at the interior door, dropped them in the dark post office, couldn't find them, and had to go back to turn on the lights. They had gone under the counter. By the time she was out on the street, Gregory was nowhere to be seen.

The Ford was shining in the street lamp. She walked around it, marveling at how brand new it looked. He had washed all the mud off and polished it. Her sailor hat was on the driver's seat. He found it! It was clean as a whistle! She looked everywhere for a note, but there wasn't one.

She went inside and upstairs. She read a few more pages of Matlock's *Issues in Philosophy*, the book Gregory lent her—Gregory's book. When it made her sleepy and her eyes closed, she held it to her breast and thought of him. "Good night, my love," she whispered to herself.

The next night, Laura had Arnold Blessing's letter by her telephone chair. He had been beaten up and arrested at the rally. He had been in jail and had just gotten out. He wanted her to come to New York. He wanted to see her.

It seemed so long ago now, an episode from another lifetime. But she remembered him vividly. Remembered kissing him and letting him put his hands under her clothes. Men weren't supposed to do that. Girls weren't supposed to let them. How did men know who was a fast girl? Did they just try any girl who came along till they found one? Arnold only wanted her to come to New York so he could do it again. He would push her until she gave in. Maybe Lois let it slip that she was already ruined. It took him this long to get around to writing.

Laura put the letter back in the envelope and set it aside. It was only polite to answer, but she decided not to. There was no future in it.

CHAPTER SIXTY-THREE

Laura kept the upstairs windows open as full summer came on. Sometimes she pulled a chair over and sat looking out. She stayed up later than she should every night, and thinking Gregory might come to the door, she lay awake listening for Plutarch's hooves and the sound of wagon wheels. Another letter came for Mr. Gregory Haines. She brought it to the back room and put it in the cubbyhole marked USPO Unclaimed. In six weeks she could place the advertisement in the newspaper for unclaimed mail. Undoubtedly, there were enough clues in the letter to answer any questions she might have about Gregory, but she couldn't bring herself to open it.

Letters can be about anything, she told herself. It could be the head of the philosophy department asking him to come back. No, it would have to be a man's handwriting with a University of Chicago envelope. The handwriting could be his mother or his sister. That must be it. She could always go to Mr. Croft in private and ask him about Gregory, just to know the facts. It was clear that he knew something about him. No, she could never do that. As the days went by without seeing Gregory, it began to dawn upon her that she was going unclaimed, as much as the unread letters in the back room.

Gregory went by the post office one night in a flatbed motor truck with cargo under a tarp. She only noticed it was Gregory because he stopped for a dog crossing the street, and there were no other vehicles out that late. When she saw him, her heart stopped. She did not breathe for a moment. He didn't look up. He kept going.

Autie came in one day for the Croft mail.

"Elijah's under the weather," he said.

Laura had been expecting to see him sometime, but it was a shock when he walked in the door. She had not seen him since he left for Fort Riley with his new wife.

"I guess you can't get away from here very often," he said, looking around the post office. "I'm sorry we left off writing, but I hear a lot about you from Mom, and she probably tells you what's going on at the farm."

"Not much, really."

"Well, you knew I left the army."

"Yes, I knew that."

"And you knew about Margaux. Mom said you were there."

"Yes," Laura said, lowering her eyes. "I know you brought her back."

"We're living in the cottage now. Everything's going pretty well. I'm working for Dad for the time being, straightening out the finances of the farm. God, it's a mess. Dad isn't much on record keeping."

Autie leaned on the counter. Laura stood on the other side, as if she were waiting on a customer and hearing another life story.

"I wish you'd come to dinner on Sundays," he said. "You aren't working Sunday nights, are you?"

"No, but I like to be alone and get ready for Monday."

"Then how about Saturday nights? We always hike up the hill for dinner with Mom and Dad every Sunday night and most Saturday nights."

"I'm tired from the week on Saturday night," she said.

"Oh come on."

The real reason was she didn't want to take a chance of missing Gregory, but she said the next truest thing, "Well, I have the feeling your wife doesn't want me around."

"No, that's just how she is with everybody. She was always standoffish."

"I'm a little embarrassed saying it, but does she know we had a thing for each other?"

"No, I never mentioned anything."

"Then she just doesn't like me, I guess."

"No, that's not it. I don't know much about the details. Well, I know you'll keep it to yourself. Margaux had some trouble in the past. Every week Mom takes her up to Baltimore to talk to a psychiatrist, a woman doctor. The only one in the country, I think. Mom found her. We all think it's done her some good. The doctor says it might take some time for her to get out of the depression, and there's something else she has, but I can't remember what they call it. Something like shell shock. I saw some of that firsthand in the war. It can happen to anyone who's had bad experiences."

Autie looked around vacantly for a moment, to all appearances as if what he was describing was just then happening to himself.

"She takes everything too hard, and bad memories come back. Something like that. Well, you probably know what I mean."

"I know. I don't think about the past anymore."

Laura was going to say that she had no reason to think about the past anymore. It was the present that was driving her crazy.

Every night that summer before she went to sleep, Laura lay in bed looking toward the curtains stirring in the open window. Gregory wasn't coming tonight. It might be tomorrow night. How many nights had she said it might be tomorrow night? That was the insidious way hope worked to keep you hoping. Waiting for the next day. It was wreaking havoc on her equilibrium. There was no reason for her to have fallen in love with Gregory Haines after one meeting and one night in his house. But she had. If she were Autie, she would have done the same thing, take Margaux back. Even after she'd been with that awful artist. Loving is loving. Maybe she loved Gregory because she wanted to be the only one who would. But maybe he didn't need her for that. Maybe he was fine by himself. She also had tried being alone and failed at it. She didn't want to be postmistress anymore. How could she be so lonely? Nobody else in the world seemed to be.

Elijah came the next morning for the Croft mail. He said he never felt better and speculated that Autie just wanted an excuse to get out on the road. Laura told him there was a letter in today's batch for Delphina from the Washington Square College of New York University. It was a thick one. That meant she was accepted, but she didn't tell him that. It would spoil the surprise.

Delphina would be very excited when she came in this afternoon. She would give notice. She was going to be a college girl in a big city, walking with college boys across the clipped, green grass of quadrangles. She'd be attending classes, taking notes, having long, intelligent conversations, developing friendships, meeting boys, and getting dreamy, and just being young. Delphina's time had come. Without jealousy or envy, but with a sorrowful eye toward the turning of seasons, Laura felt that her time had passed, not gently by, but yanked out from under her.

CHAPTER SIXTY-FOUR

Laura wished she had thought of the idea two months ago, but she was happy enough to have it now, while it was still warm. It wouldn't work so well in winter. On Saturday afternoon after she closed the post office, she went across the street to the hardware store and bought a compass. Next thing, her father's astronomy binoculars were too big and heavy to take to the woods. There was a good pair of field glasses at the store, but it cost too much money, so she bought a telescope. It was a child's telescope, but she looked through it and thought it would do. She paid a dollar for the compass and telescope and went home very pleased with step one of her plan.

Step two was getting her bearings. For that, Laura took out the aerial map of the postal routes and laid it over the top of her desk. Under the light of the desk lamp, with her reading glasses on, she located the pencil point she had made the night she first met Gregory Haines. There was a roll of tracing paper somewhere. She went through the drawers of her desk but didn't find it.

Laura checked to make sure she still had change in her skirt pocket and ran down the stairs and around the corner to the dress shop. She didn't want to get stuck talking with Mrs. Butler, who could go on forever, but she needed the tracing paper to make a good map. Mrs. Butler was just locking up, but she went back in and came out with a roll of just the thing.

"Oh, this is much more than I need."

"Well, just take what you want and bring the roll back," said Mrs. Butler. "You don't owe me anything. Mr. Butler has a Grange meeting tonight, and I have to get his dinner up. We can talk tomorrow."

Laura returned to her map feeling lucky. It was going to take time transposing accurately from the geological survey, and Mrs. Butler was a tough gossiper to get away from. For the next two hours, Laura drew carefully in pen over the perimeters of the area she wanted, marking the landmarks and highlighting the roads and paths she could make out. The better idea of superimposing a grid came to her, so she started over. She wanted to finish the map before dinner, but time got away from her while triangulating and calculating distances.

Just before nine o'clock the map was finally finished. The telephone rang upstairs. Laura ran up and told Alice she couldn't talk tonight. She didn't feel well and was going to go to bed early, and no, Alice didn't have to come over. By the time Laura had finished checking over her map, it was ten-thirty. She wanted to get a good night's sleep, but she wanted to lay out her clothes and find the bird book before she went to bed.

Sitting down with her Campbell's Beefsteak Tomato Soup, cheese, and crackers turned out to be the last thing Laura did that night. She was almost too excited to go to sleep.

It was a good thing she set the alarm clock. She woke up to it from a deep sleep and instantly remembered the plan for the day. The hot bath made her feel ready for bird-watching in the woods for Gregory Haines. Light breakfast. Two eggs over easy, toast, bacon, oatmeal. She decided to take an apple along.

In front of the full-length mirror, Laura turned around and examined herself in her lucky outfit, the riding jodhpurs, knee boots, white blouse, and short leather jacket that she had worn the day she met Gregory. She almost forgot the sailor hat.

Despite the deliberations that had gone into the trip and the patience she had applied the night before to its planning, Laura's heart quickened when she got out of town in the Ford. She had to calm herself down and remember to breathe. It might be a long day. She might not find the lodge. Gregory might not find her. The car could get stuck in the sand again. Laura tried to prepare herself for nothing happening, the way nothing ever seemed to happen right when a good plan was all laid out. But this time she let herself hope, based on the condition of the car, the accuracy of the map, and the mathematical calculations her father would have looked over with approval. The engine sounded good, and the tires had plenty of tread and new inner tubes. It was hard to imagine driving back with nothing to show.

In the woods, in the mixed terrain of old-growth oaks and scruffy pines, she pulled over at the road she thought she had taken last spring. She checked her map and counted the off-shoot paths and figured she would be about right if she took the next road that went off to the east. A few hundred yards down, it began to narrow and turn into sand like the one last spring, and she stopped when she saw ahead of her a mud hole in the middle of it. She got out of the car and walked over. There were signs of boot prints and horse tracks all around it, and she quickly deduced it was the same place.

That was disappointing, but it meant she was close. It was morning, she had the map, and she had the compass. There was time to try a few headings. According to the map, she only had to cover one hundred eighty degrees of area to a depth of four hundred yards. It would be prudent to come back and start from the car each time.

Laura took the bird book and telescope out of the car and put on her sailor hat. With the compass before her on a north heading, she set out walking through the light brush. There wasn't a way to estimate the yards, so she gave herself twenty minutes on her wristwatch to each end point, aware that it was going to vary with the terrain. The variables could only be reduced by so much.

At each end point, Laura gave herself ten minutes to sit down and wait for something to happen. She wasn't very interested in birds, but she looked through the telescope. Nothing to see but tree limbs and leaves. She wished she had a cigarette to smoke. She liked smoking with Lois and Mother in the apartment. Maybe she should take up the habit to kill time in places like this.

She made three exploratory headings, starting from the car each trip. Before the sun started to go down, there was time for one more, which would complete one quadrant of the map. That was disappointing because it was the quadrant of highest probability. She hoped there were three other Sundays of good weather. It was still a good plan. She didn't have to succeed the first time. That would be too good to be true.

Completing her last heading, Laura gave Gregory more wait time at the turn-around point, but there was no sign of him or the lodge. When she got halfway back to the car, she heard a horse neigh up ahead. Her heart leaped, and it was all she could do to keep herself from running. What luck. What fantastic luck! She could see Plutarch's head through the brush.

Laura came out of the woods onto the road. It wasn't Plutarch. It was a different horse, with a man in a uniform on him. Then a second man. Maryland State Police. They wheeled their horses when they saw her and got down out of the saddles.

"Is this your car, miss?"

"Yes," she said, trying not to let her voice tremble.

"You're under arrest. Don't try to run away."

"I'm not running away," she said quickly. "Why am I under arrest? Why? What have I done?"

"Transporting liquor."

"I don't have any liquor."

The taller of the two handed the reins of his horse to the other one. They were both big men but lean. The shirts of their uniforms were taut, without a crease, and the black chinstraps of their brimmed hats were pulled tight across their square chins. Laura watched as the tall one took two green bottles out of the saddlebags on the horse, went around to the passenger side of the Model T and put them on the floor.

"We found these in your car," the other one said.

"But he just put them there."

The two troopers smiled at each other.

"That's the way it goes," said one. "You got any on you?"

"No, I don't have any on me. You can't do this."

The tall one put a finger to his badge and smiled. Then the other one smiled too.

"We're going to have to search you, ma'am."

"No, you can't do this."

The shorter one moved to grab her. The tall one said, "Nah, leave her alone." Then he looked at Laura and said, "Look ma'am. I know you don't want to get run in for trafficking liquor. We're just doing our job. You could be carrying money from a drop. You're going to have to take off your clothes."

Laura backed up against the car and brought her arms to her chest.

"It's better if you cooperate," said the shorter one.

They were waiting.

"You can't make me take off my clothes," she said. "That's illegal."

They just looked at each other and shrugged.

"We don't run into too many lawyers out here," said one.

They just looked at her and waited. She didn't know what she could do but take off her clothes. Maybe they'd let her go. If they forced her, they would tear them. Then she couldn't get back in the post office without people seeing her in torn clothes. If they held her down and tore them off it would only excite them. Then they would rape her.

Laura lowered her eyes. "Are you going to rape me?" she said quietly. Before she needed to separate her mind from what was happening to her, she wanted to get her facts straight.

The tall one looked at the shorter one. She could tell they were smiling at each other.

"Sounds like she wants it," said one. "What do you think?"

"I think she wants it."

"Well, it was her idea."

"The back seat looks good."

"I kinda like that pile of leaves over there."

"Please stop," said Laura, holding her arms tighter around her.

"Why don't you make it easy on everybody and take 'em off?"

Laura started to get out of her jacket. Then she stopped and held her arms around herself again.

One nodded to the other. The tall one undid the strap over his gun and took it out, but he didn't point it at her. Instead, he came over to the car. He stood right beside her and pointed it at the front tire.

"Hey—" said the other one. "That's property of the state of Maryland now."

The tall one fired twice in rapid succession into the ground beside the tire, and Laura jumped.

"Bootleggers' cars can get shot up pretty bad in our business," said the other one. "You wouldn't want that to happen to your car, would you?"

"No," she said in a voice barely audible.

"Then maybe you'd better get out of those clothes."

She didn't want her car full of bullet holes. Because of her, because she had taken it to the woods where it didn't belong, it had gotten stuck in the mud and gotten all dirty. She didn't want her poor car shot full of holes. In meek submission, Laura took off her jacket. Her sailor hat fell to the ground. The troopers started laughing. Then the short one held up his hand to say something. Laura stopped at the second button of her blouse.

"This is only going to work out right for you, lady, if nobody hears about it. No arrest and you keep your car, but nobody hears about it. Understand? You don't want anyone to know you've been a bad girl, do you?"

"No," Laura said.

"What's that?"

"No."

"No what?"

"I won't tell anyone."

"All right. Back to what you were doing."

Laura felt sick to her stomach. Her fingers fumbled with the buttons. She couldn't undo them. The tall one got up from where he was sitting on a log and came toward her.

Birds, some kind of birds suddenly flew up from the ground as a horse and rider burst out of the brush and onto the road about fifty yards down. Gregory on Plutarch. They came at a trot, Gregory reining in the horse from wanting to run. They came up to the side of the car, and Gregory leaned over to touch Laura's shoulder and look at her face.

"Put your jacket on, Miss Eklund," he said. "You might want to sit in the car."

He waited until Laura was in the car, then turned Plutarch to face the two dismounted troopers. He had a rifle slung over his shoulder, but he did not take it off. The troopers had their hats off and were holding them in their hands.

"We came across the car," said one. "We were just checking it out."

"What were the shots?"

"Fired in the air, sir. She tried to get away," said the other one.

"You men move on," Gregory said.

"We will. Thank you, sir."

They put on their hats quickly and were in the saddle and down to the first turn of the road, as if Gregory had given them a count of ten.

Gregory dismounted and let the reins drop. Laura opened the door and got out of the car. He did not step back very far, and they were standing close.

"This is so embarrassing," she said, looking down at her boots. "I was bird watching. I heard it was a good spot. A lot of birds are migrating now. That's why I came out here, bird watching because they're migrating birds, they fly over—"

Then she burst into tears. Gregory immediately stepped forward and put his arms around her. She shivered and trembled. He held her tighter. She let herself go and wailed. She cried against his shoulder, against his neck, and against the wounded side of his face, holding onto him, gasping for breath between sobs, and suddenly she threw up all down the back of his coat. He only held her in a stronger grip and made soothing sounds. She realized he was holding her up, and her legs were almost dangling. She had not been held in strong arms with her feet off the ground since she was a small child, and she stopped crying and closed her eyes remembering the comforting arms of her father.

When she could finally speak, she said, "I was so scared. I was so scared."

"There's nothing to be afraid of now," he said. "I'm here. Nobody's going to hurt you."

"You can let me down," she said. She didn't want to call him Mr. Haines, but she did not want to say Gregory, as much as she wanted to. She looked around helplessly.

"I don't have anything to wipe off your coat," she said. "I'm so sorry."

He stopped her from using her hands. "It's nothing," he said.

Gregory took off his coat, turned it inside-out and used the soft cotton lining to clean her face. He didn't stop until Laura had to smile at how assiduously he was going about it. She had to bring a hand up to her face to stop him.

"There," he said. "Clean as a whistle."

"But what about you?" she said.

"I'll clean up later. It's getting dark. We've got to get you home. Let's get your car turned around. Do you know your way back?"

"I think so," she said.

"I'll lead you to the main road."

"No, I can do it. I don't want to put you to any more trouble," she said.

"It's less trouble than worrying about you," he said with a smile. "The easiest thing is taking you back to the lodge for the night, but you've probably had enough of the woods for one day."

"Can we do that?" she said.

It just came out of her mouth. Her nervous system was haywire. She put a hand out and touched his arm. She had already been held in his arms, against his chest. What was touching an arm?

"Do you mind? Be honest with me. You can say no."

He laughed. "I liked having you over the last time."

Gregory mounted up. Laura got in the car, started it up, and followed Plutarch. She saw where she had gone wrong. There was another road that branched off. Because of a dirt mound blocking the view from the main road, it didn't look like a road at all, but it opened up on the other side of the mound and eventually dead-ended at the lodge. The wagon was there and the truck she had seen Gregory driving. In the fading daylight, Laura could see it was a small clearing with a stream bordering one side. There was a large garden.

"Pete keeps the deer out," Gregory said when he saw her looking at it. "When he isn't asleep."

Pete came around the corner of the lodge and bounded up to her, smiling with all his teeth out. He still looked menacing, and Laura was still jittery, so she only put her hand out to touch his nose.

The night at the lodge was exactly like the first time, except they had a washup in the stream, sitting on separate rocks. She wore his clothes again. They had Campbell's Beefsteak Tomato with cheese and crackers, and

Gregory made a very fine salad from the last of the garden. They made the bed together and talked a little after dinner, sitting on the hearthrug before the fire. He was in the middle of explaining how philosophy had changed since the turn of the century when she started crying again for no reason. He moved over and put an arm around her without hesitating.

"I don't know why I'm being so silly," she said.

"You aren't being silly, Laura. You've had a frightening experience."

"They couldn't just arrest me, could they—Gregory?"

"Well, they can arrest anybody. But they have to have a good reason. They can get into serious trouble if they aren't careful."

"I should have told them I was a federal employee."

"There's that too, but I meant something else."

"Well, you better tell me before it happens again."

Gregory got up and went back to his chair and moved it closer. He looked like he wanted to be evasive.

"Shouldn't I know? I want to be able to defend myself. What kind of trouble do they want to stay out of?"

"You're Mr. Croft's daughter."

"Not his real daughter."

"Well—effectively you are. In the eyes of the world."

"I don't see where that puts me with respect to the law."

Gregory paused again, laughed with his skewed mouth, then fell silent, and a serious expression came to his strange face.

"If it had been Mr. Croft who rode up instead of me," he said, "those two men would not have left the woods alive."

Gregory went to his pile of bedding by the fire with Pete, and Laura went to the bed. She looked out from under the covers and said, "Good night, Gregory."

He said, "Good night, Laura."

She didn't want to tell him that he got another letter from Chicago. It could wait. There was already enough to keep her sleepless that night. Between the upsetting events of the day, which she understood perfectly well as an abuse of authority, and the scrap of information Gregory had just given her, for which she had no referent, she thought she would be awake half the night. But as the blaze in the fireplace sank into the quiet red of coals, the silence of the woods stole in through the open windows of the lodge and mixed her unfinished thoughts with sleep.

CHAPTER SIXTY-FIVE

Gregory got her up at five o'clock and cooked her a wonderful breakfast. She assured him she knew exactly how to get back to the main road and made him stay at the lodge. As she let the Ford warm up, he said, "I'm not doing anything next Saturday night. How about you?"

"Nothing," she said.

"Can I make dinner for you? I mean something more complicated than soup."

"I'd like that."

"Want me to come get you?"

"No, I can come out. That's better for you if you're cooking, isn't it?"

"All right then."

He tapped twice on the frame of the car window, and Laura made a slow turn out of the clearing. She put on her sailor hat and waved out the window as she started up the road, feeling she had never been so happy in her life.

Her beautiful black Ford—not shot up and not property of the state of Maryland—got her home with plenty of time to take a hot bath. She lay under the gentle, soapy water with her face tilted up so that her ears were under, blocking the sounds of the awakening town outside the window. She closed her eyes and dreamed. She dreamed as much as she had cried yesterday. Gregory and Laura. Laura Eklund Haines. Laura Haines. Mr. and Mrs. Haines. Don't the Haines have beautiful children? How did you meet? Oh, it's a funny story. She knew he was in love with her. It had to be true.

Laura hurried downstairs. Oh no. Three mail sacks from the train depot today. No time to look at handwriting and wonder. No time to be the woman she was before last night. She had to think like Delphina, she had to move like Delphina, and she had to be Delphina. By seven it was sorted, logged, and bundled, and Jerry Conrow was out the door. Elijah Brown sauntered in next with the outgoing Croft mail. He said Delphina got some good news in the mail yesterday and would be in on time today.

Delphina came in that afternoon in the same businesslike way she always came in and went about her work right away. At break time, she told Laura the news.

"I have to be in New York for orientation next week, Miss Laura," she said.

Laura looked at the calendar. "You'll be very busy getting ready, Delphina, so I think perhaps your last day should be this Thursday. You'll be paid for Friday and through next week anyway."

"Oh, no, Miss Laura. That's not right."

"It's in the rules, Delphina. And you're entitled to a bonus as well. For doing such a good job."

"Thank you, Miss Laura," Delphina said modestly.

Laura felt herself full of loving and giving. It was all because of Gregory. Everything that had been hibernating inside her was waking up, and she felt it all day, one good feeling after another opening its eyes to the world. Like a field of flowers. She had never thought of herself as flowers until Gregory.

That night, right after dinner, Laura called Alice.

"Is everything all right?" said Alice with heavy concern in her voice.

"Everything's fine, Mummy. I wanted to talk to you."

"You know I always call at nine."

"I want to see you. Do you think you can come over?"

"Of course, dear. Just let me change."

"Oh, no. You don't have to do that."

"We had the Mechlins over for cocktails. Very formal. They just left. I'm all dolled up. I have to get out of this corset. I can't stand it."

"Then you haven't had dinner."

"It's all right, dear. Autie and Margaux are here with the boys, so Andrew has company. I'll be around in twenty minutes."

When Alice got to the post office in the Pierce-Arrow and Laura let her in, there was a nice little dinner waiting for her. Pea soup with croutons, chicken cutlets, and a salad Gregory had sent along with her that morning.

Laura told her about her bird watching trip to the woods and getting found by Mr. Haines. She finished the good part while Alice was eating and started into the bad part when they moved into the living room with their coffee. She began by trying to swear Alice to secrecy.

"How can I promise not to tell Andrew something?" she said. "I tell him everything. If I knew what it was, maybe I could promise to just tell him part of it, but I don't know what it is. Is it about Mr. Haines?"

"Partly."

"He already knows about your interest in Mr. Haines. I went behind your back. I'm sorry, but I had to, Laura. He said Mr. Haines is a fine man, so I didn't see a need to say anything. Has something developed?"

"I can't tell you until you promise."

"Well, I don't know what to do then. It seems important for you to tell me."

"Then just promise, Mummy. Please."

"All right, I promise. For your sake."

"It's not for my sake," said Laura. "It might put someone's life in danger."

Alice looked at her very seriously. "Then I want you to think carefully about what you want to tell me, Laura. You know the way I feel about certain things. I can't be silent about injustice or cruelty and a few other things like that. You know the kind of thing. I want you to think about what you are asking of me when you want me to promise not to tell."

Laura looked around the room at the curtains she had made for the windows, at the chair she had sewn a cover for, at the lampshades she had painted—her little attempts to make the room pretty. Her mind turned to all the vain efforts she had made in her life, including living alone. She started to cry again and could not stop herself. The trembling came back, and she slumped back into the chair quite helplessly. Alice rushed to her and pulled her down to the floor where she could hold her head in her lap.

She had never seen Laura cry. There had been tears in her eyes over Rory and tears in her eyes over Autie, more than once, and that business in Rhode Island, but she had never seen Laura break down and cry like this.

"What is it, dear? Tell me. I'll promise."

"Something terrible happened," was all Laura could say. She tried, but she could not sit up or stop crying until her sense of time intervened. It was late. Alice had a husband and should be going home to him.

When Laura sat up to say it was late and she did not want to be an inconvenience, Alice went to the telephone and called Andrew.

"I'm going to stay over with Laura tonight, dear," she said. "You'll be all right, won't you? I love you. Be back in the morning." Then she hung up the telephone and turned to Laura. "Now it will be *me* keeping *you* up. I know you have work in the morning, but I want to hear it out, and let's see what we can do about what happened. I brought a little helper."

Alice took a pint bottle of brandy out of the pocket of her skirt and laughed. "There were more places to hide bottles in my day. We didn't need to hide liquor back then. All skirts had to do was hide our gams. And I brought along these. They're very tasty."

Alice pulled a package of cigarettes from another pocket. "All we need now is Lois." As she smoothed back Laura's hair, she said, "I do wish she were here. She always has good advice."

"You do too, Mummy."

"Then let's talk. I want to hear everything that makes you cry, my darling."

They went in the kitchen to get an ashtray and decided to stay at the table with a candle between them. Before she sat down, Laura closed the little louvered doors to the living room and hallway so the smoke wouldn't get out of the kitchen. They took sips of brandy from little glasses and lit their cigarettes off the candle, and Laura told Alice everything that had happened with the state troopers. She also told her the strange thing Gregory had said about Mr. Croft. Alice listened with an unchanging face. The difficult parts made Laura choke and have to pause to compose herself, but she got through them. Relief smoothed the lines across her brow as she took a gulp of brandy and a puff off her cigarette before sitting back in her chair with her arms crossed.

After a thoughtful silence, Alice said, "You were right to make me promise not to say anything to Andrew."

"I thought you'd be fuming," said Laura.

"I am. Of course I am. I'm livid. To think of those men. I'm glad you told me, but doing anything about it is up to you. At the very least they should be removed from the state police."

"I don't want to do anything."

"I didn't think so. It's just as well. But that should be solely your decision."

"Mummy—"

"Yes, dear."

"What Gregory said about Father—"

"Oh, I could have told you that," said Alice.

"Well?"

"Well what?"

"Well, he doesn't look like he would be that way."

"That's because of your father, Laura. You know how much Andrew admired your father. He decided long ago to emulate him, at least as far as the tweed suits and quiet manner. And he really is scholarly and wise himself," Alice added quickly. "I mean, not like your father was, but that's what he turned out to be. You look bewildered, dear."

"Well, you aren't really telling me anything."

"I don't need to complicate it, dear. It only means Andrew loves you as I do—and, by the way, men take themselves too seriously. But when you think of Andrew and me, you should know we are of one mind and heart. That's what you sometimes find in a husband."

That was no help. Gregory's comment sounded very literal. All Mother just did was add her name to Mr. Croft's. And they had guns. What was the use of spending any more time on confusion and things she might never know? She had to be content with the balance of what had happened that day and night. She and Gregory would be a pair.

They finished the pint of brandy, smoked a few more cigarettes, and went to bed. Alice held Laura in her arms all night. She knew Laura would remember what had happened from time to time and cry again, and she knew she would pass her dear Laura to a man someday. But for tonight they shared one more time the never finished business of mother and child.

CHAPTER SIXTY-SIX

After talking with Alice, Laura began to look for the one mind and one heart she knew would exist between herself and her man. Gregory was not as self-conscious about his disfigurement as she had first thought. He only came to town at night because he was running liquor, not because of his face. He was a strong and confident man. She wondered what he saw in her. Maybe one mind and heart was something that came out in the wash later.

Gregory took her to the moving pictures in Chestertown some Saturday nights. He put his arm around her. They kissed one night. It was just before Christmas, and she had driven out to the lodge in a snowstorm and stayed over. He still slept on his little pallet of blankets by the fire.

On Monday, Christmas Eve, Laura closed the post office at noon and called Alice. She said she was going out to the lodge that night. Alice asked if she would still be coming for Christmas dinner.

"Yes, definitely," she said.

"We're expecting Gregory to come too."

"He's very excited about it, Mother. We'll be there. It isn't too early, is it?"

"No dear, you know I don't like big meals in the middle of the day. Especially on Christmas day. Everyone gets so drowsy. Let's say five for cocktails?"

"That sounds fine. We'll see you then."

Laura got off the phone and began laying out her clothes. Then she changed her mind. Gregory saw her in the same things all the time. Maybe something less woodsy—from the shopping expedition to New York. She went to the other bedroom and looked through the closets. There was a long black dress she liked that would hang from her shoulders and not show her tummy. No belt. It was strange not to be working in the post office at that time of day, but she didn't want to dawdle. Gregory was cooking. She liked watching him with his back turned. He was such a well-built man and so graceful in motion in the kitchen.

In the bath, Laura used her new safety razor to shave her armpits. Getting into the hollows was tricky, but the razor worked so well. She knew to be careful over the bony areas of her legs. Everything she felt over was very smooth. It would only last a day or two. She didn't like how hairy she was on her body when the only hair she cared about was on her head, where it was thinning. She felt a little spot on top that she didn't want to try to look at in the mirror. Gregory was tall, always looking down on her head. He must have noticed it. Under her belly was a real bush. She stood up out of the tub to reach for the scissors on a shelf beside the sink.

"Don't slip!" she said to herself out loud. "Not now. Of all times."

Laura sat on the edge of the tub and began to snip. Just a little trim, but she didn't want it to look trimmed. She stood up and looked down. When she dried off, she went to look at herself in the full-length mirror in the bedroom. The bush was more like shrubbery now. Neat and trim. She wished there were such easy fixes to the rest of her imperfections. All she could do was exercise vigilance. A serious, grown-up man loved her, and he should never have reason to doubt his choice. Whatever else, she wanted Gregory to think he was getting a good one.

Laura pulled the plugs on the toaster and the lamps in the living room and checked around the house. The last thing she needed was a fire. In a few minutes she was bundled up in the Ford, driving out of town, looking left and right at the Christmas candles lighting almost every window of the village. The red glow of the winter sunset was just then spreading across the western horizon.

Gregory had a turkey going on a spit in the great fireplace.
"I've never tried this before," he said.
He stood up to kiss her.
"Oh, Gregory, it's going to fall apart. Do you have any wire? Look. The drumsticks are coming off."
Laura lunged for the turkey and got it off the fire, spit and all. "Ow, ow, ow."
"Put it on the floor."
"A plate. Quick. Ow, ow, ow."
"No, just drop it."
Laura put it down on the stone of the hearth, but it fell apart anyway.
"Let me look at your hands," Gregory said. Turning them palms up, he exclaimed, "Oh, Laura!" and kissed them again and again until his face was all greasy. Then she kissed him and nuzzled against his face, kissing all over the wounded parts until her face was as greasy as his and they started laughing.

They trussed up the turkey to the spit with wire and put it over the fire again. Laura helped with baking rolls and cooking the sauce, vegetables, and stuffing. Finally, they sat down to their first Christmas Eve dinner. She thought she would be preoccupied with what she planned to do later that night and would be unable to keep her mind on anything else. But every moment with Gregory was one of a kind, and when it passed, there followed another just like it.

Late into the night they talked. When the time finally came for sleep, Gregory put more logs on the fire, and Laura went around extinguishing the lamps. She called him to the bed and lay with him in the quiet of the winter woods. Without reservation, she gave herself to him that night. Married or not, that was all she needed now, the conviction of her mind and commitment of her heart, and she slept very well after giving them.

They stopped at the post office the next day en route to Christmas dinner at the chateau. Laura took a hot bath. Gregory knelt by the tub while she was soaking, and they talked about everyone who was going to be at the dinner. He held her towel when she stood up out of the water, as if they had been lovers or married a long time.

It was very satisfying to her that they were used to each other's bodies just because of what they had done last night. From all other people on the earth, they had chosen each other and become one. And what was that but one person holding very tenderly the lives of two? She had never thought of herself as one of two. It wasn't that she had abandoned rational thought. No, she could never do that, but the way she felt since Gregory was where all roads of the rational brought her.

They drove in Laura's Model T through the farm with Laura at the wheel. The lights of the chateau came into sight soon enough through the bare branches of the winter trees. Then they were on the gravel in front of the house, pulling up to a stop, and Mr. Thompson was starting down the steps to open the door for Laura.

"Good evening, Miss Eklund," he said. "Good evening, Mr. Haines. Merry Christmas."

"Merry Christmas to you too, Mr. Thompson," said Laura and Gregory almost in unison.

It did not seem strange to Laura that Gregory and Mr. Thompson were not meeting for the first time. It was looking more and more to her that the scholarly Mr. Croft and his righthand man were in the underground liquor business. Mummy must know, but Mummy wasn't talking.

After the hanging of coats and scarves in the entrance hallway and a chorus of Merry Christmas greetings from the living room, Laura took Gregory in, smiling to everyone. Father met them, with Mother right behind. Embraces, kisses, and shaking of hands. Autie came forward holding little Edward, who was nineteen months and chubby, all eyes and ears, and such a little blond boy. Laura laughed and leaned against Gregory in his rough country tweed suit.

Laura knew Rory would assess the situation between her and Gregory immediately—if he didn't already know about it. The experienced eye. He always looked so good in formal wear, and never had he looked so well-matched as he did that night to the tall, slender, sophisticated English girl at his side. She was an earl's daughter, father in Parliament, House of Lords. The popular press had followed them across the Atlantic on the boat. Laura wondered how long it would last. Rory would always have a roving eye. She caught him glancing at her and Gregory before he came over, and she thought it was the first time Rory ever looked at her and saw the real woman she was, on the arm of an intensely masculine man who wanted what she had to give.

Only Robbie, at the side of his mother, stared at Gregory's disfigurement. Margaux said nothing when introduced but held up a hand and placed it on the damaged side of Gregory's face. Every movement in the room seemed to stop. Margaux did not take her hand away for a moment or move her eyes from his face, as if she were a prophet or soothsayer arrested by a vision. Gregory stood patiently and unperturbed while it lasted. Talk came back to life presently, and Laura took Gregory's arm with more tender feelings for Margaux than she had ever had before.

Delphina was there. Laura hardly recognized her at first. She could have stepped out of a magazine—college girl, très chic, long black hair straightened, tight-fitting cloche, long scarf down to the hem of a long black dress, utilitarian footwear. Alice held both her hands, standing off to admire the beautiful young girl.

"Gregory, this is Miss Brown," Alice said. "Just home from college in New York."

Laura was so relieved. Gregory seemed perfectly at ease meeting new people, and if he wasn't shy about it, maybe that made the difference. Or Alice had prepared them. That was probably it.

For the next hour, Laura and Gregory drifted around the room. Everyone with a drink in hand. Margaux, off to one side, watching. Father engaged with Gregory; Autie passed little Edward to Delphina as they chatted; Robbie went back and forth to the glass bowls of mixed nuts; Laura confidently took up a conversation with Rory, each with an eye toward Alice and the English girl breaking the ice. Alice embraced the English girl, who held her cigarette away at arm's length.

"Laura," said Alice, coming over to her. "Can you help me in the kitchen?"

As they walked arm in arm down the hall, Alice said, "I suppose you noticed. We don't have any help tonight. Andrew gave everyone the day off. A company in Baltimore is bringing down turkey dinners to every family on the farm. They're complete with everything. I'll show you the advertisement brochure. It's marvelous. They have heated trucks. So it's just us chickens," said Alice, laughing. "We're going to make it a buffet. Rory is mortified, naturally, but we had full staff last night for his lady friend."

"Turkey?" said Laura, sniffing as they entered the kitchen.

"I didn't want it to be just leftovers," said Alice.

Delphina came in when Alice and Laura were peeling potatoes and cutting vegetables.

"No, no, no, Delphina," said Alice. "You go back out there and talk to somebody."

"Gregory was a college professor," said Laura. "I know he'd want to know what's going on in college these days."

After Delphina left, Alice said, "So would I. Viola says Delphina thinks her parents are backward and hopeless. I know that's just college, but she doesn't know how hurtful it is to them. I'm glad you were never that way, Laura darling. You were always the same—Oh, I hope you don't take that as a criticism."

"I don't think anything could bother me tonight, Mummy," said Laura serenely. "But it isn't too far-fetched to think people can do things unlike themselves. There just has to be a good reason."

"Have you expressed feelings for each other?"

"Yes, Mummy. Gregory is a good reason."

Before Laura and Alice had gotten very far, the English girl drifted in, then Margaux. Alice sent a message out with the English girl to ask Delphina how to work the plate warmer. Then Delphina came back, and she and Margaux took charge of the kitchen. Everyone followed orders with alacrity as they worked side by side, sipping at their drinks. There was a lot of laughter, even from Margaux, and the buffet turned out very well. The men took off their jackets after dinner, rolled up their sleeves, and did the pots, pans, and dishes while the ladies reposed on the couches in the living room with their illegal drinks and immoral cigarettes.

"I think we look quite the smart set, don't you think?" Alice said to the group.

CHAPTER SIXTY-SEVEN

The outhouse was a little difficult for Laura during the cold of the new year's winter. At night Gregory went with her, leading the way down the path with the lantern. Then he would wait outside in the dark. Sometimes it was raining or snowing, but he never complained. Returning to the warm cabin was wonderful, and jumping back in bed was heavenly.

"I'm sorry I have to go so much," she always said.

His reply was always that the body had to get rid of toxins and that she should be drinking more water.

"Then I'd be running to the outhouse all the time. But thank you for buying us the toilet seat, Gregory."

One night when they were getting ready for bed and Laura was trying to decide if she had to go or not, he said, "Maybe we can put in a septic system, and I can build you a bathroom."

"Make sure it's big enough for the bathtub."

"All right, big enough for the tub. A tub for two."

"Well, Gregory, what I'd like to know is, why didn't you do it before this?"

"I didn't expect to be here that long."

Laura felt she had been waiting for an opportunity like this. He still got letters from Chicago. He put them on the mantelpiece and didn't look at them, but they were always gone when she came over the next night. She had moved in with Gregory after Christmas.

"Where did you expect to be?" she asked innocently.

"I don't know."

"Didn't you go home after the war?"

"For a little bit. Then I went from one hospital to another and ended up at Johns Hopkins. I came out here one day. I had an idea to go crabbing. Buy a boat, do something like that, but I was running out of money."

"Gregory," Laura said, very seriously. "I want to come with you one night."

Gregory put his book down and took off his glasses. "You can't, Laura. It's dangerous."

"Well, if it's dangerous, I don't want you doing it."

"It's not really dangerous, sweetheart. But your father would question my judgment if I brought you along."

"He doesn't have to know about it."

"I'm sorry. I won't do anything behind his back."

"I worry about you, Gregory."

"I know you do, and I worry about you driving out here every night and getting up so early to go to work. But it won't be forever. Just till I get on my feet."

Laura saved what she was going to say for when they were in bed and she was lying beside him.

"I wouldn't care if it was forever," she whispered.

Whatever the drive at night and the early drive in the morning took out of her, the lodge restored in the hours she lived there. It was always warm and cozy, and with more and more of her things brought over from town, it felt like home to her. Gregory did all the cooking and came up with some wonders over the open fireplace. He was always affectionate. He fondled her when they talked philosophy lying on the floor in front of the fire, and Laura got over her bias for learning by the written word and fondled him back as they worked each other out of their clothes. They soon became so familiar that Laura felt there was nothing left to the anatomy and physiology of the human male that she did not know. The mental processes of the male would take longer. She was willing to admit that.

Alice knew. Laura told her everything, and she repeated her concerns every time the two had lunch together in the post office, sitting at Laura's desk, whispering while the new assistant postmistress, Mrs. Eskin, bustled around them.

"I'm terribly worried," said Alice. "You're very fertile ground, dear." She leaned close to Laura and whispered, "Do you know how many sperms are in a drop of semen? Lois told me. It's appalling."

"We're careful, Mother. You shouldn't worry."

"You've never been careless, Laura, but I think you might be getting too starry-eyed over Gregory. He hasn't asked you to marry him, has he?"

"I would have told you."

"Well, do you think he will?"

"I don't know, Mother. We're just happy being together."

"That's fine, dear. I know young people are doing things now that we never did in my day, but certain things haven't changed, and you have to think about what you would do if you got pregnant. Have you thought about that? Would you want to have a baby?"

"Of course I would."

"Oh, I know that. But what if you weren't married?"

"I don't know. He'd marry me. I know that."

"What if—for some reason—he didn't?"

"Oh, I don't know, Mummy. I'd go away somewhere. I don't want to talk about it."

"But you should be thinking about it, dear. I really am terribly worried."

"I will. I'll think about it."

"Maybe if you weren't living with him, he'd ask."

"I don't want to play games, Mummy."

"No, of course not. You're an intelligent girl."

"I don't really care if we're married or not. As long as we're happy."

"Of course, dear. I know how you feel," said Alice. "You've lost some weight, haven't you?"

"I don't know," said Laura, as if it were a topic that had never crossed her mind.

"I don't care about that anymore either. Gregory accepts me for what I am. I never thought anyone would."

"Well!" said Alice. "I guess I don't count. Andrew doesn't count. Your father doesn't count. Everyone you've known all your life up to Gregory Haines—with the exception of your difficult grandmother—doesn't count?"

It made them both laugh.

"I so miss talking to you at night, darling," said Alice. "I wish you had a telephone out there. It must be dreadfully quiet."

"We like it that way," said Laura.

Before Alice left, she made Laura promise to think about what she had said. Very confidentially, she told Laura a few ways to have fun in bed without involving the introduction of gametes to each other. When pressed, she credited her knowledge of men to Lois. "Who else?" she said.

CHAPTER SIXTY-EIGHT

On the first nice Saturday in March, Captain Armstrong Croft (retired) addressed the troops in front of the Kastelje. He was outfitted in his old army tunic, field cap, puttees, and boots from the Great War. The air around him was redolent with mothballs, but he was glad everything still fit. Before him in formation stood Lamont's three boys, Earling's two, his Robbie, and the two Banks girls.

"All right men," he said, "let's take a look at you. Tools at rest. That means hold them down, like this—"

He changed hands on the wooden handle of the scythe he was holding and lowered the blade to lay along the side of his boot. The two big boys with scythes and the smaller boys with long-handled weed cutters did the same. The two girls obediently dropped their grass clippers to their sides.

Margaux threw open a side-hinged window on the second floor of the cottage and stuck her head out under the thatched roof.

"Send Annabelle and Emma inside, Autie. They don't want to be in the army today."

Annabelle curtseyed and bent over to put her grass clippers on the ground. Emma followed her sister's lead, and they scurried toward the white door with red trim. Margaux appeared again in the window frame. "There are ticks in that field," she said, closing the window after her.

Turning back to the boys, Autie took stock of his diminished command. One twelve-year old, two eleven-year-olds, two ten-year-olds, and Robbie, almost eight.

"Our backs are to the river, men," he said. "So what do we do now?"

"Cut the weeds," said Jack Eldridge.

"That's right. We attack where the enemy least expects it. Shoulder arms, follow me."

He led them around the Kastelje. The front of the cottage faced the river, the back looked up the hill to the rear of the chateau. As they came around the side, Autie could see two women up there standing beside the flagpole. One was his mother, the other one looked like Laura. They waved and disappeared over the rise and into the chateau. To the left of Autie's band and into the distance was the goose field and marsh along the river, and just out of sight farther down was the Galena bridge.

"Now you men with weed cutters, step forward."

As the younger boys did so, Autie pointed toward the split rail fence along the road that came around the hill from the chateau.

"I want you and you to swing around the enemy's left flank and get at the high grass over there by the fence. That will be the diversionary attack. You other two, you will advance on the right flank by the cottage in an encircling movement, and I'll lead the main attack up the middle. When we've taken the grass, we'll bring the tanks up—that's Mr. Banks and the plow."

Captain Croft looked at his watch. When the second hand reached twelve, he blew the whistle that hung from around his neck. "Over the top, men. Mind the ticks."

About an hour later, Autie had his woolen tunic and cap off. He had never used a scythe before, and the day was getting warm. Laura's Ford was coming down the road from the chateau. He gave the boys a break. Robbie started into the house with the other boys behind him, and they were promptly put out at the end of a broom.

"She said we have ticks," Robbie said.

"Well, you boys sit over there."

Autie went to the door and talked to Margaux. He came back and told the boys that the field kitchen would soon bring lemonade and cookies up to the line, and they could rest on their arms for now. Laura pulled her Ford over on the grass and got out.

"I brought Margaux something for her new garden," Laura called. "Do you want to help me, Autie?"

She opened the back door and leaned in to get something off the floor. "Here, take this," she said, passing him a very heavy wooden flat of strawberry plants. "There's one more."

"Thanks," he said. "We were talking about strawberries."

"I know. Mother told me. Gregory's been growing them. We really have too many."

"Well, let's put them down."

"I want to show you something first," said Laura. "Where do you want the center of the garden to be?"

They put the flats down beside the car, and Autie walked her out to a spot in the middle of the space they were clearing. Laura had him sit down on the ground with her as she described how Gregory had built circle tiers for their strawberries.

"We've got a big brick pile out there," she said. "Really old ones. Gregory thinks it might have been an old mill from revolutionary days. I can bring you all the bricks you need for the tiers if you want to do it that way. I measured the diameters of the three tiers, based on six feet for the first tier, and I counted out the number of plants you need, based on those dimensions. You have full sun here. Gregory and I have hardly any. That's when he thought of the pyramid idea. He's not really much of a gardener. I guess that will be my job around the house. Gregory does everything else. I'm not much of a gardener either, but I learned a lot from Mother, and it's nice to grow your own food, and we, I mean Gregory and I, both like strawberries. I'm sorry, I've been talking too much."

"Oh no, not at all," he said. "It's gets pretty quiet around here."

"Well, however Margaux wants to do it. It's her garden. You don't have to do a pyramid, you have so much space. I know Gregory and I wouldn't want anybody coming out to our place and telling us how we should be doing our gardening. I hope Mother won't say anything. She hasn't seen it yet. It's too early, but I know she'll have an opinion. She went to that horticultural school in England. Did you see the photograph of her in the beekeeping outfit? She just showed it to me the other day. I never knew she went to school for it. Did you?"

Laura put her hair behind her ears again with a quick motion of her hand and looked sideways toward the goose field and the marsh. Autie was glad she had let her hair grow out from that awful Dutch Boy thing. He had to admit she looked good, smiling all the time now. Why did he waste all that time trying to figure out if she was beautiful or not? Maybe she wasn't back then, but she was now. The corduroy jacket with the sleeves too long probably belongs to that fellow Haines. Living out in the woods with him since Christmas. Mom didn't approve, but she said he's done wonders for her. She must be doing wonders for him too. Well, you can't begrudge him. Why hasn't he married her? He should have by now. Maybe there was something he hadn't made up his mind about.

"I'd better go," Laura said. "I have to check over Mrs. Eskin's work at the post office and get back to Gregory. He said he's cooking something special for dinner."

They stood up and walked back to the car. Annabelle and Emma were in and out of the house with trays for the boys.

"You look very handsome, Captain Croft," Laura said, standing with her back against the car, smiling. "You smell of mothballs though."

"I thought I'd get these things out and see if they still fit," he said, looking down a little sheepishly at his brown woolen trousers and puttees.

"Well, I think mothballs is the perfect place for your army days, Autie," she said, laughing as she got into the driver's seat.

Autie watched Laura drive up the hill. She turned out pretty good, he thought as he went back to work, remembering the chance he once had with her.

Kenneth Banks came down to the Kastelje in his Ford, driving slowly because he had a cart hitched to it with Diligence following behind. Every family on the farm had an automobile of their own. Andrew had gone into the new Ford dealership in Cecilton with his checkbook and bought four new Model Ts on opening day.

Kenneth and Autie took the old plow off the cart and a tangle of old harness that Kenneth thought would work.

"Only me and Elijah ever plowed manual," he said. "And ain't no horse alive on this farm that's pulled a plow neither. Elijah say for me to git the Persh'n. Plowing's in the breed, he say."

Kenneth hardly moved his lips when he talked, and Autie had trouble understanding him. The battered felt hat with the wide brim was so low on his head that it obscured any visual hints his face might have given to his words.

"Your ma's horse," he said.

"Oh, the Percheron."

As the boys looked on, Autie and Kenneth hitched up Diligence. With Kenneth at the plow, the job was finished in a matter of a few minutes. It was only a kitchen garden, but it would have taken Autie and the boys a few days to turn it by hand with shovels. Kenneth went over it with what he said was a one-section wooden harrow that he found in one of the barns. Afterward, the earth looked nicely turned and tilled when Margaux came out to look. Kenneth touched the brim of his hat for her.

He unhitched Diligence and put the plow back on the wagon with Autie's help. When Annabelle and Emma came out of the cottage to join the boys, Autie handed out the silver dollars the children always got, and after the little award ceremony, Kenneth took his two girls and the Eldridge and Cooper boys home in his Ford. Because it was getting late, Autie and Robbie walked up the hill with Diligence to save Kenneth a stop at the stables.

Remembering the time Robbie got thrashed for tracking mud into the house, Autie was careful to brush off the boy's boots when they got back to the Kastelje. He told Robbie if his mother ever came after him with a belt again, to just run. Sometimes she wasn't herself was all he could say about it.

Margaux called them to dinner, and Autie had to give up cleaning the boots. They pulled off a few ticks and came in barefoot without their pants. After a quick trip upstairs to wash and dress in clean clothes, they passed inspection and sat down to the table.

"We left everything dirty outside," said Autie.

"I'll get it tomorrow," said Margaux. She ladled out two bowls of pea soup from the pressure cooker on the stove and brought them over. It was thick and rich, and she set down a basket of warm rolls in the middle of the table. "Dip the bread in your soup, Robbie."

While Autie and Robbie were doing that, she sat down beside Edward in his highchair and helped him through a bowl of soup and half a roll.

"You're only Belgian on my side," she said to Edward, as if she were speaking to him alone and disavowing any responsibility for the other 50 percent.

They had fried chicken, egg noodles, and a very large salad. For dessert, there were cherry and apple pastries. Margaux encouraged them to eat everything she had cooked. She was supposed to go to the market every day and make a list of every personal encounter she had. It was part of a weekly report on her daily activities she kept for the doctor. At first, it was stressful, but when Alice taught her how to drive, she found taking the Ford into Cecilton was to her liking, and she began to enjoy shopping.

"But it's very expensive," she said. "There at the market. We get fruits and vegetables now from all over the country, but they don't have endive, so I want to grow our own endive."

"We have to get seeds," said Robbie.

"Your father will get seeds. Or your bonpapa will get them."

"I'll look around," said Autie.

"What else are we going to plant, Ma'ma?"

"Everything," said Margaux.

"We made a big garden, didn't we, Dad?"

"We sure did."

"What if the deer eat all the plants, Dad?"

"We're going to build a fence around it," said Autie.

"Deer can jump high, can't they Dad? The fence will have to be fifty feet high."

"I don't think deer can jump fifty feet, Robbie."

"Then the fence will keep them out if it's fifty feet high."

"Robbie," said Margaux. "Are you done your dinner?"

"Yes, Ma'ma."

"Then go to your room and read your books for school."

"Can I play the gramophone?"

"No. Read your books for school."

"We should get a radio, Dad," said Robbie, getting out of his chair. "Johnny Kaplan at school has one. We could put a radio in the living room and listen to shows."

"Robbie," said Margaux.

Without another word, Robbie left the table and ran up the stairs to his room.

Margaux wiped Edward's mouth with the corner of his bib.

"I don't know why in America people let children talk so much at the table," she said.

"That's how children learn."

"No, they don't learn like that. Children talk nonsense. Whatever comes into their heads. They learn by listening to adults talk."

Autie moved his eyes from her disturbed and beautiful face to the empty plates in front of him.

"We don't talk very much," he said.

"We think," said Margaux, not unkindly. "That's just as good."

"I just wish—" He couldn't finish what he was going to say.

"You wish what?"

"I don't know. You're hard on Robbie sometimes. He doesn't understand. Why did you strap him with the belt the other day?"

Margaux looked around the room. "I don't know why I do things," she said.

Margaux put Edward to bed and sent Autie into the living room to read while she did the dishes and cleaned up the kitchen. At seven-thirty she went up to put Robbie through his face, hands, and teeth regime before bed. She kissed him and tucked him in for the night. Autie called up "good night" from his winged armchair. Margaux came down, and they read quietly together in the living room. She brought him coffee and squares of chocolate. Sometimes the expressions on her face brought to mind the officer candidates at Fort Riley when they were lost on maneuvers, trying to orient themselves to what was around them with the wrong map.

Outside her bedroom door, Margaux turned her face away, and Autie kissed her cheek.

"Are we going to your parents' tomorrow night?"

"Only if you want to."

"Yes."

"I'll let Mom know."

"Is Laura coming with her man?"

"I don't know."

"What was she doing here today? I saw you out the window. I don't want her around here."

"She brought you strawberry plants for your garden. She was thinking of you."

"I bet," said Margaux, closing the door.

Better to leave it at that. Autie stood for a moment at the closed door of the little room under the eves that she had taken for herself, then he walked quietly past Robbie's room to his bedroom down the hall. At least she could call Laura by name now. It was hard to tell if she was out of the depression she was in last month. There was some progress, he supposed. It was her own choice to do all the work of the household. She was up early every morning to get Robbie ready for school. After that it was out shopping with the car in Cecilton. Then the cooking and cleaning. Now that she had a garden, she'd be working out there all summer. She insisted on doing everything herself. That couldn't be coming from the doctor. It had to be her.

The Tudor house in Boston wasn't much bigger than the Kastelje. He remembered following Mom around the house, making beds and washing clothes. Cooking and cleaning, whatever it was, she sang all the time. Her heart was in it. Nurse was there to help out, but there were always people dropping in and extra work he probably wouldn't have noticed as a child. Dad wasn't around much because of the bank or meetings. No, there was story time on the green couch. He hadn't thought of that in years. They all sat on the couch together, and Dad read the stories. Maybe it was something he could try with Robbie and little Edward. He thought he remembered Mom holding a baby, but he couldn't think who that would have been.

Autie lay in bed thinking. He remembered Margaux in Paris, hardly four years ago. She was a tough nut right from the start, but he didn't mind it then. All the money he went through trying to impress her. No mystery why that worked. She never told him why getting to America was so important. She hadn't tricked him into anything. He knew she didn't love him then. He thought that would change once she got to know him, but in the meantime, he had a pretty girl with a French accent to bring home, along with the medals he bought on the street. The amount of thought that went into both of his overseas acquisitions was probably about the same. The only difference was he could leave the medals at the bottom of a drawer.

Getting Margaux back from New York didn't fix anything. It was just picking up the pieces. Like putting a puzzle back in the box and starting over. Some people look for edges, some people look for shapes, some people look at the picture on the box of what it's supposed to look like. As far as he could tell, aside from the story of the German lover, there were no edges, no interlocking shapes, and no picture. But he could see Margaux was busy with the puzzle of what she was. After that, his thoughts were fragmented and incomplete. He fell asleep, and the whole mess became pieces of his dreaming.

CHAPTER SIXTY-NINE

Alice, in her most casual evening wear, looked with great pleasure down the dining room table to Andrew, attired in another of his tweed suits.

"It's so nice, having these Sunday night dinners together, don't you think?"

She patted Autie's hand on her right and Margaux's hand on her left. There was general agreement from Laura and Gregory, opposite each other in the middle, and no notice taken by Andrew, who was engaged with Robbie on one side of him and little Edward in a highchair at the other end of the table.

"It's such a shame Rory can't be here," Alice continued. "Don't you think it's time he came home, dear?"

"I beg your pardon?" said Andrew, looking up.

"Try to pay attention, dear. I asked if Rory couldn't come home."

"He was just here at Christmas."

"I mean home for good."

"That's up to him," said Andrew. "I dare say he might find the attractions of London more entertaining these days. Not to mention, it's against the law to drink here."

"I'm sure you could find something for him and his English girl to do around here. The title has a connection with land, doesn't it? Yes, I think it does. She must come from an estate like ours."

"No, I think she lives in London," said Autie.

"Were you talking to her, Autie?" asked Laura.

"No, Rory told me."

"I thought she told Gregory she lives in the country, didn't she, Gregory?"

"Well, the affluent often live in the country and keep a house in the city," said Gregory. "Or the other way around."

"I thought she was charming," said Alice.

"She was a good sport in the kitchen, wasn't she, Mother?" said Laura. "I've learned so much about cooking from Gregory. He used to do it all—didn't you, Gregory, but now I do some—that is, when he lets me. He doesn't like me to be on my feet after all day at the post office. It's really an art, getting everything ready at the right time. I keep thinking how useless I was at Christmas. It was a good thing you were there, Margaux."

"Delphina did the work," said Margaux, as the attention of the table turned to her.

"We all did a fair share, it seemed to me," said Alice. "A woman should always know her way around a kitchen, no matter what her station in life may be, don't you think?"

"Gregory says I'm getting very good," Laura assured Alice. Then turning to Margaux, "Autie says you're a very good cook."

"I cooked from when I was very young," said Margaux, "for a bakery."

"How good it must be to have the skills to cook if a time comes when you freely choose to," said Alice brightly. "That makes all the difference, doesn't it, Margaux?"

"Some."

The new maid, Celeste, came in with a tray and placed baskets of little toasts on the table. Mr. Thompson followed her with a bottle of wine for Andrew's inspection.

Alice spoke up. "We're starting with a parsnip and celery root bisque, then Waldorf salad, a Bourbon-glazed baked ham, and something new for dessert—ice box cake. I hope that is agreeable to everyone. Viola does quite well with the ham."

Laura laughed and asked Gregory across the table if ham was all right with him. Then she turned to address Alice and the company at the same time. "Gregory and I eat mostly vegetarian these days, Mother. I never thought about it one way or another, but one night I suddenly couldn't remember the last time we had meat. I suppose it's because Gregory cooks so well, I just hadn't noticed anything missing. So this will be a real treat.

You like ham, don't you, Gregory? I'm sorry, I should know something like that, shouldn't I? How embarrassing. It's just that food isn't so important with us. Some nights we get so caught up in conversation we forget about the time and then it's just Campbell's Beefsteak Tomato soup and cheese and crackers. I can't remember when we actually planned a meal. Well, I know Gregory must be thinking ahead because it's usually waiting when I come home from the post office. I think—"

"What do you usually make for dinner, Margaux?" Alice said as politely as she could with a glance toward Laura.

"Ham," Autie interjected.

Everyone laughed. Andrew looked up from his grandsons for a moment, realized he had missed something, and went back to poking breadsticks into little Edward's tummy to amuse him.

"I thought you liked ham," said Margaux.

"I do." Autie smiled around the table. "She does it very well."

"We didn't have things like that in Belgium. At least not our family. You learn to cook what you have." Margaux directed it to Alice beside her and to Andrew at the far end, as if they were the only ones at the table worth talking to. Then she looked at Gregory and said, "Mr. Haines, were you in Belgium during the war?"

"Yes, he was," said Laura.

"Just in the south," he said.

"Did you know any Belgian soldiers?"

"No, they passed through our lines in small groups attached to the French. But we never talked. It was late in the war."

"I had brothers in the army. Since the beginning. We never heard from them."

"Still not?"

"No, I have no family contact," said Margaux. "This is my family now."

"Thank you, Margaux," said Alice. "We feel the same about you, don't we, Andrew?"

Andrew caught on and signaled Mr. Thompson, who walked with formality around the table, filling everyone's glass, including a small one he produced for Robbie. Andrew raised his glass, then the others followed.

"Let us drink to Margaux. May she have a long and happy life as an American Croft. To Margaux, with much love."

After drinking to Margaux, in the lull that follows a toast as everyone takes a sip, Laura caught Alice's attention and announced some news.

"Gregory and I are going to Montreal, Mother."

"Oh, that's wonderful, dear."

"To Montreal," said Autie, raising his glass.

The others raised theirs, and Laura waited until the glasses were down before she continued.

"Gregory has business there, but he said it would be unbearable if I didn't come along. So we're going sometime in the next few months or so, whenever we get around to it. I'm so excited."

"You'll have a chance to use your French."

"I don't know that I'll dare, Mother. Gregory is fluent, so he'll be doing the talking. He has a very good accent. He laughs at mine sometimes. I practice my French on him in bed."

That caused a blush, and Laura looked down with a smile that made no attempt to retract or qualify her statement.

"Well!" said Alice, breaking the momentary pause. "I understand the French Canadians have no ear for how French should be spoken, so even I might pass muster. You should speak French with Laura, Margaux."

"I prefer to listen."

"Oh, we should," said Laura. "But that reminds me. Did you see the strawberry plants I dropped off, Margaux?"

"Oui. Merci bien."

Laura looked at Gregory for help.

Gregory picked up the ball and went on in French to say that it was no trouble at all, and if she needed more plants, he and Laura would be happy to bring more to the cottage.

Margaux listened with her full attention on Gregory. They went on and exchanged a few more sentences that had the tone of a private conversation and went by too fast for Alice. Then Margaux said in English, "Your accent is very good. Better than mine. I speak Flemish French. You noticed. No one else would."

Alice was surprised to hear so much out of Margaux. Perhaps it was due to the wound Gregory had suffered in the war, but it seemed that everything that had to do with him was of interest to Margaux. He had her respect. So did Andrew for some reason. It was strange that Laura seemed oblivious to everything but signs that Gregory was accepted into the family, and she beamed with pride whenever it happened.

In bed that night, Alice said she thought Margaux was doing much better. "Laura was a bit excessive, didn't you think?"

"That's just exuberance. Remember that?"

"Certainly, but I was never—excessive."

"Well, you can't blame her. But you're right about Margaux. We've never heard that much out of her."

"She really does prefer to listen, Andrew. We knew that. But I do hope it's a good sign. At least for Autie's sake. He's been through so much with her. And those poor little boys, too. I hope she has more children. A few girls would be good for her, don't you think?"

"Don't try to rush things, Alice. She doesn't strike me as very interested in motherhood."

"Well, I hope she didn't take any lessons from you tonight, dear. You looked the perfect simpleton, teaching Edward how to play with his food. But you did very nicely with the toast to Margaux. I think it boosted her spirits. I'm glad you were paying attention. Now then, what is this trip to Montreal, dear? Laura never mentioned a word of it to me."

"First I've heard of it," said Andrew.

Alice lay on her back beside him, looking up into the darkness. The windows of the bedroom were open.

"There aren't many geese out there, are there?" she said.

"They aren't migrating now."

"I'm so worried about Laura. She's going to get pregnant. I just know it."

"You have to leave her alone, darling."

"It's not like her to be this way."

"I think you mean it's not like her not to be the way she used to be."

Alice rose up on one elbow and turned to him. He had his eyes closed.

"But Andrew, look at what she's doing. She's playing house in the woods and screwing."

Andrew opened his eyes with surprise. "I've never heard you talk that way. Did you get that from your friend Lois?"

"Oh, for heaven's sake, Andrew. That's exactly what it is. They're playing house and screwing. It's all she wants to do now. She tells me about it. She says they're careful, but I know she's going to get into trouble."

"You have to leave it alone, Alice. You raised her to think independently, and now she's doing just that."

"I know," said Alice, "but there are certain realities of life for women, Andrew. We can't get around that. That's my point. She wants to get married and have children. It's what she's always wanted. I'm so worried she's going to ruin her chances for happiness going about it backwards this way."

"Well, she's happy now, isn't she?" said Andrew.

"It's so frustrating to talk to you sometimes."

"No, I understand," said Andrew. "It puts you in a bind. Laura's become independent—just what you wanted her to be—but you don't think she's making the decisions you feel an independent woman should be making."

Alice lay back on her pillow again. After a while, she said, "Gregory works for you, doesn't he?"

"Well, am I right about Laura?" Andrew asked.

"Yes, dear, you're right. What you pointed out is exactly what's bothering me. Now, what about Mr. Haines?"

"We should be getting to sleep."

"Andrew?"

"Yes, he works for me."

"Couldn't you talk to him? Find out his intentions?"

"No, I can't intrude on his personal life. They're both adults, Alice. Laura is almost thirty. She's not the girl she was when we got her. You did a good job raising her. Put your faith in that. Gregory is a good man, and I'm sure he has nothing but the best feelings for her. Apparently, they have a life together. You have to trust that they'll make decisions between them considerate of each other. I know she parades it around, but that's only because for once she has something going with a man outside of her imagination."

Alice lay back and thought about what Andrew had said. Much of it was true. She had gotten used to Laura depending upon her. It wasn't the first time she'd thought Andrew would have been better as the one closest to Laura. But that wasn't the way it was, and she could only do her best.

"Thank you, dear. I think I can sleep now," said Alice, despite the doubts she was beginning to have about herself. She kissed him and pulled the covers up. "I'm glad we aren't living in the woods."

"As am I," said Andrew. "You're only young once."

"I'm glad we're still screwing though," she whispered.

CHAPTER SEVENTY

Delphina came home from college that summer and worked at the chateau, helping in the kitchen, waiting at the table, and teaching Celeste the fine points of her job as the new maid. In turn, Margaux taught Delphina how to make pastry as she had learned it from childhood and from her years in Paris. The shop, the dough, and the oven had worn her down with oppression in those days. Now they gave a teaching purpose to her life. She found she enjoyed teaching an intelligent person she respected.

"Teaching is almost futile with children," she told Delphina. "They resist, or they use what they learn just to show off."

While the dough was rising or the creations of the flour board were baking, Margaux and Delphina sat outside smoking cigarettes when Viola wasn't around. They were both slender and lithe, and almost the same age. Delphina had cut her hair short in a boy style like Margaux. Getting together seemed a natural result of being the youngest two of the adults in the house.

Being on one side or the other of the swinging door between the kitchen and the dining room mattered very little to either one that summer. Delphina was as often sitting with Alice in the living room that summer, conversing as a college girl home on vacation, as she was waiting on the table as a servant. Likewise, Margaux was baking in the kitchen as much as she was sitting in the dining room being waited on.

With Delphina back, Margaux spent more time up the hill at the chateau. Little Edward played in the house as his brother had before him, and Robbie joined in when Elijah brought him home from school.

When the boys weren't around, Delphina and Margaux talked freely on the back porch off the kitchen and shared cigarettes. They had New York in common. At first, Delphina thought it might be a delicate subject, but Margaux was the one who brought it up. She asked Delphina where she lived in the city.

"In the Village," said Delphina. "In Lois's building. Mrs. Croft got me in. I share a room with two other girls."

"I wouldn't like living with other girls," said Margaux.

"I don't mind. They're nice. We're in the same classes at school."

"Have you been to the jazz clubs?"

"I don't have time for that," said Delphina.

"He took me up there to Harlem. That Karensky. He wanted me to dance at the clubs. For money. So he could stay home and paint pictures all day. He was a pig."

"I'm sorry," said Delphina.

"Have you been with a man?"

"No."

"You should stay away from men up there. They're no good."

"There are some nice ones at school."

"At school maybe. The ones who come to Lois's apartment are full of themselves."

"They would be too old for me anyway," said Delphina, laughing.

"I think she's very wise. That Lois."

"Yes, she's very wise."

Delphina took another cigarette out of the package. Margaux took one too and lit them both.

"I have a boyfriend," said Delphina. "Well—had one, I mean. From school. Mama and Papa don't know about him."

"He's white, isn't he."

"Yes, but don't tell anyone."

"I thought he might be. It's so stupid, how it is in this country. It doesn't matter what color you are. People are just people. It would be better if you could tell them apart by color, if kind people were green, mean people were red, orange meant stupid, yellows were smart, as many colors as you need. Then you would know where you stood right away."

"That could get confusing too, Margaux."

"Not as much as it is now."

"Anyway, he's not my boyfriend anymore."

"Why not?"

"He was too dependent on me. I couldn't love a man like that." Delphina laughed. "He'd have to be better looking."

"You're lucky," said Margaux.

"Now, why do you think so?" said Delphina, crossing one of her long legs over the other and leaning back against the next step to the porch.

"You'll have different men in your life. Then you'll pick the one you'll love."

"Well, that's what everybody does," said Delphina.

"No," said Margaux. "Sometimes you love first. Then you have the other ones."

It was nice to be home—at night, after dinner, in the house she grew up in, with Mama and Daddy and the people she had known all her life still around, as if time had stopped and waited for her to come back. Being in the country was good, too. No noise, no police car and fire truck sirens, no trams, no honking horns, no lights at night, and so many stars never seen through city skylights.

Mama read her magazines, while Daddy looked over his charts from the farm. The clock ticked on the mantelpiece. It was so quiet that Delphina thought she could also hear the ticking of the clock in the kitchen. Daddy liked to have a fire in the fireplace every night, even in summer, and fussed over it in a way that tried her patience. Everything about her parents used to annoy her so much. It made her feel nostalgic for annoyance now.

"The captain talkin' bout gittin' us all radios now," said Elijah, getting up to tend the fire. "That'll put a stop to all this readin'. That for sure."

"There are funny shows the magazine books talk about," said Viola. "Do you know any of them, Delphina?"

"No, Mama, we don't have a radio. We're too busy studying."

"Good for you, girl," said her father. "Put you nose to them books good. That way you don't end up like us."

"That's no way to talk, Elijah," said Viola. "We're doing as well as anyone. We have a car and a telephone and indoor plumbing and always food on the table. That's more than some people can say. What about the poor souls down south?"

"They can come up here where it safe, Viola. Then nothin' hold 'em back but theys own 'maginations. A girl like Delphina show what anybody can do. Here she is, a college girl. Doin' good there, ain't you, Delphina?"

"Yes, Daddy. I got As in all my classes, both semesters."

"See there, Viola?"

"I know that's good, Delphina. I'd just feel better if you had a man. Someone from around here."

"That the last thing she need, Viola," said Elijah. "Delphina don't need no man a'tall right now, least ways not one from 'round here. When she do, she'll git one a' them smart college boys."

"You should read my magazine books, Elijah. Those college boys—they're not so smart, drinking and carrying on the way they do, sitting on flag poles, driving fast cars around wild, drinking illegal, dancing in contests until they fall down, and such outlandish things. Ever since that war's been over with and the boys come home with crazy ideas in their heads. The girls are just as bad. White girls wearing their hair in pigtails! Imagine that! The churches are speaking up about it, don't you know. For what little good it will do. Girls don't listen anymore. They're drinking and smoking cigarettes too, and doing whatever they want to do, just like the college boys. I hope you're not going around that big city in skimpy clothes like they do and getting into trouble, Delphina."

"No, Mama."

"Well, I ain't familiarated with what's in them magazine books you readin', Viola, but strikes me as jus' part a' bein' young, what young people doin'. Young people gotta 'speriment. You don't understand that cause you never that way. Don't know how I ever come to be mixed up with such a old-fashion woman as you, Viola, like you was born in them clothes you got on now."

"Daddy, that's mean," said Delphina.

"She know I love her, girl. Don't you, Viola? Jus' like you is. That what I meant to say."

"That's better."

"We're so glad to have you home, Delphina," said Viola.

They both smiled at her proudly.

Soon enough, she would be back in the city she found so exciting, so progressive, vibrant, and alive. The streets were teeming with people from all walks of life and all corners of the earth, with so many young people free of the old constraints—the committed, who organized and rallied, angry over the world that was handed to them, and the pleasure-seekers, who lived by anything goes. Again, in the fall, she would thread her way through the streets every day, from the apartment to the university, where she would sit in class and listen to inspired, learned men. And soon enough, she would be doing some of what Mama read in her magazines. When she had time.

Delphina went to sleep that night listening to the faint sounds of the cows in the barn, the pigs in the sty, the chickens in the coop, all settled down but marking around themselves the breathing circles of their living presence, while they lasted on this earth, as every living thing *struts and frets his hour upon the stage*. Macbeth, act 5, scene 5. She hoped all the reading she had done in her life would lead to more than just more reading.

CHAPTER SEVENTY-ONE

Autie made do with an office in his bedroom at the Kastelje. The new filing cabinets and the boxes of documents Dad sent down from the chateau took up a good deal of space, but he fit them around the bed, dresser, and desk. The room was in the front of the cottage, so he could see a little of the river through the window. The breeze off the water, the thatched roof, and the black and white tile of the ground floor kept the whole house cool during the summer.

When he had the furniture arranged and the filing cabinets set up, Autie sat at the desk and looked around the little room. Not out the window. He couldn't afford distractions anymore. He was thirty-one years old. There was a chance to make something of himself, and he couldn't let it slip through his fingers. He couldn't work the way he had in the past, he couldn't keep being what he had been.

The manual came first. It was on top of the new Remington portable typewriter in the case at his feet, and he was determined to read every word of it before the machine came out of the box. How long it would take to master it, he was not sure. Learning to type was going to be hard. The book that came with the typewriter had pictures of the finger positions and practice exercises. It sat on top of the pile of books he had bought in Baltimore on basic accounting and the business of farming.

It was a lot to learn on his own, but there was no other way now. All his life, a world of possibilities had been handed to him on the silver platter of books, private lessons, then Phillips Exeter and Princeton. Even the army had sent him to school. He had dropped everything placed in his hands. He had emptied the cup of his best years and he had filled himself with wasted time.

The frustration of the SOS office in Paris came back to him when he first set the typewriting machine in front of him on the desk, but by then he had read the manual, he understood how it worked, and he knew what it could do. With the book of finger positions laid flat beside it, he rested his fingers on the keys and started to tap.

Within a week he felt at one with the machine and could put the book aside. It had proved to be an easier task than he thought. But there were long hours of accounting study after that, then bookkeeping study, and finally a trip to the new stationery store in Cecilton, where he knew exactly what ledgers to ask for.

It was surprising to see that an interest in the work came naturally from learning it. When he rolled his chair away from the desk and considered what he had undertaken, it seemed to him that his first exercise of perseverance had revealed a simple but underappreciated truth, that at the core of every human life, even his, is the ability to learn. It pleased him very much to have discovered it in himself, even though he knew desperation lay at the bottom of it. If he and Margaux had been happy together, or, more to the point, if she had ever been happy with him as he was, it never would have happened. If that were true, it might only mean other truths remained to be discovered.

By August, he had gone through most of the boxes and straightened out the old records from Danforth. He decided it would be important to get a clear picture of what his parents started with when they came down from Boston to take up dairy farming. By September he was caught up with the more recent records of the farm, and by October, he had a good accounting system set up for current operations. Whenever he had time, he entered incomplete records and fragments of past years into the system.

As he went over his new ledgers, it became apparent that the farm had been a losing venture. He was glad to see his idea of switching half the cultivated acreage from corn to soybeans had paid off well. With milk production up, he projected their first profitable year. It wasn't by much, and Dad would still have to put money in for one or two other things he wanted to try, but that didn't look like a problem. There seemed to be plenty of money. Where it was coming from was the question.

Out in the garden, Margaux was pulling the last of the carrots and turnips while Edward wandered around munching on a dirty carrot. Autie undid the latch on the fence.

"Keep on the path," said Margaux.

"I'm going up the hill to talk to Dad," Autie said, stepping over to her carefully.

Margaux stood up, holding a batch of carrots by the greens and brushing the dirt off with her other hand.

"Are you going to tell him your idea?"

"We have to talk about the farm first."

"That's good. Show him about the soybeans."

"I will."

"And tell him what you think—what you told me. Use the same words. And when you tell him your idea, don't let him poo-poo it. People are making money. Tell him about the shop girl who made ten thousand dollars in one day."

"He knows that, Margaux."

"Well, you tell him you want to make money too."

"All right."

"I'm only saying these things to you because you don't stand up for yourself. You can still be respectful and stand up for yourself."

Autie walked up the hill feeling a little worn down by his wife. She still looked like a young girl, but she could be tough. He hadn't brought any of the farm paperwork along, so he was going to talk off the cuff. That would show he knew the books.

He found his father in the study with the door open and went in. Pulling a chair up to the desk as Father closed the cover on a ledger, Autie asked if he had time for a little talk.

"Sure. Not doing anything special," said Andrew.

"I've been working on the October books, Dad. We came out on top. I think it's the first time."

"What did I tell you?"

"I don't know what you mean, Dad," Autie said with a look of consternation. "You didn't want to do soybeans."

"Oh, I meant you thinking the farm didn't need any help. And now the first thing you thought of is paying off."

"Well, Keener and Brandt down the road were the first to go with soybeans and did pretty well, so I thought we should try. We still have land to spare."

"If you think we should plant more, then that's what we'll do."

"I calculate that we'd need to put in twenty more acres for a yield big enough to sell to the industrial oil market. We'll have to buy feed for the livestock if everything we grow goes for oil, but that's where the money is, Dad. Industry needs it. I don't know what for, but I think it's the right move to make."

"Then go ahead, boy."

"Thanks, Dad. Got to get back."

Autie stood up and turned to go, but stopped. "There's something else, Dad. Do you have time?"

"Sure, son. Sit down."

Autie sat down again. Andrew pulled the new intercom closer.

"Mrs. Brown? I have Autie here. Could you send Celeste in with some coffee? Press the bar on the bottom if you want to speak, not the red button on the side."

"Viola's still getting the hang of it," he said in an aside to Autie. "What's on your mind?"

"Well, all the work I've been doing, Dad, you know, going back through the years and putting it into a regular accounting framework."

"I knew you could get the place on the right track, son. You know your mother likes having you here. It's a good place for Margaux and the boys. You're free to do whatever you want, of course, but don't rule out staying long-term and really making a go of it."

"I haven't, Dad, but that wasn't what I wanted to ask about."

Celeste came in with the coffee. Andrew cleared space for the tray on his desk. Celeste set it down, curtseyed, and quietly closed the door behind her.

"She's a sweet girl," said Andrew. "She's one of the Jackson girls from Cecilton, Emmet's daughter. The one who works on tractors."

"Oh sure. I know him. But back to the farm. Twenty-some years is a long time to hold onto a losing farm, Dad. You've put money into it every quarter to pay the bills, buy new equipment, and maintain the buildings, not to mention the house. I can give you an expense report for every year since you started."

"That would be grand," said Andrew. "I always wanted to get around to doing that."

"What I mean is, the farm never made a profit until this month. Where's the money coming from? I always thought it was the farm."

Andrew reached for the silver box that held his cigarettes. He offered it to Autie and then took one himself.

"No, it wasn't the farm," he said.

"Then what is it?"

"That's my part of the business," Andrew said gently.

"So you gave me the losing end."

"I gave you the part that needed help, son."

"Maybe I can help with the other end too."

"We'll see."

"Can you tell me what it is?"

Andrew drank some coffee and took a few draws on his cigarette.

"Your mother's family was well off," he began. "You knew that. And you know my family was in textiles in Massachusetts. Well, the mill burned down when I was ten years old. We got some insurance money out of it and when the parents died some years later, I was on my own. So I went to South Africa and got into mining, did reasonably well and sold out—which still provides me something of an annuity. Then I went into mercantile trade. I never wanted to use your mother's family money, you see." He paused to look up to the domed ceiling of the study. "Artifacts from China bought the farm. African ivory built this house."

"Is that still going on?"

"We have a few ships under Panamanian registry. Yes, still going on."

"Is Rory in on any of this?"

"No. He's on his own."

Autie sat back and considered where to go next.

"You're running liquor with Haines, aren't you?" he said.

"What brings you to that conclusion?" his father asked calmly, not looking surprised by the question.

"There always seems to be plenty in the wine cellar. And what business would Haines be in where he can make a living out in the woods along an uninhabited stretch of coastline these days?"

"Well, I hand it to you, son," Andrew said with good humor. "You should work for the prohibition people."

"It's just between us, Dad," said Autie holding his ground. "Is Haines going to Montreal to open a land route?"

"No, I haven't the faintest idea why he's going up there, Autie."

"Anyway, it's a messy business, Dad. You read the papers."

"Nobody's gotten hurt," said Andrew. "That's the way I look at it right now."

Margaux would want to hear everything said, word for word, and he still hadn't broached his idea.

"All right, Dad," he said. "Thanks for being honest with me. I won't bother you about it. I wouldn't want to be involved in that kind of business anyway. I want to bring up something else I've been thinking about. There must be a sizable cash flow—legal cash, I mean, from this annuity of yours and whatever cargo you're using the ships to carry." He paused, trusting a straight answer from his father.

"A fair amount," said Andrew.

"I can put it to work for you. I've been watching the stock market. It looks like '23 is shaping up to be a good year."

"I've heard it's been up and down. Down recently."

"I mean for the issues I'd like to get into, and it looks like '24 is going to be better for them. You aren't already in it, are you?"

"No," said Andrew.

"You read all these newspapers, Dad. You know it's trending up. We're going to have a booming economy in a year or two, and we've got a chance to get in on the ground floor. We don't have to go in with much at first. If you show me your books, I'll see what you can spare, then I can invest in a few good stocks to get us going."

"Yes, I've read the newspaper stories," said Andrew, tapping the tip of his cigarette on the edge of the ashtray. "Shop girl makes ten thousand in one day. Bootblack on Wall Street makes million on tips from customers. I don't pay much attention. For every lucky one there must be a thousand unlucky ones. Is that a business you want to get into?"

"You can't think of the market as pure speculation, Dad. It's a lot more than that." Autie leaned forward in the chair. "We built up industrial capacity in this country to meet the war demand. The factories and production lines are still there, and there are good, financially sound companies making use of that capacity to produce everything from automobiles to vacuum cleaners. They need capital investment to realize their growth potential. That's why they go public. We can study companies that look promising and invest wisely. A good portfolio of strong securities across different sectors of the economy can be useful in a number of ways." He thought he said it well and sat back.

"You've been doing some reading, I see," said Andrew.

"Not just newspapers, Dad."

"Well, I'd be the first to admit I'm not up on it."

"But that shouldn't stop you from seeing you could get into the market in a sensible, informed way."

Andrew sat back and considered. Autie didn't know what his father would say, but he had made his best pitch. He could let it stand the quiet of a few moments.

"You want to create a financial arm to the business, is that it?"

"That's what I was thinking," said Autie, leaning forward. "I don't want to take chances any more than you do, Dad. I want to build something. For both of us. If it works, we can incorporate all the businesses under one umbrella. Losses in one sector can offset gains in another. That can go back and forth to our advantage now that we have to factor in taxes."

"I have to think about it," said Andrew. "You didn't expect an answer today, did you?"

"No."

"Then let me ask you this, Autie. Would setting up something like this have an influence over you and Margaux staying here? I'm sure she takes an interest in what direction you take, and she wouldn't like to see you sacrifice opportunities elsewhere for the sake of remaining here working the farm. I bring this up because having you here means a great deal to your mother. Another thing. Would an arrangement like this put you in a better position with your wife?"

"Yes, on both counts," said Autie without hesitation.

"Then I'll agree to it," said his father. "In principle. I'll have to look things over. I want to do that myself."

"I understand."

"Then we'll start with a limited amount of capital. I'll give you enough to work with, and we'll see how you do with it."

"Thank you, Dad. This means a lot to me."

The two stood up and shook hands. Autie walked down the hill to the Kastelje feeling pretty good. He was glad Father had leveled with him. It shouldn't be hard to put some protections up around the legal part of the business, but still, Haines worried him. Margaux didn't have to know about that part of the business. She liked Haines. Maybe anyone who got shot up in the war was all right in her book.

When Margaux heard word for word what had transpired in the study at the chateau, she said she was very proud of him. Robbie came home from school, and Autie took him and Edward down to the river to look for arrowheads while Margaux made dinner. She called them up as the sun was going down. They brought along some driftwood from the beach, and Autie got a good fire going. It was shrimp that night, on wild rice, with vegetables, biscuits and gravy, and pastries for dessert.

After dinner, Margaux put Edward to bed and helped Robbie with his homework. She made Autie sit down with the newspaper while she did the dishes and cleaned up the kitchen. Then Robbie went to bed and Margaux sat with Autie in the living room in front of the fire. He began choosing the first stocks he would buy, writing down their highs and lows, price/earnings ratios, dividends, and yields. Margaux read and looked up from her book to gaze into the fireplace at the driftwood burning down to coals.

When it was time to go to bed, they walked up the stairs to the landing. Margaux turned to Autie in the hallway, in front of her bedroom door. "You can come in here with me if you want."

He lay beside her that night for the first time in almost a year and remained very still on his side of the bed with his hands over his chest. It was good enough to be in the room. This was his reward for successfully negotiating the deal with Dad. A parable from the book of business, where everything was give and take. Give and receive came from a different book. That was as far as he cared to think about holy scriptures and the present situation. The only mystery was the illegible handwriting on the wall.

CHAPTER SEVENTY-TWO

From Montreal, Laura and Gregory took a night train to New York. Laura was trying to undress lying down in her berth when they got to the border and was obliged to put everything back on when the train stopped. She and Gregory stood in the narrow hallway while US customs searched their bunks, asking questions about their stay in Canada and reason for their visit. All they really seemed to care about was liquor. That was the only interruption. After that, Laura slept soundly through the night, knowing Gregory was in the berth below.

She woke up quite refreshed, so she knew it was still possible for her to put things out of her mind when she had to. She told Gregory she couldn't just sleep all the time. They had a nice big breakfast in the dining car and drank coffee and smoked cigarettes. She was glad to find the simple and ordinary pleasures of life still there. The panorama of upstate New York spread out across the windows; the rolling hills, church steeples, little villages, and farms with red barns and metal silos went by. Hay was stacked in the fields, fenceless acres of rye and wheat, and now and then, a tractor and harvester turning at the end of a row. In the near distance, a pasture of black-and-white cows swept past. In the foreground, just off the rock of the railroad bed, a farm boy on a mule waved at the train and passed quickly out of view like the short life of a fly.

In the day coach, Gregory gave her the seat by the window. He seemed not to care about the bad side of his face showing to the aisle or the looks it drew from other passengers. A one-legged man Gregory's age lurched past their seats with a jerking of his crutches, and Laura noticed the grim look he and Gregory exchanged. The war to end all wars had been over for five years. The topic on everyone's lips had gone out of business. Europe had dropped out of the newspapers. But every town must have its amputees from shot and shell and men blinded by poison gas. Most people probably preferred that they stayed out of sight or stayed in the hospitals, wheeling through the wards in their chairs or groping along the walls with their hands. Or not come home at all. The mentally broken and physically maimed belonged to a little heap of dust swept under the rug. What were her little problems compared to what Gregory lived with every day?

It suddenly struck her that Autie kept the same respectful distance from Gregory and the war that she had noticed in Rory at Christmas. Rory was only home for the holidays, and he had never cared much for the war anyway, but Autie and Gregory were thrown together at dinner every week, and as far as she knew, the war was never brought up. Autie should have been proud of his medals and full of stories, but even when Gregory wasn't around, he never mentioned the war. That seemed very strange when she recalled Autie at seventeen, arrogant and yearning for adventure. Silence was probably a worthwhile lesson to take to heart when the adventure had bad parts to it.

"I don't know why anyone would want to live in the city," Laura said quietly.

Gregory opened his eyes and put his arm around her. Presently, he said, "You have to be young."

"Funny, though. I didn't like it when I was young, when I was up there at the apartment with Mother. I'm very happy where we are. I *am* happy, Gregory. I really am."

"It'll be good to get back," he said. "Are you going to be all right? Maybe we should get someone in for a couple of weeks to help out."

"No, I'll be all right. It's just this. But I'll be all right in a little while. You know I love you, don't you Gregory? I wouldn't be living with you if I didn't. I wouldn't have done anything if I didn't love you."

"I know," he said gently. "Why don't you try to sleep? I can move over a little, and you can put your head down."

"No," she said. "I want to look outside. But I don't feel like talking, if that's all right."

"I understand," he said. "I was just thinking though. You like talking to your mother, don't you. When we get back, I'll show you how to use the ship-to-shore radio. Do you think we could get it to tap into the telephone line?"

Laura laughed. "No, Gregory. Wireless transmission is completely different. We'd have to get the telephone company to run a wire out to the lodge to get telephone service."

"Well, there's a string of poles by the old iron furnace going to Boundary Creek. Couldn't I splice a wire into that? Or would I electrocute myself?"

"No, you wouldn't electrocute yourself," said Laura, laughing again. "It's low voltage, but the telephone company has to do that. We would have to lease a telephone from them anyway."

"Well, you're so good with figuring out things—"

"No, Gregory. I can't make a telephone. And two tin cans with six miles of string wouldn't work."

"Well, you know I'm no good with that kind of stuff. They've got us over a barrel, don't they?"

"Sure do," said Laura. "Especially when you live in the woods."

"Well, I'm glad one of us is smart."

"Oh, no, Gregory, you're the smart one," said Laura, suddenly concerned that she had hurt his male pride. "I only know about technical things. My father was always interested in science. I got it from him, but I only know the basics. Philosophers—that's you—have to explain what it all means when science and practical applications like the automobile, radio, and moving pictures begin to change our lives. Your time is too valuable to waste on learning to be useful."

"I think I'll go back to saying I'm glad one of us is smart," he said frankly.

Laura was beginning to feel the way she had felt at first with Gregory, when they only talked about things in the air and laughed so much. She let him move over, and she lay down with her head in his lap, feeling better about everything. If they had a telephone, she could talk to Mother again every night or when she needed to. It wouldn't be too difficult putting a telephone in.

They changed trains at Grand Central and again in Baltimore, arriving at Cecilton station at eight o'clock that night. Laura was surprised but very happy to see Alice standing by the Pierce-Arrow in a yellow cloche and a long black cloak.

"Welcoming committee!" Alice shouted.

Laura dropped her small carry bag and rushed over to her.

"Gregory called from Baltimore," said Alice, pulling Laura to her exuberantly. "We wouldn't have known when you were getting back otherwise."

"I'm so glad to see you, Mummy."

"I'm so glad to have you home again, dear," said Alice, holding Laura very tightly.

Gregory brought their bags to the car and embraced Alice with one arm.

"Thanks for coming out, Alice."

"Mother, could I have a moment with Gregory?" Laura asked.

"Certainly, dear. I'll go inside. Just toot the horn. Take all the time you need. I'll find one of those wonderful fashion magazines that make women feel so badly about their bodies. Don't worry about me."

Alice took the steps up to the station door briskly, and Laura turned to Gregory with her eyes lowered. She said nothing until she had held him for a moment.

"I think I want to stay here for the night, Gregory. Nothing has changed. I just need to be alone for a night."

"I understand."

"I want to talk to Mother. Thank you for calling her."

"I'm glad she came. I'll make the house warm and cozy for you. You just come out when you're ready. All right?"

"I'll miss you tonight. It was nice to be with you all day and every night for a week. I hope you liked it too."

"I did. And I'll miss you tonight too."

"You understand, don't you?"

"I understand," he said as Laura leaned up to kiss him.

At the post office, Gregory transferred his bags to his truck. With a kiss and a hug from Laura and a pat on the back from Alice, he had the old truck started up after a week of sitting and was on the road to the woods. Alice carried Laura's suitcases up the stairs. Laura turned on every light on the floor and looked into every room.

"Oh, I'm so glad Mrs. Eskin watered my African violet," she called from the bedroom.

"Isn't there something you want to tell me?" Alice called back.

They met in the living room. Alice put her arms around Laura and felt for her hands.

"I've been to Montreal," Alice said. "So I know all about that. What I want to hear about is *this*."

Alice brought Laura's left hand up between them. Laura looked a little sadly down on the gold ring on her fourth finger.

"We didn't get married, Mummy. We just bought rings. We're going to tell people we're married. It'll be easier that way."

"Well," said Alice. "I'm glad. I wouldn't want to be deprived of taking charge of your wedding—when you have the real one, that is."

"I don't know when that will be."

"Well, I hope Andrew and I will still be around when you get to it, dear. We should build a fire under Mr. Haines, don't you think? He knows you would accept an offer, doesn't he?"

"He knows, Mummy."

"Laura, what's wrong, dear?"

When Laura had nothing to offer but a hesitant silence, Alice went to the telephone table and called Andrew. Laura heard her say she'd be staying over for the night. There was nothing she said after that except that she loved him, so he must not have had any questions.

Laura said she felt better talking at the kitchen table, so they went in, and Laura started the water on the stove for tea.

"I don't have any food in the house," she said, looking around the cabinets.

"We can go out for breakfast tomorrow morning," said Alice. "Let's try the hotel. I've heard the food is very good there. Then we can go to the market."

"I'll be going back to Gregory tomorrow."

"Oh, of course. Then what's the matter, dear?"

"I had an abortion, Mummy," said Laura, looking down at the stove.

"Oh, darling, no."

Laura came back and sat down across from Alice, doing her best to keep tears out of her eyes.

"Gregory said it wasn't the right time to have a child."

"He didn't make you, did he?"

"No, we talked it over."

"Then you agreed?"

"I had to, Mother. He was right."

"Then that's the way you must think about it, dear."

"He has some things he has to work out for himself. It's just that—"

"I know," said Alice. "You wanted the baby."

"I did, Mummy. I wanted it so badly."

"I know, dear."

Alice put out her hands and took Laura's.

"The water, Mummy."

Laura got up quickly to catch the shrill whistle of the teakettle. She hadn't faltered so far, and Alice could see she was trying very hard not to give way.

"Did it go all right?"

"The doctor was very nice. I bled a little the next day, but it stopped by itself. I don't know what they do with the—I guess it's only an embryo at that point. I didn't see it. I guess I could find a medical book with pictures and see what a six-or-eight-week embryo looks like, but I'd probably cut out the picture and take it home under my coat and look at it every night, or put it in a frame for the mantelpiece—"

"Oh Laura, stop."

Alice got up and held Laura in her arms, and Laura finally cried, trembling and holding onto her.

"You did it for Gregory," Alice said. "That's what you have to remember when you feel this way. He knows. He won't forget. You'll get married, and you'll have children when the right time comes, and it will make up for all of this."

"You can't know that, Mummy," Laura blurted out.

"I know from my own experience, dear. I lost Andrew once. I thought he was dead for four years. And I had two daughters who died when they were babies."

Laura broke away and stopped crying.

"Why didn't you tell me?"

"I'm telling you now."

"How did you bear it, Mummy?"

"You'll see for yourself, dear, in how you bear the loss of your own. You're a strong girl, and you'll find out how true that is. Now let's sit down, have some tea, and you can tell me about Montreal."

Laura went back to Gregory the next evening after closing the post office at five o'clock. In the silence they had kept on the train from Montreal, she had felt the beginnings of a gulf between them. It did not fail to materialize, but in the next days and weeks at the lodge, there seemed to be so many rope ladders strung over it, so many boards thrown across the chasm, so many lifelines of daily life tossed between them, that Laura put aside her fears of becoming distant.

Gregory was the way he had always been. When the weather began to get cold and rainy he built a shed for the bathtub. They had electricity brought to the lodge, and put in a regular telephone line. A small electric range would have fit nicely beside the large fireplace, but they decided they liked sitting by a fire at night without looking at an appliance, so he built another shed for the electric stove. Alice came out and said the lodge looked quite civilized without any loss of its charm. On the anniversary of the first night they slept together, Gregory surprised her with an extravagant dinner and a package of French rubbers. He had someone get them for him in Baltimore. Laura read the directions on the package out loud, and Gregory had to define some French words Laura had never heard before. There were so many funny little things about their life together that she could never tell anyone about, not even Alice.

She worried every night, whenever Gregory went out on the boat or drove the truck into town. She knew he carried a gun. Before or after Sunday dinners at the chateau, he always managed to deliver a bundle of money to Father's study. It was thousands every time. She helped him count and wrap it. The newspapers always had stories of Prohibition crackdowns, more agents being hired, and more people thrown in jail. Gregory kept telling her she shouldn't worry.

During the day while Laura was at the post office, Gregory read his philosophy books, tended the garden, cooked, and built things out of scrap wood. Inspired by his success building the two sheds, he started carving driftwood he found along the river and decided that becoming an artisan in wood was a good cover for living out in the woods. Laura thought his work was real art and brought some of his pieces to Alice, who was delighted to use some of the smaller ones in her dining table centerpieces.

Laura continued to fulfill her duties as postmistress, jumping up from her desk for anyone with two pennies to buy a stamp. She was cheerful and conversational with everyone but always closed the doors promptly at five o'clock. Just outside those doors her faithful Ford waited, ready to convey her back to the lodge every evening. As much as living in two places was impractical, she did not feel divided in the slightest when Gregory greeted her at the door, or when she shed her work clothes and all formalities to sit down to hearty meals made by the man who loved her, or when she lay down by his side every night. It was not one place or the other. Gregory was where she lived.

CHAPTER SEVENTY-THREE

EARLY SPRING 1924

Autie, standing at the counter in the post office, said that was the thing about having a regular life. There was nothing to talk about.

"Just living day to day," he said. "Sometimes it seems hardly worth your while to try to say anything about it at all. You do have to wonder where the time goes, though."

"I know," said Laura. "When Sunday dinner comes, and Father asks what I did this week, I can't think of anything. But maybe it's because I talk to Mother every night on the telephone. I should write down what I do every day in a diary. It would be the most boring book. Reading it would serve anybody right for snooping. Same thing every day. Worked at post office. Came home. Washed clothes. Made dinner. Went to bed."

"Well, how's married life?"

"That's the part I wouldn't be writing down." Laura laughed. "Do you want to come in the office and sit down?"

"Sure, I've got a little time."

"Just go on back, Autie. I'll see if Mrs. Eskin is finished her lunch."

When Mrs. Eskin was in place holding down the counter, Laura came back to the office and took her seat at the desk, feeling as fine and free and breezy as she ever felt.

"I was going to ask you the same thing," she said, laughing.

"You first."

"All right," she said thoughtfully. "Well, Gregory is perfectly wonderful. I could give you a million instances, but I can't really."

"I don't think I'd be able to remember a million either."

"You're making fun, but, no, they're just private little things I shouldn't be talking about."

He could see Laura was working up to the old intensity he knew from before he left for the army.

"I guess they're ordinary enough. You and Margaux probably have the same, I'm sure all married people do. But what I'm trying to say is, Gregory's had plenty of time to, you know, get used to me, or become complacent, or take me for granted, whatever you call it. But he never does. He's attentive, he talks to me. And he always listens so well. He's very affectionate, and he's always doing little things to show how he cares about me. I'm sorry for going on. I guess I just can't say enough about him."

"Don't worry about it."

"He's not so concerned about his face anymore. I think he's become reconciled to it and won't let it rule his life."

"Well, that's because of you probably."

"Oh, do you think so? I hope it's true," said Laura eagerly.

"He's sure isn't shy and retiring on Sunday nights. And he charmed the pants off Rory's new girl last Christmas."

"Oh, Rory. I hope he doesn't bring home a new one every year."

"Well, that's Rory. He's still got his looks, and so far they're still on par with the ladies who go for him."

"Margaux doesn't like him, does she?"

"I wish it wasn't so obvious."

"Oh, it really isn't," said Laura. "She's so quiet. But I can tell."

"She's not so quiet at home," said Autie with a wry smile. "She says she sees right through Rory."

"I'm afraid to ask what she thinks of me," said Laura, posing a bold question. "She doesn't particularly like me either, does she? No, don't say anything. I know it's true. But you can tell I'm trying with her, can't you, Autie?"

"Oh sure. Everybody's trying. She's just not good with people."

"She's still going to the doctor in Baltimore, isn't she? Mother mentions it. That's how I know."

"They make a little outing out of it. That's probably helping as much as the doctor—getting out of the house and going out to lunch with Mom."

"Is all this because of—do you mind me asking—I really shouldn't."

"No. Go ahead."

"Well, that man Karensky. I was never so shocked. He's the one who painted my portrait years ago."

"Don't ask me. I don't know. I don't think anybody knows why she went off with him. Including the lady psychiatrist. He asked Margaux to pose for him. That's all she told me. I think he drugged her. She didn't seem right when I brought her back. She was like a dishrag. It's just my opinion, but I was there, and I saw how she looked."

"Oh, I'm so sorry for you, Autie." Laura reached across the desk to put her hand on Autie's without a second thought. It was a natural thing to do.

"It's my own fault. I should have left the army and come back with her from Fort Riley when she had Edward. That was a big mistake. If I had stuck with her, maybe she wouldn't have gotten unglued."

"You can't blame yourself, Autie. Everyone's been so good to her. She had your mother here, and they did a lot of things together. I didn't see much of her because I just got the job and moved out, but I thought she was fine."

"Well, I'm glad I'm at home now. I can tell she's better."

"I hope so, Autie—so how are you doing in the stock market, mister?"

"Everything's going up," said Autie, brightening with the happier topic.

"Do you think Gregory and I should get into it?"

"If you have money to spare, I would."

"Gregory handles all the money," said Laura, "but I can ask."

"Well, just let me know if I can do anything to help get you started. I'm following some good companies right now. I'd love to talk more about it, but I'd better be getting back. Margaux might be looking for me. She drives now. Mom taught her. I don't want her coming out looking for me." He laughed as he stood up.

"Then get going. I don't want her to hate me any more than she already does."

"She doesn't hate you."

There was no one in the post office but Mrs. Eskin, so Laura gave Autie a quick hug inside the door. Then she stood at the window, waving as he drove off.

Autie was glad he didn't run into any search parties on his way home. Sometimes Margaux had to know where he was every minute. Sometimes long stretches went by when she couldn't have cared less where he was or whom he talked to. Living with an unusual person made him think how easy most people were to live with.

Maybe the weekly sessions with the psychiatrist should include the husband, with one hour for her on the couch, one hour for him, then a session together. It wasn't such a crazy idea. Part of Margaux's problem might be him, and he was getting off scot-free. That didn't seem fair.

When he got home, Margaux was in the garden. He went through the gate, careful to walk on the paths because she was watching. She stood up from the tiered strawberry pyramid. He put an arm around her and kissed her on the cheek.

"You've been with that Laura Haines," she said. "I can smell her on you."

She broke off abruptly and went back to brushing the winter straw off the little green bunches.

"I had to go to the post office."

"You've been gone one hour and a half."

"We talked a little."

"I hope you don't talk about me."

"No, we talked about other things."

"What things?"

"She goes on about Gregory. You know how she is."

"I like her better married," said Margaux, not looking up. "You can talk all you want to her, but since you sleep in my room now, there's no need for you to touch her."

"All right," said Autie. "Are we going to get any strawberries?"

"No strawberries," she said. "For another year I have to clip the buds. The plants aren't strong enough."

"What else are you putting in this year?"

"I don't know yet. I need your mother to tell me what she needs. She said make a Belgian garden this year. I told her that means three vegetables and two are cabbage."

Autie laughed.

"I'm not trying to be funny. You should go back to work now. I'll be in the kitchen making dinner."

Autie went in the open red-and-white front door of the Kastelje. He loved the cottage now. He'd been afraid of moving out of the chateau and living with Margaux and the boys on their own, but it was turning out to be less of a minefield than he had expected. There hadn't been many flare-ups, just small ones, the kind that only blow your toes off.

He'd been found out. Margaux had a good sense of smell. He should have known. And he should have known she wouldn't take it lightly. Margaux took nothing lightly. But it was worth it to get out of the office and go for a drive. Laura had changed a lot. She'd grown up, and he had to admit it was nice to put his arms around a big, solid girl.

Being allowed back in the bedroom with Margaux took the edge off, but lovemaking had slipped to minor importance since she came back from her fling, whatever it was, in New York and left him out in the cold. Getting along was more important. Wanting a pretty girl had gotten him into this mess in the first place. Hopefully he was beyond that. It had gotten him a person difficult to understand, and now they were just two people trying to live together without falling apart. Laura Eklund would have been so much easier. Unless the one difficult to live with was him.

That night he lay awake in bed beside Margaux. She was fast asleep. She must have gotten better at turning her mind off. Not like the early days. Not a sound. He wondered if they would stay together. Nobody was calling quits so far. Sometimes he wanted to be free. She hadn't said she wanted to die for a while. What's stopping her? It would be his fault now. Maybe it was the boys. Maybe she was beginning to love him, Robbie, and little Edward. That's what it was beginning to feel like when the kids were in bed and they were downstairs reading. It must be confusing if she believed people could only love once. Then again, sometimes the wrong people find each other. Incompatibility didn't necessarily mean not loving. They didn't talk easily. She might never tell him any more than she already had. Maybe she had talked to her German. Or maybe the German could intuit better than he could. How long would it take to get good at something like that? It could consume all the years of growing old together. They might run out of time anyway. Which one would die first? Who would be the one to draw a last breath and say, We tried, didn't we?

CHAPTER SEVENTY-FOUR

There was a nice-looking lady in a smart traveling outfit waiting patiently behind elderly Camden Nast, who was taking his time counting out pennies on the counter.

"You need two more, Mr. Nast," said Laura. She should have just given him two pennies from the slush money. Now he had to go through all his pockets, trousers, vest, shirt, and coat.

"I'll take you over here, ma'am," said Mrs. Eskin, coming out of the back room.

"Thank you very much, miss," the lady said, stepping out from behind Camden Nast and meeting Mrs. Eskin at the corner of the counter. "I wonder if you can help me? I'm looking for someone who takes general delivery at this post office."

"Well, we know pretty near everyone in town and surrounding, so that shouldn't be too hard," said Mrs. Eskin, smiling easily.

Mr. Nast produced the two pennies due and put his roll of stamps into a pocket.

"Thank you, Mrs. Haines," he said on his way out the door. "You be good now."

"You'll have to ask the postmistress, ma'am," said Mrs. Eskin. "I wouldn't know about that."

"What is it, Mrs. Eskin?" Laura asked, straightening up from picking up the pennies that got away when she was sweeping them off the counter into her hand.

Mrs. Eskin directed the lady to Laura and disappeared into the back room as if she wanted to get out of the way of a truck.

"I'm so sorry to bother you," the lady said, coming over to face Laura.

"Not at all," said Laura. "I believe I overheard you inquiring of one of our customers."

"Yes. If it isn't too much trouble. My name is Joanna Haines. I'm looking for my husband, Mr. Gregory Haines. I understand he lives in this postal district."

Laura tried not to register the shock, but it must have showed in a flush of blood to her face.

"I'm sorry. Are you unwell, miss?"

"No, thank you, Mrs. Haines," said Laura. "I just had a candy. It stuck in my throat. I'm quite all right now. Yes, Mr. Haines comes in for his mail. We hold it for him because he lives outside our delivery route. We don't know where he lives though. I don't think anyone does. You may certainly leave a note for him."

"Do you know when he'll be in?"

"No. It might be a month or more. We never know when he'll be in."

"My husband is very recognizable," said Joanna Haines. "He was wounded in the war."

"His face, yes. I've seen him," said Laura.

"Oh, that's good. Then I really have found him," said Joanna Haines, with a happy sigh of relief. "I've been mailing letters to several different places I thought he might be. This was my last hope. Thank you so much—"

"Miss Eklund."

Joanna Haines looked at Laura quizzically for a moment. It was the first time Laura thought to put her left hand with the wedding ring under the counter.

"I thought I heard the elderly gentleman address you as Mrs. Haines."

"No, I'm Miss Eklund. He must have gotten mixed up, hearing you just mention your name to my assistant."

"That would have been a funny coincidence," said Joanna Haines, returning to the happiness her face had expressed at the news that her search was over. "I don't care how long I have to wait. I'm so happy I've found him. If you wouldn't mind doing me an enormous kindness, Miss Eklund, could you telephone me when he comes in? I'll have my bag sent over to the hotel. I only have one, but I see you have a nice little dress shop in town if I'm going to be here for any length of time."

"I'd be happy to do that for you, Mrs. Haines," said Laura.

"Thank you very much, Miss Eklund. You won't mind me checking in every so often, will you?"

"Not at all."

When Mrs. Haines left the post office, Laura went to the door to watch her walk over to the hotel. She called Mrs. Eskin to the front and said she did not feel well and had to go upstairs and lie down. She sat down in her chair beside the telephone table and took a deep breath.

Gregory answered after a few rings. He must have been inside reading.

"Gregory," she said, "your wife is here."

There was silence on the other end. Laura thought she might as well get it over with. She wouldn't be able to stand it very long.

"She's staying at the hotel. She wants me to telephone her when you come in to get your mail. She said she doesn't care how long she has to wait."

Gregory finally spoke. She didn't feel any better or worse for what he said. "I'll come to town," he said.

That was all. Laura went to lie down in the bedroom. She didn't know what to think. She didn't know what was going to happen next. What were her chances? Laura tried to picture Joanna Haines in her mind, wishing she had not been so overcome by shock and had taken a good look at her. Trim. Pretty. Shapely. Intelligent face. Blonde hair, cut short in the style. She might have guessed that from the handwriting on the letters if she had tried. She would have known Gregory was married if she had gone against the rules and read the letters. It was perfectly obvious now.

The people at the hotel knew her as Mrs. Haines after she and Gregory came back from Montreal. They would point out the coincidence to the real Mrs. Haines. Gregory could tell his wife he had found his true soul mate and send the wife back to Chicago. She was young and pretty. She could find someone else.

Laura got up suddenly. Gregory was coming to town. She had to look her best. She scanned through her closets, pulling out his favorite dresses, looking in the full-length mirror, getting in and out of six or seven, and finally deciding. She put her hair up in a French twist and touched perfume here and there.

When Laura got to the window of the living room, Gregory was coming down the street in his truck. She made herself wait upstairs. Mrs. Eskin could call up and tell her he was here asking for her. After a few minutes, she went back to the living room window. The truck was parked not outside the post office but in front of the hotel, and Gregory was nowhere to be seen.

At five o'clock, Mrs. Eskin called upstairs to say she had closed the post office and everything was locked up.

"I hope you feel better," she said.

"Thank you," Laura called back. "Good night."

Another hour passed with Laura sitting by the corner of her window in the quickly fading daylight. Gregory came out of the hotel. Joanna was behind him. He held the door for her, and she got in. He came around the front of the truck and stepped up on the running board, pausing for the moment when he might have turned around to look toward the second-floor window of the post office where he had first seen her that night more than a year ago.

But he didn't turn around. He was not coming to get his mail, as advertised in the unclaimed mail advertisement she had placed. He was not standing below, removing his hat and holding up a newspaper to her in the window, and she was not going to fall in love with him. Gregory got in the driver's seat. The truck started, the headlights turned on, and they drove off.

Laura's mouth dropped open as if the earth had rent and was falling away under her feet, but no sound came from the hurt welling up inside her. She didn't know how long she stood frozen at the window, staring agape and suffering without the ability to make a sound.

In a daze she emptied her purse on the floor, took a large denomination bill and went down the stairs. She crossed the street and walked two blocks to the grocery store. It was closed, so she went around the back and broke a window with a stone. It was a small stone, and she slashed her arm on the broken spears of glass as she reached in to unlock the door. There was a light on over the meat counter, enough to see down the aisles to the cellar stairs. Down in the utter darkness of the dirt-floor basement, Laura felt around for the crates she knew would be there. When she found them, she grabbed two bottles of whatever it was Gregory delivered there at night. She left a bloody twenty-dollar bill on the counter and got out of there.

In the kitchen, she took off the pretty dress she put on for Gregory and cut it up with scissors. She wrapped up her bleeding arm with a length of it and went into the living room in her underwear, where she sat in the telephone chair with a bottle and started drinking it down in gulps.

Alice called at nine o'clock. "What's wrong, Laura?" she said.

"Everything's wrong. Everything's wrong."

"I'm coming over right now."

Alice called Andrew to the living room.

"It's Laura. I'm going over there. Keep her talking."

Andrew took the phone from her right away.

"Don't drive fast, Alice," he said after her.

"Laura, are you there? Laura?"

"What? Where's Mummy?"

"Mummy's coming over. She's leaving right now. Just stay where you are. Tell me what you're doing right now. Laura? Tell me what you're doing."

"I'm drinking stuff."

"What stuff?"

"A bottle of stuff."

"Where did you get it?"

"The grocery store. I paid for it with my own money. I broke a window."

"Is it liquor?"

"I got it out of the cellar."

"How much have you had?"

"The bottle's all gone. It's not working. I have to get the other one."

"No, Laura, stay right where you are and talk to me," he said calmly. "We haven't talked in a long time, have we? You know what I think you ought to do first? I think you should throw up. You probably feel like throwing up, don't you?"

"I don't like throwing up."

"Laura, listen to me. You have to throw up. It will make you feel better. Get on your hands and knees and throw up."

"I can't."

"Laura? I'll tell you how to do it. Hold the phone to one side. Put a finger in your mouth and tickle your throat."

"I don't want to."

"It will make you feel better."

"I don't want to feel better."

"Laura, Mummy's on her way."

"I have to drink the other bottle. I don't want to waste money. I bought it with my own money."

"Laura. Stay right there. Mummy won't know where you are if you go away from the telephone. She's coming. She's on her way. Can you sing something for me? You have such a beautiful voice. Everybody says so. Did you know that?"

When Alice got to the post office, she found the door unlocked. The interior door to the house was wide open, and she ran up the stairs. Laura was in her underwear, facedown on the floor in a puddle of vomit. It looked like her dress was wrapped around her arm. She was singing fragments of a children's song as Alice turned her over. Her eyes were half open, showing only the whites and crescents of the iris under the upper lids. The song turned into mumbling. Alice picked up the telephone.

"Andrew? I've got her," she said. "No, you stay there. I'll call you in a few minutes when I know what's going on."

Alice looked at the bottle. Imported scotch. One hundred proof. It looked like she drank the whole thing. "Laura, we have to get you up," she said, sitting down on the floor and setting her back against the chair for leverage. It was only then that Alice noticed the dress had been cut and wrapped around Laura's arm as a bandage and that the carpet was soaked with blood. She was a heavy girl. Alice got her up to a sitting position but couldn't bring her around. She reached for the telephone and called Andrew.

"I'm going to need you, dear. Try not to wake anyone in the house. Bring a blanket or two."

Inside of twenty minutes, the old Silver Ghost pulled up in front of the post office behind the Pierce-Arrow.

"We've got to get her to a doctor, Andrew. It's her arm. Look at it. I think she nicked an artery." Alice undid the blanket she had wrapped Laura in enough to expose the injured arm.

"That's what it is all right," said Andrew, hastily retying the cloth around her arm, tighter to act as a tourniquet, and tucking in the blanket. "There's blood up the steps too. The hospital in Chestertown. She's going to need plasma."

"How are we going to get her down the stairs?"

"I'll carry her."

"Andrew, she's too heavy."

"You go ahead of me. We'll take the Pierce."

Andrew picked up Laura as if she were no heavier than the blanket and was going for the stairs before Alice could get herself off the floor.

"Be careful. Be careful, Andrew. One step at a time. Oh, her head. Andrew."

Andrew stopped and deftly jolted Laura in his arms so that her head fell forward between her hunched shoulders.

On the way to Chestertown, Alice sat in the back seat with Laura, with her head in her lap, checking her breathing and making sure the airway was clear.

"Watch for deer, Andrew."

"I know. I'm only going forty-five. We'll still get there in forty minutes. Do you know what caused all this?"

"No, she was nearly out cold when I got there. It must be something with Gregory."

"That's probably right."

"Maybe you could go a little faster," Alice said. "I think she's going into shock."

Andrew brought the car up a few marks on the speedometer.

"Remember the last time we did this?" he asked, over his shoulder. "Lamont Eldridge and the collapsed lung. We got him there in time, didn't we? We'll get Laura there in time too."

The darkness of the road made the lights of the hospital welcoming when the car entered the bright circular drive in front. An orderly came out immediately to determine the nature of the emergency, then two others with a stretcher removed Laura from the car and carried her inside. Following along as far as the nurse at the desk, Alice and Andrew noticed the blood on her dress and wrap, and on his herringbone tweeds.

"We look as bad as she does," Andrew whispered.

"That's not funny, dear."

"I'm sorry."

"Push back your hair, darling. What name do we give?"

"Laura Croft," said Andrew, stepping up to the front desk and brushing back his hair with blood dried on his hands.

Alice leaned against Andrew's shoulder on a couch in the waiting room and fell asleep. Andrew watched the second hand on the clock on the wall opposite. There wasn't enough information to think out the situation at hand, beyond knowing what lay before them that night. They had to clean up the blood at the post office. There might be blood in a direct line from the grocery store to the post office they'd have to take care of. They had to get home and change clothes because Alice would want to go back to the hospital. They had to get in touch with Mrs. Eskin to work the post office.

Shortly after two o'clock in the morning, a doctor came through the doors. He said Laura would be all right. The arm took stitching on several layers of skin because the glass had taken some meat off the bone, but it was a clean wound, and the six units of plasma she had received would help counteract the alcohol poisoning.

Alice was back at the hospital when Laura woke up around eight that morning. Andrew, from a little earlier in the day, was sitting on the floor in the back room of the post office sorting the mail from the train depot, getting up every few minutes to bring a batch for Mrs. Eskin to enter into the logs at Laura's desk.

When Elijah came through the kitchen door at the chateau with the Croft mailbag that morning, he said to Viola, "Don't put no breakfast on for the Crofts yet, Viola. Mr. Croft, he over workin' at the post office just now, sittin' on the floor sortin' mail, and the missus pass me in the Pierce car goin' south on the county road like a bat outta hell. You guess good as mine."

CHAPTER SEVENTY-FIVE

A week later, Laura returned to work at the post office with her arm still heavily bandaged but well hidden under long sleeves. She could hardly keep her eyes off the door. One day Gregory would come into town to put his wife on the train. Then he would come around to the post office, walk in with a weary smile because it had taken him so long to explain to Joanna that he loved someone else. Joanna would understand and tell him she would not complicate his life any further and return to Chicago. With Gregory hers again, she would roll up her sleeve and show him the wound she had inflicted upon herself for love of him. She spent hours as she worked through the next days, thinking of what she would say, trying to come up with something good before the day came when he jingled the bell on the door.

Andrew drove out to the lodge in the old Silver Ghost and spoke with Gregory. He brought back a note from Joanna Haines addressed to Laura Croft. It was closing time at the post office when he handed it to Laura.
"Would you like me to stay?" he asked.
Laura was trembling a little, he noticed, and she had to pause to steady her voice.

"No, Father. I don't want to read it now."

"I could have your mother come over when she gets back from the psychiatrist in Baltimore."

"She'll be tired from Margaux."

"You know she never gets tired, Laura. Except perhaps with me." He smiled a small smile that he felt was in keeping with the topic but respectful of the circumstances.

"I'm sure that's not so, Father," said Laura. She hugged him and remembered the same smell of tobacco, shaving soap, and wood-fire smoke that her own father had when he was alive and she was young.

"Thank you for what you did," she said.

After her dinner, Laura sat down in her chair by the telephone table and turned the letter over in her hands. It was in the same handwriting as Gregory's unclaimed mail. Mystery solved. But was it ever a mystery? Was her capacity for self-deception so boundless that she never thought Gregory was married? No one who had ever wanted to love and be loved could blame her for that, no one who had been overlooked, no one who once saw a chance could be blamed for taking it.

Laura picked up the book she had taken out of the library the day before Mrs. Haines came into the post office. It was about creating rustic home furnishings. She was going to make a chair for Gregory.

Mother called at nine o'clock.

"We just got home," she said. "We had a flat tire. I fixed it myself. Those drills Andrew put me through since we got the first car finally paid off. I was surprised I remembered how to do it. You know I hardly pay any attention to him. Laura, I want to ask you, are you all right, dear?"

"Yes, Mummy, I'm fine."

"Did you read the letter?"

"No, I might read it tomorrow. I'm not up to it now, but I'm fine."

Laura heard Alice call Andrew and then the sound of her hand covering the mouthpiece.

"Laura," said Alice, coming back on, "Andrew says you should read it now. Laura dear, I'm going to hang up now. I'll give you half an hour, and if you haven't called me back, I'm getting in the car."

"You don't have to do that, Mummy. I'll read it, and I'll call you back."

Laura put down the telephone and picked up the letter. She was aware of her heart beating and her rate of respiration. If she had reason to fall to the floor, she wished her heart would do her the kindness of stopping altogether.

> *Dear Miss Croft,*
>
> *In the many talks we have had this week, Greg has told me about the love you have for each other. He will always cherish it and hold you forever in his heart. I am glad of it and hope very much that he does, for you are the reason he is able to return to me now.*
>
> *Though the war did not take his life, it destroyed the dear man I knew from childhood and married eight years ago. He came home angry and bitter, finding no comfort in the life he had longed for in so many letters written before he was wounded. He fought with me and with everyone who tried to help him. He did everything he could to put an end to the love that I and others felt for him.*
>
> *I am so deeply indebted to you and so painfully aware of your sacrifice in giving him back to me. As Greg and I begin our family and restore the happiness we had, none shall hold so firmly a place in our hearts as you, dear Laura. Please forgive my informality, but Greg has told me so much about your loving and generous nature that I feel close to you as I would a sister.*
>
> *We will be at the train station tomorrow morning at 8:00 am to begin our trip home. Greg and I would like very much to see you. If you cannot bear it, I will understand. You have given so much, it is hard for me to ask any more of you.*
>
> *With my deepest gratitude,*
Joanna Haines

It was written in beautiful script, in the hand of a mature woman accustomed to writing polite thank-you notes. Laura put it down in her lap. She looked at her bandaged arm and wept for that hurt part of herself that did not show to the world.

The telephone rang.

"You've been crying, Laura," said Alice.

"It's over with Gregory, Mummy. I'm back where I was."

"No. You're not, dear. You're a different person. A better person. Do you want me to come over?"

"It won't do any good. I think I should be alone."

"Do you *want* to be alone?"

"Yes, I think I do."

"Are you going to the station tomorrow?"

"No, I couldn't do that."

"That's perfectly understandable. If you change your mind, I'll go with you. You can call any time. I'll probably be up all night anyway."

"There's no need to do that, Mummy. I'll be all right."

"You're not to do anything foolish, dear. I'll come over right away."

"I won't do anything foolish," said Laura. "I'm finished doing foolish things. I won't ever do a foolish thing again."

"Oh, darling, don't say that. I'm so sorry for you. Things will get better. You have to believe that. You're an intelligent, beautiful girl. You're older and wiser and experienced in the world now."

"The world of misery?"

"Oh no, darling," said Alice. "You can't think of it like that. You've been with a man now. You've lived as a husband and wife. You know everything about sharing a life and what you need. Gregory just wasn't the right one."

"But he was, Mummy."

"Well, he was already taken. I know you'll find someone else, dear. You're so perfectly made for a happy life with a man."

There was quiet on the line.

Then Laura said, "Mummy, I want to go to bed now."

"Of course, dear. You must be very tired."

Alice got off the telephone with Laura and sat thinking in her comfortable chair in the living room. It had a footrest that came out from under, but she did not feel like availing herself of every comfort her life had to offer just then. Andrew put his book down and looked over to her.

"Is she going to the station?"

"No, she says she's not."

"Maybe it's best."

"Andrew," said Alice abruptly, "is it me?"

"I don't know what you mean, dear."

"I haven't done well with Laura, have I?"

Andrew set his book aside, took off his glasses and put them down. He got up from his chair and moved to the couch.

"Come over here and sit with me, Alice," he said.

"No, Andrew, I have to think of what to do."

"We can do that together. Come over here."

"No, Andrew, you'll only distract me."

"Then I'll pick you up and bring you over here."

"I'm only doing it because I know you can," said Alice, coming to sit with him.

Andrew put his arm around her, and finally she lay down across the couch with her head in his lap.

"Now then, what are you thinking?" he asked.

"I've failed Laura," she said. "I can't get through to Margaux. I killed Elizabeth, and my body wasn't strong enough for the other one. She didn't even live long enough for us to name her."

At that, Alice came close to tears as she waited for Andrew to say something. There was really nothing he could say against the preponderance of evidence.

"I've never been able to change your understanding of what happened in the past, Alice," he said quietly, "so I won't try again. But I remember how Laura was when she first came here, and I know how Margaux was. You've been the Rock of Gibraltar for Laura, probably the same for Margaux. All rocks have to do is be rocks, Alice. With Margaux, Autie has to take the lead, but we can still do something for Laura."

Alice sat up and dried her eyes on Andrew's shirt cuffs.

"Do you think we should bring Laura back here?"

"No, that's not what I'm saying."

"I'm trying to be practical now, Andrew."

"I realize that. I've been thinking too, and I might have something. But it depends upon you believing in the influence you've had over her."

"All right. Let's say I do. What's your idea?"

"We send her away on a European tour. It's a common thing to do these days. You take her over for two months, six months, whatever it takes for her to forget Gregory Haines or meet someone else. Either way, it'll buck her up. The way she is now, she won't be able to face the talk around here until her situation changes or her skin thickens."

"Oh, Andrew, I couldn't bear to be away from you that long."

"I think it's the only solution to the situation, dear."

"I know. You can join us over there whenever you can get away."

"That wouldn't fit in with the plan, Alice. It would only make her feel like a third wheel and accentuate her sense of isolation, just when she might be coming out of it."

"But I'd miss you so much."

"I'll miss you too, but you know I'm right."

They agreed on it, and Alice went to bed wishing they could pack up and leave that night and spare Laura the painful staring into the dark she must be doing. It might not be any consolation, but it would introduce a host of new stimulants into her mind. At the same time, as Alice drew the covers back and Andrew got into bed beside her, her thoughts flew ahead to the loneliness of the nights that now lay before her in the plan taking shape.

"Maybe Rory knows someone in London who would be good for her."

"That's a start," said Andrew. "But you shouldn't come home until you're sure the mission has been accomplished."

"What if we're away six months, and we haven't met anyone, and she's still on tenterhooks?"

"Then you keep going."

"What if your plan backfires, and we go to Athens, and I develop an unwholesome attraction to a Greek goat boy? You'd be sorry then, wouldn't you?"

"I'd come after you."

"Of course I would know that. We would hide in caves until you gave up and went away."

"Oh, I wouldn't bother looking through caves," he said. "You'd get tired of living in caves soon enough, or bored with your goat boy. I'd be at my luxury hotel in Athens waiting. I'll leave a candle in the window for you."

"Oh, Andrew," said Alice, completely at a loss. "I wish you hadn't thought of a tour, but I'm afraid you really are right. She'd never be able to take the scandal in town."

"Now we have to do it, don't we? How will I bear being away from you? I'll end up taking her to the ends of the earth—that's how far she said she would go on loving Gregory Haines. To the ends of the earth. Oh, Andrew."

He let silence wander through the dark bedroom for a few moments. Alice hoped he was thinking of a reason the idea wouldn't work, but when his voice came back, she knew she was as good as throwing confetti from the rail of a liner casting off in New York harbor.

"You would do anything for her, wouldn't you, Alice?"

"Of course I would."

That put an end to the tour question, and Alice resigned herself. Then she had another thought.

"Andrew, I have to ask. Did you know Gregory was married?"

"No, I didn't pry into his private life."

"Then how did you know he was all right for her?"

"We had some talks. I came across him along the river one day, a little up from the sandbar, but still on our land. He was going to shoot himself. I persuaded him not to do it. Well, actually, I took the gun away from him. I'm not as good with verbal modes of persuasion as I should be by now. So we talked. He was out of money and had nowhere to go, so I helped him out. I had no idea he'd get together with Laura. I don't think I could have dreamed it up, but there it was. He got better, she got better. So I stayed out of it and didn't ask questions."

Alice abruptly sat up. She was only a dark outline against a dark background, but he would have recognized her silhouette anywhere, going back thirty-four years and forward for as many as he was not privileged to know.

"Why didn't you tell me all this, Andrew?"

"I did."

"When?"

"The day I met Gregory."

"I don't remember that at all."

"You were doing something. I doubt you were paying attention."

"Well, Andrew, I'm sorry, but you're going to have to let me know when you're saying something important."

CHAPTER SEVENTY-SIX

Alice grabbed Laura's hand and pulled her through the crowd pressing to the rail of the *SS Leviathan*.

"There they are," she shouted above a blast of the horn.

Laura looked along Alice's arm. Far below on the dock, in a sea of upward-turned faces in every contortion of sending up their loudest goodbyes, stood Andrew and Autie. Laura waved, and they waved back. Alice put confetti from her pockets into her hands.

"Throw this at them. Here. I'll give you mine too."

Laura threw as far as she could into the air. Then they waved feverishly as the ship pulled away from the dock, waving as long as their arms could stand it and as long as the arms on shore could be seen waving back.

"Well, we're off," said Alice, turning to Laura and hugging her. "Let's go to our rooms. I don't know where they are now. Do you remember?"

"It's this way, Mother," said Laura, taking her hand.

They pushed through the dispersing mob on deck and followed a line of others going down metal steps.

"This is our floor, Mother."

They stepped carefully over the high rim of the watertight doorway into a beautifully carpeted hallway, brilliantly lighted by ensconced lamps.

"We're 423 and 425," said Laura, looking at the numbers on the doors. "No, it's on the other side."

Going back through the doorway, Laura bumped into a gentleman coming the other way. She got through before him, but he came up square against Alice.

"Excuse me," he said courteously. "I'll let you go first."

"Thank you, sir," said Alice.

"Miss Sheffield!" he exclaimed.

"I beg your pardon?"

"It's Miss Sheffield, isn't it?"

Alice turned to face him.

"It was," she said. "Many years ago."

"Richard Griswold," he said, as if his amazement extended to his own name. "Lieutenant Griswold, Royal Marines. Also many years ago."

For a moment Alice was struck dumb, but almost instantaneous with hearing the name, the features she had found so handsome long ago came up from the river bottom of the past and surfaced on the face before her. His hair was gray now, the blue eyes a little more watery, but the rest was the same, as fit and trim in the leisure attire of an English gentleman as it had been in red military. Laura came back through the door on the other side and stood behind her.

"China," he said. "The motor launch on the river."

"Oh, yes," said Alice. "Lieutenant Griswold. My memory has not gotten so poor that I would not remember. It's just that I never saw you in civilian attire or thought of you without an Asian backdrop."

"Well, I never saw you in anything but ill-fitting borrowed missionary garb," he replied, "but I could never forget your face."

"Nor I yours, but you must forgive me, Lieutenant Griswold. I am not looking at faces these days with the interest I had then."

Alice reached for Laura and brought the dumfounded girl to her side.

"May I present my daughter, Laura Croft. Laura, Lieutenant Griswold of the Royal Marines."

"It's a pleasure, Miss Croft," he said briskly. "Not a lieutenant any longer though. I retired as a full colonel after the war. Then you must be Mrs. Croft."

"Quite right."

"Croft wasn't the name of that bounder you were with, was it?"

"I answer to his name proudly, sir," said Alice, without defiance or pretension.

"Oh, I'm sorry, madam. I meant no offense. I respected the man highly, very highly. A man's man to be sure."

"I will convey to him your compliments," said Alice.

"You wouldn't be related to Rory Croft, would you?"

"Why yes. What a surprise. He's my eldest son."

"I know him from the City. A very fine man."

"He is?" said Alice skeptically.

"Very well thought of in financial circles. We're great friends. Will he be in Southampton?"

"I certainly hope so. He's planning our whole trip."

"It'll be great fun to see his face when we get off the ship together—oh, I think they want to get by," he said, stepping to one side of the passageway for latecomers from the deck. "I'd like very much to converse further with you, Mrs. Croft, Miss Croft. Perhaps at dinner. I'm traveling with my son."

"I believe we're assigned the first night," said Alice, "but we'll watch for you. Late seating?"

"Very good. See you then."

He took Alice's hand, brought it to his lips graciously, let it go, and went down his corridor.

In Alice's stateroom, Laura closed the door behind them and let out all the shock and bewilderment she felt in one word, "Mother!"

"He was just an acquaintance," said Alice.

"Sit down, Mother. There's more to the story, and I want you to tell me."

"No, I'm sorry, but I'm not going to tell you anything, dear. I don't mind for myself, I'm an open book. But I cannot intrude upon your father's privacy without his explicit permission."

"You're not an open book at all, Mother."

"Then get what you can out of Mr. Griswold. I can't be responsible for that."

"You're being cruel to me, Mother."

Alice put her arms around Laura tenderly.

"Your father and I had a past, you know. When we're dead and gone, you can go through all the letters, diaries, and papers you find. I give you leave to do that after both of us are out of the way. You can read everything then. They're probably not so different from what you must have about yourself, locked up somewhere." Then she laughed and said, "I haven't seen hide nor hair of that little red leather-bound diary you kept as a teenager. I was so tempted to read it sometimes—but I didn't."

"I still have it," said Laura. "I'm glad you didn't read it. It was just silly things."

"I wouldn't have been the least bit shocked, dear."

Alice helped Laura dress for dinner in one of the new dresses they had bought in Baltimore for the trip. Laura was being difficult.

"I'm not an heiress, Mother."

"It's just for the boat, darling."

"And I don't want so much of my bust showing."

"You have a very fine bust, dear. You can wear a scarf over it if you want. Men are attracted by modesty, too. But you'll have to do better with your countenance. Can you try to look proud and detached?" Alice gave another pull on the sash of the dress. "Oh, I know what you're going to say, but please just try. It's only for a few dinners. We can let our hair down once we get to England."

"I wouldn't count on that, Mummy. You know what Rory says about England."

"We'll just keep our heads down," Alice assured her. "But for now we're shipmates with these ladies and gentlemen for five days, and we must put our best feet forward."

The first night at sea justified the trouble they had taken to dress but seemed to Alice to serve no other purpose as far as Laura's romantic possibilities were concerned. They were assigned to the captain's table, an honor shared by an assortment of elderly titled English returning to England and middle-aged Americans in the business of business, flouting America's new importance in the world. Some conversations struggled to stay afloat for longer than a minute or two. At every other table in the great dining room of the ship, as well as everywhere else the American stock market was a permissible topic, Alice and Laura found the chatter was as vociferous as a tickertape machine.

The next four nights at the dinner table with Richard Griswold and his handsome son, Eliot, were everything Alice could have hoped for Laura. The two were on their way home after an American tour in celebration of Eliot's completion of an advanced degree in economics at Oxford. After dinner they walked the upper deck every evening, Richard offering his arm to Alice and Eliot offering his to Laura as they reached the top of the stairs and came out to the sea air and the stars overhead. Richard and Alice walked one direction, Eliot and Laura the other.

The second night out, Richard and Alice paused at the same time, without prompting from the other, at a place along the railing that stood in direct line with a splendid high white moon trailing its light along the water to the ship.

"It feels as if we've been here before, Mrs. Croft," he said. "Standing at the railing of a ship."

"Do call me Alice," she said.

"Then please call me Richard."

"I don't remember it as a ship exactly," she said lightly.

"Well, a water craft anyway."

"It was certainly a step up from the sampan."

"I wanted to kiss you then. I thought you wanted me to."

He said it as lightly as she had spoken, but with an undertone that Alice took to be suggestive of an imminent revisiting of the past in order to rectify a regrettable omission.

"No, not really," she said. "I was already in love with Mr. Croft. Not that I did not find you very well-bred and interesting, but that was as far as it went, as I recall." Turning to him, she declined to lower her eyes as a younger woman might when she added, "And I do not wish to mislead you now, Richard."

There was a moment when she feared he would rashly take her in his arms and kiss her, which one part of her recognized as a sovereign right of impetuous passion. The other part of her did not want to be rude.

"You need say no more, Alice," he said. "I'm sorry if I've been overbearing and presumptuous. I'm afraid I've been rather desperate for companionship lately."

"I thought the English were famously good at concealing such things."

"Well, you see, my wife passed away a year ago."

"Oh, you poor man. I'm so sorry to hear that."

"But you're right about English restraint. I suppose we've been in America too long. Very frankly, I was stunned to see the behavior going on."

"Oh, many Americans are stunned as well," replied Alice. "Morals have gotten very loose since the country devoted itself to temperance."

Just then, Eliot and Laura appeared among the few late-night strollers, coming toward them, arm in arm. If Alice was not mistaken, Laura seemed to be leaning into the young gentleman a little. From then on, Alice was pleased to see the lean became more pronounced every evening, like the listing of a ship in peril on the sea.

Alice did not want to analyze anything when she and Laura stayed up late in her cabin, sitting in the berth in their nightgowns, sipping very tiny amounts of very good brandy and smoking cigarettes like college girls. Eliot was such a lucky break. Laura was in no frame of mind to actively look for a replacement for Gregory, but the persistent presence of Eliot forced her into acknowledging that a smart, good-looking man her age was romantically interested in her, and it could not be ignored. Calling any attention to it would only awaken her loyalty to Gregory and the lost cause. Anything to distract from that.

Alice even allowed herself to be the lightning rod in their sessions before bed. But sometimes she had to defend herself.

"Mother, you're flirting with Mr. Griswold," Laura said, frowning with disapproval on the third night of the voyage.

"Of course I am," Alice replied tartly. "It's just having fun. You don't do it with just anyone, naturally, but you can sharpen your skills with a man like

Mr. Griswold, who knows it doesn't mean anything. He does it too. I'm sure you noticed."

"I saw that right away."

"Good to spot it, dear."

"But I never thought you would flirt back at him."

"We knew each other before this trip, dear. And we're not young. That makes all the difference."

During the day, Alice and Laura lounged in their deck chairs reading, sometimes played shuffleboard, roamed the ship, shot at clay pigeons off the stern, or partook of other shipboard diversions. Richard mingled with the other passengers, but Eliot seemed to be always at Laura's side. He wrote up an itinerary of interesting sites for their stay in London, which Alice thought would be very helpful and promised to keep under advisement. She cautioned him, however, about stepping on Rory's toes.

"He's had a month to plan everything for us," she said. "He has us on a very tight schedule both in England and on the continent. I think he has us booked positively everywhere from London to Vienna."

Eliot was in plus fours with a tweed jacket, sitting on the deck with his knees up beside Laura's deck chair.

"Would you like some company?" he asked in Alice's direction. "On your tour, I mean."

"With Rory, it's always the more the merrier, so I venture to say yes, we'd love to have you, Eliot. I would invite your father also, but I think he has business, doesn't he?"

"Oh, he'd drop everything," said Eliot.

When Eliot went off to get Laura a lemon ice, Laura sat up and took off her sunglasses.

"Mother, we hardly know them."

"It's perfectly all right, dear. Rory will be with us all the time."

"I think you're going to have trouble with Mr. Griswold, Mummy. He's really in love with you."

"Oh nonsense. We're just friends."

"I think you should cable Father and tell him he's on the boat."

"There's no need to do that, Laura. I'll tell him when we get home. He'll think it's very funny."

Laura put her sunglasses on again and lay back in her chair, seeming to be a little out of patience with her mother. Alice replaced her sunglasses and lay back in her deckchair as well. It was so lovely in the sunshine and sea breeze as the gleaming liner steamed on to England. There was less and less to worry about with Laura now. The ardor of her new admirer was putting more dents into her despondency as each day went by. Alice began to worry rather more about herself and Andrew; what scrutiny they would come under as they grew older. It had never dawned on her before. She drifted into a little nap, thinking this trip might be the last time she had the upper hand over any of her children.

CHAPTER SEVENTY-SEVEN

Rory met them in Southampton. Laura spotted him as they came down the gangplank, and the surprise his face registered was gratifying to all members of the debarking party. There was Mother on the arm of a friend from the City, and Laura on the arm of what looked to be a well-cut university man. In a few moments Rory had made his way through the crowd and was embracing those members of his family and hardily shaking hands with Mr. Griswold and Eliot.

"Gosh, it's good to see you," he said to everyone.

Laura smiled her sunniest smile, and Alice beamed through her introduction of Eliot and an explanation of their chance meeting aboard ship.

"All right now," said Rory. "I'll get the baggage together and hail a cab to the train station. About an hour to London. I've put you up at the Lord Exeter."

"I thought we were staying with you," said Alice.

"Oh no, you wouldn't want to do that."

"But I wanted to see your place."

"It's just a little flat, Mom. You'll like the Exeter."

"It's the best hotel in London, Alice," said Mr. Griswold. "Not far from our townhouse. Perhaps we could join you for dinner."

"Love to have you," said Rory.

Getting into the cab, Alice moved over to Rory in the back seat.

"I'm glad for a chance to talk to you, dear. Mr. Griswold and his son intend to join us on the trip—I'm afraid for the better part of it."

"Won't upset the plans at all," he said. "There's already one extra fellow, a friend of mine, along for the ride as far as Copenhagen, and a lady he might bring. So that's seven of us so far. We may pick up a few along the way."

"And what about you, dear?" Alice asked. "Will there be a lady along?"

"Nope, just yours truly."

Laura bent around Alice and laughed. "No consort?"

"Not this time, sweetheart," said Rory. "Consort backed out. I'm on the loose this trip."

For the rest of the ride to the hotel, Laura and Rory chatted and laughed around Alice in the middle. Alice thought something very strange had happened crossing the Atlantic. The devastation on the land, wrought by Gregory Haines, had been replaced with a flowering of the plain. What Laura had done for Gregory, apparently Eliot had done for Laura. Rory was as devilishly handsome as ever, but Laura stood right up to him—no more lowered eyes, no more inviting him to clonk her on the head, no more waiting to be squashed.

The object of the tour had been achieved. The boat was enough to do the trick. She could go home to Andrew. At dinner that night at the hotel, Alice gave Eliot a good looking over while he and Rory talked finance and economics. Laura followed the discussion carefully and raised intelligent questions, laughing at an amusing remark from Rory and looking on with thoughtful consideration when Eliot enlightened Rory on a point of capital investment. Alice watched Laura take in stride the two good-looking men at the table as well as any woman who had seen it all. She was ready to fly all right.

At breakfast the next morning, before Laura made her appearance, Rory began to fill Alice in on the social calls they had to make on his friends and business associates while they were in London. He was very explicit on the rules.

"Ladies never take their hats off at afternoon tea, but you may at luncheon. Never leave your coat in the hall. It implies you have the run of the house. Never thank a servant. It's considered rude to call attention to the dress or adornments of anyone present. Do not touch anyone to catch his or her attention. Only sparing use of the handkerchief at the dinner table. When you pass someone you know on the street—"

"I'm never going to remember this, Rory."

"Don't worry, it gets to be second nature. I cut down the list, and we'll have time to work on it because we're getting out of here day after tomorrow. Little change of plans. We're going to the continent first."

"Oh for heaven's sake, Rory. Your father wanted me to pay a call on Mr. Norman before anything else."

"At the moment, that isn't in the cards, Mom. Montagu has to watch who he's seen with. You know, financial stuff. Dad's known over here. I'm supposed to make myself scarce too. I know you're not wild about him anyhow."

"Well, all right. It's one less obligation."

"So we do the continent first."

"Oh, Rory, I wanted so much to see Briarwick College," Alice said with a frown.

"That's still on the agenda, Mom, just on the way back."

Alice had been looking for the best time to tell Rory and Laura that she was going home. She buttered another muffin for Rory and decided the change of itinerary didn't matter. It would be nice to walk around her old school by herself anyway. She could see them off to the continent, go see Briarwick College, and take the next boat home.

"Rory dear," she said, "Has the bank approved this holiday you've arranged?"

"Oh sure. My boss is all for it. Montagu gave him a ring."

"How long can you be away?"

"As long as I need to be," said Rory. "Just politics, Mom. Nothing to worry about."

"What is that supposed to mean? No, let's not get into it. You can discuss it with your father. Unless it involves a woman."

"No, nothing like that."

He was smiling and as sure of himself as ever, but Alice could tell he was in a corner of some kind. Whatever it was, it sounded like Rory and Montagu Norman were in the same boat. She had every confidence in Montagu, despite the eccentricity, but she had heard enough. It was Andrew's business, not hers.

Any concerns Alice had that deserting the tour would cause a commotion were allayed in the next two days of their London stay. In the course of the obligatory social visits, Rory picked up more recruits, and by the time they were ready to embark for the continent, the party had grown to twelve. Six men, six women. He was a natural leader with unfailing enthusiasm and was lots of fun. England was definitely the place where an American would draw a crowd, and undoubtedly a place an American would not like to wear out his welcome.

Alice spoke to him on their last night in London. Eliot and Laura had left the restaurant to walk around town in a long swing back to the hotel.

"Rory dear," she said, putting a hand over his on the table. "I'm going to beg out of the tour. I've had a very nice week with you, and we'll see you at Christmas. Laura's doing fine now, and she doesn't need me."

"Aw, Mom. You can't drop out now."

"I've heard the rules you've given the recruits—no maids, no valets, no chaperones."

"That's for everybody else. Not you."

"Rory, it's for young people. I'm thrilled you're leading it, and nothing could be better for Laura. But it's not for me. My presence would only inhibit Laura, and I doubt Mr. Griswold will come along if I'm not on the tour, so you get rid of two old birds with one stone. You'll have so much more fun without me, and I want so much to go home. Please."

"Well, I can't arrange anything for you now. Everything's closed."

"I'm perfectly capable of booking my own passage, Rory."

"All right. If that's the way you want it."

"Thank you, Rory."

"But you'd better ask Laura how she feels about it."

"She'll understand. She'll do just fine on her own. You know what happened with Gregory, don't you?"

"Not the details."

"Let's just say she's a mature woman now. I'm going to trust you to see that nothing interferes with the natural development of this relationship with Eliot. They seem to be getting on very nicely, and it's come at a very important time of her life."

"That's her affair, Mom. I'm not going to get involved. It'll take its course."

"I don't mean for you to get involved, Rory. I just want you to watch out for her and be a sympathetic ear. You can at least promise me that you aren't going to leave her somewhere."

"Mom, I'm not going to leave her anywhere," Rory said with exasperation.

"Well, you weren't always very nice to her."

"That was years ago."

"I know, dear. I can see you're more responsible now," said Alice. "And I know Laura doesn't hold anything against you. Go and have a little fun now, and we'll talk to your father when you get back—if you're getting tired of England. He's good at thinking of what to do."

Alice waited for Laura in the hotel. Eliot dropped her off early because they were leaving the next day. When they were sitting on Laura's bed in their nightgowns, Alice told her she was leaving the tour. Laura took it well when Alice said how homesick she was and how much she wanted to be with Andrew. Alice was the one with tears in her eyes this time. In her own bed that night, falling asleep, she cried softly for losing another daughter and for herself, at the end of her season and the falling of her leaves.

The trip to Briarwick brought another great sadness of time forever gone to Alice. She was accommodated for the night in the castle. The next morning, she walked the grounds of the college where she had worked and learned agricultural science almost forty years ago, before motor tractors were invented and before she knew Andrew. She did not remember having dreams then, when she was here. Working in these fields was just part of what she was doing, going from one thing to another. It was nursing after that, going to China, and then Andrew. That was surely when her life really began, with the advent of Andrew. Before that, not a bead had moved on the abacus from one side to the other.

More days at sea. Alice walked the decks, took her meals over tedious hours of polite conversations, and read in her deckchair. She hoped Andrew would not be angry with her for letting go of Laura. She wondered if the worries they shared over her were not a mainstay of the bond between them, and if Laura, married and living in England, would deprive them of a great deal to talk about, if nothing else. How foolish this would all sound if he were here in the next deck chair. All she had to do was get across the damn ocean.

Alice stayed a night at the apartment in New York. Lois recommended a telephone call to Andrew, but Alice wanted to surprise him. They smoked cigarettes and drank and talked the night away. Alice was dead tired the next morning, but the thought of being with her husband in her own bed that very night, if she pushed, spurred her through a quick breakfast and a run to the train station. By late afternoon she was in Baltimore. By nightfall, the cab was turning off the main road to pass through the brick pillars with bronze plaques. The lights were on in the Eldridges' house, the Coopers', the Browns', and the Banks' as the cab drove through the farm. Alice's state of excitement was joyfully unbearable. Then the headlights of the cab lit up the chateau, and Mr. Thompson was coming down the front steps in his cutaway jacket.

Andrew met her in the front entrance with his newspaper in one hand and his glasses in the other. There was a flurry of Celeste, Lilly, and Cassie bursting out of the kitchen and rushing past them upstairs to prepare her room. Once they were alone in the living room, Alice fell into Andrew's arms and his newspaper fluttered to the floor. She was never so happy to see him.

"Oh, Andrew," she whispered. "The last three weeks seemed like an eternity."

He held her just as hard as she held him before they released each other, and he said, "I didn't want to get my hopes up, but I expected you home any day. You came alone, didn't you?"

"I left her in very good hands, and she's very happy. I'll tell you all about it tomorrow. Laura has a new man. Eliot. He's English."

"Good to hear it. Good to hear it. Mission accomplished."

"I want to go right to bed, dear. I was up all night with Lois, and I'm bushed. It's only nine-thirty. You don't have to come up if you want to read your paper."

"No, no. I'm coming."

"Don't step on your glasses, dear."

Alice and Andrew ended up talking until after midnight. Alice told him about Eliot and also about Richard Griswold. At first, he found it very amusing, but then he said he was glad Lieutenant Griswold had made it through the war.

"I liked him," he said. "I was worried after the Somme and started checking the casualty lists in the English papers. I was behind a year when I started looking, but I thought the chances of getting killed were only then going up significantly."

"I hope you would have told me," said Alice.

"I'm glad I didn't have to."

"He's quite the same as he was."

"Handsome as ever, I suppose?"

"Very much so. British handsome. Not like you. Well, I'm here, aren't I?"

Andrew moved to the center of the bed and put his arms around her. After a while Alice sighed deeply.

"The trip made me feel old, Andrew. The children aren't children anymore. They've completely grown up." Alice sighed again. "The best years of our lives are behind us."

Andrew stroked the hair away from her forehead and lay back. The quiet was gentled by their breathing and the sound of the wind in the early summer leaves of the woods.

"Well. There's age. That's true. Nothing we can do about that," said Andrew. "But I'm glad to be here and have you. I wouldn't want to go back. I wouldn't want to be what I was."

"Me neither." She was surprised at how quickly it came out. She searched for his hand and it was there beside her. She could feel his smile in it and his voice came softly.

"Well, then maybe we can say that even if our best years are behind us, our best selves are with us now."

Alice turned on her side and nestled against him. "You couldn't have said it better, dear. Let's hope it's true. Good night, my love."

PART SIX

CHAPTER SEVENTY-EIGHT

EARLY SPRING 1925

Rory and his party wintered in Rome. Before that, Laura's letters had come with postage stamps from France and the Low Countries, Norway, Sweden, Denmark, Switzerland, Austria, Spain, and Portugal.

Alice and Andrew were at breakfast in the sunny dining room, looking through the morning mail.

"Now look at this one, Andrew," said Alice, holding up an envelope with a large, colorful stamp, replete with draped flags and coats of arms.

Andrew looked up from his mail, over the rim of his glasses.

"What's that one?"

"Lichtenstein."

"The smaller the country, the bigger the postage stamp, don't you think? It makes me want to take up stamp collecting, just to test the theory. Is she having a good time?"

"The time of her life, I think," said Alice. "The shorter the letter, the better the time, just like the stamps. This is the shortest one yet. I can't imagine why it took so long to get here.

> *Dear Father and Mummy,*
> *Not much time to write. Eliot is waiting downstairs. We're about to leave for Rome to Christmas there. Sorry can't be with you. We've lost a few, but Rory picked up a few along the way, and what an international bunch we are now! Big adventure yesterday in the Alps. We climbed to the top of the mountain where they have the St. Bernard dogs. It was snowing hard. A blizzard really. Rory was determined to get to the monastery up there. Eliot and I were the only ones brave enough to go with him. Well we made it without being rescued by the dogs, and they made us very welcome for the night—the monks, not the dogs! I didn't*

know monks drank so much!! We all laughed a lot. I miss you, Mummy. You too, Father. Your loving daughter, always thinking of you, Laura.

"What do you think of that, dear? Heavens, I'm glad I didn't go."
"Well, I'd say Eliot seems to be holding his own," said Andrew.
"Wouldn't it be marvelous, Andrew?"
"Yes, it would. He sounds like a nice young man."
"I wonder if Laura would want to live in England. It wouldn't be the worst thing, I suppose. I can easily see her as mistress of the Griswold family estate since Richard's wife died and Eliot is the only child. Oh dear, Andrew, what if Richard marries again? He seemed very susceptible on the boat. Any presentable lady with the idea of catching him would have no obstacle. And then what? Laura could have a mother-in-law who doesn't like her."
"Well, you'd better hurry over there and marry Griswold before someone else does."
"Andrew, please," said Alice. "I wish you would take this more seriously."
"I'm sorry. What you brought up is certainly possible, but as it is contingent upon Laura marrying Eliot, and Richard meeting someone suitable to marry, let's not entertain possibilities two steps beyond uncertainties." Andrew put down the letter from Montagu Norman he was reading and took off his glasses. "I know you have Laura on your mind, but I've been thinking more about Rory at the moment," he said.
"You aren't worried about what I told you, are you? Whatever the trouble is, I'm sure it doesn't amount to much. I definitely saw a change in him. He doesn't have that reckless streak anymore, and I was left with the impression that he'll be summoned back to England when the time is right. He didn't seem worried, and you know nothing gets him down for very long. That much hasn't changed."
"Well, Montagu says he's doing well. But I'm not sure if I altogether trust Montagu. He can be a bit wild himself. I wouldn't want Rory involved in anything that would damage his reputation. A good reputation is important in the financial world, and if he runs afoul over there, it might ruin his chances here. Something like an extradition treaty exists with reputations."
"Can't you find something for him to do, dear?"
"Not much around here for a man not cut out for living in the country. It's different with Autie. He always had more of the farm in him, and then he

married a country girl. I'll talk to Rory when he gets back. Not that I don't believe he's changed, but I'd like to see it for myself."

Andrew picked up the letter from his friend in London and looked it over again.

"Nothing but good things about him, two years in a row."

At Alice's signal to the little window, Celeste came through the swinging door from the kitchen with more coffee. They silently watched her pour. She was a small girl with a round face, round eyes, and delicate hands.

After she left, Alice said, "She's very good now, isn't she? Delphina did a marvelous job training her."

"No complaints from me," said Andrew. "I hope she stays. I didn't like losing Delphina."

"It wasn't quite like that, dear. We sent her off to school. You wouldn't want her to come back here with a college degree and be a maid again, would you?"

"No, of course not."

"Well, unless we're going to put everyone who works for us through school, you should give Celeste a raise to make sure she stays."

"I'll look into it," said Andrew. "So where are you off to today, darling?"

"I'm going down the hill to help Margaux paint the master bedroom. She liked my idea of mixing just a little violet into the white. I wanted to do that in the Tudor house, remember? I think it's going to look marvelous."

Alice leaned into Andrew and whispered, "I think she's pregnant."

"Oh, that's grand."

"I'm not sure, and she hasn't mentioned it, but I think so. Maybe this will be the turning point."

"That would be nice," said Andrew. "It's been pins and needles with them, hasn't it?"

After breakfast, Alice went upstairs to change. Andrew took the flag out of the dark metal box in the back hallway and went out the little door to the rear of the house. It was a mild morning without mist on the river, and he could see clearly the commanding Georgian mansion of Flodhöjder on the other side. He raised the flag and lashed the lanyards to the cleat on the pole. With a sorrowful heart, he directed his salute toward the bare flagpole at Flodhöjder, to the spirit of Peter Eklund and to the ghosts of the American and Swedish flags that no longer flew.

Alice came up behind him dressed in her dungarees with a white painter's smock over them and yellow rubber gloves in her hand.

"Why don't you have lunch with us, Andrew? We can have a picnic."

"What time would that be?"

"Around one."

"I have to talk to Mr. Thompson on the West Coast this morning. It's the last chance I have before he sails for China. Let me see." He paused a moment to think. "Yes, I can call him at eleven, that's eight his time. All right, I think I'll be finished by one."

"Just let Viola know before you bury yourself in your office. Picnic lunch for four."

Then Alice was off down the hill to the Kastelje.

"Let's not talk about the stock market, shall we?" she tossed over her shoulder.

Alice set up luncheon on the picnic table in front of the Kastelje while Margaux went down the flagstone steps to the river to gather reeds for a centerpiece. When she came back up, they spotted Andrew by the flagpole, starting down the hill from the chateau with Bow-wow, the collie, and Henry, the Chesapeake Bay retriever. Margaux called to the second-floor window under the thatched roof, and Autie stuck his head out long enough to signal that he was on the telephone and disappeared again.

"I don't mind," said Margaux. "He's making a lot of money."

"That's what Father says. You must be very proud of him."

Margaux shrugged her shoulders. "That's what he should be doing."

Alice saw Henry picking up speed down the hill. "Watch your knees, dear. The dog doesn't have much sense." She took Margaux's arm and tried unsuccessfully to draw her behind the safety of the picnic table as Henry hit the bottom of the hill at full tilt. He brushed the corner fence post of the garden, slammed into the rain barrel and careened off in a wide loping circle around the cottage before coming to an abrupt stop in front of Margaux.

"You're very brave," said Alice.

Margaux looked down with a stern expression at the panting dog standing attentively at her feet. He was still quivering all over with energy and his tongue was hanging from the side of his mouth, but the eyes were fixed on her.

"He knows me," she said.

Alice came out from behind the picnic table and sat down on the bench to pet Henry's big, curly head. Looking up the hill she noticed Andrew had not altogether recovered from his last collision with Henry. He told her he didn't mind admitting that age probably had something to do with his bad knees. He thought he must be sixty or sixty-one. Sixty-two at the most. It was always an approximation.

He greeted them with a gentle smile.

"Hospitality," he said, handing a bottle of wine to Margaux.

"Autie's on the telephone," said Alice. "I think we'd better start without him. We really have to finish painting today. We have the doctor tomorrow, Margaux."

"No. We're not going," said Margaux.

"Oh," said Alice, taken aback.

"I've had enough."

"Well, Margaux, that's certainly up to you, but I wonder if you should think about it."

"I've thought about it. Could you call her for me?"

"Of course, dear," said Alice. "What should I say?"

"You can say I'm fine now. I don't need to go anymore."

Andrew, acting as if he had not heard anything that had to do with him, sat down at the green picnic table and looked under to see that his feet were not disturbing Bow-wow, hoping that his presence over a table setting would remind the ladies that he was a busy man.

"Well, dear, all right then," said Alice. "I'll let her know. You can always start again if you feel the need."

"Thank you, Mother."

Margaux opened Andrew's bottle and poured four glasses while Alice finished arranging the table. Autie came out of the house looking pleased and sat down across from Andrew.

"Just made four thousand dollars, Dad."

"That's wonderful, Autie, but this is a picnic," said Alice.

"Is anything coming up in the garden yet, Margaux?" Andrew asked.

"Only the leafy greens. And the endive. I was happy to see that. Thank you for finding seeds for me." Turning to Autie, she said, "Do you like this chicken? I'll make it for you."

"Viola makes the best fried chicken," said Alice.

They all agreed on that. Margaux lit a cigarette and smoked all through the luncheon. She opened the bottle of wine that had come down from the house with the picnic basket and had two more full glasses. Alice was used to it from their weekly trips to the doctor in Baltimore, when they had lunch after the sessions. Alcohol did not seem to have any detrimental effect on her. But it didn't seem to do her disposition much good either. It looked like Autie was keeping track with his eyes.

Alice drove up to Baltimore the next day in the Pierce-Arrow alone. She wore the walking dress she usually wore. It was perfect for striding around the city, and it went so well with the gray cloche she liked. The book she had along to read when Margaux's sessions were extended stayed in the car.

Dr. Perrigan was surprised the patient was not along, and Alice told her what Margaux had said.

"That's very unfortunate, Mrs. Croft," she said. "I felt we were making significant progress. Won't you sit down?"

"Yes, thank you," said Alice. "Well, perhaps enough progress has been made."

Dr. Perrigan took a place on the patient's couch with a look of concern on her face.

"I will speak frankly with you, Mrs. Croft. In this sort of case, when the source of the trauma has not been removed and the patient is expected to adapt to it, the treatment needs to be ongoing."

"I'm afraid I'm not sure what you mean," said Alice. "The source of the trauma is quite removed."

"Specifically," said Dr. Perrigan, "I mean to say the rape."

"Yes, what about it?"

"Your daughter-in-law lives in subjugation to her rapist—your son."

"I beg your pardon?"

"Perhaps you were unaware that he raped her before they were married."

"That is quite preposterous."

Dr. Perrigan looked down with her eyebrows raised, as if she pitied Alice's limited ability to understand a very simple matter.

"Mrs. Croft," she said, "I don't know what you have been told, either by your son or your daughter-in-law, but in here, with me, in a safe and professional setting, patients are uniquely free to speak honestly. In the outside world they are likely to resort to lies and made-up accounts. For the patient, the objective of treatment is to gradually acquire the ability to honestly confront her innermost anxieties, first here, and then in the outside world."

"I assure you, Dr. Perrigan," said Alice. "That is not beyond a layman's comprehension. Apparently, however, you have been deceived as to the beginnings of my daughter-in-law's difficulties. She was raped by a party of German soldiers when they invaded Belgium in 1914. To be honest, we have no confirmation of that, only the fact of the child born in 1915. My son did not meet Margaux until he was assigned to Paris in 1919. Since then he has devoted himself to her care and to the son he did not father—at some cost to his own emotional well-being."

Alice took a checkbook out of her coat pocket and gave a pleasant face to Dr. Perrigan. "Let's settle up now, shall we?" she said.

They parted cordially. It was difficult to tell if Dr. Perrigan believed she was correct in her assessment of the patient or if she had been taken in. But her final words to Alice at the door seemed justified in either case. "She'll bear watching."

Alice related to Andrew that night, while getting to bed, the exchange she had had with Dr. Perrigan.

"I thought you were brimming over with something at tea and dinner," said Andrew.

"I couldn't say anything on such a private topic with the servants near, naturally."

"Something like what Autie tells me about Wall Street."

"Whatever are you talking about, dear?"

"Well, he goes up there for meetings with his brokers. He says there are plenty of analysts and experts predicting the market and a lot of talking goes on, but the real business takes place on the floor of the exchange."

"I still don't know what you mean," said Alice.

"Well, here we have all this room in the house, but the bedroom turns out to be where the real business takes place."

"That may be a very astute observation, Andrew," Alice said, "but a perfect waste of time. Now what are we to think about Margaux? I'll take motions from the floor."

"There's nothing really to think about," said Andrew. "She's finished with the psychiatrist. Are you going to read?"

"No, I couldn't tonight. I'm too agitated."

Andrew reached to turn out the light on his side of the bed, and Alice turned off hers. Andrew lay on his back and waited for the meeting to reconvene.

"Then explain it to me, Andrew," said Alice.

"Explain what?"

"The way you see it."

"All right. Well—I understand the facts exactly as you explained to Dr. Perrigan."

"Then why do I feel so unsettled, Andrew?"

"Let me think—well, because it seems to me all we've done is match pieces of a story to the calendar. Very little has come from Margaux, and Autie seems to be in the same position we are."

"Well, doesn't that bother you?"

"Not very much. Why should I know something she wouldn't want me to know?"

"You can say that because you've never been close to anyone, Andrew. Maybe Peter Eklund, but you've never really had friends."

"But that's very much to my point, Alice. You like to know everything about a person. You like to be taken into confidence. Intimate talks, long stories, and keeping secrets."

"That's what women do, Andrew. That's how we get to know each other."

"But you aren't accepting something very basic about Margaux. She doesn't like any of that. She doesn't want anyone to know her or her personal business. It's still a mystery why she went off with that artist fellow, and why she came back, for that matter. And we shouldn't try to get it out of Autie, either. He may not know any more about her than we do."

"But she's been living with us, Andrew."

"Not anymore. And I suspect her idea of moving to the cottage was to give her an easier place to keep her private life private, without us and servants constantly around."

"Well, if you're right, there's nothing to be done about it."

Alice turned over in a huff, pulling the sheet and blanket with her, wishing it didn't frustrate her so terribly when Andrew was right.

"No," said Andrew, "there's still plenty of room for getting to know her. You can wait for times when she wants to talk, and simply accept what she wants to tell you. Can I have some of the blanket?"

"I'm sorry, dear. Here."

Andrew got up to straighten out the sheet and blanket, then hastened back under the covers.

"I'm afraid she'll just tell me stories," said Alice. "Or truths that sound like stories. I won't be able to tell the difference. What good does it do her to have people get the wrong idea about her?"

"I don't think she cares about being misunderstood. A strong personality doesn't care very much about that." After a moment, he added, "Do you know where I learned that?"

"From me?"

"No, I'm sorry, darling. Peter Eklund."

"Oh," said Alice, a little crestfallen.

"I don't think it ever occurred to Peter Eklund to wonder if people had a good opinion of him or not. But I've learned other things from you. More important things."

"I'm glad to hear it, dear."

"I don't know why she put up with the psychiatrist for so long. Maybe to show she was making an effort."

"Or throw us off the track."

"No, maybe she just wants to deal with her problems in her own way. She met you halfway with going to the sessions. Now you have to leave her alone to sort things out. Don't worry, she'll do it."

"All right. I hope everything you say is true. You're generally right. I don't know how you became so wise."

"It must be what I learned from you."

"That's very sweet to say, dear." Alice turned on her side and put her head on his shoulder. "It's only because I love her as if she were my own daughter. That's why I worry. She drinks a bit, doesn't she?"

"I didn't notice."

"I know. Good night, dear."

CHAPTER SEVENTY-NINE

The next letter from Laura came from Greece.

"They're yachting around the islands," said Alice. She turned the letter over and looked in the envelope. "I think they're getting shorter. Do you want to hear it?"

Andrew nodded consent and put down his glasses as Alice took a sip of her breakfast coffee and began to read.

Dear Mummy and Dad,

We're in Greece!! Rory leased a yacht and it turned out some of the gang are great sailors so we didn't have to take on a crew. There wouldn't have been any room for them anyway. We're sixteen now. Ten girls and six boys. Last week it was the other way around. Rory, Eliot, and I are the only ones we started with. We got into trouble with honest-to-goodness pirates the other day but the boys captured them and made them take off all their clothes. Imagine how fast they jumped overboard with ten girls looking at them!! I'm afraid we're spending an awful lot of money. Hugs and kisses from the gang. Your loving daughter, Laura.

"Honestly, Andrew, I think Laura's lost her senses."

"I thought that was what the trip was meant to do," said Andrew. "Apparently she isn't upset over Gregory Haines so much anymore."

"Yes, I think he's quite out of her system. But don't you think you should send Rory a cable about the money?"

Andrew looked out the big window and thought for a moment.

"I probably should," he said. "But I don't want to. No, I don't think I will. They need to have some fun."

"But this can't go on forever, dear. They've been away for months without any responsibilities."

"I believe that's the point."

"I don't see how that can be the point, dear."

"This might be the best time of their lives, don't you see."

"I wouldn't say Rory has suffered any privation of best times, Andrew."

"No, I'm thinking about Laura and Eliot. They're learning how to have fun with each other. It'll see them through the bad times, and I think bad times are coming."

"You read too many newspapers, dear."

"What I mean to say is, it's the right time of her life to marry someone, and if having fun together is part of the courtship, all the better. We had a little of that ourselves."

"Now *that's* what we should have done," said Alice, greatly amused. "Send them on a sampan trip down a river in China on short rations."

"It was fun, wasn't it," replied Andrew, smiling away his concerns about the future for the time being. He liked looking at Alice when he caught her remembering the past they had come through together, and because she was the same woman he had loved since the time they were now recalling.

Two weeks later there was another letter from Laura for Alice to read at breakfast.

> *Dear Mummy and Dad,*
> *They wouldn't let us land in Turkey, so we're bound for Majorca. On my birthday the gang was going to blanket-toss me thirty-two times, but on the third time I went in the drink. They said I was forty feet in the air, and I believe it!! Then Rory blindfolded me, and the boys lined up for kisses. I had to guess who was who, and I didn't get a single one right!! They threw me in the water again for that!! I'm fantastic friends with Lizzy Saunders from Richmond. The gang calls her "Lizard." Eliot is very angry with me now for not knowing his lips. I have to go find him. Rory says he's going to put him off on a desert island if he doesn't shape up. I love you two so much. Your loving daughter, Laura*

Alice took off her glasses and looked at her husband, utterly speechless.

Three more weeks passed before another letter came. There was a photograph enclosed of a group of a dozen young women, arm in arm among Roman ruins, attired in white togas.

> *Dear Mummy and Dad,*
> *We're back in Rome. We had a Vestal Virgin party in the forum the other day. That's the photograph. You should be able to pick me out. I'm not the only one who should have been disqualified!! The polizia kicked us out, so we went downtown in our togas, and you should have seen the looks we got on the tram. Nothing on underneath!!*
> *I want to go to Vienna. Love you, Mummy. Love you too, Dad. Your loving daughter, Laura.*

"Dear me," said Andrew, blinking his eyes.
"Don't you think it's time to lower the boom?"
"Maybe you're right, Alice. But it's going to be an adjustment for her to come back here."

"Oh, but she's not. Don't you remember the long letter after her visit to the Griswold estate?"

"Oh, that's right. You said she sounded down to earth for the first time."

"I'm just afraid that after all the gallivanting around the world she'll suddenly be asked to manage a household and staff. Richard sounded perfectly willing to have her as mistress of the house, and she's already done that for her father. Of course, Eliot won't give her any trouble. Well, we'll be going over for the wedding. We can stay on a bit if she needs us."

"I wonder who that is," said Andrew.

Alice turned to the window and saw what Andrew was looking at, a car just coming around the curve at the woods and starting down the drive to the chateau.

"Western Union car," said Andrew, rising from his chair.

Alice put a hand on his arm. "No, dear, let the staff."

Andrew resumed his seat and waited, watching the car approach and pull into the gravel yard in front of the house.

"Are you worried about Mr. Thompson?" Alice asked.

"Not especially, no."

"Well," said Alice, "we'll know soon enough."

In precisely the interval of time that Alice would deem soon enough, Lilly appeared with a silver platter bearing the telegram.

"You open it," said Alice. "I'm too nervous. Hurry though."

"Overseas cable. From Laura," he said, eyes quickly scanning the heading and sign-off.

> *Mummy / Dad // Up all night in Milan // Serious talk //*
> *Have accepted marriage proposal // Rory // To Paris few days*
> *// London to pack // Home next boat // Gloriously Happy //*
> *Laura*

"It sounds like she's going to marry Rory," said Andrew, taking off his glasses.

Alice was stunned. Finally, she said, "It must be a mistake."

"No, that's what it sounds like to me."

Alice stared at him in disbelief.

"I don't know how you can be so calm, Andrew. You never thought he'd be good for her."

"Well, my dear, the thought had occurred to me that Eliot might not be the only ball in play. On the other point, nothing convinces me that Rory has changed more than hearing he wishes to be the husband of Laura Eklund, wouldn't you say?"

"Oh, I suppose so," said Alice, still distraught, as if a zeppelin, aloft with the gases of a thousand groundless hopes, had suddenly plunged from the sky for no other reason than it was never meant to be up there.

"In any case, it settles my idea for a wedding gift," said Andrew.

"I beg your pardon? Am I hearing things? When have you ever gone shopping for a wedding present? Andrew?"

"I'm sorry, darling. I've been talking to Karl Eklund."

"I thought you wanted nothing to do with him."

"Well, I heard he was carrying a lot of debt and was going to sell out to a land development company. I didn't want to see that happen, so I gave him a call the other day. If it's all right with you, I'd like to accept his asking price for Flodhöjder."

"Oh, Andrew. How much is that going to cost?"

"About a quarter to half a million."

"Well, I'm sure you know what you're doing. But it seems like a very big wedding present."

Celeste slipped in and out of the dining room to refill their coffee cups, glancing at the mail to see how far they had gotten.

"Thank you, Celeste. We'll be ready for breakfast shortly," said Alice.

"I had my own ideas for the property," Andrew resumed, "but I'd be just as happy to give it to Laura and see an old injustice righted. Getting back the estate her brother cheated her out of would be a good reason for her to persuade Eliot to settle over here, which was my thinking when it looked like it was going to be Eliot. I knew you'd like that."

"Oh, certainly I would, Andrew," Alice said, brightening with the possibilities she was beginning to see. "And now there's a much better chance of having both Laura and Rory close by."

"But a little more complicated."

"I don't know what you mean, dear."

"What about Autie and Margaux?"

"What about them?"

"As you said, it's a very big wedding present, even if we put the property in Laura's name only."

"Well, Autie and Margaux will get this place," said Alice. "Eventually."

"That's not what our wills say. It was half Rory, half Autie. When we added Laura, it went to equal thirds."

"We'll just change our wills so that Margaux and Autie get our place. That's fair, isn't it? It just means Rory and Laura get their inheritance now. Autie and Margaux later."

"It's not that simple," said Andrew. "Aside from the difference in valuation now and say, twenty years from now, Karl let the farm run down over there. We'll have to put money into it."

He looked out the window. Laura marrying Rory. What about the day in his office when he threatened to disown his son if such a thing ever took place? Hard to imagine that much had changed. Alice never saw that side of Rory. Laura didn't have two cents to rub together so Rory wouldn't be marrying her for money. They'd been traipsing around Europe together for almost a year. He must have a pretty good idea of what she was like. He was thirty-four. Old enough to know what women expected in a man. Old enough to know he'd have to settle down. Were they to believe he already had? It will be nice to see spring back again. It looked like the woods needed it. He turned back to Alice.

"I just don't want trouble between the boys."

"I'll leave that to you, dear," said Alice. "I know you'll keep everything even. I wonder if Laura wants a big wedding. I was going to take Diligence to the farm for eggs this morning and see if Liza has any paintings for me, but I suppose I should go down the hill first and tell Autie and Margaux the news."

"Alice," said Andrew, making sure he had her attention by taking off his glasses, "don't mention anything about Flodhöjder."

"I can't even pronounce it, dear," she said. "Are we finished with the mail? Let's get going with breakfast."

Margaux was rolling out dough on her pastry board when Alice came around the corner of the Kastelje. It had been raining, and the hill was muddy. Knowing how finicky Margaux was about her floors, Alice left her Wellingtons outside and came into the kitchen in her stocking feet.

"What are you doing here, Mother?" Margaux said without lifting her eyes.

Alice told her the news.

"That's very funny," said Margaux, with only the slightest lift in the straight line of her mouth. She rolled up her dough in wax paper and put it in the icebox. Wiping her hands on her apron, she went to the hall and called up the stairs to Autie.

"He's working on his stock market. He'll be down. Do you want any of this?"

"Thank you, no," said Alice.

Margaux refilled the wine glass on the corner of the pastry board and sat down, offering a cigarette to Alice before lighting one for herself. It was obvious that she was pregnant now; there was no hiding it in the dress she wore. But Alice was trying to keep in mind what Andrew had said. She wouldn't say anything about it until Margaux did. The announcement of an upcoming wedding might coax out the announcement of a baby on the way.

"No, that's very funny," said Margaux. "Rory and Laura Eklund. I always thought they were perfect for each other. It's no surprise to me."

"Well, to be perfectly honest, Margaux, Father had to help me make sense of it."

"Father is a smart man."

"He said he expected it might happen on their trip. It started out so well with Eliot. The young man I told you about. I thought it was going to be him."

Autie came down the stairs with his shirttails hanging out and his glasses up on his head.

"Hi, Mom. What's the occasion? Can I have some coffee, Margaux?" He clumped down in a chair at the table. "The newspaper print is so small on the market pages. It's wearing out my eyes."

"You should see an eye doctor, dear," said Alice.

"No, I don't do it all day. Just mornings. So, what's new on the hill?"

"We've heard from Laura. She sent a telegram this morning."

"What happened? Did they run out of money?"

"She's going to marry Rory."

"What?"

"He's proposed. She accepted. That's what it sounds like. They're coming home in a month or so."

"Are you sure you read the cable right? I thought she was still getting over what's-his-name. And Rory? What the hell? It's got to be a mistake."

"No, your father read the telegram. He wouldn't get it wrong."

"I can't believe it," Autie said, sinking into a mental effort that pulled his brows together over narrowing eyes.

"I'm glad," said Margaux.

"She's gone crazy. Of all the stupid things to do."

Alice wasn't sure if she should stay or go. The news had been duly delivered. No one was going to ask why he or she was the last to know, but it seemed to touch a nerve with Autie and Margaux.

"Well, it's her business," said Alice. "We just have to accept it and be happy for them."

"I don't care either way, personally. It just doesn't make any sense."

"It makes sense," said Margaux.

"How do you figure that?"

"You put two people like that together and that's what happens."

Margaux lit another cigarette and poured the last of the bottle into her glass.

"It's eleven o'clock. I've got to go back to work, Mom," Autie said, standing up to go, not looking at Margaux.

Alice watched him go up the stairs. After she heard the door close, she turned back to Margaux and said, "I wonder why he's so upset."

"He wanted her for himself," said Margaux. "Anyone can tell that."

That night in bed, Alice asked Andrew if he thought that was true. She lay down with her head on his shoulder and told him the whole story of her visit to the cottage, word for word. "Do you know if Autie has an attraction to Laura?" she asked. "I mean now."

"How would I know?"

"He's up here in your office all the time. Don't you ever talk?"

"Not about Laura."

"Well, you had all that time before he went overseas, when Laura and I were—oh, I don't remember, Rhode Island, New York?"

"We just talked about the army, as far as I remember."

"The way Laura acted at the time, you would have thought they were engaged. Maybe it wasn't all one-sided, but why would Autie marry Margaux if he were thinking romantically about Laura? He must have known she was waiting for him to come home from France."

"That's all in the past, Alice. It might be easier to understand if you just look at the present."

"I don't see where that gets us."

"Well, Margaux probably knows Autie better than anyone else. So the simple explanation is—she may be right."

After a quiet moment, Alice said, "That just leaves us with another problem, doesn't it?"

"That's where you always go wrong, darling. We aren't the ones left with a problem."

CHAPTER EIGHTY

Following a walk-through of the house, accompanied by Karl Eklund, Alice and Andrew withdrew with him to the study, and in the presence of their attorneys, settlement on the property was made. Andrew and Alice Croft took possession of Flodhöjder in the soon-to-be official name of Laura Croft. Karl's wife, Camille, did not make an appearance, having gone on ahead with the baggage to their new home in upstate New York. In the afternoon, Andrew and Alice returned with Autie and Elijah Brown for a closer inspection, with an eye toward restoration of the new acquisition to its former condition. Elijah's brother, Jacob, and the farm manager took Elijah and Autie to the garage and stables first, and then to the farm, leaving matters of the house to Alice and Andrew.

In the main hallway, the butler assembled the staff for Alice to review while Andrew looked around the house. Standing at attention, easily identified by the differences in their livery, was a cook and sous-chef with two helpers for the kitchen, a head housekeeper, a lady's maid and gentleman's valet, four chambermaids, one footman, and another footman who doubled as a groom and driver. All were of northern European extraction. Alice suspected that Autie's report from the farm would bear out that Karl Eklund had not gotten on well with his Negro tenant families.

They compared notes over drinks in the living room at the chateau later that evening.

"Let's not still be talking about this when Margaux comes up for dinner," said Alice quickly. "I think she might be sensitive on the topic."

"Won't take long, Mom. What about the house, Dad?" said Autie.

"Very good shape."

"Well, they had to keep the house up for all the entertaining Camille did," said Alice. "But Laura won't know what to do with the staff."

"That's up to her and Rory. For now, we'll have to keep everybody on. How about the farm?"

"Pretty bad," said Autie. "The herd was sold off and most of the machinery. Elijah said it wouldn't be too hard to get the dairy operation running again, but I think we're better off going with soybeans. There's still time to get a crop in for this year, but I don't know how we're going to get all that fallow pastureland plowed unless you want to give them a lot of very expensive machinery."

"No, I don't think we should do that," said his father.

Autie seemed relieved to hear it and settled back more comfortably in his armchair. "I can ask around the farms on that side of the river and see if we can get some help."

"All right. Well then, I'll leave that to you, son. I know it's going to take a lot of work. Keep track of your hours over there."

"I hope they know what they're getting into, Dad. Maybe you should have asked Rory if he wants to be a farmer. Somehow, I doubt it."

"You'd do better with Laura," said Alice. "She quite capable, and I'm sure Rory isn't going to want her continuing at the post office."

"Then what's Rory going to do?" Autie asked.

Andrew and Autie looked at each other with blank expressions.

"I'm sure he'll find something with a financial house in Baltimore," said Alice. "Or you could teach him the stock market, Autie."

"He wouldn't want to learn it from me, that's for sure."

"No, he's been in banking, Alice," said Andrew.

"Well, he doesn't have to do anything right away. I think I hear Robbie."

A few doors at the back of the house banged. Presently, Robbie appeared in the hallway outside the living room, looking back and calling, "Come on. Come on!" Then little Edward ran up behind him.

"Mom's coming," said Robbie, flopping on the couch.

"She can't run anymore," said Edward as Alice picked him up and hugged him.

Alice turned toward Autie with a questioning look.

"Not saying anything yet," he whispered.

Margaux came in from the hallway, and Andrew stood up, then Autie.

"No need to do that," she said.

"It's just good manners," said Alice. "Andrew can certainly use the exercise."

Margaux took the chair beside Autie and looked at what he was drinking. Alice rang for Celeste just as Margaux asked, "Can I get one of these?"

After putting the boys to bed, Autie came downstairs to the cozy little living room of the Kastelje. Margaux had her sewing basket out and was doing needlework under the bronze standing lamp. In the halo of its light, her short black hair and her arms, hands, and concentration were the same as he first saw them, through the swinging doors of the pastry shop in Paris.

By now everyone understood that she liked her privacy, but he didn't know what she had against letting it be known that she was pregnant, which would soon be plain to anyone. At least they stayed off the topic of Rory and Laura and the wedding present at dinner. It was clear to him that while Margaux thought it was very funny that Rory and Laura Eklund were getting married and viewed it as a logical step in the ruination of both, she took the wedding present of Flodhöjder very seriously.

When he had made himself a little tea and sat down with her to read the sections of the newspaper he had skipped over during working hours, she asked, "Did you see everything over there?"

"You mean the farm?"

"The farm and the house, yes. The wedding present."

"I just looked over the farm. Mom and Dad went through the house," he said.

"How much did your father pay for that?"

"About four hundred thousand. That's mostly for the house and land. The farm isn't up and working. Karl sold the cattle off to pay his debts, so the dairy's shut down."

"Is he going to put money into it? Your father."

"The house doesn't need anything. It'll be the farm."

"How much?"

"I don't know yet."

"Your brother is getting your inheritance," Margaux said. "You understand that."

"It will work out in the end, Margaux. Dad's fair."

"The end can come at any time."

"Then it would be Mom," said Autie. "She's fair too."

"What if they die at the same time, and you're left out?" replied Margaux. "I want you to go talk to your father. He has to make it in his will so that you get this place. Rory will try to take it. And the same money he spends for this wedding present should go to you. If he says anything about it, you ask him how much he is spending to have those two going all over the world doing silly things for a year."

"I can't do that," Autie said patiently. "I know you respect Dad, Margaux, and I know you trust him to make everything even. Maybe he's already changed his will. I don't see why you want me to confront him with demands."

"Just to be sure. He'll know it's me who wants to know, so you don't have to worry he'll think badly of you. We understand each other."

"I don't know why you keep saying that. You hardly say two words."

"Your father and I don't have to talk. We read each other's faces. That works just as well. Your mother is different. I love her, but for all our talk, she doesn't understand me. She probably thinks I manipulate you."

"That isn't what she thinks at all," said Autie.

"Well," said Margaux, "I hope not. I'm not smart enough to manipulate anybody. That's why I have to be direct."

She ripped out a seam and began again on a new line of stitching.

"If you want a good example of a manipulating woman," she said, "it's that Laura Eklund. She looks at everyone with that sad face and droopy eyes and gets them to do things for her."

Then Margaux stopped sewing and looked up at him.

"Don't talk behind my back to Laura Eklund when she comes home."

CHAPTER EIGHTY-ONE

Andrew was the first to spot the airplane high over the pasture. He was on the old stallion, General. Autie was on Alice's big Percheron, Diligence, and little Edward was on his pony, Chicklet. The airplane passed overhead, banked, and came in low at the far end of the field.

"He's going to land," said Andrew, dismounting quickly. "Don't move, Edward." He grabbed the reins of the pony, but before he could get to Edward, the boy had scrambled down and was off at a run toward the airplane touching down. It came on fast, bouncing on its wheels, eating up the grassy yardage ahead of it at a good clip.

"Oh Jesus, Dad!" Autie cried. Then he shouted after Edward.

Andrew jumped into the saddle, wheeled General, and spurred the old horse into a gallop. He overtook Edward with only seconds to spare, leaned down and yanked the boy off his feet by the collar of his jacket. At the same time, the pilot gunned the engine, and the airplane jerked off the ground with a roar, right over General's head.

Catastrophe averted, with Edward in his arms, Andrew rode back to Autie, who was still standing by the split rail fence, holding Diligence and Chicklet. When they came up to him, Autie pulled his boy roughly off General. He shook Edward by his little shoulders and shouted in his face.

"Didn't you hear Bonpapa? Never, never, never do that again. Do you understand me?"

"I didn't hear, I didn't hear," Edward cried.

Andrew got down and tied the reins of the three horses to the fence. He didn't feel he had to add anything. They watched the airplane make another pass over the field. Then it came in low again for another landing attempt. It touched down, bounced once or twice, gave up speed on the uneven ground, and finally taxied to a stop. Mounting up, Andrew, son, and grandson rode at a walk toward the airplane as the flaps went up, the tail rudder wagged, and its balsa frame shuddered.

The engine shut down. Two great wooden blades came out of the spinning circle of air around the nose of the plane and abruptly halted on the hub between them. Edward never took his eyes off the airplane, and as he got closer, they widened to take in every detail of the upper and lower wings, the double-seated, red-painted fuselage, the black-painted tail, and the aviator.

It looked like a bear was climbing out of the open cockpit of the long two-seater, but it proved to be a man, outfitted in a padded brown leather jacket with fur collar, leather flying helmet, padded trousers, and short, fur-lined brown boots. "Anyone hurt?" he said, clambering off the lower wing to the ground.

"No casualties," reported Andrew.

The pilot took off his flying helmet and goggles. Andrew, Autie, and Edward approached to shake hands with him.

"You almost got your little noggin knocked off," said the pilot, bending down to Edward first. Then standing up to take Andrew's hand, he added,

"Quick thinking, sir. I wouldn't have seen him over the cowl. Couldn't miss a horse and rider though. John Hollyhock at your service."

"Andrew Croft. Autie, my son. Edward, grandson."

"Good to meet you," said the pilot. "I can't steer much on the ground either. Good thing I had enough speed to lift off."

"We've seen a few airplanes go over once in a while," said Andrew, "but none ever landed. Any trouble with your aircraft?"

"No, sir. I'm working my way down the coast and thought I'd see if anyone around here wanted to take a ride. Five dollars a head. Thrill of a lifetime, and you get your money back if you get killed." He laughed in a good-hearted way.

"Well, I think we can take you up on that," said Andrew to the irrepressible delight of little Edward, who promptly began to jump up and down.

"Where did you start from?" Autie asked.

"Binghamton, New York, six o'clock this morning. Going south for the winter."

"Like the geese," said Edward.

"Yup, just like the geese," he said with a nod to Edward. "I set down here also because I'm running low on fuel and thought I'd better start looking for a place to spend the night."

"Well," said Andrew, "We've got gas pumps on the farm, and you're welcome to spend the night with us. We can talk over your prospects in the area over dinner. How's that sound?"

Pilot Hollyhock readily agreed to the offer. As it was a long way back to the house, and the pilot said he had a rather hefty bag with him, Andrew went on ahead on General, saying he would send a car from the farm. He left Autie and John Hollyhock leaning against the fuselage of the airplane smoking cigarettes while little Edward climbed over the wings and through the rigging like the monkey bars at school.

Within half an hour, Elijah Brown showed up at the edge of the pasture in the Model T. Pilot Hollyhock and his bag took the back seat, and Edward sat up front with Elijah. Before they started off for the chateau, Autie made Edward sit still for a moment.

"Edward, pay close attention to me for a minute." He spoke to the boy through the window of the car, glancing to the back seat as he did with a conspiratorial eye. "We aren't going to tell Mommy how the airplane landed, are we?" he said. "No, we're not. Because if Mommy ever found out you almost made an airplane crash, she would never let you ride your pony with Bonpapa ever again."

"All right, Daddy."

"You have to promise."

"I promise."

Autie looked to the back seat. John Hollyhock solemnly raised a hand as if he were taking a sacred oath of high office.

"I promise," he gravely repeated.

Elijah took his cue, and the car pulled away, leaving Autie to ride back to the stables on Diligence, with Chicklet following. On the way, looking over the fields and passing by the houses, barns, and sheds of the farm, Autie was grateful for the peace and quiet he rode through. It would have been different if a little boy had just been killed. There would be an ambulance and state police. The farm families would be out on their porches, standing, watching the cars go by. It was more than enough to remind him that he had to be careful. Robbie and little Edward were bound to get into things. He remembered when he and Rory started a fire under the front porch of the Tudor house. As he rode toward the chateau, he kept repeating under his breath, "That would have been terrible."

John Hollyhock had passable evening dress in his bag for just such occasions and made a good appearance at the dinner table that night. He was in his early thirties, with thinning brown hair cut close, gray eyes, and a European nose that might have shared the ancestry of Alice's.

"Mr. Hollyhock," she naturally inquired, "do you by chance have any ties to the Sheffields of Boston?"

"I don't believe so," he replied.

"I'm sorry—I asked the wrong question," she said, remembering that her nose was a legacy of her mother's side. "Have you any connection to the Wellsleys?"

"Of Boston? No, I come from the West. I was born and raised in Arizona. We go back a long way there, before it became a state. I'd still be there now, ranching, if the war hadn't come along. That's when I started flying. I didn't so much care for what I heard of the trenches, but I liked the idea of becoming a pilot. It seemed much safer up in the clouds. In training anyway."

"Yes, my son Autie—I believe you met him today—gave us his own account of life in the trenches," said Alice. "Simply dreadful."

"Well, I got lucky. I applied for the air corps, and they took me."

"Did you get there before it was over, Mr. Hollyhock?" Andrew asked from the far end of the table.

"Oh yes. I was one of the first pilots shipped over to France, sir. They trained me a few hours on a French SPAD and sent me up the same day. They had us up every day too. Rain or shine. The only thing that made a difference was cloud cover."

"I imagine if the target area was reported to be clearing, local conditions would not deter operations."

"Quite right, Mr. Croft," said Mr. Hollyhock. "Have you ever been up, sir?"

"No, I've never been in an airplane."

"Would you be interested?"

Andrew looked at Alice. He had no trouble deciphering her expression. "Yes, I think Mrs. Croft and I would be most interested in going up."

In the living room after dinner, Edward and Robbie were added to the list of the interested. The possibly interested list began with Autie and Margaux and expanded quickly to include a very democratic mix of members of the chateau staff, families on the farm, local distinguished persons, shopkeepers, and tradesmen in Cecilton and Galena. At that point, it became apparent to Alice and Andrew that it would be fun to provide the experience of a lifetime to anyone within their reach who cared to risk their lives to have it. They decided to put up notices in the post office in Cecilton and the hardware store in Galena. The rest would be left to Alice on her telephone and word of mouth.

They engaged Mr. Hollyhock's airplane and his services for a week to start with, at one hundred dollars a day as a retaining fee, and five dollars for each ten-minute ride. It was likely to be a large expenditure, but Andrew liked the man, and he knew from what he read in the newspapers that the arrangement was a barnstormer's dream come true. As he told Alice that night in bed, he had never seen little Edward so interested in anything as he was in the flying machine and the man who dressed like a bear to fly it. He prudently withheld the story of Mr. Hollyhock's first landing attempt, fearing that Alice might feel it necessary to restrict his future outings with children.

John Hollyhock came down a little too early for breakfast every morning of his stay. Andrew was accustomed to his coffee and his quiet contemplation of the view through the window, followed by the pleasant company of Alice and going through the mail. But it would only be for a week, he thought, and Hollyhock seemed to be a right enough fellow. Before Alice joined them, they talked about the last war, with Hollyhock invariably stressing the importance of air power.

"It was so easy to see from the air," he said in justification of nearly every point he made. "The massive effort it would take to breach those trench lines. But what were we doing every day in our airplanes? Why, we were flying right over those trenches. We'd jump twenty miles behind their lines sometimes. Think of what we could have done with massed air power. No one was sharp enough to see the possibilities. Instead of that—and I admire Pershing, I really give him credit—but he let the British and French make us fight the same, completely discredited way they were fighting. We only won by the application of sheer numbers on the ground—and at the cost of very high casualties."

"I don't know how it could have been otherwise," said Andrew. "I mean, if you're right in thinking that no one could see an alternate way to win."

"That's true. That's true. But just watch when airplanes get better. Well, it's all behind us now, but the smart ones learned something from it."

"Most likely the losers," said Andrew in a bemused but prophetic tone.

"That's right," said Hollyhock. "That's exactly right. The Huns are going to come after France again, you know. Just give them a few years. France just gets under their skin something terrible."

"France gets on my nerves too, sometimes," said Andrew. "Let's wrap it up now."

"Aw, I'm sorry Mr. Croft."

"No, it's only because Alice should be down soon, and she doesn't like hearing talk about the war at breakfast."

"Well, can't blame her. Nobody likes to hear it these days. Once the war was over, people wanted to forget about it. Never saw a topic drop dead so fast."

"No, I do quite a bit of thinking about the last war," Andrew said thoughtfully. "I think you're right. We're probably in for another one."

"Another what?" said Alice, at the dining room entrance. "Good morning, Mr. Hollyhock. Good morning, dear."

"Another good day for putting the most adventurous of the environs into the skies," said Andrew.

"Yes, it looks very nice out," said Alice, sitting down at her place at the table and signaling to Celeste at the window. "Although it was quite thrilling for yesterday's bunch to go up through the clouds into the sunshine. Before you leave here, Mr. Hollyhock, you must take us on a cloudy day. How many adventurers have we had so far?"

Celeste was in and out with the coffee in the time it took Mr. Hollyhock to consult a small leather notebook in his breast pocket.

"One hundred and six," he said.

"I thought it was one hundred and five," said Andrew.

"I took Eddie up again. He's born to fly, Mr. Croft."

"Oh, that's what I wanted to bring up, Mr. Hollyhock," said Alice. "Ever since you explained the parachute to him and regaled him with your war stories of abandoning the airplane while in flight, he's been expressing his desire to take a jump for himself. I must tell you right now that his mother won't stand for it. If she ever heard of such a thing, it would be the last Mr. Croft and I would ever see of our grandchildren."

"Well, the only way to prevent it—I'd have to tie him up."

"Then tie him up."

A sharp look from Alice and a very straight line to her mouth when she regarded Mr. Hollyhock told him he'd be wise to tie up little Edward on his next trip to the skies.

There was no report of little Edward jumping from the airplane that week, and Alice was never troubled at breakfast or dinner by the ponderous war conversations that took place between Andrew and Mr. Hollyhock before she came down to breakfast. But she knew Andrew took pleasure in the company of a man's man, and she overlooked small incursions of war talk into the customary discourse of the household. She also overheard little Edward repeating every story Mr. Hollyhock told him to Celeste, Lilly, Cassie, Viola, and anyone else obliged to listen.

She knew, for instance, that John Hollyhock had flown with the celebrated Eddie Rickenbacker. That once his parachute did not open, and he was saved in his fall by the snow on a giant fir tree, when he slid right down the side of it and landed miraculously on his feet. That once he shot the wheel off a German airplane, landed, got out of his plane, and the enemy's wheel hit the ground just at that moment at his feet. Also sound practical advice for everyday living: that if the engine catches fire, you put your airplane into a steep dive, and the wind might put out the flames before you burn to a crisp.

After a week of living in the chateau and flying for hire every day, John Hollyhock said his goodbyes and flew on toward warmer weather. Alice lay in bed the night he left, thinking back for no special reason on Hollyhock's stories.

"Andrew," she said, "Autie doesn't have any stories like that, does he?"

"Not that I've heard."

"I know he was in the trenches, and that was dreadful, I'm sure, but don't you think there would have been one or two little funny things that happened? You remember that funny one you told me about the rats in South Africa. I know prison wasn't any fun, but still, you had a funny story."

"Well," said Andrew sleepily, "there's every reason to believe nothing funny happened in the trenches in 1918."

"But he was away three years and only one year was the war."

"If you're trying to forget something big, you have to forget the little things too," said Andrew. "The little things only lead back to the big ones."

"That's true, but he doesn't even have his medals out, Andrew. I thought when he had his own house, he'd put his medals on the mantelpiece or in one of the glass cabinets in the living room. You should speak to him. Maybe he's just forgotten about them."

"No, Alice. What did I just say?"

"He doesn't want to remember."

"Let's leave it that way."

"It's such a shame. I know the boys would be so proud of his military career."

"I expect they may be proud of him in other ways." After a pause, he added, "We aren't taking our usual points of view on this one, are we?"

"Well," said Alice, "we don't always have to be consistent, do we?"

CHAPTER EIGHTY-TWO

Autie walked up the hill to talk privately with his father. The market was up and down on low volume. His first round of telephone calls to New York was over. The little jumps in radio smelled like a pool, but he went in with two thousand anyway. If it kept going up, the little guys would jump in. Then he'd sell just before the big guys pulled their money out and let radio crash.

Not a bad strategy as long as he was right about what was behind the climb. The earnings could go into Caterpillar and Westinghouse. They didn't move much but they were solid. Maybe he did have a knack for spotting a pool but he didn't want to make a habit of it. It might be a good way to make money but it caused havoc and undermined trust in the market. Halfway up the hill he stopped to take a piece of paper and pencil out of his back pocket. He had to remind himself to look at copper on the commodities exchange. It might give him some insight on what was going on with Anaconda.

They sat down in Andrew's study, and Autie came right out and said he was uneasy about the wedding gift to Rory and Laura.

"I thought you might be," said Andrew. "You've put a lot of work into the farm over there to give them a good start. As far as that goes, are we still agreed on the salary until Rory comes back to take over?"

"That's fine, Dad."

"Then what is it?" he asked with a concern that Autie knew was genuine.

"Well—fairness, Dad. I know you built the cottage for us, gave me the farm to run, and set me up in the market, but it's not the same thing."

"How are we doing in the market, by the way?"

"Just fine."

"That's all yours, you know."

"I thought we were going to incorporate."

"No, I spoke to Jack Bowman in Wilmington about it. He understands your point about gains covering losses. He thought it was the way to go too, but for reasons of my own, I want to keep the businesses separate. I'll manage the house here and the import business. If you want, you'll stay on salary as farm manager, but I retain ownership. The securities business is entirely yours. That's how I'd like to do it."

Andrew sat back in his chair. On the other side of the desk, Autie was still leaning forward with his fingers tapping the armrests of the chair.

"Am I supposed to return the capital you put into the stocks?" he asked.

"No," said his father. "That's yours."

"You're giving it to me?"

"Is that agreeable to you, son?"

"You put in half a million."

"I want you to have your own show to run. You don't have to tell me now. You can go home and talk it over."

"No, I don't have to do that, Dad."

Andrew leaned forward with his hand out, and they shook hands across the desk.

"Feel better about the situation?" Andrew asked.

"Sure, Dad. I appreciate it very much. With two kids, I have to think of their future and make the right moves. I lost a lot of time staying in the army longer than I should have. I could kick myself for that."

"No, I wouldn't regret anything," said Andrew. "What you learned in the army is figuring into what you're doing now, isn't it?"

"Hard to see it that way most of the time. But there's one other thing, Dad. Kind of along the same lines. Have you and Mom written up anything about the house and estate?"

"Do you mean a will?"

"Yes."

"Yes, we've always had wills, and we've always changed them when circumstances changed."

"Well, they've changed, Dad."

"Not yet. As of now, it's still one third, one third, one third."

"Laura's one-third?"

"Your mother has always thought of her as a daughter, Autie. And Laura never got the inheritance she should have had from her father. But I want to see if this marriage actually goes through. If it does, then you get clear title to this side of the river in the will. I want you to give Rory whatever from the house that holds sentimental value for him. You'll have to work that out between yourselves, but there won't be any question of the chateau and land. All right. Are we straight?"

Autie said he thought so and stood up.

"I'd better get home for dinner," he said.

Andrew followed him out of the study, through the library, the black-and-white tiled passage to the living room, and to the small door at the back of the house. They walked out to the flagpole. The sun was just starting to go down over the river, so Autie helped his father bring the flag down and fold it. A few geese were coming in for a landing in the field below, and there was the marsh beyond, full of honking geese bedding down for the night.

"Call me tomorrow, Autie," said Andrew. "I want you to tell me if Margaux is all right with everything."

"I will, Dad. Thanks. Tell Mom good night for me."

"And good night from us to you and yours in the cottage, my boy."

CHAPTER EIGHTY-THREE

Laura Eklund sat in her wedding dress on a little settee in front of the mirror in her old room at the chateau. She heard the tires of another car crunching the gravel outside as it came to a stop in front of the house. If she looked out the window, she would see Mr. Thompson in his cutaway, holding doors for ladies and gentlemen who might have last seen her selling stamps in the post office and must have heard all about Gregory jilting her.

This was her wedding day. In an hour she would be Mrs. Rory Croft. Her face became wet with tears at the thought. She wished she didn't have such a deep tan from the months on the yacht, but she wasn't going to powder up like a Japanese girl. It would only run, and she wouldn't look very happy like that.

They had been home only a week. Mother said it would take at least a month to put together a splendid wedding and tried to talk her into it. A decisive, confident daughter was something new to her. And how could she not see that she and Rory were really in love? Not only that, they were familiar and used to each other. How they smiled across the dinner table every night. Proof positive.

She bought the dress in Paris. Mother hadn't seen it. Wouldn't she be surprised. Even Mother wouldn't have a spare wedding dress lying around. People were going to talk about it, maybe more than they were still talking about the man with the airplane. It was a mix of silk and satin, off shoulder, full sleeve. The right side crossed the front to a tie closure on the left waist. It outraged the seamstress to cut off two yards of fabric and hem it at the ankle, but it was the only way for a five-foot-four heavy girl not to look like she was hammered into the ground.

So much had changed since she last slept in this room, the night before they left on the boat for England. She would not have thought herself strong enough that night, if the thought could have occurred to her then, to be marrying Rory Croft. Now all she had to do for the guests gathering below in the living room was to be Laura Eklund for a short ceremonial walk with Father, who would give her away. The minister standing in front of them would swear her to vows and proclaim her Mrs. Rory Croft. For their children, it would be best to leave out some parts of the story. They probably wouldn't care. As far as they would know, their parents never had a life before they met each other. You never catch on to that until the next generation comes along.

Becoming Rory's wife made perfect sense if you could see that fate was different than chance. All the while fickle chance had batted her this way and that way, fate had been moving the ground under her toward a destiny. Flodhöjder was hers. The first boy she kissed was hers. Beyond that was whatever would come. She was young enough to have ten children. Well, maybe eight. Chance might pare that down even to one, and she would still be happy. She would be to Rory the wife she had been to Gregory, and Rory would find himself, as Gregory had. She wasn't worried about that. And she would find herself too, if she could ever calm down and stop being so excited by every dream coming true.

There was a light tap at the door, and Alice announced herself.

"Just a moment, Mummy."

Laura stood up and moved the settee to the side for a good view of herself in the mirror. It would be most effective to be facing the mirror when Mother came in. Then turn around. Everything looked about as good as it could be.

"You can come in now."

When Alice's face came into the mirror, Laura turned.

"Oh!" Alice exclaimed.

"Do you like it, Mummy?"

"It's breathtaking."

"Is it too much?"

"No, no. It'll wake up the geezers down there, darling. I know you don't like to make an impression on anyone, but it's your wedding day. You aren't trying to be Luisa Casati."

"Who?"

"Oh, you know, that Italian marchioness or something—before the war. The one in the magazines I showed you. She wore those wild dresses."

"I don't think this is wild at all."

"No it suits the new you."

"I wish I wasn't so heavy."

Alice stood off to look at the dress, her hands holding Laura's.

"Don't give it a thought, dear. The dress is lovely, but you have to stand up straight. There. Turn around. See how radiant and queenly you look?"

"A little top heavy."

"No, the cleavage makes you look luscious."

"Oh please, Mummy."

"That's just what you want, dear. Especially for Rory. I could tell you stories."

"I don't want to hear any more stories about Rory."

"That's right, dear. He's yours now. Is this the veil?" With two fingers, Alice picked up the light brocade headband and slipped an arm under the sheer two-layer tulle. "How lovely. All the way to the floor!"

"It's called cathedral length, Mummy."

"Turn around and let me fix it. I love your hair short like this, dear. Let's leave a little showing."

"It was getting too impractical living on the yacht with long hair."

Laura sat down at her vanity table before the three mirrors, carefully arranging her dress, and Alice busied herself adjusting the headband.

"I remember when I got married," Alice said casually, "I was so preoccupied with expectations of the evening, I just wanted to get the wedding over with."

"If you want to know if anything other than expectations await Rory and me tonight, the answer is no, Mother dear."

"Well," said Alice, "from your very brief letters home, we got the impression that the tour was getting somewhat bacchanalian."

"Oh no. Not really. Everyone had little flings. That's all. I was with Eliot most of the time. We didn't do anything. He was really a boy, Mummy. After being with Gregory for so long, I knew I wanted a man. And after all the flings Rory's had with girls, he wanted a real woman. That's what he said."

"Is this too tight?"

"No, that's fine," said Laura, touching the back of her head with one hand. "It really was fate, I think. He was the first boy I kissed. Remember that hypothetical situation I brought up when I was sixteen? Well, that was Rory. He kissed me on the stairs. My birthday party was going on downstairs. It was his first kiss too. I think that's very nice because I always thought I would marry the first boy I kissed, and fate made it turn out that way. So, yes, Mummy, tonight is going to be a big night. We haven't done anything but kiss." Then she laughed. "I think he's very eager to get me out of this dress and see what he's got."

"Well, you take it off yourself. Don't let him touch this lovely dress. Do you want me to send Lilly over tonight? She's very good at folding fine fabrics to be put away. When you have a daughter, she'll want this for her own wedding day."

Laura laughed again. "Oh Mummy, I have so many people over there. What am I ever going to do with them?"

"You'll have to start entertaining."

"No thanks!"

"Rory might want to. You know how sociable he is."

Music began to drift up from the grand piano in the living room below.

"That's Lois," said Alice. "She's very good, isn't she? I'm so glad she could come. Don't worry. She dressed for the occasion."

"I know how Rory is, Mother. He knows me too. I've learned not to compare myself to other women. Now I know why you never did."

With the headband of the veil in place, Laura stood up to spread the tulle. Alice hugged her tightly.

"I love you so much, Laura, dear," she whispered. "It made me so happy to have you as my daughter. I know Rory will be just as happy having you for his wife. There's nothing I could want for you more than that. Don't try to say anything now, dear. We have to go."

"I love you, Mummy."

Laura composed herself and turned toward the door. With Alice at her side, Laura stepped slowly and carefully down the stairs along the wall where Rory had kissed her in the dark many years ago. At the bottom of the staircase, with a hand on the polished baluster was Andrew Croft, formally attired in a black suit, waiting to take her arm, looking up so proudly.

END, BOOK ONE

ACKNOWLEDGMENTS

Much credit for bringing this novel to publication goes to:

My sister and first reader, Carolyn E. Miller, who read the manuscript when its chances were 50/50. Her questions and encouragement were vital to continued work.

Judith M. Meloy, for her undaunted good spirits when—expecting each draft she read to be the last—printed out and took the next one to the couch.

Tom Locke, copy editor. Tom's painstaking and detailed edits were invaluable. Equally so were his comments as a reader that often sent me back to the drawing board. Taking an interest in the content was above and beyond, and much appreciated.

Dan and Jim Pratt of Pratt Brothers Composition for a layout fraught with last minute changes, good taste in cover design, and especially for all the tinkering that went on with a photograph and copy that didn't make the cut.

Tracy Jones for proofreading. We didn't think she'd find anything, but of course, she did. Her private assessment of the book was as heartening as a *NY Times* review.

Presiding over all aspects of content and production, my brother, Jeffrey B. Miller coordinated and managed the project. It is hard to imagine a publisher more devoted to working with the writer and freelancers to bring out a book that reads its best and looks well cared for. Getting to know the professional side of Jeff's life has been one of the rewards of writing.

ABOUT THE AUTHOR

ERIC B. MILLER was brought up in a small town in New Jersey. Formal education included degree programs at Denison University and Hollins College. As a young man, he worked on farms in Maryland, Virginia, and Belgium. Back home after some wanderings, he spent twenty-three years in family business, then eighteen years with American Red Cross blood services.

Little Known Stories was written as a reflection on the life and death of his wife, Lisa, and their forty-one years together. *Hula Girls* was his first published novel.

Tidewater is first of a two-part series.

Reuniting after fifty years, Eric and Judith M. Meloy, accomplished academician, educator and writer, live and work together in Vermont and New Jersey.

Made in the USA
Columbia, SC
24 October 2024